THE CHRONICLES OF
MALUS DARKBLADE
VOLUME TWO

IN THE WORLD of Warhammer, no race is as cruel and treacherous as the dark elves, and no member of this race is more infamous than Malus Darkblade. Having been possessed by an ancient daemon, he was been tasked with retrieving five missing artefacts, and in this second omnibus, we see the continuation of Darkblade's unholy adventures.

In *Warpsword*, Darkblade's quest leads him to the dreaded city of Har Ganeth and the legendary Warpsword of Khaine. Time is running out and as Darkblade becomes embroiled in religion and assassination, the daemon within is becoming stronger.

In *Lord of Ruin*, Darkblade must return to the ancient daemon Tz'arkan's lair. But can he be trusted to honour his part of the bargain to return his soul or will he try to trick the dark elf one last time?

And finally the original Darkblade comic strip, exclusively reprinted, reveals some of the dark elf anti-hero's earliest adventures.

A WARHAMMER ANTHOLOGY

THE CHRONICLES OF
MALUS DARKBLADE
VOLUME TWO

DAN ABNETT
& MIKE LEE

A Black Library Publication

Warpsword and *Lord of Ruin* copyright © 2007 Games Workshop Ltd.

This omnibus edition published in Great Britain in 2009 by
BL Publishing,
Games Workshop Ltd.,
Willow Road, Nottingham,
NG7 2WS, UK.

10 9 8 7 6 5 4 3 2 1

Cover illustration by Clint Langley.
Map by Nuala Kinrade.

A CIP record for this book is available from the British Library.

ISBN 13: 978 1 84416 783 8

Distributed in the US by Simon & Schuster
1230 Avenue of the Americas, New York, NY 10020, US.

See the Black Library on the Internet at
www.blacklibrary.com

Find out more about Games Workshop
and the world of Warhammer at
www.games-workshop.com

Printed and bound in the US.

THIS IS A DARK age, a bloody age, an age of daemons and of sorcery. It is an age of battle and death, and of the world's ending. Amidst all of the fire, flame and fury it is a time, too, of mighty heroes, of bold deeds and great courage.

AT THE HEART of the Old World sprawls the Empire, the largest and most powerful of the human realms. Known for its engineers, sorcerers, traders and soldiers, it is a land of great mountains, mighty rivers, dark forests and vast cities. And from his throne in Altdorf reigns the Emperor Karl Franz, sacred descendant of the founder of these lands, Sigmar, and wielder of his magical warhammer.

BUT THESE ARE far from civilised times. Across the length and breadth of the Old World, from the knightly palaces of Bretonnia to ice-bound Kislev in the far north, come rumblings of war. In the towering Worlds Edge Mountains, the orc tribes are gathering for another assault. Bandits and renegades harry the wild southern lands of the Border Princes. There are rumours of rat-things, the skaven, emerging from the sewers and swamps across the land. And from the northern wildernesses there is the ever-present threat of Chaos, of daemons and beastmen corrupted by the foul powers of the Dark Gods. As the time of battle draws ever near, the Empire needs heroes like never before.

CONTENTS

FOREWORD

MALUS DARKBLADE'S MURDEROUS guile has sustained him for a surprisingly long time. He wasn't the first character I created and wrote for the Black Library (for the record, the first was Gilead, in a short story, followed by a short eldar comic strip, followed by – *ta da!* – the first Gaunt story), but he was definitely an early essay in character generation and series building.

At first, he seemed an unpromising and one-dimensional fellow. He was all leering bombast and cruelty, a villain just crying out for a damn good come-uppance. I thought I might be able to squeeze a story arc or two out of him before he became too tiresome. I was wrong.

There was a reason for this, naturally. Not me being wrong, I mean. I refer to Malus's initial, unpromising 'thin-ness'. I manufactured him to be the lead in a comic strip. This was early days, BC in Black Library terms, and I was finding my feet. Novels, and the necessarily more complex characters that propel them, were still a way off.

Point of order: okay, before you write in, I fully appreciate that comic book characters can absolutely be as fully rounded and complex as characters in a novel. I wasn't dissing comics (would I?). It's a sophisticated and sublime art form yadda yadda yadda...

The fact of the matter is, Malus *was* a cheap and shoddy comic book character. I deliberately lashed some less-than-subtle characteristics together in the hope of setting up a big, melodramatic persona, who was so in your face he'd carry the strip for a while. He wasn't supposed to be all sophisticated and stuff. The strip was six pages an episode, six pages a MONTH. There wasn't any time to waste with la-di-dah character development. Darkblade had to, excuse my French, grab you by the balls from page one and never let go. He had to be as immediate as Judge Dredd, as Desperate Dan... as a *cattle prod*.

Oddly, I warmed to him. It's hard to hate such a total bastard. He was a curious mix of Macbeth, Blackadder, Han Solo and Hans Gruber (the 'terrorist' leader in *Die Hard*, as played by the fabulous Alan Rickman). I found myself simultaneously wanting to hurt him, and willing him to hurt others.

What helped immeasurably, of course, was the injection of someone *else's* talent, in this case the entirely gifted and splendid Kev Hopgood, who drew the strip all the way from its inception to its ultimate demise, and did it brilliantly. Let's be clear, Mr Hopgood is a major art talent. Unassuming and understated, he is sometimes overlooked. I believe Kev to be one of the best comic artists the UK has produced in the last twenty years. He's certainly one of the most underrated. His style is utterly distinctive, his storytelling is immaculate, and his contribution to the genre is significant (for example, his long run on *Iron Man* at Marvel, during which he created *War Machine*. He CREATED *War Machine*, people, and the character's still in use today!).

Working with Kev, Darkblade took off. I suddenly saw sustainability, durability; I saw a character that might have depth. I saw a character that might have character... If you know what I mean.

Darkblade ran... and you'll have to help me out here, because I'm writing this in the house, and my archive copies of stuff are ten minutes up the road in my lock-up, and I've had a glass of wine, so I really shouldn't go and check... Darkblade ran for four 'books'. It might have been five. We were either in the middle of the fifth when *Warhammer Monthly* was canned, or the sixth. Or the fourth. Hell, I don't know. The point is, there was a fair bit of material under our collective belts, a fair head of steam. Kev and I had taken the character a long way (eg, hell and back), and we'd summoned up the confidence to take him even further. If you like Malus (why wouldn't you, and, besides, you did buy this book), then I suggest you go seek out the old comic stories if you haven't already read them. I'm sure you can pick them up in graphic novel form on Amazon or Ebay. The French edition is especially nice (large format) though, of course, you'll need to be able to read French. I urge you to do this because I think the series stands up really well, and, more particularly, you'll get to relish Kev's art. It's great. He created *War Machine*, you know.

By the time the strip went away, I'd been living with Malus for quite a few years. When he was created, year numbers started with a '1'. That's a long time to engage with a character.

I believe it was the inestimable Lindsey Priestley who suggested that Malus might make the transition from comic book to novel. I think she noticed the depth we'd bred into him. It was an inviting idea, but I baulked, because I was busy. Gaunt and Ravenor were taking up all my time, and I couldn't quite see how I might find room for the three or four month diversions that writing Malus novels would require.

For the second time in Malus's 'life', what helped immeasurably was the injection of someone *else's* talent. Enter Mike Lee – gentleman, scholar, acrobat (oh, wait, think I may have gone into a Pink Panther riff). Mike is an American author, whom I first met in San Diego. His work for you, dear Black Library readers, needs no introduction, but I will take this opportunity to aim you at *Fallen Angels*, his first Horus Heresy novel. It's aces. Mike is aces too. His wife is lovely (her art is hanging on our walls), he writes like a dream, and even though I made him laugh and cry 'like a little girl' (his words, not mine) at

Baltimore a couple of years ago, I hold him and his craft in the highest esteem (and I have no doubt that most of you assume, as a given, that people often cry when they meet me).

Mike's given the Darkblade books the depth that Kev gave to the comic series. Like Kev, he's taken my flimsy, one-dimensional creation and made it solid and phlegmatic.

In fact, he's making me look bad (note to self, ditch Lee, raise game).

So, anyway, welcome to the second Darkblade omnibus (if Mike and I can get our act together, there will be more... We've only just scratched the surface of Malus continuity). We hope you enjoy your stay. If you do, then will your thanks towards Kev, and towards Mike. Kev, for the pictures, Mike for the mind pictures. I believe in credit where credit is due, and in the case of Darkblade, Kev and Mike should be above the title in big type, and my name should be much smaller, and have the words 'also featuring' in front of it.

Dan Abnett
Maidstone, May, 2009.

WARPSWORD

Chapter One
BAG OF BONES

TWO FULL MOONS hung low in the evening sky, gleaming like burnished pearls in a band of indigo just above the sharp mountain crags to the west. Their light cast a shimmer of faded gold across the restless surface of the Sea of Malice, and the wind blowing in from the water was cold and damp. Tendrils of mist coiled along the rocky shore, reaching tentatively northward through the rustling fields of yellow grass and touching lightly on the dark stones of the Slavers' Road. As the night wore on the mist would thicken, swallowing the road entirely and pressing hungrily into the dense forest of dark pine beyond.

The small group of druchii walking along the winding road eyed the swelling fog with a kind of weary dread. After many days of travel along the seacoast, they knew that the wind and the mist would sink through their light summer cloaks like an assassin's knife and settle deep in their bones. They were all young and strong – and had demonstrated so on more than one occasion since leaving their homes – but their muscles ached and their joints were stiff after weeks of sleeping on damp, cold earth. So when one of their number spied a small, cleared area with a fire pit at the edge of the tree line the band stopped in their tracks and spoke amongst themselves in low, hushed tones.

Their leader, a tall woman with finger bones plaited in her black hair, turned and looked along the road to the north, searching for a sign that their destination might only be a short way away. She wanted to press ahead a bit further, but when the man who'd first spied the clearing walked to the fire pit and pointed out a stack of ready firewood tucked beneath a nearby pine, that settled the debate. With a last, searching glance to the north the woman joined her compatriots by the fire pit, throwing back the folds of her cloak and shrugging her travel bags from her shoulders. Lengths of wood clunked and rattled as they were tossed into the pit and the druchii murmured easily amongst themselves, pleased at the thought of a warm fire to keep the fog at bay.

Preoccupied as they were with flint and tinder and unwrapping what remained of their meagre rations, none of them noticed the lean, haggard figure step quietly from the concealing mist close to the shore. Droplets of water glittered like shards of broken glass on the dark surface of Malus Darkblade's heavy, fur-mantled cloak and ran in thin streams across his worn and split-seamed boots. His long black hair hung loose in a thick, matted tangle, almost indistinguishable from the wolf-fur that weighed upon his narrow shoulders. Moonlight limned the hard lines of his weathered face, sharpening the bony angles of his cheekbones and the dagger-point of his pale chin.

Shadows pooled in the hollows of his cheeks and the sunken orbits of his eyes as he studied the four men and two women forming a circle around the fire pit just a few yards away. As he watched, one of the druchii stuffed a wad of tinder beneath the piled logs and took up his flint, scattering a stream of thin red sparks with a few deft strokes before bending low to blow gently on the smouldering wood shavings. Within moments a tongue of fire rose from the tinder and licked along the cured wood, and the druchii all leaned forwards expectantly, reaching out with slim, pale hands for the warmth that was soon to follow. Malus smiled coldly, scarcely noticing the offshore breeze caress his face with cold, damp fingers. A few moments more, he thought, nodding to himself. They'd taken the bait, but now he had to set the hook.

Within a few minutes the druchii had a roaring fire going, filling the clearing and painting the sides of the dark pines with flickering orange light. The druchii ate meals of hard biscuit, dried fish and cheese, and stretched their feet wearily towards the blaze. After a long, hard day of travel the men and women seemed to come unclenched at the heady sensation of warmth and food in their bellies. None of them noticed Malus's approach until he limped like one of the walking dead into the circle of the firelight.

Conversation stopped. Several of the druchii straightened, hands reaching for their swords. Their faces were carefully neutral, but Malus could see the calculating gleam in their eyes. They were sizing him up, deciding whether to treat him as predator or prey. Malus reached both hands from beneath the folds of his faded cloak and showed his empty palms. 'Well met, brothers and sisters,' Malus said carefully. The words came out in a low, hoarse voice – after two and a half months of living like an animal in the woods along the Slavers' Road he'd had little use for conversation. 'Might a fellow traveller share your fire for a while?'

Without waiting for a reply, he unclasped his cloak and pulled it from his shoulders. Beneath, Malus wore a ragged shirt of blackened mail and a battered kheitan of human hide, cut in a rustic style common to the north country. A broad, straight northern sword and a set of knives hung from his belt above a set of faded and torn woollen robes. His black boots were ragged as well, the soles pulling away from their pointed tips. But for a large ruby ring glinting brightly on his right hand and a plain silver band glinting on his left, he looked like a half-starved autarii or a crazed mountain hermit.

Malus spread the cloak carefully on the ground and shrugged a plain cloth bag from his shoulder. Sharp, measuring stares flicked from Malus's face to the stained brown canvas bag and back again. All of the travellers carried similar bags, kept close by their sides. Like Malus, the other druchii were dressed simply: plain robes and kheitans, light armour or none at all, and a single sword or broad knife to deal with encounters on the road. Had they horses and clinking bundles of slave irons they could have been traders on the way to Karond Kar in anticipation of the autumn flesh harvest.

After a moment the leader of the small band leaned forwards with a soft rustle of layered wool and studied Malus thoughtfully. Her hair was drawn back in a series of tight braids, accentuating her long face and severe features. The woman's brass-coloured eyes shone like polished coins in the firelight. 'Have you travelled far, brother?' she asked.

The highborn met the woman's gaze and struggled to conceal his surprise. The woman's eyes marked her as a high priestess of Khaine, the Bloody-Handed God. They set her apart even among other members of Khaine's temple as especially favoured by the Lord of Murder.

Malus nodded slowly. 'From Naggor,' he replied, thinking to describe his route down the Spear Road past Naggarond but holding back at the last moment. Say no more than you must, he cautioned himself. 'And you?'

'From the temple at Clar Karond,' the woman replied, and then nodded to two men to her right. 'And they from Hag Graef.'

Malus continued to nod, keeping his face carefully neutral and giving the two men only the briefest of glances. His mind raced and a fist tightened around his heart. A voice hissed inside his head, like a blade drawn across naked bone.

'I warned you of this, little druchii,' the daemon said, its voice dripping with contempt. 'They will recognise you any moment and your pathetic scheme will come undone.'

* * *

'AFTER TONIGHT YOU will not be able to return to Hag Graef,' his mother had told him, her voice cutting through the howling wind as the city burned around them. 'You must seek the Warpsword of Khaine in the city of Har Ganeth. Your brother Urial awaits you there, seeking to make the sword his own.'

And so he had travelled north and east, slipping from the corpse-choked Vale of Shadow with food taken from the ruins of the Naggorite camp. He moved at night and stayed off the roads whenever he could, knowing that his kin would be sniffing for his trail as soon as they were able. Once the fires had been put out and order restored in the city, his half-brother Isilvar would send his troops into the Vale to check every bloated and torn body to see if he lay among the fallen. When they realised he'd escaped, word would spread, and every druchii in the Land of Chill would be watching for him. For the man or woman who delivered Malus Darkblade – living or dead – into the clutches of the Witch King would reap a drachau's ransom in wealth and favour. Not because Malus had led an army against his former home, but for the crime of taking the life of his father Lurhan, the Vaulkhar of Hag Graef, and by extension a sworn vassal of Malekith himself. No one slew the Witch King's property without his leave, and for that Malus had lost everything – rank, property, wealth and ambition, all stricken from him with a single stroke of a sword.

He had thought himself clever, but in the end he'd played right into his enemies' hands. Now Isilvar was Hag Graef's vaulkhar and possessor of not only Lurhan's wealth, but Malus's as well. His half-sister Nagaira had conspired with Isilvar; together they'd known more about Malus and his secret quest on behalf of the daemon Tz'arkan than he'd realised. They knew of the five relics he needed to find in order to free the daemon from its prison and reclaim his stolen soul. They knew he would seek the Dagger of Torxus in the tomb of Eleuril the Damned, and so they'd arranged for Lurhan to get it first. And he, blind to everything except recovering the relics and ridding himself of the daemon, had done their bidding like a trained dog.

It had taken a week to reach the Slavers' Road, and two weeks more to reach Har Ganeth, City of Executioners. Malus had stopped there, hesitating warily before the city's open gates and sombre streets.

The gates of Har Ganeth never shut because the City of Executioners hungered for flesh and blood. It was Khaine's city, seat of the temple's worldly power, and no one came or went from it without the approval of the priests who ruled there.

Malus knew they would be watching for him. His half-brother Urial would have seen to that, if nothing else. Urial had every reason to hate and fear Malus, and desired the warpsword for reasons of his own. It figured into an ancient prophecy, one that the crippled highborn believed to be his birthright.

Malus had reason to believe otherwise. Prophecies were often slippery things, and had a tendency to turn in the hand of those who thought to wield them.

Nevertheless, he knew nothing of the city and hadn't a coin to his name to bribe anyone with, so he had no confidence that he could slip quietly into the city and remain hidden beneath Urial's very nose, much less go poking through the temple fortress in search of a sacred relic. More than once he found it bitterly amusing that before, when he had everything to lose he would have just charged headlong into the city, convinced he could think his way out of any mess he found himself in. Now, however, since he'd lost everything, he found himself much more circumspect.

He needed more information about the city and its inhabitants, he'd decided. So he retreated into the wooded foothills north of the city and waited for someone to leave.

The first thing he'd learned was that, unlike every other city in Naggaroth, few people came and went from Har Ganeth. It was almost a week before a lone traveller emerged from the city gates and headed west on horseback. Malus shadowed the solitary figure until nightfall, when the man left the road and built a fire at a campsite along the edge of the tree line. After watching the man for half an hour, Malus walked into the camp and offered to share some of his wine in exchange for a spot close to the fire. After sampling Malus's wine, the man grudgingly agreed.

He was a stranger to the city, as it happened – visiting a cousin in Har Ganeth who kept a chandler's shop close by the temple fortress. As Malus had feared, every stranger entering the city had to report to the temple straightaway and receive the blessing of the priestesses, or else he took his life in his hands. There were only three sorts of people in the City of Executioners: servants of the temple, guests of the temple and sacrifices to Khaine. A druchii caught on the street – by day or night – without the temple's blessing could be slain out of hand as an offering to the Lord of Murder, and the people of the city were zealous in their devotion to the Bloody-Handed God.

The man knew nothing about the temple fortress. Only members of the cult were permitted to enter, leaving the devout to worship at any one of a dozen smaller shrines located across the city. He had heard a recent bit of gossip, though. There were rumours throughout the city that a holy man had appeared before the temple elders bearing signs and portents that the culmination of a great prophecy was at hand. What that meant the man could not say, but there were acolytes in the streets exhorting the faithful to prepare themselves for a time of blood and fire, and bloodied skulls began to appear in piles on every street corner. Fearing that soon his head would be added to one of the piles, the man fled for his life.

The news filled Malus with dismay. They finished the wine in dreary silence, and then he stabbed the man in the heart and went through his belongings for anything useful. Spite feasted on man and horse that night, and Malus had bread and sausage for a week after.

As the days passed Malus settled into a grim routine, stalking travellers leaving the city and learning what he could from them. Sometimes the conversation ended at the point of a knife; other times he chose discretion and slipped away into the darkness once the wine was done. Once he nearly had the tables turned on him, and it was only the Dark Mother's own luck and his familiarity with the forest that allowed him to

escape with a whole skin. Little by little, his knowledge of the
city grew, but nothing he learned helped solve the most crucial
riddles of all: how to avoid the notice of the temple without
winding up an unwilling sacrifice, and how to find the
Warpsword of Khaine.

It never once occurred to Malus to ask either Tz'arkan or his
mother Eldire for help. The silver ring he wore had been a gift
from his mother, one of the most potent sorceresses and seers in
the Land of Chill. He could use it to speak with her on nights
when the moon was bright. As for the daemon, it had never
passed up a chance to tempt him with tastes of its supernatural
powers – but after the night in the burning city, its behaviour had
changed. It was warier now, questioning Malus's every move and
offering nothing unless asked. The daemon feared Eldire's power
for some reason, and that both pleased and troubled Malus.

As the summer wore on the pattern of travel changed. Druchii
began heading for Har Ganeth – singly at first, and then in small
groups of up to half a dozen, arriving at all hours of the day and
night. They came down the Slavers' Road from the west or crossed
the Sea of Malice in boats, and they all travelled surreptitiously,
without fanfare or finery. They came from all walks of life, as near
as Malus could tell: highborn and lowborn, princes, bakers and
thieves and everything in between, and once they entered Har
Ganeth, they didn't emerge again. Malus found himself thinking
about Urial and his prophecy once more, and wondered whether
there might be something to it after all.

Seeking answers, Malus headed down the road and looked for
a solitary traveller to share a bottle of wine with.

The first man he found welcomed him like a long-lost brother
and barely took a sip of wine before trying to cut Malus's throat.
He'd laughed like a lunatic as they'd rolled across the damp
ground, wrestling over the man's serrated knife. When Malus
had finally gained the upper hand and searched the body afterwards he found a brown canvas bag filled with body parts:
hands, ears, noses and genitals, many still sticky with gore.

Malus approached a second man a day later, and received
another warm welcome. This time he was ready when the

druchii leapt at him with a knife. He, too, had a bag full of
freshly severed bits of flesh. In a fit of pique Malus tossed the
druchii's head into the bag and took it with him.

After that he watched the people on the road much more
closely. Man or woman, young or old, they all carried a sword or
a broad-bladed knife and a stained bag hung from shoulder or
belt.

Was there some holy ceremony in the offing, calling the faithful to the city to present their offerings to Khaine? He'd never
heard of such a thing before. One thing was clear, however: the
travellers seemed happy to kill any stranger they met except those
carrying bags of their own. Malus had no idea why that mattered,
but finally a glimmer of a plan began to take shape in his mind.

'WINE, BROTHERS AND sisters?' Malus pulled a clay bottle from
a second carry-bag and offered it to the group. One of the men
from Hag Graef leaned forwards and took the bottle eagerly.
Malus caught the man's eye as he surrendered the wine, but
saw no glint of recognition there.

'I hadn't realised there were any followers of the true faith
living at the Black Ark,' the temple maiden said.

The true faith? What did that mean, Malus thought? 'I hadn't
known of any in Karond Kar either,' he answered. 'I suppose
that makes us even.' Eager to change the subject, he nodded his
head eastward. 'We'll be in Har Ganeth by midday tomorrow.'

The other travellers from the Karond Kar murmured in
approval. 'We should have listened to you after all, holy one,'
the second woman said to the temple maiden. 'If we'd continued on we would have reached the holy city by midnight.'

'Let's go then,' one of the men declared. 'We have a sacred
duty, do we not? The heretic and his minions could be battling
with the faithful even now—'

The temple maiden cut the man off with a curt wave of her
hand. Her gaze never left Malus. 'You look as if you've been wandering in the mountains for weeks,' she said to the highborn.

Malus affected a shrug, his mind churning. The heretic? That
had to mean Urial. Who else had recently come to Har Ganeth
shouting about the end of the world?

'I... well,' Malus stammered, looking away. 'I confess that I've tarried a while on the road, holy one.' He reached over and hefted the bloodstained sack. 'There are meagre pickings on the Spear Road this time of year, and I didn't want to reach Har Ganeth with a poor offering for the god.'

Several of the faithful nodded their heads approvingly. He'd taken a wild guess about the contents of the bag, and the gamble had paid off. The temple maiden considered him for a moment more, and then leaned back against a fallen log and resumed her meal.

The man from Clar Karond eyed Malus. 'Have you seen many other faithful on the road, brother?'

'Oh, yes,' Malus nodded. 'They've come from all over. I'd wager there are thousands in the holy city, ready to fight the heretic.'

At the news, the man's eyes glinted with a savage light. 'At last! The day of reckoning is at hand. We've suffered the heretic's lies long enough!'

'I couldn't agree more, brother,' Malus said with feeling. The man from Hag Graef passed the bottle back to him and he took a hearty swallow. This was going to work. If he kept his wits about him he could slip into the city with the rest of the faithful and no one – least of all Urial – would be the wiser.

Grinning broadly, the man from Clar Karond reached for the wine. 'With so many of the true faith returning to the city the streets must be busy indeed,' he said. 'We have a place prepared for us at the home of Sethra Veyl. Where will you be staying?'

'With my cousin,' Malus replied. 'He is a chandler, with a shop close to the temple fortress.'

The man from Clar Karond froze, his hand still reaching for the bottle. His grin faded. Suddenly Malus noticed that everyone else had fallen silent.

The temple maiden rose to her feet, a curved dagger in her hand.

'Seize the heretic,' she hissed.

Chapter Two
EYES OF BRASS

MALUS BIT BACK a curse. So much for blending in with the herd, he thought bitterly. Thinking quickly, he grabbed his bag of offerings and rose slowly to his feet.

'Where I choose to stay inside the city is my business,' he said sharply, fixing the temple maiden with a steely glare. 'Just because I'm careful doesn't make me one of the enemy. Obviously you're as concerned about infiltrators in our ranks as I am, or you wouldn't be asking all these questions.'

Malus saw the two men from Hag Graef hesitate, their weapons half-drawn. They looked to the temple maiden for guidance.

She paused, the muscles in her jaw clenching as she wrestled with her bloodlust. The maiden opened her mouth to speak, but whatever she meant to say was lost as her female companion shrieked like a scalded slave and threw herself at Malus.

The woman's serrated dagger whistled through the air as she slashed at Malus's throat. He blocked the stroke with the stained bag of offerings, and the razor-edged blade split the damp cloth like wet paper. Withered, rotting body parts flew across the campsite, some landing in the fire with a sizzle and a flare of sparks. Malus planted his back foot and snapped the empty bag at the woman's eyes, checking her advance. Then he reversed his grip on the wine bottle and smashed it against the side of her head. She fell with a howl of rage and her companions took up the cry, rushing across the damp earth towards Malus with weapons held before them.

Malus back-pedalled, cursing fiercely as he dragged his broad sword from its scabbard. The zealots rushed at him from both sides, swinging wildly with swords and knives. The highborn blocked a knife stroke with his half-drawn sword and then twisted wildly to the left to dodge a downward slash of a sword that struck sparks from his shirt of blackened mail. With a roar he freed his blade and drove the zealots back a step with a fierce swipe at their eyes, but less than a second later they were back on the attack, hemming Malus in with a net of glinting steel.

What the zealots lacked in martial skill they made up for in utter fearlessness, apparently unafraid of losing their lives in the process of bringing Malus down. They kept up their relentless advance, forcing Malus to remain on the defensive against the flashing points of sword and knife. He could tell that the zealots were gauging his reflexes, and the attacks were falling into a deadly rhythm. The two men from Hag Graef pressed him from the right, while the temple maiden and the man from Clar Karond circled to his left. One of the men from Hag Graef reached in with a long thrust to Malus's neck. As he swept the blade aside with a quick shift of his sword, the temple maiden's dagger flickered in at the same moment and dug into his side. Mail rings popped and the dagger point carved a furrow through his leather kheitan, but the armour stopped the worst of the blow. Snarling, Malus aimed a savage blow at the maiden's neck, but she nimbly leapt back out of the highborn's long reach. As she did, the second man from Hag Graef stepped in and sank his dagger into Malus's right thigh.

The blow was overextended and weak and the point of the blade sank only a few inches into the muscle of Malus's leg, but the fiery explosion of pain made the highborn stumble.

The man from Hag Graef showed his red-tinged blade to his fellows and cackled with glee, showing crudely filed teeth.

Malus met the man's frenzied stare and let out a furious bellow, swinging at the hand holding the bloodstained blade. The man leapt back, just as the temple maiden had done, but the move was wasted, because the highborn's attack was only a feint. Checking his blow at the last moment, Malus reversed his swing, just as the man from Clar Karond rushed in on his left. The man was at full extension, slashing low with his knife, and Malus's heavy sword buried itself in the side of his head. The druchii staggered beneath the blow, a choking, bloody rasp hissing past his shattered jaw. Then he let go of his knife and gripped Malus's sword in his bare hands, trapping it in a death grip.

The zealot fell, blood pouring from his ravaged face and hands, and pulled Malus along with him. Without thinking, Malus put his boot in the man's face and took hold of his sword hilt with both hands, but he was not fast enough to pull his weapon free. The dagger-man from Hag Graef tackled him around the waist, knocking the highborn off his feet.

Malus hit the ground with a roar, feeling the sword wrenched from his grip. The zealot's dagger was trapped beneath the highborn for the moment. Malus pounded and clawed at the druchii's head, but the zealot tucked in his chin and closed his eyes tight against the highborn's stabbing fingers.

The highborn changed tack, fumbling for his dagger, but the temple maiden and the remaining zealots swept down on him, weapons ready. 'Hold his arms,' she ordered. The maiden ran a pink tongue over gleaming white teeth. 'I want him to watch while I sip from his living heart.'

Malus thrashed and kicked, but the men from Hag Graef seized his wrists and pulled his arms back over his head. The maiden knelt and with one hand hiked up Malus's mail shirt until the leather kheitan was exposed. Her saw-edged blade would make quick work of the tough leather. She set the point of the knife just beneath Malus's ribs and flashed the highborn a lustful smile. 'Servant of the false Swordbearer,' she hissed, 'you were a fool to think you could face us alone. You placed your faith in a false prophet and now you will pay the price.'

The highborn tried to wrench free one last time, drawing muffled curses from the zealots, but their grip was like iron. Finally he subsided, shaking his head. 'Alone? I think not,' Malus said coldly. 'Let me show you where I place my faith, temple whore.' The highborn drew a lungful of air and bellowed. 'Spite!'

There was a shrieking hiss, like water poured on a hot forge, and a huge, dark shape burst from the deep shadows beneath the trees. The nauglir was small for its breed, no more than twenty-four feet long from blunt snout to tapered tail, but its gaping jaws held fangs as long as daggers and its taloned forepaws were as broad as a man's chest. It propelled itself forwards on two powerful hind legs, shaking the earth with its tread. Lean, cable-like muscle rolled fluidly beneath its armoured green hide as it charged like a lion at the stunned zealots. The woman from Clar Karond was rising to her feet, blood streaming from the side of her face as the cold one reached her. Her scream was cut off with a thick, wet crunch as Spite's jaws closed on her torso and bit her in half. The war beast never broke stride, throwing the lower half of the druchii's body high in the air with a sharp toss of his head and a thunderous roar.

The temple maiden met Spite's hunting bellow with a shriek of her own, but it was like a war scream in the face of a howling storm. She leapt to her feet, dagger ready, but the dagger-man from Hag Graef let out a terrified scream and ran for his life.

Spite was on them in moments, clawed feet crashing down to either side of Malus and the zealots holding him. Gobbets of flesh and poisonous slime dripped from the cold one's jaws as it snapped at the man still holding Malus's arm. The highborn cursed and screamed along with his foes, rolling on his side and pulling at his trapped arm for all he was worth. The cold one would just as easily bite off Malus's arm in the heat of the moment and never know the difference.

The man from Hag Graef refused to let go of Malus, yelling his own curses at the scaly war beast and the temple maiden alike. Spite lunged at the man, snapping his drooling jaws, but the zealot ducked at the last moment and narrowly avoided losing his head.

Still screaming in fury, the temple maiden tried to drive her knife into the cold one's neck, but she didn't reckon on the thickness of the nauglir's leathery hide. The serrated blade sank barely a couple of inches into the dark green scales and was caught fast. Spite snarled and rounded on the maiden, but the woman anticipated the move and leapt backwards, out of reach of the war beast's jaws. Or so she'd hoped.

Just as she made her move Malus caught her ankle with his free hand and checked her flight. The maiden stumbled, but Spite caught her before she hit the ground. Her scream of rage turned into a rising shriek of pain as the nauglir shook her like a rat in a terrier's jaws and then flung her at the man still holding Malus's arm. Both zealots went tumbling across the ground, the impact nearly wrenching the highborn's arm out of its socket before the druchii's grip was broken.

Spite leapt after his stunned prey, bloodstained jaws gaping, and Malus fumbled his dagger free as the man pinning his legs saw his chance to escape and tried to get clear. The zealot rolled to his feet, eyes bright with hate, and Malus threw his dagger left-handed, burying it in the man's throat.

By the time Malus staggered to his feet the only sound in the clearing was the crackle of the fire and the brittle crunch of bones. Spite stood over the remains of the temple maiden and the man from Hag Graef, devouring clothes, flesh and bone in quick, snapping bites. The highborn gave the cold one a wide berth while it fed, looking for the man who'd fled towards the Slavers' Road. After a moment he caught a glimpse of a pale face, several hundred yards along the road to the north-east. He could not see any details, but Malus could imagine the man running as hard as his legs would take him, casting terrified glances over his shoulder every few yards for fear that the terrible nauglir had given chase.

'Spite!' Malus called. The cold one looked up from its meal, steam rising from the hot blood coating its snout. It snapped its jaws once, scattering streams of gory slime, and then loped heavily towards the highborn like a faithful hound.

Malus pointed down the road. 'There, beast of the deep earth,' he said coldly. 'Smell his fear? Hunt, Spite. Hunt!'

The nauglir raised its snout, nostrils flaring, let out a rumbling growl and started off at a ground-eating trot. It wouldn't be long before the zealot cast a glance over his shoulder and saw nothing but red eyes and dagger-like teeth.

Malus turned back to the corpses of the faithful and bit back a snarl of dismay. 'Damnation,' he said wearily, reclaiming first his dagger and then his heavy sword. 'One day I'll have a plan that works to perfection. The shock of it will likely kill me.'

'You were a fool to think they would be deceived, little druchii,' Tz'arkan sneered. 'All cults are born of secrets and deception, the better to identify outsiders. One wrong word, one wrong look, and your skull will be sitting atop a pile on a Har Ganeth street corner.'

'And what would you have me do?' Malus shot back. 'March into Har Ganeth and ask them politely for the sword?'

The daemon's presence slithered against his ribs like silk. Malus had come to think of the sensation as Tz'arkan's version of a smile. 'Why not? It was meant for you, after all.'

Malus let out an involuntary snarl and began searching through the zealots' bags. One of them was bound to have a bottle of wine. 'I'm not interested in your riddles,' he growled. 'I am not bound by fate or prophecy – least of all yours.'

Back in ancient times, when the druchii still ruled lost Nagarythe, the cult of Khaine was outlawed for its violent excesses and refusal to acknowledge the authority of cursed Aenarion, king of the elves. In those days, the faithful who worshipped the Bloody-Handed God clung to a prophecy that one day the Lord of Murder would send his chosen servant to lead the druchii to eternal glory in a time of blood and fire.

Urial thought he was that man, chosen by Khaine for his purity and devotion in spite of his physical deformities. He certainly fit the criteria set forth in the prophecy. But then, so did Malus.

The Scourge was destined to take up the Warpsword of Khaine. If Urial was indeed the figure of prophecy, he was going to be very surprised indeed when Malus pried the blade out of his half-brother's cold, dead hands. He had to have that blade, and to the Outer Darkness with the rest.

'Your mother has filled your head with lies,' Tz'arkan hissed.

'You sound jealous,' Malus replied absently, tossing aside the last of the bags. No wonder the zealots were such miserable wretches. Not a drop of wine among them. It was unnatural.

'I have never lied to you,' the daemon said querulously. 'I have shared my power with you when you needed it, even when it caused me great pain to do so.'

'And you've destroyed me into the bargain,' Malus snapped. 'No wealth, no rank, no prospects – I've lost it all thanks to you.'

'Trinkets,' the daemon sneered. 'Cheap gewgaws unfit for one such as you.' Tz'arkan slithered gently beneath Malus's skin, setting the highborn's teeth on edge. 'Have you ever considered that perhaps this quest is but a test?'

'A test?' Malus spat. 'Of what?'

Again, came the silky, scaly rustle of the daemon's smile. 'Malus, dear Malus. Think for a moment. I am not born of flesh. I am Tz'arkan, Drinker of Worlds. I am eternal. Do you honestly think I suffer in my crystal prison to the north?'

The answer seemed evident. 'Of course.'

'Foolish druchii. To you, a millennium of entrapment is a horror beyond imagining, but to me? It is an eye blink. If I remain bound to that crystal until the sun goes dark in the heavens it would be about as onerous as wiling away a long afternoon.'

The highborn paused. 'So you do not truly care if you are freed?'

Tz'arkan laughed. 'I will be free, Malus. That is beyond doubt. The question is whether you will be able to free me.'

Malus frowned. 'Now you're speaking in riddles.'

'No, you're being obtuse. Must I spell it out for you? I care nothing for pitiful little worlds, or the nations of pale grubs that writhe upon them. I am like unto a god, Malus. You could be, too. If you are worthy.'

The highborn laughed, shaking his head in amazement. 'And you expect me to believe that? You'd make me a god, just like that?'

He expected the daemon to sneer at him. Instead, Tz'arkan's reply was strangely sombre. 'How else do you think gods are born?'

The thought brought Malus up short.

He's lying, the highborn thought. He must be. He's trying to get the upper hand again now that Eldire has allied herself with me. And yet... it all made a terrible kind of sense.

Malus thought it over. 'All right,' he said slowly. 'Give me my soul back.'

'What?'

'You heard me,' the highborn said. 'If this isn't about your freedom, there's no need to hold my soul to compel my cooperation. Give it back, and I'll get your relics for you.'

The daemon writhed within Malus's chest. 'Impertinent druchii! I offer you power undreamt of, and you insult me!'

'I'll take that as a no,' Malus said, pleased at the thought of discomfiting the daemon. Slowly but surely, he was learning how the game was played.

Tz'arkan roiled like a storm inside his chest, but Malus gritted his teeth and tried to focus on the matter at hand. He had thought that with a bag of bones and a quick wit he could pretend to be a pilgrim and bluff his way into the city, but he'd underestimated the tensions running within the cult. It sounded as if the temple was on the verge of civil war.

Still, now he knew more about the situation than he did previously. He knew that the faithful were flocking to Har Ganeth to stop the false Swordbearer, which was encouraging. He also knew that the zealots were gathering at the house of Sethra Veyl.

Deep in thought, Malus walked over to the remains of the temple maiden. Spite hadn't left much. Her head and part of one shoulder lay amid the pieces of the man she'd landed on. The maiden's face was frozen in a rictus of hate, defiant until the end.

The highborn knelt, studying the face. What he needed was an extra layer to his disguise, something that would make the zealots think twice about suspecting him.

'All right, daemon,' he said thoughtfully. 'Forget giving me the power of a god. Right now I'll settle for a pair of brass-coloured eyes.'

Tz'arkan had obliged without hesitation. That was a bad sign.

The pain had been immense, and it seemed to last for hours. There was a point when Malus thought that the daemon had decided to take him literally and turn his eyes to molten metal. After a while longer he wasn't thinking much of anything, hugging his arms tightly around his chest to keep from clawing his own eyes out.

The fog had reached the wood line and the fire had burned down to embers by the time the pain subsided. His face was flushed and each eye blink sent shivers of agony through his body.

Malus could hear Spite moving around the clearing, nibbling idly at the remains of the zealots. After some thought, the highborn rolled painfully onto his hands and knees and crawled towards the embers of the fire. Even the dull red light of the coals sent needles of pain into his eyes, but after some searching, he managed to find the maiden's offering bag. Malus called the cold one over and fumbled his way into the saddle. Then he pointed Spite up the road towards Har Ganeth and gave the nauglir its head.

They rode through the night. Malus swayed in the saddle, holding his eyes tightly shut. Well past midnight, his parched throat felt so tight he could barely breathe, and he groped behind his saddle for a water skin. The highborn drank deep of the brackish liquid, and then on impulse he poured a little into each eye. The pain was so sudden and sharp he cried out, but afterwards his eyes felt much better.

False dawn was colouring the mountains to the east when they reached the City of Executioners. The sea breeze shifted, carrying with it the burnt copper tang of blood, and Malus slowly opened his eyes.

The city shimmered like a ghost in the pearlescent light.

Har Ganeth, the Fortress of Ice. Before the druchii built Karond Kar at the mouth of the Slavers' Straits, Har Ganeth had been the northernmost city in the Land of Chill. Its walls and towers had been built from the purest white marble, quarried from the mountains near the Houses of the Dead. The Fortress of Ice was cold and cruel and everlasting, a symbol of the merciless druchii heart.

That had been before Malekith had given control of the city to the temple of Khaine, before the night of slaughter centuries past when the streets had turned to rivers of blood.

Walls of stone towered thirty feet above Malus, their sheer faces painted in layers of crimson from foot to crown. The bloodstained walls could be seen for miles, but up close, with the dawn light wakening the white marble beneath, Malus stared in wonder at hundreds upon hundreds of bloody hand prints, layered one on top of another to create subtle shades and murderous hues. The red sheen looked fresh. Malus was tempted despite himself to touch it, to add to it, deepening the mosaic of slaughter one thin layer more.

The city gate was unusually broad and low, wide enough for six mounted knights to ride comfortably abreast but not with their lances held high. An enormous gatehouse loomed overhead, its wide face pierced by arrow slits and murder holes. Oil gutters hung like arched tongues from the carved mouths of dragons and basilisks, ready to pour searing death on any invader. The gates of Har Ganeth were long gone, however, and its portcullis dismantled. The gateway yawned like the wide mouth of a leviathan, ever hungry for more prey.

There were no guards upon the battlements, no green light of witchfires burning behind the arrow slits. Beyond the gate Malus saw streets cloaked in eddies of pale fog.

Somewhere in the distance, a voice cried out in anger and pain. Malus put his heels to Spite's flanks and entered the City of Executioners, seeking the house of Sethra Veyl.

Chapter Three
CITY OF RAVENS

MALUS SOON LOST count of the dead.

They lay everywhere in Har Ganeth's streets and gutters, contorted by pain and violence and left to cool in drying pools of gore. Some were piled in narrow alleys like old rubbish; others lay slumped against the red-tinged marble walls, having painted the stone with bright swathes of their own blood. Most were druchii like him, although more than once Malus caught sight of the corpse of a slave, stripped naked but for his collar of service. Every victim had been hacked to death. Many bore the gruesome wounds of axe or draich, the great two-handed swords favoured by the temple Executioners. There were men and women, young druchii and old. Some died fighting, with swords and daggers in hand and mortal wounds to head and neck. Others simply ran and took their wounds in the back. The end result was the same.

Many of the victims had been beheaded. Their skulls had been added to pyramids of similar trophies, some stacked as high as a mounted man along the sides of the roadway or next to the door of a business or home. Nearly all of the piles of skulls rested in thick layers of dirty grey dust. The sight puzzled Malus at first, until he noticed that there was a gruesome stratum to the pyramids. The heads nearest the top were the freshest, of course, still cased in tattered flesh and skin. Closer to the bottom vermin and the elements had stripped them clean, leaving a layer of bleached bone at the very base. In time, even those sturdy bones crumbled, pressed down by the weight of the bones above and ground into pale dust.

The city stank like a battlefield. In the open squares it was bad enough, but climbing the narrow, winding streets towards the upper districts was like walking through a dimly lit abattoir. Spite grumbled and sniffed at the heavy odour of rotting blood and spilled organs, and Malus fought the urge to cover his face with a fold of his cloak. Even in the brutal battles on the road to Hag Graef he'd never seen the like.

The City of Executioners had been built on commanding ground on the shore of the Sea of Chill. At first just a collection of forbidding spires rising into the sky from atop a broad, granite hill, over the centuries the city had spread like a mantle of white stone down the hill slopes and along the flat ground around the hill's base. When Har Ganeth was given over to the temple by edict of the Witch King the temple in the lower city had been abandoned and the elders seized the districts surrounding the crown of the high hill. Many of the city's richest citizens had been turned out of their homes, and the buildings demolished to create the massive temple fortress that surrounded the drachau's stained white towers in a fist of dark stone. No matter where one stood in the lower city one felt the ominous shadow of the temple of Khaine.

Like all druchii cities, Har Ganeth was a warren of narrow, twisting streets and alleys, purposely designed to confound intruders. Tall, narrow buildings channelled would-be invaders into dead ends and cul-de-sacs where they would find themselves at the mercy of citizens waiting on wrought-iron balconies high overhead. But for a few main thoroughfares meant for commerce or war, no road was wide enough to admit more than two riders abreast, and in many cases the streets were narrower still. Sunlight rarely found its way into these claustrophobic lanes, and even in daylight every other house was lit by an intricately wrought, iron lamp hung outside the heavy oak door.

Upon entering Har Ganeth, Malus had found himself in the city's merchant district. Eddies of pale fog swirled around Spite's flanks as Malus led his mount past shuttered warehouses and through market commons littered with trash. Next came the slave quarter, with its broad squares and ironbound cages. The first of the city's many shrines lay just off the quarter, and it was here that the highborn saw the first signs of slaughter. Malus couldn't help but wonder how much flesh was bought at the markets and marched across the square just to bleed on the altar of the Lord of Murder.

The narrow streets of the artisans' quarters lay past Khaine's shrine, and further still were the flesh houses and blood pits of the entertainment district. Every lodging-house and tavern was tightly shut, their stoops empty of the indigent or the drunk. There were no signs of exhausted revelry, only piles of leering, tattered heads. For weeks he'd fantasised about a bath, bottles of wine and a soft bed in such a lodging-house, but the eerie stillness of the district drove all temptations from his mind.

Beyond the neighbourhood of lodging-houses and taverns the road began to climb the wide hill. The tall, shabby houses of the lowborn rose around him, and the way ahead became difficult. Malus's hair stood on end as he led Spite into the close-set streets. The narrow windows were shuttered and the overhanging balconies were empty, but he could not shake the sensation that he was being watched. The highborn drew his heavy sword and rested it in his lap, suddenly wishing he'd thought to put on the plate armour bound up in rolls of cloth and hung from the back of Spite's saddle.

The more scenes of carnage he passed, the more his wariness grew. Some of the bodies still steamed in the chilly morning air, suggesting that the killers were close by. The thought of a running battle with a mob of fanatics – on their home ground – set the highborn's teeth on edge.

He knew, from his conversations with travellers, that the highborn districts lay around the top of the hill, but he wasn't certain how to get there. How long could he wander down the maze-like streets before he stumbled across an armed band looking for more trophies to stack outside their door? Would his appearance give the attackers pause? Malus had no way of knowing. Nothing he'd seen so far made any sense to him. For the first time since the long, harrowing trip back from the Chaos Wastes, Malus felt vulnerable and exposed.

It wasn't as if he could go door-to-door and ask the way to the house of Sethra Veyl. Briefly he contemplated heading straight for the temple and simply presenting himself there – surely with a heresy simmering in the city the priestesses wouldn't scrutinise any offer of help too closely. The solution was simple and direct, but it gave Malus pause. There had to be a reason why the faithful were being lodged in houses in the city proper. Perhaps the temple ranks had been infiltrated? If so, how could he be certain that the priestess he spoke with wasn't a secret ally of Urial? With no other recourse open to him he nudged Spite onward, ears straining for the sounds of movement from the alleys or the balconies overhead.

As the dawn broke to the east Malus heard the first stirrings of life, high up in the shadows of the eaves along the street. Feathers rustled and bits of loose stone rattled down the stained facades of the houses. To Malus, far below, the shadowed ledges up near the slate roofs seemed to bob and writhe with invisible life. Then, with a querulous squawk and the beat of heavy wings, an enormous raven launched itself from the shadows and swooped low over Malus's head before alighting at the peak of a pyramid of fresh trophies. The carrion bird glared impetuously at the passing highborn before cocking its sleek head and contemplating its resplendent red feast.

Within minutes the air was black with gore-crows, flapping and calling to one another as they soared down the city streets. They passed so close to Malus that he felt the wind of their wings against his face, and they showed no fear at all of Spite. Once the cold one stepped right over a sprawled body covered in hungry ravens, and the birds paid no attention whatever to the lumbering nauglir.

The constant chatter of the birds made Malus uneasy. Some of the ravens even croaked at Malus in passable druhir. 'Sword and axe!' one bird called. 'Skulls! Skulls!' cried another. 'Blood and souls! Blood and souls!' croaked a third. Their eyes glittered cruelly as they jabbed at torn flesh with their dagger-like beaks.

He kicked Spite into a trot and rode on. Every house looked just like the next: stained walls and iron-banded doors of dark oak, without sign or symbol to identify who lived inside. At every turn Malus chose the uphill path, scattering ragged clouds of squawking birds before the nauglir's one-ton tread.

When Malus heard the ringing clash of steel and the screams of wounded men he turned Spite in the direction of the sounds without hesitation, his previous fears eclipsed by the morbid celebration of the birds.

He headed up a long, straight lane, certain the fight was dead ahead. Moments later Malus reached a dogleg and found himself abruptly heading downhill. Snarling, he pulled on the reins and turned Spite around in the cramped space to retrace his steps, and headed down another road that appeared to circle the hillside in the general direction of the battle.

That ended at a cul-de-sac piled with old bones and bare, white skulls. A lone, elderly druchii stood at the rail of an overhanging balcony, glaring down at Malus as he brought Spite about. The cold one knocked over piles of bones and crunched them underfoot, snapping irritably at the pall of fine dust kicked into the air. Snarling, the highborn kicked the nauglir into a canter, eager to be out from under the old man's silent stare.

He nearly missed the knife-slit of an alley as they careened back along the street. Malus caught the path out of the corner of his eye and reined Spite in roughly, causing the war beast to growl angrily and back-pedal along the cobblestones. The alley seemed to point in the direction of the fight, and was barely wide enough for the cold one to wriggle through. The fit was so tight that Malus had to draw up his feet and rest them on the saddle's cantle as the nauglir stalked down the narrow passage.

The alley intersected another street that seemed to climb the side of the hill at an angle. Malus reined in, cursing the damn labyrinth under his breath. Then he heard the unmistakeable ring of steel slicing flesh and a man's agonised shout just ahead. 'Slowly now, Spite,' Malus said quietly, prodding the cold one's flanks with his spurs.

They turned up the cross street and followed only a few dozen yards to the first bend. Predictably, the road came to a dead end just ten yards farther on. It was there that the killers had cornered their prey.

Five men had been backed up against the sheer wall at the end of the lane; only one of them was still standing, and he bled from a score of deep wounds. There were six druchii arrayed against him, locals, Malus guessed, by the similarity of the dark robes they wore. Their pale faces were streaked with patterns of dried blood – the five-fingered sigil of the Bloody-Handed God – and they wielded a mix of axes, clubs and knives. Their intended victim wore a highborn's kheitan and a breastplate of steel, and he fought with a knife in one hand and a long-hafted axe in the other. Despite his wounds, the man roared like a nauglir at his attackers, whirling his axe in a lethal pattern that drove the locals back. They had good reason to be wary of him; four others were already splayed out on the cobblestones, hacked open by the man's ferocious axe work.

As Malus watched, the locals gave ground before the man, staying just far enough back to avoid the reach of the axe, but close enough to threaten him if they got a chance. All they had to do was wait, the highborn thought. The axe wielder was already white as Har Ganeth marble, his robes dark and heavy with his own blood. Soon enough he would slow, and falter, and then the knives would strike home.

The highborn was just about to turn away when he saw the pile of cloth bags set neatly side by side along the sheer wall behind the beleaguered axe man. He was one of the faithful.

Malus slid quietly from the saddle and stepped close to Spite's head. He pointed to one of the locals. 'That one,' he told the cold one. 'Hunt!'

The cold one's jaws gaped wide as the war beast crept with surprising stealth towards the unsuspecting man. The highborn picked out a victim of his own and stole quietly up behind him, his broad sword raised.

At the last moment Spite's prey stiffened. Perhaps Khaine had sent him a premonition, or perhaps he'd simply caught a whiff of the nauglir's carrion breath. He whirled, weapon ready, and barely had time to scream before the cold one's jaws bit him in half. Blood and entrails splattered across the cobblestones as the nauglir latched onto the druchii's lower torso and began to feed.

Malus struck at the same moment, striking the man's head from his shoulders with a single, sweeping blow. The headless body collapsed, bright arterial blood pumping from the severed neck, and the highborn leapt at the next man in line with a savage scream.

The surviving attackers recovered with surprising speed and two men turned on Malus, deeming him the greater threat. One of the locals, teeth bared in a bloodthirsty snarl, rushed at the highborn with a sweeping diagonal cut aimed at the point of his right shoulder. At the same moment the second attacker swept in wide from the left and swung his bloodstained club at Malus's knee. Laughing hatefully, Malus gauged the speed of the axe and dodged backwards at the last second. Then he slapped the weapon aside with a hard stroke from his blade. It sent the man's axe into the path of his companion, snapping his shin with a brittle crack. The club wielder fell face first with an anguished shriek, and Malus finished off the axe wielder with a backhanded stroke that opened his throat to the spine. The highborn turned back to the fallen man and took a moment to kick him in the side of the head. Then he turned back to the wounded zealot, but his foe was already down, blood pumping from a half dozen brutal wounds.

Smiling in satisfaction, Malus went back and finished off the druchii with the broken leg. He gave the axe man a comradely grin. 'It's well for you that I came along when I did, brother.'

The zealot was still standing over the body of his fallen foe. His head hung low and his shoulders trembled. Rivulets of bright blood shone against the pallid skin of his face and hands. He took a single, racking breath. 'You... you saved me, holy one,' the man breathed.

Malus bent to wipe his sword clean on the dead druchii's hair. 'Well, I confess I had a question to ask you–'

Had the zealot not been half-dead from blood loss his first stroke would have split Malus from crown to navel. As it was, the highborn heard the faint scrape of the man's boot and battlefield instincts threw him to the side. The axe came whistling down and split the dead druchii in two, but the zealot scarcely skipped a beat. He pulled his weapon free and leapt after Malus, his expression a rictus of madness and hate.

There was no time for confusion or shouted commands; the axe was a crimson blur, reaching for Malus's head, neck and chest. The zealot's skill was incredible, and it was all Malus could do to parry the rain of razor-edged blows. The street rang from the clash of axe and sword, like the tolling of a madman's bell.

Malus gave ground, his anger rising with every step. The axe blade sang past the highborn's sword and sliced through the sleeve of his upper left arm. He felt warm blood soaking into the fabric of his robes. 'What kind of gratitude is this?' he snarled.

But the man only redoubled his attacks, howling in fury. The zealot leapt forwards, feinting at Malus's neck and then sweeping upwards to smash his skull. It was all the highborn could do to throw himself back out of the weapon's reach. He felt the edge of the blade nick his chin in passing.

'He can still answer questions without his arms,' the daemon suggested in its silky voice.

'True enough,' Malus gasped. Just then the man aimed a vicious backhanded cut at the highborn's head. Malus dropped to his knees and the swing of the heavy axe pulled the man off balance. Before he could recover the highborn hacked off the man's foot just above the ankle.

The zealot screamed and fell, still swinging at Malus. The axe scored a glancing blow to his right arm, popping mail rings in a long, ragged cut. Furious, the highborn rounded on the bleeding man and chopped off his right hand. Steel rang on the cobblestones as the axe cartwheeled across the street.

'Kill me!' the zealot moaned, trembling with shock and despair. 'Give me back my honour, holy one! I've done nothing to offend you.'

No, you just tried to turn me into sausage, Malus thought furiously. He leaned over the man. 'I care nothing for your honour, you fool,' he hissed. 'I just wanted to ask you a question. You brought this on yourself.'

'I did this? How? If you hadn't come along those men would have killed me. We'd been fighting for nearly an hour!'

The man was obviously delirious. Malus was frankly surprised the zealot had any blood left to lose. 'Just tell me: where is the house of Sethra Veyl? That's all I want to know. Tell me...' Malus paused, trying to think of a suitable threat. 'Tell me... or I'll let you live.'

'No!' the man wailed, his eyes widening in horror.

'I can tie off your stumps; find a torch and cauterise the wounds. I could see to it you lived a long time.' He couldn't believe what he was saying.

The man looked at Malus as if he was a monster. 'All right, all right! His house is in the highborn quarter, near the city armoury. A house with a white door.'

'A white door, you say?' Malus snapped. 'That should be easy to spot in this blood-soaked place.' He rested the point of his sword against the man's neck. 'If you're lying...' The highborn paused. 'I'll... Oh, never mind.' He finished the man off. The zealot died with a grateful look in his eyes.

Shaking his head in wonder, Malus turned and called for Spite. 'In Har Ganeth you spare your foes and kill your friends,' he muttered. 'What do I do when I meet Sethra Veyl? Offer to burn his house down?'

* * *

By SHEER LUCK – good or bad, Malus could no longer say – the next uphill street he found took him straight to the high-born quarter. The streets were starting to come to life; servants were emerging from the forbidding homes on errands for their masters, heading to the market or perhaps to restock the house's supply of slave flesh after a night's revelry. The servants moved with purpose, shoulders hunched and eyes downcast, never meeting another's eye or tarrying on the street for more than a moment. They wove gracefully among the piled skulls and the fresh bodies, and gave the fat, presumptuous ravens a respectful berth.

It took another hour of searching to find the city armoury, where the spears and armour of the city's militia were stored in anticipation of war. Using that as a point of reference Malus began exploring each nearby street, until at last he found a house with a spotless white door.

Malus dismounted, going over his story one last time in his head as he pounded his fist on the oak door.

Several minutes passed. Finally Malus heard the sound of a bolt being drawn back, and the door's spyhole opened. A dark eye regarded him dispassionately.

'Greetings brother,' Malus said. 'I've come a long way to answer the call of the faithful. I was told there would be a place for me here.'

The eye regarded him a moment more, and then the spyhole snapped shut. Larger bolts rattled in their housings and the door swung open. A young woman in startlingly white robes stood in the doorway. A long, fresh cut traced a red line down the side of her pale face, still seeping a thin line of blood. Her expression was eerily serene. 'Welcome, holy one,' she said in a measured voice.

Malus paused. Do I step inside or draw my sword, he thought?

He decided on the former. Stepping just inside the doorway, he found himself in a small, walled courtyard full of armed druchii. They all wore white robes, like the woman's, and little or no armour, but every one of the zealots had a bared blade in hand. They studied Malus with barely concealed belligerence.

Malus studiously avoided the stares of the assembled druchii, focusing on the wounded woman instead. 'I will need a place for my nauglir,' he said. It occurred to him that nearly every zealot he'd seen on the road had been travelling on foot.

'It will be seen to,' the woman said. 'There are nauglir pits in the quarter, with people we can trust.' She motioned to one of the armed men, who bowed and ran across the courtyard to a flight of steps that led into the house proper. 'Your arrival is propitious,' she told him. 'The heretics have learned how many of the faithful have slipped into the city over the last few weeks and they have decided to move against us.'

Malus nodded. 'I saw a bloody battle on the way here. The heretic's servants cornered five of our men and slew them not far from here. Where is Sethra Veyl?'

The woman's serene expression darkened. 'Dead, holy one. The heretics sent assassins in the night and slew Veyl while he slept. Tyran the Unscarred is the new elder, and he vows that the atrocity will not go unavenged.' A thought struck her. 'I should take you to him, holy one. You may be of great use to his plans.'

'Of course,' Malus said smoothly, considering the possibilities. Anything he could do to gain the zealots' confidence would make his position that much more secure. 'We will have to act quickly,' he said. 'Take me to the elder. If the heretics are on the move, then Urial must be close to claiming the sword.'

'Indeed,' the woman said with a fierce smile. 'The elders cannot deny him much longer. Soon he will take up the holy blade and we will sweep the heretics away on a tide of blood. If Tyran's plan succeeds, you will open the way for the Rite of the Sword to begin. Think of the rewards you will reap when the true faith is reborn and the Swordbearer takes his place at the head of the temple!'

Chapter Four
KEEPERS OF THE DEAD

THE WOMAN USHERED him into a large, empty chamber on the top floor of the house, and left him to wait as she announced his arrival to Tyran the Unscarred. A variety of swords, axes and knives hung from three of the room's walls, and the floor had been dusted with talc. The room was clearly meant for practice and perhaps meditation, although it was strange to find it at the top floor with the master's quarters. There was no fireplace to warm the open space, and the woman had made no attempt to offer Malus food or drink. Cold, hungry and deeply confused, he walked to the tall windows that dominated the north wall of the room and glared down at the city streets below. Suddenly he was envious of all the damned ravens and their sleek, black wings. At that moment he wanted to fly from Har Ganeth as fast as he could.

'This place is a madhouse,' he muttered darkly. 'Urial is the hero of the faithful and the temple elders are the heretics? Is everything turned backwards in this cursed city?'

'Heresy is mostly a matter of perspective,' Tz'arkan replied, clearly amused. 'The true faith is the one ruthless enough to wipe out all its rivals.'

'Or the one that has the support of the State,' Malus said. 'The heretics in the temple fortress have the support of Malekith, and Urial has sided with the opposition. How interesting.' The highborn tapped his lower lip thoughtfully. 'I wonder how long this has been going on for.'

'How long has he believed himself to be the Swordbearer?'

Malus nodded. 'A good point. Urial survived Khaine's cauldron and was marked by the Lord of Murder, but perhaps the temple elders balked at the idea of a cripple emerging as the heir to their precious prophecy.'

'As well they might, for we know who the true Swordbearer is.' The highborn grimaced. 'I'll take up that cursed sword because I must, and the prophecy be damned.'

Tz'arkan chuckled. 'A prophecy cares not what you think of it, Malus. It is like a map, showing the road ahead. You can curse it all you want, but the road remains unchanged.'

'Indeed?' Malus replied. 'Eldire thinks differently.'

'The witch knows nothing,' the daemon spat. 'She intends to shape you to her will, little druchii. You are her pawn, and she will cast you aside the moment you are no longer useful.'

Malus laughed scornfully. 'Next you will tell me that the sun is warm and the night is dark. You will have to do better than that, daemon,' the highborn sneered. 'At the moment she makes a far better ally than you. For one thing, she doesn't hold my soul in her clutches.'

'No,' Tz'arkan replied, 'but she sent you to me. Think on that.'

The highborn's smug grin faded. Before he could reply, the door to the practice room swung open. The druchii woman beckoned to him from the doorway. 'Tyran wishes to speak with you.'

Malus nodded curtly and joined her. She eyed him curiously. 'Are you troubled, holy one?' she asked.

'No more than usual,' he muttered. 'Life is never at a loss for ways to vex me, it seems.'

* * *

SHE LED HIM to a tapestry a short way down the corridor and without preamble pulled it aside, revealing a narrow opening and another stairway climbing into darkness. The zealot bowed slightly, gesturing for him to precede her. Frowning warily, he stepped across the threshold and peered upwards. Pale light shone steadily from under another door at the top of a short flight of stairs.

Malus climbed the wooden steps carefully, feeling them creak beneath his boots. A breath of sorcerous power brushed across his face, setting his black hair on end and causing his cheeks to tingle. Tz'arkan tightened painfully around his heart, and cold threads of daemonic energy withdrew from Malus's extremities, receding like a tide back into his chest. The sudden absence made his entire body ache. When had he gotten to the point that he only felt Tz'arkan's power by virtue of its absence? What will be left once I drive the daemon out, he mused?

He paused at the top of the stair, his throbbing fingers brushing the door's cold, iron latch. Another wave of power brushed against him, invisible as the wind. He was reminded of his mother's sorcery at the top of the witch's convent at Hag Graef. Tz'arkan isn't the only power in the world, he reminded himself, and where the soul is lacking there is always hate to sustain me. With hate, all things are possible.

Malus thumbed the latch and pushed open the door, letting in a blaze of cold, biting sunlight.

The door opened onto the tower's flat roof, providing a panoramic view of the eastern highborn quarter and the white-capped sea off to the south. The dark bulwark of the temple fortress rose to the west, a permanent stain against the summer sky. A sea breeze whistled fretfully over the battlements and across the flat expanse of the roof, carrying to Malus hints of pungent incense and snatches of whispered chants from the ceremony unfolding only a few score paces away.

A block of polished black basalt sat at the exact centre of the roof, its head and foot oriented to face east and west respectively. The body of a man lay on the block, his pale face stained

with dark blood and his hands wrapped around the hilt of a
gleaming draich. His body was attired in the clothes in which
he had died: simple white robes, similar to the other zealots,
but his were soaked in red from a gaping wound that ran from
his shoulder to his hip.

Three women danced slowly around the corpse, their thick,
white hair billowing like banners in the wind. Each wore a
witch's black headdress, and their naked bodies were sleek and
voluptuous. Sweat glistened on their powerful arms and
gleamed coldly from white throats and heavy breasts as the
witches swayed to a rhythm only they could hear. Their eyes
were like shadowed pools, depthless and dark, and their full
lips moved, whispering words of power that he could feel
pulsing against his skin. With a start, he saw that their slender
fingers were tipped with long black talons, and their white
teeth were sharp and fanged like a lion's. All at once Malus was
reminded of the dreadful statues lining the road to the Houses
of the Dead.

'Are they not magnificent? They are true blood-witches,' his
guide whispered in his ear. Malus hadn't even heard her
approach. 'Heshyr na Tuan, the Keepers of the Dead. No one,
not even Sethra Veyl, knew any still existed.' The zealot's voice
was tinged with awe. 'This rite hasn't been performed in thousands of years. It is a great honour just to witness it.'

And in full view of the temple fortress, Malus thought, looking up at the watchtowers looming at regular intervals from
the black walls. Honour or not, he suspected that Tyran
wanted to send the temple elders a message. More than a half-
dozen zealots stood in a tight bunch just to the left of the
doorway, dividing their attention between the fortress walls
and the hypnotic movements of the ritual. They were taut and
alert, as if expecting a flight of arrows to rise from the fortress
battlements at any moment.

One man stood apart from the rest, about halfway between
the ongoing rite and the doorway where Malus stood. His
back was to Malus and he was bare to the waist, revealing
broad, powerful shoulders and strong arms that could have

been sculpted from pale marble. The man's black hair had been pulled back from his face and bound with a rough leather cord. A long, curved draich rested in one hand, its polished edge gleaming like ice in the sunlight. For all that he stood with the ready poise of a skilled and experienced swordsman, his bare skin bore not a single scar.

'That would be Tyran, I presume,' Malus said softly.

'Yes,' the guide replied. 'We will wait here for a few moments. The rite is almost complete.'

Malus wasn't certain how the woman could tell. The blood-witches continued their slow dance around the corpse of Sethra Veyl, staring at the body with their hooded eyes and whispering supplications to the Lord of Murder. As he watched, however, the trio suddenly stopped. One stood to either side of Veyl's body and the third stood just behind the man's head. The blood-witches reached towards the corpse, stretching their long, taloned fingers, and the woman at Veyl's head bent with a bestial grin and pressed her lips to his.

The corpse convulsed, arms and legs spasming as if in the throes of death. The blood-witches withdrew, throwing back their heads and letting out an ululating howl that set Malus's teeth on edge. Then with a furious roar Sethra Veyl sat bolt upright, his bloody face twisted in an expression of hatred.

Several of the druchii witnesses drew back with startled shouts. Tyran, however, spread his strong arms as if welcoming a lost brother, and let out a joyful laugh.

'Arise Sethra Veyl!' Tyran shouted. 'Shake off the black veil of death and heed your vow to Khaine!'

The risen corpse glared at Tyran. Veyl's face worked spasmodically, as if wishing to hurl curses at the laughing druchii but unable to make its mouth form the words. Nothing but a choked rattle escaped Veyl's bloodstained lips as he slid from the stone and raised his two-handed blade.

After a moment the corpse gave up trying to speak. Veyl's dark eyes glittered with bitter humour. Malus suddenly wondered if the dead elder wasn't trying to curse Tyran, but to impart some dark wisdom from Khaine's blood-soaked realm.

The realisation barely had time to sink in before Veyl rushed soundlessly at Tyran, his sword flashing in a complex pattern of deadly blows.

The speed of the attack shocked Malus. Whatever else could be said of the zealots, their dedication to the arts of war was astonishing. Tyran was motionless, and the highborn wondered if he too was stunned by the ferocity of the corpse's assault. If so, there would soon be another corpse for the blood-witches to dance for.

But just as the corpse's long blade sliced for Tyran's throat the bare-chested zealot exploded into action. One moment his sword was hanging calmly from his hand, and the next he was past Veyl's onrushing form, his draich held high. Malus barely registered the ringing sound of steel against flesh.

Veyl staggered to a stop, still frozen in mid-swing as if confused. Then Malus heard a wet, slithering sound, and the upper quarter of the corpse's torso slid off at an angle and fell to the floor with a spray of clotted blood. Incredibly, the rest of Veyl's body remained upright for a moment more before toppling forwards and spilling steaming organs across the slate tiles.

With an ecstatic shriek the witches fell upon Veyl's bisected form, pulling away robes and tearing into the shorn flesh with fang and claw. Tyran turned gracefully on his heel, lowering his sword slowly to his side, and Malus was struck by the eerie, serene look on his handsome face.

Tyran approached the crouching witches, moving as if in a trance. The blood-witches eyed him over their carrion feast, their chins dark with blood. They studied Tyran with large, leonine eyes.

Tyran held out his left hand. 'Give me my due,' he said, 'in Khaine's holy name.'

One of the blood-witches smiled, showing bloodstained fangs. She reached into Veyl's ruptured chest and pulled forth his heart. Tyran took the organ respectfully, threw back his head and squeezed the heart's contents into his open mouth.

There was a subtle change in the air. Malus felt the sudden absence of an electric tension that he hadn't realised was there. A sigh went through the assembled zealots.

'Now Tyran possesses a part of Veyl's strength,' Malus's guide whispered, more for her own benefit than his. 'It was ever thus, when an elder died in ancient days. Truly our time of reckoning is nigh!'

When the last drop of blood was gone, Tyran turned to the looming walls of the distant fortress. Slowly and deliberately, he raised his blade and his grisly trophy high over his head. 'The call of blood is answered in sundered flesh!' he cried.

'Blood and souls for the Lord of Murder!' the faithful answered.

Tyran lowered his sword and returned the heart to the waiting blood-witches. His face, neck and upper chest were streaked with dark blood. At that moment he noticed Malus. Tyran favoured the highborn with a calculating smile. 'Ah, here is our new pilgrim,' the zealot said. 'How was your journey, holy one?'

Malus paused but a moment, uncertain how to respond. Tyran's eyes were dark, not brass-coloured like Urial's or like those belonging to the other favoured servants of the temple. How did one address such a man? Malus knew with icy certainty that if Tyran wished, the zealot could split him like a gourd before he even realised he was in danger. 'My travels were profitable,' he said carefully, 'although pickings between here and the Black Ark were poor.'

Tyran studied Malus thoughtfully. 'It looks as if you travelled through the mountains to get here,' he said. 'Did you take to hunting autarii for your offerings?'

The highborn shook his head. 'I have no skill at catching ghosts, elder.' He offered his stained bag to Tyran. 'I gathered what offerings I could along the road, but I confess that I spent more time out of doors than I'd intended.'

Tyran took the bag and emptied its contents onto the roof beside the hungry blood-witches. They eyed the collection of body parts with feline disdain. Tyran did not seem much impressed either. 'You say you came from the Black Ark of Naggor?'

The highborn took a slow breath. 'I did. The temple there is small, but there are still a few of us who honour the old ways.'

'I didn't know there were any.'

'Didn't Veyl tell you, elder?' Malus asked. 'He was expecting me.'

Tyran considered this. 'What of the rest? Surely you are not the only true believer at the ark?'

'The others are dead, elder,' Malus replied. 'Perhaps you have heard the news of the feud between the ark and Hag Graef? The Witch Lord lost his entire army against the forces of the Hag. It was a tragedy for the ark, but a glorious day for Khaine.'

Tyran's smile turned cold. 'It's a convenient story, holy one, but your manner is strange, and you could easily be a heretic spy.'

Malus forced himself to remain calm. 'You would not be the first man to mock my rustic manners,' he said, 'but why would the heretics bother with spying on you when you hold your rites in plain view of the fortress?'

The zealot's smile faltered, and Malus felt his guts clench. Then Tyran threw back his head and laughed.

'Well said, holy one,' he replied. 'Forgive my impertinence, a man's heart blood is heady stuff, and it's left me addled. Welcome to the house of Sethra Veyl. What is your name?'

'My name is–' he caught himself saying 'Malus' and paused. 'I am Hauclir. Tell me,' he said quickly, eager to change the subject, 'is it wise to provoke the temple with such displays?'

Tyran's expression darkened. 'Do you fear the heretics and their slaves?'

'Of course not,' Malus replied, 'but neither are we in a position to challenge them openly. Otherwise we would have destroyed the heretics long ago.' The highborn was making it all up as he went along, his pulse pounding in his chest.

The zealot shrugged. 'They already know we're here. The fact that they sent a handful of assassins last night instead of turning out the temple guard tells me that they don't wish to provoke a confrontation. If they did, they couldn't be certain of killing us all, and then they would have to explain to their worshippers why they tried to wipe out the Swordbearer's disciples.'

'And what news of Urial?'

Tyran chuckled. 'They remain cloistered in the Sanctum of the Holy Blade. When he and his sister came through the Vermillion Gate there were far too many witnesses for the temple elders to hush it up. Urial presented his sister as the Bride and declared himself Swordbearer in front of almost a hundred witnesses. So they've made a big show of honouring his claim and have spent the last three months using the scriptures to discredit him.'

'And?'

A gleam of triumph shone in the zealot's dark eyes. 'They have failed. Our sources in the temple say that the elders have already been forced to admit that Yasmir is indeed a living saint of the Bloody-Handed God. So now I expect they are panicking.'

Malus very much wanted to know why the temple elders would be panicked over such a thing, but he feared that the question might give him away. 'Which is why they killed Sethra Veyl.'

Tyran nodded. 'It was a clumsy, crude gesture, which speaks to me of the elders' desperation. They seek to thwart Khaine's will by silencing his true believers, as if that would spare them from his wrath.' The zealot stepped forwards and put his bloodstained hand on Malus's shoulder. 'That is why I wanted to speak with you.'

'Is there some rite you need me to perform?' Malus asked, praying fervently that there wasn't.

The zealot laughed. 'I like you, Hauclir. For a priest you've a fine sense of humour.' He took another step closer and lowered his voice. 'No, I need you to lead a band of true believers into the temple fortress and kill the bastards who were responsible for last night's attack.'

Chapter Five
THE ASSASSIN'S DOOR

THE DOOR LAY at the end of a narrow street that only knew the touch of sunlight for about an hour each day. Tall houses, the homes of highborn lords, rose to either side of the close-set lane. Malus noted that the windows facing the street were tightly shuttered. Clearly the local nobles wanted little part in the temple's clandestine affairs.

He cursed himself for not anticipating Tyran's plan. In retrospect, the druchii's interest had been obvious. Veyl's death had to be avenged and the zealot leader needed expendable men for the job. Malus was new to the city, of uncertain provenance, and had no patrons to argue on his behalf. If he died in the depths of the temple fortress the zealots would scarcely feel the loss.

The highborn turned away from the mouth of the narrow alley and looked over at his two companions. The zealots were nearly invisible in the deep shadows of the rubbish-strewn passage, their faces concealed in dark woollen wrappings and shrouded by close-fitting hoods. They seemed utterly relaxed, poised and ready for action at a moment's notice. The prospect of certain death seemed to affect them not at all. For the first time, Malus found himself wondering what rewards the cult promised in return for their devotion. He'd never shown any interest in the temple as a child; many highborn families cultivated strong ties to the cult for political reasons, but the children of Lurhan the Vaulkhar had little need for such affiliations. What do you think awaits you beyond the veil of death, Malus thought? Splendid towers and vassals? A thousand virgins? Feasting halls and an eternity of battle? He could still vividly remember the night he walked in Urial's sanctum and trod on the threshold of Khaine's realm. The highborn wondered if the true believers would be quite so sanguine if they knew what awaited them.

Like the zealots, Malus had been forced to don the robes of a dead temple assassin. The black woollen robes had been carefully cleaned and patched during the day to conceal the fate of their previous owner, and Malus had been forced to scrub the dirt of the road from his face and clean his tangled nest of hair, which caused him no small amount of apprehension. The grime had served to conceal the grey cast of his skin and the thick, blue-black veins that climbed all the way up his right arm, across his shoulder and up the side of his neck. He'd been able to conceal the corrupting touch of the daemon's curse for a time by a simple act of will, but the more he'd opened himself to Tz'arkan's gifts, the more the taint had spread. Now gauntlets covered his hands and he kept his own scarves bunched tightly around his throat. Over his robes he wore the assassins' lightweight kheitan of human hide and a shirt of fine black mail. Two short, broad-bladed swords were buckled to a wide belt at his waist. Malus nodded to the pair and pulled his hood up over his head. 'The sun is setting,' he said quietly. 'It's time.'

Without waiting for a reply he turned and slipped out of the alley, the sound of his movements lost amid the noise of the bustling avenue at the other end of the shuttered street. Horses trod across the cobblestones, men shouted to one another or cursed their slaves, and servants chattered together as they hurried to complete their masters' business before the sun went down. By day, Malus found Har Ganeth was much like any other city in Naggaroth. It was during the hours of the night that it became a very different place indeed.

The Assassin's Door was made of bolted iron, with a small spyhole covered by a cage of steel bars. There was no latch or knob; the flat, tarnished surfaces of the metal plates were inscribed with ancient, rust-stained carvings of leering skulls and piled bones.

Malus raised his fist and pounded on the rusty iron, calling to mind the strange words Tyran had told him to say. Somehow the witches had got the password from the temple assassins. He wondered if they'd made the men talk before or after they'd died.

There was a sound of scraping metal immediately and the spyhole cover opened. A pair of dark eyes studied Malus and his companions warily.

The words tumbled from his lips, spilling out in a rush. The phrase was in an archaic form of druhir, the language of scholars and theologians. Perhaps it was a proverb of the temple, or an exhortation of the god – he simply concentrated on repeating the words as they'd been given to him. 'Khaine's will is done,' the highborn finished. He had no idea if it was the right thing to say, but it seemed appropriate. 'We have returned from the house of Sethra Veyl and must make our report.'

The spyhole shut so quickly that Malus feared he'd made a mistake. Then there was a rattle of heavy locks and the highborn relaxed slightly as the Assassin's Door creaked open. Without hesitation Malus stepped through the widening gap into the chill darkness beyond.

He found himself in a narrow tunnel lit by a pair of flickering tallow lamps. Long shadows flitted and danced along the curved, soot stained walls. A small, pale face peered around the edge of the iron door as Malus and the zealots stepped hurriedly inside. The druchii who pushed the door shut was no more than a boy, clad in stained white robes and wearing a brass hadrilkar fashioned in the shape of a ring of linked skulls. The young novice shot home the door's heavy locks and then sat back down on a wooden stool beneath one of the guttering lamps. The highborn noticed a second, empty stool and reasoned that someone had run ahead to warn the elders that their assassins had returned. With a nod to his companions, Malus set off down the tunnel at a swift pace.

The plan that Tyran and the other elders had devised was a sketchy one, but the zealot leader was very specific in his orders: only the temple's master of assassins and the elder or elders who ordered the death of Veyl were to be slain. Of course, no one knew which of the elders had sent the temple assassins to Veyl's house, nor did anyone know what the master of assassins looked like, or where he could be found. Finally, after lengthy debate, Tyran concluded that once Malus and his companions reached the temple their targets would invariably come to them. The elders and the master of assassins would want to hear their report of the attack, delivering them into the zealots' hands. There was a straightforward, audacious simplicity to the plan that Malus couldn't help but admire, although bitter experience left him appalled at the number of ways that the whole thing could go disastrously wrong.

Within a few dozen steps the zealots were swallowed in reeking darkness. Malus was forced to slow his pace and move more carefully, his senses straining to penetrate the cavernous blackness that surrounded him. His hands clutched the twin hilts of his stabbing swords, and not for the first time he wrestled with the notion of turning on the two men with him and cutting their throats. After more than two months he was finally within the walls of the sprawling temple fortress. He could leave the zealots' corpses rotting in the darkness and lose himself in the temple's maze of tunnels. Tyran and the true believers would simply think him dead, and if he went back and killed the boy at the assassin's door then there would be no one to describe him to the temple guards.

It was a tempting notion, but again, experience told him that things wouldn't be quite so simple. He had reason to believe that the blade he sought was kept within the Sanctum of the Sword, but he had no idea where that would be or how to get inside. Finding out would take time, which he suspected was in short supply. Urial was eager to claim the warpsword for himself, and it would be reasonable to assume that he and Tyran were plotting to force the temple's hand. Why the temple would be reluctant to accept Urial as Khaine's chosen one still intrigued Malus. What sort of agenda did the temple elders have, and how could it be turned to his advantage?

The highborn walked straight through the trailing edges of a dusty cobweb, the invisible tendrils clinging to his face and the rim of his hood. He snatched at the strands in irritation, slowing his steps even further. I'm out of my element, he thought angrily. The intrigues of the temple were similar enough to politics in the Hag that he had a sense of what was happening, but the rules of the game were altogether stranger and more confusing than he was accustomed to. He needed more information before he could make his own play for the sword.

As preoccupied as he was, it was some moments before he was aware of a shifting orange glow outlining the far end of the passage up ahead. Malus resumed his brisk pace, quickly composing himself before stepping through the arch and finding himself in a vaulted, fire-lit gallery that stretched to either side of the highborn for as far as his eye could see. Pillars of white marble, stained and streaked with centuries of soot, rose more than thirty feet into the air, supporting thick stone arches worked in the shapes of fearsome, imperious blood-witches.

Don't gawk, he reminded himself fiercely, forcing himself to lower his eyes and study the gallery with feigned indifference. Red coals glowed and popped in the base of iron braziers set every dozen feet or so along the gallery, outlining narrow archways that opened off the gallery on either side. Many of these archways were dark, but in a few Malus saw rearing shadows and flickering candlelight glowing against the walls of narrow cells.

Acolytes of the temple shuffled quietly through the shadows, their heads bent in contemplation. They were pale-skinned, young and fit, and the highborn noticed that many of them moved with exceptional grace and speed. All at once Malus was reminded of his former retainer Arleth Vann, himself a former temple assassin who'd forsaken his oath and found his way into the highborn's service. The last he'd seen of Arleth Vann he was being dragged away into the darkness with two crossbow bolts in his back.

Such a waste, Malus thought bitterly. Like the rest of his retainers, Vann's honour had been ruined when Malus had slain his father at Vaelgor Keep. When the highborn had returned to the Hag at the head of the Naggorite army, the former assassin had done the only thing he could do to escape the stain of Malus's crime: he'd slipped into the Naggorite camp and tried to kill his former master. But for the timely arrival of a band of autarii scouts, Vann would have succeeded. Malus vividly remembered the touch of Vann's razor-edged sword at his throat. The man had most likely died in the forest outside Hag Graef, coughing up his life's blood and cursing Malus's name.

A figure in dark robes entered the gallery from a shadowy archway opposite Malus. For a moment the highborn was speechless, thinking he was looking at a ghost. The druchii's alabaster skin, pale hair and brass-coloured eyes resembled Arleth Vann's in eerie detail, as well as the paired swords that hung at the man's hip. Another young novice accompanied the assassin. He pointed at Malus and his companions and then backed away into the shadows, his head bowed.

The temple assassin stepped forwards, holding out his hands at waist height, palms up. 'The blessings of Khaine be upon you, brothers,' he said. 'This is a glorious day indeed. When you didn't return this morning we believed you had fallen to the blades of the heathens.'

Malus mirrored the assassin's gesture. 'Far from it,' he replied, speaking softly and counting on the hood to muffle his voice. 'The fools never saw us. We merely had to be patient in order to slip away while their leaders bemoaned Veyl's fate. In the process we heard much of the heathens' plans, and need to make our report.'

The assassin nodded. 'Master Suril has been summoned, as have the elders. Follow me.'

Malus relaxed slightly as he fell into step behind the temple assassin. As far as he was concerned, the hard part of the plan was over.

Their guide led the highborn and his companions back the way he'd come, up a narrow, spiral stairway that climbed past several more gallery levels until they emerged into a narrow room lit with pale witchlight. The transition from fire and shadow to the pale green light left Malus momentarily disorientated, a feeling that only deepened when the guide pushed open a tall door and led the men outside into the deep orange glow of the setting sun.

They exited through a portal built into the side of the fortress's thick wall, which emptied them out at street level at the end of a broad avenue lined on either side with some of the most palatial buildings Malus had ever seen.

Hidden behind the high walls of the temple fortress, the homes confiscated from the city's highborn by the order of the Witch King had not been transformed into dour vaults of worship. If anything, they had been made grander and more opulent than before. Long, roofed porches had been built along the fronts of most of the homes, with pillars of veined marble carved in the shapes of manticores, dragons and hydras. Windows had been broadened, and balconies built from soft stone instead of hard, ruthless iron. Malus saw door facings fashioned from gold and silver, wrought in intricate styles that could only have come from the hands of expensive dwarf slaves. The air was cool and smelled of incense. Priests and priestesses strolled casually along the street, wrapped in thick, red robes and kheitans of fine elf hide set with gold, rubies and pearls. The raw display of wealth and power nearly stopped Malus in his tracks. He'd known, like all druchii, that the temple of Khaine was universally feared. What he hadn't ever stopped to consider was that it was also very, very rich. Malekith's support had benefited the cult enormously.

The guide led them swiftly along the broad street, his eyes carefully downcast as he passed the high officials of the temple. He led them to the third house on the left, climbing a broad set of marble steps to a pair of gold-ornamented doors that slid open silently at his approach. Human slaves held open the doors and bowed from the waist as the druchii filed inside. Beyond was a spacious entry hall filled with expensive statues, some bearing the refined but effete style of the craftsmen of Ulthuan. They'd probably been tithed to the temple some time in the past by a noble seeking the elders' favour, Malus suspected.

They crossed the hall, the soles of their boots whispering across piled rugs, and climbed another flight of stairs. The druchii crossed another room lined with statues and hung with expensive tapestries, and were ushered into a small chamber set with a low table and half a dozen wooden chairs. A tray containing a plate of fruit and a bottle of wine sat on the table. The guide bowed to the men once more and left the room, closing the door behind him. Immediately the two zealots began a careful check of their weapons. Malus eyed the wine greedily, certain it would be a fine vintage and fighting the temptation to open it and find out.

He was still contemplating the bottle when the door swung open again and a small crowd of red-robed druchii bustled hurriedly into the room. The zealots immediately dropped to one knee, palms out, and Malus followed suit a moment later.

'Arch-Hierophant Rhulan will be along momentarily. In the meantime we shall hear your report,' a woman said in a harsh, businesslike voice. Malus looked up to see a tall, narrow-shouldered priestess striding purposefully towards him, walking with the aid of a slender, silver-chased staff. Her hair was white and bore the headdress of a witch elf, but she wore the heavy robes and ornamental kheitan of a temple dignitary. A short, broad man, also swathed in crimson robes came in behind her. A ring of gold glinted on each of his stubby fingers, and a pair of dark eyes glittered like chips of obsidian beneath a pair of jutting brows. A pair of temple novitiates bearing scrivener's easels, ink and quills and sheets of parchment attended him.

'It would not be proper to begin without Rhulan,' said the last man to enter the room. He was of middle height and whipcord-thin, with a long, pointed face that reminded Malus of a fox. His red robes were not as heavy as the others, and his kheitan was noticeably devoid of ornamentation. To Malus's surprise, the man carried no obvious weapons, but he had no doubt that he was looking at the temple's master of assassins.

'In the absence of the Arch-Hierophant I am the voice of the temple,' the woman snapped, 'and I will hear what these men have to say.' The two druchii exchanged heated stares, but after a tense moment the man deferred with a bow. 'Now then,' the woman said, turning back to the assassins, 'we watched the heathens dispose of Veyl this morning,' she said, 'so we know your mission was a success. What I want to hear is why you are only now returning to the temple?'

Malus quickly took stock of the situation. The two temple elders and the servants were closer, but less dangerous than the man by the door. He would have to kill the master of assassins at once, and that would leave him in a position to cut off the others' retreat. Then they could lie in wait for this Arch-Hierophant to arrive and deal with him at their leisure.

Suddenly an idea occurred to Malus. He considered his circumstances for a second time, and then smiled within the depths of his hood. Yes, there was an opportunity here.

The female elder leaned in close to Malus, near enough for him to feel her hot breath. 'Answer me, hound! You were told to return at once. Why did you tarry, when there is still more of Khaine's work to be done?'

Malus looked up, meeting the elder's glare. He smiled a killer's smile. 'Please accept our apologies,' he said. 'We would have been here sooner, but it took hours to get the blood out of these robes.'

The elder's face twisted into a bemused frown. She opened her mouth to speak, but the words were lost in a torrent of blood. The elder staggered, dropping her staff and fumbling at the gaping cut in the side of her throat with one hand while clawing at Malus with the other. But the highborn was already on his feet, blood dripping from his sword, and he charged across the room at the man by the door.

For a split second, the temple elders and their servants were frozen in shock, just as the highborn hoped. The zealots leapt into action a fraction of a second behind Malus. There was a whickering sound, and one of the stocky elder's novitiates let out a startled cry and collapsed with a thrown dagger jutting from his chest. Malus saw the remaining novitiate draw a pair of long daggers from his belt, but the highborn knew the man wouldn't have them ready in time. He would be on the master of assassins in another three steps.

To Malus's surprise, the fox-faced druchii still hadn't reacted to the sudden attack. This is their master of assassins, he thought?

Then came the blow against the side of Malus's neck, clipping him beneath the ear. His vision disappeared in a burst of white pain and the highborn fell face-first onto the piled rugs. Both swords tumbled from his nerveless fingers. He realised, too late, that he'd made a fatal mistake.

Malus rolled weakly onto his side as the stocky druchii stepped back from the highborn's stunned body and met the rush of one of the black-robed zealots with his bare hands. The zealot's daggers were a blur of motion, but the master of assassins slapped them aside with contemptuous ease and drove his stiffened fingertips into his attacker's throat. Bone crunched and the zealot fell to the floor, writhing and choking for breath.

The surviving novitiate leapt at Malus, intending to finish the highborn off, but was intercepted in mid-stride by the last zealot. As the two druchii began a whirling dance of razor-edged steel, Malus tried to drive the numbing paralysis from his body by sheer force of will. He fumbled for his blades with leaden fingers, knowing that he had scant moments to spare before the druchii by the door regained his senses and raised the alarm.

His fingertips brushed the pommel of one of his swords, and the physical contact seemed to focus Malus's energies. Groping, he drew the weapon quickly into his palm and rolled onto his knees. There was a grunt and a crack of bone and the surviving zealot tumbled across the rugs, his right arm twisted at an unnatural angle. Malus straightened and saw the fox-faced druchii with his hand on the door latch. The novitiate was sinking slowly to the floor, blood pouring from a wound over his heart, and the master of assassins was turning to face Malus once more, the rings on his fingers glittering coldly.

Malus's thin lips compressed into a grim line as he reversed his grip on his short blade and hurled it at the fox-faced elder just as a pair of fearsome blows hammered into his chest. The next thing he knew he was bouncing off the far wall, his ribs afire with pain. Expensive statues crashed to the ground, snapping off delicate arms and sweeping dragon wings.

Move, move, Malus thought desperately, biting back a groan of pain as he lurched to his feet. The master of assassins was advancing on him slowly and deliberately, reaching for Malus with his small, lethal hands. Desperate, the highborn glanced around for a weapon. He snatched up a stone arm and hurled it at the master's head, and then followed it with a piece of broken wing and a length of barbed tail. The master of assassins batted them easily out of the air, closing inexorably on the highborn.

Malus dodged the first blow at the last moment, ducking behind the statue of a rearing griffon. The second blow shattered the statue into pieces, lashing the highborn's face with chips of razor-edged stone. The highborn stumbled, landing hard on a scattering of stone limbs and wings.

The druchii master yanked back the highborn's hood and seized Malus by the hair the moment he hit the floor. 'Your technique is disgraceful,' the master of assassins hissed, his free hand poised to strike. 'Your every breath is an insult to the glory of Khaine.'

'I'm… flattered… you noticed,' Malus grunted, his face contorted in a grimace of pain. 'What I lack in… skill… I make up for… in… treachery.'

The highborn rolled to the side, lashing out with the stone limb he'd snagged during his fall. Bone snapped like kindling as he struck the master in the left ankle, bringing the master of assassins to his knees. Shouting in rage and pain Malus struck again, lashing out at the hand that held him and breaking the stunned druchii's wrist. He tore himself free of the master's grasp and swung a backhanded stroke that caught the druchii against the side of the head. There was a sickening crunch, and the master fell lifelessly to the floor.

Malus staggered to his feet, gasping for air. He struck the master twice more for good measure, and then tossed the bloodied stone arm aside. The man might have been a master at killing victims through stealth and guile, but he wouldn't have survived ten seconds on the battlefield.

Across the room the surviving zealot had struggled to his feet, his broken right arm clutched close to his side. Malus glared at the man. 'You might have helped,' he hissed through clenched teeth. It felt as if at least one of his ribs was cracked.

The zealot's eyes widened. 'And deprive you of the honour of the kill?' he said, aghast.

'Ah,' Malus said. 'That. Of course.'

The fox-faced elder still leaned against the door, pinned there by Malus's sword. The highborn limped over and pulled the weapon free with a grunt of pain. Just as the elder's body slid aside the door swung inward, and Malus found himself face to face with a druchii in rich, crimson robes, overlaid with a brass breastplate studded with rubies and pearls. Upon the elder's brow was a circlet of gold inlaid with garnets in the shape of tiny, glittering skulls. Like the female elder Malus had killed, the man held a short staff, this one chased with red gold.

The elder's face went pale with shock. There was a faint rustle of woollen robes behind Malus. He took a deep breath, switched his sword from his right hand to his left, and spun just as he heard the sound of the zealot's approach and drove his short blade through the man's chest. The zealot doubled over at the force of the blow, and his life left him in a single, gurgling gasp. The highborn pushed the corpse away and turned back to the stunned elder.

'Step inside, Arch-Hierophant,' Malus said, indicating the far table with a sweep of his blood-spattered hand. 'Take some wine. You and I have much to discuss.'

Chapter Six
BALANCE OF TERROR

ARCH-HIEROPHANT RHULAN filled one of the brass goblets on the table to brim full with thick, plum-coloured wine and took a deep draught before turning back to face Malus. He had the face of an ascetic, with long, drawn features and a scrawny neck that bobbed furiously as he drank. The temple elder said nothing at first, surveying the room's grisly contents.

The highborn studied the man's reactions intently. Rhulan's eyes lit first on the female elder, lying close by in a spreading pool of dark blood. His thin lips pursed in a fleeting smile, and Malus could not mistake a smug gleam of satisfaction in Rhulan's brass-coloured eyes. The elder's gaze passed over the dead scribes and the contorted shape of the dead zealot, seeking out the slumped form of the fox-faced elder and grimacing in evident dissatisfaction. Malus could see the gears turning in the elder's mind as he took in the carnage, gauging new political equations within the temple. Judging by your reaction it would appear that I've handed you quite an opportunity, Rhulan, the highborn thought to himself.

It was only when the elder's searching gaze fell upon the battered form of the master of assassins that Rhulan was truly taken aback. Wine sloshed from the rim of his cup as he shot Malus a worried glance. 'You're not of the temple,' he said. 'Of that I'm certain. Who are you?'

'Who I am is not important,' Malus declared. 'My identity will not alter the situation you've found yourself in.' Unable to resist any longer, Malus walked stiffly to the table and helped himself to some wine. His ribs were aching madly, sending shooting waves of pain across his chest.

'And what situation would that be?' Rhulan snapped. The shock of what he'd seen was wearing off, and the elder was beginning to recover some of his composure.

'Save your bluster, holy man,' Malus shot back. 'The only reason you're still alive is because I'd rather bargain with you than kill you. Your city – nay, your very religion – is under siege by a small army of fanatics who believe you're denying Khaine's holy will, and they must be at least half-right, because you seem powerless to act against them directly.'

It was a feint, meant to upset Rhulan and get him talking, but Malus was inwardly shocked when the elder gritted his teeth and accepted the insult in silence. The highborn studied Rhulan intently. You truly are desperate, he thought. You suspect the zealots are right but you're trying to silence them. Why?

'How is it you bear the blessing of Khaine, but side with these heretics?'

Malus chuckled coldly. 'Rhulan, you shock me. How long have the zealots opposed the will of the temple? Did you honestly think that they could have survived as long as they have without the support of some among the priesthood? The temple fortress itself has been infiltrated, Arch-Hierophant. How else do you think I got in here?' It was another bluff, but judging by the look of terror that came over the elder's face, it was an allegation with bite to it.

'Who?' Rhulan stammered, his hand tightening on his cup.

This is almost too easy, Malus thought. He smiled. 'In due time, Arch-Hierophant. Let us first consider the crux of your problem. How are you dealing with Urial?'

The elder bristled. 'The man is deluded,' Rhulan snapped. 'We should have arranged for his death long ago. I knew that sooner or later he would try something like this.'

'Why then is he still within the Sanctum of the Sword if his claim is not legitimate?'

The knobbly muscles in the elder's jaw bunched tightly, like clenching fists. 'There is the matter of his sister,' Rhulan conceded, 'and his lineage. The situation is very complicated.'

Malus glanced at the thick liquid in his cup. He took a small taste and winced: too sweet by half. 'You accept that she is a living saint. The zealots know this.'

Rhulan shifted uncomfortably. 'Of that there can be no doubt,' he admitted. 'No one like her has been seen among the druchii since Nagarythe was lost,' the elder said, his voice tinged with wonder. 'There is much she could teach us once this... incident is resolved.'

'Is it your desire for Yasmir that keeps you from dismissing Urial's claims, or is he truly what he pretends to be? You must realise that the longer this draws out the more you play into the zealots' hands.'

Rhulan glared at Malus. It had been a long time since anyone had dared speak to him so brashly. 'His claim is compelling enough to demand exhaustive study before a decision can be made.'

Malus cut the man off with a sweep of his hand. 'The fact of the matter is that you think he might be right, but you don't want to hand him the sword, and I suspect your reasons have nothing to do with the will of Khaine.'

A tense silence filled the room. Rhulan had gone very still, his dark eyes narrowing warily as he studied Malus. The high-born took a sip of his wine contemplatively. I've hit a nerve, the highborn thought. What then was the temple's agenda?

'The temple keeps its own counsel in matters of the faith,' Rhulan said carefully. 'You said you had a bargain to make. I am listening.'

Malus fortified himself with a sip of the cloying wine and nodded curtly. 'Your position is untenable, Arch-Hierophant,' he said. 'Time is running out. You've been able to deny Urial so far, but his allies are preparing to take matters into their own hands.'

'How?'

The highborn shook his head. 'First things first. I can deliver the zealot leaders into your hands, but in return you will agree to grant me sanctuary in the temple fortress. Once we've dealt with the heretics inside the city, I can begin ferreting out their sympathisers within the temple fortress, leaving you to focus your efforts on Urial and his sister.'

Rhulan didn't reply immediately, contemplating the depths of his cup. 'I would need to discuss this with the council of elders,' he said.

Malus startled the man with a bark of laughter. 'Rhulan, ten minutes ago you were certain that the heretics couldn't possibly have agents within the temple fortress. Are you absolutely certain you can trust the elder council? The fewer people who know of this arrangement the more likely you are to turn the tables on the zealots.' Malus took a step towards the man. 'Choose, now.'

'All right!' Rhulan snapped. 'I accept your bargain. Woe betide you if you play me false.'

'I could say the same, Rhulan,' Malus replied, setting his cup aside. He searched for his second blade amid the bodies, and then held the weapon in his hand as he considered the two dead elders. 'Do not look at this as an adversarial arrangement, Arch-Hierophant. We both stand to benefit from this. When we're done the zealots will have been dealt a crippling blow, the temple will be cleansed of heretics and Urial will no longer be a problem.'

'And what of you? What do you stand to gain out of this?'

Malus smiled as he walked over to the body of the female elder. 'One thing at a time, Rhulan,' he said. 'Let's focus on you for the time being.' He grabbed the woman by the hair and pulled the head upright. The short blade flashed downward, biting into the corpse's neck, but it was too light for such butcher's work. Malus had to hack his way through the flesh and vertebrae, grimacing at the artlessness of the decapitation.

'What in the name of Khaine are you doing?' Rhulan gasped.

'I can't return to the zealots empty-handed,' Malus explained. Holding the grisly trophy by his side, he made for the fox-faced elder. 'For your part, I want you to stay here and help yourself to some more wine while I make my way back into the city. Wait half an hour before sounding the alarm, and then tell whomever you must that you arrived late to the meeting and found things as they are now.'

'Very well,' Rhulan said, uttering a sharp sigh as he reached for the wine bottle. 'How will we communicate? Will I find you skulking in my chambers tomorrow night?'

Malus chuckled. 'Nothing so dramatic. I still have some more enquiries to pursue among the zealots. When I have news worth sharing I will pass you a message through the shrine in the highborn quarter. Pick a trusted servant and have them check the offerings at the shrine each night.'

'And what will he look for?'

The highborn grunted in pain as he went to work again with his sword. 'Tell him to look for a head that's missing the tips of both ears,' he said, holding up the fox-faced elder's skull. 'I expect I'll have plenty of candidates to choose from in the coming days.'

SCREAMS AND THE clash of steel lingered in the air over Har Ganeth, echoing like the cries of ghosts beneath the gleaming moons.

It was less than a mile from the Assassin's Door to the house of the late Sethra Veyl, but Malus spent more than three hours getting there. Armed bands were prowling the streets with swords and axes in hand, looking for offerings to the Blood God. Armed and armoured highborn with retinues of well-armed retainers passed gangs of commoners wielding meat cleavers and knotted cudgels, each gauging the strength of the other like packs of hungry wolves. The night was still young, but many of the roaming bands already sported one or two bloody trophies. From what Malus could tell, there seemed to be an unspoken rule to prey on solitary travellers rather than engage in big street battles. It was certainly safer for the killers that way.

He moved with care, using his dark robes to melt into the shadows whenever he heard a group of druchii approach. There was no way to be certain if the marauders would spare even a temple assassin once their blood was up. Once, the highborn stepped into a shadowed alley and found himself face-to-face with a white-robed zealot. The true believer was splattered with gore, and half a dozen trophies hung from his broad leather belt. The zealot had glided silently towards Malus, raising his stained blades, but at the last moment he recognised the highborn's face and bowed deeply, stepping past Malus and resuming his own hunt along the city streets.

Malus didn't begrudge the delay. It gave him time to think. Now that he had a way into the temple, he had to make good his part of the bargain and deliver the zealots into Rhulan's hands. Once that was done, he could bend his efforts to penetrating the confines of the Sanctum of the Sword and locating the damned warpsword. As he crept through the confines of the highborn quarter he considered his options. There was still much he did not know, but for the first time Malus saw a clear path to his goal. For the moment at least he had the upper hand, and he intended to make good use of it.

It was near to midnight by the time he turned onto the narrow street outside Veyl's white door. A pile of torn and headless bodies lay in a heap in the middle of the lane and a single bloodstained zealot stood guard outside the door, his dripping blades crossed over his chest. He bowed to Malus as the highborn approached, and stood aside as Malus pushed the door open and disappeared into the courtyard beyond.

The small square was all but empty; clearly the zealots had been turned out into the night to reap offerings in the name of Khaine. To Malus's surprise, he found Tyran standing near the steps of the house, speaking to a small group of new arrivals.

When the zealot leader caught sight of the highborn his eyes lit up with interest. 'Well met, holy one,' he said gravely. 'You return alone.'

Malus nodded, pulling back his hood. 'My companions died in glorious battle,' he replied. It seemed like the proper thing to say.

'And you did not,' Tyran observed, the unspoken question clear in the tone of his voice.

The highborn pulled aside his cloak. Moonlight glimmered on pallid flesh and dark, dried blood as Malus pulled his trophies from his belt and held them up to Tyran. 'Someone had to return with the good news,' he said.

Tyran took a step forwards, peering closely at the three bloodstained faces. 'I see Aniya the Harrower,' he said, pointing at the head of the female elder, 'and this is Maghost,' he said, glancing at the fox-faced man. He frowned at the pulped mess of the third trophy. 'And this?'

'The master of assassins, as you commanded,' Malus replied. 'He wasn't as accommodating as the other two.'

A slow smile spread across Tyran's face, his suspicions forgotten as he considered the news. 'The temple Haru'ann is broken, while ours is nearly complete,' he said. 'This is a great victory for the faithful.' He beamed at Malus. 'Truly you are blessed, holy one! You have hastened the day when the Sword-bearer shall walk among us.'

'Such is my fervent hope,' Malus said with convincing sincerity. 'What is our next move?'

Tyran took the heads from Malus, smiling proudly into their vacant eyes. 'Now we can contest with the temple for the hearts of the people,' he said. 'The surviving elders will be in disarray, and the assassins will be paralysed until they choose a new master.' The zealot leader indicated the new arrivals with his free hand. 'More and more true believers arrive each day,' he said. 'We are strong enough to make our case openly in the city streets.' The zealot leader beckoned for the waiting druchii to join them. 'We can even count another blessed soul such as yourself in our ranks.'

Malus was scarcely listening. 'Good news indeed,' he said, absently, pondering what the Haru'ann might be, and how that figured into Tyran's scheme.

Tyran bowed to one of the hooded figures. 'Holy one, this is Hauclir, a true believer from Naggor,' he said, indicating Malus. 'Truly, it is a powerful omen that two blessed souls from feuding cities should be brought together in the common cause for the glory of Khaine.'

The zealot reached up with a pale hand, drawing back his hood. His long, white hair glowed like a ghostly shroud in the moonlight, and his brass eyes shone like hot coins as he fixed Malus with an enigmatic stare.

'Truly the ways of the Lord of Murder are mysterious indeed,' Arleth Vann said, staring into his former master's eyes.

'PREPARE YOURSELVES, OH servants of Khaine! The Time of Blood approaches!'

The zealot stood on a block of dirty white stone, his twin swords glittering in the sunlight as he held them up to the afternoon sky. Twin pyramids of stained skulls rose to either side of the true believer, offering a welcome meal to a murder of nodding ravens that listened with cursory interest to the zealot's fiery speech.

Barely a handful of druchii paused to listen to what the true believer had to say, thinking at first that he was a novitiate of the temple preaching to the citizens outside the marble-columned shrine of the highborn quarter. A steady stream of men and women were passing through the small square in front of the low building, bearing offerings to be deposited before the altar at the far end of the shrine. A pair of true novitiates stood at the entrance to the dimly-lit building, fingering the ceremonial sickles hanging from their belts and glaring at the zealot across the square with naked contempt.

Malus had positioned himself at the mouth of a narrow street leading into the square, allowing him a clear view of both the shrine and the zealot's energetic sermon. The man had been at it for an hour. Not long after he'd begun, Malus caught sight of a messenger dashing down the steps of the shrine and heading north, towards the temple fortress. The highborn figured they wouldn't have to wait much longer.

For the past three days the zealots had sent men and women into the city, declaiming their beliefs to the people of Har Ganeth. Prior to today, the zealots had stayed on the move, wandering the city streets and spreading the word but not providing the temple with a stationary target to vent their displeasure upon. Today, Tyran had decided to give them their wish, sending a man to preach the true faith outside every shrine in the city.

'The Bride of Ruin awaits in the Sanctum of the Sword!' the zealot declared to his sparse audience. 'She waits for her mate, but the temple elders deny her. They defy the will of the Bloody-Handed God, and soon they will suffer his wrath!'

Malus surveyed the square, trying to spot the other zealots lying in wait for the temple's response. Dressed in typical robes and unadorned kheitans, they were invisible among the steady stream of servants and retainers traversing the square on their masters' business.

Malus knew that Arleth Vann was out there somewhere, and the thought made his blood run cold.

He'd nearly given himself away when the assassin had shown himself that night. For a moment Malus had panicked, thinking he'd walked into a devilish trap. Surprisingly, it was the daemon that had stayed his hand, banishing the cold terror with a voice of iron and bone. 'Look in his eyes, Darkblade,' Tz'arkan had commanded. 'Look! He is as shocked as you are.'

And it was true. For a fleeting instant they had eyed each other warily, but then Tyran invited the new arrivals to join him inside, and Arleth Vann had simply turned away, falling into step with the zealot leader and not giving Malus a single backwards glance. His mind reeling, Malus had staggered to the spare, unfurnished cell set aside for him in Veyl's house and sat with his back against the stout wooden door, his straight northern sword naked in his lap. He'd sat in the darkness for hours, sleep dragging at his exhausted mind as he tried to decide what was going to happen. Were they waiting for more of the zealots to return before they confronted him? His instincts had told him to run while he could, slipping into the city before Arleth Vann could betray his identity to Tyran. Except that the zealots were his bargaining chip with Rhulan. If he broke his agreement with the Arch-Hierophant he doubted he could get anywhere near the Sanctum of the Sword. He was entangled thoroughly in a web of his own making. So, he'd waited in the darkness, wondering how and when Arleth Vann would try to take his revenge. The next thing he'd known he was blinking at the first rays of daybreak, his eyes gummy from sleep, his charade still intact.

He'd seen little of his former retainer since then. Tyran spent the next few days sending the zealots into the city, sniffing for news of the death of the elders. Malus caught glimpses of the former assassin at dawn and dusk, coming and going from the house like one of the city's ubiquitous ravens. The highborn did not know where Arleth Vann slept, or even if he slept at all, but it was clear that when he was at the house he spent much of his time in Tyran's company. It was a situation that troubled Malus no end, but he hadn't the slightest idea what to do about it, not when the former assassin could betray him whenever he chose. So the highborn had kept his distance, passing cursory messages to Rhulan that did little more than state the obvious: the zealots were agitating the people of the city to force a confrontation with the temple.

It took two days before Malus realised he wasn't in immediate danger. No one had moved against him, indeed, Tyran treated him no differently than before. Belatedly, Malus realised that Arleth Vann might be just as wary of him. After all, he was a renegade himself, an assassin who'd broken his oaths and abandoned the temple in years past. The cult's treatment of prodigals was legendary. They never forgave nor forgot those druchii who betrayed their trust. They would spare no effort to capture or kill Arleth Vann if they knew he was in the city. A few judicious words spoken in one of the city shrines would be enough. It was a tenuous stalemate.

But why was he here, Malus wondered? Had he been a zealot all along, nursing his heretical beliefs in secret, or did he track me here, seeking to finish the job he'd begun in the Valley of Shadow? The only thing he knew for certain was that he couldn't wait for Arleth Vann to show his hand. He had to find a way to kill the man without betraying himself into the bargain.

Movement at the edge of the square caught Malus's attention. A trio of black-robed men were making their way towards the ranting zealot, sunlight glinting on the edges of their long, curved draichs. Malus straightened, reaching for his sword. The temple had heard Tyran's message and here was the answer the zealots had expected.

The three warriors were not merely swordsmen: they were Draichnyr na Khaine, peerless slayers of men renowned for killing foes with a single, perfect stroke of their huge swords. He had seen men like them at work when Urial had led the warriors of the temple into battle against their sister Nagaira. Their reputation was richly deserved. The highborn set off after the men, sliding his long sword from its scabbard and concealing it beneath his cloak. He noticed two other cloaked figures on the move as well, stalking after the temple executioners like lean, hungry wolves.

'Even now the cowards in the temple fortress set their dogs upon me!' the zealot cried from his pedestal, pointing at the approaching swordsmen. 'Why? Because they do not wish their lies to be known! They have deceived you, brothers and sisters! They have tricked you, and stolen from you, and twisted the words of the Blood God to feed their own greed! The Bride of Ruin has come! The Time of Blood is nigh, sons and daughters of lost Nagarythe! Will you stand tall before the Scourge or be swept aside?'

'Heretic!' the lead executioner thundered, causing the zealot's small audience to scatter. 'You blaspheme in Khaine's holy city and impugn the honour of his devoted servants.' He raised his sword. 'Even the Lord of Blood repudiates you. Your skull is not fit to lie at Khaine's feet. After we've split you like a steer you'll be thrown into the sea for the fish to eat.'

Malus was less than ten steps from the rearmost of the executioners. He reached up to his cloak clasp, unfastening it and letting it fall to the cobblestones. Out of the corner of his eye he glimpsed his compatriots readying themselves as well. The highborn's hand tightened on the hilt of his blade as he drew in a deep breath and shouted in a voice fit for a battlefield.

'The Swordbearer has come! Blood and souls for the Swordbearer!'

To their credit, the executioners reacted to the surprise assault with speed and deadly skill. The man in front of Malus whirled at his shout, his draich making a fan of reflected light as it spun in a defensive circle around the swordsman. To his left, Malus heard the sharp ring of tempered steel and then the sound of a man's death rattle. A body hit the cobbles with a muted thud, but the highborn didn't dare look away from the warrior facing him. One wrong move and the executioner would strike his head from his shoulders.

Shrieking a terrible war scream, Malus rushed at the warrior. The executioner's curved blade paused in its circling movements, and for a split second Malus was reminded of Tyran, standing frozen in the face of Sethra Veyl's furious assault. He means to let me commit myself, and then strike the killing blow, Malus thought. He held his blow as he rushed ever closer, dropping the point of his sword as he went. If the executioner didn't react quickly he would be run through.

At the last possible moment, the executioner exploded into a blur of motion, sidestepping the highborn's thrust and aiming a blow at Malus's neck. But as the warrior committed himself to the motion Malus checked his advance, planting his leading foot and pivoting into a short, vicious cut across the warrior's midsection. The heavy sword bit into the executioner's thick kheitan and the hard muscle beneath, spinning the druchii half around with the force of the blow and throwing off his attack. Before the warrior could recover Malus pulled his blade free and drove its point into the side of the man's throat. Bright blood jetted from the wound and the executioner staggered, choking on his own fluids. Eyes bright with hate, the warrior swept his long blade around in an off-balance strike to Malus's head, but the highborn tore his sword free and blocked the blow easily, before lashing out with a backhanded stroke that decapitated the mortally wounded man.

Malus stepped out of the way as the headless body toppled over, quickly taking stock of the situation. A second executioner lay dead, his torso split by a terrible wound that ran from his collarbone down to his waist. The headless body of the zealot who attacked him lay several steps away. The leader of the executioners and another zealot circled one another warily, each searching for a weak spot in the other's guard. Malus took a step towards them, thinking to strike the man down while his back was turned, but then remembered the true believers' strange sensibilities. Far be it from me to deny the man an opportunity to die, Malus thought sourly, and left the zealot to his fate.

The highborn turned back to the man he'd slain, snatching up his bloodstained head. Moving swiftly, he sheathed his sword and pulled out a short knife as he walked over to one of the trophy pyramids by the preacher's stone block. With his back to the rest of the square, he reached up and sliced off the tips of the executioner's ears, before putting away the knife and pulling a folded strip of oilcloth from his belt. The cloth note went between the executioner's teeth in a single, deft move, and then Malus ostentatiously set the skull atop the pile.

Just then the highborn heard the sound of a blade striking home, and turned to see the executioner staggering away from his foe, clutching at a terrible wound in his chest. His long draich fell from nerveless fingers as he stumbled towards the shrine. The novitiates at the top of the stairs looked on in horror as the warrior fell onto his face and died.

'The Time of Blood is at hand!' Malus said again, repeating the words that Tyran had told him to say. He eyed the city dwellers still standing in the square, his face alight with righteous wrath. 'Shake the temple doors and command them to hearken to the Swordbearer! The Scourge is here, and he will strip the souls from the unworthy and fling them into the outer darkness!'

The people of Har Ganeth looked into Malus's eyes, and he saw that they believed him.

Chapter Seven
THE EXECUTIONER'S BLADE

THEY CAME FOR him that night.

It was well past midnight when the door to Malus's cell creaked open. His mind registered the noise, but it took precious seconds for him to force his exhausted body to awaken. By the time his eyes snapped open there was pale green light seeping into the room from the open doorway and he could see the shapes of men and women outlined in the corridor beyond. His hand closed on the hilt of his sword, but he knew instinctively that he was far, far too late. He was also so deeply exhausted that it was difficult to give much of a damn.

Malus lay there on his travel-worn bedroll, blinking stupidly in the witchlight for several long seconds. No one moved. 'If you've come to kill me, get on with it,' he growled. 'Otherwise let me sleep.'

Someone chuckled. 'Tyran sent us,' a woman's voice said. 'He wants to talk to you.'

Gods below, Malus thought, sitting stiffly upright. Did the bastard ever sleep? 'All right, all right,' he growled. 'Let me find my boots.'

He could feel them studying him as he collected his gear. Every inch of him ached, and his muscles refused to work as they should. He could sense their amusement as he fumbled clumsily with belt and sword. The zealots showed not the slightest sign of discomfort or fatigue.

For people who thought of themselves as the true worshippers of Khaine, the zealots had a strange notion of piety. Unlike the practices of the temple, with its devotionals and its catechisms, the only display of righteousness the zealots respected was the perfection of the killing arts. When they weren't out in the city ambushing temple warriors by day or collecting skulls on the blood-spattered streets each night the true believers were in the courtyard or the practice rooms of Veyl's house fighting with one another. Hour after hour, sparring with heavy wooden weapons or even live steel, the zealots devoted themselves body and soul to the craft of ending life as swiftly and irrevocably as possible. The temple's fearsome executioners were layabouts by comparison.

The more the zealots suffered the deprivations of hunger and exhaustion the more serene they became. They thrived on suffering, mortifying their flesh through exertion rather than by scourge or blade. Malus had thought himself a hard man before being thrust into the world of the zealots. Now he felt like an old, tired man trying to keep pace with a pack of lions. *Give me the tender mercies of Slaanesh any night,* he thought grimly. *At least she expected her worshippers to sleep off their devotions.*

Malus fell into line with the waiting zealots and followed them upstairs. The master's chambers were dark and silent. The highborn's tired mind registered fitful glimpses of dark hallways and turgid shadows cast by banked braziers. Before he knew it, he was climbing a familiar, narrow stairway and emerging onto the roof. A brisk wind off the sea blew salt mist into his face and banished the last vestiges of sleep. He took a deep breath of the briny air, looking out over the polished pewter surface of the Sea of Chill, and then to the west, where the moons peered bright and curious over the far mountains.

The zealots drew back their dark hoods and moved silently across the roof, settling down into a rough circle facing Tyran the Unscarred. The zealot leader's head was uncovered, his hair glistening with tiny drops of sea-spray. His draich lay across his folded knees, and he studied Malus thoughtfully. 'Come and join us holy one,' he said, 'we have much to discuss.'

Malus considered Tyran's words for signs of danger. It was possible the zealot leader was toying with him. If so, Malus thought, he would be made to regret it. 'A strange place for a meeting,' he mused, approaching the seated zealots.

Tyran shrugged. 'For a city dweller, perhaps. I've spent most of my life living under the open sky, moving from one city to the next or following armies on the march. This is as natural to me as a temple cell is to you,' he said. 'Besides, only a faithless heart hides itself behind walls of stone. We have nothing to fear from man nor beast, for the Lord of Murder is with us.'

The highborn bowed deeply. 'Well said.' He sat heavily on the slick roof tiles, wincing at the flare of pain from his stiff joints. Several of the zealots chuckled quietly, their faces hidden in shadow. Now fully awake, Malus surveyed his companions more carefully. There were six of them besides Tyran. He recognised nearly all of them, including the lone hunter he'd encountered on the streets on the way back from the temple fortress and the woman who'd first welcomed him into the house nearly a week ago. She returned his gaze with a frank, playful stare.

At the far end of the circle Malus found himself staring into a pair of brass-coloured eyes. Arleth Vann studied him with the expressionless interest of a rock adder. With an effort, Malus looked past the former assassin and focused on Tyran.

'Each day brings us closer to Khaine's triumph, brothers and sisters,' the zealot leader said with a fierce smile. 'Word of the Swordbearer and his bride spreads through the city, and the temple elders remain in disarray. Their assassins have gone into conclave, debating the choice of a new master, and the Haru'ann remains broken. The apostates have never suffered such setbacks before, and they are paralysed with fear: fear that the Time of Blood is indeed at hand and their lies are about to be exposed.'

Murmurs of approval rose from the assembled zealots. Tyran regained their attention with a raised hand. 'Their fear is so great that our allies within the temple fortress report that some of the apostates are considering recanting their decadent ways and joining with us for the greater glory of Khaine. One of them is a temple elder.'

The zealots glanced at one another, their eyes widening in surprise. One of the men snorted in disgust. 'They think to erase a lifetime of apostasy now that the hounds of Khaine are baying at their door? Let them offer their necks to the axe if they are so repentant.'

'Indeed,' Malus said. 'They knew all along what lies they were spreading. It's the fear of discovery that motivates them, not true faith.'

Several of the zealots nodded, muttering in agreement. In fact, it was fear of discovery that motivated Malus. Who was this elder? Was it Rhulan? What if the elder hoped to buy his survival by exposing the highborn's scheme?

'The ways of the Lord of Murder are mysterious and terrible,' Tyran replied, shaking his head. 'Like you, I have no mercy for those who turn aside from the holy path of slaughter, but there is a great opportunity here if we are bold enough to seize it.' The zealot leader folded his arms. 'So, after careful thought and prayer, I have decided to help this elder escape the clutches of the apostates.' He stared at each of the assembled druchii in turn, 'And I have chosen you to perform the rescue.'

Malus frowned. 'Entering the temple fortress so soon after our last effort will be very difficult,' he said. 'They will be watching for infiltrators at every door and gate.'

Tyran nodded. 'Of course. That is why the elder is going to come to us.' He met the zealots' confused expressions with a crafty smile. 'The confrontations across the city today have created an opportunity for us to exploit,' he said. 'Tomorrow, the temple elders will enter the city and appear at certain shrines to reassure the people and demonstrate their divine authority. The elder who wishes to join us has arranged to appear at the shrine here in the highborn district at noon.' Tyran smiled. 'Naturally, he will be under heavy guard, which itself provides us with another chance to demonstrate our righteous wrath. Your task is simple: slay the elder's bodyguards and escort him here, where we will test his devotion and plan our next move.'

Startled gasps rose from the zealots. Several prostrated themselves before their leader. 'This is a great honour,' the female druchii said, her eyes alight at the prospect of such a battle.

'If you succeed the rewards will be greater than you know,' Tyran said portentously. 'I believe Khaine has handed us this opportunity for a reason. If we prevail tomorrow, it will be a sign that our final victory is close at hand.' The zealot leader turned to Malus. 'Hauclir, I want you to lead this holy mission. Arleth Vann will be your lieutenant. You are both blessed by the Lord of Murder; together I know that you will prevail against the apostates.'

Malus felt his heart clench. He could feel Arleth Vann's reptilian gaze resting on him like the point of a knife. 'It… it's an honour to serve,' he managed to say.

The zealot leader nodded. 'After your exploits in the temple fortress, I have no doubt you will succeed,' he said, and then rose fluidly to his feet. 'You have ten hours, brothers and sisters. Prepare yourselves as your hearts dictate. Tomorrow the eyes of the Blood God will be upon you.'

As one, the zealots stood and took their leave of Tyran. Malus remained seated, lost in thought. Tyran was right in one sense; tomorrow would indeed present a golden opportunity, one that Malus could ill afford to ignore.

The question was, if he only had one chance to strike would it be better to kill Arleth Vann or the turncoat elder?

RAIN BLEW IN thin sheets across the small square outside the shrine, causing the passers-by to huddle inside their oiled cloaks and making life thoroughly miserable for the crowd waiting for the elder's arrival. Word had gone out just after dawn, when well-escorted town criers had walked the city streets, announcing that the elders of the temple would come before the people to denounce the words of the heretics that blasphemed against Khaine's holy cult. The announcement made things somewhat easier for Malus and the zealots, giving them much-needed concealment as they waited for the elder to arrive.

The highborn glanced up at the weeping grey sky and frowned. 'He's late,' the highborn muttered.

'He's probably offering sacrifices to Khaine to stop the rain,' the female zealot replied quietly. Her name, Malus had learned that morning, was Sariya. She was very young, the daughter of a highborn family in Karond Kar. 'The Lord of Murder forefend that his chosen servants get their feet wet walking down the street.'

Malus grinned at the girl's acid tongue. The zealots all stood together at the edge of the crowd, waiting for the highborn's instructions. He'd told them that he wouldn't know what they would do until nearly the last minute. There were simply too many unknowns: how large would the elder's escort be? Would he stop to speak to the crowd, or march straight into the temple? How closely would his guards hem him in? Until he saw firsthand what he was dealing with, he had no idea how to respond.

Malus fingered the hilts of a pair of heavy throwing knives beneath his sodden cloak. Shortly before dawn he'd finally decided on their target.

'More likely he's being hampered by his escort,' the highborn muttered darkly. 'A large contingent would have a hard time getting organised and moving quickly down these cramped streets.' He slowly scanned the assembled druchii, looking for anything untoward. 'That, or they are waiting to hear back from their informants to see if the square is safe to travel through.'

Sariya gave Malus a sidelong glance. 'My, holy one, you're a font of cheery news.'

'The true faith is not an easy one,' the highborn replied with a wry smile, 'but it is realistic.'

He turned to Arleth Vann and caught himself just before he asked if the former assassin had seen anything. The druchii was looking away at the time and didn't catch Malus's startled expression. Sariya's banter had almost caused him to forget himself. He's no retainer of mine, the highborn thought angrily, quickly looking away.

The tramp of armoured feet carried across the rain swept square from the east. Heads turned. Malus stood on his toes to peer above the throng and caught sight of a rank of four executioners, their lacquered armour gleaming wetly in the weak light. They marched with their draichs unsheathed and raised before them like a hedge of razor-edged steel. Their faces were grim and their dark eyes fixed on the crowd as if viewing them from across a battlefield. Malus paid no attention to the executioners, instead straining his ears to gauge the weight of the marching feet echoing across the cobblestones. He bit back a snarl. It sounded like a full company of swordsmen, possibly as much as two hundred men. The temple wanted to send a very clear message to the people of the city.

'Damnation,' Malus muttered, considering his options. There weren't many to choose from. From where he stood, it looked as if the swordsmen were marching directly at the assembled crowd, evidently intending to create a cordon for the elder between the audience and the shrine. After a moment he thought he understood what the temple contingent was planning.

'All right,' the highborn said, turning his back on the crowd and addressing the zealots in low, urgent tones. 'Here's what we're going to do.' Malus took a deep breath. 'Arleth Vann, take Sariya and get inside the shrine as quickly as you can. The rest of us will work to the front of the crowd and attack the executioners once the elder shows himself. When the fighting starts, he'll retreat inside the shrine, where you'll be waiting for him. Kill his escorts and take him straight to Tyran. We'll keep the executioners distracted until you get away.'

Malus looked first to Sariya, and then at Arleth Vann, making certain they understood their instructions. He met the former assassin's gaze and the druchii nodded curtly, acknowledging the order as he'd done countless times in the past. 'Go,' Malus said, and the two zealots headed swiftly away, circling around the edge of the crowd to get past the oncoming line of executioners.

The highborn turned back to his remaining men. 'Spread out and work your way up to the front of the crowd,' he said. 'No one acts until I give the order.' With that, he turned on his heel and started easing his way through the muttering throng.

Within moments Malus found himself fighting his way upstream against a press of people being pushed in the opposite direction. The executioners were using their blades to force the crowd to give ground, eliciting angry murmurs from the spectators. A long double line of armoured warriors was extending itself for twenty yards across the square in front of the shrine. A large block of troops was assembled near the mouth of the street the escort had emerged from, securing their line of retreat.

The tramp of feet fell silent, followed by the rattle of harnesses as the swordsmen adjusted their line. Malus stopped short behind the foremost line of spectators, first eyeing the warriors and their brandished blades and then trying to catch a glimpse of the steps to the shrine. He just caught sight of two hooded figures slipping inside the entrance to the building, and knew that Arleth Vann and Sariya were in position.

Movement near the mouth of the eastern lane caught the highborn's attention. All he could see over the line of troops was the tip of a gold-topped staff and a voluminous crimson hood. Was it Rhulan, he thought? There was no damned way to tell.

He watched the figure move along behind the line of executioners as he eased his sword from its scabbard beneath his cloak. Malus shifted slightly, taking up position almost directly behind a tall, scowling man who was glaring irritably at the temple soldiers.

Malus watched the elder begin to climb the temple steps, just as he'd anticipated – the man would need the extra height to address the crowd over the soldiers. The highborn took a deep breath and lowered his right shoulder. 'Blood and souls for the Swordbearer!' he roared, and shoved the unsuspecting man at the executioners as hard as he could. Taken by surprise, the spectator flew at the swordsmen with a startled shout, his arms flinging wide for balance, and the surprised executioner in front of him reacted out of instinct. A draich carved a flickering arc through the rain and the spectator screamed, blood rising in a fountain as the sword split him nearly in half.

The highborn struck at just that instant, while the executioner's blade was still deep in his victim's body. 'They mean to kill us all!' he shouted, stabbing his sword into the executioner's exposed throat. The swordsman reeled backwards, blood pouring down the front of his armour. More shouts and the clash of steel echoed up and down the line, adding to the pandemonium.

Malus leapt into the gap opened in the executioners' line, hacking left and right with his heavy blade. He struck the man to his left a heavy blow on the side of his helmet and then cut open the hamstring of the man on his right. The executioner collapsed with a scream, clutching at his leg, and the rest of the swordsmen lost their self-control and attacked the shouting crowd.

A draich swept down at Malus, but the swing had little real power and the highborn swept it aside with ease. The tight ranks of the executioners made for an imposing wall of men and steel, but it left the warriors with little room to use their long blades properly. He hacked at the man in front of him, feinting at his head and then altering the course of the blow to smash his heavy sword into the executioner's fingers. Two severed digits tumbled from the man's right gauntlet. Malus half-knocked the draich from the man's grip with a savage swipe and then smashed his sword into the executioner's face.

In the space of an instant the square had become a raging battlefield. The executioners lashed out at anything that moved, and spectators in the crowd were fighting back in an effort to save themselves. Screams and the stink of spilled blood filled the air. The executioner Malus had struck fell to his knees, his helmet crumpled by the highborn's savage blow. He stepped in and slit the man's throat with his sword, laughing like a madman in the ringing tumult. Malus felt the daemon respond to the terror and pain around it, writhing and squirming around the highborn's hammering heart. For a fleeting instant he was tempted to ask the daemon to share its power, just for the sheer joy of spilling blood. This was his element. He'd known it since the day he'd rescued the army of the black ark from the ambush at Blackwater Ford.

The line of swordsmen was disintegrating. Without orders, some men advanced into the crowd and others gave ground, splitting the force into isolated knots of struggling warriors. The cobblestones were black with pools of blood, men slipping and stumbling over fallen bodies or spilled entrails. As Malus watched, an executioner overbalanced and fell to the ground, only to be set upon by a trio of druchii who pounded his head and back with pieces of stone torn from the square itself.

A muffled shout drew his attention to the east where Malus caught sight of an executioner in ornate armour brandishing a rune-inscribed draich and shouting orders to the block of swordsmen covering the eastern road. Once they entered the fight the battle would be over in moments. The highborn spun in place, looking everywhere for signs of Arleth Vann and the temple elder.

There! Malus saw a pair of dark-cloaked figures herding another druchii with a crimson cloak towards the lane on the south side of the square. No one was paying any attention in the chaos of the battle. This was the only chance he was going to get.

Drawing one of his throwing knives, Malus cut back through the seething mob, staying low and skirting struggling opponents as he closed the distance with the fleeing trio. A bloodstained man grabbed at Malus's arm, bleeding from a head wound and babbling incoherently. Malus stabbed him in the leg with an angry snarl and shoved the man away.

They were nearly at the mouth of the street. Malus picked up his pace, running up to the edge of the mob. It would be a long shot, he realised with a grimace. The highborn took a deep breath, drew back his arm and hurled the knife as hard as he could at the elder's retreating form.

The knife was just a dark blur against the grey mist as it arced towards its target. It struck the red-cloaked figure just beneath the left shoulder blade. Malus watched as his victim staggered under the force of the blow, and then took two more stumbling steps before falling face-first onto the cobblestones. Malus watched Arleth Vann turn at the sound. The two cloaked figures paused only a moment, staring at the fallen body. Then they turned and made good their escape.

A tremendous shout echoed from the other side of the square as the reserve block of executioners charged into the fray. Malus couldn't see what had become of the remaining zealots. Perhaps they had already broken free, or maybe they lay among the dead littering the cobblestones. Either way, they were no longer his problem.

Malus headed south, pushing aside other fleeing city folk as he fled the oncoming executioners. As he approached his fallen victim, however, he was gripped by overpowering curiosity. Was it Rhulan? Had he made the right choice? On impulse, he skidded to a stop beside the body and pulled his knife free, before rolling the corpse over to peer inside the depths of the hood.

His heart clenched. 'Mother of Night,' he cursed, looking into Sariya's lifeless eyes.

Chapter Eight
REVELATIONS

BLOOD FLOWED IN the streets of Har Ganeth, and the sounds of battle rang out all across the city as the warriors of the temple vented their fury on any druchii unlucky enough to be caught in their path. Men were chased down and hacked apart, their entrails spread for the ravens and their heads set aside as offerings to the Bloody-Handed God. Slaves were hunted and torn apart like wild animals. Market squares turned to charnel houses as the servants of the temple sought to drown their rage in rivers of blood.

An elder of the temple had been taken, so the rumours said, seized within the holy grounds of a city shrine while his bodyguards were slaughtered by a howling mob. Never in the history of the temple had such a crime been committed. It was an insult too great to be borne. Trumpets sounded from the temple walls all through the afternoon, and a flood of black-robed druchii streamed into the city streets with bared blades held in their hands, half-mad with anger and grief. The witch elves joined them late in the day, their muscular bodies painted with sweat and blood, and their eyes wild with murderous ecstasy. They sniffed the air and howled like wolves, their faces twisted in masks of bestial hunger, and when they could not find any more victims to kill on the city streets the brides of Khaine drove the temple servants to break down the doors of the lowborns' homes and flesh houses.

That was when the fighting began in earnest. For hundreds of years the people of the city had prospered under the terrible rule of the temple and bled for the Lord of Murder when necessary. The daylight was given over to the mundane needs of the city, but at night the streets were a place of holy communion, where sacrifices could be made to the Lord of Murder without fear of feud or reprisal. Highborn families would offer up clutches of slaves in hopes of a good flesh harvest or to call down a curse upon their enemies. Lowborn families, hungry for wealth and power, were forced to turn out their own kin in hopes of winning the Blood God's favour. One and all, they were prey to the armed bands that roamed the streets from dusk to dawn in search of victims to sate the eternal hunger of the temple.

The streets were given over to the Lord of Murder so that the houses of the citizens would remain inviolate by the unspoken rule that had allowed the city to survive for centuries. So when the servants of the temple tore down the doors of the lowborns' houses they did not find fearful victims waiting for the executioner's blade, but were welcomed with axes and spears like any other invader.

Malus Darkblade, the architect of the day's bloodshed, wandered the streets of Har Ganeth all through the afternoon, his face a mask of hate and his blade wet with blood. He staggered like a drunk and killed every living thing that crossed his path, furious with himself and with the city of madmen he found himself in.

Arleth Vann had anticipated him, forcing the elder to exchange his cloak with Sariya. Had it been a trap all along, designed to force his hand and show his true intentions to Tyran? Malus couldn't be sure, and wasn't certain it even mattered any more. The elder was doubtless safe at the house of Sethra Veyl, telling the zealot leader everything he knew. If Rhulan had told the elders of Malus's deal then he was certain to be exposed.

All this had gone through Malus's head as he'd crouched over Sariya's body. Then the fleeing mob surged around him, filling his ears with cries of anger and pain, and he let himself be caught up in it.

When he came back to his senses he was sitting in an alley surrounded by corpses. The sounds of battle raged in a small square just a few yards away. Malus listened to the clash of steel and the screams of the dying like another man would listen to the patter of rain or the whisper of wind in the trees. His robes were stiff with blood and his sword felt glued to his hand with layers of crusted filth. The stench of the battlefield filled his nostrils. His stomach rumbled and he recalled that he hadn't eaten all day.

A shadow passed over Malus's face, and he felt the beat of wings against his cheeks. The raven settled on the head of a man doubled over on the alley floor next to Malus. The bird studied him with one yellow eye and let out a croaking laugh. 'Blood and souls! Blood and souls!' the dreadful bird cried.

Malus took a half-hearted swipe at the damned raven, sending it squawking into the air. Exhausted, he slumped onto the bloodstained ground, rolling onto his back and staring up at a thin bar of cloudy sky between the alley's close-set buildings. He felt the daemon move within him, slithering against his ribs like a contented cat. The sensation repelled him.

His rage spent, the highborn wearily considered his options. There was a very real risk that his dealings with the temple had been exposed. Certainly Arleth Vann suspected him, but the former retainer might well have done that on nothing more than general principles.

The zealots were the key to the Sanctum of the Sword. He had to deliver Tyran and the other true believers into the hands of the temple, and that meant returning to the house of Sethra Veyl. Perhaps there were other ways to reach the warpsword, but they would take time to unearth, and time was one commodity he had in short supply.

I've got to go back, he thought grimly. I have to know what they're planning. Let Arleth Vann make his accusations. I've talked my way out of worse situations before.

Another shadow fell across Malus's vision. For a moment he thought the raven had returned, but then a bloodstained face and a pair of shoulders loomed into the highborn's view. A grimy hand reached for his hair, and a gore stained hatchet glinted in the fading light.

Malus rolled onto his side with a snarl and stabbed the man in the chest. The druchii, wearing the stained robes of a tradesman, groaned weakly and toppled onto his side. The man had a clutch of severed heads tied to his belt and a leather bag bulging with looted coin, gold earrings and silver bracelets. Malus had to admire the man's opportunism in the midst of chaos. The highborn helped himself to the bag and struck off the man's head for good measure.

A croaking laugh echoed down the alley. The raven looked up from its meal and eyed him knowingly. 'Gore-crow! Gore-crow!' the bird called mockingly.

Malus hit the bird squarely with the tradesman's head, sending it croaking angrily skyward in an explosion of greasy feathers. The damned skulls were good for something after all, he thought to himself.

THE HIGHBORN DISTRICT was relatively quiet after the bedlam of the lower quarters. Even in the depths of their anger the temple followers evidently knew better than to menace the city's well-armed nobility. Still, the tall houses were dark and tightly shuttered and the streets were largely deserted as Malus found his way to the house of Sethra Veyl.

There were no zealots standing guard outside the white door when the highborn arrived. Malus pounded on the door with the pommel of his blade, but got no reply. 'Open up, damn your eyes!' he roared over the wall, his previous anger returning. 'Since when do true believers cower behind stone walls?'

Within moments there was a rattle of bolts and the door opened. A white-robed zealot stood in the doorway, clutching his sword in a white-knuckled grip as he glared at Malus. 'No one enters tonight, holy one,' the man said, 'not even you. Tyran's orders.'

'If Tyran wishes to keep me out he can tell me himself!' Malus snarled, advancing on the man. The zealot raised his blade, but the highborn slapped it aside with his own and then shoved the man rudely in the chest. The true believer fell backwards onto the cobblestones and the men with him gave ground, stunned at Malus's bloody visage. To them he was the very image of the divine, anointed in the red wine of battle.

Malus raised his blade and levelled it at the astonished guards. 'Those of you who are ready to offer up your heads to Khaine need only stand in my path and I will give you gladly to the god.'

But the man Malus had struck wasn't so easily cowed. He sprang gracefully to his feet, a fierce expression on his face. 'Let us see who has the greater devotion, then,' he said, edging forwards with his sword held ready. 'I'll go to the Lord of Murder laughing with joy, knowing you'll soon be following me.'

'Enough!' cried a husky, female voice from across the small courtyard. 'Put aside your blades and let the man from Naggor pass. I can see the spirits of the dead that surround him. He has offered up a great bounty to our god this day, and punished the ranks of the blasphemers.'

The zealots reluctantly parted to allow Malus to pass. A woman waited on the steps leading up to the house, her pale face gleaming from the depths of a wide, black hood. The blood-witch studied Malus with a frank, predatory stare.

Malus made his way slowly across the courtyard, noticing for the first time that it was conspicuously empty. The zealots that had camped in the open space had all vanished, taking their meagre possessions with them. The highborn frowned up at the woman. 'Where is Tyran?' he asked.

'Elsewhere,' the blood-witch replied. 'When word of the elder's disappearance reached the temple the remaining leaders could not contain the fury of their servants. Once night has fallen and their bloodlust has been spent they will return to the fortress and the elders will send them against the houses of the true believers no matter where they lie.'

'And the elder who has joined us?'

The blood-witch smiled, showing her leonine fangs. 'He has proven worthy, holy one, and eager to witness the Time of Blood. Our Haru'ann is complete, while the temple remains in disarray.'

Malus paused, trying to puzzle out the full import of the blood-witch's words. If she knew so much and yet allowed him into the house then clearly the zealots still trusted him. Or perhaps they simply had no time to deal with him because something much more important was afoot. What was this damned Haru'ann everyone kept talking about?

'What would Tyran have of me?' he asked.

The blood-witch shrugged. 'When you did not return with the others it was assumed that you found a glorious death in the riots,' she said. 'Those of us who have no role in what is to come will take to the streets tonight and offer up tokens of devotion to the Bloody-Handed God.' She smiled again, her feline eyes glowing in the fading sunlight. 'I will dance with many men tonight, take many mates and bathe in their fluids. You may dance with me, if you wish.'

'That... that's quite an honour,' Malus managed to say, quite taken aback by the woman's feral gaze, 'but I am not worthy of your attentions. For one thing, I'm filthy.'

The blood-witch threw back her head and laughed. The sound both aroused and frightened Malus at the same time. 'Go then, as the Lord of Murder wishes,' she said. The blood-witch descended the steps, reaching up to gently trace a curved talon along the line of his jaw. 'Another night perhaps,' she said softly. 'Remember me, holy one. I might not recognise your freshly scrubbed face when we meet again.'

MALUS STRODE SWIFTLY down the deserted hall, his mind racing. Tyran was making his move tonight, of that he was certain, but what was his plan?

He reached the sparsely furnished cell that had been set aside for him and dashed inside, not bothering to shut the door behind him as he started gathering up his possessions. There was no way he was going to find the zealot leader before he set his plan in motion. The best he could do was to bluff his way into the temple and tell Rhulan what little he knew. Malus figured he could improvise the rest as the situation developed. It was not as if he had any other choice.

The highborn went to roll up his bedroll and realised that after everything that had happened he was still holding on to his sword. Malus stared at the long blade in irritation. Put the damned thing away, he thought. You wouldn't have made it this far if the zealots wanted to kill you.

Then a chill went down his spine as a dark shape moved through the light at his back. Malus whirled just as Arleth Vann struck.

The assassin was nearly invisible in the dimly lit room. The only warning Malus had was a glint of witchlight on metal as one of Arleth Vann's blades caught the light streaming in from the corridor beyond. The highborn raised his blade and narrowly parried a stroke that would have sliced open his throat. Pure, desperate instinct caused him to sweep his blade downwards and parry the assassin's second sword as it stabbed for his stomach.

Malus gave ground quickly, trying to circle around to the cell's doorway so he would be backlit by the corridor lights, but Arleth Vann anticipated this and darted swiftly to the side, aiming a flurry of blows at his former master's head and neck. The highborn parried stroke for stroke, but was forced inexorably backwards as he warded off the assassin's attacks. Malus fumbled for one of his throwing knives as the assassin shifted position again and melded back into the darkness.

The highborn pulled the dagger free as quietly as he could, reversing his grip on the blade with a flick of his wrist. He crouched low, sliding warily to the left. 'I continue to underestimate you, Arleth Vann,' he hissed. 'I never expected your little surprise in the Valley of Shadows, and here you nearly pulled the same trick on me again. Surely you realise that there's no honour left to reclaim by killing me. As far as the world knows, I died with the army outside Hag Graef.'

For a moment there was only silence. Malus waited, his ears straining for the slightest sound. Then there was a faint hint of movement and Arleth Vann spoke in a sepulchral whisper, like wind soughing through the cracks in a tomb. 'Would that I thought so as well,' he said, 'but in the absence of honour, the need for vengeance remains.'

Malus fixed on the source of the voice and hurled the dagger with all his strength, before bolting for the open doorway. He heard the discordant ring of steel behind him as Arleth Vann knocked the dagger aside and bit back a savage curse. He reached the shaft of light thrown by the hall lights and dashed for the relative safety of the corridor, only to be hauled roughly off his feet as Arleth Vann seized his bloodstained cloak.

The highborn crashed to the floor, swinging his sword wildly over his head. He felt the blade bite home, and Arleth Vann hissed a sibilant curse. Reaching up with his free hand, Malus undid the clasps of his cloak and rolled quickly to the side just as a curved sword thudded into the wooden floor where he'd been.

'What vengeance?' Malus spat, scrabbling backwards across the floor. 'I could understand such feelings from Silar or perhaps Dolthaic, even that rogue Hauclir, but you? I gave you a new life when you fled the temple. You owe me everything. It was you who was false. You swore fealty to me, when in secret your first loyalty was to these fanatics!'

There was a whirring in the air. A spinning shape passed through the weak light, and Malus caught sight of the hurled sword a moment too late. He moved to block the weapon but misjudged its trajectory. The back of the curved sword smashed into his right forearm. The highborn felt the bones break and cried out in pain. Then another blow knocked the broad sword from his nerveless fingers. Arleth Vann's hand closed around Malus's throat. His second sword hung poised above his head.

'My loyalty to you and to the temple was one and the same!' Arleth Vann snapped. 'I sought you out, across the length and breadth of Naggaroth. I served you for years, watching and waiting in secret because I was certain that you were the one. When the autarii foiled our attack in the Valley of Shadow I thought that it was Khaine's will, and I rejoiced.' The assassin bent lower, until Malus could see the anger and despair gleaming in his brass-coloured eyes. 'Then I returned to Har Ganeth to find your brother Urial in the Sanctum of the Sword, and I was forced to admit my mistake. I'd found the right house, but chosen the wrong son.'

Malus wrestled with Arleth Vann's choking grip, but the assassin's fingers were locked around his throat like a vice. Slowly, remorselessly, Malus's former retainer lowered his sword and placed its point above his master's racing heart. 'I do not know how you gained Khaine's blessing since I last saw you,' Arleth Vann said, 'but whatever piety you may have found here, I know you for the deceiver you truly are. You destroy everything you touch, Malus Darkblade. For the sake of the faith, and for the sake of blessed vengeance, your life ends here.'

Sparks swam in Malus's vision. Desperate, he switched his grip to Arleth Vann's sword wrist, but the blade sank inexorably lower, driven by a ruthless engine of hate. The assassin's words rebounded in the highborn's brain. I served you for years, watching and waiting in secret because I was certain that you were the one.

Arleth Vann's blade pierced his skin. Icy clarity focused the highborn's mind. You know what to do. Act now or die!

'Tz'arkan!' Malus growled under his breath. 'I have need of your strength!'

His body spasmed as his veins burned with a torrent of black ice, driving Malus deeper onto Arleth Vann's blade. A wave of crystalline agony tore a strangled scream from Malus's lips as the bones in his right arm re-knit. The darkness receded as the daemon's energies kindled his vision, and the highborn saw the look of fear and wonder spread across Arleth Vann's face.

Malus put his right hand on Arleth Vann's chest and with a single shove the druchii flew across the small room. The highborn flew upright as if weightless, his limbs burning with foul energies. It tasted like wine on his lips. How had he gone for so many months without the daemon's touch? The power was intoxicating. Malus heard laughter ringing in his ears, and thought it was his own.

He advanced on his former retainer, gliding like smoke across the floor. His eyes were molten, gleaming in the faint light. Malus channelled the daemon's seething power into his voice as he spoke.

'It is you who were deceived, Arleth Vann. Your faith deserted you in your time of trial and you doubted the Blood God's will. I am the Scourge, the anointed son of Khaine, and the Time of Blood is nigh.'

Arleth Vann looked up at Malus and cried out in awe. 'My lord!' he said, abasing himself at the highborn's feet. 'Truly I have failed you. My life is forfeit. Strike me down for my weakness and cast my soul into the Outer Darkness.' He drew a dagger from his belt with a trembling hand and offered it up to the highborn.

The gesture stunned Malus, rendering him speechless. What sort of madness was this religion that it drove men to offer up their lives like lambs? 'Put away your blade,' he snapped. 'I have no use for martyrs, Arleth Vann. If you would redeem yourself, then serve me as you once did, body and soul.'

Arleth Vann straightened, looking up at his master. Tears gleamed like gold in the reflected glow of Malus's blazing eyes. 'I swear it,' he said, 'body and soul, until death's release.' He bowed from the waist, pressing his forehead against the wooden floor.

Malus's eyes narrowed in triumph. Only then did he become aware of the laughter, still echoing within his mind.

'Now you accept your fate, Malus,' Tz'arkan said. 'I knew it was only a matter of time.'

'TELL ME OF the battle,' Malus said, peering out through the narrow window at the twin moons rising on the eastern horizon. 'What happened to you after the attack on my tent?'

Arleth Vann shrugged, the motion eliciting a grimace of pain as he dabbed at the cut oozing blood down the side of his left leg. 'There is not much to tell. The autarii nearly killed me. Had one of those bolts struck a finger's width more to the right it would have pierced my heart,' he said. 'I lost consciousness as I was being dragged from the camp. I awoke later, in a flesh house near the Slavers' Quarter. Silar had arranged for a chirurgeon to tend me, but it was many weeks before I was fully recovered.'

'What became of Silar and the rest?'

'Scattered like ravens, my lord,' Arleth Vann replied. 'They lost nearly everything when word came that you'd slain your father. All that treasure Silar had worked so hard to ferry from Karond Kar fell into Isilvar's hands when he seized your property. The new Vaulkhar was going to have us slain on the next Hanil Khar, but then he learned that you were heading for the city with an army from Naggor at your back. So we were given the chance to regain our honour if we returned to the Hag with your head.'

Malus nodded to himself, tasting bile in the back of his throat. 'I would have done the same, of course. It was by luck alone I survived.'

'We returned empty-handed, but Isilvar grudgingly credited us with causing enough of a diversion that the main attack was carried home successfully,' Arleth Vann said, wrapping a makeshift bandage around his leg. 'So we were given our freedom, such as it was. I think he wanted to seem magnanimous to the court, because he was still trying to win over many of the city's highborn. At any rate, Silar and Dolthaic left for Clar Karond, hoping to sign on with a corsair. Hauclir vanished. For all I know, he's still out there hunting for you.'

The highborn frowned. 'Did Isilvar not think me dead?'

'He said as much, but I doubt he truly believed it. We knew better. Scouts had turned up the body of Bale's only son, but you were nowhere to be found.'

'So how did you find my trail?'

Arleth Vann turned to face Malus, a bemused expression on his face. 'Your trail? I didn't come here looking for you, my lord. Word had spread among the true believers that Urial had appeared in Har Ganeth with the Bride of Ruin. The faithful were commanded to return to the Holy City and stand by his side as he petitioned the temple to perform the Swordbearer's Rite.'

Malus turned and approached the kneeling assassin, considering his words carefully. 'Arleth Vann, you have known me for many years.' He spread his hands and smiled sheepishly. 'You know I was never a worshipper at the temple. It was no accident that Khaine led you to me. I have need of a guide to illuminate the path I'm on.' He knelt beside his retainer. 'What is the Rite of the Swordbearer, and why would the temple be loath to perform it for Urial?'

'The Warpsword of Khaine is bound within ancient, powerful sorceries, wards that can only be undone by a special rite, and only in the presence of the prophesied one,' Arleth Vann said. 'Only the Haru'ann can perform the rite itself, which is why the temple–'

'Wait,' Malus said, raising his hand. 'What is the Haru'ann?'

Arleth Vann looked shocked. 'The Haru'ann is the council of elders that serves the Grand Carnifex,' he said. 'There are five members of the council, each bearing a sacred duty to the temple.'

Malus remembered the blood-witch's words outside the house. *Our Haru'ann is complete, while the temple remains in disarray.* Suddenly he knew what Tyran was planning.

While the temple turned out its warriors for an assault on the houses of the faithful, the zealots were going to sneak into the temple and perform the Swordbearer's Rite themselves, delivering the sword into Urial's hands.

Chapter Nine
CITADEL OF BONE

THE PIECES ALL fell into place. Malus realised that Tyran had manipulated the elders of the temple masterfully. The zealot leader would call on his agents in the temple fortress to admit him and his zealot council while the warriors of Khaine fought the bulk of the true believers in the city streets. There would be nothing to prevent them from reaching the Sanctum of the Sword and performing the Rite of the Swordbearer for Urial.

Malus rose and began to pace the room, considering his next move. 'Where are Tyran and the elders now?' he asked.

Arleth Vann shrugged. 'I don't know, my lord. I brought the elder here and found Tyran waiting for me in the courtyard with a cadre of warriors. They took charge of the elder and left immediately.'

The highborn bared his teeth. 'Likely he's gone to ground somewhere close to the temple, waiting for the right time to make his move, or he could be inside the temple even now, having slipped inside with the returning warriors.' Malus took a deep breath. There was only one viable course of action to take. 'I have to speak to Arch-Hierophant Rhulan,' he said. 'Can you get us inside the temple?'

Arleth Vann cinched the bandage tightly around his leg and eyed Malus with a frown. 'You wish to speak to the blasphemers? Why?'

Malus steeled himself, wondering if what he was about to say would spark off another fight. 'Because we must sound the alarm and stop Tyran and his men before they reach the sanctum.'

The retainer stared at Malus for a long time, his expression unreadable. 'Why would we want to do that?' he asked at last.

'Because Tyran has thrown his lot in with Urial,' Malus replied, 'and my half-brother will stop at nothing to get his hands on the warpsword.'

The assassin shook his head. 'He isn't the chosen one. The rite will not work for him.'

'Do you think that will sway him?' Malus asked. 'He thinks that he stands upon the brink of everlasting glory. He believes Yasmir is his for the taking. When the rite fails he won't fault himself, but Tyran and his council. He believes that he is the prophesied one, and he will stop at nothing to fulfil his ambitions, even if that means destroying the cult in the process.'

Tz'arkan wrapped tightly around his heart, his voice rasping softly in the highborn's ear. 'Speak for yourself,' the daemon hissed.

Arleth Vann considered the highborn's words at length, his expression troubled. Finally, he nodded. 'There is a way,' he said. 'It's known to few people even within the temple, so we should be able to reach Rhulan's chambers unobserved. The path is long, however, and it will take time.'

'Then let's go,' Malus said, eyeing his half-packed possessions and deciding to leave them behind. His truly valuable items – namely the Octagon of Praan, the Idol of Kolkuth and the Dagger of Torxus – were buried in a saddlebag strapped to Spite's back. He could get another bedroll and water bottle later, if need be. Right now, every minute counted.

If they moved quickly they could catch the zealots' leaders all in one place, far from any hope of assistance, and he could hand the temple elders a great victory. In the back of his mind, however, Malus harboured an even more ambitious plan. If he could reach the sanctum as the zealots were performing the rite, his presence would allow it to conclude successfully. Then he could make his own play for the relic, perhaps with the daemon's help.

The highborn smiled grimly as he worked. It would be worth it just to see the look on Urial's face.

ARLETH VANN LED Malus out into the darkened streets, heading south and east away from the fortress. Malus kept pace with his retainer, sword in hand and scanning the streets and alleys with care. The sounds of fighting still echoed in the lower parts of the city, and he could see the flickering glow of fires on the horizon near the warehouse district. Based on what he'd witnessed over the course of the afternoon, when the temple warriors were unleashed on the zealot strongholds around the city, things would spiral rapidly out of control.

The assassin led Malus out of the highborn district, following a zigzag course through twisting lanes that led inexorably down the long hillside. Along the way the pair slipped past armed bands of city dwellers, spattered with dried gore and drunk on bloodlust, in search of more heads to hang from their belts. Each time Arleth Vann slipped silently from one pool of shadow to the next, moving like a ghost past the exhausted druchii.

They moved quickly through the city's entertainment district. The flesh houses were tightly shuttered and many of the ale rooms had been looted over the course of the day. Many of the looted buildings sported piles of fresh, severed heads outside their broken doorways and windows. Malus imagined the proprietors letting the looters drink their fill and then descending on the drunken thieves with clubs and meat cleavers, determined to recoup their loss in flesh if not in coin.

After almost an hour Malus found himself in the lowborn district, near the city's great warehouses and tanneries. The acrid stink of the tanners mixed with the smoke of burning buildings, causing his eyes to water. Malus thought he heard the call of a single trumpet from high up the hill, and imagined the great gates of the temple fortress gaping like a dragon's maw, ready to unleash the temple's wrath upon the city.

He was so focused on the distant sound that he almost walked right into Arleth Vann. The assassin had stopped in a pool of deep shadow a few feet back from the mouth of a narrow alley and was studying a dark, shuttered house across the street. Malus crouched beside the retainer, eyeing the building. To his eyes, it looked very old and decrepit. The witchlamps over the door had long since expired, and at some point in the past one of the three iron balconies had given way, leaving only deep gouges in the stonework where the iron railings had once been. The door, Malus noted, was dark oak, and its iron hinges were thick and free of rust. 'What is this place?' he whispered.

Arleth Vann gave him a sidelong glance. 'This house is the reason why the temple chose Har Ganeth for their own.' He edged forwards and peered carefully up and down the street. 'I see no guards. Perhaps they were caught up in the fighting, or maybe the temple has grown lax over the years.' The assassin shrugged. 'Follow me.'

Moving quickly and quietly, the two druchii slipped across the moonlit street. At the door, Arleth Vann laid his hand on the dark wood and pushed. It slid open noiselessly, revealing abyssal darkness beyond.

Malus shot Arleth Vann a worried look. 'No guards and no locks?'

'No obvious ones,' the assassin replied, 'but the house is tightly warded, my lord. Be assured of that.'

The retainer stepped cautiously into the blackness. Malus followed, apprehension tickling his guts. As he crossed the threshold he felt a prickling sensation along his neck and scalp. Tz'arkan stirred. 'Old magic,' the daemon whispered. 'It tastes of rot and the grave. Be wary, Darkblade.'

Darkness, cold and dank, enveloped Malus. He stopped and waited for a moment, allowing his eyes to adjust. The entry hall of the old house was high ceilinged, like most druchii homes, and three narrow windows allowed only a trickle of moonlight past their grimy panes. Everything appeared to Malus in different shades of night. The ghostly arch of a stairway rose on his right, a fainter shade of black than the ebony surface of the floor. High overhead the perfect vault of shadow was smudged by a grey blob that Malus took to be an ancient witchlamp holder.

Arleth Vann turned back to Malus, his alabaster face hovering in the darkness like a disembodied spirit. 'There is a door at the base of the staircase. We'll follow it into the cellars,' he said, and disappeared into the gloom.

Malus lost sight of the assassin almost at once. Cursing to himself, he focused on the half-seen staircase, crossing the stone floor with care. After a few moments he reached the base of the stairs and worked his way along the wall until he almost bumped into Arleth Vann's nearly invisible form. Malus heard the creak of a door, and felt a gust of colder, wetter air against his cheek. He wrinkled his nose at the smell of damp earth and old rot. The doorway itself was a pool of darker shadow against the iron-grey of the wall. He sensed rather than saw Arleth Vann slip inside, and moved quickly in his wake.

Without warning, Malus's eyes were dazzled by an explosion of pale green light. He hissed a curse, trying to shield his eyes from the small globe of witchlight that burned in the palm of Arleth Vann's upraised hand.

'I never knew you were a sorcerer!' Malus exclaimed, blinking in surprise.

Arleth Vann shrugged. 'The temple teaches its assassins a few simple cantrips: how to make light, how to silence rusty hinges, things of that nature. Nothing like the knowledge possessed by someone such as Urial.'

They were in a narrow, enclosed stairway that led down to another ironbound door. Arleth Vann descended slowly, testing each of the stone steps with a tentative boot before proceeding. 'One of these steps activates a poison trap,' he muttered, 'so follow my moves exactly.'

'You seem to know a great deal about this place,' Malus said, attempting to follow in the assassin's footsteps.

Arleth Vann shrugged. 'This was how I escaped the temple, many years ago.' He paused at the third step from the bottom, testing the riser carefully with the point of his boot. 'This is the one,' he said, stepping carefully over the trap and continuing to the door. There was a grating of metal as he turned the iron ring and pushed it open, letting in a blast of frigid air that sank right into Malus's bones.

The doorway opened onto a stone landing lit by a flickering green glow. The assassin doused his witchlight and stepped through the doorway. Malus followed close behind Arleth Vann, watching his breath turn to vapour in the chill air. His boots skidded on the dark stones, which were rimed with glittering frost. Arleth Vann caught his arm at once, helping his master steady himself. 'Careful, my lord,' he said quietly. 'You wouldn't want to take a fall right here.'

Malus steadied himself and looked around. The landing was barely three paces square and looked out over a cavernous space at least thirty feet deep. From where he stood he could see that the upper half of the space was square shaped and bounded with finished stone blocks. Another narrow staircase descended from the landing, following the rough wall towards the chamber floor. The source of the light came from below, radiating upwards in a flickering, ghostly nimbus.

Malus freed his arm from his retainer's grip and carefully approached the edge of the landing. Below, he saw a wide ribbon of dark, glossy stone, wide enough for four men to walk abreast, leading to a tall archway set into the side of the great hill. The archway was at least fifteen feet tall at its apex, and appeared to be formed from huge, polished bones the likes of which he'd never seen before. It looked as if arch and roadway had been excavated from the cold earth. The piles of rock and soil cleared from the path formed raised banks to either side of the road, packed down to rock-like hardness over the passage of centuries. Four iron spikes, each twelve feet long, had been driven into both banks alongside the road, making a rough octagon pattern with the roadway passing through its centre.

Corpses were impaled on each of the iron spikes, their dark, shrivelled bodies stacked one on top of the other so that Malus couldn't tell for certain where one body ended and the next began. They had all been bound hand and foot, their limbs twisted in the throes of long, agonising deaths. They had hung from the iron spikes for a very long time, and colonies of grave mould covered the corpses, emitting the pale light that filled the eerie space.

Malus glanced in wonder at Arleth Vann. 'What is this place?'

'Hundreds of years ago, when the city was first founded, a druchii named Cyrvan Thel built this house,' the assassin said in a hushed voice. 'Several years after the building was complete, Thel decided to add a lower level for a wine cellar, and the workers uncovered the roadway. The paving stones resisted every attempt to remove them, including sorcery, so Thel ordered the workmen to follow their course and see how far they went. That was how they came upon the archway. When the workers broke through into the tunnel beyond a breath of foul wind rushed out that killed them in an instant. Thel, being a devout man, took this as an omen. When the air had cleared enough for a slave to survive without ill effects, Thel and a handful of retainers entered the tunnel to see where it led.'

'And what did they find?'

'The Vermillion Gate,' the assassin replied. He pointed to the arch. 'The passage leads deep into the heart of the hill, to a circular chamber that might sink all the way to the heart of the world itself. A flat-topped spire rises in the centre of that chamber, spanned by a bridge of ancient bone, and on top of that spire sits the dreadful gate. No one knows who built it or why, but it is old beyond all reckoning.' He turned to Malus, a fearful look in his eyes. 'It leads to the very heart of the Lord of Murder's realm.'

The highborn was taken aback. 'Khaine is a druchii god. How can that be, if the gate was made in a time before Nagarythe was lost?'

Arleth Vann spread his hands. 'Thel looked upon the gate and thought it had been set here in anticipation of our coming, a gift from the Blood God to his chosen people. He took word of his discovery to the elders of the cult, and they came from across Naggaroth to look upon the gate. When they beheld it for the first time, they knew that from that moment forwards the hill and everything upon it must belong to the cult. Shortly after, the Witch King gave Har Ganeth to the temple of Khaine.'

Malus stared at the archway of bone and a feeling of dread turned his guts to ice. 'Urial spoke of the Vermillion Gate,' he said, 'on the way back from the Isle of Morhaut. He used it to reach Har Ganeth.'

The assassin nodded thoughtfully, as if the highborn had answered a worrying riddle. 'Some of the texts in the temple library claim that a true disciple of Khaine can call upon the power of the gate no matter where in the world he may be. He can reach the cavern beneath the hill in a single stride, if he makes the proper offerings. Spirits guard the gate from the unworthy, and if they are not provided for they will exact a terrible price from those who cross the threshold.'

'He rewarded them amply,' Malus growled, thinking of the slaughter on the main deck of the battered corsair, 'and from what little I saw he timed his crossing so that there was a crowd of worshippers waiting on the other side.'

The assassin shrugged. 'Every new moon the temple elders gather at the gate to perform sacred ceremonies of veneration. If Urial had emerged from the gate – with Yasmir in tow, no less – it would have seemed most portentous indeed.' He turned and headed for the narrow staircase leading to the cavern floor.

Malus followed warily, picking his way across the landing and then down the long flight of stairs. The risers glittered with frost. When he reached out a hand to steady himself along the wall he found that it was covered in a thin layer of ice.

Malus felt a prickling along his skin as they made their slow descent. The chamber was thick with sorcerous energies.

The highborn cleared his throat. 'About Urial–' he began.

Arleth Vann cut him off with an upraised hand. 'Quiet,' he said, his voice barely a whisper, 'we are about to pass the guardians.'

The stairway ended at the edge of the roadway. Up close, Malus saw that the stones of the dark path were like blocks of obsidian, polished to a mirror hue. It looked as if every stone had a flaw to it: a faint, pale smudge in each stone's centre. When he bent a little closer, however, he saw that it wasn't a blemish on the surface: there was something within each of the stones. The shapes were blurry, but there was just enough play of light and shadow for the objects to take on the quality of living faces.

Puzzled, Malus started to bend even closer, but the daemon's voice rasped in his ear. 'If you value your sanity, mortal, look no further,' Tz'arkan said coldly. 'There are some things no druchii – not even you – were meant to know.'

The highborn straightened with a start. Arleth Vann was already some distance away, approaching the first of the iron poles with his head bowed and his hands tucked into his robes.

Malus moved as quickly as he dared, hurriedly following suit just as the assassin reached the first set of poles. Suddenly a chorus of thin wails filled the air, rising piteously from the blackened mouths of the bound corpses.

A thrill of terror coursed down Malus's spine. He had heard that sound once before, in the depths of Urial's tower.

The highborn glanced fearfully at the pole to his right. Pale mist was leaking from the slack jaws and gaping eye sockets of the impaled figures. The tendrils danced and wove about in a spectral wind, taking the shape of pale, spindly figures with long fingers and emaciated faces. Their eyes were orbs of purest jet, soulless and cruel. 'The maelithii!' Malus breathed.

'Be not afraid,' Arleth Vann hissed. 'Avert your eyes and walk the ancient path. They are bound to do no harm to those who bear the blessings of Khaine.'

Malus averted his eyes, focusing on the black stones at his feet. They would not be fooled by his magically altered eyes.

He imagined the maelithii swarming over him, sinking their black fangs into his flesh and feasting on his life force. When they were finished with him his skin would be the colour of a deep bruise, the blue-black of a corpse lost for months in the snow.

The vengeful spirits whistled and howled above Malus's head, drawing ever nearer. His legs began to tremble. There was no way to fight these spirits: swords passed straight through them and left the arm numb and frozen to boot. He fought the urge to turn and run for the staircase, wondering how much further he was from the archway.

One of the maelithii let out a shrill cry and swooped close enough to Malus for him to feel veins of frost spreading through his black hair. Other maeliths began a cacophony of wailing in reply. They've found me out, he thought!

Malus felt a needle of ice pierce his cheek, and just as swiftly he felt the daemon uncoil in his chest like a startled viper. Tz'arkan howled a challenge at the maelithii that set Malus's teeth on edge and the baleful spirits withdrew, wailing plaintively.

The highborn quickened his pace, not caring if he trampled Arleth Vann in the process. The sounds of the maelithii receded behind him with every step. Then without warning he was surrounded in a flare of witchlight. When Malus looked up he found himself standing beside his retainer, just past the tall arch of polished bone.

Arleth Vann was looking back the way they'd come, eyeing the eight maelithii circling above the centre of the octagon. 'They seemed interested in you for some reason,' he told Malus, 'and then they cried out in fear. I've never heard the like.'

Malus looked back at the tormented spirits. 'They tried to claim something that belongs to another,' he said grimly.

The assassin frowned. 'I don't understand.'

'Count yourself fortunate,' Malus replied. He gestured down the dark passage. 'Let's go.'

* * *

THE PASSAGE SEEMED to go on forever. Arleth Vann's witchlight just barely reached the rounded walls to either side. To Malus's eyes they appeared to be made of dark, grainy stone, like granite, but worked in loops and strands as if the tunnel had been woven out of the stone rather than carved. He couldn't fathom how such a thing had been done, much less why. The strange patterns created many corners, niches and crevices among the coarse weave of the stonework, and over the centuries the worshippers of Khaine had filled those recesses with offerings to their god. Skulls by the thousand leered at the two druchii as they went deeper into the hill. Skeletal hands seemed to reach for them in the flickering aura of the witchlight. Malus saw leg bones and vertebrae, ribs and shoulder blades, all arranged to blend almost seamlessly with the fluid lines of the stonework. The dead pressed in on Malus from every side, setting his heart to race. He tried to focus on something else, and remembered the question he'd started to ask outside the archway.

'Why doesn't the temple want Urial to have the sword?'

Arleth Vann paused, turning to look back at his master with a rueful grin. 'Had you ever taken an interest in religion, my lord, you wouldn't have to ask such a question,' he replied. 'As far as the temple is concerned, they've already given the sword to another.'

'Another!' Malus exclaimed. 'Who?'

The assassin shook his head. 'Who else? Malekith, of course.'

'They think Malekith is the Scourge? How can this be?'

To Malus's surprise, Arleth Vann threw back his head and laughed. 'As clever a man as you are, my lord, I'm amazed you'd have to ask such a question. How do you think the temple of Khaine came to exist?'

Malus frowned. He didn't much care for the assassin's patronising tone. 'Malekith used the cult to consolidate his rule after Nagarythe was lost,' he snapped. 'They had every reason to hate most of the old houses, who worshipped Slaanesh and had persecuted them for hundreds of years. Malekith raised them up, made them the state religion, and in return they helped him break the power of the warlocks and assassinate any rivals to his throne.'

Arleth Vann nodded. 'Just so, my lord, but you must understand that the cult in those days was not like the temple as it is now. When you think of the temple, you envision people like your half-brother Urial, but back then they were true believers like Tyran. They were utterly devout, dedicated to the pure teachings of the Lord of Murder and the heirs of centuries of persecution.'

'They were fanatics,' Malus said, 'and I suppose they cared little for Malekith or his power plays.'

The retainer gave one of his rare smiles. 'Now you begin to see. The elders of the cult saw much to gain in Malekith's offer, however – power, legitimacy, wealth and influence – but they had to find a way to convince their followers that the alliance served the will of the Blood God.'

'So they claimed Malekith was Khaine's Scourge.'

'Indeed. For almost as long as the druchii have lingered in Naggaroth the temple has taught its followers that Malekith is their unquestioned master because he is the chosen Scourge of Khaine. When the time is right he will come to Har Ganeth and wed the Bride of Ruin. Then he will take up the Warpsword of Khaine and usher in the Time of Blood. Anything else is heresy.'

Chapter Ten
FAITH AND MURDER

MALUS STARED DUMBFOUNDED at his retainer. 'You mean to tell me that all of this is built on a lie? The temple followers sold out their faith for the sake of political favour?'

Arleth Vann nodded. 'Does this trouble you?'

The highborn cocked his head thoughtfully. 'Actually, it's rather reassuring. These motives at least make sense to me, but clearly not all of the faithful believed the elders' pronouncement.'

'No,' the retainer said. 'The elders built a compelling case, of course, pointing to numerous obscure prophesies that seemed to support their claim. A devious mind can make the words of an oracle fit anything he wants if he tries hard enough, but it wasn't enough. Several cult leaders and their disciples saw through the elders' arguments and refused to take part in the alliance, regardless of the benefits. The debates raged for years, but the nascent temple continued to grow and gain legitimacy. Finally, the true believers saw that their power was waning fast. If they didn't act soon, the elders and their blasphemy would be too deeply rooted to eliminate.'

'So they fought.'

The assassin nodded. 'They fought. At the culmination of a weeklong holy festival – the Draich na Anlar – the schism leaders gathered their followers and attacked the elders in the midst of their consecrations. Somehow, the attempt failed. Some scholars suggest that the schism leaders were betrayed, while others point to divine intervention. At any rate, the five true believers that entered the temple to kill the blasphemous elders were never seen or heard from again. Other confrontations across the city degenerated into a chaotic riot that killed thousands. Fighting raged through the city streets all through the night, and by daybreak the White City was stained with rivers of blood. Afterwards the temple elders tore the city apart looking for the schism leaders and their allies, dragging those they found into the street and decapitating them on the spot. This is how Har Ganeth came to be known as the City of Executioners.'

'And the survivors?'

Arleth Vann shrugged. 'They fled the city, spreading out all across Naggaroth and beyond to keep the true faith alive. They knew that one day the true Scourge would appear, and there would be another day of reckoning with the blasphemers.'

'So the zealots returned to their roots, worshipping in secret as they'd been doing since time out of mind.'

The assassin nodded, resuming his course down the long tunnel. 'It was the proper way, regardless. Khaine is not meant to be worshipped in a temple, but on the battlefield or by the side of the road. We are exalted by testing our strength against others and taking their lives with skill and daring.'

Malus fell into step behind his retainer, thinking back to the constant training and superlative skill of the zealots. 'So Khaine is actually a god of combat?'

'No, he is a god of death,' Arleth Vann replied. 'What is the greatest power a man can have in this world?'

Malus shrugged. 'The power of a king.'

The assassin let out a snort. 'A king can die on the field of battle like anyone else. Think again.'

'Damned sorcery, then.'

The retainer shook his head. 'No, it is simpler than that. The greatest power in this world is the ability to end life. The one thing every man shares, whether he is a slave or the Witch King himself, is a beating heart. The power to stop that heartbeat in a single stroke is what brings us closer to Khaine. We become gods, holding the lives of those around us in the palms of our hands. Do you see?'

'I believe so,' Malus said. 'That is the purpose of the executioners, I suppose?'

The assassin nodded. 'In the days before the temple, every worshipper of Khaine was an executioner: a Sword of Khaine. The true believer killed his opponents with a single, perfect stroke, making it a gesture of worship and enhancing his power with every foe he slew in battle. It was only after the temple was founded and the elders required acolytes to devote themselves to sinful practices like tithe collection that the executioners became an isolated sect.'

'And the temple witches?'

Arleth Vann cast a sidelong glance over his shoulder at Malus. 'They suffered the worst degradations of all. Once, they were Khaine's bloody oracles and the enforcers of the Blood God's divine will. They had the power to summon back the souls of the fallen and partake of their powers. And now? Now they are degenerates, aping the glories of their forebears with drugs and pitiful necromancies. You have seen true blood-witches, my lord. Can the witches of the temple compare to their terrible majesty?'

'No,' Malus admitted, 'certainly not. So what happened?'

The assassin shrugged. 'The blood-witches tried to stay apart from the fray during the early years of the schism. The brides of Khaine did not concern themselves with such petty conflicts. After the true believers were driven from the city and the elders hemmed the rest of the cult into temples, their prestige gradually diminished. There hasn't been a true blood-witch serving the temple for at least two thousand years.'

As they walked, Malus began to notice narrow doorways cut into the ropy stonework of the tunnel walls. The door-frames were made of glossy white marble and carved with intricate runes in archaic druchast. Next to the strangely flowing weave of the walls the newer construction still seemed crude and awkward by comparison. 'What are these?' he asked.

'Those? They are tombs,' the retainer said. 'The temple has always interred the faithful, despite the Witch King's edict of cremation. Perhaps the elders venerate the spirits of the dead in the hope they will intercede on their behalf when Khaine returns in his wrath.' He gestured at the doorways with a sweep of his free hand. 'The entire hill is honey-combed with tomb complexes, and they reach far into the earth.'

The two druchii walked on in silence for a time, journeying down the dark road past the doorways of the dead. Some quality of the stone swallowed their footsteps, and for a while it felt as if they had left the physical world behind, trudging like ghosts through some forgotten underworld. Malus considered the implications of everything Arleth Vann had told him. It did go a long way towards explaining the temple's odd behaviour... but his mind kept drifting back to his meeting with Rhulan, and the wary look on the elder's face. *Urial's claim casts the entire history of the temple into doubt,* the highborn thought, *which was ample reason to keep him in seclusion and look for a way to silence him. However, that would be self-evident to anyone familiar with temple dictum. There's something more going on here,* he thought. *The elders have a secret that no one, not even the zealots, suspect.*

Arleth Vann stopped. Malus looked around and saw that they had reached a point where two curving stairways – one ascending, the other descending – were carved into the living rock to either side of the dark road. 'We'll go no further into the hill. The Vermillion Gate is close by, and it is always well-guarded by a cadre of witches and executioners.'

He pointed to the climbing stairway. 'Here is where the journey becomes difficult.'

Malus eyed the staircase. 'More spirit wards?'

Arleth Vann shook his head. 'No. Just hundreds and hundreds of stairs.'

MALUS LOST ALL track of time as they trudged up the winding stairway. The journey passed as a blur of echoing steps and shadowy landings that opened onto ancient galleries and maze-like passageways leading to mouldy tombs. The temple hill was a labyrinth vaster and more convoluted than anything he had ever seen; even the tower of the mad sorcerer Eradorius seemed smaller and less complicated by comparison. The highborn mused between gasps for breath that crossing paths with Arleth Vann had turned out to be a great boon. Alone he might have been fumbling about the hill and its passageways until the seas ran dry. He breathed the dry, dusty pall of bone dust at every turn, as centuries of temple servants rotted to dust in the niches and alcoves beneath the great temple. The dust made his nose itch and left the taste of the grave in the back of his throat.

At last, they emerged into a well-lit chamber glowing with the green fire of witchlamps. They were in a large space with low, vaulted ceilings, practically an underground plaza compared to the tight passageways and the narrow, enclosed staircase they'd travelled. Malus fought the urge to rub the ache from his trembling legs. 'Where are we?' he asked quietly.

'We're in the vaults beneath the temple proper,' Arleth Vann replied, eyeing the many passageways leading off from the chamber. 'From here we can reach almost every major building within the fortress, including the elders' private chambers.'

Malus nodded, gritting his teeth against the burning ache flaring from his knees. 'All right. Where are we likely to find Rhulan at this point?'

'When the elders are not conducting their rites, they typically retire to their chambers,' the assassin replied. 'No doubt to reflect on matters of the faith,' he said with a sneer.

'Yes, but this is no typical night. An elder has deserted the temple. The story on the street might be that the man was kidnapped, but I imagine the rest of the elders know the truth of the matter. Their warriors have taken to the streets to fight the true believers, and their sacred council remains broken. Where do the elders normally go when they meet in conclave?'

'The council chambers within the Citadel of Bone,' Arleth Vann replied, 'but if the elders are meeting there they will be well-guarded.'

'I thought the temple assassins were supposed to be invisible,' the highborn snapped.

'When the situation demands,' the retainer answered coolly. 'Can my lord say the same?'

Malus gave the man a hard stare. 'Just get us as close as you can. We'll improvise from there.'

'You mean we'll kill whoever gets in our way.'

'That is what I said, yes.'

Arleth Vann gave another of his ghostly smiles. 'It is good to know some things never change. Follow me, my lord.'

THE ASSASSIN QUICKLY led Malus out of the well-lit tunnels beneath the temple and into noisome passageways dripping with slime and tangled with dense layers of cobwebs. He made no effort to relight his sorcerous lamp, forcing Malus to crouch low and follow the almost undetectable sound of the retainer's footfalls. From time to time their path crossed better-travelled corridors, and once or twice the highborn caught snatches of whispered conversations as the servants of the temple went about their nightly tasks. Each time, Arleth Vann would pause at the junction and listen for several moments, gauging the servants' movements, before darting silently across the passageway into the darkened tunnel mouth opposite. Malus felt like a rat inside the walls of some vast city house, scuttling from shadow to shadow to avoid the master's house serpents.

After nearly half an hour, Arleth Vann stopped a few feet shy of the end of the passage and drew his twin blades. He turned to Malus. 'From here on out, I go ahead,' the assassin whispered. 'Wait three minutes and then follow after me.'

Malus frowned. 'Three minutes? How will I know where you've gone?'

The assassin looked at Malus over his shoulder. 'Look for the trail of bodies,' he said in a hard voice. Then he stepped out of the corridor and slipped off to the right.

Malus drew his own sword. His limbs felt leaden after the long climb through the heart of the hill, and the prospect of more fighting filled him with a weary kind of dread. I should drink of the daemon's power, he thought. Just a little, to lend me strength and take away this damned fatigue.

No sooner had the thought occurred to him than a wave of trembling wracked his body. His insides twisted with need as he thought about the glorious, icy vitality of the daemon's power. 'Mother of Night!' he breathed, dropping to one knee. The hunger felt bottomless, and his mind recoiled in terror from it.

It was several minutes before the trembling passed, leaving Malus feeling even weaker than before. His face and neck were bathed in cold sweat, and his guts felt tied in knots. The highborn clenched his sword tightly, focusing on the strain of his knuckles and the hard weight of the sword hilt digging into his palm. With an effort of will, he forced himself back onto his feet. A terrible sense of foreboding pressed down upon him. Had the daemon's recent silence been nothing more than the infinite patience of a predator, knowing its prey was but a single step away from ruin? Blessed mother, have I gone too far, Malus thought? Am I now beholden to the daemon, body and soul?

The daemon slithered across his ribs. 'Are you unwell, Malus?' Tz'arkan's voice slid into his ears like sweet poison. 'The temple elders await. Do you wish my aid?'

Yes, Malus thought. He bit his lips to keep the words from slipping past them. His mind roiled with horror and revulsion. Another wave of trembling passed through his taut frame.

'Come now, don't be proud,' the daemon whispered. 'I can feel your weakness, little druchii, your need. If you go before the elders like this they will see how weak you are. Let me make you strong again.'

Malus tasted blood on his tongue. He bit deeper into his torn lip, letting the pain kindle the fires of his hate. With hate all things are possible, he told himself. 'I... want nothing from you,' he gasped, sending a trickle of blood coursing down his chin. 'Nothing, you hear?'

The daemon chuckled, his manner smug and easy. 'That's an easy thing to say when you're alone and in the dark,' Tz'arkan said. 'You have no idea how pitiful you look. If the elders see you like this they will laugh in your face. Is that what you really want?'

Growling like a wounded beast, Malus forced his body to move: one step, and then another. Hate seethed in his heart, a weak fire compared to the icy torrent of the daemon's power, but it propelled him nonetheless. He bared red-stained teeth and spat onto the stone floor. 'They will see what I choose to show them,' the highborn said, feeling a little of his old strength return, 'nothing more or less.'

'Of course,' the daemon said in a patronising tone. 'I should have guessed you'd say such a thing. Perhaps you can manage a little longer without my help, but mark me: there will come a time very soon when you will find yourself in dire need of my power. Ask, and it will be yours.'

Malus staggered from the dark passageway, blinking owlishly in the light of the corridor beyond. Not ten feet to the right a temple servant lay on his face in a pool of spreading blood. The man had died without the slightest sound.

The highborn drew a shuddering breath, horrified that suddenly he felt unequal to the task before him. He'd thought he'd gained the upper hand over Tz'arkan, and the whole time the daemon had simply bided its time, like a spider sitting in the centre of its invisible web.

All is not lost just yet, the highborn thought. I still live. I still have my sword and my mother's ring; and my hate, always my hate. Dark Mother, let that be enough!

Licking bitter blood from his lips, Malus set off in the assassin's wake.

ARLETH VANN WAS true to his word. The assassin left a trail of slaughter that a blind man could have followed. Malus passed more than a dozen temple servants in corridors and at junctions, each laid out on the floor as if slain in mid-stride. At one point he passed a trio of corpses propping one another upright, and Malus was struck with the image of the pale-faced assassin weaving his way through the close knit group and slaying them so quickly that they fell almost as one. The man's supernal skill filled Malus with admiration even as it reminded him of his own wretched state.

Finally Malus found himself at the end of a long corridor built from pale marble that glowed beneath globes of witch-light. An open doorway waited at the other end, beyond a pile of armoured guards. The highborn picked his way through the tangle of steel-clad bodies, his boots making tacky sounds as he crossed an enormous puddle of congealing blood.

Beyond lay a narrow chamber, dominated by a short ramp that led upwards to a large, echoing chamber. Arleth Vann waited at the base of the ramp, surrounded by half a dozen dead servants. The assassin was pausing to clean his twin blades with a cloth rag appropriated from one of the corpses. His pale face was spotted with blood and eerily serene. The roar of scores of angry voices rolled down the stone ramp from the chamber beyond, washing over Malus in seething waves.

'Where... where are we?' Malus stammered, raising his voice to be heard above the cacophony.

'Just beneath the council chamber,' Arleth Vann replied. 'This is the room where they remove claimants who fail to persuade their case before the council.'

At that moment a projectile hit the top of the ramp with a wet thud and bounced down the slope past the assassin. Malus caught the furious expression on the face of the severed head as it rolled across the floor.

The retainer looked up from his work. 'Are you well, my lord? You look–'

'I expect I look as if I'd crawled from a tomb, considering the route you took us through,' Malus snapped. 'It's a wonder I can see after all the webs I walked into.' He looked down at the grisly trophy and gave it a savage kick. The spiteful gesture heartened him a little. 'I'm fine,' he said, injecting a touch of steel into his voice, 'merely vexed at the foolishness of priests.' Without another word he moved past his retainer and climbed the ramp, his sword held at his side.

For a moment Malus was certain Arleth Vann had led him wrong. He found himself near the point of an oval chamber, ringed by a gallery that rose in tiers for at least twenty feet. Men and women crowded the tiers shouting and shaking their fists at the brawl that raged on the chamber's floor. The air stank of blood and shook with the inchoate thunder of an arena in the city's entertainment district. Not ten yards from where Malus stood more than a score of druchii pushed, pummelled and slashed at one another. At the centre of the fight two older men grappled with each other, their faces twisted with bestial hate. Broad bladed knives trembled in their white knuckled fists as they wrestled for the advantage. Each man wore rich, red robes and kheitans of fine leather studded with gold and precious stones. Their retainers were only slightly less bedecked themselves, their struggles having left a fortune in gilt and gems scattered across the marble floor. Wounded men stumbled or crawled away from the raging fight, clutching at their wounds and screaming encouragement to their respective sides. A handful of corpses lay forgotten underfoot.

Malus looked up at the gallery, realising that the shouting throng was made up of still more richly attired elders and their servants. Six large thrones were set around the perimeter of the chamber at the lowest gallery tier. Three of the seats were empty, although they were surrounded by elders and their retinues like hounds standing over a freshly killed deer. At the apex of the oval chamber, in a throne that surpassed all the rest in size and extravagance, sat an ancient druchii in vestments of hammered brass inlaid with diamonds and rubies. A mask of gold worked in the shape of a leering skull concealed his features, but his gnarled fists shook as he leaned forwards in his chair, shouting encouragements or curses upon the men fighting below. Malus caught sight of Rhulan sitting on the throne to the elder druchii's right. Of all the assembled elders, he seemed least interested in the fight. A gold mask lay in his hand as he leaned to one side and conferred with one of his followers.

The highborn looked over at Arleth Vann, who emerged from the ramp behind Malus. 'This is how the temple council conducts its affairs?' he shouted.

Arleth Vann shrugged. 'You must admit it's more entertaining than any drachau's court,' he shouted back.

The highborn shook his head irritably. 'To the Outer Darkness with this,' he snarled. He pointed at the reeling brawl. 'Make me a hole,' he said to the assassin.

Arleth Vann nodded grimly, raising his short blades. He glided swiftly towards the fight with Malus close behind and cut his way through the crowd like a thresher harvesting grain. Men fell away to either side, struck down by the assassin's flickering blades, and the rest recoiled in shock from the sudden assault. Within moments Malus reached the battling elders, each man lost in his own single-minded struggle. The assassin stepped aside with a bow. Malus walked up to the two men and swung his heavy blade, decapitating both elders in a single stroke.

Blood erupted in a bright fountain from the two slain men, their bodies falling against one another in a grisly embrace. The severed heads bounced audibly on the stone floor in the sudden, shocked silence.

Gore dripping from his blade, Malus turned, regarding the assembled elders with cold, brass eyes. 'Now that I have your attention,' he said, his voice echoing in the council chamber, 'I've come to bring a warning to the council. You must sound the call to arms and hurry to the Sanctum of the Sword. While you squabble here like dogs over a corpse, Urial and his supporters are closing their hands around the Warpsword of Khaine.'

Murmurs of shock and snarls of derision echoed from the assembly. At the far end of the chamber the Grand Carnifex of the temple rose portentously to his feet. To his right, the Arch-Hierophant turned pale, his dark eyes shifting from Malus to the leader of the temple and back again.

The Grand Carnifex's voice was a liquid rasp, bubbling up from old lungs thick with corruption. 'Who are you?' he said, his words carrying across the chamber in spite of the mask he wore.

'A servant of Khaine,' Malus answered. 'A man with a dire warning, and beyond that, what does it matter? Your enemies are on the verge of destroying you, Grand Carnifex: you and this house your predecessors have built. Will you act, or shall we sit here and waste precious time with introductions?'

The entire chamber resounded with a single intake of breath as the audience recoiled in shock at Malus's words. Steel rang as swords leapt from gilt scabbards, and a number of the temple elders barked at their retainers to make a way for them to reach the chamber floor. Then Rhulan leapt to his feet, calling out in a carrying voice. 'How do you know this?' he asked, looking meaningfully at Malus.

The highborn met the elder's gaze and nodded respectfully. 'Because I have spent the last four days at the feet of Tyran the Unscarred, the leader of the zealots who oppose you,' he answered. 'I have sat in their councils, and I know that they have agents within the temple itself.' He surveyed the outraged elders coldly. 'They have been in close contact with Urial since the moment they entered the city and everything they have done has been in preparation for this very night.' He raised his bloodstained sword and pointed at each of the empty thrones in turn. 'Do you think this was all some sort of accident? A stroke of cruel luck? No. They struck directly at the Haru'ann, sowing confusion and discord while they formed a learned council of their own. Now, with all your warriors pounding at the gates of empty houses across the city, they have slipped inside the temple and are performing the Rite of the Sword-bearer even as we speak!'

'Let them!' A woman shouted. Her voice was an angry rasp, cutting jaggedly through the tense atmosphere. Malus saw a young priestess in the third tier of the gallery face the Grand Carnifex. 'We know Urial is not the Scourge. The ritual will fail, and we will have the opportunity we've been waiting for to denounce him!'

'If the rite fails the heretics will find fault in the men per-forming the rite, not in their would-be saviour,' Malus shot back. 'This can only end in death,' he snarled, looking to the Grand Carnifex. 'You know this.'

'I say this is the work of the heretics!' said an older druchii to Malus's left, leaning over the first tier railing and pointing a long finger at Malus. 'They've already sent assassins against us once. Perhaps they sent this loudmouth to draw us to the sanc-tum so they could slay us all!'

Malus gave the elder a cold stare. 'If you fear for your life, elder, then by all means run and cower beneath your over-stuffed bed.' He met the Grand Carnifex's dark gaze. 'This is a matter for warriors.'

'This is nothing of the sort!' snapped the young priestess. 'If this is true, the zealots have handed us an opportunity! Let them try to complete their ritual. When it fails they will return to their followers and fall upon one another, looking for someone to blame. This crisis can solve itself in a single stroke.'

Malus watched the Grand Carnifex glance at the priestess, and for a brief moment he caught a flicker of uncertainty in the ancient druchii's eyes. He is afraid, Malus thought with a start.

'I have heard enough,' the Grand Carnifex declared. 'Sum-mon the guards. We will march to the sanctum and offer prayers to the Lord of Murder for a bloody deliverance from the works of heretics.' He held out his hand and a retainer appeared from behind the tall throne to press a huge, rune carved axe into the Carnifex's palm. 'If there are trespassers within the sanctum we will offer them up as sacrifices to our lord.'

The Grand Carnifex rose to his feet. Ropy tendons stood out taut as steel wires beneath the skin of the elder's neck and arms as he levelled the axe at Malus. 'If not, I will strike off your head and pour your blood upon the sacred stone,' he declared. 'As you said, stranger, this can only end in death.'

Chapter Eleven
WARPSWORD

THE SKY OVER Har Ganeth was the colour of blood as the doors to the Citadel of Bone yawned open and Malus followed the elders of the temple into the battle torn night. More buildings were burning in the city below, sending towering plumes of cinders into the sky, and the air reverberated with the distant clash of arms. Malus knew that the streets would be choked with corpses come the dawn, but the madness and slaughter in the city was nothing more than a mummer's show. The true battle would be fought between a few score men and women within the towering structure barely thirty yards from the council chambers.

Witchlight globes swung from long, iron poles as a vanguard of temple executioners led the way, their bared blades glittering coldly as they fanned out into the deserted lane outside the gleaming citadel. Behind them came the temple elders, led by the Grand Carnifex in his grinning skull mask. The remaining officials and their retainers jockeyed for position behind their leader, brandishing broad knives and ornamented axes at the prospect of reaping fresh skulls for their hungry god.

All except for Rhulan. The narrow-faced elder had dutifully slipped on his skull mask, but let the mob sweep past him until he fell in among the guards escorting Malus and Arleth Vann. The executioner escort eyed Rhulan curiously as he paced along beside the highborn, but made no move to intervene.

'Why didn't you warn me?' the elder hissed. Unlike the Carnifex, his voice was muffled beneath the weight of his mask.

'There was no time,' Malus replied. 'The zealot leaders guarded their plans with care. No one was told until late this evening.'

Rhulan said nothing for a moment, staring into the night. Then the death's head turned back to Malus. 'If Tyran and his lieutenants die tonight, then their agents must be slain as well. We must sweep them all up in a single stroke. You understand?'

I understand that our arrangement is at an end, Malus thought grimly. 'I suspected as much,' he said coldly. It was unavoidable. Tyran had forced his hand, just as he'd forced the elders' hand.

If Tyran and Urial were stopped, Rhulan would force him to reveal what he knew about their network within the temple. Once they realised he was bluffing, he was finished.

Malus eyed the white stone of the temple rearing into the flame-shot sky like an upraised blade and thought he could sense the sorcery at work within. Somehow, in the midst of battle, he would have to make his move.

'Once you have the sword, what then?' the daemon whispered. 'Will you cut your way through the elders of the temple and into the city beyond?'

'First things first,' muttered Malus. Rhulan shook his head, thinking the words were meant for him.

'Fear not,' the elder said. 'However many agents this Tyran has, he could not have slipped into the temple undetected with more than a token force. There are nearly a hundred of us. We can bury the heretics in bodies if we have to. The zealot uprising ends tonight.'

'And Urial?' Malus asked. 'Surely you knew he would attempt this, sooner or later. The temple thought he was marked by Khaine from the moment he emerged from the sacrificial cauldron.'

'We knew nothing of the sort,' the elder snapped. 'Yes, clearly he was blessed by the Lord of Murder, but none of the witches could divine his destiny. Certainly no one believed that Khaine would anoint a cripple as his Scourge. His ambition has got the better of him.'

The highborn cocked his head at the quaver in Rhulan's voice. He studied the elder with narrowed eyes. 'You aren't so sure.'

'Do not presume,' Rhulan said archly. 'You heard me. He is a cripple. It's inconceivable that he could be Khaine's chosen one.'

'Then why do you sound so afraid?'

Just then a howl of challenge, fierce and joyous, rang out from the front of the great temple. 'Weep, unbelievers, for the great reckoning is at hand! The faithful stand in the presence of the sword and the Time of Blood draws nigh! Your wickedness will soon be revealed for all the people to witness, but see the gift of Khaine's mercy we bear in our hands. Come and redeem yourselves on our hungry blades!'

The procession of elders stumbled to a halt in a welter of angry shouts and bellowed curses. Seeing his chance, Malus nodded his head at Arleth Vann and quickened his pace, diving into the milling press of the elders and working his way towards the Grand Carnifex. Rhulan shouted something that Malus didn't catch. Then there was a rush of pounding feet as the highborn's escorts swept wide of the crowd and ran ahead to join the semicircle of warriors forming a cordon between the Carnifex and the five white-robed zealots that stood in his path.

They seemed like living shards of the shimmering, blade shaped tower that rose behind them. Moonlight shone on their unbound hair and glinted on the edges of their fearsome draichs. The zealots' dark eyes were alight with holy purpose.

They were ready to shed their blood in holy sacrifice to the Lord of Murder. Malus thought he'd never seen five more dangerous warriors in all his life.

The Grand Carnifex however was not impressed. He raised his enchanted axe skyward and his voice trembled with rage. 'Be silent, unbeliever! Your every breath defiles this sacred place!' The elder spread his arms wide and commanded the executioners. 'Split their bodies asunder and cleanse this holy earth in libations of blood!'

With a shout the temple guards raised their long swords and charged at the waiting zealots, who met them with triumphant shouts and an intricate dance of death.

Malus watched in horrified wonder as the five zealots wove their way among four times their number of foes. Their swords were a gleaming blur as they rushed, ducked and spun, seeming to glide past a flurry of fearsome sword strokes and bypass their opponents' heavy armour with swift, precise blows. Executioners collapsed, clutching at the stumps of severed arms or hands, or doubled over from disembowelling strokes that slipped beneath the edge of their breastplates. Screams of anger and pain reverberated in the red tinged air, some cut short with a ringing note of steel.

The fight was over in moments. With a clatter of steel plates the last executioner stumbled away from the pile of fallen bodies, one hand outstretched towards the gleaming temple of Khaine. His draich tumbled from his fingers as he fell to his knees, and then toppled lifelessly to the ground.

One of the five zealots lay among a score of fallen temple guardsmen. The rest were streaked with splashes of gore, but their white robes made it plain that none of the blood belonged to them. Their leader raised his dripping blade to the Grand Carnifex and smiled.

'Your men are forgiven,' the zealot said with a smile. He'd just killed four men in as many seconds and wasn't even short of breath. 'Why do you hesitate, Grand Carnifex? Do you fear that the Bloody-Handed God has no cold mercy in his heart for one such as you? I assure you that he does.'

To Malus's surprise, the Grand Carnifex threw back his head and laughed. It was a terrible, bubbling sound, full of hatred and black fury. The Carnifex reached up and pulled away his ceremonial mask, revealing a ruin of broken bone and deep, twisted scars. The master of the temple was ancient, marked by hundreds of years of brutal war. The fearsome blow of a battle-axe had caved in the right side of his face, twisting his mouth into a feral, gap-toothed sneer. The tip of his nose was nothing more than a nub of ragged flesh, and his forehead was a patchwork of ancient scars, one on top of the other. The zealot leader met the Carnifex's baleful gaze, and Malus saw the briefest flicker of fear.

The Grand Carnifex hefted his enchanted axe. 'My god knows nothing of mercy, you moon-eyed fool,' he hissed. 'He does not forgive. He cares nothing for redemption. He simply hungers, and I live to see him fed.'

That was more like it, Malus thought. He drew his sword. 'Blood and souls for Khaine!' he roared, and the elders took up the shout just as the Grand Carnifex charged the zealot leader.

Malus glanced at Arleth Vann. 'Stick close,' he shouted, drawing one of his throwing knives.

The assassin shook his head. 'You can't possibly expect to fight these men, my lord. They are the best warriors Tyran has, and they have no fear of death. Their skill–'

'I'm not going to fight them, you fool. I'm going to kill them,' Malus snarled, and charged into the melee.

The zealots had resumed their deadly dance, reaping a red harvest among the elders and their retainers. They were constantly in motion, whirling and cutting with their long, curved swords as they wove among the howling mob. Their skill was transcendent and glorious in its purity and lethality. They were living works of the killer's art. Anyone who stepped within reach of their whirling blades was dead in seconds.

Malus watched the nearest zealot decapitate a howling acolyte and then spin gracefully on his heel to eviscerate a charging priestess. When he did the highborn struck the swordsman dead from fifteen paces away, burying his throwing knife in the back of the zealot's skull.

Shaking his head, the highborn peered through the melee for his next victim. Five yards away the Grand Carnifex fought the zealot leader in single combat. The master of the temple was already wounded in half a dozen places, but the speed and ferocity of his attacks was undiminished. Knowing better than to intercede, the highborn turned away and spotted a third zealot, hemmed in by a circle of wary elders. They pressed the swordsman from all sides, like wolves surrounding a mountain lion. When the zealot attacked they gave ground, providing him no opening to employ his deadly blade, but giving the druchii behind him a chance to strike at the swordsman's back.

Malus timed his move just as the zealot made another fierce rush. The elders fell back as before, but the highborn came up behind them and caught one of the men by the scruff of the neck. The elder let out a cry as Malus shoved him onto the zealot's blade. The razor edged sword sank deep into the man's chest and Malus continued to push the dying elder forwards, trapping the draich beneath the man's collapsing form. The zealot had just enough time to shout a bitter curse before the highborn split his skull like a melon.

A savage howl rang though the air. The highborn turned to see the priestess who had gainsayed him in the Citadel of Bone raise a bloody axe and a zealot's severed head to the burning sky. A deep wound scored her left shoulder, but her face was lit with a savage grin.

That left the zealot leader. If he knew his companions were dead the fanatic gave no sign. The swordsman held his draich before him, its point aimed at the Carnifex's throat. His body was taut, like a steel trap wound and ready to strike. The temple leader glared forbiddingly at the young warrior, flexing his two-handed grip on the haft of his great axe and shifting slightly from foot to foot. Blood flowed freely from deep wounds in his arms, chest and legs.

The two warriors faced each other for long moments, neither one presenting an opening to the other. No one moved. The temple elders observed the fight with reverent silence. Malus stole a glance at the temple and suppressed a snarl. His hand strayed to the other throwing dagger at his belt. 'Get it over with, for the Dark Mother's sake,' he muttered under his breath. 'I don't have time for this.'

It was the zealot who lost the test of wills. Thinking his foe was weak from blood loss and perhaps coveting the glory he'd gain from slaying the master of the temple, the swordsman exploded in a blur of motion, aiming a fearsome blow at the Carnifex's neck. The temple master was anything but weak, however, and as the long sword sang through the air he struck it with a backhanded blow from his axe. The enchanted steel broke the sword in three pieces. Then the Carnifex's return stroke sliced the man's head from his shoulders.

The temple master bent and plucked the zealot's skull from the ground. 'Take the heads of the others,' he ordered, tying the trophy to his belt. 'When this is done we will pile them high on the temple altar.'

Malus surveyed the grisly remains of the battle. Nearly two score of their number lay dead or dying, and he knew the worst was yet to come.

'Let us be swift,' the highborn said. 'We can catch Tyran and his heretic council as they attempt to perform the rite.'

'Blood and souls!' cried the axe wielding priestess, and the rest of the elders took up the shout. Their blood was up, and they rushed towards the temple in a ragged mob, eager to show their devotion to the Lord of Murder. The mob quickly left the Grand Carnifex behind as they swept up the white steps of the temple and through the tall, narrow doorway. Malus paced along behind them, checking to make sure that Arleth Vann was close by. He nodded to himself. This was going to work.

The temple was built from the same alabaster stone as the rest of the city, but there the similarities ended. The work of dwarf slaves – scores, perhaps even hundreds of them – was evident in the intricate design. The building centred on a single, narrow spire that rose like a sword into the burning sky, built from a broad, octagonal base supported by a cunning network of graceful buttresses that soared more than thirty feet into the air. The white marble was fitted with joins so precise that the whole structure looked more like a sculpture than a building, carved from the summit of the hill by the hands of a god. The temple was a symbol of wealth and power that could humble a drachau, much less a man such as Malus. He stared up at the great spire and could not help but feel a surge of black-hearted avarice.

The highborn raced up the temple steps, listening to the cries of the elders echoing angrily in the cavernous space beyond. Doors of dark oak plated in brass had been swung wide, providing a glimpse of the red shot blackness beyond.

Malus crossed the threshold and tasted blood in the air. Sorcerous energies pressed against his skin, pulsing in time to a rhythm he could not hear. Tz'arkan writhed in his chest, reacting hungrily to the power reverberating through the temple.

The space beyond was cavernous, lit by dozens of braziers that painted the walls and ceiling with leaping crimson shapes and menacing shadows. Pyramids of skulls, hundreds of them, were arranged in complex patterns across the black marble floor. Overhead, a red-tinged haze of smoke spread the bloody glow of the fires. The air reeked of rot and the sweet smell of cooking flesh. Malus's eyes burned and his throat ached, and for a moment it was as if he had been cast back in time, and was struggling through the red tinged realm of Urial's tower in the Hag.

At the far end of the chamber Malus saw another broad staircase, rising to another narrow doorway. He turned to Arleth Vann. 'Where do we go?' he asked.

The assassin nodded at the stairs. 'The temple has three sanctums. This chamber is reserved for acolytes and visitors. Up the steps yonder we will come to a smaller chapel where the temple priests and the elders make sacrifice and worship. Beyond that lies the Sanctum of the Sword.'

Malus nodded and started loping towards the stairs. 'When we reach the sanctum, I'll need a clear path to the sword. Do whatever you must.'

'I understand,' the assassin replied grimly. 'Khaine's will be done.'

The air grew thicker as Malus neared the steps to the second chapel. He felt a buzzing in his ears, like the distant shouts of a multitude. Again, he found himself reminded of Urial's tower, and steeled himself for what might lie ahead.

'You will need my power,' the daemon whispered. 'Take it, or you will die.'

The highborn paused, halfway up the broad stairway. 'No,' he hissed.

'Now is not the time for pride, Malus. You are weak. You know this. I can help. If you do not partake of my power you will be defeated. They are much too strong for you.'

A shudder wracked Malus's body. All at once he felt shrunken and starved, his muscles shrivelled and his bones aching from fatigue. Unbidden, he thought of Urial and his sorcery, and of Tyran's fearsome swordplay.

'I have my hate,' he whispered. 'I have my wits. They will suffice, daemon. They always have.'

'You know that isn't true. How many times would you have been lost had it not been for me?'

Malus bared his teeth, forcing doubt and fear from his mind by sheer, bloody-minded will. Then he heard the war screams and the shrieks of dying men coming from the chapel at the top of the stairs, and ran towards the sound.

The chapel was a smaller, oval-shaped chamber some eighty paces across, surrounded by roaring braziers that sent columns of scented smoke spiralling upwards to the peak of its arched ceiling. Between each brazier were deep, arched niches filled with stacks of gilded skulls, and a pile of similar, unadorned trophies lay in deep drifts around the raised dais at the far end of the room. A pall of shifting, reddish steam hung above the marble platform, rising from the brass mouth of an enormous cauldron sunk to knee height within the dais itself. Terrible power seethed from the vessel, its bubbling liquid hissing and spitting as if stirred to life by the desperate battle being fought nearby.

Another, narrower stairway rose beyond the dais, climbing towards a towering sculpture of the great god Khaine on his

Dan Abnett & Mike Lee

terrible brass throne. A doorway lit with crimson light gleamed at the base of the fearsome statue, and a fierce melee raged within feet of the glowing portal.

Another rearguard, Malus thought angrily. The crowd of temple elders and their retainers had swept up the short flight of stairs and swarmed around the fight just before the doorway. He couldn't see much of what was happening thanks to the haze of boiling blood rising from the cauldron, but he could clearly hear the clash of steel and the screams of the dying.

The air hummed with power. Malus felt pains shoot through his insides and a hot tear trace its way down his cheek. The drop broke over his lip and he tasted blood. Almost there, he thought. Just a little closer!

Malus pushed his way through stragglers on the near side of the dais and clambered onto it. He found himself looking down into the seething surface of the cauldron, where small skulls and delicate bones rolled in the dark, boiling liquid. He caught Arleth Vann climbing up beside him and shook his head. 'Go around the side,' he ordered in a rough voice. 'I'll draw the attention of the rearguard. You come in and attack them from the rear.'

The assassin nodded and dropped back off the dais. Malus turned back to the cauldron, took a deep breath, and leapt into the pall of steaming gore. Sword held ready, the highborn cleared the gaping maw of the sorcerous vessel and landed in a crouch on the other side.

He found himself looking over the heads of shouting elders as they tried to force their way up the narrow staircase and join in the fight. Figures pushed and stumbled over the bodies of the dead, and pale hands dragged bloody corpses away from the battle, leaving them to fetch up against the foot of the dais. Malus stood, peering intently at the swirling fight near the top of the stairway. A single figure spun and stabbed within a raging circle of temple elders. He caught sight of a long, tight braid of glossy black hair, and slim, alabaster arms moving in a swift, steady rhythm of slaughter.

Then the crowd recoiled under a fierce onslaught, and it seemed that the entire front rank of the elders simply collapsed like threshed wheat. A pale, blood spattered face appeared, and Malus found himself staring into Yasmir's violet eyes.

She wore the ritual garb of a temple witch: a long crimson loincloth of silk held by a girdle of golden skulls that wrapped around her slender hips. Her torso was bare, decorated with streaks and loops of sticky blood, as were her long arms and her long, delicate fingers. A torc of golden skulls surrounded her slender throat and bands of gold and rubies gleamed at each wrist. Beneath the angular headdress of a temple witch her oval face was serene and achingly beautiful, like a flawless sculpture animated by the breath of the Blood God himself. Two long, needle-like daggers flickered in her dripping hands, licking through the air like adders' tongues to turn aside stabbing blades and pierce deep into yielding flesh.

When her eyes met his he felt a cold shock transfix him. It was like looking into the eyes of death itself, and at that moment he wanted nothing more than to sink into her embrace.

The crowd of elders surged back up the stairs, only to lose three more men to Yasmir's flickering blades. As they fell she extended a small foot and took a single step forwards. Her eyes never left his.

'She is coming for you, Malus,' Tz'arkan whispered. 'Accept my power, or she will kill you!'

If she reached him he would die. Her eyes told him that. He could feel her desire like a cold breath against his skin. Malus's hand tightened on his sword, but it felt no better than a bar of lead.

Three more elders leapt at Yasmir, striking at her almost simultaneously. They died before the blows were halfway to their target, stabbed through throat, eye and heart. She took another small step as the dead fell at her feet.

Malus couldn't take his eyes off her. Another few steps and she would be almost close enough to touch. Yet he could not move, transfixed by her violet gaze like a bird before the gliding serpent.

'Hear me, Darkblade, this is the moment of truth! The Bride of Ruin approaches, and without me you cannot prevail. Take what I offer you! Take it!'

A terrified cry went up from the elders, and they fell back before the onslaught of the living saint. One man realised he could not escape and simply sank to his knees before Yasmir, accepting a dagger point in his eye with a prayer upon his lips. Others at the base of the stairs turned and ran.

Less than ten feet separated them. Suddenly the very air resounded as if struck by the hammer of a god, and Malus sensed that the Rite of the Swordbearer had been completed. Somewhere beyond the red-lit doorway he knew that Urial was reaching for the Warpsword of Khaine, and the thought of being thwarted so close to his goal kindled a spark of bitter hate in his breast.

Death approached, bearing her dark knives, and damnation lay coiled in his breast. What could he do?

With a cry of despair three elders fell and poured out their blood on the marble steps, and Yasmir leapt like a deer onto the edge of the dais. Malus drew a shaky breath, gazing into her face. 'Hello sister,' he said.

That was when Arleth Vann appeared, crying out the name of the Blood God as he leapt at Yasmir's back. Quicker than lightning his short blades jabbed at her throat and arms, but she whirled with uncanny speed, flowing like water around his strokes and stabbing the assassin once, twice, thrice. Her long braid uncoiled like a whip, brushing Malus's cheek.

Without thinking he seized that thick rope of hair, and the spell was broken. His hate blazed like a furnace and he pulled with all his might, twisting into the motion and dropping to one knee. Yasmir was pulled from her feet, crashing into and over Malus and falling headfirst into the seething fluids of Khaine's cauldron.

Tz'arkan writhed and screamed in rage, raking along the inside of Malus's ribs, drawing an involuntary shout of pain from the highborn even as he bared his teeth in triumph. Arleth Vann sank against the side of the dais, one arm pressed tight against his chest. A trickle of blood leaked from the corner of his mouth. 'The will of Khaine be done,' the assassin gasped.

The way to the sanctum was clear, and Malus knew that speed meant everything now. Tyran and his ritual mates would be nearly spent from the exertions of the rite. He would deal with Urial now, and claim the warpsword for his own.

With a howl of bloodlust he leapt over Arleth Vann and charged up the stairs, his sword held ready.

A shadow loomed in the doorway just as he reached it. He felt an icy shock transfix him as his half-brother Urial stepped through the portal, clad in gleaming black armour. His brass-coloured eyes gleamed with triumph and his thin lips were drawn back in a savage smile.

Malus tried to raise his sword, but his body refused to obey. He staggered slightly, still off-balance, but something held him upright.

The highborn looked down at the length of dark, gleaming steel that pierced his chest. A thin line of blood ran down the surface of the warpsword, filling the runes etched along its surface.

'Looking for this?' Urial asked, and plunged the blade deeper into Malus's chest.

Chapter Twelve
FROM THE CAULDRON BORN

MALUS FELT HIS heart clench in agony as the long blade slid between his ribs. His chest spasmed and he gasped, coughing up blood. Urial's sepulchral laugh rang in his ears.

'Glory to Khaine, greatest of gods!' Malus's half-brother shouted, his pale face alight with triumph. 'Truly it is a gift to find you here at the moment of my exaltation.' The former acolyte stepped closer, his twisted left foot dragging slightly across the polished marble. His withered right hand was tucked against his breastplate, its deformity hidden within a shell of dark steel armour. Urial's gaunt, hawk-like face was lit with a savage grin and his thick, white hair spilled unbound around his shoulders. He looked like a sorcerer prince out of the ancient legends, radiating icy cruelty and implacable power.

'It is fitting that you be the first to die,' Urial said, his voice almost a whisper. 'After all you and that whore Eldire have done to me, this will be sweet indeed.' He smiled, flexing his good hand on the warpsword's hilt. 'I'm going to split you from crotch to chin and let you bleed out on these steps. Then

I'll command the blood-witches to call you back, and I'll look you in the eye as I feast upon your liver.' His grin hardened into a sneer. 'Once I've eaten of your spirit Darkblade you will be no more. I will take your strength – such as it is – and what is left will be lost to the Abyss forever.'

With a single, fluid motion, Urial jerked the warpsword free from Malus's torso. A wave of pain spread like ice through the highborn's body, so great it took his breath away. Blood leaked from his gaping mouth as he swayed on his feet. Then his knees buckled and Malus fell backwards, landing on his back and sliding limply down the marble steps. His sword, clutched in a death grip, rasped and rang as it was dragged along in his wake.

Malus fetched up at the base of the dais, his labouring heart sending cold waves of pain rippling through his chest. Tz'arkan stirred, and for a brief moment the agony subsided. 'I'm here, Malus,' the daemon whispered. 'Ask, and I shall heal you. The wound is deep, and you will die unless I intervene.'

It was hard to think and harder still to breathe. 'Not… possible,' Malus rasped, bloody froth collecting at the corners of his mouth. 'The prophecy…'

Urial looked out over the temple elders and raised the bloodstained sword, savouring their cries of dismay. Behind him came a slow procession of white-robed zealots, stiff and exhausted from their labours. Tyran led the way, his draich unsheathed by his side. He looked down at the crowd of elders and gave them the serene smile of an executioner. 'The Time of Blood is at hand!' the zealot leader proclaimed. 'Weep for the end of your world, you faithless curs! Khaine's truth gleams from the edge of the Scourge's blade. Prostrate yourselves at his feet and beg for his forgiveness!'

'Yes. Plead for a clean death to wash away your sins,' Urial hissed at the stricken throng. He brandished the warpsword at the crowd like a burning brand. 'When the cauldron spared me you knew that I was blessed by the Lord of Murder. You knew the prophecies of old, and yet you refused to believe the signs that were before your very eyes, because I was a cripple,' he spat, 'a bent and twisted man, unfit to wield a dagger, much less this sacred blade!' Urial took another slow step down the stairs. His face was taut with murderous rage and his eyes gleamed with savage glee.

'I say to you that these withered limbs were a warning, revealing your blindness and lack of faith! You chose the pleasing lie over the grim truth of Khaine's will, and you will reap the bitter fruit of your faithlessness!' The Swordbearer gave a bloodthirsty laugh. 'I have claimed the sword, and soon I shall take my magnificent bride. Then the world will burn – oh, how it will burn! – and we shall rise on a tide of blood as high as the stars themselves.' Urial levelled the warpsword at the temple elders. 'But these glories are not for the likes of you. The blood-witches will call you back and we will feed your guts to the ravens!'

'Be silent, heretic!' thundered the Grand Carnifex.

The crowd of elders fell away to either side from the fearsome master of the temple as he strode into the chapel and climbed onto the dais beside the bubbling cauldron. The Carnifex's face was a mask of fearsome, righteous rage, and fresh blood dripped from the long blade of his rune carved axe. The severed heads of the zealots slain outside the temple were clenched in his left fist, and his gold covered kheitan was smeared with dark splashes of gore. He was the image of an avenging hero, anointed in sacred blood, and the ferocious glare he laid upon Urial stopped the Swordbearer in his tracks.

'You are an abomination, Urial of Hag Graef,' the master of the temple proclaimed. 'You claim that the cauldron gave you back as a gift from Khaine, but I say the Lord of Murder spared you to test our beliefs, not fulfil them!' The Grand Carnifex surveyed the assembled elders, fixing each one with a stern glare. 'The will of the Bloody-Handed God is clear to the faithful: Malekith is his chosen Scourge, who will lead the faithful to glory!' He cast the severed heads into the cauldron and raised his axe to Urial. 'You are a deceiver and a false prophet,' he declared. 'You have defiled the holy sanctum and laid hands on the sacred blade of the

Scourge.' The master of the temple stepped from the dais onto the steps, taking his axe in a two-handed grip. 'I condemn you and repudiate you, and it is my joyous duty to slay you in the Blood God's name!'

To Malus's surprise, Urial smiled and shook his head. 'The first man that dies by this blade is my half-brother. You aren't fit to bleed on my boots, you fraud.'

'Slay the blasphemer!' Tyran cried, and two zealots answered with a lusty roar, charging down the steps past Urial and brandishing their deadly blades. The Grand Carnifex met them with a howl of righteous fury, his axe whirling in deadly patterns as he advanced on Urial.

The charging zealots reached the Carnifex first, their blades flickering like lightning. The master of the temple gauged their advance, and with skill born of countless battles he shifted his stance and sidestepped to the left, meeting the left-most attacker blade to blade. The zealot's sword snapped as it met the temple master's ensorcelled axe, and the Carnifex responded with a lightning return stroke that split the man's torso crosswise, just beneath the ribs. His sudden dodge threw off the rightmost attacker's stroke just enough to spoil the man's killing blow, but not enough to fully escape the reach of the long blade. Malus felt the hot droplets of the old druchii's blood as the zealot's sword tore a deep cut through the Carnifex's side.

A torrent of blood and spilled organs tumbled down the steps around the temple master's feet as the two halves of the slain zealot emptied their contents onto the stairway. 'Blood and souls for Khaine!' the Grand Carnifex shouted, pivoting smoothly to meet the remaining zealot's charge. The old druchii parried a deft swing at his upper thigh and struck back with a reverse stroke at the zealot's head, but the robed warrior ducked nimbly beneath the blow. The zealot stepped into the temple master's guard with a blurring backspin, aiming an eviscerating cut at the Carnifex's midsection, but the old druchii gave ground and parried the blow against the long haft of his axe. The swordsman skidded slightly in the thick blood coating the stone steps, but with preternatural agility he checked his motion and leapt backwards, getting swinging room for his two-handed blade and chopping downwards into the Carnifex's right leg. The long sword bit deep into the meat of the temple master's thigh, but like an old, grizzled boar the Carnifex bellowed in rage and pressed the attack. Twisting slightly to trap the sword in the wound, the old druchii lashed out one-handed with his axe and hacked off the zealot's right arm just above the elbow.

The zealot let out a sharp hiss of pain, blood pumping from the severed limb, but his left hand tore the draich free from the temple master's leg and the swordsman got the long weapon into a defensive stance as the Carnifex lurched forwards. Drops of hot blood scattered like rain as the old druchii unleashed a barrage of blows against the zealot's faltering guard. On the third, ringing stroke the rune-carved axe snapped the draich just above the hilt and the curved blade buried itself in the zealot's face. Drunk on pain and slaughter the Grand Carnifex pulled the axe free and rounded on Urial. Laughing like a madman he ran his tongue along the edge of the gore-stained blade. 'The blood of slain warriors is sweet,' he proclaimed, 'but cowardice is bitter! I can smell your blood curdling to vinegar, Urial. The true Scourge of Khaine would not cower and leave others to fight on his behalf.'

The elders of the temple shouted their approval and the zealots responded with a maddened cry as the two sides threw themselves at one another. Robed figures poured around the dais like a black wave, surging up the stairs alongside their master as white-robed zealots rent the air with bloodthirsty howls and rushed to meet them. Blades flashed and rang and more blood poured down the black stairs as the battle was joined in earnest.

Amid the mayhem Malus felt strong hands grab his shoulders and try to pull him upright. Crying out in pain and coughing up more blood, the highborn tried to twist in the unseen grip and came round to find himself staring up into Arleth Vann's bloodstained face. 'Let go of me!' he croaked.

'Let go! You have to get to the Grand Carnifex. When Urial falls, you must claim the sword and bring it to me.'

The former assassin shook his head. 'It's hopeless,' he said in a dull voice. 'Urial has the warpsword. Not even the master of the temple can prevail against him.'

'But you can,' Tz'arkan whispered in Malus's head, 'with my help. Take it, Malus! Quickly, before it's too late!'

The highborn shook his head angrily. 'I don't need your damned help!' he gasped. His knees weakened and he slumped against Arleth Vann, who struggled to hold him upright. The ache in his guts belied his defiance. His lungs felt heavy, as if a great weight was pressing down on them, and a numbing coldness was spreading across his chest. Hissing in frustration, he tried to push himself back upright and catch a glimpse of Urial among the swirling melee raging on the stairway.

Urial and the Grand Carnifex raged at one another like demigods less than fifteen feet away, their sorcerous weapons striking showers of angry sparks as they clashed again and again in a flurry of artless, brutal blows. The master of the temple lashed at Urial relentlessly, but the former acolyte wielded the warpsword one-handed and blocked the Carnifex's two-handed blows with ease. Still, the Swordbearer was giving ground, falling back towards the sanctum one slow step at a time. Malus would have taken this as a good sign were it not for the vicious smile on Urial's gaunt face.

The master of the temple was weakening. Bleeding from deep wounds, any of which would have been enough to kill a lesser man, the old druchii was slowing a little with each murderous stroke. Whatever strength the Grand Carnifex had stolen from his foes was nearly spent, and Malus realised that with every step he took towards Urial he became more isolated from his fellow elders. He was already a solitary black figure in a surging sea of white.

With a bloodthirsty howl the old druchii feinted at Urial's waist, and then checked his swing and made a vicious, backhanded blow at the Swordbearer's knees. Again, Urial blocked the heavy blow with frightening speed, as if he was swinging nothing more than a willow-switch. The Grand Carnifex stumbled slightly, and Urial flicked his blade across the temple master's face, scattering a thin spray of blood. The old druchii barely flinched from the blow, redoubling his attack with a swipe at Urial's sword arm. Laughing, the former acolyte swayed back, letting the axe blade whistle through empty air. Then he straightened and slashed open the temple master's left arm from wrist to elbow.

Urial was toying with him, Malus realised, his heart sinking. He fumbled at his belt for his remaining throwing knife, but the hilt of the blade was slick with his own blood and slipped from his fingers. His bitter curse was lost amid the cacophony of screams and clashing blades echoing in the steamy air.

The Grand Carnifex reeled as Urial raked his blade across the old druchii's forehead. Another stroke sliced off the temple master's left ear. The wounded elder swayed on his feet, his chest heaving. Blood had soaked through his robes, making them gleam dully in the reddish light. Malus saw Urial say something to the Carnifex, but the words were lost in the tumult. The temple master responded with an angry shout and aimed a powerful stroke right at the centre of the Swordbearer's chest.

Urial blocked the blow easily, a smug expression on his face; one that turned to a look of horror as the canny old druchii hooked the blade of the sword with the beard of his axe and pulled the former acolyte off his feet. The Swordbearer crashed against the Grand Carnifex, his mouth gaping like a gaffed fish as the old druchii closed a powerful hand on Urial's narrow throat. The axe rose heavenward, trembling in the temple master's hand, and then plunged downwards into the former acolyte's left shoulder. Urial screamed in pain and fear as the sorcerous blade pierced his black armour and bit into flesh and bone.

For a moment, Malus thought Urial had dropped the sword. He saw the bloodstained blade dip, but then it flashed upwards, piercing the temple master's midsection and rising underneath the ribs until the point erupted from the elder's right collarbone. Both men froze for several long moments, and then the old druchii sagged, sinking to his knees.

A cry of horror went up from the temple elders as they saw their master fall, turning to wails of terror as Urial gritted his teeth and levered his blade upwards, splitting the old druchii's chest open like a slaughtered steer. The blood-stained axe fell from the temple master's lifeless hands, his ruptured body toppling onto its side.

'Blessed Mother of Night,' Malus hissed, as the zealots redoubled their attack and the temple elders recoiled in horror. He saw Urial searching the melee intently, and knew who his half-brother was looking for. The highborn looked to Arleth Vann. 'This is about to become a rout,' he snarled. 'We've got to get out of here!'

The former assassin nodded and without warning heaved Malus back onto the dais. Groaning in pain, the highborn pushed himself across the black marble, close enough to brush the lip of the brass cauldron in passing. He heard an exultant shout over the din: had Urial seen him? Fighting against waves of crushing pain he forced himself to crawl across the dais and into the crowd on the other side.

Shouts of panic and the frenzied cries of the zealots rang out behind Malus, and he felt the crowd around him surge backwards, like a black tide receding towards the far doorway. He let himself be borne along in the press, until he realised that the shouts of the dying were spreading around the sides of the dais like fire through tinder. Tyran and his men were closing in like a pack of wolves. Snarling angrily and spitting streams of dark blood, the highborn threw himself forwards, using the blade of his sword to batter his way through the panicked elders. He stumbled and kicked his way through piles of weathered skulls. 'Stand fast!' he managed to shout. 'Avenge your master and slay the unbelievers!'

If his words had any effect on the panicked elders and their men he could not say, but the men and women in front of him gave way rather than feel the bite of his sword. Arleth Vann appeared at his side, swords bared and facing back the way they'd come in case the zealots pressed too close.

They had forced their way through the far doorway within moments. Malus paused at the threshold and risked a backwards glance just as a great wail of despair went up from the servants of the temple. He saw that the zealots had swept past the dais and were wreaking a terrible slaughter among the panicked and demoralised elders. On top of the marble platform, shrouded in crimson steam, Urial the Forsaken stood before the great cauldron where he'd been sacrificed as a crippled babe, only to be reborn as one of Khaine's chosen. He held the Grand Carnifex's severed head over the mouth of the great vessel, letting streams of dark blood fall into its hissing brew. The Swordbearer's eyes were fever bright with divine madness, and his hateful gaze was fixed hungrily on Malus.

Then the contents of the cauldron erupted, showering Urial and the zealots with a rain of steaming fluids as Yasmir burst from the cauldron's depths. Heat shimmered from her naked form, and blood ran like quicksilver from her alabaster skin. Her raven hair had gone snowy white, and when her eyes opened Malus saw they were luminous and golden. They transfixed him, sinking like hooks into his labouring heart.

Yasmir smiled, revealing curved, leonine fangs. Long, black talons gleamed in the ruddy light as she gripped the edge of the cauldron and climbed gracefully onto the dais. The newborn blood-witch extended her sleek arm and beckoned to Malus, summoning him to her side.

Malus was already fleeing, stumbling like a child into the lesser sanctum with his own eyes screwed fearfully shut. He could still feel her stare upon him, like hot metal searing his skin.

He felt someone grab his arm as he stumbled on the broad stairway. After a dozen steps he dared open his eyes again and saw it was Arleth Vann at his side. Rhulan eyed him fearfully from the centre of the room. The Arch-Hierophant stood next to a slender female elder with a shaven head, her scalp tattooed in myriad intricate patterns that seemed to shift restlessly in the firelight. He had a fleeting memory of her in the Citadel of Bone, sitting in a throne almost directly across from the seat of the Grand Carnifex. She had to be the fifth member of the temple's Haru'ann. Malus suddenly realised that with the death of the Carnifex she and Rhulan were the only senior temple leaders still alive. They were surrounded by a thin cordon of temple retainers under the watchful eye of the young priestess that Malus had seen earlier.

'What has happened?' Rhulan asked, although from the look on his face it was clear that the elder already suspected the worst.

'We've failed,' Malus said bitterly. 'The Grand Carnifex is dead, and we're next if we don't get out of here.'

The tattooed woman gave Malus a look of contempt. 'You expect us to surrender the temple to a gang of heretics and thieves?' she snapped, her voice thick with a rustic northern accent.

'That's not a matter of debate,' the highborn shot back. 'You've already lost the temple. Your only choice is to stay here and throw your lives away or retreat and find another way to strike back.' He looked to Rhulan. 'We need real troops, and quickly. Are there any warriors left here at the fortress?'

Rhulan shook his head. 'We sent every swordsman and witch into the streets, hoping to overwhelm the zealots. If we sound the recall, the troops in the highborn district could be here within the hour.'

'By then it will be too late,' Malus snarled. He turned to ask something of Arleth Vann, but the question died on his lips. The highborn glanced back at Rhulan. 'What about the temple assassins?' he asked.

The Arch-Hierophant frowned. 'They have withdrawn into their tower to select a new master,' he said. 'After that they will swear vengeance upon the man who killed their former master and will not rest until he has been slain.'

Malus grinned. 'Is that so?' he asked. 'Well, then, I've got a proposition for them. If they want their vengeance they'll have to stop Urial from getting his first. Let's go.'

Chapter Thirteen
AMONG THE DEAD

AT THAT MOMENT a chorus of terrified wails erupted from the inner sanctum as the temple elders' courage finally gave out. The stream of wounded and demoralised temple servants pouring into the outer sanctum suddenly became a raging flood as scores of panicked druchii fled before Urial and his fearsome bride.

'Go!' Malus shouted at Rhulan. 'Gather your retainers and make for the temple doors.' Then he turned to face the tide of retreating temple servants and raised his bloodstained sword.

'Stand fast!' he roared, his face a mask of implacable rage. The shout was almost lost in the surf-like roar of the rout, but the leading rank of fleeing druchii saw the highborn's furious expression and pulled up short. He took a step towards the fearful elders. 'Turn and face the enemy! Defend your elders and the sanctity of the temple, for Khaine is watching!'

Each word was like a dagger, digging into Malus's chest. His lungs felt thick and swollen, and they couldn't seem to hold enough air. The daemon was right, Urial had wounded him badly. His chest heaved and he turned his head to spit a gobbet of blood onto the marble floor, but instead of fear, Malus felt only a black, boiling rage.

He stepped fearlessly into the press, forcing frightened men to either side. 'Skulls for the Blood God!' he cried, bloody foam flecking his thin lips. The front rank of temple servants turned with him, raising their weapons as Malus forced his way through the crowd towards the narrow door.

He knew that if he could reach the door they could hold it almost indefinitely. The battered temple retainers could form a tight ring around the portal and slay the zealots one at a time if they tried to fight their way through. The doorway was less than twenty feet away, but the path was crammed with thrashing, black-robed figures that contested each and every upward step. Malus snarled like a trapped wolf, laying about the men before him with the flat of his sword and eyeing the doorway with mounting dread. If the zealots could reach it before he did then all would be lost.

'Stand fast!' Malus shouted again, and succeeded in rallying the men closest to him. 'Drive for the door!' he ordered, and the men around him tried to force their way upwards, against the tide. The fleeing druchii pushed back, yelling and cursing. A temple retainer in front of Malus stabbed wildly at the highborn, and Malus split his skull without a moment's hesitation. He stepped into the gap the fallen man left behind and continued to press forwards. 'Hold them at the door!' he repeated. 'We'll stop them here!'

Had they been soldiers, accustomed to following orders amid the chaos of battle, the plan might have worked, but these were elders and temple acolytes, many of whom had not spilled another's blood except in temple rituals. The death of the Grand Carnifex and the slaughter visited upon them by the vengeful zealots had ground their courage to dust. Malus was halfway to the door when a chorus of thin cries rose to challenge his shouted commands.

'The Swordbearer is come! All hail Urial, the Scourge of Khaine!'

Men screamed as their fellow temple brethren turned on them, crying out Urial's name and stabbing their kin in hopes of saving themselves. The throng pressed with renewed vigour against Malus and his handful of rallied troops, but this time it was with knifepoints and axe-blades as well as elbows and fists.

The highborn heard the brittle snap of bones as the man in front of him was struck in the back by a retainer's axe. He fell with a gurgling scream, and his assailant pulled his weapon free with both hands and set upon Malus with a fevered gleam in his dark eyes. Malus blocked the frenzied axe-stroke with his upraised blade and then smashed the man in the face with the round pommel of his sword. The retainer staggered, fetching up against the men behind him, and Malus chopped his sword deep into the turncoat's neck.

A dagger lashed out from Malus's left, scoring a narrow track along his left bicep. He coughed and spat more blood, his breath coming in wet, rattling gasps. A short sword chopped at him from the right and Malus blocked the clumsy strokes without conscious thought. The crowd at the top of the stairs surged forwards. A man fell towards Malus, and he stabbed the druchii in the chest, unable to tell whether he was friend or foe. Then he saw it: a white sleeve spattered with red, holding up a bloodstained draich in front of the doorway to the inner sanctum. The zealots had seized the doorway to the sanctum, and there was no holding them back.

Another dagger reached for Malus. Unable to discern who held it in the tangle of bodies he took a swipe at the man's hand and severed a pair of fingers. Something sharp jabbed at his lower leg, causing him to shout in surprise. He stole quick glances left and right and saw the men beside him putting up a fight, but the weight of numbers had shifted against them. If they stayed where they were they would be overcome within minutes.

Malus gathered in as much breath as he could. 'Warriors of the temple!' he cried. 'One step back!'

The elders and their men eyed Malus with bewilderment, but their ragged line fell back a step. Several of the oncoming druchii overbalanced and fell at the feet of the retreating temple loyalists, and Malus was heartened to see his men despatch the turncoats with swift, merciless blows. The highborn risked a quick glance over his shoulder and saw Arleth Vann right behind him, his swords held low and to either side of his body. Malus noticed the rivulets of blood running from beneath both of the assassin's sleeves and dripping from his clenched fists, but the highborn had no doubt that his retainer could still fight and kill on command. 'We're retreating to the door!' he shouted. 'Watch our backs and keep the bastards from flanking us once we're off the stairs!'

Arleth Vann nodded grimly and turned his back on Malus, surveying the chapel floor.

'Warriors of the temple! One step back!' Malus commanded, and the retreat began in earnest.

The eighty paces back to the doorway were the longest steps of Malus's short life. Every loyal temple servant between Malus and the doorway was dead within moments and there was nothing in front of him but a bloodthirsty mob howling for his head. A man charged headlong at him, brandishing an axe, and the highborn dropped to one knee and stabbed the turncoat in the groin. Another rushed in and slashed for his face with a short sword. Malus pulled his sword from the axe man and blocked the sword stroke, forcing his assailant backwards with a jab to his face. He regained his feet and stepped backwards, taunting the men in front of him to try their luck against his blade.

And so it went: step, parry, kill and step again. As the temple loyalists came off the steps the mob spilled onto the chapel floor and lapped around the ends of the ragged line, slowly forcing the retreating fighters into a tight knot of weary men. The piled skulls on the chapel floor were a boon to the loyalists, breaking up the turncoat attacks so that they couldn't press the defenders from all sides. True to his word, Arleth Vann kept the line of retreat open, slaying every turncoat who crossed his path.

When they were slightly more than halfway to the doors, Malus was panting like a dog. Red spots swirled at the corners of his vision as he struggled for breath. He'd picked up a dagger from a fallen turncoat and fought on two-handed, blocking with the heavy northern sword and stabbing foes with the knife. He'd lost track of the number of men he'd killed. The rest paced in his wake like wolves, sensing that he was weakening and waiting for the right moment to strike. The highborn gasped like a landed fish, hardly daring to glance away from his opponents to see how well the rest of the loyalists were faring.

With each, halting breath he felt the daemon shift inside him, saying nothing but reminding him of its presence. Malus caught himself with the daemon's name on his lips, more than once, knowing that a single word could fill his lungs with fresh air and turn his blood to deadly ice. Each time he pushed temptation away with a snarl, although whether from fear or sheer, bloody-minded spite he could not say.

It was only when the turncoats redoubled their attacks that Malus knew they were nearly to the door. He heard the tempo of fighting increase to either side of him, and the three men who had been testing his defences for the last few minutes decided to rush him all at once. Two men held short, stabbing swords, while the druchii on the far right hefted a large, single bladed axe.

The axe man nearly got him, rushing forwards just as Malus tried to blink a swarm of bright spots from his eyes. He sensed more than saw the looming shape of his assailant and on instinct alone he leapt forwards and to the right, placing himself within the arc of the axe man's swing. Malus's attacker tried to adjust his aim by pivoting further to his right, but the move was a second too slow and his aim was poor, and the weapon struck one of the swordsmen in the back of the head instead. Before the axe man could recover Malus stabbed him twice in the chest and neck. Then he threw himself at the last swordsman, who was stepping over his fallen mate and thrusting his weapon at the highborn's throat. The turncoat's shorter blade meant he had to overextend himself in order to reach his target and the highborn made his foe pay dearly for it, side-stepping the thrust and chopping his sword deep into the side of the man's neck.

Malus risked a quick look backwards and saw the doorway only a few paces distant. Someone – probably one of Rhulan's men – had pulled the doors partly shut, so only one or two men could slip through at a time. Already there were only a bare handful of loyalists led by Arleth Vann remaining on the interior side of the door, barely keeping the escape route open. The highborn would have laughed out loud if he'd had the wind for it. Instead he turned back to the bloodthirsty turn-coats, and found himself face to face with one of Tyran's zealots. The swordsman held his gore-crusted draich at the ready, a rapt smile on his face.

I can't beat him, damn it. I can barely breathe, he thought. Still, he leapt at the man with a rasping shout, holding his dagger close and feinting at the zealot's face to gauge his prowess. The swordsman was clearly spent from his exertions performing the Swordbearer's rite, because his killing stroke was just barely slow enough for Malus to block the blow with the flat of his dagger. Malus retreated from the swordsman, chest heaving, and the zealot glided after him, his expression hungry and intent.

Malus angled his course to head for the doorway, hoping his memory and blurred eyesight hadn't deceived him. He threw another short jab at the zealot's eyes, and pulled back just in time to avoid having his sword arm taken off at the elbow.

The zealot laughed. 'You disgrace yourself, blasphemer,' he said. 'I had hoped you would be a worthy foe, but you puff and stumble like a drunkard. Why don't you throw down your swords and accept Khaine's cold mercy?'

A ghostly grin came and went from Malus's bloody lips. 'Because I know something you don't.'

The zealot frowned. 'Such as?'

'Such as my retainer is about to stab you in the side of the neck.'

The swordsman whirled, raising his blade in a blurring defensive move. Malus leapt at the same time, catching the zealot's left arm at the crook of his elbow and shearing straight through it. The zealot staggered, but before he could regain his senses the highborn finished him off with a thrust to his neck.

Arleth Vann finished off the turncoat in front of him and took a step back, reaching Malus's side. He gave his master an accusatory look. 'I heard what you said,' he declared sternly, 'suggesting I would interfere in a sacred duel!'

'I'm a bit surprised he fell for it myself,' Malus replied. He grabbed the assassin by a blood soaked sleeve and pulled him back through the doorway. Wide-eyed druchii stood to either side of the threshold, their hands gripping the edges of the tall, oak doors.

'Shut them! Hurry!' Malus ordered. 'They're almost upon us!'

The retainers leapt to obey, pulling hard on the heavy panels. Frantic, bloodstained faces appeared in the narrowing gap and hands pounded fearfully on the closing doors. A pale hand shot through the gap, reaching desperately for Malus. With a curse the highborn stepped to the side and brought his sword down on the offending limb, severing it in a spray of blood. The loyalist's agonised shriek was lost in the heavy thud of the doors slamming shut.

Malus turned and sought out Rhulan, who stood ashen faced at the foot of the temple steps. 'Can you seal it?'

The temple elder started at Malus's voice, as if lost in a reverie. 'Seal?' he asked, blinking owlishly.

'The door, damn you!' the highborn snapped, his voice so sharp that Rhulan and his retainers flinched at the sound. 'Do you know some sorcery to lock the doors?'

'Oh, yes. Of course.' Rhulan strode forwards, raising his right hand. 'Step away from the doors,' he said.

Malus and Arleth Vann cleared the steps, and the rest of the temple servants scattered to either side. The heavy doors began to swing open almost immediately, giving vent to a chorus of fierce cries and pounding fists. A severed head rolled through the widening gap, bouncing wetly down the wide steps to stop at Malus's feet.

Then Rhulan straightened to his full height and spoke a single word of power that crackled in the air like the lash of a whip. He made a fist with his upraised hand and the twin doors slammed shut with a thunderous boom.

Malus nodded in weary satisfaction, revising his opinion of the frail-looking Rhulan somewhat. He quickly took stock of the motley band of loyalists who'd escaped the debacle within the temple. Rhulan had six men and women standing in a loose circle around him, and Malus saw the tattooed elder standing a short distance away, surrounded by her own coterie of retainers and hangers-on, including the axe-wielding priestess he'd seen fighting earlier. Four more loyalists stood near Malus at the foot of the steps. They were all that remained of the meagre force he'd led out of the building.

Out of the hundred druchii who'd followed the Grand Carnifex from the Citadel of Bone, less than twenty remained. Malus shook his head bitterly and tried to curse, but all he could manage was a wet, wracking cough that sent spasms of pain through his chest. He swayed on his feet, but Arleth Vann steadied him with a bloodstained grip.

'Are you well?' Rhulan asked, his face paling further.

With an effort, Malus bit back a sharp-tongued reply. He spat another mouthful of blood onto the ground and took a strangled breath. 'Well enough,' he managed to say.

'We haven't long,' the elder said, his voice hollow. 'What do we do?'

The daemon stirred. 'Listen to him,' Tz'arkan whispered. 'Time is running out for you, little druchii. You must choose.'

A sharp spike of pain lanced through Malus's chest, almost doubling him over with its intensity. Again, Arleth Vann's grip steadied him, but Malus jerked his arm away. With nothing but bitter rage to sustain him, he forced himself upright.

'We go talk to these assassins of yours,' he said through clenched teeth, 'and then we put an end to these fanatics once and for all.'

AFTER THE IVORY eminence of the Citadel of Bone and the dwarf-wrought glory of the temple, Malus had no idea what to expect from the sanctum of the temple's holy assassins. A razor-edged keep wrought entirely of steel? A palace of ruby and garnet? Many fanciful visions passed through his mind as Arleth Vann shepherded him across the temple grounds.

It turned out to be a hole in the ground.

More accurately, it was accessed by a long, spiralling path, almost a hundred and twenty paces across, that wound its way deep into the earth. Large witchfire globes surrounded the perimeter of the wide spiral, throwing shifting patterns of light across the narrow pathways. The path was wide enough for only one traveller at a time, and it was formed of dark, crimson glass that glimmered like fresh blood in the sorcerous light.

Rhulan took the lead. The temple retainers – even the fearsome priestess with her bloodstained axe – looked to one another apprehensively as they fell into line behind their masters. Even Arleth Vann seemed hesitant to begin the descent, although Malus suspected that he had very practical reasons for avoiding his former comrades. He didn't expect that the silent knives of Khaine nurtured any compassion for those who broke their oaths and deserted the order.

The descent seemed to go on forever. It was fully five minutes of slow, methodical pacing before they'd completed the first circuit and began to sink below the earth. Malus gritted his teeth, one hand pressed against the wound in his chest, and expected to hear the sounds of pursuit at any moment. He couldn't imagine that Urial would be delayed overmuch by Rhulan's ward, nor would he waste a single moment in setting the hounds on his trail.

It was almost another five minutes before they were fully below ground. What in the Dark Mother's name was taking so long, he wondered? Were there traps for the unwary? Poison needles or voracious spirits? Everyone ahead of him seemed to be studying the path at their feet with intense interest. Concentrating on keeping his breathing even, Malus followed suit, watching the gleaming red stones for telltale pressure plates or tripwires.

On and on they went. The smell of damp earth filled his nostrils, and when they had passed beyond the light of the braziers their path was lit with the faint effulgence of grave mould, glowing from niches on the glistening stone walls.

He soon lost track of time. One step led to the next, their pace neither speeding up nor slowing down. A tight band of pain began to constrict around his chest, and from time to time a drop of blood would slip past his lips and fall heavily to the pathway. His breath bubbled in his throat, as if he was caught in the grip of a terrible ague. He heard the daemon whispering in his ears, but the sound was strangely faint, like the murmur of the tides, and he paid it little heed.

After a time Malus began to sense that their curving path was shrinking, drawing tighter and tighter with each revolution. He took heart, realising that they must be close to their destination, but he was careful not to get complacent and take his gaze from the perilous floor.

Not long afterwards he watched his steps glide across a narrow threshold, and looked up to see that they had reached a small, circular chamber carved from dark stone. Globes of witchlight gleamed from the walls, worked into carvings of dragons and leering daemons. Double doors stood on the opposite side of the circle. Rhulan gave the party a single backwards glance, his expression clearly indicating that they should wait here, and then went to stand before the doors. He spoke not a word, nor rapped upon the wooden panels, but nevertheless one door swung silently open, allowing him to slip inside.

After Rhulan was gone many of the loyalists sank wearily to the stone floor. Some checked their injuries, while others slumped into an exhausted stupor. The tattooed elder drew apart from the rest and sat with her back to one of the curving walls, closing her eyes as if to meditate or pray. The axe-wielding priestess sat, and then stood, and finally began to pace like a caged lion, her expression distant and vengeful.

Malus declined to sit as well, not so much out of nervousness, but because he wasn't certain he could get up again if he did. It was bad enough that Arleth Vann had to see him in such a weakened state; he would be damned if anyone had to carry him. The assassin leaned against the wall beside the entryway, resting his head against the carved stone. His gaunt features were scabbed with dried blood, and the front of his sleeves and kheitan were stiff and dark with gore.

The highborn glanced back the way they'd come. 'All that caution, and not a single trap or alarm,' he said. 'It appears that the assassins are less fearsome than their reputation suggests.'

Arleth Vann looked up at him, a bemused expression on his face. 'What are you talking about?'

Malus pointed back at the curving path. 'All that checking for traps,' he said, 'totally unnecessary.'

'Traps?' the retainer said. 'That was a labyrinth, my lord. A journey of meditation. Who lays traps in a labyrinth?'

The highborn blinked. 'Oh, well, no one, I suppose.' He frowned. 'What assassins' order forces you to walk a labyrinth to reach them?'

Arleth Vann studied his master for several moments, uncertain whether or not he was being mocked. 'We are not mere cutthroats, my lord,' he said at last. 'The Shayar Nuan are a holy order, much like the executioners or the temple witches.'

Malus raised an eyebrow at the name. 'The Blessed Dead? Is that what they call themselves?'

'That is the name we call ourselves,' the assassin said. He gave Malus one of his ghostly smiles. 'Now that you've heard it I have to kill you, of course.'

The highborn glowered at his servant. 'You speak as if you are still one of them.'

Arleth Vann shrugged. His brass-coloured eyes were haunted. 'We are Shayar Nuan when we emerge from the cauldron, my lord. Nothing can take that away.'

'I don't understand. I thought the cauldron was reserved only for sacrifices.'

The assassin sighed, trying to find a way to explain. 'Yes and no, my lord. The witches of the temple bathe in the cauldron. It is the source of their terrible allure and ageless vigour,' he said. 'That power is indeed born from sacrifice: prisoners, criminals, the weak and the crippled, as well as every neophyte assassin. It is the final rite of passage. We die, yet live on in service to Khaine.'

Malus peered closely at the assassin. 'You don't mean to say you're actually dead?'

'It's a metaphor, my lord. You're familiar with the term?'

'Don't get flippant with me,' Malus snarled weakly. 'In case you've forgotten, I was stabbed with a sword not too long ago, and I'm not in the mood.'

'Your pardon, my lord,' the retainer replied.

'Besides, with everything else I've seen in this damned city, I wouldn't be at all surprised.'

'No, I suppose not,' Arleth Vann replied. 'All right, consider this: how do you kill a man who is already dead?'

Malus considered the question. 'Cut off his head and limbs and burn the bits. It's the only way to be certain.'

The assassin's brow furrowed. 'I begin to see why your father never considered sending you to the temple,' he said. 'Let me be blunt: the greatest power a man can have is the ability to take the life of another. That is the central tenet of the executioners. If a man is already dead, however, not even the blessed swords of Khaine can touch him. He is a ghost, fearing nothing of this world or the next.'

Malus grunted, touching off a spasm of coughing. 'Interesting,' he said, wiping his mouth with the back of his hand. 'If I recall, you said that the order was a recent invention, not originally part of the Lord of Murder's cult.'

Arleth Vann eyed the other Khaineites warily. 'That is so,' he admitted softly. 'The Witch King needed a way to eliminate threats to the state without risking open war with the noble houses, and the temple needed a new reason to justify its authority after the last of the warlocks had been killed.' He shrugged. 'In the past, those who survived the depths of the cauldron were taken by the witches and trained in the ways of the cult. Many became priests, and others lived as exalted oracles or scholars. The temple elders gave them a new calling: the art of stealth and silent murder, a combination of the witch's magic and the executioner's skill.'

'And Urial was trained in these arts?'

The assassin shook his head. 'No, according to all reports, he was a voracious scholar and a potent sorcerer, but that was all.

His deformities precluded him from mastering the arts of combat. As far as I know, he was never considered for inclusion into the order, nor could he truly be considered a priest, for even elders like Rhulan must be ready and able to march to war. Honestly, I don't think anyone quite knew what to do with your brother.'

'It's a pity they never asked me. I could have offered a number of pointed suggestions.' Malus studied the closed doors. 'Do you think they will help us, now that Urial has the sword?'

Arleth Vann shrugged. 'Truly, it's hard to say. Like the blood-witches of old, the order professes to take no interest in the affairs of the temple. Indeed, much of the witches' prestige and authority has been ceded to the assassins over the centuries. They may see Urial as usurping Malekith's role as the Scourge, or they may not care who wields the warpsword so long as Khaine's will is done.'

Another sharp jolt of pain stabbed through Malus. His breath was coming in shallow draughts, and shadows crowded at the edges of his vision. He knew that time was running out. Where was Rhulan? What was taking so long?

'It appears they need some persuading,' he said grimly, and lurched towards the doors.

Arleth Vann let out a startled shout, but Malus was at the doorway before anyone could react. He placed his hands against the cold, damp oak and pushed.

The doors opened easily, giving way to cave-like darkness. Without hesitation, Malus plunged through. He walked blindly forwards, expecting any moment to smash into a wall or plunge off the edge of a pit. He dimly heard Arleth Vann shouting his name, but he paid no mind.

After only a few moments he saw a dim light up ahead. A few steps later he could make out three figures, two standing and one kneeling before them. Malus guessed that the kneeling figure had to be Rhulan, and a dozen strides later, his suspicions were confirmed.

The Arch-Hierophant knelt in a circle of faint luminescence that seemed to emanate from the very air itself. Two robed figures stood before him, their faces hidden within deep hoods.

Rhulan glanced back fearfully at Malus's approach. His eyes widened as he recognised who it was. 'Blessed Murderer! What are you doing here? You were supposed to wait!'

'Time is more precious than gold at the moment,' Malus seethed, 'and we are growing poorer by the second.' He faced the hooded men. 'Are you among the elders of the order?'

One of the figures stepped forwards. 'The elders are in conclave,' a young man's voice replied. He reached up and drew back his hood, revealing the boyish features and dark eyes of an initiate.

Malus pointed at Rhulan. 'Do you not know who he is, boy?'

'Of course,' the initiate replied, 'but he has brought no blood tithe and nor have you. Not even the Grand Carnifex may speak to the elders without a suitable offering. The commandments of the order are clear–'

The highborn's hurled dagger struck the initiate in the forehead with a meaty thunk. The boy's body quivered for a moment, his mouth frozen in mid-sentence, and then the corpse collapsed to the floor.

Malus turned to the second hooded figure. 'All right,' he said coldly. 'There is my blood tithe. Take me to the elders.'

Rhulan let out a strangled gasp. The hooded figure considered the dead acolyte for a moment, and then faced Malus. 'Your tithe is… acceptable,' he said, 'but the elders are choosing a new master. They will speak to no one until their sacred duty is complete.'

'Do you not realise that a usurper has stolen the Warpsword of Khaine and killed the Grand Carnifex? If we do not move against him quickly he will seize the temple and then the city beyond!'

The figure said nothing.

Furious, Malus tried another tack. 'Are you not bound to avenge the death of your fallen master?'

'Yes,' the figure replied.

'Well it was I who slew him!' the highborn declared. 'I beat the fat oaf's brains out with a hunk of broken marble. If your damned elders don't get off their arses and do something about Urial, he'll kill me and rob them of their revenge.'

Someone shouted angrily. Malus couldn't be certain who it was. The room started to spin. A fierce jolt of pain shot through him, but with a shout of rage he fought to stay upright. The highborn groped for his sword, but powerful hands seized his arms and pulled him from his feet.

Malus never felt himself hit the ground.

HE WAS FLOATING through darkness. A hot wind hissed across his face and strange sounds echoed in his ears.

Visions came and went in brief, red flashes. He saw stone walls and robed men, twisting passages and narrow stairs. After a time he realised he was being carried, but he could not guess where or why.

Sometimes the sounds resolved themselves into voices, echoing in close, dark spaces. Sometimes they whispered, sometimes they shouted. He tried to answer them, but no words would come.

The next thing he knew, he was cold. No, he was laying on something cold. He tasted blood. There was another red flash, and Malus flinched, blinking in the sudden glare. Arleth Vann loomed over him, his pale face mere inches from Malus's own. Brass-coloured eyes peered deep into his.

Malus tried to speak. The sounds that came in response to his efforts were barely recognisable. 'Where... are... we?'

The assassin's face receded. The torchlight painted a wall of rock to Malus's right, revealing deep niches set at regular intervals from floor to ceiling. Skulls and piles of bones shone dully in the flickering light.

'Among the dead,' Arleth Vann replied. Then darkness closed in once more.

Chapter Fourteen
CONTEMPLATING THE ABYSS

A HOT WIND blew over Malus, tangling his unbound hair and blowing fine, rasping sand across his face. Flat plains stretched for miles, lifeless and inimical.

He lay on his chest, facing north, staring at the broken line of iron dark mountains that reared up from the edge of the burning world. Malus knew that one of the mountains had a cleft in it, as if it had been split by the axe-stroke of a god. At the foot of that mountain, in a dead and withered wood, there was a road of dark stones that led to an ancient temple.

He'd tried to do his part. He had tried to gather up all five of the lost relics, but in the end he'd failed. It was too much: too much for any one man to do.

Now the sands were running out. They were stolen from him by the desert wind, streaming away into the pale white sky.

He tried to rise to his knees, but his body refused to obey. A hot pain burned like a coal beneath his skin, stealing his breath away. He'd crawled for miles upon miles, trying to reach the temple and beg the daemon to release his tainted soul. Terror gripped him as the hour drew near, when Tz'arkan would claim his soul for all time.

A hand, cool and strong, gripped his shoulder. Sharp, writhing pain made him cry out as he was turned onto his back. Harsh, white light burned through his clenched eyelids. Then a shadow covered him, blotting out the merciless sun.

He felt a caress along the line of his blistered cheek. The skin was rough, calloused at fingertip and palm.

'Do you suffer, my lord?' her voice, throaty and deep, reminded him of the slave cruise, and the time before the daemon's curse.

'I have to get to the temple,' he croaked, his breath coming in bubbling gasps. His clumsy fingers pawed at the ragged tear in his robes. 'I'm hurt,' he said, bitter tears carving tracks through the grime caking his face. 'There is a daemon inside me–'

'Hush, my lord,' she said, 'the corruption has made you mad. I shall not let the daemon have you. Do not fear.'

Gentle fingertips probed at the tear. Malus opened his eyes and looked up into Lhunara's face. She smiled, causing the blood-filled orb that had been her right eye to bulge from its ruined socket. Blood and vile fluids seeped from the terrible wound in her skull and maggots writhed in the rotting brain matter, disturbed by the terrible heat.

Her fingers wriggled into the tear and then the open wound beneath. He felt the cold digits grasp the inside of his ribs and he screamed as she flexed her arms and pulled his ribcage apart. Flesh and bone parted with a rotten, tearing sound.

She lowered her face to the gaping hole and started to feed, tearing at his organs like a wolf, and it was all he could do to open his mouth and scream.

HANDS SHOOK HIM, gently at first, and then insistently. 'Wake up, my lord. For the Murderer's sake, wake up!'

Malus awoke, his rising scream silenced by a spasm of wracking coughs. His body was cold and damp, and his joints ached from lying on unyielding stone. He rolled onto his side, spitting clots of blood and phlegm from his mouth and struggling for a decent breath.

He lay on a mortuary slab in a small, rectangular cell. Its previous occupant, some withered temple elder from centuries past, had been dumped unceremoniously on the rough-hewn floor. Long niches lined the walls, filled with the tattered skeletons of favoured retainers and allies. A small oil lamp guttered from one of the higher niches, shedding a dim yellow light onto the ancient crypt. The air was dank and thick with dust, coating the back of his aching throat.

Strong hands gripped his shoulders, touching off a thrill of terror as he relived the last moments of his nightmare. He tried to fight back, but a fist of agony clenched around his left lung, leaving him near senseless with pain. Arleth Vann pulled his master back down onto the slab, studying him with concern.

'You had a nightmare, my lord,' he said quietly. 'It must have been a terrible one. I don't think I've ever heard you scream before.'

Malus wiped his face with a trembling hand. 'That's just because you haven't spent much time with me lately,' he replied, attempting a half-hearted smile. 'I've had occasion to hone my vocal skills over the last several months.' He pushed aside the retainer's hands and tried to sit up. 'Where in the Dark Mother's name are we?'

'Deep in the tombs,' the assassin replied. 'By the time we'd emerged from the assassin's sanctum Urial had already broken through the temple door and was well on his way to seizing the entire temple fortress. The great gates had been opened and a large force of zealots had slipped inside, reinforcing Urial's small band. They were killing every slave they could find and rounding up all the remaining acolytes. It was all we could do to sneak past their hunting parties and lose ourselves in the catacombs.'

Malus winced as another stabbing pain shot through his chest, but he refused to lie back down again. 'How long have I been out?'

'You've been in and out for most of a day,' the assassin said. He nodded to the narrow doorway over his shoulder.

'Rhulan and the rest are in the antechamber beyond. They haven't stopped bickering since we got here.'

The highborn muttered a curse. 'An entire day,' he said bitterly. 'Urial grows stronger with every minute. Do we know what is happening on the hill?'

Arleth Vann shrugged. 'I made a trip to the surface a few hours ago, hoping to get some food and water from the kitchens and maybe some hushalta,' he said. 'Urial is in complete control of the temple, and he's closed the fortress gates to the temple warriors still out in the city. Much of Har Ganeth continues to burn, and I could hear sounds of fighting in the highborn district.'

Malus nodded thoughtfully. 'A damned brilliant plan,' he admitted. 'Urial holds all the advantages.' He tried to slide his legs off the slab, grimacing in pain. 'If we don't do something very soon, all will be lost.'

Arleth Vann reached for the highborn. 'My lord, I'm not sure you should be moving,' he said. 'Your wound...' He paused, his face troubled.

Malus stopped. 'What about my wound?'

The retainer considered his words carefully. 'The warpsword pierced between your ribs and punctured your left lung,' he said. 'There was bloody froth on your lips, and you were gasping for air. Most men die from such a wound, even with the aid of a chirurgeon. Indeed, there were times during the morning when I was certain that you were about to take your last breath.'

'But?' the highborn enquired.

Arleth Vann started to reply, but words failed him. Helplessly, he pointed to the cut in Malus's robe.

Malus looked down, realising for the first time that his kheitan had been stripped off and his robe loosened. He felt a twinge of dread as he reached up with tentative fingers and pulled the dark cloth aside.

Arleth Vann had evidently used some of his plundered water to clean Malus's wound as best he could. The skin on the left side of his chest was mottled with dark, indigo-coloured bruises from his breastbone all the way to his navel. The puncture was a neat line almost as long as his finger, running between his fifth and sixth ribs. The ache in his back told him that a similar wound was present there as well.

The skin around the puncture was almost solid black. The injury itself was sealed shut, bound by a rope of thick, black tissue that wept a pale, foul smelling liquid.

Mother of Night, Malus thought, his blood running cold. What has Tz'arkan done to me?

Arleth Vann pointed hesitantly at the highborn's wound. 'I... I've never seen anything like that, my lord,' he said. 'What is it?'

Corruption, he thought, remembering Lhunara's words. The daemon's grip on his body was far worse than he'd imagined possible. Suddenly he remembered the stab wound he'd received in the battle on the Slavers' Road. He ran a hand over his thigh, finding not so much as a scab or scar. It was all he could do not to cry out in fear.

I'm teetering on the abyss, he thought. One more step, and I'm lost!

Belatedly, Malus realised that Arleth Vann was watching him, his expression growing more disturbed with each passing moment. He groped about for an explanation. 'It's... it's the blessing of Khaine,' he said. 'Am I not his Scourge?'

A cruel chuckle echoed in Malus's head. It was all he could do not to clench his fists and try to beat that sound out of his skull. 'What of you?' Malus asked, eager to think about something else. He studied his retainer's filthy, tattered robes and blood-stained skin. 'I saw what Yasmir did to you with her knives.'

The retainer averted his eyes, apparently willing to accept Malus's explanation, although his expression remained troubled. 'The wounds in my arms will heal,' he said simply. 'The witches teach us techniques to speed the healing process and knit torn flesh. As for the rest...' He reached up and pulled back a flap of his own robe. The faint light gleamed off polished rings of fine, close-set mail stitched to the inside of the assassin's clothes. 'They weren't as bad as they looked.'

Malus hazarded a weak chuckle. 'I thought you and your kin had no fear of death.'

The assassin shrugged. 'I don't fear death, my lord, but that's no reason to make things easy for my foes.'

Suddenly a heated exchange of words echoed from the antechamber beyond the tiny crypt. 'Speaking of making things easier on our foes,' Malus said. He drew as deep a breath as he could manage, and was both surprised and frightened to discover that he was breathing much easier than before. Then slowly, painfully, he pushed himself off the stone slab. His legs threatened to give way beneath him. Arleth Vann leaned forwards, reaching for him, but Malus waved him away. Another deep breath, and a measure of strength returned. The highborn adjusted his robes, cinching them tight, and then headed for the doorway.

Two more oil lamps threw fitful light on a rectangular chamber some thirty paces long. More crypt entrances, many still sealed by thin wooden doors, lined both of the long walls of the room, while larger entryways opened onto subterranean darkness at either of the short ends of the chamber. Alcoves had been carved into every free space on all of the room's walls and piled with skulls and cloth-wrapped bones. Ancient statuary lay in broken, moss-covered piles in each of the four corners, their original appearance long lost to the mists of time.

Rhulan stood in the centre of the room, glaring hotly at the young priestess who'd fought so well in the battle at the temple. Her hands were open in supplication, but Malus could see a steely glint in her eyes. There was a hint of anger and desperation in her voice. 'We deserve answers, Arch-Hierophant,' she said. 'If Urial is not the Swordbearer, how could this have happened?'

All eyes were on Rhulan. Every one of the temple loyalists sat on the bare stone floor, watching the exchange with hope and dread in equal measures. Even the tattooed elder had taken keen interest in the argument, sitting with her back to one of the piled sculptures, a pair of broad bladed knives lying naked in her lap.

'Does the writ of the temple not teach us that Malekith, lord and Witch King, is Khaine's chosen Scourge?' the priestess continued. 'Was the blade not bound by chains of sorcery, warding it so that only the Swordbearer could draw it forth?'

Malus saw a glimmer of fear in Rhulan's eyes. His lip trembled as he struggled for an answer. It looks as if he's living his worst nightmare, the highborn thought.

'No ward is perfect,' Malus interjected, causing everyone to jump. Startled faces turned to regard the highborn as if he'd risen from the dead.

'Urial is a potent sorcerer in his own right,' Malus continued, leaning against the doorframe for support, 'and has he not spent years studying the temple's lore? He's had plenty of time to uncover a means to circumvent the magic protecting the sword.'

'But the sword is meant for the Scourge alone.'

Malus studied Rhulan carefully. The elder was clearly very nervous. He knows that the sword has passed through many hands over the centuries, the highborn thought. Have they told the faithful it was passed directly from Khaine to the hands of the temple? 'The sword may be meant for the Scourge, but cannot others bear it? Wield it, even? After all, how long had the elders kept it before they came to Har Ganeth?'

The priestess glanced at Malus, her brow wrinkling in thought. 'Are we certain he is not the Scourge?'

'I am,' Malus said with utter conviction. He eyed Rhulan. I'm not so certain about the Arch-Hierophant, though.

'Malekith is the chosen one,' Rhulan said weakly, 'so it is written.'

'Then you had best get the blade out of Urial's hands before the Witch King learns of this,' Malus said.

'Why is that?' the tattooed elder asked, fixing Malus with a penetrating stare. 'This is a matter for the temple to resolve.'

Malus shook his head. 'Not if word of this coup makes it to the other cities,' he said. 'Malekith cannot see it as anything less than a challenge to his authority. He will have to take the sword from

Urial, if only to prove that it is his by right. If other members of the temple decide that Urial is the true Scourge, the resulting feud could tear Naggaroth apart.'

'Blessed Murderer!' Rhulan said, placing a trembling hand over his mouth. 'What are we going to do?'

'We're going to fight them,' Malus said grimly. 'You should have been out in the city hours ago, rallying the faithful behind your banner. In a battle like this, the side that seizes the initiative will triumph, and I guarantee that Urial has already started moving against you.'

The priestess frowned. 'Urial can't possibly stop us,' she said. 'He has his zealots, but we have a small army at our command.'

'Urial has more than just his true believers,' Malus said. 'He has an entire city to call upon. Everything the zealots have done up to this point is to turn the citizens of Har Ganeth against the warriors of the temple. They goaded the temple into a campaign of fire and slaughter, and then they locked them out of their safe refuge, leaving them at the mercy of the people they savaged. Once Urial shows the people that he has taken up the sword and condemns the warriors of the church for their crimes, the streets will run red once more.' He pointed to the two elders. 'You must escape the fortress and rally the faithful. Denounce Urial and blame yesterday's bloodshed on the zealots, and then hunt down the heretics remaining in the city and turn your attention to retaking the fortress.'

The elder gave Malus a stricken look. 'We can't fight Urial,' he said.

'Why not?'

'The bearer of the warpsword cannot be defeated in battle,' the elder replied. 'So it is written.'

Malus started to argue, but then he understood. You think Urial really is the chosen one, he thought. You know the truth about the prophecy, and you're trapped between the Witch King and the man you believe is the true Scourge.

'Leave Urial to me,' the highborn said. 'I will remain behind with a handful of volunteers and strike the usurper directly while your forces hold his attention at the fortress gates.'

Rhulan said nothing for a moment, his dark eyes narrowing as he considered Malus's plan. Finally, he nodded. 'So be it.' He turned to the assembled loyalists. 'Mereia and I must join our brothers and sisters in the city. Who will remain behind and take the battle to the usurper?'

'I want no more than a dozen,' Malus said. 'We will have to strike hard and fast. Even then, there is little chance that many of us will survive.'

The priestess turned to the highborn, raising her chin haughtily. 'I will stay,' she said. Other druchii rose to their feet, singly or in small groups. Malus counted only ten, but he wasn't going to press the issue.

Rhulan surveyed the volunteers and nodded. 'The blessings of the Lord of Murder be upon you, brothers and sisters,' he proclaimed. 'Khaine's will be done.'

'Khaine's will be done,' the faithful answered.

Mereia, the tattooed elder, rose smoothly to her feet. 'How will we escape from the fortress?'

Malus looked to Arleth Vann.

'Take the winding staircase and follow the ancient road to Thel's house,' the assassin said. 'Even if there are guards watching the passage, you could still slip past them in the darkness. You could even call the maelithii down on them if you could fight your way to within sight of their iron anchors.'

Rhulan nodded. 'Then let us go. Every moment is precious.' As Mereia and their escorts gathered up their weapons, the Arch-Hierophant stepped close to the highborn.

'Are you certain you are capable of this?' he asked, studying Malus's face intently. 'Your wounds are grave.'

'I have suffered worse,' Malus said evenly. 'Never fear, Rhulan. I will fulfil my part of the plan. See that you do the same.'

'The fate of the temple – perhaps Naggaroth itself – rests in your hands. So far, Urial has yet to put the sword to the test, and if we can deal with him before he reveals the sword to the people then no one ever has to know this happened,' the elder said quietly. 'How will you separate Urial from the sword?'

Malus shrugged. 'I don't know for certain, but I expect it will involve a bit of bloodshed.'

'Remember what I said,' Rhulan whispered. 'Everyone knows the sword cannot be defeated in battle. You must find another way to best Urial and take the blade from him, and once in your possession it must never be used, by you or anyone else. Swear it!'

The highborn gave the elder a bemused look. 'As you wish, Arch-Hierophant.'

Rhulan nodded. 'Good. Very good. When you have the sword, bring it to me, and you will be well rewarded.'

Malus fought to keep his expression neutral. What are you playing at now, he wondered?

Before he could inquire further, a faint sound echoed from the dark passageway to Malus's left. Everyone in the antechamber froze upon hearing it.

'What is that?' the priestess whispered, clutching her axe.

The sound faded, but the echoes still lingered in Malus's mind. Setting his jaw, he slowly drew his sword.

'It sounded like a howl,' he said.

Chapter Fifteen
THE ABODE OF THE DEAD

THE CRY CAME again – a thin, almost despairing sound that wound faintly down the corridors of the crypt. The Khaineites shared apprehensive looks.

Malus looked to Arleth Vann. The assassin drew his twin blades, his expression tense. 'Whatever it is, it's coming this way,' the retainer said.

'Could it be a wight or a guardian spirit?' the highborn asked.

Rhulan answered, a quaver of fear in his voice. 'We built these tombs to contain the dead, not give them free rein.'

'Then I believe Urial has come looking for us,' Malus growled.

Mereia rose gracefully to her feet. 'What do we do?'

'You and Rhulan get out of here. Now.' Malus said. 'We'll buy you as much time as we can.'

The howl echoed down the eastern passage once again – then dissolved into a chorus of shrieking, gobbling cries that seemed to draw nearer by the moment. Galvanised by the horrific sounds, Rhulan, Mereia and their escorts dashed for the western corridor. The tattooed elder gave Malus a comradely nod as she passed. 'Kill one for me,' she said, drawing a vicious grin from the highborn.

Rhulan's parting look was far grimmer, as he paused at the mouth of the passageway and turned his gaze on the highborn. 'Remember what I said,' he said. 'The future of the temple depends on it.'

'I'll do what must be done,' Malus said gravely. 'Count upon it.' Providing I live through the next ten minutes, he thought.

He was in no shape to fight, of that alone he was certain. The wound in his chest ached when he moved, and his limbs felt clumsy and weak. Unbidden, he thought of the daemon. A taste, just the merest taste of Tz'arkan's power would make all the difference.

Could he take one more sip from the font of corruption without losing himself forever? He could bargain with the daemon. He could ask for just enough to get through the next battle, and no more. He could do that, couldn't he? If he died here, in the depths of this goddess-forsaken crypt, his soul would belong to the daemon anyway. Was it not better to live in corruption than to die and be enslaved forever?

The cries of the hunters drew nearer, and Malus felt all too keenly just how trapped he'd become.

More sounds emanated from the darkness: wet, slithering sounds, punctuated by the dry scrabbling of claws. One of the loyalists let out a frightened cry and shrank from the passageway. 'Blessed Murderer deliver us,' he said, his voice cracking with strain. 'We're all going to die!'

The words sent a tremor through the assembled Khaineites, but the axe-wielding priestess let out a derisive snort. 'Speak for yourself, wretch,' she said, spinning the haft of her weapon in her hands. 'I'm going to live long enough to make the bastards pay for what they've done.'

Arleth Vann chuckled. 'Never underestimate the power of sheer, bloody-minded spite,' the assassin said. 'Isn't that right, my lord?'

Malus thought it over. A wolfish smile spread across his face. 'Truer words were never spoken,' he said, hefting his sword. 'We'll meet them at the threshold,' he said, the words coming briskly as a plan of action took shape. 'Whatever's coming, I'd rather face them one at a time.'

The loyalists took heart from the highborn's fierce demeanour, readying their weapons and rushing to form a tight semicircle around the open doorway. The sounds of the approaching hunters stalking down the narrow passageway grew louder and more terrible: a cacophony of slithering, galloping, clawing madness that sent chills down the highborn's spine. Suddenly he was reminded of the twisted Chaos beasts that he fought in Urial's tower, many months past. As bad as those things were, this sounded a great deal worse.

The roiling tide of unnatural motion swept down on them in an avalanche of unsettling noise. Then it suddenly stopped. The druchii stared vainly into the cave-like darkness, more unsettled than ever.

An eerie stillness hung in the air, setting Malus's nerves on edge. He glanced at the man on his right. 'Fetch me one of those lamps,' he whispered, barely loud enough to be heard. The loyalist nodded and quickly snatched a lamp from the base of a broken statue. The brass vessel was hot to the touch as it was pressed into the highborn's hand.

'Let's see what we're dealing with,' Malus said, hurling the lamp down the passageway.

The palm sized lamp tumbled end over end, its tiny flame guttering until it struck the stone floor and broke apart. Orange fire whooshed into life as the wick ignited the spreading oil, revealing the hunters in all their horror.

There were three of them, their bulk so great that they could not stand side-by-side in the narrow, bone strewn corridor. Firelight shone on glistening, gelatinous flesh, shot through with thin, black veins and throbbing with unnatural strength. They had lean, powerful bodies similar to those of lions, their broad paws tipped with glossy, black claws, but their heads were like bloated octopi. The closest one to the fire reared back on its paws, its soft, bulbous skull pulsing with rage as it lashed the air with eight long, whip-like tentacles. Hundreds of suckers lined each tentacle, each one fitted with a barbed hook for trapping and shredding prey. At the centre of the mass of tentacles a cruel, glossy beak snapped furiously at the offending flame, unleashing a torrent of thin shrieks and gobbling cries.

The man beside Malus screamed like a child, and the Chaos beasts attacked.

The lead hunter bounded over the pool of flame and leapt for the screaming man, as if drawn by the sound. Its tentacles made a whirring sound in the air as they lashed at the terrified druchii. One slashed across the man's face, shredding the skin and muscle beneath as if they were rotted cloth. The stench of brine and rotted meat filled Malus's nostrils, making him gag. More tentacles wrapped around the hapless druchii, in the blink of an eye, enfolding him and pulling him from his feet. Wet, tearing sounds emanated from within the writhing web of fleshy ropes, and the druchii's frenzied screams of agony made Malus's blood run cold.

'Kill it!' Malus cried. 'In the Dark Mother's name, kill the thing!' He slashed at the beast's shoulder with his sword, but the creature's gelatinous flesh was deceptively strong, and his blade rebounded as if he'd struck solid oak. Arleth Vann darted at the thing, unleashing a flurry of stabbing blows. The blades sank barely an inch into the creature's flank, producing thin streams of clear, foul-smelling ichor.

Blows rained down on the creature from all sides. The priestess aimed a fearsome, two-handed blow at the creature's bulbous skull, but the axe blade left only a shallow cut in the heaving flesh. Undeterred, the Chaos beast continued to rip its victim apart. Blood poured from between the thrashing tentacles.

More tentacles whirred through the air, this time from the left side of the doorway. Malus heard a strangled scream and turned to see another man lifted from his feet by a second Chaos beast that clung to the wall of the passage like a spider. One broad paw had reached around the edge of the threshold and flattened itself against the wall of the chamber for support, and Malus saw that the base of the creature's feet were also lined with hooked suckers. The beast lifted its victim off the ground as if he was a child, wrapping one tentacle around the druchii's sword arm and ripping it off in a spray of hot blood.

'Mother of Night!' Malus cursed fearfully. They didn't stand a chance against these things. 'Run!' he shouted to his dwindling band. 'We can't stop them!'

The loyalists needed no convincing. They broke and ran for the western passage with barely a backward glance. Malus, Arleth Vann and the priestess were the last to break away, leaving the creatures to consume their prey. Though powerful, the beasts didn't seem to be much smarter than hunting hounds, easily distracted by the smell of blood, which suggested that their handlers were probably somewhere close by.

They were barely halfway across the antechamber when the third beast raced along the right wall of the passage and bounded heavily into the chamber, its tentacles waving sinuously as if it was tasting the air for prey.

The priestess let out a defiant scream and the beast oriented on her at once. Thinking quickly, Malus let out a war scream of his own and the beast turned to face him, spreading its tentacles wide and showing its clashing beak. The highborn raced for the nearest wall as the beast gathered itself and leapt with a keening wail.

It landed less than five paces from Malus, reaching for him with a blur of fleshy whips just as the highborn grabbed up the second of the three oil lamps and flung it at the creature's head. The lamp burst apart, covering its bulbous skull with blazing oil, and the beast recoiled with a tortured shriek as its wet flesh sizzled in the flame. The highborn took no time to savour the hurt he'd caused. The moment the beast was distracted he ran for the western passage as fast as his feet could carry him.

Malus plunged into near-total darkness without the faintest idea where he was going. He sensed he was in another narrow corridor, the twin of the passageway to the east. Somewhere up ahead he heard faint shouts, so he gritted his teeth and ran towards the sound. His feet struck a pile of spilled bones and he stumbled through the remains, cursing under his breath. Thin howls echoed behind him as the hounds began sniffing for new prey.

He reached a crossroads lit by patches of grave mould and paused, his heart hammering in his chest. The shouts seemed to be coming from everywhere at once, overlaid with the unsettling cries of the Chaos beasts. Thinking quickly, he glanced at the stone floor and saw hints of wet tracks following the passage to the left.

The highborn ran on, swallowed once again by suffocating darkness. The passage curved before he knew it and he bounced along the wall for several feet before it straightened out again. A piercing cry rang out behind him. It sounded as if one of the hounds had reached the crossroads, just a dozen yards or so away. Malus broke into a run, not caring if he ran headlong into another wall.

After another dozen yards the passageway opened into a larger, broader antechamber, bordered by half a dozen crypts and connecting three other passageways. Malus's heart leapt when he saw a small globe of green witchfire glowing at the mouth of the southern corridor. Arleth Vann beckoned to him urgently. 'Hurry, my lord! They're right behind you!'

An impertinent reply rose to his mind, but Malus elected to save his laboured breathing for more important work. Sharp daggers of pain shot through his chest as he struggled to breathe, and whenever he stood still it felt as if the chamber would start to spin. Focusing his will, he took the deepest breath he could and ran on.

The assassin took the lead, racing down the twisting passageway as fleet as a deer. Arleth Vann pulled steadily away from Malus, even as the sounds of the pursuing hounds drew closer. He could hear their wet, slithering strides and the click of their claws on the stone as they bounded steadily closer.

Malus could only utter a breathless curse as the retainer darted around a sharp corner up ahead, taking the faint light with him. The sounds of pursuit echoed all around him, and he found himself dreading the whip-like touch of the hounds' lashing tentacles against his back.

He was so focused on the sounds behind him that he missed the turn ahead, crashing against the wall hard enough to lose what meagre wind he had. He rebounded from the stone and reeled like a drunkard with the gobbling cries of the hunters punishing his ears.

He staggered a handful of steps around the corner, and found another long corridor glowing with patches of mould. A broad, jagged fissure ran across the passageway.

Arleth Vann was nowhere to be seen.

Grunting against the pain and loss of air, Malus lurched down the hall. He could hear the whirring of the tentacles. The hounds were just around the corner.

'My lord!'

Malus started at the sound. The assassin's voice was coming from the fissure. 'Down here!' The retainer said. 'Quickly!'

There was no time to argue. The first hunter rounded the corner with a wailing roar and Malus threw himself at the fissure. Fierce pain bloomed in his chest as he hit the stone floor and half-slid, half-rolled into the jagged opening. Clawed tentacles scraped the stone just a hand span behind him.

Malus felt a powerful sense of vertigo as he tumbled over the edge. The fissure was no mere cleft in the ground. It was a narrow crevasse, plunging deep into the earth. Arleth Vann let out a warning shout as Malus flailed desperately at the close-set, irregular walls. Pain bloomed in his knees and elbows as he managed to wedge himself tightly enough to stop his fall. His boots hung over empty space, leaving Malus giddy with fear.

'My lord!' the assassin cried from above. 'Are you all right?'

'Just fine,' Malus snarled. 'These jagged rocks managed to break my fall.'

A sharp howl echoed in the darkness and clawed tentacles lashed against the sides of the crevasse as one of the hunters tried to reach its prey. 'Keep going down!' the assassin shouted. 'The beasts won't be able to reach us.'

A tentacle slapped the wall of the crevasse less than a hand span from Malus's head. The highborn frantically groped about with the toes of his boots, trying to find some kind of foothold, but nothing gave him enough purchase.

Then Malus felt a sharp impact as one of the beast's tentacles struck him in the cheek. Another tentacle brushed against his neck. With a desperate shout the highborn relaxed his limbs and plummeted into blackness.

STRONG HANDS PULLED at Malus's shoulders, rolling him onto his back. His eyes fluttered open, and then snapped shut as a jagged pain lanced through his chest. The highborn bit back a tortured groan, hearing the sound echo in the space around him.

'My lord?' Arleth Vann said. The assassin bent close, examining Malus's chest. 'You're bleeding again. I think you tore your wound open in the fall.'

'Where in the Dark Mother's name are we?' he panted, forcing his eyes open again and peering around in the subterranean gloom. Faint witchlight played on smooth walls and square beams, hewn from living rock. The stone ceiling of the passage was split crosswise by a ragged cleft, its edges still spilling a faint spray of earth from his long, uncontrolled plunge.

'We're safe, for now,' the assassin said. 'The hunters can't fit into the cleft, and their handlers won't abandon the beasts to come after us alone. They might even think we're dead.'

Gritting his teeth, Malus tried to sit upright, but another flare of sharp-edged pain forced him to abandon the effort with a frustrated snarl. He pressed his hand to his left side and it came away sticky with fresh blood. 'They may not be all that far wrong,' he snarled, 'but that doesn't answer my question. Where in the Dark Mother's name are we?'

'We're outside the Lodge of the Delvers,' Arleth Vann said, reaching his hands under Malus's arms. Slowly, carefully, he pulled the highborn upright. 'There may be only a handful of people left in the temple who even know this place exists.'

Biting back waves of pain, Malus allowed himself to be pulled to his feet. The passageway was low-ceilinged, brushing the top of his head. The corridor itself ran as straight as an arrow, receding into blackness to the right. To the left, it ran for thirty paces and ended at a pair of stone doors hung on hinges of gleaming iron.

Arleth Vann helped Malus down the passage, towards the waiting portal. As they came closer, Malus could see that the surfaces of the doors were elaborately carved with underground scenes. Short, stout figures with braided beards came and went in fantastic scenes of subterranean splendour, bringing riches from the deeps and crafting them in works of cunning and art in a wondrous city chiselled from stone. It was like nothing the highborn had ever seen before.

He reached out and touched the surface of the doors, and the massive stone slabs swung inward on perfectly balanced hinges, revealing a broad, low-ceilinged room. A number of bare stone tables stood inside the chamber, each one short and broad. Four were arranged on each of the long sides of the room, their feet facing another, more ornately carved table in the room's centre. Another set of double doors stood at the chamber's opposite end.

Malus frowned. 'This is where the temple keeps its dwarf slaves?'

'In a manner of speaking,' the assassin replied. 'This is where the builders of the temple were entombed.'

The retainer helped Malus into the room, leading him to the central table and leaning the highborn against it. 'The elders entombed their dwarf slaves?' Malus asked, unsure at first if he'd heard the assassin correctly.

Arleth Vann nodded. 'It was a singular honour, a reward for their labours. Surely you noticed the craftsmanship of the building?'

'I had rather a lot on my mind at that point, but, yes, I noticed,' Malus replied irritably.

'That was just after the schism,' the assassin said, surveying the room appreciatively. 'With the dissenters driven out or slain, the first elders began work on the great temple in earnest. Over a hundred and twenty dwarf slaves laboured to build it, and construction took almost half a century. When the building was complete and the warpsword installed in its sanctum, the elders had the dwarfs build this splendid mausoleum for themselves. They told the delvers that their work had earned them a place of everlasting honour among the faithful, and that their spirits would be venerated for all time.'

'And then?'

Arleth Vann paused. 'Once they had completed the crypt the elders had them all killed and interred within.'

'Mother of Night,' Malus gasped. 'A hundred and twenty dwarfs, cut down in their prime?' The waste of so much valuable chattel staggered the imagination. A highborn could build and outfit a raiding ship for the cost of just one dwarf slave. Short of dragon eggs there was no more expensive commodity in all of Naggaroth.

The assassin shrugged. 'Bad for them, but good for us. The lodge was built deep below the hill – deeper even than the Vermillion Gate – and no one has come here for millennia. Only a few records of the place remain in existence, buried in the archives of the temple library.' He nodded to himself. 'It's a perfect base of operations, really: defensible and difficult to reach, but close enough for us to reach the passage leading to Thel's old house and communicate with the loyalists in the city if we need to.' He sighed. 'Now I've just got to get back up into the tunnels and lead the rest of our people down here past those damned beasts,' he said. 'This could take time. Will you be all right until I get back?'

Malus had nothing to say. When Arleth Vann looked over at his master he found the highborn had passed out once more.

Chapter Sixteen
DARKNESS AND DOUBT

'THE WOUND IS grave, my lord.'

Malus's eyes fluttered open. He was lying on the stone slab in the antechamber of the dwarf tombs. Someone had stripped away his kheitan and robes, and gooseflesh raced along his bare shoulders and back.

Firelight danced along the walls and limned a robed and hooded figure at work beside one of the long tables at the highborn's right. Malus heard the sound of metal ringing faintly on stone as the figure laid out a series of small tools. The voice he'd heard was familiar, but he couldn't place it.

He tried to rise, fearful that the figure would see the daemon's taint upon him, but ropes pulled tight at his wrists, shoulders and forehead. Memories of his days in his father's tower sent a cold thrill of panic racing up his spine. 'What is going on?'

'There is an infection,' the figure said. 'Your lung has collapsed, and the wound is... corrupted. Something must be done quickly, or you will die.'

A shiver of fear wracked his body. He knew what the figure was trying to say. 'You are going to have to cut the infection away,' Malus said, unable to keep a note of dread from his voice. 'Have you any hushalta?'

'No,' the figure said, holding a small, curved blade up to the light. 'You must brace yourself for what must be done, my lord. It is the only way.'

The figure turned towards him, reaching for his chest with a long-fingered hand. Orange light shone on the blade's razor edge. Malus could feel the wound in his side begin to throb and his heart quicken in fearful anticipation.

'I will work very quickly,' the figure said. Fingers played across Malus's ribs, fluttering like spider's legs over the raw, bleeding wound. 'You may scream if you wish. It will not trouble me.'

Malus opened his mouth to reply, but the words were lost in a terrible groan as the figure's bare fingers pressed into the cut and spread wide, enlarging the tear. Hot blood welled up in the wound, flowing down his side as the knife went to work. A spear of white-hot pain lanced again and again into his chest, stealing his breath away. Just when it seemed he could take no more he saw the figure straighten, holding up a lump of pink, glistening meat in its hand. The hooded face looked down at him.

'You see? Almost the size of a fist. As I said, very grave.'

A shudder passed through Malus. 'I feel... cold...'

'Of course,' the figure replied, tossing the flesh onto the floor. 'That is to be expected, but it is a small price to pay for your health, is it not?'

The figure raised the knife again, but this time its bloodstained hand pulled at the hem of its own robes. With a flick of its wrist it pulled its robe open and revealed bare, gleaming ribs stained black with corruption. Nearly all of the internal organs were missing, save for a wrinkled sac of flesh pulsing close to the breastbone.

'Nearly done,' the figure said. As it spoke, it reached up into its chest cavity and cut away the tattered, oozing remnant. 'The wound is painful, but it will heal, and then you and I will be stronger than ever.'

Malus tried to move, but the bonds held him fast. He screamed, shouting curses at the figure as it bent low and pushed the corrupted tissue into the highborn's gaping wound. At once, he felt the alien flesh wriggle and squirm inside him – and worse, he felt his organs heave and rise up to meet it.

The hooded head turned, close enough for Malus to see the face sheltered within. It was *his* face, pale and perfect, devoid of any daemonic taint. Only the eyes – black orbs like shards of the Outer Darkness itself – suggested the depths of the corruption that seethed within.

Tz'arkan smiled, showing jagged, obsidian fangs.

'You'll be a new man before you know it,' the daemon said with a gruesome chuckle.

'CAREFUL! CAREFUL! HOLD him tight!'

Malus awoke with a shout, struggling against the grip of the four druchii who held him pinned to the stone slab. Arleth Vann loomed over him, pressing a hand to his clammy forehead and forcing a small vial between his lips. 'Drink,' he said, his voice hard and unyielding.

The taste of burnt copper flooded Malus's mouth. He gagged and tried to spit the hushalta out, but the assassin cursed fiercely and covered the highborn's mouth. Glaring at the retainer, he reluctantly swallowed the healing draught and forced himself to relax.

Arleth Vann studied Malus's eyes closely for a moment, and nodded in satisfaction. 'All right. You can let go,' he told the druchii, and the loyalists withdrew. They eyed Malus fearfully as they returned to sentry positions on either side of the dwarf lodge's entryway.

Malus raised a trembling hand and pressed it against his side. The wound ached fiercely. He pulled open his grimy robe and peered at his ribs, discovering the cut scabbed over and beginning to shrink. The black bruises remained, however, giving him the look of a week-old corpse. His mouth still tingled with the sharp taste of copper, and his joints creaked like dried leather. 'Water,' he said hoarsely.

The retainer lifted a leather water bottle to the highborn's lips, and Malus drank greedily. It was warm and brackish, but he savoured it like rare wine. When his fierce thirst abated somewhat, he glared at the grim faced assassin. 'You've been drugging me,' he croaked.

'You were going to die otherwise, Scourge or no,' Arleth Vann replied.

Malus drew a deep, slow breath, his eyes narrowing as he tested the extent of his injury. 'How long have you kept me out?'

'Three days.'

'Mother of Night!' Malus seethed, grabbing a handful of his retainer's robe. 'Have you any idea what you've done? Rhulan has been waiting outside the wall all this time! You may have damned us all!'

'Rhulan is not at the wall,' the assassin replied. 'In fact, I can't say for certain that he's even in the city any more.'

The highborn's anger faded. 'He hasn't rallied the warriors of the temple?'

Arleth Vann shrugged. 'If he tried, they evidently didn't listen,' he said gravely. 'I made my way out through the house of Cyrvan Thel the night after we reached the lodge, hoping to locate some food and other supplies,' he explained. 'The city had gone mad. Bloody riots were raging in the streets and much of the city was burning. From what I could discern, the temple warriors are holed up in scattered pockets all across Har Ganeth, cut off from one another by the raging mob. Certainly no one is directing their efforts to regroup and reach the temple.'

Malus took his hand away from Arleth Vann and slowly, painfully, he forced himself upright. The pain gave him something to focus on beside the rising tide of dismay that lapped at his brain. 'So Rhulan and Mereia ran afoul of the riots,' he said.

'It is possible. There are bodies everywhere,' the assassin replied. 'Or they might be trapped with one of the isolated warbands and can't find a way to communicate with the rest.'

The highborn gave his retainer an appraising stare. 'You don't think so,' he said.

Arleth Vann weighed his reply carefully. 'If he isn't dead, I think he's escaped the city,' he said with a sigh. 'Perhaps his courage failed him. Who knows? You heard him in the crypts. He thought Urial couldn't be beaten.'

'Damnation,' Malus spat. 'I thought at least Mereia would have been made of sterner stuff. We needed that diversion to help us reach Urial.'

The assassin straightened and set the water bottle on a nearby table. 'In a way, the temple warriors may be serving us better in the city than they would outside the temple gates,' he said. 'As long as the fighting continues, Urial must divide his forces between the temple fortress and the riots in the streets. He doesn't dare ease up on the pressure and allow the warbands to link together.'

Malus considered this. 'How easily can you move about the catacombs?'

'I can come and go as I wish, so long as I'm careful,' the assassin replied. 'The tunnel network is just too vast and interconnected to patrol effectively. I still hear Urial's hunters prowling through the crypts, but in truth they are poor trackers. So long as one is patient and quiet, they can be circumvented.'

'All right,' the highborn said with a sigh. He suddenly felt completely drained, as if the mere effort of sitting upright had consumed every ounce of his energy. 'How many of us are left?'

'Eight, counting you and me,' Arleth Vann replied. 'After the flight from the crypt I was able to find out where six of the volunteers were hiding and led them down here one at a time. Khaine alone knows what happened to the other two.'

The highborn nodded. His eyelids were getting heavy. He realised that it was because of the damned hushalta. 'No more mothers' milk,' he mumbled. 'No time to waste. Find where Urial is hiding... how he's being guarded...'

Arleth Vann said something in reply, but the assassin's voice seemed to fade into the distance as the healing drug pulled him under.

* * *

WHEN HE AWOKE again, Arleth Vann was gone.

Malus was ravenous. He took that as a good sign. The high-born lay on the stone slab in the centre of the dwarf lodge for several long minutes, gauging the stiffness of his limbs and the degree of pain in his chest. Finally, he summoned his resolve and swung his legs off the side of the table.

His knees nearly gave way beneath him when he slid to the stone floor. The sentries at the door stirred as Malus caught himself on the edge of the table. 'I'm all right,' he said, waving them back to their places. In point of fact, he felt anything but.

Malus looked around the chamber. Several small oil lamps flickered on three of the long side tables, and the assassin's water bottle still lay nearby. The door opposite the lodge's entrance stood open, and he thought he heard faint sounds echoing from beyond.

He reached for the water bottle and took several deep draughts, wincing at the vile taste. 'What time is it?' Malus asked the sentries.

The loyalists looked to one another and shrugged. 'Night time, I think,' one of them said. 'I no longer know what the hour is.'

Malus nodded thoughtfully. Then, gritting his teeth with effort, he walked towards the open doorway.

Beyond the low threshold he found himself in a long, irregular chamber that stretched off to his right. The features were a strange mixture of square-cut pillars and straight walls connecting small, rounded niches that had been carefully shaped to resemble natural caverns. In each niche the stone floor rose up to form a squat, rectangular tomb, inscribed with angular dwarf runes and overlaid with arcane magical sigils that glittered in the lamplight. There was no gilt-work or precious gems, no grave goods or mummified slaves, but the sheer scope and craftsmanship of the crypt was staggering. The caverns and their connecting passages had been hollowed out of solid rock, and the crypts constructed with surpassing skill.

Malus could see that the four tombs closest to him were open. He limped slowly to the nearest one, noticing a name inscribed at the foot of the stone coffin in druchast. *Thogrun Hammerhand*, it read, *Stonemaster*. A broad-shouldered dwarf clad in a slave's simple woollen robes lay in the coffin. His red beard was thick and stiff as wire, and his skin was the colour of granite. Only the faintest signs of decay could be seen around the stonemaster's seamed eyes and rounded nose. It was as if he'd been laid in the coffin only a few days before. The edges of the gaping cut that bisected the stone-master's throat were only just beginning to shrivel. A veritable pall of sorcery hung over the figure, encasing it in a tight weave of magical energy.

More sounds echoed through the chamber from its far side: the scrape of stone, mutters, and faint, tired sounding curses. Frowning, the highborn sought out the source of the noise.

The room curved slightly to the right, following a logic that perhaps only a dwarf could appreciate. Malus walked past nine more crypts before the walls of the room narrowed to form a short, broad entryway into a connecting chamber. Two loyalists worked in front of the entryway, hauling heavy, rectangular stone panels into place to form a kind of defensive breastwork facing back the way Malus had come. They looked up at the highborn's approach and paused in their labour, wiping their faces with grimy rags.

Malus reviewed their work and nodded appreciatively, noticing that the stone panels were the thick lids used to seal the dwarf tombs.

'I see my retainer has been keeping everyone busy,' he said.

One of the men nodded. 'This is the last of them, my dread lord,' he said, a little breathlessly. 'There are more like this going all the way back to the prime chamber. We didn't have much to work with, since this place is practically built like a fortress already. A handful of people could hold off an army down here if they wanted to.'

Malus considered the crude fortifications and had to agree. With multiple, well-protected bastions to retreat to, they could take a fearsome toll of Urial's zealots if discovered. His half-brother's Chaos-spawned monsters were another matter, but he didn't think it wise to point that out. 'Where is our camp?' he asked.

The loyalist gestured over his shoulder. 'Five chambers further back, my lord,' he said, 'just outside the prime chamber. There's some food and water there if you're hungry. Your man brought in supplies a couple of days ago.'

Malus nodded again and carefully picked his way over the defensive barriers. 'With luck, we won't have to put these to the test,' he said, 'but carry on, all the same.' The men went back to work as the highborn disappeared into the chamber beyond.

The grave lodge wound back and forth through the rock beneath the hill like the track of a serpent. Each burial chamber was slightly curved, running away at an angle from the one before it. Possibly it was a technique to allow such a large number of tombs to fit within the stone confines of the region, but Malus suspected there was a ritual purpose to the layout, as if the curving lines of the chambers formed a sigil or sacred rune carved into the undying rock. At each entryway the druchii had built a defensive position using the lids of the tombs found nearby. One or two oil lamps sputtered in each chamber, providing just enough light to travel by.

By the time he'd passed through the second burial chamber the sounds of work behind him were swallowed by the stone walls, leaving Malus wrapped in funereal silence. For a brief time he felt truly alone, passing from shadow to shadow like a ghost amid the broken tombs, and it soothed him after a fashion.

'Did you have pleasant dreams?' whispered the daemon inside his head.

Malus paused at the entrance of the next burial chamber. Was it the fourth, or the fifth? He hadn't been keeping track. 'I dreamt of stuffing you into a chamber pot and throwing you into the deep sea,' he growled.

Tz'arkan chuckled. 'Dreams of vengeance and spite. I should have expected no less.' The daemon uncoiled itself within the highborn's breast. 'What of your wound? Are you healing well, little druchii?'

Malus's hands clenched into fists. 'You should know better than I, daemon. Soon I'll be no better than the wretches confined in these tombs, infused with so much sorcery that not even the worms will touch me.'

Obscene laughter raked along the inside of Malus's ribs. 'Such childishness! Such vanity! Your body has recovered from a mortal wound in less than a week. There are men who would think that an awesome gift, one worth almost any price.'

The highborn entered the next chamber, picking up his pace. 'The difference is that I see through your deceptions,' he replied. 'Every time I open myself to your power I let you increase your hold over me.'

'I have your soul, Darkblade.' The daemon sounded genuinely amused. 'What greater hold over you do I need?'

'Then why this?' Malus pulled open his robes, revealing the glossy, black scabs on his chest and the deep bruises in his flesh. 'Your gifts are making me into an abomination!'

Tz'arkan sighed. 'No, they are making you worthy of the fate that awaits you. Do not dissemble, Malus. I know your heart's deepest desires. You crave power. You dream of the day when all of Naggaroth bows before you.'

Malus continued on in silence, stalking angrily past the dwarf tombs.

'Did you think that mere treachery and cunning would be enough to supplant one such as the Witch King? You will need power beyond that of the greatest druchii heroes. That is what I offer you, yet you reject it at every turn.'

'I don't feel stronger, daemon. I feel... hollowed out.' Malus said. 'I feel twisted and diseased. You're corrupting me.'

'To what purpose?'

'To enslave me! What else?'

The daemon laughed. 'Stupid, stupid Darkblade! Why would I do such a thing? I know your fate. I laid its foundations millennia ago. In that sense, you were a slave to my wishes from the moment you were born. For the sake of argument, let's assume you are right. Let's say that I am subverting your will with each touch of my power. Tell me then: how is it you continue to resist me, even as your body weakens and your foes gain in strength? Have you lost one whit of your obstinate personality since you entered my temple in the north?'

Malus held his tongue. Part of him hungered for the daemon's power, like a drunkard ached for the taste of wine. If Tz'arkan didn't know it, he wasn't about to volunteer the information.

'Nothing to say? I thought not,' the daemon replied smugly.

The highborn crossed the dimly lit burial chamber and entered the next. Things were different here. More lamps burned along the curving chamber, outlining a meagre camp of bedrolls and cloth bags lying haphazardly in a dense cluster in the centre of the room. The priestess and a druchii novitiate lay wrapped in their cloaks, sleeping soundly on the stone floor. It struck Malus that after all this time he still didn't know the young priestess's name.

'So what will you do, Malus?' Tz'arkan asked. 'Will you continue to suffer needlessly, or will you allow me to renew your strength?'

Moving silently, the highborn picked his way among the snoring loyalists and sought out the far end of the room. Another set of defensive barricades had been placed there, but Malus also saw that a large stone door sealed this portal. Runes had been carved into the door's surface and inlaid with molten silver. Powerful charms and spirit wards radiated from the barrier, tingling across the highborn's skin.

Malus climbed over the barricades and carefully pushed the door open.

There were no oil lamps within. He pushed the stone door wide, letting the illumination at his back flow into the small room before him. It was similar to the burial niches he'd passed along the way, fashioned like an artificial cavern and containing a single tomb. Unlike the rest, the stone coffin was still sealed, and its surface was covered in a profusion of layered sigils and spells. *Gothar Grimmson*, the inscription read, *Ironmaster*.

Malus stepped inside the prime chamber and, after a moment, pushed the door closed. Darkness and silence swallowed him whole.

'How do I know you're telling me the truth?'

The daemon chuckled. 'Lies are for the weak and the stupid, Darkblade. I have little need of them. I have said this before, and I will say it again: I have never lied to you, ever.'

'You haven't told me the entire truth, either.'

'That, Malus, is a very different thing,' Tz'arkan replied archly. 'I've told you everything you needed to know at the time.'

'So what aren't you telling me now?'

The daemon paused. 'Nothing of import, I assure you.'

Malus smiled coldly. 'Then you'll understand if I look for answers elsewhere.'

'What does that mean?' the daemon hissed.

Wrapped in concealing darkness, Malus raised his hand and felt for the cold silver band that circled the finger of his left hand. The sentry had told him it was night outside, and as near as he could reckon the moon would be waxing bright.

Of course, Eldire hadn't bothered to explain to him how the damned ring actually worked. Lacking any other ideas, he clenched his fist and focused his will into a single word.

Mother.

Malus felt a ghostly breeze touch his face. He smelled the faint scent of ashes. Suddenly the daemon wrapped tightly around his heart, making him wince.

'Malus, what are you doing?' Tz'arkan asked sharply. 'What foolishness is this?'

The daemon's grip was relaxing and its voice fading. A strange, silvery glow, like faint moonlight, began to fill the small chamber. Malus felt his aches diminish, yet at the same time his body turned leaden and cold.

The light intensified, pushing back the shadows and drawing the sharp outline of a figure standing next to the ancient tomb. From one moment to the next the figure took on more and more solidity, swelling from little more than a silhouette to a tall, square-shouldered woman wearing the black robes of a seer. Long, white hair hung in a thick braid to below her waist, bound at the tip with a band of gold. She was statuesque and regal, with a face that was both beautiful and coldly forbidding. Wreathed in pearlescent light, she studied her surroundings with detached interest, entirely unfazed by his sorcerous summons.

'Eldire,' Malus said, inclining his head respectfully.

She turned at the sound of his voice. 'Hello, my son,' she replied. Her voice sounded clearly in the room, although it had a curious echo to it, as if she was speaking from the bottom of a well. Eldire's body remained somewhat ethereal, like a ghost's, and he could see the faint outline of the dwarf tomb through her vaporous form.

'It has been some time, Malus,' Eldire continued. 'I had begun to fear the worst.'

The thought made Malus chuckle. 'As if a seer of your power would have any need to worry.'

'Nothing is ever certain, child, especially where divination is concerned,' she said coolly. 'We deal in possibilities. Where you are concerned, the threads of fate are more tangled than most.'

The highborn frowned. 'That doesn't sound encouraging.'

'On the contrary, it means you are finally attempting to create your own fate instead of having one shaped for you,' she said. 'Of course, this necessarily means that things are less certain than they were before.'

'So you're saying I'm flirting with disaster.'

'More so than usual, yes,' Eldire said. Her lips quirked into the briefest of smiles.

'I'll try to take heart from that.'

'Good,' she said, turning to regard the tomb beside her. 'Now perhaps you can explain what you are doing in a dwarf crypt when you should be at Har Ganeth looking for the warpsword.'

And so he explained as best he could, describing how he'd finally gained entrance to the City of Executioners and then found himself caught up in the holy war waged between the temple loyalists and Tyran's zealots. He told her of the debacle in the sanctum and their retreat into the catacombs.

Then he spoke of the wound he'd been given, and the power of Tz'arkan's hold over him.

'He claims to be strengthening me,' Malus said bitterly. 'It makes some sense, come to think of it, but is it the truth? What other reason can there be, if not to enslave me completely?'

Eldire considered all that Malus had said. 'The daemon speaks the truth, as far as it goes,' she said carefully. 'It is true that Tz'arkan has stolen your soul, and that corrupting your body would not gain it any more influence over you than it already has, but I do not think it seeks to control you at this point. It intends to *become* you.'

A chill coursed down the highborn's spine. 'What do you mean?'

'Tz'arkan is transforming you, slowly and surely, to become a daemonhost,' the seer replied. 'Normally such a process takes a great deal of time, but your case is hardly normal, is it?'

'So the daemon seeks to… what? Wear me, like a glove?'

'In a manner of speaking, yes. Your soul will be destroyed, and Tz'arkan will take its place.'

Malus looked down at his chest. 'If the daemon's energies can heal me like this, how far gone am I?'

Eldire glided silently forwards and reached a ghostly hand towards the wound. Her expression darkened. 'You walk a knife's edge, my son,' she said. 'Chaos energies seethe within your flesh, but you have not yet been wholly consumed. Your will remains strong, and while it does you can keep the daemon at bay a little longer.'

Malus nodded, even though he felt anything but strong. Did he dare tell her how his limbs trembled at the thought of the daemon's power? He craved the icy rush of Tz'arkan's gifts, and he feared, deep in his bones, that he could not beat his half-brother without them.

'The battle ahead will be difficult,' he said. 'How will I be able to confront Urial alone and defeat him when he wields the warpsword?'

'How should I know?' Eldire asked irritably. 'I'm hundreds of leagues away. I've never set foot in Har Ganeth, much less examined the sword. You will simply have to find a way.'

Malus sighed, folding his arms tightly across his chest. 'Why couldn't you simply turn up and solve everything with a bit of arcane insight, like the sorcerers in all the legends?'

She leaned close. 'If we could truly do that, my son, we wouldn't have need of people like you,' the seer replied. 'Find a way. Your soul depends on it.'

'With hate, all things are possible,' he said, wishing the saying still had the power to reassure him.

Eldire smiled, brushing an insubstantial hand against his cheek, and then stepped away. She studied the tomb once more. 'Why so much effort for dwarfs?' she asked.

'It was a reward for building the temple,' Malus said sourly. 'A hundred and twenty prime dwarf slaves. Such a waste of very expensive flesh.'

The seer extended a long finger, tracing the sigils inscribed into the tomb. 'Dead, but their spirits remain,' she said. 'These are powerful wards of binding. A great deal of sorcery was invested in these tombs.'

'Who can fathom the wisdom of priests?' Malus asked with a shrug.

'Indeed,' Eldire admitted with a sigh.

'Has word reached the Hag about Urial?'

'No, not yet,' she said. 'If the priestesses at the temple know it, they are keeping the news to themselves. You are right of course, once Malekith learns that Urial has the sword, he will march on Har Ganeth. A fast rider could reach the Hateful Road from Har Ganeth in less than a week.'

Malus imagined Rhulan galloping down the Slavers' Road for all he was worth. 'And Isilvar?'

Eldire looked back at Malus. 'The Drachau has proclaimed him a hero for saving the city,' she said. 'His power grows by the day.'

'As powerful as Lurhan?'

'No, but powerful enough, in time,' she said. 'Forget him and Hag Graef, my son. Your future lies elsewhere.'

'My future is mine to decide, mother,' Malus said. 'You told me that. When the time is right, I will return to the Hag. I have unfinished business there.'

Eldire opened her mouth to respond, but thought better of it. She shrugged. 'As you wish, child. First, however, you must deal with Urial. That, I fear, will be challenge enough.'

With that, she was gone. There was no gesture of farewell – Eldire simply faded like a ghost, taking the penumbral light with her.

Malus was swallowed in darkness and doubt.

Chapter Seventeen
SECRETS OF THE SWORD

WHEN ARLETH VANN returned to the lodge he found Malus sitting on the tomb of Gothar Grimmson, picking at a few scraps of stale bread and a piece of stringy meat spread out on a greasy cloth in his lap. An oil lamp sputtered on the top of the stone coffin, near the dwarf's feet.

The highborn glanced up as the assassin slipped quietly into the small crypt. 'Where did you find this awful stuff?' he asked, grimacing in distaste. He pulled a thread of the dark, stringy meat from the cloth and reluctantly put it in his mouth. 'If I didn't know better I'd say you robbed the temple kennels.'

'Nothing so fancy,' Arleth Vann replied.

Malus paused in mid-chew. 'Do I want to know?'

'Almost certainly not.'

The highborn eyed the rest of the food with dismay. 'Damnation,' he muttered wearily, and forced himself to continue eating.

'How are your injuries, my lord?'

'Better,' the highborn answered, hoping he sounded sincere. 'Or well enough for me to get out of this damned mausoleum, at any rate. What have you learned?'

The assassin glanced back into the chamber beyond, checking to see if anyone might be listening. Apparently satisfied, he sank to his haunches and steepled his fingers under his chin while he collected his thoughts.

'It's getting harder to move around the temple grounds,' he began. 'The zealots have killed most of the temple novitiates and slaves, and converted the rest. Those that remain have been given a brand in the centre of their foreheads in the shape of a sword. I think Tyran has done this to make infiltrators easier to spot.'

Malus considered the news. 'Are there still zealots in the fortress grounds?'

'Yes. I'm not certain how many, but most of them know one another on sight at this point.'

'I see,' the highborn replied. He pulled out his dagger and began sawing at the stale bread. 'Any news of the temple assassins?'

Arleth Vann shook his head. 'Incredibly, they remain in conclave. I suppose Urial's move has complicated their decision somewhat.'

'That doesn't sound good. If they were solidly for Rhulan and the loyalists they would have made up their minds by now.'

The retainer shrugged. He drew his own stained cloth parcel from the folds of his robe and unwrapped it across his knees. There was a piece of flatbread inside and a handful of small, dried fish. 'That's true, but at least they aren't actively opposed to us yet.'

'True enough,' Malus said. He stopped sawing at the bread and inspected his work, surprised that he'd barely made an impression on the stale lump. Frowning, he set the bread on the top of the tomb and hammered at it with the pommel of his knife. The blows made no mark at all. He held the lump up to the lamplight. 'If I could put a strap on this I'd use it as a shield,' he muttered darkly.

Arleth Vann pulled a small bottle of water from his belt and set it by his knee. Then he reached into the voluminous folds of his left sleeve and produced a small, clay jar. The assassin broke the wax seal around the lid of the jar and pulled off the lid, sniffing experimentally. Satisfied, he dipped one of the fish in the jar and popped it into his mouth, chewing contentedly.

'What have you learned about Urial and Yasmir?'

The assassin frowned, switching back to business. 'Nothing good, I'm afraid. It appears that your half-brother has taken his bride-to-be and retreated back into the Sanctum of the Sword. Only Tyran and a few other zealots are allowed inside to confer with him, and the temple is heavily guarded.'

Malus leaned back against the foot of the coffin. 'How heavily guarded?'

'I can only guess based on what I was able to overhear, but I would say at least a dozen zealots stand guard at the entrance to the sanctum, and twice that number on the stairs leading from the chapel on the ground floor.' The assassin shook his head. 'We can't fight our way through all that without raising an alarm.'

The highborn stared at the stone floor. He knew that there was a way. With the daemon's help he could carve through the true believers like a whirlwind, but Eldire's words dogged him. *You walk upon a knife's edge.*

'Surely there are secret passageways leading into the sanctum? Every other building on the hilltop seems riddled with them.'

Arleth Vann shook his head. 'The sanctum was created specifically to safeguard the sword and serve as the site for the temple's holiest rites. There is only one way in and out.'

Frustration gnawed at Malus, setting his teeth on edge. He leaned his head back and knocked it lightly against the tomb. 'There has to be another way in. Think, damn you!'

'Not unless you know a way to dig through dwarf-crafted stone,' the assassin replied grimly.

Malus froze. 'What did you say?'

The assassin frowned. 'I wasn't trying to be impertinent. I just said that unless you know a way to dig through dwarf-crafted stone–'

'That's it!' Malus said leaning forwards intently, 'Dwarf-crafted stone.' The highborn tapped his lower lip thoughtfully. Slowly, he turned and looked back at the tomb. 'Blessed Mother of Night,' he whispered in wonder.

Arleth Vann eyed his master warily. Surreptitiously, he picked up the jar of yellow sauce and sniffed it suspiciously, before setting it down again. 'Is everything all right, my lord?'

Malus stared thoughtfully at the foot of the coffin. 'Why is this room called the prime chamber?' he asked.

The assassin shrugged. 'That's not its real name. Dwarf burial rites are very secret affairs. Bodies are prepared in the antechamber yonder, away from the prying eyes of all but their kinsmen, and then laid to rest in their crypts.' He looked around the small room. 'I called this the prime chamber because there's just one tomb in here, unlike the others.'

'So this slave was someone important?'

'Most likely. A master of his craft, perhaps.'

Malus nodded, feeling his heart quicken. 'And the sanctum is made of stone? All of it?'

Arleth Vann could not help but give his master a condescending stare. 'Of course, my lord. Dwarfs don't build with wood. Every bit is cut stone, cunningly fitted together. What *are* you driving at?'

Once again, Eldire's words echoed in Malus's ears. *Why so much effort for dwarfs?*

The highborn reached up and touched the inscription on the tomb. 'Tell me,' he said, looking back at his retainer with a dawning smile, 'if the temple was built entirely of stone, what did the elders need with an ironmaster?'

Arleth Vann's eyes narrowed warily. 'I don't understand.'

'Gothar Grimmson here is an ironmaster, not a stone carver,' Malus said. His mind raced as he began putting the pieces together. He rose to his feet and began to pace the small room. 'What if the sword Urial took from the sanctum isn't the actual Warpsword of Khaine?'

The assassin was too stunned to speak for a moment. 'That's absurd,' he sputtered.

'Is it?' Malus asked. 'You said that the sanctum was built to safeguard the sword, but from what? The relic had been in the possession of the elders for centuries. Why the sudden need to enshrine it under layers of sorcerous wards?'

'I...' The retainer's voice faded as he wrestled with the notion. 'I don't know. Perhaps the elders feared the schism leaders would try to steal the sword at some point.'

'Or perhaps they already had!' the highborn exclaimed. 'You said that the five zealots who volunteered to kill the temple leaders were never heard from again. Doesn't that seem odd to you? If they had been caught or killed, wouldn't the elders have wanted to make a public spectacle of their deaths?'

'I suppose so.'

'Then it's reasonable to assume they weren't caught. So what happened to them?' Malus spun on his heel, his stride quickening along with his thoughts. 'What if they realised that their assassination attempt was doomed to fail, and decided on another course of action? Perhaps they couldn't kill the elders, but they could deprive them of the cult's most prized relic! So they took the sword and vanished.' The highborn nodded to himself. 'That's why the elders sent their warriors rampaging through the city afterwards. They weren't looking for the zealot leaders so much as they were looking for the warpsword itself!'

'But we know the assassins never returned from the fortress,' the retainer said. 'So where did they go?'

'Where else? Through the Vermillion Gate.'

Arleth Vann froze, a rebuttal dying on his lips. 'Blessed Murderer,' he swore softly. 'Of course.'

'One can imagine how frantic the elders were when they learned the sword had been taken,' Malus said. 'How could they claim to be the true servants of Khaine without the blade in their possession? What would become of their alliance with the Witch King? The elders may have survived the assassination attempt, but the zealots had dealt them a mortal blow all the same.

'Then a very strange thing happened. Days turned to weeks, and weeks into months, and nothing more was heard about the sword. If the zealots had it, they would have used it to discredit the temple publicly. So the elders realised they'd been given a sort of reprieve. For the moment, no one in Naggaroth knew of the warpsword's fate, so they hatched a desperate plan to save themselves.'

'They made a copy of the blade,' Arleth Vann said, his voice tinged with wonder.

'Exactly,' the highborn said. He patted the foot of the tomb. 'They had Gothar here make a perfect copy of the relic, and then made a grand show of installing it in the temple. The sanctum wasn't built to safeguard the sword at all, but to protect the temple's darkest secret.'

'That's why they killed the dwarf slaves,' the assassin said. 'They had to silence Gothar so he couldn't betray them, and murdered the rest to camouflage the act.'

'The elders even went so far as to bind their spirits into these tombs so that no sorcerer could question them later,' Malus said with admiration. 'That's why the elders kept Urial at arm's length all this time. Even if he had been the true Scourge, they couldn't give him what they didn't have.'

'So Rhulan and the other elders knew the truth?'

'Yes. That's why he told us we couldn't fight Urial directly – because the legend says the bearer of the warpsword can't be defeated in battle. If we put the lie to that claim, the rest of the deception would have begun to unravel.'

The assassin nodded thoughtfully. 'It all makes sense,' he said. Although from the sound of his voice he was loathe to believe it. Suddenly he straightened. 'Do you think Urial knows he doesn't have the real sword?'

'Honestly? I don't think so,' Malus said. 'Not yet, at least. Until the blade is put to the test he has no reason to think it is a replacement.'

'That's why Rhulan hasn't rallied the temple warriors. He doesn't dare spur a real confrontation with the zealots, despite the fact that he knows he has a good chance of defeating them.' The assassin shook his head ruefully. 'What madness!'

'Indeed,' Malus said. He continued to pace, tapping his chin furiously. 'Mother of Night,' he swore. 'The sword could be anywhere in the world. How are we going to find out where the assassins took it?' The rush of triumph he'd felt as all the pieces of the puzzle clicked into place turned to bitter frustration. For a moment he thought he'd found a way to cheat the daemon and claim the sword without having to confront Urial or Yasmir at all. He struggled with a flood of hopeless fury, so preoccupied that at first he didn't notice Arleth Vann had spoken. Malus caught the questioning look in the assassin's gaze and paused in mid-stride. 'What?' he asked.

'I said that I think I know a way,' Arleth Vann replied.

THE ASSASSIN'S RIGHT hand shot up and the small party froze in place. Malus and three of the surviving six loyalists settled onto their haunches, hands tightening on their weapons. Darkness flowed towards them as Arleth Vann closed his left hand, muffling the small globe of witchfire he'd conjured.

For several long moments Malus heard nothing but the sound of his own heart labouring in his ears. Then he heard a faint, keening wail, skirling out of the blackness somewhere up ahead of them. Two of the druchii behind Malus shifted nervously at the ominous howl. One let out a fearful moan.

'Hsst!' Malus whispered threateningly. 'Not a sound!'

No one moved. Malus caught himself holding his breath, straining to hear the telltale signs of discovery. A minute passed, and then another.

Finally Arleth Vann relaxed, opening his hand and filling the narrow tunnel with cold light. He turned his body slightly so he could glance back at Malus. 'The Chaos beasts are hunting somewhere up ahead, but they don't seem to be in our path,' he whispered to the highborn.

Malus nodded. He hadn't the faintest idea how the assassin could tell, but he knew better than to argue with the druchii's keen senses. 'How far to the citadel?' he asked.

'Another few minutes, if all goes well.'

'Let's go, then.'

The retainer rose silently to his feet. Malus followed suit. Behind him, the axe-wielding priestess – whose name he'd finally learned was Niryal – and two more loyalists made ready to move. They had been working their way through the tunnels beneath the hill for more than an hour, climbing from the deepest levels where the dwarf lodge was located and taking a circuitous route to the subterranean chambers of the Citadel of Bone. They had been forced to crouch in the darkness and hold their breath many times, while Urial's hunters prowled nearby, but so far the assassin had succeeded in leading them away from the horrific beasts. Arleth Vann's assessment had been correct; the monsters were fearsome killers but very poor trackers. Had the zealots turned a pack of nauglir loose in the tunnels the loyalists would have been in serious trouble.

Not for the first time, Malus wondered how Spite was faring in the war-torn city. Was he still being fed and boarded in the highborn district's nauglir pens, or had hunger or misadventure driven the cold one into the streets? He had no real fear for the nauglir's safety – the warbeast was more than a match for any but the most heavily armed warbands prowling Har Ganeth's streets. It was the safety of the relics in the cold one's saddlebags that gave the highborn cause for concern. He was haunted by visions of the cold one clawing its way through the doors of its pen and tearing its saddlebags off in the process, or having them ripped open in a fight and spilling their contents onto the street.

One thing he was coming to realise about sorcerous relics was that finding them was only half the challenge. *Keeping* them for any length of time was just as hard, if not harder.

If the zealots had stolen the sword and escaped through the Vermillion Gate hundreds of years ago, Malus hadn't the faintest idea how to track them, but Arleth Vann knew of a library in the Citadel of Bone that might contain some useful clues. All they had to do was slip past Urial's hunters and zealot patrols and infiltrate one of the most important buildings in the temple fortress undetected. As ever, the assassin volunteered to make the attempt alone, but Malus had insisted on sending a small party instead. There was simply too much at stake to risk sending a single man, even one as skilled as Arleth Vann. If anything went awry and Urial guessed their interest in the library, the would-be Scourge could place it under such heavy guard that they wouldn't be able to get anywhere near it – or worse, lay a sorcerous ambush to catch them unawares the next time they tried to reach it.

Holding the globe of witchlight over his head, Arleth Vann set off down the narrow, bone-strewn corridor. Many of the crypt passages had been thrown into disarray by the passage of the Chaos beasts. Skeletons had been scattered from their shelves and crushed to powder beneath the hunters' leonine paws. Some of the fresher ones even had the skulls and long bones split open in a vain search for meat. The assassin picked his way carefully among the drifts of bone and rotted cloth, leaving Malus and the loyalists to follow in his footsteps and watch every dark niche and side passage with a growing feeling of unease. No one spoke, but everyone shared the same sense of dread. The longer they spent in the tunnels, the greater the chance that the hunters would catch their scent. Sooner or later their luck would run out.

Arleth Vann moved unerringly through the maze of tunnels, pausing only occasionally to check his bearings at corridor junctions or antechambers. From what Malus could tell Niryal and the other temple servants were just as disorientated as he was. All he knew for certain was that they were close to the surface. The corridors showed signs of frequent traffic and were largely free of cobwebs and layers of dust. The highborn was surprised at how eager he was to get above ground, even for a short time. It had been almost six days since he'd been out in the open air, and the claustrophobic weight of the catacombs was beginning to tell on his nerves.

Long minutes passed, and Malus's impatience grew. One passageway led to another and every sound set the highborn's teeth on edge. They heard no more hunting howls echoing in the blackness. Did that mean the beasts had moved further away, or were they creeping stealthily closer, waiting until the very last moment before rushing at their prey in a cacophony of terrible, whistling shrieks?

Finally, Malus could take no more. He quickened his steps slightly, enough to catch up to Arleth Vann and pluck at a corner of his robe. The assassin stopped.

'You said just a few more minutes,' Malus whispered.

'We're nearly there,' the retainer replied. He pointed into the darkness ahead. 'There is a chamber just a few more yards that way. Beyond it will be a ramp leading up into the citadel's lower rooms.'

Malus took a deep breath, forcing himself to relax. 'All right,' he said, 'lead on.'

The assassin slipped quietly along the corridor, and within a few minutes more Malus saw the glow of the witchlight expand to fill a broad chamber just ahead. It was a rectangular room almost twenty paces across on its long sides, and its walls and corners were piled with skeletons and crumbling skulls. Passageways led off to the left and right, and a long, sloping ramp led upwards from the opposite side of the chamber. Arleth Vann stepped to one side as he entered the room, and Malus rushed past with the loyalists hot on his heels.

'Wait, my lord!' the assassin hissed in warning. 'Something's not right–'

Frowning, the highborn turned to ask what he was talking about, but his question went unasked as a chorus of high-pitched screams shattered the dank air.

Chapter Eighteen
INTERROGATING THE DEAD

FOR THE BRIEFEST instant, Malus froze in horror as the high-pitched shrieks reverberated across the dimly lit chamber. The attackers charged from the shadowy passageways, but instead of the rapacious Chaos beasts they expected, their foes were in the shape of men. They wore grey robes and kheitans beneath long shirts of blackened mail, and their skin and hair were smeared with a thick layer of soot or ash. Each man carried a short, cruelly hooked spear or a short, stabbing sword with a serrated edge, and their expressions were contorted in snarls of feral bloodlust.

Malus knew that these were not sorcerous monsters that shrugged off the touch of sharpened steel, and the knowledge filled him with murderous vigour. The highborn raised his sword and met the enemies' charge with a bloodthirsty laugh. 'Blood and souls for Khaine!' he cried, and rushed at the oncoming men.

The first man he reached lunged at Malus with his spear, his eyes widening in surprise at the highborn's reckless charge. Malus slapped the spearhead aside with the flat of his blade and then smashed the heavy sword into his attacker's face with a backhanded strike. Bone crunched as the keen edge struck the man just beneath his nose and split his skull in half. The corpse lurched on past the highborn for several more steps before collapsing to the floor.

The clangour of battle filled the air as the loyalists threw themselves at their foes. An ashen-faced attacker screamed as Niryal ducked beneath his spear thrust and hacked off his right leg just below the knee. Arleth Vann drew one of his blades and danced through the onrushing foes sweeping in from the left, toppling two men in a spray of bright crimson.

Two druchii rushed at Malus, holding their saw-bladed knives in an underhand grip. Still laughing furiously, he charged the first man, driving him back with a swipe at his face. The second man saw an opportunity and lunged in from the right, bringing up his blade in a disembowelling thrust, only to find he'd fallen into the highborn's trap. At the last moment Malus pivoted away from the thrust and severed the man's knife-hand with a short, powerful stroke. Hot blood sprayed across Malus's face as the maimed warrior reeled backwards, but the highborn had already turned his attention back to the second knife wielder. The druchii slashed at Malus's throat, but the highborn blocked the knife stroke easily, deflecting the smaller weapon away with his heavier blade. Before the druchii could recover Malus planted his left foot and lunged, driving his double-edged sword into the man's throat. The point of the blade grated against the druchii's spine and the mortally wounded man dropped lifelessly to the floor.

Suddenly Malus felt something curved and sharp circle his left ankle. He glanced left just in time to see one of the druchii leering triumphantly at him before hauling back on his spear. The weapon's curved billhook pulled Malus off his feet. Instinct and battle-hardened reflexes made him rotate in midair, letting him take the fall on his back instead of his sword arm, but the spearman was a quick and cunning fighter, stepping in swiftly and smashing his billhook against

Malus's sword-hand. The highborn roared in pain and rage as his sword was sent spinning end over end across the room.

The spear swept around again, this time angling for Malus's neck, but the highborn caught the haft with both hands and pulled the druchii towards him. As the man stumbled forwards, Malus kicked the druchii hard in the groin and then smashed a heel against his attacker's left knee. The man fell hard, his face locked in a grimace of pain, and Malus pulled the spear from his hands. The highborn reversed his grip on the weapon and buried the spear's point in his foe's temple, and then crawled clear of the twitching body and scrambled for his lost blade.

Men were running past him. The ashen-faced attackers were in full retreat, demoralised by the ferocity of their foes' counterattack. There was a whirring of steel through the air and then a meaty *thunk*, and one of the fleeing druchii let out a strangled gasp and fell to the floor with Arleth Vann's sword buried in his back. Malus reached his sword and lurched to his feet, but by then the rest of the attackers had vanished, their footfalls receding swiftly into the darkness.

Arleth Vann dashed to his victim and pulled his sword free with a muttered curse. Malus took stock of his party and found that none of the loyalists had been injured in the brief fight. He turned to his retainer. 'Who in the name of the Outer Dark were they?'

'Beastmasters,' the assassin replied. 'The temple employs them to provide animals for festival games and to train its warriors.' He glanced down the left passageway, concern on his face. 'We must have surprised them as much as they did us, but they'll be calling the hunting beasts to them at any moment. We need to get inside the citadel, now!'

'Lead on,' Malus said, and Arleth Vann darted up the ramp without another word.

The ramp ran up through a series of large storerooms, switching back upon itself with each new level. They passed dusty crates and cracked clay urns that had once held expensive ink, bales of rotting cloth and sheaves of incense sticks that thickened the air with cloying, spicy scents. They saw no one as they raced for the upper levels of the tower, although in places Malus noticed a line of fresh boot prints running ahead of them through the layers of dust.

After several long minutes they reached the chamber and the top of the ramp, their noses clogged with dust and strange scents. A pair of broad, iron-banded doors stood at the other end of the room, and one of the heavy panels was slightly ajar. Arleth Vann rushed down an aisle of crates and pulled the door wider, as if he feared it might slam shut at any moment. Malus glimpsed a large, dimly lit room, beyond, piled high with more supplies. Stairs rose along the high, stone walls into the tower proper.

The assassin breathed a sigh of relief and doused his sorcerous light. 'We're in luck. The fools didn't think to bar the door. Quickly now!'

Malus and the loyalists filed through the doorway and Arleth Vann pulled the heavy door shut behind him. A broad, wooden wheel was mounted on a spindle set into the stone wall next to the doorway. The assassin grabbed the wheel's spokes and leaned against it, pushing with all his strength. Bemused, the highborn joined him on the wheel's opposite side and pulled, grimacing at the flare of pain in his chest. At first the wheel refused to budge. Then, inch-by-inch, it began to turn. There was a building screech of rusted iron, and then the doors trembled with a muted *thud*.

'That's it,' Arleth Vann said breathlessly, leaning against the wheel. 'The dwarfs built this to secure the citadel in times of war.' He pointed at the top of the threshold. 'Iron rods can be lowered into slots on the top of the doors, fixing them in place. The beasts can't get to us now.'

'How are we supposed to get back to the lodge?' Malus asked.

To his surprise, Arleth Vann gave him one of his ghostly smiles. 'Honestly, I have no idea. I'm more or less making this up as I go.'

Malus winced. 'Ah, well, that's comforting.'

'Would it help if I told you that it may not be a problem?'

'And why is that?'

'There's a good chance we'll all die once we reach the library.' The highborn stared balefully at his retainer. 'I think you spent too much time with Hauclir back at the Hag. He's been a bad influence.'

Arleth Vann straightened. 'Really? That's interesting.'

'Why?'

'He said the same thing about you.'

Malus frowned. 'Impertinent wretch.'

'That's funny. He said the same thing–'

'Enough!' the highborn growled. 'Let's go see this damned library!'

Arleth Vann gave Malus a sketchy bow and dashed off, heading for a staircase on the far side of the room.

They climbed two more floors before they emerged into a corridor lit with globes of witchfire. The air smelled fresh, and Malus drank it in like wine. They were finally above ground.

Muted shouts echoed from one end of the corridor. Malus turned to Arleth Vann. 'What's that?'

'Urial must have men guarding the citadel,' the assassin said. 'The beastmen are raising the alarm.' He glanced down the opposite end of the passageway and seemed lost in thought for a moment. 'We'll take the servants' stairs,' he said after a moment. 'This way!'

Malus and the loyalists raced after the assassin, dashing through a maze of corridors before reaching a set of tightly curving stairs that led up into the higher levels of the tower. They climbed for a long while, their panting breaths echoing hollowly in the dark, cramped space. The highborn expected a wave of screaming zealots to sweep down on them from above at any moment, but many minutes later they left the staircase and emerged unchallenged into a brightly lit hallway. Arleth Vann raised his hand in warning, crept silently to the end of the passageway and peered into the space beyond. He motioned for the group to join him a moment later.

They crept from the passage into a large, open room not unlike a highborn's entry hall. A sweeping staircase rose to a gallery overlooking the room, and a circular platform sat in the centre of the chamber, piled high with severed skulls. Incense hung heavy in the air, attempting to mask the stench of rot rising from the putrefying trophies. A pair of heavy, gilded doors stood shut in a shadowed alcove beneath the gallery, opposite an open archway that led to an antechamber on the far side of the tower. The marble floor was covered in scraps of cheap brown paper. Malus frowned and stirred a pile of papers with his toe. Each sheet was covered in fine, archaic script. 'What's all this?' he asked quietly.

'Petitioners' writs,' Arleth Vann replied. 'Members of the temple may petition the Haru'ann for access to the libraries, and if their request is granted they are given a scrap of paper marked with the elder's signature and a verse or two from the *Parables of Sundered Flesh*. Then the petitioners are left here to wait and meditate upon the verses until the librarians call their names.' He gestured at the pile of grisly trophies. 'Many petitioners bring offerings in hope that the librarians will expedite their access, but the keepers of the sacred texts are rarely impressed.' The assassin pointed to the double doors. 'This level contains nothing more than histories and copies of sacred texts,' he said, indicating the gallery overhead. 'What we want is up there.'

Arleth Vann crossed the chamber and climbed the staircase two steps at a time. Malus went after him, noting that Niryal and the other loyalists followed with considerable reluctance. Priestesses and mere novitiates were not welcome in this place.

The gallery was furnished with thick rugs and plush, high-backed chairs arrayed in twin ranks before a single door of blooded oak. Side tables set off in the far corners were set with silver goblets and bottles of wine, clearly meant for the pleasure of the temple elders. Arleth Vann turned to Niryal and the loyalists. 'Wait here,' he said.

To Malus's surprise, Niryal glared at the assassin. 'We know our place,' she said. 'It is you who overstep your bounds. This is not proper!'

'You are welcome to complain to the Grand Carnifex,' the assassin said coolly. He pushed the door open and stepped into the room beyond as if he belonged there. Malus followed close behind.

The upper library was huge, its curving walls lined with bookshelves that stretched as much as three storeys high. Long ladders of blooded oak ran on tracks of polished brass that circled the towering shelves, allowing apprentice librarians to scurry up and retrieve volumes for their patrons. Thick rugs were piled on the stone floor around ranks of wooden carrels, their working surfaces brightly lit by a cluster of large witch-light globes suspended on a chain from the centre of the vaulted ceiling. The air was thick with the smell of dust, old leather and ancient paper. It reminded Malus of his half-sister Nagaira's former library back at the Hag. 'These places are nothing but trouble,' he muttered darkly.

Arleth Vann moved quickly to the far side of the room. There, beyond the furthest rank of work carrels, the rugs abruptly stopped at an expanse of polished black marble. A large circle of arcane sigils was carved into the stone, and beyond that stood a series of tall, wooden cabinets arrayed in a rough semi-circle. The assassin studied each cabinet in turn before settling on the fourth in line and pulling its wooden doors open.

There were dozens of polished skulls inside, resting on shelves lined with black velvet. They all looked very old, and many were bound together with intricate nets of gold and silver wire.

'What is all this?' the highborn asked.

Arleth Vann looked over his shoulder at his master and smiled faintly. 'These are the real treasures of the library,' he said. 'Sacred texts are well and good, but the temple has always placed its greatest faith in the wisdom and insight of its elders. These cabinets contain the skulls of more than four hundred of the greatest men and women of the temple, stretching back for more than four thousand years. Their spirits remain tied to their skulls with powerful spells, so that they can continue to serve the faithful long after their deaths.'

The assassin reached into the cabinet and reverently lifted one of the skulls from its resting place. Malus noted that several spots on the shelves were empty, and thought of the skull that Urial had showed him in his quarters on the *Harrier*. A thought occurred to him. 'Why didn't Urial forsake the temple like the other zealots? He had to have known that the temple elders didn't dare acknowledge him even if he had been the true Scourge.'

Arleth Vann shrugged. 'I suppose it was greed. You've seen the wealth and luxury that the temple elders enjoy here. I suspect that Urial kept the zealots at arm's length for years, knowing he would need them when the time came to make his play for the sword, but looking to build his influence in the temple at the same time. Perhaps he seeks to reconcile the two in some fashion, letting him have the best of both worlds.'

Malus gave a cynical grunt. 'So much for the purity of faith,' he said. 'At least the Slaaneshi are honest about their appetites.'

The assassin shot the highborn a warning glare. 'Don't blaspheme,' he said, 'especially not in the presence of four hundred very pious, very savage ghosts.'

'Point taken,' Malus replied, watching his retainer carry the skull into the magic circle. 'For an assassin you seem to know a very great deal about the temple and its history,' he said.

Arleth Vann paused, staring down at the skull. 'I never wanted to be an assassin,' he said quietly. 'This is where I wanted to be, among the books and the old bones.'

'You wanted to be a librarian?' Malus said, not bothering to hide his disdain.

The retainer shrugged. 'I grew up here. My parents gave me to the temple when I was just a babe, like so many others. I grew up in the cells near the Assassin's Door, and when I was five I was given to the librarians to carry books and run errands. I took to letters well and could write by the time I was seven.' He looked up at the shelves. 'I was also good on the ladders, which the elderly librarians appreciated. I prided myself on getting up and down as quickly and quietly as possible.' His expression darkened, 'and that was my undoing, in a way. The librarians assigned me to a temple witch who was working on an important project, and she thought my skills were going to waste fetching books and picking up rubbish. So she spoke to the master librarian and at ten years old I began my tutelage with the temple assassins.'

Arleth Vann knelt and gently laid the skull in the centre of the circle. 'Once I entered the assassins' order, I was forbidden to enter the library, of course. So at night I would sneak into the crypts and slip back into the citadel, where I would spend hours poring through the old tomes. That's how I learned about the schism, and the deception the elders have practised for millennia. The truth is here, scattered in vague references and small details spread through scores of unrelated books.' He stood and pointed to one of the carrels near the back of the room. 'I was sitting right there the night I put all the pieces together. That was both the best and the worst night of my life. Nothing was the same after that.'

'So you threw in your lot with the zealots.'

The assassin gave Malus an indignant look. 'We're not talking about some petty highborn intrigue, where one's allegiance shifts with the wind. I was a servant of Khaine, and I had been practising heresy from the moment I entered the temple. So what other choice did I have but to leave Har Ganeth and seek the wisdom of the zealots?'

'That's why they sent you to Har Ganeth in search of the Scourge?'

'No,' the assassin replied, 'for all that you have seen of Tyran and his schemes here in the city, the true cult is not as dogmatic and rigid as the temple. Masters wander the land, practising their devotions and perfecting the killing arts, and aspirants to the cult must seek them out for instruction. When the master deems the student worthy, he or she is sent out into the world alone to worship the Bloody-Handed God and wait for the coming of the Scourge.' The assassin smiled faintly. 'Unlike most true believers, I wasn't content to simply wait for the Time of Blood to announce itself. I began searching for signs of the Scourge in every city I came to.'

'Why?'

The assassin shrugged. 'Redemption, I suppose, or revenge against the temple. At any rate,' he said with a sigh, 'that was how I found myself in a seer's hut outside Karond Kar several years ago, wagering my soul in a game of Dragon's Teeth in exchange for a divination. The woman was utterly mad, but her visions were true. She told me that the Scourge would be born of a witch in the City of Shadow, and would dwell in the house of chains.' He shook his head ruefully. 'The old wretch tried to serve me poisoned wine afterwards. The city folk had warned me she was a poor loser.'

Malus considered this and tried to hide his discomfort. He'd never inquired about Arleth Vann's beliefs when the assassin had served him at the Hag, and now he found all this talk about service and devotion more than a little disturbing. 'I hope you aren't expecting some kind of divine forgiveness from me,' he said, 'because I don't do that sort of thing.'

The assassin shook his head and chuckled softly. 'Khaine forfend!' he said. 'No, I simply serve, my lord. If the Lord of Murder wills it, I will find my own redemption. Speaking of which,' he said, drawing a deep breath, 'we're wasting time. Urial's men could be searching the citadel as we speak, and I don't know how long this summoning will take.'

'I thought you said that the assassins' order only taught you minor sorceries,' Malus said.

Arleth Vann nodded. 'That's right, but I've observed similar rituals many times in the past.'

'Meaning you've never done this before.'

The assassin hesitated. 'Strictly speaking, yes.'

'Mother of Night,' Malus cursed. 'What happens if the summoning goes wrong?'

'Well,' Arleth Vann said carefully, 'there is a very small possibility that I could lose control of the magical forces and cause a minor explosion.'

'Ah,' the highborn said, 'in that case, I'll wait in the gallery.'

'Very well, my lord.'

Malus turned on his heel and strode swiftly from the room, pulling the oak door shut behind him. Niryal and the two loyalists stood at the gallery's edge, peering over the rail at the space below. The priestess turned at his approach. 'Did you find what you were looking for?' she asked.

'My man is still searching,' the highborn replied. 'It shouldn't be long.' He joined her at the rail. The two temple servants stepped away, retreating to the top of the stairs.

Niryal resumed her watch, her expression troubled. She was tall and lean, with weathered skin stretched taut over hard, cable-like muscles. Faint scars marked the backs of her hands and the side of her thin face and neck, and her small mouth was set in a hard, determined line. 'How am I to address you?' she asked.

Malus gave her a sidelong look. 'What?'

Her dark eyes met his. 'You have a retainer – a man with the blessing of Khaine upon him and the swords of an assassin, no less – but for Rhulan, none of the other elders had any idea who you were. You know next to nothing about the temple, but you know things about the warpsword and about Urial that no one else does.' She looked him up and down. 'You dress like a beggar but shout commands like a highborn, and somehow you spent several days in the company of Tyran and his zealots, and then arrived unannounced in the council chambers to deliver an anonymous warning to the Grand Carnifex.' She cocked her head inquisitively. 'So, who… or what… are you?'

The highborn spread his hands and managed a smile to mask his concern. 'As I said to the council, I'm a servant of Khaine. What else matters?'

Niryal arched a whip thin eyebrow. 'I can think of a great many things, but let's start with this: how can you be so certain that Urial is not the Swordbearer after all? The more I think about it, the more trouble I have believing that he found a way to circumvent Khaine's will and claim the blade for himself.'

Malus hesitated. 'Malekith is the Scourge of Khaine, so it is written.'

'Yes, but written by whom? All I know is that the Witch King is in his tower at Naggarond, and Urial is here with the warpsword in his hands. I saw it with my own eyes, just as I saw him slay the Grand Carnifex in single combat. The Grand Carnifex! How can that be possible if Urial isn't Khaine's chosen one?'

The highborn's eyes narrowed warily. 'Because Urial is a sorcerer of fearsome power, and he has coveted the warpsword for many years. The Arch-Hierophant realised this. Why can't you?'

Niryal leaned close to Malus. 'The Arch-Hierophant has fled the city,' she whispered. 'I heard your retainer say so.'

Malus stiffened. 'Rhulan is a coward,' he hissed.

'Or he has no faith in you, and if he does not, then why should I?'

Out of the corner of his eye, Malus saw the loyalist sentries watching from the stairs drop into a crouch. He caught the warning movement a moment too late. Before he could react he heard shouts of alarm from the chamber below. The highborn gave a silent snarl as he saw a trio of temple beastmasters standing just inside the room. One of them locked eyes with Malus and levelled a short spear at his face.

'Damnation,' Malus cursed quietly, and the air shook with hoarse war screams as the beastmasters charged for the gallery stairs. Five of Tyran's zealots followed hot on their heels, their gleaming draichs held high.

'Stop them on the stairs!' the highborn shouted to the loyalists. The stairway was just wide enough for two men to walk abreast. If they could keep their foes off the gallery floor the zealots would be at a disadvantage with their long blades. As he raced past Niryal, Malus shot a nervous glance at the door to the upper library, but there was no hint as to what was happening on the other side. All he could do was hope Arleth Vann learned what he needed quickly. They couldn't hold out for long.

The beastmasters flung themselves at the loyalists, jabbing fiercely with their spears in an effort to drive them back. One of the men started to give ground, but Malus reached the top of the stairs and grabbed a fistful of the retreating man's robe, forcing him back. The highborn stood close, just above and behind the two loyalists, looking for an opportunity to strike.

One of the beastmasters blocked a spear thrust with his sword and then drew a ragged cut across his opponent's weapon arm. Seeing an opportunity, the second beastmaster feinted at the man in front of him and then threw a lightning quick thrust at the overextended swordsman, but Malus's sword flashed down like a thunderbolt, biting deep into the beastmaster's forearm. Bones snapped with a brittle crack and the beastmaster's howl of pain turned to a choked gurgle as his opponent recovered from the feint and stabbed him in the throat.

The dying beastmaster sagged to his left and tumbled off the stairs. His companion stepped forwards into the gap, aiming a low blow at his foe's legs. The loyalist tried to block the thrust, but the stroke was ill timed and the steel spearhead dug a deep gouge along his thigh. Screaming in pain, the temple servant slashed wildly at the beastmaster's head, but the warrior ducked beneath the blow and drove his spear deep into the loyalist's abdomen. Malus saw the sharp, steel point burst from the man's back and the loyalist died with a terrible groan.

Growling like a wolf, Malus kicked the dead loyalist in the back, sending the corpse crashing into his killer. The beast-master shouted angrily and pushed the corpse off the stairs, but as he tried to pull his spear free of the falling body Malus swept down the stairs and split the man's skull. The beastmas-ter collapsed, blood spilling down his shattered face, and the highborn pivoted on the ball of his foot and drove his blade into the third beastmaster's chest.

The second blow nearly got him killed. Just as Malus pulled his sword free from the dying man he caught a flash of steel, and instinct caused him to fall backwards, away from the draich's blurring strike. The sword flashed through the space where his head had been, continuing downwards to slice across the highborn's forearm. He grimaced at the sudden flare of pain, but there was no time for concern – the zealot continued to press his attack, reversing his curved sword and slashing upwards at Malus's neck. The highborn rolled right, feeling the razor edged steel hiss through the air a finger's breadth from his jawbone. Then there was a meaty *crunch*, and hot blood sprayed across his face. He opened his eyes in time to see the zealot fall off the stairs, the top of his head shorn away by the stroke of Niryal's axe.

Legs pumping furiously, Malus scrambled backwards up the stairs. The zealots pressed forwards. On the highborn's left the surviving loyalist was also retreating, blood flowing from a deep wound in his shoulder. Niryal stood over Malus, her bloody axe swinging in vicious strokes to keep the enemy at bay. Then movement on the floor below caught the highborn's eye. Zealots and black robed temple converts were streaming into the room and adding their weight to the group pushing up the stairway.

'Fall back!' Malus shouted angrily. 'Back to the library!'

The wounded loyalist stole a glance at Malus upon hearing the order, and the mistake cost him his life. His opponent leapt forwards with a shout and brought his powerful blade down at the juncture of the man's neck and shoulder. The blow chopped through collarbone and ribs, splitting the breastbone and tearing through his vitals. Blood burst from the man's open mouth and he fell without a sound. Whether by luck or design the loyalist's body collapsed against the front rank of zealots, slowing their advance long enough for Malus to scramble to his feet and race for the library door.

The door latch was icy cold to the touch. Malus pulled the door open and a blast of freezing air lashed at his face. Frost glittered on the inside of the door, and the chamber was suffused with a shifting blue glow. At the far end of the room, Arleth Vann stood before the elder's skull, which floated in the air several feet above his head. Blue flames burned from the skull's eye sockets, and it was attached to a wispy body that twisted and writhed as it hung in the air.

Malus raced across the room, feeling the invisible tension of the sorcerous struggle seethe across his skin. Arleth Vann's back was arched and his head was thrown back, his mouth working silently as he waged a battle of wills against the elder's spirit. Niryal stumbled through the door behind Malus, her eyes going wide at the scene playing out before her.

'Into the circle!' Malus shouted to her as he stepped across the mystical lines. Power surged and crackled around him. He felt a wave of freezing cold against his face, and his hair stood on end. A seething crackle filled his ears. The highborn turned to find the priestess right on his heels. As she stepped into the circle they were buffeted by a cyclone of unstable energies. Arleth Vann's head snapped forwards, his face etched with strain and his eyes wide.

'Release the energy!' the highborn shouted into the building storm. 'Let it go!'

The door to the library burst open as the first of the zealots charged in. In half a dozen strides the swordsmen were halfway across the room. Malus started to shout at the assassin again when he heard Arleth Vann howl in agony and the world exploded in a blast of bluish flame.

Chapter Nineteen
REVERSALS OF FORTUNE

A CLAP OF thunder smote Malus's ears and he was yanked off his feet by the power of the blast, like a leaf caught up in the wake of a raging wind. He heard screams and the sound of splintering wood, and then he crashed into something hard and unyielding, knocking him senseless.

When his vision finally cleared, long moments later, he found himself sprawled beneath a pile of shredded, smouldering books at the base of one of the library's many bookshelves. The ringing in his ears began to fade, replaced by the groans of wounded men.

A hazy, bluish light hung in the air, seeming to emanate from the very stones of the floor, walls and ceiling. The witch-light globes had shattered in the blast, and drifts of shredded paper hung like fine ash in the unearthly glow. Everything caught in the blast had been destroyed. The study carrels had been smashed to pieces like a ship's rail hit by a catapult stone, and the hundreds of books lining the shelves around the room had been mulched by a storm of wooden shrapnel. The tall cabinets containing the skulls of former elders were likewise crushed, spilling a rain of bone fragments onto the floor.

Niryal lay against one of the bookshelves to Malus's left, covered in debris but apparently unhurt. As the highborn staggered to his feet he saw Arleth Vann rising in a daze on the opposite side of the room. The assassin's face was lined with pain and exhaustion, and his eyes were wide with horror at the devastation he'd wrought. The arcane circle laid in the floor was gone, its lines of silver obliterated by the release of magical energy. Malus reckoned that the only reason he and his companions were still alive was because the destructive force radiated outwards from the edge of the circle and dragged them along with it.

Their foes had not been so fortunate.

The zealots closest to the circle could not even be said to resemble men. Their swords had shattered and their clothes had burned away, but their bodies had simply melted like candle wax, leaving nothing but piles of steaming, red mush behind. The next rank of men had caught the full fury of the blast's shrapnel, riddling and slicing their bodies into tattered, dripping rags. Only those closest to the narrow doorway had escaped death, although the door itself had been torn to flinders and hurled into the gallery beyond. Bodies writhed on the floor, clutching seeping wounds or mangled limbs.

His breath turning to vapour in the unnaturally cold air, Malus cast about for his sword and found it embedded in a pair of thick, leather-bound tomes still resting on their shelf at roughly chest height. The highborn yanked the blade loose, spilling the torn contents of the books onto the glowing stone, and stumbled through the debris towards the wounded men with a grim look on his face.

'Blessed Murderer,' Niryal gasped, her face pale and furious as she surveyed the desolation. 'What have you done?'

'What was necessary,' Malus snapped, reaching the first pair of wounded men and despatching them with short, vicious strokes. Steaming sprays of blood arced heavily through the blue tinged air with each upswing of the double-edged blade. 'Would you rather have let these blasphemers kill us?'

'Of course!' the priestess cried. 'Our lives mean nothing compared to the knowledge within these walls–'

Malus rounded on her, levelling his dripping sword at her face. 'Don't start,' he warned. Nearby, a zealot rolled onto his stomach and began crawling towards a nearby blade. The highborn caught the movement and fell upon the wounded man, hacking remorselessly at his head and neck.

'None... of... this... is... yours!' Malus said, emphasising each word with a vicious sword stroke. The zealot collapsed, and the highborn searched for another victim. 'Every book, every damned skull, all of it belongs to Urial. Do you see?'

'What I see is another bloody disaster!' the priestess shot back. Somehow she'd managed to keep her grip on her axe during the explosion, and she pointed the curving tips of its twin blades at Malus. 'Everywhere you go, you leave death and ruin in your wake.'

Malus stepped over to an unmoving form and studied it. Quick as an adder he stabbed the man in the throat and was rewarded with a bright fountain of blood. The man began convulsing, and the highborn grunted in satisfaction. 'Didn't I say I was a servant of Khaine?' he replied, giving her a challenging stare.

'What servant of Khaine would leave his god's temple in ruins?' she said.

'One fighting a war,' the highborn replied. He pointed through the doorway with his sword. 'If you think that usurper in the sanctum is the true Scourge, then go to him and see how he rewards your misguided beliefs.'

The two druchii exchanged furious stares: Niryal trembling with anger, and Malus cold and still as stone.

A pile of debris shifted, revealing a badly wounded zealot. A bloody groan bubbled from the warrior's lips.

Niryal's face twisted in a bitter grimace. Hefting her axe, she took three swift strides and buried the heavy blade in the wounded man's chest. The priestess pulled her weapon free, spattering the surrounding books with spots of bright crimson, and then stalked from the room with a single, hateful glare. Moments later Malus heard the wet, butcher's sound of her axe cleaving into the survivors in the gallery.

Malus turned to Arleth Vann. The assassin's gaze still wandered through the ruins of his childhood, drifting from one devastated pile of books to another. The highborn joined him, picking his way carefully through the wreckage.

'Do not mourn,' the highborn said softly. 'You did what had to be done.'

Arleth Vann seemed to notice him for the first time, peering out of his bleak reverie. 'She was right,' he said, his voice hollow. 'You can't imagine what has been lost, my lord: so much knowledge... so much history!'

Malus took his retainer by the throat, pulling him close. 'Knowledge is illusory,' he growled. 'History is but prologue. Everything kept in this room was meant to shepherd the temple to this point in time. It served its purpose, Arleth Vann. The Time of Blood is nigh.'

The assassin stared at Malus, a stricken expression twisting his pale features. He nodded slowly. 'Yes, of course. You have the right of it, my lord.' Arleth Vann spoke intently, as if trying to convince himself. 'What's past is past.'

'Well said,' Malus replied. 'Did you learn anything from the elder?'

Arleth Vann glanced at the ruined circle. The elder's skull sat upright at its centre, miraculously unharmed by the blast. 'It was harder – much harder – than I expected,' he admitted, 'but, yes, the elder finally shared some of his knowledge.'

'And?'

The assassin breathed a misty sigh. 'There is no way to track the zealots through the gate,' he said. 'To do that would require a personal connection with one of them, like the blood of kinship or the power of a sorcerous oath.'

Malus growled deep in his throat. 'That is not helpful.'

Arleth Vann interrupted the highborn's protests with a raised hand. 'We have no tie to the zealots, but we do have a powerful connection to the sword itself.'

'What tie?'

'Why, you, of course,' the assassin replied. 'You're the Scourge. The blade is fated to be wielded by you during the Time of Blood. That destiny binds you to the warpsword, and with it you can navigate your passage through the Vermillion Gate.'

Damned fate! Malus thought bitterly. He imagined he felt the daemon swell with pleasure inside his chest. 'Then we shall leave at once,' he said brusquely, 'provided we can get back into the crypts.'

'We can't go back the way we came, obviously,' the assassin replied, his voice slowly regaining its strength as he shook off the strain of the ritual and its cataclysmic end, 'but if we move quickly we can slip out through the ground floor and find another entry point in one of the nearby buildings.'

'What about the guards?'

The assassin managed a faint chuckle. 'They're all up here and more will be coming any minute. Urial could not have helped but sense what happened here.'

'I shouldn't be surprised,' Malus said. 'Let's get out of here. Once we've reached the lodge, however, I've got another errand for you.'

'As you wish, my lord,' the retainer replied, stifling a weary sigh. 'May I ask a question?'

'Make it quick.'

Arleth Vann nodded in the direction of the gallery. 'Would you have let her go to Urial if she'd wished?'

Malus didn't dignify such foolishness with an answer.

THE FOUR REMAINING loyalists filed silently from the prime chamber, all of them casting troubled glances over their shoulder at Malus and the tomb of Gothar the Ironmaster. Niryal was the last. She hadn't said a single word since leaving the Citadel of Bone, but Malus could plainly see the anger and doubt warring behind her eyes. The conflict had only deepened when he'd told them his theory about the warpsword.

He could tell that they wanted to believe him, because it meant that there was still a chance to restore the rightful order in the temple and gain some vengeance in an otherwise hopeless situation. The fact that the temple elders had lied to the faithful about the sword for centuries hadn't made much of an impression yet, but that would come in time. Providing that any of them survived.

There was no telling what they would find on the other side of the gate. Malus had wracked his brain, trying to deduce where the zealots would have taken their prize, but he couldn't think of a single place that made any sense. He wanted some idea of what they would be up against when they emerged on the other side of the gate.

A shiver passed through Malus, making him cast a worried glance at the chamber door. Fortunately, the temple servants were gone, having been told to gather up their meagre camp and make ready to depart. The highborn wrapped his arms tightly around his chest and breathed deeply, trying to keep his knees from trembling.

Malus ached for a taste of the daemon's power. The need had come upon him as they slipped from the citadel and crept across the temple grounds. Maybe it had been the brush with sorcery in the library, or the after-effects of the battle, but as he'd walked he felt his muscles shrivel like old roots and his guts turn to ice. It was by sheer willpower alone that he forced himself to complete the long journey back to the lodge. He'd told the loyalists his plans while leaning against the tomb so they wouldn't see his body tremble.

Just a taste, he thought. Just a small taste. Eldire said all wasn't yet lost. My will is still strong.

Another wracking shudder passed through him. He felt his knees buckle and couldn't get his hand out in time to keep himself from landing hard on the stone floor. Malus bit back a stream of vicious curses, appalled at his own weakness.

'It will only get worse, little druchii,' the daemon whispered, sliding like oil across his brain. 'This is but a taste of the ordeals to come, unless you let me help you.'

'You're corrupting me,' the highborn growled wearily, 'chewing out my guts from the inside, like a rat. Do you think I can't see what you're doing?'

'Malus, you brought this on yourself,' the daemon replied, 'the ordeal in Lurhan's tower, and all those times afterward, when we returned to Naggaroth from the sea. You were too greedy, taking too much of my strength at once.'

'Don't put this on me!' the highborn shouted angrily. 'I did what I had to in order to survive! I took nothing but what I needed at the time.'

'If that's the way you insist upon looking at it, then I can't make you think otherwise,' Tz'arkan replied, 'but all that is in the past. You are what you are, and nothing can change that. Why make yourself miserable, and risk your continued existence into the bargain, by wallowing in this wretched state? Let me restore your strength. You're going to need it for what lies ahead.'

Malus clenched his fists. It all sounded like sweet reason. Why bother fighting it when he was already so far gone? What would be the point? If you're already damned, better to go out in a blaze of glory than shivering and whimpering in a corner. 'What does lie ahead?' he asked, desperate to change the subject. 'What do you know?'

'I know there will be struggle, of course, hard, desperate fighting and rivers of pain. It is your fate, little druchii.'

'Fate,' Malus spat, feeling a little of his old hatred flare to life. Mentally, he huddled around its wan flame. 'You mean the grand trap you built for me.' Suddenly, a thought occurred to him. 'How does Khaine fit into all this?'

'What are you talking about?'

'Your plan,' the highborn said. 'What does a daemon of Slaanesh have to do with the Scourge of Khaine? And how is it that one of the five relics used to bind you just happens to be the talisman of Khaine's chosen one?'

The daemon didn't respond at first. Malus took that to be a sign he was on to something.

'The sword has not always been called the Warpsword of Khaine,' Tz'arkan said. 'It is very, very old, and has had many names in its time.'

'What was it called when it was being wielded by the Chaos lord who bound you?'

'What's the point? You don't have the mouth parts to pronounce it properly anyway.'

The highborn put that unpleasant mental image aside. 'My point is that the relic wasn't handed down to the cultists by Khaine himself. It fell into their hands sometime after you were bound in the far north.' Malus's mind began to race as he considered the implications. 'They were meant to keep it until the day I would come and claim it. So, is the prophecy of the Scourge also part of your plan? Did you plant that seed as well as the sword?'

Tz'arkan chuckled gleefully. 'Who can understand the machinations of fate, Darkblade? Certainly not you. How could I possibly manipulate so much while trapped in my crystal prison hundreds of leagues distant?'

'I don't know. I was hoping you would tell me.'

'Then you are destined for disappointment, I fear.'

Malus relaxed a little. With his mind fully engaged, the aches in his body seemed to abate. 'All right. Let us suppose that Khaine handed down the prophecy of the Scourge, and you somehow inserted this relic into the legends, knowing that one day I – or some other misbegotten bastard like me – would come along to claim both. Aren't you courting Khaine's wrath in all this?'

The daemon sighed. 'Such a clever little beast you are sometimes. All right, as a token of pity for the sad state you are in, I will tell you this much: the Blood God does not care who spills blood in his name, or why, only that it flows.'

Malus considered this. 'Then, in truth, anyone can wield the blade.'

'Anyone? Hardly.'

'Obviously it isn't meant solely for the Scourge of Khaine, which means that I have no more a tie to the damned thing than anyone else.'

'No, but I do,' the daemon said. 'I have felt its bite, and it remembers the taste.'

The highborn's eyes widened. 'Then you knew that the sword in Urial's hand was a fake.'

'Of course. I knew it from the moment he stabbed you.'

'And it never occurred to you to tell me?'

'Certainly it did,' the daemon purred, 'but where would be the fun in that?'

Malus bared his teeth at the daemon's gleeful laughter, huddling against the stone tomb of the ironmaster as he felt another of the tremors begin.

HE WAS DOZING fitfully when Arleth Vann finally returned.

Malus awakened to a gentle tapping on his boot. The highborn opened his eyes to find the assassin crouching a polite distance away. Arleth Vann's pale face was smudged by soot and mottled with spots of dried blood.

'Where have you been?' the highborn asked, trying to rub the exhaustion from his face.

'In the city, of course,' the assassin replied wearily. 'Things have taken a turn for the worse.'

'Worse for us, or for them?' Malus winced. 'Never mind, the answer's obvious.' He tried to stand. 'Help me up.'

Arleth Vann pulled him upright, a worried frown creasing his face. 'Is it the old wound?'

'That and more, but I will survive,' the highborn said. 'Now tell me what's happened.'

The assassin nodded and headed for the doorway with Malus following close behind. 'Sometime this morning – most likely just after dawn – the temple warriors abandoned their holdouts and tried to fight their way out of the encirclements Urial threw around them.'

The highborn shook his head, bemused. 'Why now, of all times?'

Arleth Vann shrugged as they passed through the first of the burial chambers. The two temple loyalists resting there saw Malus on the move and rose to their feet, picking up cloth bags containing their supplies and falling into step behind the highborn.

'There are rumours on the street. Most people think that the holdouts ran out of food several days ago, so they had the choice of breaking out or starving to death. Others say that penny oracles in the merchants' district have had visions of a terrible army bearing down on Har Ganeth from the west.'

Malus hissed thoughtfully. Could the Witch King already be on the move, he wondered? 'Anything's possible,' he admitted. 'Were the breakouts successful?'

'Eventually,' Arleth Vann said. 'The fighting lasted all day, and there are rumours that hundreds of warriors and witches were slain. What little of the warehouse district hadn't burned before was put to the torch, it seems. Over the course of the day the isolated warbands managed to link up and fight their way to the city gate.'

The highborn stopped in his tracks. 'The *city* gate? Not the fortress gate?'

Arleth Vann nodded. 'They retreated about half a mile up the Slavers' Road to the west and they're building a camp by the shore.'

'Those fools,' Malus spat. 'Urial controls the entire damned city! It will be a hundred times harder to dislodge him now. Unless...'

'Unless perhaps those penny oracles were right and the temple witches have foreseen that Malekith is on the way.'

'Damnation,' Malus said. 'If it's true, then we're nearly out of time. If Urial is still in control of the city when the Witch King arrives, the die will be cast and there will be no stopping the war that will follow.' With a muted growl he leapt back into motion, speeding though the succession of chambers with long, impatient strides.

'Honestly, my lord, I'm surprised you care,' Arleth Vann said, moving swiftly to keep pace. 'Would a holy war not serve Khaine's purposes?'

The highborn gave his retainer a hard look. 'Under the circumstances, I believe that's for me to decide.'

'Of course, my lord.'

Malus continued on, rushing through the last of the crypts and coming to the open doorway of the lodge's antechamber. A familiar, acrid reek filled his nostrils, and he heard one of the accompanying loyalists let out a surprised curse at the smell. A sharp, drawn-out hiss sounded from within the antechamber, like steam whistling from a cracked kettle.

Though small for its breed, Spite took up nearly a third of the large, rectangular antechamber. Arleth Vann had left it resting on his haunches just inside the lodge's main doors, and even with its powerful tail tucked along his side, the nauglir was long enough to brush the ends of the long tables on either side of the room.

Malus raised a warning hand. 'Wait here,' he said to Arleth Vann and the loyalists. Spite, hearing his voice, rose onto its clawed feet and turned its huge, blocky snout in his direction. Nostrils flared wide as Spite tasted his master's scent.

The highborn slowly crossed the room, studying the cold one carefully for signs of danger. Before he'd sent Arleth Vann into the city to fetch Spite he'd applied a fresh coat of vrahsha to both his and his retainer's skin from a small vial tucked into his robes. The salve disguised a druchii's scent, but not the daemonic corruption that Malus knew was spreading through his body.

Spite's nostrils flared as it tasted Malus's scent. A low grumble rose from its chest.

'It's all right, you great, dumb beast,' Malus said lightly, 'it's me.'

The cold one lowered its head slightly. Venomous drool fell in long, ropy strands from its huge jaws. Spite growled threateningly as the highborn took another step forwards. Scales grated over stone as the nauglir uncurled its tail. The powerful, cable thick muscle brushed the room's centre table in passing and smashed one of the corners into powder with a sharp *crack*.

Malus stopped where he was, suddenly wary of getting within the cold one's reach. 'Where did you find him?' he asked.

'In the stables where Tyran's men left him,' the assassin replied. 'He'd broken out of the pen days ago and just seemed to be settling there.'

The highborn looked the nauglir over and noticed a number of recent wounds on the warbeast's armoured hide. None looked remotely life threatening. To his great relief, the saddle and bags on the cold one's back still looked intact. 'Has Spite been fed?'

'Oh, it's eaten well,' the retainer assured him. 'There were bits of flesh and pieces of broken bone all over the pen. It probably ate the attendants first, and then started hunting the locals over the last few days.'

Malus nodded. If Spite was well fed, this was as safe a time to approach the beast as any. Taking a deep breath, he took another step forwards.

The cold one settled slightly onto its haunches, assuming a defensive stance, another bad sign.

'What do you think you're doing?' Malus said to the warbeast. 'It's me, and I don't have time for your nonsense. There's hard riding to be done.'

He took another step forwards. Spite's jaws began to open, one slow inch at a time.

The highborn realised that Spite was getting ready to attack, and felt an overpowering rush of frustration. 'Now you listen here, you great lump of scales,' Malus snapped, levelling an angry finger at the one ton warbeast, 'I didn't come all this way to get made a meal of by my own mount. Now *stand*, and let me look at you!'

Malus's commanding shout rang from the chamber walls, startling the cold one. Spite jerked back, nostrils flaring, and snapped at the air with a bone-jarring crunch of dagger-length fangs. For an instant the highborn feared that the warbeast would turn and dart out of the antechamber into the tunnel beyond, but then it paused, blew steam from its nostrils and settled obediently onto its haunches.

Inwardly the highborn breathed a sigh of relief. 'That's better,' he said, and walked up to the nauglir. He circled the cold one and looked him over, checking talons, teeth, eyes, flanks and tail. Once he was convinced that the beast was essentially unhurt, he moved to check his possessions. 'Help me with this armour,' he called out to Arleth Vann.

Moving warily, the retainer joined Malus at Spite's side and helped remove the leather bags containing the highborn's plate harness. Arleth Vann worked quickly and efficiently, unwrapping the armour plates from their oiled cloths and then helping Malus into his old kheitan. Within minutes the highborn was buckling his sword belt over his mail fauld and almost feeling like his old self again.

'You said that fighting in the city lasted until around sunset,' Malus said, pulling on his armoured gauntlets, 'what time is it now?'

'About two hours past sunset, my lord,' the assassin replied.

Malus grimaced. The first light of false dawn had been paling the sky over the fortress when he, the assassin and Niryal had escaped the Citadel of Bone. 'We've lost a great deal of time,' he said. The highborn glanced at the lodge's main doors. 'Where's Niryal? She and one of the other loyalists were standing watch.'

Arleth Vann frowned. 'I didn't see anyone when I came in, my lord.'

Malus froze. A cold knot of dread tightened in his guts.

Suddenly, Spite turned, pointing his snout towards the tunnel outside and growling threateningly. At once, a chorus of gibbering howls answered.

Chapter Twenty
BLOOD AND SOULS

'BAR THE DOOR!' Malus shouted, grabbing Spite's reins and leading the cold one deeper into the room. Arleth Vann and the loyalists leapt to obey, giving the hissing nauglir as wide a berth as possible. The three druchii reached the doors and pushed them shut. Then they picked up wedge-shaped pieces of stone they'd broken from the dwarf crypts and began jamming them as tightly as they could into the narrow space beneath the stone panels.

'What did you see?' the highborn asked his retainer as he guided Spite around the far end of the room's central table.

'I saw at least one of the hunting beasts,' the assassin replied, using a hammer looted from one of the tombs to drive the wedges home. Flecks of stone flew with every sharp blow. 'Worse, I saw witchlights.'

'How many?'

'At least a dozen,' Arleth Vann said grimly.

'Mother of Night,' Malus whispered. That many lights could mean fifty men or more. 'Any sign of Niryal or the other sentry?'

The retainer shook his head. 'If the assassins finally decided to join Urial they could have taken both of them and left no one the wiser. They probably let me through because I had Spite with me.'

'And they know we're trapped,' the highborn said grimly.

Something heavy smashed against the doors with a thunderous crash, causing even Spite to jump. Stone dust puffed through the doorjamb, and a gibbering howl echoed outside. Malus heard the scrape of thorny tentacles lashing against the stone.

'Get back,' Malus ordered, drawing his sword. Arleth Vann and the two loyalists retreated behind Spite. The nauglir was back in a defensive pose, growling ominously, its long tail extended. The highborn patted the cold one's neck as his companions drew their weapons and formed a small semicircle behind him.

They heard another fearsome crash, and a sharp crack of breaking stone.

'That won't hold for long,' Arleth Vann muttered.

'I don't suppose there's a secret passage out of here that you haven't told me about?' Malus asked.

'If there was, don't you think the dwarfs would have taken it?'

'Good point.'

Another blow struck the doors, and this time the druchii could see a pair of cracks spreading upwards and downwards from the centre of the leftmost panel.

Malus tried to think past the frantic sound of his pulse pounding in his ears. 'Perhaps we could hide in the tombs? Pretend we're dwarfs?'

Arleth Vann shook his head. 'It wouldn't work, my lord, Spite's too tall for a dwarf.'

'There is that,' Malus deadpanned. 'I suppose we'll just have to find a way to kill the bastards then.'

With a thunderous *crack*, the leftmost door exploded in a shower of dust and fragments, and the lean form of one of the Chaos beasts came tumbling into the chamber. Dust caked its damp, gelatinous hide, and its claws raked across the stone as it skidded to a halt. Tentacles lashed the air hungrily and one of the beast's fist sized eyes focused on the highborn, only a few yards away.

Spreading its fearsome, barbed whips and hissing through its glossy beak, the hunter gathered itself to leap. Malus slapped his hand against the nauglir's neck and shouted 'Hunt, Spite! *Hunt!*' just as the creature pounced.

The Chaos beast was swift as a hunting cat, but the nauglir let out a bellow that shook dust from the ceiling and met the fearsome creature mid-leap. The hunter was huge, but Spite's body was a third again larger and much more massive. The two creatures crashed together and the hunter was propelled backwards, its tentacles lashing furiously at Spite's armoured hide as the cold one dug its claws in and tore at the beast's throat. They landed with an earth-shaking crash, smashing two of the side-tables to pieces just as a wave of screaming druchii charged through the broken doorway.

They were a mismatched band, armed with an apparently random mix of weapons and armour. Black-robed temple servants brandished short swords and heavy axes next to knife wielding druchii in plain robes. One woman with the leather jerkin of a butcher hefted a gore-crusted cleaver beside a highborn wearing full armour and wielding paired swords. The only thing the mob had in common was the sign of the Blood God branded on their foreheads and the mindless look of bloodlust that burned in their dark eyes.

Their savage charge ran headlong into the path of the two wrestling beasts. Spite's lashing tail smashed three city folk off their feet, hurling their broken bodies back onto their companions. Lashing tentacles cut like saws through the enemy ranks, the barbed hooks ripping off hands, legs and faces with indiscriminate fury. Showers of blood and torn flesh burst among the charging druchii, but the survivors paid the carnage little heed. They saw Malus and his men across the room and scrambled past the thrashing creatures, their faces alight with the prospect of slaughter.

Malus bared his teeth at the oncoming mob. 'If they want a battle we'll give them one,' he said, raising his sword. 'Blood and souls!'

'Blood and souls!' the warriors of Khaine shouted, and the slaughter began in earnest.

The attackers were largely unskilled, making mistakes in their frenzy that no experienced soldier would have. Howling zealots raced around to either side of the large, central table that Malus had situated his men behind, thereby breaking the force of their charge, but some were so eager for bloodshed they scrambled atop the table itself. The highborn let them come, ducked low out of the reach of their shorter weapons, and hacked off their legs at the knees. Three city folk died that way, spilling huge gouts of blood onto the flat stone as they toppled off onto the heads of their compatriots.

To Malus's left, Arleth Vann slew every foe that came within reach, blocking with one sword and coolly despatching each opponent with a single thrust or cut from the other. To the highborn's right, the two surviving loyalists staggered against the frenzied assault of the zealots, but grimly held their ground, lashing at their foes with red stained swords.

With the tabletop clear Malus turned his attention to his right, using the corner of the table to keep the zealots at a distance where their knives and axes couldn't reach him. It was like slaying cattle. The frenzied city folk rushed at the loyalists, clashing blades, and Malus stabbed them in the throat or chest, dropping them to the ground. Whatever had robbed the attackers of their reason served to blind them to the murderous efficiency of the highborn's tactics.

The thrashing struggle of the huge beasts continued near the door. Spite's neck and flanks were criss-crossed with countless furrows from the hunter's barbed scales, but the nauglir had the Chaos beast by the throat, keeping its fearsome black beak at bay. The two creatures struggled to overbear one another, but Spite's greater bulk and long tail gave the cold one a powerful advantage. The nauglir found its feet and bore down with its jaws, forcing a strangled screech from the hunter. Its thick skin was more than enough to stave off sword and axe blows, but could not resist the fearsome might of the cold one's powerful bite. Runnels of clear ichor flowed off Spite's jaw as the warbeast lifted the hunter off the floor and shook it like a terrier shakes a rat. Tentacles flailed and bones snapped. Then Spite jerked his head and flung the creature across the room. It smashed into another of the long preparation tables, shattering it beneath its weight, and the hunter went limp.

Spite's bellow of victory shook the antechamber, drowning out even the zealots' frenzied screams. Barely a handful of attackers were left, out of the score or so who had charged into the room, and Malus felt his spirits lift. If this was the best the zealots had available, then Malus and his followers could easily fight their way out to the gate.

The druchii woman with the two-handed cleaver charged at one of the loyalists with a piercing, bestial shriek, foam flying from her thin lips as she swung her filthy blade at the man's neck. The loyalist tried to parry the blow, but the heavier weapon knocked his blade aside and deflected into the man's shoulder. Before the butcher could pull her grisly weapon free Malus leaned in and took off the top of her head with his long sword. Bone and brain sprayed into the air, but the highborn looked on in shock as the frenzied druchii jerkily pulled her weapon free and tried to strike another blow before collapsing to the ground.

There were only two attackers left on Malus's right. On the left Arleth Vann duelled with the armoured highborn, blocking the noble's clumsy, frenzied attacks and darting in to strike at unprotected joints or exposed gaps in his plate harness. Leaving the assassin to finish the highborn, Malus edged in beside the wounded loyalist and took the battle to the zealots.

A man rushed at Malus with a bloody woodsman's axe held high. The highborn pivoted on his left foot as the blow fell, allowing the blade to pass harmlessly by, and stabbed the onrushing zealot through the heart. Sneering in disdain, Malus pulled his sword free and rounded on the second man, who was raining blows on the uninjured loyalist with a knotted club in one hand and a short sword in the other. The zealot was so intent on his victim that he never saw Malus step up beside him and split his skull from back to front, spraying the loyalist fighting him with bits of blood and bone.

On the other side of the table the armoured highborn slumped against the flat surface with a groan, succumbing to blood loss and a score of deep wounds. Arleth Vann stepped close, slicing his swords across the noble's neck in a scissoring motion, and the man's head went bouncing across the floor.

Malus himself leaned back against the other side of the table, panting like a hound and trying to ignore the dull pain throbbing in the side of his chest. Bodies were heaped everywhere, bleeding out onto the floor. The fight had lasted less than half a minute.

The loyalist who'd been struck by the cleaver was bleeding badly, the shoulder and sleeve of his robe already soaked and dripping. The other man appeared unhurt, as did Arleth Vann. All things considered, it could have gone much worse, the highborn thought.

Malus pushed himself away from the table and walked over to the body of the Chaos beast. The creature's neck was ripped open, revealing strange, yellowish muscles and a backbone that looked as if it belonged in a shark rather than a lion. Stepping carefully through the spreading pool of gluey ichor, the highborn raised his sword and began hacking at the flesh, working from the inside out. It was tough going, but within a few minutes the large, octopus-like head rolled free. He bent and picked the thing up by its tentacles, and walked to the shattered doorway. Grunting with effort, he took two quick steps and hurled the trophy through the doorway.

'We'll let them think on that for a bit,' the highborn said grimly. He turned to Arleth Vann. 'You check that one's arm. I'll look over Spite.'

They worked quickly, unsure what awaited them outside the lodge. A cursory check showed that Spite had dozens upon dozens of shallow cuts from the beast's tentacle hooks, but nothing that the nauglir's legendary constitution could not handle. Malus had moved on to check the state of his saddle-bags when Arleth Vann joined him. 'The man's wound is deep,' he said quietly, 'and I've no means to close it. He'll die in a few minutes, maybe less.'

'Then we'd best get this over with quickly,' the highborn said. 'Let's take a look outside.'

The two druchii crept up to the doorway and peered into the tunnel beyond. Globes of witchlight filled the wide passage with ghostly luminescence, forcing Malus to squint into the cold glare. What he saw made his heart sink.

There were scores of white-robed zealots filling the tunnel, their robes and blades stained with smudges of soot and streaks of old blood. They stood in a packed group behind two more of the terrible Chaos beasts, which lashed at the air with their tentacles as if angered by the sight of their mate's severed head. A handful of beastmasters circled the creatures, holding their short spears and prods ready. They threw black looks at the broken doorway of the lodge, as if anticipating their own measure of revenge for their slain kin.

'Mother of Night,' Malus cursed softly, 'they must have pulled every zealot from the city back into the fortress.'

'With the temple warriors gone, why not?' the assassin replied, his face grim. 'They sent in those city folk just to take our measure and keep us occupied.'

'Well, what are they waiting for?'

As Malus said the words, a ripple of motion passed through the packed ranks of the zealots. Men stepped aside, bowing their heads as Urial moved through the crowd. A trio of blood-witches attended the usurper, and Urial carried the copy of the warpsword in his hand. The mere sight of the weapon seemed to leech the strength from Malus's limbs, reminding him of the wound he'd been dealt and of the daemon's poisonous touch.

The would-be Scourge of Khaine reached the front rank of the men and stopped. Urial eyed the head of the dead Chaos beast and laughed.

Malus fought a black tide of despair. He looked upon the assembled zealots, and the merciless arithmetic of the battlefield showed him the future as clearly as any seer could. There was no way they could prevail against such numbers, to say nothing of the sorcery of Urial and the blood-witches.

'We'll have to fall back,' he said. 'We can't possibly hold them here. We'll use the fortifications at each burial chamber to slow them down, bleed them–'

'No,' Arleth Vann said quietly.

'What?' Malus demanded, his expression incredulous.

'Don't be a fool, my lord,' the assassin said. 'You know better than that. We could fight them all the way back to the prime chamber, trade ten lives for each one of ours – twenty if you count Spite – and they would still have men left over. That's without counting your half-brother, much less the blood-witches.'

'Have you any better ideas?' Malus snarled.

The assassin nodded. 'When they attack, you mount Spite and ride straight through them. We'll cover your back as long as we can.'

'You can't be serious,' Malus said.

'Of course I am!' Arleth Vann said hotly. 'You have to escape and find the sword, for Khaine's sake! Otherwise the temple – even Naggaroth itself – could well tear itself apart.'

'Why would you do such a thing?' the highborn asked, torn between revulsion and awe. 'The temple owes you nothing.'

Arleth Vann turned away, eyeing the crowd of zealots and the leonine blood-witches. 'Do you remember what I said about seeking redemption, about a good death outweighing a bad life? What better chance than this to cleanse the taint from my honour?' He looked back at his lord. 'There's no glory in living as an outlaw, my lord, no matter what the bards say.'

Malus was surprised at how much the comment stung. 'You've been a highborn retainer for the last five years,' he growled.

'That didn't change who I was,' the assassin replied, 'but this will.'

The highborn bit back his anger. Fleeing the battle felt like cowardice, but the assassin's logic was unassailable. He could either stay and die – or worse, fall into Urial's clutches – or he could fight his way free and locate the sword. 'Damnation,' Malus snarled, and then turned and made his way to Spite.

Nearby, the two loyalists watched Malus intently. The wounded man was pale and shaky, using his left hand awkwardly to press a soaked bundle of cloth against his wounded shoulder. Their expressions were bleak.

'We're breaking out,' Malus told the men as he grabbed Spite's reins. 'I'm going to provoke the zealots into charging us, and then I'll counter charge with my nauglir and open a hole in their ranks. Stay close behind and keep our flanks clear, and we'll fight our way through. Understand?'

Both men nodded. The look in their eyes said they understood completely.

Malus nodded, and then headed Spite towards the doorway. The zealots hadn't moved. Urial appeared to be speaking to the assembled force, but Malus couldn't hear what his half-brother was saying. He's probably ordering his men to take me alive, he thought. I expect he and the blood-witches have something special planned.

The highborn turned to Arleth Vann. 'Are you ready?' he asked.

'I suppose I've been waiting for this for a long time,' the assassin said calmly. 'Farewell, my lord. When the Time of Blood comes, perhaps you and I will meet again.'

Malus didn't know what to say. He shook his head fiercely. 'If you see the Lord of Murder before I do, you march up to his throne and tell him I'm coming. Tell him that when I get there I'm going to kick his brass teeth straight down his throat.'

Before the assassin could reply, the highborn drew a deep breath and shouted into the tunnel. 'What are you waiting for, brother? More men, perhaps? I think these dead bakers and butchers had more courage between them than you and all your ilk!'

Malus heard Urial laugh. 'Is that you, brother?' the usurper asked. 'I was certain you'd died. The last time I saw you, that man of yours was dragging your limp body away from me as fast as he could.'

'What can I say, brother? He's a very pious man, and was afraid I'd hurt Khaine's Scourge.' Malus said, his voice dripping with contempt. 'Fear not, I set him straight. I told him all about the night on the *Harrier*, and what that damned skull of yours told me. Say, did the skull ever speak to you alone, or did you just forget to mention that to the temple elders? That was part of the prophecy, correct?'

'Shut your blasphemous mouth!' Urial snapped, the heat in his voice so strong that Tyran and the closest zealots gave the usurper questioning looks.

'How are things with your new bride? Is she still spurning you? I expect so,' Malus said, smiling despite himself. 'The Bride of Ruin is not meant for the likes of you, brother. She will never think of you as anything but a withered, pitiable man.'

The highborn's taunts were drowned by Urial's wordless shriek of rage.

Arleth Vann chuckled, readying his blades. 'You always did have a way with words, my lord.'

Malus swung into the saddle. 'Perhaps I'd have made a decent priest after all.'

The assassin smiled ruefully. 'I don't know if I'd go that far–'

A roar shook the tunnel as the zealots charged. Blades glinting, they flowed in a furious tide past the Chaos beasts, charging for the dwarf lodge at the command of their lord.

'Now?' Malus said, looking to Arleth Vann.

The assassin shook his head, peering into the tunnel. 'Not yet.'

Shouts of bloodlust echoed in the antechamber. The sounds of pounding feet filled Malus's ears.

'Now?'

'Not yet.'

Malus could make out individual voices in the thunder of the war shouts. He could hear the slap of boot heels on stone.

'We did decide to fight them in the tunnel, correct?' the highborn said pointedly.

The assassin looked at Malus and nodded solemnly. 'Go, my lord, and Khaine be with you.'

'Not if he knows what's good for him,' Malus growled. He put his boots to Spite's flanks. 'Charge!'

The warbeast leapt forwards with a bone jarring roar, its shoulder striking the edge of the right door and smashing the heavy panel from its hinges. Malus ducked at the last moment as they crossed the threshold, feeling the top of the doorframe scrape along his backplate.

When he looked up again he saw that they were rushing at the front rank of zealots, less than ten yards away. The charge of the white-robed druchii faltered as the nauglir bore down on them, its blunt jaws clashing together as it smelt the blood on the zealots' robes. Malus howled like a wolf as they plunged into the press, his blade falling left and right as he lashed out indiscriminately at the bodies flashing past.

Zealots screamed, flung like bloody dolls into the air by the nauglir's jaws or smashed aside by the beast's armoured shoulders. A blade struck Malus on the left thigh and glanced from the steel plate. On his right, the highborn slashed down at an upturned face, splitting the druchii's skull like a melon. He twisted his waist and cut to his left, knocking aside a blood-stained draich and slicing open another man's forehead.

The cold one plunged on, leaving torn and broken bodies in its wake. Zealots struck at the nauglir from all sides, opening deep wounds in the beast's muscular flanks, but the pain only enraged the cold one further. A zealot leapt for the nauglir's face, aiming a lightning thrust at Spite's left eye, but the cold one's training took over and the beast snapped at the flickering motion. The huge jaws bit off the swordsman's right arm at the elbow and spat his twisted sword onto the tunnel floor.

Malus looked over his shoulder to see how Arleth Vann and the others were keeping up. The wounded loyalist was already dead. His headless body lay only a few yards from the lodge's broken doors. The assassin and the last remaining warrior fought side-by-side close to the cold one's lashing tail.

Roars of rage turned to screams of anger, pain and fear. Men fell back to either side of the thundering cold one, stunned by the ferocity of the sudden attack. A tight semicircle of zealots formed between the nauglir and Urial. Malus smiled fiercely and aimed Spite directly for them.

The swordsmen held their ground, ready to die to protect their lord. Malus did everything in his power to give them their wish.

Spite let out a bloodthirsty roar and lunged at the man to his right, catching the swordsman's right arm and torso and biting them in half. The zealot to the cold one's left saw his opportunity and slashed with all his might at the nauglir's bent neck, but Malus anticipated the move and blocked the stroke with his sword. Hearing the sound, Spite jerked his huge head and smashed the zealot to the ground, where the beast crushed the screaming man beneath a clawed foot.

Malus caught a flicker of movement in the corner of his eye and instinctively dodged to his left. The movement saved his life, a draich glancing from his right pauldron as a zealot leapt onto Spite's flank and grabbed hold of Malus's saddle. Snarling, the highborn elbowed the man in the face, and then slashed open his throat as he reeled from the blow.

More zealots were closing in on both sides as the attackers recovered from the surprise charge. Urial stood just five yards away, surrounded by the fierce blood-witches. Letting out a battle scream, the highborn kicked Spite's flanks and charged.

Zealots were thrown left and right by the lunging warbeast, and Malus raised his sword for a decapitating stroke as he bore down on Urial. The blood-witches scattered, hissing curses, but the usurper stood his ground. With less than two yards between them, Malus saw his half-brother smile.

Suddenly Urial raised the sword in his left hand and shouted a word that smote Malus like a physical blow. Spite stopped dead in his tracks, roaring in pain and confusion. It took all of Malus's skill as a rider not to be thrown from the saddle by the force of the sudden stop.

'Forwards, Spite! Forwards!' the highborn roared, but the warbeast could only shake its head and bellow in pain, as if pressed against a wall of fire.

Urial laughed. 'He won't move, not if his life depends on it,' he said. 'Did you think me a fool, knowing you had your damned cold one with you?'

Malus shouted in impotent rage. Men were closing in from behind the nauglir and to either side, like wolves closing in for the kill.

Then there was a flash of movement and Urial ducked, catching Arleth Vann's hurled knife on the side of his head rather than in his throat. The knife scored a bloody line through the usurper's scalp, and in an eye blink, the spell was broken.

'Go, my lord!' Arleth Vann shouted, racing up beside Malus with the last surviving loyalist close behind. The assassin charged at Urial, blades reaching for the man's throat.

Zealots roared their bloodlust as they closed in on Spite. Malus gritted his teeth and once again spurred the nauglir forwards. 'Run, Spite, run!' he yelled, knowing that Urial could renew the spell at any moment.

Arleth Vann was determined not to give the usurper a chance. His short swords wove a pattern of death before him, stabbing at Urial's face and neck. Urial parried the attacks with unnatural agility, wielding his large sword as if it was a willow wand. Though no warpsword, it was clear that the dwarf ironsmith had imbued the weapon with considerable power.

Swallowing bitter bile, Malus spurred his mount past Urial. A lone voice cried 'Blood and souls!' as the last temple warrior charged at the witches. His sword sliced at one blood-witch's head, but she dodged the blow with unnatural speed, and her two compatriots fell upon the man from either side. His fierce shouts turned to a gurgling scream as their talons slashed open his throat. The witches bore the struggling man to the ground, and like lionesses, began to feed.

The last Malus saw of Arleth Vann, he was trading blows with his half-brother, circling and stabbing, leaping and slashing within a closing ring of zealots. Cursing venomously, he turned away and tried to guide his mount past the waiting Chaos beasts.

Unlike the zealots, the beastmasters knew very well how dangerous a charging cold one could be. They scattered like quail at the thundering nauglir's approach, shouting commands to the hunters in a strange, savage tongue. The air filled with the hunters' obscene, gibbering cries as they were unleashed upon Malus and Spite.

There was no point trying to fight. Malus knew all too well how useless his sword was against the monsters' hide. He bent low in the saddle and cried, 'Race like fire, beast of the deeps! Show these slugs how you can run!'

Rumbling like a cauldron, Spite obediently lowered his head and stretched his legs into a full, earthshaking gallop.

Malus angled their flight to pass the beasts on their right. The closest hunter flared its tentacles and screeched at the nauglir, but the cold one lunged at the Chaos beast and struck the creature a powerful blow with its shoulder. The hunter was knocked sideways, tentacles lashing, and the highborn was slapped on the side of his head by the back of one of the beast's fleshy whips. The blow nearly took his head off, throwing him hard to the left and almost pitching him from the saddle. Another tentacle brushed against his leg, the barbs scraping against his armour.

Suddenly, Spite lurched and bellowed in pain. The cold one's body slewed to the left, struck on its rear flank. Blinking tears of pain from his eyes, Malus glanced back and saw another of the hunters sinking its claws into Spite's powerful rear leg, much as a lion would pull down a gazelle. The highborn looked into the creature's right eye and heard the whirring of its tentacles as it reached up to pluck him from the saddle.

Malus hauled on the reins and planted his right heel in Spite's side, and the obedient warbeast slashed its tail to the left. The powerful motion flung the clutching Chaos beast over the nauglir's back, smashing it against the side of the tunnel. 'Go!' Malus shouted, spurring his mount forwards once more.

With the howls of the hunters echoing behind them, Malus and Spite raced down the broad passage. Darkness engulfed them, and the sounds of battle faded.

He gave Spite his head, trusting the cave-born nauglir's senses as they raced down the passageway. Arleth Vann had shown him where the tunnel ran, and he knew that after a hundred yards it ended in a large, empty chamber that once housed the dwarfs while they worked on their tomb. A spiral ramp at the west end of the chamber led up to the road of black stones that would take Malus to the Vermillion Gate.

When the echo of Spite's footfalls suddenly stopped, Malus knew he'd entered the housing chamber. He slowed the warbeast's pace and guided him to the left, allowing the nauglir to pick his way through the debris-strewn room. When he felt a breath of moving air against his cheek, he nudged the cold one's flanks. 'Climb the ramp,' Malus said, trusting it was there even though he couldn't see it. 'Up!'

With a grunt, the cold one padded forwards and sure enough, Malus felt them begin to climb. The ramp was just broad enough for the cold one to work its way up, and the highborn lay flat against the nauglir's back and tried to stay out of the way.

After several long minutes, Malus found he could see vague outlines of the ramp around him. They were almost at the top, where the road's glowing fungus shed a modicum of light. Two turns later Spite edged out into the main passageway, and the highborn breathed a sigh of relief.

He turned Spite's nose to the left, heading deeper into the hill, and let the warbeast lope down the tunnel. They rode on in silence for some minutes, until Malus began to feel the tingle of eldritch power against his skin. They were drawing close to the ancient gateway.

Moments later Malus found himself riding through a long, underground plaza, its ceiling lost in darkness high overhead. Stone statues flanked the long chamber, their features worn smooth over uncounted millennia. A heavy silence hung in the enormous chamber, and even Spite seemed to feel its weight.

The plaza led them to a large, semicircular gallery at the edge of a wide, natural pit. Here, statues of beautiful, fearsome

blood-witches bore lamps of witchlight and robed executioners carried elegant swords of white marble. A slender bridge of
stone ran from the gallery to a circular spire of rock that rose
from the centre of the pit. The top of the spire was flat and
capped with paving stones of glossy, black marble, and upon
those stones rose an arch of seamless, reddish stone.

Taking a deep breath, Malus led Spite onto the bridge. He
had no idea if the span would support the cold one's weight,
and it was just barely wide enough to accommodate it. A cold
void yawned beneath the bridge, leading perhaps to the heart
of the world itself.

'Easy, Spite, easy,' he said. The nauglir seemed to understand,
taking one slow step at a time as it edged its way across the
abyss.

Nearly five minutes later they were just over halfway across
the span, and Malus was starting to breathe easier. Then he
heard the sounds of pounding feet behind him and turned just
in time to see the Chaos beast leap at Spite with a chilling
howl.

Chapter Twenty-One
RED SKIES

THE CHAOS BEAST landed square on Spite's back, its talons sinking deep into the nauglir's hindquarters. The cold one roared in surprise and pain and instinctively turned to bite its attacker. The nauglir's right hind leg slipped from the bridge, and to Malus the world seemed to lurch vertiginously to the right. He threw himself to the left, away from the bottomless chasm, just as the hunter lashed at him with a pair of tentacles.

One of the barbed whips wrapped around his left arm and another wound around his waist. Screaming in fear and rage, Malus hacked at the tentacles with his sword, but the rubbery skin was barely marked. With no apparent effort the beast dragged him out of the saddle.

Malus looked down and saw nothing but emptiness and shadow. Then Spite's jaws snapped at the hunter and caught the tentacles in his fearsome maw.

The cold one's teeth parted the whips like thread, splashing Malus with sticky ichor. Still screaming, he fell like a stone, hitting the edge of the span and tumbling over it face-first.

By an equal mix of pure luck and desperation, Malus caught the raised edge of the span with his left hand and seized it like a drowning man. His legs swung past and he rocked like a pendulum over the pit as the two beasts raged above him. He heard the sounds of talons on stone as he fought for purchase, clawing at the other side of the bridge with his hind leg in an effort to force himself back onto the span. A stream of broken stone trickled into the blackness, and Malus heard an ominous crack.

His ichor covered hand and arm slid across the stone. With a thrill of terror, he realised he was slipping. The highborn threw his other hand over the edge of the bridge, hoping to stop his fall without losing his sword, but he hadn't reckoned on the slickness of the foul ooze coating his arms, and the sudden motion caused his left hand to slip.

Malus's stomach lurched as he dropped. Then he felt a heavy weight cover his arm and jerk him to a stop. He hung over the pit for an instant, his legs swinging uselessly. Then the mind numbing panic subsided and the highborn had the presence of mind to let go of his sword and try to find some kind of purchase with his right hand.

The weight on his left arm shifted slightly, and Malus distinctly felt the armoured shell of his vambrace bend beneath the pressure. Pain began to build at his forearm and wrist as they took the mounting strain. Gritting his teeth, Malus pulled himself upwards with his sword hand until he was able to get the crook of his arm over the bridge's rounded edge.

A clawed hand the size of his torso slashed past him, missing his head by inches. Spite had managed to regain his footing and was reaching back to claw and bite at his attacker. In doing so the one-ton warbeast had stepped on Malus's arm.

The Chaos beast still clung to Spite's hindquarters, tearing at one hip with its cruel beak and lashing at the warbeast's face with its remaining tentacles. The nauglir's clashing jaws had bitten off several more, and the stumps sprayed the cold one with gouts of clear, briny ichor. Spite roared and lashed his tail, hoping to dislodge the hunter from his back, but the

Chaos beast only dug its claws in deeper and held on. The nauglir's foot ground down as it swung its tail, and the pain in Malus's arm intensified. He threw a leg over the edge of the bridge and pulled most of his body over. Then he grabbed up his sword and slapped at Spite's leg with the flat of the blade. 'Get *off*, you great lump of scales!'

Whether by accident or design, Spite lifted his leg and Malus yanked his arm free. The vambrace was crumpled, and a thin stream of blood leaked past the edges of the steel halves from where the armoured parts had bitten into his skin, but the highborn was not in any position to complain.

Spite shifted again, and Malus heard his jaws snap shut on empty air just above his head. A surge of terror shot through the highborn as he saw a shadow spread like a stain on the bridge around him, and out of pure instinct he rolled as far to the left as he could, just as a smothering weight of stinking flesh smashed against him.

He couldn't breathe for a moment, much less see, but then the Chaos beast drew back from its lunge and Malus saw how horrifyingly close he'd come to being impaled by the thing's beak. The shroud of flesh surrounding its mouth slid away from Malus, and without its weight to pin him he fell back over the edge of the span. Screaming, he flailed his hands and grabbed the first thing he could: a bleeding stump of wriggling tentacle. The highborn felt the clenching barbs of the thing's suckers scraping against his armoured glove as the creature screeched in his ear and tossed its head, flinging Malus high into the air.

The highborn held on for dear life as he was whipped about by the hunter's thrashings. More tentacles lashed around Malus, wrapping his legs and trying to pull him closer to the creature's rending maw. He groped at his belt, desperately trying to find some weapon he could use against the thing. The beast's strength was enormous, drawing him inexorably towards the great beak, and he had no illusions that his armoured breastplate would give the beast a second's pause before it tore him to pieces.

The monster's lunge had left it overextended, however, and Spite saw his chance. He darted forwards, closing his jaws around the hunter's neck. The Chaos beast shuddered and screamed, spraying Malus with spittle and gobs of sticky ichor.

He heard the creature's thin bones crunch as Spite bit deeper, and he knew what was soon to happen: the nauglir would break its neck with a savage shake and hurl the beast aside, just as it had down in the crypt. Frantically, he started to kick and thrash in the monster's grip, praying to the Dark Mother that it would start to weaken as its wounds began to tell.

With a fierce kick, Malus managed to pull his left leg free. He felt the beast begin to shift as Spite found his footing and started to lift. Acting on impulse, the highborn drew back his armoured leg and kicked the monster on the side of its beak. To his surprise, the monster howled and let go of his other leg.

Spite rumbled deep in his chest, lifted the hunter into the air, and started to shake. Malus heard bones crunch and felt the beast go limp. As the nauglir was wrenching the hunter back over the bridge the highborn took a deep breath and let go.

For a horrifying moment, Malus was certain he'd miscalculated. Rather than being thrown back onto the bridge, it seemed as if he was being hurled along its length, his arms flailing wildly as he began to plummet downward. At the last moment his left hand struck the edge of the bridge and he grabbed hold, his shoulder flaring in pain as it took the brunt of the impact. Without hesitating, Malus kicked up his feet and swung roughly over the edge of the span, just in time to see Spite hurl the broken body of the Chaos beast into the abyss.

Panting and giddy with terror, Malus rolled carefully onto his back and savoured the sensation of lying on something that wasn't writhing or clawing at him. Further back on the bridge, Spite lifted his snout and roared in triumph, and the highborn felt the curved bridge start to shift.

'Damn me,' Malus breathed, rolling onto his knees. He could see wide cracks spreading along the length of the bridge, racing towards him from the weakened section where the nauglir still stood. 'Spite!' Malus cried, waving his arms. 'Go! Move!'

The cold one looked curiously at his master. It blew a gobbet of ichor from its nostrils and shifted its weight, edging its way towards him.

'No! Not this way, you thick lizard! Back! Go back that way!' he yelled. He scrambled down the bridge, waving his hands wildly at the heavy cold one. Grumbling, the nauglir finally got the message and turned around, walking ponderously towards the Vermillion Gate.

The bridge groaned and crackled with each hair-raising step, but Malus managed to recover his sword and creep onto the spire without further incident. He fell to his knees beside the cold one, trembling with exertion.

'Well, I think it's safe to say we won't be going back that way,' he gasped.

The nauglir rumbled and turned to sniff at the red stone arch. After a moment, Malus managed to catch his breath and staggering back to his feet, he went to check on his cold one's injuries. He counted more than a dozen deep gouges torn by the hunter's beak, and applied a healing salve from his saddlebags to each before climbing back into the saddle.

No sooner had he taken up the reins than he heard a commotion at the gallery behind him. Malus turned in the saddle to see about a dozen zealots standing at the foot of the bridge, glaring angrily at him. Apparently they'd seen the damage to the middle of the span, and had no interest in testing its strength.

The highborn gave the zealots a mocking salute with his sword, and then nudged Spite towards the arch. Taking a deep breath, he addressed the daemon. 'I don't suppose you know anything about this gate?'

'I know a bit,' Tz'arkan admitted.

Malus bit back an angry curse. 'Well, why don't you tell me how it works?'

The daemon shifted within his chest. 'There's little to tell. Cross beneath the arch and fix your destination firmly in your mind.'

'I don't have a destination, as you damned well know,' Malus snapped.

'Don't be churlish, little druchii,' Tz'arkan sneered. 'I will guide us to where we need to go.'

They rode towards the archway. Malus studied it closely as they approached. There was not a single rune or sigil anywhere along its length. Whatever magic worked upon it was invisible to his uneducated eye. He could feel its power though, washing over him in pulsing waves that made his ears ring and set his teeth on edge.

As they passed beneath the arch, the highborn expected to see a portal of smoke or light, but nothing appeared. 'Are you sure you know how this works?' he said.

Then the world turned the colour of blood, and Malus felt himself twisted inside out.

TZ'ARKAN HAD NEGLECTED to mention the pain.

Malus was blind, plummeting through howling darkness, and it felt as if ravens were feeding on his organs. The highborn felt their sharp beaks tear at his heart and lungs, worrying out little pieces and pecking thoughtfully at his quivering flesh as if savouring a fine meal. He could not move, could not scream. All he could do was suffer the ravages of the carrion birds for what felt like an eternity.

Then there was a clap of thunder, a hot wind smote Malus in his face, and Spite was stumbling down a shallow hillside of loose stone and parched dirt.

The nauglir bellowed in confusion and pain. Malus reeled in the saddle, feeling sticky moisture on his face. His stomach heaved, and for a terrifying moment it felt like something was trying to force its way out.

Spite skidded to a stop at the base of the hill and Malus all but fell from the saddle. He landed hard on his knees and vomited a fountain of dark blood and glossy, black feathers onto the lifeless ground.

'Mother of Night,' he groaned, wiping his mouth with the back of his gauntlet. The armoured glove came away slick with blood. Gasping for breath, he straightened and tried to see where he was.

The hillside behind him emptied onto a dry and desolate plain under a swirling sky the colour of blood. Towering black mountains reared above the northern horizon, their iron flanks painted with chiaroscuros of jagged yellow lightning. The hot wind seemed to blow from every direction, shifting crazily around the compass at the whim of some lunatic god. It moaned and whispered in his ears with a susurrus of strange voices, hinting at things that he only dimly grasped, but the pieces he understood turned his guts to greasy ice.

A city of black iron and blasted stone sat on the plain like a vast, black spider. Tall, blade-like towers reared hungrily into the crimson sky behind ruined walls and craggy battlements. Pillars of inky smoke rose here and there across the cityscape, wreathing the ancient buildings in a pall of suffocating fumes and ash. Off to the east, huge, hulking shapes the size of citadels writhed and lumbered along the horizon, reaching skyward as if to grasp the fickle lightning, and bellowing in madness and rage.

The gate had sent him into the far north, into the Chaos Wastes. Nowhere else in the world could such a vision of torment exist.

Why had the zealots brought the warpsword here, he wondered? What had possessed them? Was it fear of discovery by the temple, or had the blade itself chosen its resting place?

'Where is the sword, daemon?' Malus croaked, his throat ravaged by his ordeal. 'Enough with your damned games. Just tell me where to find it so we can quit this accursed place!'

'It is yonder, I think,' Tz'arkan said. Malus knew the daemon meant the foul city on the plain.

'You *think*?'

'What am I, a hound that sniffs out swords?' Tz'arkan spat. 'The gate is not so precise as I imagined, or else my control was not quite as perfect as it might have been. We are in the proper area, and I feel a source of great power to the north. What else could it be?'

'Here? In the Wastes? It could be a great many things.' Before Malus could expound further, however, Spite looked back the way they'd come and sniffed the hot air warily.

The highborn looked back over his shoulder. Up the long, rocky hillside, perhaps two hundred yards away, a knot of horsemen regarded him from the hillcrest.

Malus glared sidelong at the nauglir. 'You and your damned bellowing,' he muttered, climbing to his feet. As he did so, the horsemen kneed their mounts forwards, walking them carefully down the treacherous slope.

'Time to be going,' the highborn said, reaching for his saddle. He swung himself onto Spite's back and kicked the nauglir into a trot. His mind racing, he led the warbeast out onto the plain.

The cold one's feet kicked up puffs of grey dust as the nauglir trotted across the wasteland towards the ruined city. The horsemen easily kept pace with the cold one, fanning out expertly into a semicircular formation once they came down off the hillside. Malus studied them intently as they rode, but he could make out few details except for the spears that rose above the riders' heads and the skill with which they rode. As near as the highborn could reckon there were at least a score of them. That either meant a large patrol or a small raiding force. Malus wasn't certain which possibility he preferred.

Spite made good time at first, but as the minutes wore on the highborn noticed that the great beast began to tire. His gait became uneven, and Malus let out a curse. The nauglir was going lame from the deep wounds in his hind legs. It was much harder to lame a nauglir than a horse, but with only two legs to drive it along, when it happened the effects were often much worse. The highborn snarled. He didn't dare stop to let the beast rest, but if he didn't slow down the cold one would eventually collapse. Having little choice, he reined in and slowed Spite to a walk.

The riders gained ground steadily, although they did not seem especially eager to get within spear distance of the lone druchii. The closer they got, however, the more they hemmed Malus in to left and right. Soon their intentions were clear: they were herding him closer to the city on the plain.

Malus considered his options as they rode on. As far as he knew, the sword was somewhere in the city, and it was entirely possible that whoever led those riders might know where it was. However, he doubted that anyone in this goddess-forsaken wasteland would have any interest in helping him. It was far more likely that they were herding him along like a prize cow for slaughter. That left fighting or running, and at the moment he couldn't manage either, unless he called upon the daemon.

With Tz'arkan's help he could wipe out the riders to the last man, with or without Spite, but at what cost?

Do I have a choice any more, Malus thought?

Behind him, the riders blew a strange, skirling horn. Malus's heart quickened, thinking the riders were about to charge, but when he looked back they were still keeping their distance a few hundred yards away.

They were only a few miles from the city. The highborn knew that he had to act soon. He had no intention of becoming a prisoner to these Chaos twisted savages. The more he thought about seeking the daemon's help the more he felt his body ache for the taste of Tz'arkan's power. How much more potent would it be here, with the energies of Chaos raging through the very skies? How like a god he could be!

Malus had the name of the daemon on his lips when they crested a gentle rise in the landscape and saw the riders waiting ahead of him.

There had been no warning of their approach, no horns or telltale dust clouds. They had mastered the terrain with devilish cunning, using its folds to manoeuvre directly into his path. Just like that, the trap closed shut around him. Horsemen from the trailing patrol had already reached the rise to either side of him, cutting him off from escape. The riders in front were less than a hundred yards away, waiting patiently.

He studied the men awaiting him as he guided Spite down the shallow slope. They were broad shouldered, powerful men, wearing animal furs and bits of ragged chainmail. Bracelets of silver or hammered brass adorned their arms, and steel helmets with mail skirts rested on their shaggy heads. Their skin was swarthy, almost like brown leather, and their bodies had been twisted by years of living beneath the boiling sky. Malus saw ram's horns sprouting from the forehead of one warrior, while another stared at the highborn with a single, catlike eye set in the centre of his forehead. Another man had two heads upon his neck, one broad and flat-nosed and the other shrivelled, scaly and bestial. Even their horses showed signs of terrible mutation, with cloven hooves and mangy bodies thick with cable-like muscles. Fangs protruded from their slack mouths, and their lolling tongues were long and forked like serpents'.

As he drew nearer, three of the riders kneed their mounts forwards upon some unspoken command. Each drew weapons that glinted in the bloody light. The man with one eye readied a long, curved sword and a steel buckler, while the two-headed man brandished a pair of long handled axes. A third man with piercing blue eyes and a ragged, drooling hole where his mouth should have been, uncoiled a long whip in his left hand and hefted a short, stubby mace in his right.

None of the other riders moved. Malus looked back at the men behind him, and saw them observing the scene from the rise many yards away. The highborn questioned whether this was some sort of challenge. He'd heard that some tribes of marauders favoured trials by combat, pitting their champions against those of their enemies. If that was their intent, he was happy to indulge them and see where it led. At worst, he could call the daemon's name and fight his way free if he had to.

The three riders spread out, edging their mounts forwards. Spite, smelling horseflesh, quickened his pace and let out a hungry roar, but the mutated animals were unfazed by the nauglir's hunting cry.

Malus realised that they were all going to attack him at once. He guessed that was supposed to be some sort of compliment. He drew his sword and decided to change the rules of the game.

Kicking his heels into Spite's flanks, Malus turned the nauglir hard right and charged at the two-headed man. The cold one closed the distance in an eye blink, but the horseman reacted with amazing speed, kicking his mount into a gallop and dodging nimbly out of the nauglir's path. Then he darted back at Malus, slashing at him with both deadly axes. Caught by surprise at the deft manoeuvre, it was all the highborn could do to get his sword up in time to block the flurry of strokes. Even so, the rider's last blow rang hard against Malus's pauldron, drawing a hiss of pain from his lips.

Malus reined Spite around, but already the two-headed man was darting away, his horse responding to his commands as if they were of one mind. The highborn started to lunge Spite after the horseman when a blur of motion to his right caught his eye. The one-eyed swordsman was charging at him from the flank, his sword gleaming redly. Malus cursed and twisted in the saddle, blocking the horseman's blow, but the attack had tremendous power behind it, nearly knocking his sword from his hand.

The one-eyed rider swept past, and Malus felt something wrap around his sword arm and haul backwards, wrenching the limb painfully in its socket. The blue-eyed man was behind Spite, hauling on his own reins and trying to pull the highborn from his saddle.

Gritting his teeth with pain, Malus wrenched his reins and applied his left boot, and Spite lashed out with his powerful tail. The blue eyed man had just enough time to comprehend his mistake before the muscular appendage slammed into his horse's side, splintering ribs and shattering the man's leg. The horse collapsed with a strangely human scream, but the wounded warrior held onto his whip with both hands, still drawing Malus with him towards the ground.

Hot pain lanced from the highborn's shoulder across his narrow chest as he heeled Spite around. He looked over his shoulder and saw the one-eyed swordsman sweeping in on his left flank, while the two-headed axe man was coming up fast just behind and to the right. He yanked at the whip wrapping his arm, but the braided rawhide bound him fast.

Facing the prone marauder, Malus kicked Spite into a trot. The blue-eyed warrior tried to roll aside, but the whip trapping the highborn worked against him as well. The marauder let out a terrible, gobbling cry as the nauglir crushed him underfoot.

Hooves thundered to Malus's left as the one-eyed swordsman swept in, aiming a mighty stroke for the back of the highborn's neck. Malus gauged the man's approach, and at the last moment he kneed Spite hard and threw up his left arm. The nauglir sidled towards the onrushing horse, closing the distance faster than the swordsman expected and throwing off his aim. The flashing sword smashed into the back of Malus's shoulder, hard enough for the highborn to hear the pauldron bending. Then Malus closed his hand around the marauder's wrist and dropped his arm, trapping the sword against his chest.

The one-eyed swordsman let out a savage curse and tried to ride past, but he was far too close to the cold one to escape. The nauglir's jaws closed on the horse's head and crushed it like an egg. The animal collapsed, throwing its rider forwards, and Malus let the man go. He rolled admirably with the fall, tumbling to a stop more than a dozen feet away. Spite leapt at the man like a cat upon a mouse. The swordsman barely had time to scream before the nauglir's bloody jaws clamped down and bit him in half.

Malus was just turning to look for the third rider when a pair of blows struck him from behind. One hit square between his shoulder blades, rocking him in the saddle, while the other struck a glancing blow against his head. Pain bloomed behind

Malus's eyes and his body went slack. The next thing he felt was the jarring shock of hitting the dusty ground.

Vague noises came and went as he slowly regained his senses. He heard the sound of hooves and the roar of the cold one, both noises reverberating oddly in his head. He opened his eyes and saw the two-headed man swinging wide of the cold one and angling back towards him.

He tried to sit up, shouting as a spike of pain lanced through his skull. He felt hot blood running down his cheek and the back of his neck. Malus saw a glint of metal on the ground nearby and dimly recognised it as his sword. He rolled over and crawled towards it as the two-headed man kicked his horse into a gallop, bearing down on him. The ground shook as the horse drew closer, and Malus knew that there was no way he was going to reach the weapon in time.

As the thunder loomed over him Malus threw himself flat and rolled onto his back, looking up at the marauder leaning down out of his saddle to strike with his axe. The blade blurred through the air. Malus reached up and crossed his arms, forming an X, and the haft of the long blade crashed against them. The highborn grabbed the leather wrapped haft and held on for all he was worth. The marauder, already at the limit of his balance, came out of the saddle and hit the ground hard, close to Malus.

Malus yanked hard on the axe, pulling it from the marauder's hands, and then rolled drunkenly to his feet. His opponent was on his back, still clutching his second weapon. Without hesitation the highborn charged at the man, bringing his axe down on the marauder's head. The two-headed man brought up his axe and blocked the highborn's blow, but Malus twisted his weapon and hooked the beard of the axe around his opponent's haft, pulling it out of the way. He rushed in, hammered an armoured boot into the marauder's groin, and then broke several of his ribs. Grabbing his axe with both hands, he twisted the weapon out of his stunned opponent's grip and methodically cut away both of the warrior's heads.

The highborn straightened, his chest heaving, and looked for someone else to kill. The knot of riders at the base of the depression had not moved during the fight. Now one of their number slid gracefully from the saddle and approached Malus. He was a huge, broad shouldered warrior, with dark tattoos spiralling across his powerful chest. His skin was the colour of polished mahogany, and one of his eyes glowed a nacreous green, like trapped witchlight. Two large broadswords hung from a wide leather belt at his hips, but the man made no move to draw them.

A trickle of blood ran down Malus's cheek and touched his lips. He spat it into the dust. 'If you don't want to die empty-handed you'd best draw one of those blades,' he growled.

To his surprise, the warrior halted and addressed him in passable druhir. 'You were magnificent, holy one. Whom do I have the honour of addressing?'

The highborn frowned. This was just about the last thing he expected.

'I am Malus, of Hag Graef, a warrior of the druchii.'

The man bowed deeply. 'You bear the blessing of the Lord of Murder in your eyes.' He straightened and said gravely, 'You have come for the sword.'

The frankness of the question stunned Malus. 'Yes. Yes I have. How did you know?'

'It was foreseen,' the warrior said with a dreadful smile. His teeth were filed to jagged points. 'You are the Scourge. We have been waiting for you for a very long time.'

Chapter Twenty-Two
THE AGELESS KINGS

THE DARK-SKINNED warrior turned to his companions and shouted something in a foul, debased tongue. The warband erupted in cheers and savage howls that were echoed by the riders at the crest of the rise.

Malus frowned thoughtfully, considering what he'd heard. 'Who are you?' he asked.

The tattooed marauder bowed again, in a passable impersonation of a druchii retainer. 'I am Shebbolai, the chieftain of the Tribe of the Red Sword. We serve the Ageless Kings in the City of Khaine, yonder.'

At first Malus wasn't sure he'd heard the man correctly. The City of Khaine, he thought. 'Who are these Ageless Kings?'

'Servants of the Bloody-Handed God, who brought the great sword out of the hands of the blasphemers and kept it safe for many centuries, awaiting the day when Khaine's Scourge would walk out of the wasteland to claim his due.' The chieftain gave Malus another sharp-toothed smile and beckoned to him. 'Come, we must waste no time. The kings will want to see you at once.'

Malus was taken aback. Was it possible that the five assassins still lived after all this time, guarding the sword until the coming of the Time of Blood? It seemed incredible, but who knew what strange forces were at work here in the Wastes?

Slowly, painfully, the highborn recovered his sword. He looked at the bodies of the men he'd slain. 'Who were these warriors?'

'The champions of the tribe,' Shebbolai said proudly. 'Not even I could have defeated them all at once.'

Malus didn't think that spoke very highly of Shebbolai or the rest of his tribe, but the highborn judiciously held his tongue. On impulse he went to each of the men, struck off their heads, and carried the trophies over to Spite. The marauder chieftain watched, nodding in approval.

The highborn stuffed the heads into one of the empty sacks that had held his armour, and hung it from his belt like any zealot pilgrim. He took Spite by the reins and looked the cold one hard in the eye. 'Hunt, Spite,' he said. 'See what you can eat in this damned wasteland and wait for my call.' Then he slapped the nauglir on the neck and sent it loping off to the east. Whoever these Ageless Kings were, he wasn't about to trust them completely, not with his cache of Tz'arkan's relics at stake.

Malus turned back to Shebbolai. 'I'll take his mount,' he said, pointing to the two-headed man's horse.

The warrior nodded. 'He's yours,' the chieftain said. 'The horse and all three men's wives. It is your right.'

'Just the horse will do,' the highborn said, fighting to suppress a look of pure horror.

SHEBBOLAI LED THE party through a ruined gate at the southern edge of Khaine's city, past towers of bleached skulls that rose more than thirty feet into the crimson sky. The city itself was huge, easily the size of Hag Graef, and looking at the sleek, black stone of its construction Malus couldn't help but see the hands of elves in its making. Certainly the Ageless Kings hadn't built it. The crumbling structures groaned under the weight of ages, perhaps going back as far as the Great War against Chaos or even earlier.

Malus and the marauders rode down deserted streets piled with broken stone. He found himself catching movement out of the corner of his eye more than once, but when he turned to look, he saw only a shadowy alley or an empty doorway. Piles of ancient skulls stood at every corner, reminding the highborn of Har Ganeth, hundreds of leagues distant.

'How did your tribe come to serve the Ageless Kings?' Malus asked.

Shebbolai chuckled, letting his horse find its own way along the avenue beside Malus. 'By conquest, of course. Long, long ago my tribe wandered these plains like the other tribes, but the Ageless Kings came from the cold lands and slew our chieftain and nearly all of his warriors with the power of the red sword. Then they took the wives and children of the tribe and brought them here, to the City of Khaine. We have served them ever since.' The marauder twisted in his saddle and pointed back to the plains from whence they had come. 'We rule all the land from east to west, and many tribes pay us tribute in flesh and treasure to cross our territory.' Shebbolai smiled proudly. 'Other tribes must journey for many leagues in search of wealth and glory to heap at the feet of the Old Gods, but we need only stretch out our hands and the tribes bury their faces in the dirt and give us all they have. There is no tribe more powerful or more favoured by the gods than ours.'

'A tribe's glory is wrought in battle, is it not?' Malus asked.

Shebbolai's smile faded. 'We fight from time to time, but few of the tribes dare to challenge the power of the sword. The Ageless Kings tell us to bide our time and wait for the coming of the Scourge, and then we will drown ourselves in hot blood!'

The highborn nodded thoughtfully. 'The Ageless Kings are wise,' he said. 'Tell me, how many of them are there?'

'The legends say there were five at first, but now only three remain,' the chieftain said. 'Once they rode alongside the tribe, bearing the red sword before them, but for many hundreds of years they have kept to the god's temple here in the city.' Shebbolai extended a hand. 'There it is, yonder.'

Malus saw a squat, square tower rising from a pile of ruins just ahead. Perhaps it had always been a temple or a citadel for one of the city lords. Now its sloped flanks were adorned with thousands upon thousands of skulls. The sheer scale of the offerings stunned the highborn. Not all of the temples in Naggaroth combined could equal it.

The closer they drew to the temple the more people Malus saw: hideous, twisted wretches, clothed in rags and bits of fur, who watched the passage of the chieftain and his retinue with hard, feral stares. Many of the buildings near the temple were inhabited, but few were in good repair. Whatever wealth the tribe had accumulated, it hadn't gone towards providing the marauders with luxury or comfort. As they rode through the more populated streets Malus could sense an undercurrent of tension rising out of the squalor, and wondered how he might turn that to his advantage.

Before they reached the temple the riders passed through a broad plaza. Princes and generals in ages past might have reviewed their armies in such an expanse. Now, however, it was a forest of iron poles bearing the rotting, headless corpses of thousands of sacrificial victims. The stench of decay was immense. Malus gritted his teeth and tried to keep his expression neutral as they worked their way through a miasma of death.

Malus studied the bodies closest to the narrow path. 'Many of these look quite fresh,' he observed. 'It seems you've been fighting recently.'

Shebbolai's expression darkened. 'Just the killing of dogs,' he said gruffly, and spoke no more.

Beyond the plaza of corpses the riders reached a broad flight of stone steps leading up to the tower. As they reined in, a pair of towering doors at the top of the steps groaned open, and a mob of cowering, naked human slaves spilled out. Their bodies were thin and sallow, covered with scars and weeping sores, and they raced to the bottom of the steps to take the marauders' horses and see to their needs. Malus slid gratefully from the saddle, happy to be rid of the mangy, stinking beast, and tossed its reins to one of the trembling humans before following Shebbolai up to the open doorway.

The chieftain ushered Malus across the threshold with a bow, and then returned to his fellows. A long, broad corridor stretched beyond, lit by globes of flickering witchlight. The highborn composed himself before striding swiftly down the long passageway. Tall figures in ornate, archaic brass armour stood sentinel along the corridor. The men were inhumanly strong, their bodies swollen to hideous proportions, and they held huge, double-headed axes in their broad, scarred hands. The highborn studied them as he walked past, feeling the weight of their gaze, but unable to see the expressions behind their helmets' ornate faceplates.

Malus stepped into a large, dimly lit space at the end of the passageway. A single shaft of light speared down into the centre of the chamber, falling upon a small stone altar carved of dark marble. Its square sides were anointed in fresh blood, and two grinning skulls rested upon it, their surfaces stained nearly brown by centuries of bloody libations.

Malus approached the ancient bones, noting that they were free from mutation and perfect in form. The cheekbones were sharp, the jaw lines angular. 'The two dead kings,' he murmured, reaching out to touch the remains of one of the five lost assassins.

'You are not worthy to touch the bones of the Ageless Kings!' hissed a voice from the darkness. The sound was eerie, like a keening wind whistling through bare branches and forming words Malus could understand. It echoed in the vast chamber, seeming to come from every direction at once. 'You defile this sacred place with your presence!'

Malus turned, seeking the source of the frail voice. 'Are you wraith or man?' he called out. 'Show yourself!'

Another voice spoke. Like the first, it was chillingly unnatural, like the groan of glacial ice. 'We are ageless,' it said, 'and we rule here, not you.'

The imperious tone in the groaning voice annoyed the high-born. 'You rule here? I thought you were waiting, serving the will of Khaine and guarding the warpsword until the arrival of the chosen one.'

A third voice answered, thin and creaking like old leather. 'Who are you to question us so?'

Malus took a deep breath. 'I am the Scourge,' he said. 'Your vigil is ended, for I have come for the sword. The Time of Blood is nigh.'

The echoes of his voice faded into the stillness. Malus waited, straining to locate the aged assassins in the depths of the room. After a moment he caught the faintest sound of movement to his left: a dry rustle of robes.

'Impossible,' the first voice said. 'You cannot be the chosen one.'

Malus turned to the source of movement. 'Can I not? Am I not druchii, like you? Do I not bear the blessing of Khaine upon my face? I have followed you here through the Vermillion Gate, drawn by the tie I have with the sword. How else could I have found you here in the Waste?' He held out his hand. 'Will you bring me my sword, or will you dishonour your long vigil here at its end?'

More faint hints of movement whispered in the darkness. The second voice spoke. 'You come from the temple,' it groaned.

'So did you, once upon a time,' Malus answered. 'The true believers count you among the dead. The heretics in the temple concealed the theft of the sword and have ruled unchallenged for centuries.'

'That is of no matter to us,' creaked the third voice. 'Let them rule atop their filthy hill. It will all be swept aside when the Time of Blood arrives.'

The voices were drawing closer. Malus was certain now. 'Why conceal your triumph from your fellows?' he asked. 'They might have swayed the people of the city to the true faith had they known.'

Faint shapes resolved themselves at the edges of the light. Malus saw the outlines of robed and hooded figures regarding him from the darkness. 'We are the true faith,' the first voice replied.

'Prove it,' Malus said. 'Give me the sword.'

'The sword is not here,' the second voice groaned, 'and you are not worthy.'

'You dare deny me?' the highborn snapped. 'I am Malus of Hag Graef, born in the city of shadow to the house of chains. My mother was a witch and I slew my father with my own hands. The skull of Aurun Var spoke to me through my sister, a living saint of the Lord of Murder. Have you forgotten your duty after so many centuries, or has your lust for power turned you into the very heretics you once rebelled against?'

All three voices shouted at once. 'Blasphemy!'

'A man blasphemes against the gods, not cowardly figures hiding in the shadows of a ruined temple,' Malus shouted. 'Did you steal the sword to keep it from the hands of the temple elders, or did you secretly covet its power? What are you but pathetic mockeries of the very heretics you once railed against?'

'Seize him!' the first voice shrieked. Malus reached for his sword, but huge figures loomed silently out of the shadows to either side of him. There had been more of the armoured guards standing a silent watch in the darkness of the room, and they grabbed Malus's arms and lifted him from the ground as if he was a child.

The robed figures crept slowly into the light, drawing back their hoods, and Malus looked upon them and cried out, horrified at what the assassins had become.

Their bodies were impossibly ancient, shrivelled and dried like mummies over thousands of years in the hot air of the Wastes. Two males and a woman – her paper thin lips framed a pair of yellow fangs that told Malus she had once been a blood-witch – little more than living skeletons with parchment skin stretched over sharp bones.

The man in the centre of the trio stepped close to Malus, studying him with cold, reptilian orbs that bore little resemblance to living eyes. 'You are young and strong,' the creature said, its voice whistling from the depths of dried lungs and past cracked lips. 'The people here are faithful, but their spirits are weak. We have lived on thin gruel for far too long,' the withered druchii said. 'You are blasphemous, but in a sense you are also a blessing from Khaine. Tonight we will kill you, so that tomorrow we may call back your spirit and consume it. Your energies will restore us and lend us strength for a very long time to come.'

'You would dare take the life of Khaine's chosen Scourge?' Malus raged.

The withered creature looked up at Malus and shook his head. 'The true Scourge would not have been taken so easily,' he said, and gestured to the guards.

'Take the heretic to the plaza and crucify him,' the Ageless King said.

Chapter Twenty-Three
THE BURNING BLADE

MALUS ROARED LIKE a trapped animal, thrashing and kicking in the guards' iron grip as they began to remove him from the altar room. Consumed with rage, he used their strength against them, twisting at the waist and kicking the man to his left in the side of the head. The highborn's armoured shin rang like a gong off the polished brass helmet and the guard staggered, allowing Malus to pull his arm free.

The guard on his right reacted quickly for a man of his immense size, reaching for Malus's throat with a wide, spade-like hand. Snarling, Malus ducked beneath the guard's lunge and tried to grab the bone handle of a dagger sheathed at the man's waist. The highborn's hand closed on the hilt and he drew the blade free, just as a clawed hand grasped the side of Malus's cheek and every nerve in his body exploded in icy pain.

Malus convulsed beneath the witch's agonising touch. His body arched, taut as a bow, and his face locked in a rictus of torment. Malus dimly heard a sharp, brittle *crack* near his waist and realised that the bone hilt had snapped in his clenched, quivering hand.

Armoured hands grabbed him roughly, tearing the dagger away and lifting him from the ground. His gaze was fixed. He could not move, could not breathe, could not even blink. The pain was so intense that he could barely think. Tz'arkan's name rose unbidden to his mind, but he had not the power to speak it.

The blood-witch recoiled from Malus with a frightened groan, her black eyes glittering with shock and horror as the guards dragged him away. The last thing he saw as darkness enfolded him was her white, withered face, its leathery features twisting into an expression of despair as the witch reeled from the glimpse she'd been given into Malus's soul.

In time, the pain began to recede, like a slow tide ebbing from his tortured frame. Visions of red slowly resolved into a crimson sky, painted with twisting shapes of black smoke and ashen clouds. Thunder rumbled in the distance.

Long shapes loomed at the edges of his vision. He lay on his back amid a forest of dying men, their ravaged bodies impaled upon iron stakes as tall as saplings. His body was contorted awkwardly on the wide paving stones, like a statue tumbled from its plinth. Figures moved slowly past the limits of his eye-sight, their movements perceived as no more than shifting shadows playing across his contorted form.

He thought he heard a voice rise in anger, and moans of defeat and despair. Malus could not tell if they were real or part of a dream, and his mind wandered as he stared into the shifting, crimson sky.

Once he thought he saw the blood-witch standing over him, a curved knife trembling in her shrunken hand. Shrieks and groans echoed in the turgid air, and when he looked into her eyes she wailed like a ghost and shrank from his sight. He tried to laugh but managed only a low, tortured moan.

The sky darkened. Thunder rolled like war drums, and drops of blood mixed with gritty ash fell heavily against his face. Hands gripped him around his arms and lifted him. He rose into the air, wondering if he was being offered up to the storm.

Then he was falling again, being lowered onto a frame of rough wood in the shape of an X. The hands pulled at him, stretching his contorted limbs and laying them flat against the crossbars. His head sagged between the cross-posts, sending drops of dark red streaming down into his ears and hair.

He felt his gauntlets being pulled away. Something cold and sharp pressed against his right wrist. His mind drifted, unable to make sense of what was happening.

Then the first hammer blow struck, driving the spike deep into his wrist, and Malus began to scream.

THUNDER CRASHED, VIBRATING his armour like a struck gong and startling him awake. His body jerked, and he cried out in the grip of raw, jagged pain as his broken wrists and ankles grated against the nails pinning him to beams. Agony caused his stomach to clench, and he vomited blood and bile onto the paving stones.

Darkness had fallen since the guards had nailed him to the wood and left him in the plaza to die. Lightning raged overhead, playing a nightmarish pantomime of shadows across the stones of the plaza. Blood and ashes had dried on his cheeks, forming a brittle death mask that lent a daemonic cast to his angular face.

Had it not been for his armour he would have been dead already, suffocated by his own ribcage as he hung from the upright wooden posts. As it was, the interlocking plates kept his body from sagging too far downwards, taking some of the weight off his mutilated wrists. He'd swum in and out of consciousness for hours, delirious from pain and loss of blood.

His mind was clearer now. Perhaps the last vestiges of the witch's touch had faded, or else his nerves no longer had the power to communicate the awful truth of his injuries. It was enough that he was able to notice the solitary figure outlined by the flash of lightning only a few yards away.

Grunting in pain, he managed to raise his head slightly and peer at the motionless figure. 'Sh… Shebbolai,' he whispered, his voice little more than a thready rasp.

The figure stirred. 'I thought you dead,' the chieftain replied. He stepped closer. Another flicker of lightning etched his dark skinned face in sharp relief, revealing an expression of anger and torment. 'How can this be?' he asked. 'You are the first warrior of Naggaroth to come here since the arrival of the Ageless Kings. You bested my finest warriors, and you bear the mark of Khaine in your eyes. You must be the Scourge!'

'The Ageless Kings have forgotten their duty to the Lord of Murder,' Malus rasped. 'They have been seduced by power and wealth. Long ago they ruled this land to safeguard Khaine's sword. Now they rule for their sakes alone.'

'Do not blaspheme!' Shebbolai snapped.

'You know it's true!' Malus said. He tried to look up at the bodies hanging nearby. 'On the way here you told me that your tribe rarely fought any more. Where, then, did all these men come from? They have the look of warriors, but were they foes taken in battle or members of your own tribe who rebelled against the Ageless Kings and their inglorious rule?'

'You're here now,' the chieftain said, 'and The Time of Blood is at hand! How can they deny you?'

'Because this is all they have,' Malus said. 'They've clung to life and power for so long that the struggle is all they know. They cannot return to Naggaroth, not as they are, and once I claim the sword, who will fear them? The centuries have made them mad, Shebbolai, and weak. Their time is at an end.' Malus met his eye. 'It's your time now. Of all the hundreds of chieftains who have led the red swords, it is you who will ride to battle beside Khaine's chosen Scourge.'

An expression of awe transformed Shebbolai's scarred face. 'What would you have me do?'

'Tell me where to find the warpsword.'

'It... it is not here,' the chieftain said. 'Long ago, when the kings first came here, the sword passed between them at the turning of each moon, so that all of them would share the burden of safeguarding it. One day the king who kept the sword refused to give it up, and they fought among themselves. The struggle lasted for centuries, or so the legends say.'

Shebbolai turned and look back at the temple. 'Two of the kings died during the feud. You saw their skulls in the reliquary chamber.'

'And the sword?'

'They agreed to place it beyond their grasp except in the direst of circumstances, so that they would never feud amongst themselves again. They took the sword north, into the mountains, and hid it in a cave, so goes the legend,' Shebbolai said grimly, 'as it has been passed down through the line of chieftains. It is part of our pact with the Ageless Kings, to keep their secret from the rest of the world.'

'That's all very fascinating,' Malus wheezed impatiently, 'but how am I to find this cave?'

'Follow the skulls,' the chieftain said. 'They will lead you through the gullies to the cave and its guardian.'

'Guardian,' Malus spat, 'what sort of guardian?'

The chieftain shrugged. 'The legends do not say: something powerful enough to guard the warpsword for ages and not be tempted by it as the kings were.'

'Delightful,' the highborn snarled. The pain in his wrists was starting to build once more. Gritting his teeth, he tried to take some of the weight off of them, prompting a groan of torment as he bore down on the spikes penetrating his feet just below the ankles.

When the agony subsided and his vision cleared he focused his gaze on Shebbolai once more. 'You must pass the word to those of your tribe you can trust,' the highborn said. 'When I return with the sword the reign of the Ageless Kings will end. Do you understand?'

The chieftain nodded. 'I understand.'

'Good. Now get me down from this damned cross,' Malus groaned.

But Shebbolai was unmoved. He looked Malus in the eye. 'If all you say is true, and you are the Scourge of Khaine, you should be able to free yourself.' He backed away from the cross. 'I will await your return,' he said, and disappeared into the darkness.

Malus stifled a vicious curse. He had a plan for Shebbolai and his warriors, so for the moment he needed the chieftain on his side. Plus, he thought bitterly as he tried in vain to close his fists, there was not enough mothers' milk in the world to heal him from the guards' iron spikes.

Lightning flared overhead and arced among the iron poles of the plaza. Malus heard screams and smelled the sweet odour of burning flesh. He drew a deep breath.

This would not be any mere taste. He stood at the edge of an abyss. The next step he took would be into darkness.

Thunder crashed. 'Tz'arkan!' he screamed at the bleeding sky, and his veins burned with the daemon's icy touch.

Power coursed through him in an icy torrent, banishing fear, weakness and pain. The strength of a god flowed through him. Clenching his fists, he tore them free of the iron spikes and laughed like a madman as shattered bone and torn flesh re-knit. Reaching down, he pulled the lower spikes loose with his bare hands and fell to his knees upon the gore slick stones. Malus squeezed the spikes between his fingers as if they were half-melted wax, and threw them high into the air.

He felt the lightning coming before it flared overhead. He heard the heartbeats of the men slowly dying among the forest of iron poles. He could taste the scent of each and every living thing in the city, and see the peaks of the mountains to the north despite the roiling darkness overhead.

It was like nothing he had ever felt before. The daemon did not merely strengthen and heal him. He *was* the daemon, and the daemon was him.

HE'D FOUND THE cold one a mile outside the city, tracking it through the darkness by its peculiar, acrid scent. It had growled threateningly at his approach, lowering its blocky head and snapping its fearsome jaws, but he had met its red eyes and bent his will upon the beast. The nauglir struggled against him but a moment, and then recoiled with a cry of pain. He advanced on the beast, lashing it again and again with his power, until it lay on its belly and allowed him to climb into the saddle.

Malus led Spite around the ruined city under the cover of darkness and up into the broken foothills to the north. His razor-keen senses banished the darkness and allowed him to traverse the narrow, labyrinthine gullies as if it was broad daylight.

Shebbolai had spoken true. He began to see the bones almost at once: smashed skeletons of men and horses, the long bones snapped and sucked clean of marrow and the skulls split open to get at the brains. Shorn armour and broken swords lay rusting in the dirt, enough to equip an army. For the first hour he'd amused himself by counting the skulls, trying to gauge how many souls had gone into the narrow defiles in search of Khaine's sword. Before the hour was up he'd counted a thousand, and didn't bother to continue from there.

Spite's broad feet were wading through drifts of old bones before long, crushing them and kicking them underfoot. They led unerringly upwards, many times branching off into twisting side paths, but Malus kept to the primary trail, knowing where it must eventually lead.

'Whoever lives here, daemon… has quite an appetite,' he said.

'Then let's hope he's sleeping, Malus,' Tz'arkan replied. The voice reverberated through his skull no differently than the highborn's own, as if he and the daemon were simply two spirits bound to the same body. 'Somewhere in these gullies lies the lost Warpsword of Khaine. We're not leaving until you've found it.'

The tone in the daemon's voice angered Malus, as if he was nothing more than a slave going about his master's business. For the moment, he chose to hold his tongue. Tz'arkan's power had subsided somewhat, but still flowed freely, infusing him with strength and power such as he hadn't known for months.

Up ahead the gully widened, forming a broad V that pointed to the mouth of a large cave. The gully floor outside the cave was literally carpeted with bones and the detritus of the dead. After many long months, he'd reached his goal at last.

Malus reined in Spite and slid carefully from the saddle. The nauglir shied away from him at once, retreating further down the length of the gully. He shot the beast a warning glance. 'I found you once, dragonlet. I can find you again,' he warned, and then turned his attention to the drifts of old bones that blanketed the rocky ground. It was a crude but effective alarm, providing the sword's guardian had sharp ears.

Choosing his course very carefully, Malus began to pick his way through the multitude of fallen treasure seekers. He tried not to think about the fact that many of them had probably attempted the very same thing.

'Quietly now, Darkblade,' Tz'arkan said, 'let's not wake anyone.'

'Your concern is touching,' the highborn murmured, slowly drawing his sword.

Lightning flickered silently overhead, making the landscape of bones appear to shift and slide. Disorientated, Malus tried to step over a yellowed skull directly in his path, and came down directly on it instead. The aged bone collapsed with a hollow *crunch* that seemed to echo like thunder between the gully walls.

Malus froze, not even daring to breathe. A moment passed, and then another. Still he waited, straining his ears for any signs of movement.

Two minutes passed. Only then did Malus relax, cursing his foul luck.

That was when the night air shook with an ear-splitting roar and an enormous figure emerged from the depths of the cave.

The guardian of the sword was huge. Its lower body alone was larger than a cold one, covered in scales of indigo and dusky red. Large legs, like those of a dragon, propelled it in a thunderous charge down the slope towards Malus, kicking up clouds of powdered bone with every ponderous step. Above the set of clawed forelegs where a dragon's neck and head would normally be there was instead a broad leather belt, decorated with scales of gold and a buckle shaped like a skull. Above the belt, towered the upper torso of a fearsome ogre, clad in crude armour that protected its midsection and capped its powerful shoulders. Tusks thick enough to disembowel a boar jutted from the shaggoth's thick lips, and its ice blue eyes gleamed beneath a craggy brow and a round steel helmet. In its platter sized hand, the guardian held a sword that was longer than Malus was tall, and the creature raised it angrily as it bore down on the stunned highborn.

'Mother of Night!' the highborn cursed.

'Malus, under the circumstances I think I'll let you run, now!'

The terrible sword whickered through the air. Galvanised by the daemon's shout, Malus hurled himself to the left, just out of the weapon's reach. The blade struck a pile of bones and sent shattered fragments spraying into the air. Still bellowing in rage, the dragon ogre charged past, quickly changing course to come around for another charge.

The creature was between Malus and his cold one. Frantically he cast around for other avenues of escape, but the walls of the gully were steep and sheer. 'There's nowhere to run!' he exclaimed.

The dragon ogre bore down on Malus again with a terrible crunching of bones. The highborn raised his sword warily. There was no way he could trade blows with something so massive. He would have to wear the monster down with lightning-fast strikes, much as he'd seen Arleth Vann kill the highborn in the crypt.

He crouched low as the beast charged into reach. Its sword swept down at an angle, aiming to cut the druchii in half from shoulder to hip. At the last second, Malus dodged to the left, cutting across the dragon ogre's path and fouling his swing. The creature let out a furious cry and the highborn answered with a druchii war scream as he put all his strength into a powerful cut aimed just below the shaggoth's belt.

The heavy northern sword, backed by the daemon's terrible strength, struck the monster dead on, and the steel blade shattered with a discordant clang. Malus barely had time to register his shock before the dragon ogre lashed out with a clawed forelimb and struck him a backhanded blow that sent him flying head over heels into the air.

Had the limb struck his chin it would have taken his head clean off. As it was, the shaggoth's paw had glanced off his chest and dented his thick breastplate. He felt as if he'd been kicked by a nauglir, and he gasped for breath as he hit a pile of old skulls near the side of the gully wall.

Malus rolled off the pile of bones, glaring helplessly at the monster. He tried to subdue it by force of will just as he'd done to the nauglir, but the dragon ogre was unfazed. Furious, he grabbed a skull and hurled it at the beast with all his strength. 'Curse you, creature!' he roared. 'Curse you back to hell!' The projectile struck the beast in the side of the head and shattered into pieces, leaving not a mark on the monster's thick skull.

Terror and despair raged through Malus. The daemon's gifts were useless. Had he surrendered the last vestiges of himself for nothing?

Bellowing like a bull, the dragon ogre came about, readying its massive sword.

Malus could feel Tz'arkan's strength pulsing through him. He could hear the blood rushing in his veins and feel the fury of the storm raging overhead, but not a bit of it mattered. In the next few moments the shaggoth would cut him apart.

As the dragon ogre trotted towards him, Malus's eyes turned to the dark mouth of the cave. I'll be damned if I'm going to die empty-handed, he thought.

The highborn pushed himself to his feet and sprinted up the gully. The dragon ogre bellowed angrily, surprised by the sudden move. Tz'arkan was surprised as well.

'Malus, where are you going? You're running towards the cave!'

'We still have a job to do, remember?' the highborn countered.

'You fool! It's right behind us!' the daemon said. 'You'll trap us in there!'

'I need a weapon,' Malus snarled. 'The warpsword is in there. That will do.'

Malus reached the entrance to the cave. A cacophony of pounding feet and crunching bone rose behind him as the shaggoth charged headlong up the gully.

'The Warpsword of Khaine is no pig stick to be used in brawling!' the daemon raged. 'It is a talisman of glorious power–'

'It's still a sword,' Malus said. 'Shut up, daemon!'

Malus rushed into the cave. He expected a long, carrion choked passageway, leading back into darkness. Instead he found himself in a broad, high-ceilinged cavern. The space was piled with bones and rotting bodies nevertheless, save for a cleared area near the centre of the chamber where the dragon ogre evidently slept. A plain stone altar stood on the other side of the cleared area, and upon that altar rested a sword.

The Warpsword of Khaine was a double-edged blade nearly as long as a draich, slightly wider at the point than at the hilt to give the weapon extra power to cut with. Its blade was sheathed in a scabbard of black lacquered bone, chased with gold and ornamented with fiery rubies. The weapon's hilt was long and slim, built for two hands and wrapped with dark leather. A large cabochon ruby, like a dragon's eye, gleamed at the point where hilt met blade. It glimmered with power, radiating from the entire blade in waves of invisible heat.

Malus looked upon the sword and saw the potential hidden within its depths. He saw red battlefields and toppled towers, looted cities and fallen kings. With such a blade a druchii could conquer the world.

'Malus, I forbid this!' the daemon snarled. Was there an edge of fear in Tz'arkan's voice?

The highborn dashed across the chamber. The shaggoth burst into the cavern just behind him, shaking the dank air with its furious cries.

'Then we die here,' Malus replied. 'The choice is yours.'

In truth it wasn't. Nothing the daemon could say or do would keep Malus from placing his hand upon the warpsword's hilt and drawing the weapon from its scabbard.

The hilt was hot to the touch, as if the ancient steel was still fresh from the forge. The warmth sank into his skin, suffusing his muscles with power. He drew the weapon in a single, smooth motion, marvelling at the blade's black finish. Its edge shone like fire in the gloom.

With a stentorian bellow the dragon ogre charged. Malus felt no fear. When he turned to face the onrushing beast he was smiling like a wolf.

Malus stepped into the shaggoth's charge, swinging the warpsword in a clean, perfect arc that was the virtual twin of the blow he'd struck before. The bright edges of the blade left an arc of ghostly light in the darkness as it sliced through the dragon ogre's midsection. The beast screamed, hurled backwards by the force of the blow. It landed in a broken heap close to the mouth of the cave, its armour half melted and smoke rising from the fearsome wound in its abdomen. The beast was dead, almost as if the blade had reached into its huge body and snuffed out its life like a candle.

The highborn stared at the sword in wonder. Its warmth coursed through him, banishing Tz'arkan's black ice. His heart hammered in his chest, and his mind was suffused with an emotion he hadn't felt in many months: hope.

'Good sword,' Malus said in an awed whisper. 'No wonder you wanted it for your collection.'

The daemon seemed to shrink inside Malus, dwindling in presence until it coiled like a serpent around the highborn's black heart. 'I despair of you Malus,' Tz'arkan said hatefully. 'When the final task is done there will be *such* a reckoning.'

Malus stared into the depths of the blade. A faint smile tugged at his lean face. 'I'm counting on it,' he said.

Chapter Twenty-Four
THE SCOURGE OF KHAINE

MALUS DARKBLADE RODE into the city of the Ageless Kings with a gleaming sword in his hand and a Chaos storm raging at his back.

Lightning roiled the crimson skies, etching the broken walls and crumbled towers in stark relief. Thunder rolled, matched by the terrible growl of the nauglir as it stalked down the debris-choked lanes. Tribesmen rose from the furs they had been sleeping on, clutching axes or swords, and peered into the night, sensing something terrible was at hand.

Malus rode through the plaza of impaled men, passing the crossed timbers where he himself had hung mere hours before. The dark bulk of the temple reared before him, its skull adorned flanks silhouetted in flickering displays of brazen lightning. He reined in his cold one at the base of the towering steps and regarded the sealed doors coldly. Spite reared his head at the ancient building and roared, a raw sound of fury that echoed roughly from the temple's thick walls.

The double doors swung open within moments and a troop of temple guards swarmed out, brandishing long, heavy pole arms and axes. Malus slid from the saddle and took the warpsword in a two-handed grip, savouring the heat radiating from the unearthly blade. It pulsed in time with his beating heart, quickening hungrily at the prospect of battle.

The temple guards spread out at a run and charged down the steps shouting the name of Khaine, blessed Lord of Murder.

A wolfish smile spread across Malus's grim face. 'Blood and souls,' he whispered, and ran to meet them.

He saw the battle unfold with dreadful, icy clarity, as if it was a ritual dance unfolding in slow motion. A guard rushed in from the highborn's left, stabbing with his pole arm. Malus hacked off the spearhead with a desultory sweep of his blade and cut the man in half with a backhanded stroke. Without pause, Malus swept his sword to the right to block the sweep of another guardsman's axe, before reversing the blade and cutting off both of the warrior's legs just above the knee. Armour parted like rotted paper; flesh blackened and bone splintered at the sword's ravening touch. Men's screams wove a brutal threnody around Malus as he wove among his foes, scattering arcs of hot blood that sizzled and steamed in the air.

One guardsman swept low with his pole arm, aiming to knock Malus from his feet. Before the blow could land the highborn reached out and sank the point of the warpsword into the onrushing guard's neck, and then spun on his heel and severed both arms and the helmeted head of the guard charging at Malus from behind. The highborn laughed like a drunkard, spinning and cutting with the seething blade and climbing ever higher towards the temple doors.

A guard screamed in fury and leapt for him, heedless of the long fall to the plaza below. The move caught Malus off-guard for a fraction of a second, but with the battle fever on him his foe seemed to hang languorously in the air, his muscular arms outstretched like a child's. Fluid as a blade dancer, Malus half-spun and dropped to one knee, bringing the sword up in a glittering stroke that sliced the man open from groin to chin and propelled him in a bloody arc to the grey stones at the nauglir's feet.

There was a droning sound humming lazily towards Malus. He turned and swatted the thrown axe aside, and then dashed up the last few steps to the sole remaining guard. The warrior had barely enough time to unsheath his dagger before Malus reached him.

Both men regarded one another. The armoured giant towered over the lithe highborn, his masked face looking down at the druchii as if in startled bemusement. Then the guard let out a bubbling sigh and bright blood erupted from the air holes in his visor as the highborn pulled the warpsword free from the man's breastplate. Malus stepped gracefully to the side as the giant's body crashed face first onto the stone steps and slid towards the bottom on a dark trail of gore.

A pale figure regarded the highborn from just outside the temple doorway. The blood-witch sank slowly to her knees, her marble-like eyes glittering fearfully as Malus approached her. Thin, wrinkled lips pulled back from yellowed fangs in a frightful grimace of dread.

'I knew you would return,' she groaned. 'I tried to tell the others, but they would not believe what I had seen.' The ancient blood-witch spread her hands. 'You are death and ruin given form, oh son of the house of chains, and the blessings of the Dark Gods go with you. Our time is finished. Let the Time of Blood begin.'

She raised her chin, and the warpsword seemed to leap in Malus's hands. The black blade flickered through the air and the blood-witch stiffened in the wind of the sword's passing.

Malus studied the witch coldly for a moment. A trickle of dark blood welled in a thin line across her narrow throat. The highborn stepped up to her and reached out, taking a handful of her white hair in his fist and lifting her severed head from her neck.

The highborn hung the witch's head from his belt and stalked past her still upright body, heading into the darkness of the temple beyond.

* * *

WHEN MALUS EMERGED from the temple a short while later the tribe of the red sword was awaiting him.

They filled the plaza at the foot of the temple, standing like wraiths amid the forest of impaled men. Lightning picked out steel helms and glittering mail, sharpened swords and bared fangs. Warped faces turned upwards as the highborn's armoured figure strode to the top of the stairs, and every eye beheld the steaming sword and the trio of severed heads gripped in Malus's hands.

Shebbolai stood at the head of his tribe, waiting at the foot of the broad stairs with a look of grim joy on his face. Malus regarded him balefully, and then his gaze swept across the gathered warriors. Thunder rumbled from the north.

'The rule of the Ageless Kings is no more,' Malus said, his sharp voice ringing out across the plaza. 'They forgot their duty to the Lord of Murder, and Khaine has meted out his wrath, but their taint has spread to you, warriors of the red sword. The sons of Khaine do not hide in cities of stone and turn their faces from the battlefield! The glory of the Bloody-Handed God lies in death, not in slaves, nor gold, nor stone walls. The Ageless Kings chose to cling to life, and you joined in their depravity.'

A groan rose from the assembled warriors at the highborn's harsh words. Malus cut them off with a shout.

'When Khaine sent his chosen Scourge to claim his birthright from the kings, they were sunk so far in their iniquity that they did not know him.' Malus raised the terrible blade. 'Look upon the Warpsword of Khaine and know that his Scourge has arisen!'

The warriors replied with shouts of anger and despair. Men slashed their cheeks and their chests, offering up their blood-stained blades to the highborn. Warriors turned on the weaker men of the tribe and hacked their bodies apart, throwing glistening bits of flesh and bone upon the steps of the temple.

'We live to serve!' Shebbolai cried out, his face a mask of shame and despair. 'Forgive us, dreadful Scourge!'

'There is no forgiveness in the eyes of Khaine,' Malus snarled, 'only death. Blood alone can wash away your sins.'

'Then blood it will be!' Shebbolai roared. 'Show us the way, holy one. We live and die at your command!'

The highborn looked down upon the chieftain and smiled an executioner's smile. 'Follow me, sons of the red sword. Death and glory await.'

MALUS LED THE tribe out into the wasteland, returning to the place where the Vermillion Gate had left him. He had no idea if it would make any difference, but it gave him some time to think and take stock of the forces at his command.

The Chaos warriors did not march as an army of Naggaroth, in ordered lines and divisions. They swept over the plain in a ragged mob, perhaps two hundred strong, riding swift, lean horses that moved as if they shared a single mind with their masters. Hoarse shouts and lusty war cries echoed in the darkness as the warriors followed the Scourge from the city. The prospect of battle had quickened their blood, banishing doubt and fear.

The same could not be said for Malus. He rode ahead of the unruly mob with the warpsword riding in its scabbard against his hip. With the weapon sheathed he felt cold again, the heat of Khaine's hunger leeching slowly from his muscles and leaving him wretched and weak. Every few moments his hand would stray to the weapon's hilt, as if he was warming himself by the side of a small fire.

Tz'arkan stirred within Malus. Where before the daemon's presence seemed to swell within the highborn's chest, now it caused his whole body to tremble. 'You grow overbold, little druchii,' the daemon sneered. 'You trifle with forces beyond your understanding, and you think to lead this pitiful mob to war with your brother?'

Malus looked back at Shebbolai, riding just a few yards behind the highborn, and beyond to the shifting crowd of riders spread out across the plain. 'I don't expect them to triumph,' he said coldly. 'I expect them to die, in as dramatic a fashion as possible. I will need a grand diversion if I'm to reach the Sanctum of the Sword and deal with Urial.'

It was a gamble, to be sure, and a desperate one. As fearsome as the warpsword was, Malus didn't care to pit himself against Tyran and his entire band of zealots. If he could distract them with a sudden attack inside the walls of the fortress, it might buy him enough time to reach the temple and confront Urial directly. He hoped that with his half-brother dead the zealots would accept him as the new Scourge or else lose heart and scatter into the night. Then he could deal with Rhulan or whoever was commanding the forces of the temple.

'You think that you can defeat Urial by yourself?' the daemon sneered.

Malus's hand strayed towards the hilt of the warpsword. 'With this I can.'

'You are a fool, Darkblade!'

'No, daemon. You put this sword into my hands. If you didn't think I'd take it up and use it to slay my enemies then you are the fool, not I.'

As he spoke, Malus caught sight of a trio of ragged shapes lying upon the lifeless ground and realised they'd reached the site of his battle with Shebbolai's champions. He prodded Spite into a canter and rode halfway up the shallow rise so he that could turn and regard the tribesmen. As the nauglir heeled about the riders brought their mounts to a halt and waited expectantly.

Malus drew the warpsword, shuddering slightly as the rush of heat flooded his body. 'Warriors of the red sword,' he cried, 'the hour of your redemption is at hand! Follow me and cleanse your souls in the blood of the foe! Kill every man who stands in your way!'

Shebbolai drew a fearsome, curved sword and waved it in the air. 'Blood for the Blood God!'

The night air erupted in a cacophony of bestial shouts to Khaine. Malus smiled, and focused his will upon the sword. *Open the gate*, he commanded. *Return us to the temple, you damned Lord of Murder, and we'll reap a red harvest in your name.*

An angry rumble shook the air. Whether it was thunder or the growl of a bloodthirsty god Malus could not say, for at that moment the warriors of the tribe cried out in terror and the world turned inside out.

THEY APPEARED UNDER clear skies, with a bright pair of moons overhead. The transition was so jarring that for a moment Malus was completely disorientated.

Horses screamed and men shouted in wonder and fear. The night shook with the stern cry of trumpets and Malus heard shouts of alarm echoing down the lanes of the temple fortress. Then the world snapped back into focus.

Malus and the warriors found themselves in the broad avenue between the Citadel of Bone and the dwarf-built temple. White-robed zealots were charging from every building and pathway, and the alarm trumpets continued to sound. It was as if their arrival had been expected somehow, the highborn thought. If so, his gambit had already failed.

The sounds of battle revivified the Chaos warriors, however, and already screams and clashes of steel echoed across the avenue. Malus stood in his saddle. 'Warriors of Khaine, redeem yourselves in the blood of your foes!'

With a bloodthirsty roar the marauders spurred their horses and threw themselves headlong at the zealots, and in moments a fierce, swirling melee raged along the length of the avenue. More zealots were streaming in from every direction, but for the moment the horsemen had an edge in both numbers and mobility. The highborn knew the tide would turn soon enough.

Malus put his heels to Spite's flanks and dashed for the temple.

White-robed warriors raced across his path from left and right, trying to cut him off. The highborn pulled on his reins and headed directly at the zealot on his right. To his credit, the zealot held his ground, readying his weapon to strike at Spite's head, but at the last moment Malus changed direction again, veering left and swiping his sword at the warrior as he went past. The zealot's draich bit into Spite's shoulder just as Malus took off the top of the warrior's skull.

Steel rang on Malus's left side. He glanced over his shoulder in time to see the second zealot's headless body collapsing to the ground. Shebbolai and half a dozen marauders had fallen in behind Malus, using spears and swords to kill anyone who came too close. The marauder chieftain raised his sword to the heavens, laughing like a fiend. Malus grinned cruelly and put his boots to Spite's flanks.

The doors to the temple were open as Malus reined in before the building's broad steps. Fearing an ambush, he dismounted quickly and let Shebbolai and the marauders take the lead. The Chaos warriors raced across the threshold, and almost immediately Malus heard screams and the sounds of battle. As he charged through the doorway, he found the marauders slaughtering a group of temple servants who had been stacking a new set of trophies near the doors.

'This way!' Malus shouted as he dashed across the large chamber. Shebbolai and the men followed the highborn as he raced up the stairs to the chapel. He burst into the chamber expecting at least a handful of zealot guards, but the smaller chamber was empty.

Something's wrong, Malus thought, feeling the first twinges of dread tickle at his heart. The Cauldron of Khaine seethed and bubbled on the ceremonial dais with no one to attend it. It felt like an ambush, but how could Urial have possibly expected this?

Gritting his teeth, Malus decided that it didn't matter. He was committed, one way or the other, and would have to see things through to the bitter end. Taking a deep breath, he made his way to the sanctum stairs.

Shebbolai and the marauders gasped at the towering statue of Khaine as they worked their way around the dais and climbed to the red-lit doorway. Malus gripped the warpsword tightly, drawing strength from its heat as he approached the door. He remembered all too well what had happened the last time he'd stood at that narrow threshold.

Raw power seethed from the doorway, washing over Malus's skin and making the warpsword vibrate in his hands. 'Be ready for anything,' the highborn warned the marauders, and stepped inside.

Malus was not prepared for what he found.

THE VERY AIR howled and shimmered with pain.

Malus stood at the foot of a broad bridge fashioned from skulls that crossed a sea of seething red. Heat and light rose from its surface like the glow of a furnace, searing his skin and filling his ears with the cries of the damned.

At the far end of the bridge stood another doorway leading into the sanctum, and at the bridge's midpoint, naked and gleaming in the ruddy light, stood Yasmir.

Malus looked upon her and felt smaller and weaker than he'd ever known before. She was unearthly, radiant in her lethal beauty. Her dark eyes met his and she smiled, revealing her leonine fangs. Behind Malus, one of the marauders moaned like a frightened child.

'Who is she?' asked Shebbolai, his voice full of dread.

Malus didn't know what to say. Finally he shrugged. 'She is my bride,' he said grimly, and went to meet her.

She waited for his approach, spreading her arms slightly. Had it not been for the slim, needle-like knives in her hands she might have been offering herself to her lover.

The highborn clenched the warpsword tightly. One did not fight Yasmir; one offered oneself up to die. For an instant he thought of the daemon, but he pushed the idea away. The warpsword would have to be enough.

Her gaze was inscrutable. It was as if she stared through him, seeing some vista beyond the ken of mortals. When she was within reach of his longer sword he came to a halt. His fingers flexed on the sword's leather wrapped hilt.

Yasmir made no move. She continued to stare through him as if he wasn't even there. Malus frowned. 'Hello, sister,' he said.

At the sound of his voice her expression changed. Her eyes shifted slightly, as if she was seeing him for the first time, and then she was flying at him, her daggers reaching for his throat.

Malus brought the warpsword up in the nick of time, barely deflecting the lethal strikes, but there was no time to recover, as the living saint switched targets and began a series of deadly thrusts at his face, chest and groin. She never stopped moving, flowing towards him like a dancer and making a lethal move with each and every step.

He had no time to be afraid. The warpsword seemed to move of its own accord, matching Yasmir blow for blow. Once again, he saw the fight unfold with a detached clarity, as if he was a spectator rather than a combatant. Her speed and grace were devastating. Even though he could read Yasmir's next attack his body was hard-pressed to counter it.

She drove him back steadily, keeping him constantly on the defensive. A dagger thrust sank a quarter of an inch into his throat, but he scarcely felt it. Another blow stung him like an adder just below his eye.

The next one was going to hit his hip, right where the breast-plate met his fauld. Malus waited until the last possible moment, and then pivoted on his left foot and let her thrust slide past. He continued the spin, turning it into a lightning quick backhanded cut aimed for her neck. The warpsword hissed through the air, but Yasmir was already gone, rolling forwards out of the sword's path.

Malus rushed at her, but Yasmir recovered from the roll at once and whirled, knocking aside his stop thrust, and making a blurring stab for his neck. The highborn sensed the strike and faded back, deflecting the thrust with the flat of his blade.

Two marauders charged at Yasmir, their weapons aiming for her slender back. She reversed her daggers with a flourish and stabbed both warriors through the heart, before pushing their corpses off and tucking into a tight roll towards the highborn. When she came up out of the roll her blades were reaching for his throat and a terrible smile of joy lit her unearthly face.

Malus had anticipated her attack and ducked beneath the thrust. His sword swept up at her torso and her knives fell into a cross block, trapping his sword. Malus yanked his sword clear, feinted low and then thrust at her neck, just as she twisted her body, deflecting the attack with her right hand dagger and stabbing at Malus with her left.

The point of her dagger scratched the hollow of his throat and stopped. She could reach no further with her right hand blocking Malus's sword. They were at a deadlock.

Yasmir looked into Malus's eyes. She seemed to truly recognise him for the first time. 'I cannot kill him,' she said breathily.

Malus gave her a bemused frown, and then realised that she wasn't speaking to him.

From behind the highborn, back towards the doorway at the far end of the bridge, he heard Urial's angry voice. 'What is this foolishness?'

Malus thought quickly. 'She cannot kill me because we are too evenly matched,' he said. Slowly, carefully, he stepped away from Yasmir and lowered his sword. She mirrored his moves exactly. 'As befits a bride and a groom, don't you think?'

Angry shouts from the other end of the bridge caught his attention. The marauders were retreating from a group of bloodstained zealots, and two fearsome grey figures that crawled like spiders down the stone walls above the doorway to the chapel. The Chaos beasts lashed their tentacles hungrily as they sank closer to their prey.

There was a meaty *thump* near Malus's feet and something bounced heavily off his calf. He looked down and saw Arleth Vann's bloodstained head roll to a stop at his feet.

'He told me everything,' Urial hissed. 'An assassin's body can resist torture, but his spirits are powerless to one such as I.'

Malus turned to face his half-brother, pure murder dancing in his eyes. 'If he told you where I went,' he said raising the warpsword, 'then you know what *this* is.'

Urial stood at the far end of the bridge, the copy of the warpsword clutched in his left hand. His face twisted with rage. 'It is not yours, you misbegotten cur! It is meant for *me*! I was reborn in the cauldron while you were whelped by that

Naggorite whore. If you are here it is because Khaine willed it so. You are here so that I may take the sword from your broken and bleeding body.'

Malus smiled. 'Do you want it, brother? Come then, and take it.'

Urial screamed like one of the damned and charged at Malus, his sword held ready. Behind the highborn Shebbolai roared a challenge at the zealots, and suddenly the air rang with the clash of steel and the screams of the dying.

Malus charged at his half-brother, a war scream bursting from his throat. He read Urial's every move, knowing his blade would come slashing down for his shoulder half a second before the blow fell. The warpsword swept up, knocking the blow aside. Then Malus reversed the stroke and sliced at Urial's chest. Before the blow could connect, however, Urial's form blurred, and the sword passed through the space where he had been.

Damned sorcery! Malus whirled just as Urial's blade whipped at his face from an unexpected angle. Caught by surprise, the sword sliced neatly across his cheek. Hot blood poured down his face, and Urial laughed.

Malus stabbed at his half-brother, but again, the sorcerer's form blurred and seemed to coalesce three feet to the left. Urial's sword stabbed out, glancing from Malus's armour, and the highborn spun and slashed down at the extended arm, but once again, it was like cutting at air. Urial blurred and then reformed again to Malus's right. This time the highborn was expecting an attack and was ready when Urial lashed out at his neck. Malus parried the blow and stepped in for a thrust, but again, his half-brother turned to smoke and reappeared three feet to the highborn's right. His half-brother's sword flashed, and Malus felt a spike of pain lance through his right thigh.

The highborn roared in anger, and rushed at his half-brother just as a heavy weight landed on the bridge behind him. He heard the tentacles hissing through the air a fraction too late as the Chaos beast entwined his sword arm and waist and lifted him into the air.

Hissing, gobbling howls rang in Malus's ears as the beast reared onto its hind legs and lashed at Malus with the rest of its tentacles. Barbed hooks grated across Malus's armour as he was spun through the air. He could hear Urial cursing the beast, but the hunter paid the sorcerer no mind, intent on drawing Malus towards its clashing beak.

Snarling, Malus shifted the warpsword to his free hand and slashed at the tentacles holding him. The warpsword parted the flesh whips in a spray of steaming ichor and he plunged face first to the bridge. He hit hard on his left shoulder and rolled away down the beast's right flank. Malus rolled to his feet as the Chaos beast rounded on him, and he buried his sword in the creature's neck just as two of its tentacles smashed against the side of his head. The blows knocked the highborn to the ground and he rolled clear, dragging his sword with him.

When his vision cleared Malus found himself facing back towards the chapel end of the bridge. The second Chaos beast had leapt from the wall and clung to the side of the stone span, snatching men in the midst of the melee and lifting them clear. As Malus watched, the hunter snatched one of the marauders from the battle and lifted the wriggling body high overhead, whereupon it began to pull the man limb from limb.

Tyran and Shebbolai faced one another, trading blows with their curved swords in a blur of razor edged motion. All around them zealots and marauders tore at one another with single-minded ferocity, although it was clear that with the Chaos beast on their side the zealots would soon gain the upper hand. Yasmir stood apart from the battle, watching the slaughter with dispassionate interest.

A shadow loomed over Malus. Urial's sword whirred through the air and struck the bridge where the highborn had been, but Malus had rolled away and was clambering unsteadily to his feet.

Roaring with hate, Urial charged at his half-brother, launching a series of powerful blows that Malus blocked with steady, deft strokes. Malus didn't attempt to strike back, knowing that it would only give Urial a chance to discorporate and strike him from an unexpected angle. Instead he gave ground, defending himself easily and trying to think of a way to turn the tables.

With every step Malus drew closer to the melee at the end of the bridge. On impulse he blocked Urial's next attack, and turned and ran towards the battle. Behind him, Urial laughed in disdain and lurched after him, dragging his twisted foot across the smooth stone.

A zealot struck down one of the Chaos warriors and stepped in Malus's path. The highborn cut the man in half and dashed past before the bloody halves hit the ground. He raced right for the last Chaos beast, which saw him coming and reached for him with eight thrashing tentacles. He seemed to race directly into the creature's embrace, but at the last moment he threw himself to the ground and rolled beneath the creature's head.

As he'd hoped, Urial ran headlong into the monster's clutches. The Chaos beast, not able to tell the difference between friend and foe, reached for Urial as eagerly as it had tried to grab Malus, but again the sorcerer's form blurred and he appeared three feet to the left of where he'd stood. Half mad with fury, Urial stabbed the beast in the eye, and it plunged from the edge of the bridge with a shriek. One of the last marauders leapt at Urial from behind, but the usurper twisted at the waist and sliced the man in half with a savage swipe of his blade.

There was a scream to Malus's left as the last zealot leapt at the two remaining marauders. Both Chaos warriors buried their blades in the druchii's chest, but the zealot crashed heavily into the two men, bearing all three over the edge of the bridge and into the red sea beneath. Their screams ended as they sank beneath the heaving liquid and did not rise again.

Only Tyran and Shebbolai were left. Both men circled one another warily, bleeding from scores of deep wounds on their chests and arms. Shebbolai raised his sword and charged

Tyran with a fierce roar, as Malus looked on. The zealot leader watched the man come and ducked the chieftain's swing at the last second, thrusting with his draich and taking Shebbolai squarely in the chest. The onrushing warrior impaled himself on Tyran's blade, the draich bursting from Shebbolai's back. Before Tyran could pull his blade free, the chieftain grabbed the zealot leader's wrist. Smiling madly, the chieftain pulled Tyran towards him, driving the man's sword deeper into his chest. Tyran tried to pull away, but the Chaos warrior's grip was like iron. Shebbolai's sword flashed, and Tyran's sword arm was hacked away at the shoulder. The zealot staggered back with a hideous scream and fell backwards off the bridge. Still smiling, Shebbolai sank to the ground and toppled over dead.

Urial charged Malus with a roar, thrusting at the highborn's neck. Malus blocked the thrust and swung at Urial's head, but again the sorcerer's body blurred and reappeared three feet away. The usurper's sudden counterattack nearly took Malus's head off, but he saw the blow just in time and ducked out of the way.

Malus's half-brother laughed. 'You're done for, Darkblade,' he taunted. 'I can do this all night long if I must.'

'I know,' Malus snapped, swinging at Urial's chest. The sorcerer's form blurred – but the highborn continued the swing, aiming for a point three feet to the left.

Urial screamed, staring down at the black sword jutting from between his ribs. Blood poured down the length of the warpsword, turning to steam against its hot edge.

'It makes you predictable,' Malus said, and pulled his sword free.

Urial staggered backwards, his sword falling from his hands. Blood poured in a rush down the front of his armour. He fell back, and found himself enfolded in Yasmir's slender arms.

She laid him gently on the ground, cradling his head in her hands. Urial stared up at her, a look of longing in his eyes. His mouth worked breathlessly.

Yasmir rose and walked around him, kneeling at his side. Smiling lovingly, she placed her hands at the join of his breast-plate and pulled. Rivets popped and straps broke as she tore the armour away, revealing Urial's misshapen chest. Then the living saint ran a delicate finger down the usurper's uneven sternum until she found the spot she wanted, and dug in with both hands. Cartilage popped wetly as Yasmir ripped her brother's chest open.

The last thing Urial saw was his beloved sister feeding on his still-beating heart.

As it happened, the warriors of the red sword acquitted themselves far better than Malus had ever expected. After slaying all the zealots and temple servants they could find, they opened the gates of the fortress and rampaged out into the ravaged city. Several of their bodies were found as far away as the warehouse district when the warriors of the temple made their way back into Har Ganeth.

Malus sat back in the throne of the Grand Carnifex as Arch-Hierophant Rhulan entered the council arena, attended by a handful of priests and priestesses. When the elder saw Malus, his relieved expression turned to a look of abject horror.

'You!' he exclaimed. 'What happened? Where's Urial?'

The highborn eyed the elder contemptuously. 'Why, Arch-Hierophant, don't you remember the plan? I said I would find a way to strike at the usurper directly, and so I did. He will trouble the temple no more.' He leaned back in the throne, his right hand resting on the pommel of the unsheathed warpsword. 'I would have resolved this more quickly, but the diversion I'd been led to expect never materialised.'

Rhulan gaped at Malus, his eyes widening in fear. 'It... that is, we tried, but the citizens had gone mad. We couldn't reach the temple–'

'Where is that other elder?' Malus interjected, 'the striking one with the tattoos?'

'Mereia?' Rhulan stammered. 'She... she died trying to reach one of the more isolated warbands.'

'Meaning she tried to fulfil your part of the plan and died fighting while you cowered in a basement somewhere,' Malus snarled.

'Do not presume to judge me,' Rhulan cried. 'I did what I thought best.' He looked back at his attendants, and then fixed Malus with a conspiratorial stare. 'You couldn't have beaten Urial. He had the warpsword. He couldn't be defeated in battle.'

Malus smiled coldly. 'Ah, yes, the scriptures, so, let me understand this correctly: in the interests of doctrinal veracity, you betrayed me and left me to die. Is that right?'

Rhulan began to tremble. 'No, no, it wasn't like that. We had to wait for Malekith to arrive. He could have found a way to stop the usurper.'

'Fortunately for our people, he won't have to.' Malus rose from the throne, holding the fake warpsword in his left hand. Stepping to the edge of the railing, he jumped off and landed on the arena floor. A flare of pain in his wounded leg made him wince, but he pushed the feeling aside. Actually, the discomfort was a good sign. It meant that the daemon's power wasn't healing him as well as it had been. The power of the sword was somehow counterbalancing it. He didn't know how, but he wasn't going to question it for the time being.

Malus straightened and stalked over to Rhulan. 'This, I believe, belongs to the temple,' he said, dropping the fake blade with a clang at the Arch-Hierophant's feet. 'The Grand Carnifex can return it to the sanctum, and as far as the rest of Naggaroth is concerned, it never left its home.'

Rhulan frowned. 'I don't understand–'

'I know,' Malus said, and beheaded Rhulan with the warpsword.

Men and women screamed in horror as the Arch-Hierophant's body collapsed to the floor. Malus silenced them with a cold glare. Then he levelled his sword at one of the priestesses. 'You, come here.'

Niryal stepped from the crowd. She'd put aside her axe at some point, and changed into better clothes. Unlike Rhulan, she mastered her fear, keeping her chin up as she stepped closer to the bloodstained sword.

Malus gave the priestess a murderous look. 'You weren't taken by assassins. You slew the other sentry and then betrayed us to Urial.'

The priestess never flinched. 'I was certain you were deceiving us, and, as it happened, you were.'

'Then, as soon as Urial was dead you switched sides again.'

'I serve the temple,' Niryal said.

Malus smiled. 'I thought you would say as much. That's why I'm making you the new Grand Carnifex. Of all the people in this damned fortress you're the only one whose motives I can understand.'

The other attendants gasped. Even Niryal was stunned. 'You can't do that,' she said.

Malus raised the warpsword. 'I am Khaine's chosen, Niryal, I most certainly can.' He surveyed the other loyalists. 'And they shall be your new Haru'ann. They seem a dim sort, but since they know the truth about the sword, we can either kill them or make use of them.'

Niryal struggled with her sudden change in fortunes for a moment more, and then managed to recover her composure. 'What would you have us do, holy one?' she asked.

The highborn smiled. 'That's better. You will return the counterfeit sword to the sanctum. At this point, no one who saw Urial with the blade is still alive except for us.'

'What about the Witch King? He is probably marching up the Slavers' Road even now.'

'When he arrives you'll receive him with luxurious hospitality and inform him of Urial's usurpation,' Malus said. 'Tell him that Urial and a cabal of zealots used Chaos magic to sow discord among the citizens and slay the temple elders. There was fighting in the streets for almost a week, but in the end you sent a group of volunteers through the tunnels and they managed to assassinate the usurper and the ringleaders. The Witch King will probably want to publicly execute some citizens to vent his pique, but other than that he should be satisfied with the outcome.' He raised the sword in warning. 'You will not tell him anything about me, or Yasmir. She is to remain in the sanctum until such time as the Witch King departs. After that, she may do as she will.'

Niryal thought everything over and finally nodded in satisfaction. 'It shall be as you say, holy one, but what about you?'

'I am leaving,' Malus said. 'Summer is almost done, and I have pressing business elsewhere.'

Malus reluctantly slid the warpsword into its scabbard. Spite waited in the fortress's beast pen, packed and ready to ride. Somewhere out there was the Amulet of Vaurog, the final relic the daemon required. Time was growing short.

He pushed his way through the crowd of stunned attendants, walking briskly to the door, when Niryal called out. 'I don't understand. You're the Scourge. The Warpsword of Khaine is yours. What about the Time of Blood? Are you not here to lead us into an age of death and fire?'

Malus paused. He looked back through the crowd at Niryal, his hand straying to the hilt of the burning blade.

'Perhaps,' he said with a ghostly smile, 'but not today. The apocalypse will have to wait.'

LORD OF RUIN

Chapter One
THE MOUNTAIN IN THE NORTH

The Chaos Wastes, first week of winter

THE COLD WIND shifted, blowing gusts of snow from the south-east and whispering in torment through the topmost branches of the trees. Urghal froze in place, settling on his haunches amid the snow-covered undergrowth. The beastman's nostrils flared, scenting prey, and his thin lips pulled back in a rictus of feral hunger.

Urghal swung his horned head left and right, catching glimpses of his two fellow hunters, Aghar and Shuk, as they split up and slid into concealment as well. The dense mountain forest had gone deathly silent save for the keening wind, and the beastman's long, tufted ears twitched restlessly as he strained to hear signs of movement from farther down the long slope. Heavy muscles bunched and relaxed along the beastman's broad shoulders, causing the dark, spiral tattoos etched into his thick hide to roll and shift in unnerving patterns. He breathed slowly and deeply, his clawed fingers flexing around the knotty grip of the rough-hewn club resting in his broad hands. The hunting had been poor since the herd had crept back to the cleft mountain and reclaimed their former territory. Soon the new master of the herd would begin culling out the weak and the slow and butchering them for the cook fires. Urghal had no intention of being one of them.

Silence stretched across the dark wood, broken only by the shrill buzzing of flies circling the open sores on the beastman's bony snout. Then without warning came the rustle and crash of bramble and fern, and Urghal heard the drumming sound of hooves racing over the loamy earth.

The beastman listened intently as the herd of deer stampeded up the slope directly at him. Ferns and thick shrubs were trampled and torn as the panicked animals forced their way through the dense undergrowth. Urghal could smell them now, perhaps as many as a dozen, the scent of their fear burning in his nostrils. He ran a thick, black tongue over his jagged teeth, lusting for the taste of hot, salty blood.

Twenty yards. Ten. Urghal caught glimpses of swaying branches now as the herd drew near. He heard the slight sounds of his fellow hunters readying themselves to strike. The beastman's muscles tensed like coiled springs just as the herd crashed over him like a wave.

A doe burst from the undergrowth to Urghal's left, dodging nimbly around the bole of a dark oak tree in a blur of frenzied motion. The beastman caught a glimpse of wide, terrified eyes as he sprang from his crouch and lashed out with his heavy club. The length of hardened oak smashed into the doe's side, splintering ribs and snapping the animal's spine with a brittle *crack*. The deer squealed in agony and plunged headfirst onto the ground.

Howls and hungry roars shook the air as Aghar and Shuk joined in the bloodletting, slashing at the plunging, leaping bodies with dagger and claw. Urghal smelled bitter blood in the air and bellowed cruel laughter as a huge stag burst from the foliage to the beastman's right. The stag saw the beastman at the very same moment; consumed with terror the deer tossed its antlered head and tried to spring away, but Urghal swept his bloodstained cudgel in a whistling arc, shattering the stag's gleaming antlers and smashing its skull. The deer hit the snowy earth with a heavy thud, its legs thrashing in the throes of death, and Urghal dropped his club and fell upon it, tearing at its warm throat with his teeth. The beastman ate greedily of its flesh as it trembled and died, tearing away ragged bites and choking them down whole in an effort to sate his frenzied hunger.

It was several long moments before Urghal realised how quiet the forest still was, and as the all-consuming hunger began to ebb he wondered what could have panicked the woods-wise deer in the first place.

The beastman raised his gore-smeared snout, licking his nostrils clean and tasting the frigid air once more. The wind rose and fell; over the rich scent of blood and spilt entrails he caught the faint whiff of something strange and bitter that sent a thrill down his knobby spine. His companions ate on, oblivious to everything except the steaming feast laid before them.

A premonition of fear tightened Urghal's throat. Baring his blood-slicked teeth, the beastman looked about frantically for his club and saw it lying on the bloody snow a dozen paces away. He lunged for the weapon, barking out a warning to his herd-mates just as the air shook with a thunderous roar and a huge shape leapt from the shadows beneath the trees.

The beast was massive, shaking the earth as it landed on two taloned feet among the surprised beastmen. Nearly thirty feet long from snout to tail, it filled the small clearing where the hunters had ambushed their prey. Its hide was dark green and scaled like a dragon's, and its muscular haunches were covered in scars from hundreds of deadly battles. Long, skinny forelimbs were tucked in tight against the beast's narrow chest; the creature's muscular, cable-like tail balanced its lunging motion as it snapped up a pair of deer carcasses in its huge, lizard-like jaws and swallowed them in a few crunching bites. Rivulets of blood mingled with tendrils of ropy spittle that drooled from between the creature's dagger-like teeth. Eyes the colour of spilled blood rolled wildly within deep, bony oculars as the beast searched about for more prey. Quick as a snake it lunged again, tossing the body of a deer into the air and eating it in a single gulp.

Shouts and bellows of fright echoed across the clearing as the hunters reeled from the beast's sudden assault. Urghal snatched up his club, snarling in rage. Hunger warred with fear as he watched the monster feed upon their kills. As the creature lunged for another deer, Urghal realised that it was oblivious to the three beastmen surrounding it. Its long, powerful tail now drooped, partly dragging the ground, and the flesh covering its bony head was shrunken, stretched across the skull like thick parchment. As it ate, Urghal saw its ribs standing out sharply from its flanks. It was starving, the beastman saw. He understood that madness all too well.

The beastman noticed the empty, weathered saddle strapped around the monster's back, just behind the sloping shoulders. Ragged saddlebags were strapped down behind it, their sides tattered and frayed by hard use and indifferent care. Silver rings glinted in the beast's leathery cheeks where reins had once been fitted. Then he saw the long, black-hilted sword buckled to the side of the saddle and knew that its rider had to be long dead.

Urghal bared his blackened teeth and barked commands to his fellow hunters. The creature was weak and stupid with hunger, he said. They could leap upon its back and kill it while it fed and feast off its acrid flesh for many days. Aghar and Shuk listened, and their shrunken bellies lent them courage they might not otherwise have possessed. Gripping their weapons tightly, the beastmen circled around the creature's flanks. Aghar sidled up along the creature's right side, raising his dagger for a deep thrust into the monster's neck. Shuk crept near the base of the creature's tail, ready to throw his massive bulk onto the appendage and weight it down, hampering its movement. Urghal crept up along the left side, drawing closer to the saddle. He would leap up and draw the black blade, then plunge it into the back of the monster's neck. The beast would be dead before it realised it was in danger.

Grinning viciously, Urghal turned to Shuk – and, too late, saw a dark shape leap from the depths of the forest and land upon the beastman's back with a terrifying shriek. Urghal heard the clatter of metal as the attacker pounced upon Shuk's bare torso, then saw pallid hands reach around the beastman's broad chest and plunge claw-like fingers through scarred hide and slab-like muscle. Shuk bellowed in terror and pain, throwing back his horned head and reaching over his shoulder to try and pry free his assailant, but the pale-skinned attacker clung to his victim like a cave spider, pressing close to the beastman's back.

Urghal caught a glimpse of a pale, angular face framed by loose, matted black hair as the armoured attacker lunged for Shuk's throat. Eyes as dark as the Abyss burned into Urghal's own. Bluish lips skinned back over perfect white teeth, and the figure tore open the beastman's muscular throat. Blood burst from Shuk's lips as he tried to staunch the fountain of crimson jetting from the ragged wound in his neck. Urghal watched the black-eyed monster bury its face into the gaping wound, tearing away mouthfuls of flesh like a frenzied rat.

The dying beastman fell to his knees, choking on his own blood. Urghal gripped his cudgel and bellowed a challenge – just as the scaled beast beside him turned and lunged for Aghar. The creature's whip-like tail slashed in the opposite direction, crashing into Urghal's chest. Ribs snapped like twigs beneath the powerful blow; Urghal was flung backwards across the clearing and dashed against the bole of a towering oak tree. Stunned by the double impact the beastman toppled onto his side, feeling broken bones grate together in his chest.

As his breath rattled wetly in his throat, Urghal saw Aghar charge at the black-armoured attacker. The hunter bellowed in berserk fury, and the lithe figure responded with a bestial growl of his own. Bloody mouth agape, the armoured warrior leapt to his feet with disquieting speed and met the beastman's rush head-on.

Aghar was head and shoulders taller than his foe and half again as wide. Urghal expected the armoured attacker to be smashed to the ground by the hunter's furious charge, but instead the two crashed together in a clatter of flesh and steel. A pale hand reached up and took hold of the beastman's throat, and the pair grappled for the space of several heart-beats. Savage snarls and guttural growls rose from the desperate struggle; Urghal could not say for sure from which throat the terrible sounds came. Then, with a sudden, convulsive wrench Aghar pulled his dagger-arm free and stabbed at the armoured figure again and again, the blows ringing against the smaller assailant's steel breastplate and pauldrons.

There was a muffled heavy thud and a crunch of broken bones. Aghar shuddered at the blow, his cloven feet lifting off the ground from the impact. The beastman doubled over, choking in agony from a shattered breastbone, and the black-eyed attacker grabbed Aghar's ridged horns and wrenched them around in a neck-snapping twist.

Urghal felt the cold gaze of the killer settle on him. Growling in pain, the beastman struggled to rise onto his knees. Without warning an armoured boot crashed into his shoulder, flipping him back onto the ground. The pale-skinned warrior had crossed the dozen yards between them in the blink of an eye. The beastman growled defiantly, hefting his club one-handed – but as he met the warrior's face the weapon tumbled from his stunned grasp.

Depthless black eyes, without iris or pupil, regarded Urghal with the soulless hunger of the Abyss. The warrior's mouth and pointed chin dripped with clotted gore, spattering the ornate gilt-work of his plate armour. Trickles of red flowed into the crevices and corners of three golden skulls affixed to the foe's breastplate, and a thick torc of red-gold enclosed his wiry neck. Just above the burnished gold curve of the torc jutted the rusty hilt of Aghar's dagger. The long blade had been driven clean through the warrior's throat, its broad point emerging at an angle just below the warrior's right ear.

As Urghal watched, the warrior reached up with a red-stained hand and slowly pulled the dagger free. A trickle of thick, black ichor leaked from the gruesome wound. Ropy black veins pulsed and writhed like worms beneath the skin of the warrior's throat and along the back of his hands.

The warrior let the dagger tumble slowly from his dripping fingers. It landed right beside Urghal's head, but the beastman made no move to pick it up. With a ghastly red grin, the black-eyed warrior opened his mouth and uttered a sound no living throat could possibly make, and the beastman's fevered mind shattered at the sound of it.

Urghal's cry of terror shook the black-limbed trees as the killer reached for him with claw-like hands.

LITTLE BY LITTLE, as the beastman's raw flesh filled his wasted belly, a measure of sanity returned to Malus Darkblade. His body, withered like a shrunken root by the nightmarish ordeals of his journey, began to shudder and ache as the daemon relaxed its remorseless grip. The shock of consciousness was so intense that for an agonising moment the highborn was certain that he was going to die. He fell onto his back, still clutching tattered scraps of flesh in his hands, and howled his wretched hate to the roiling northern sky.

Part of him was certain he was already dead. His mind recoiled from the few memories he had of the past few weeks, driven ever northwards by the daemon's merciless will. No sleep, no food, no rest for weeks on end, driven to lengths no living body ought to endure. Even Spite's near limitless stamina had been driven to the breaking point and beyond.

But they had reached the broken mountain. Nearby lay the pale road and the dreadful temple. Many times in the last few weeks he hadn't thought such a thing possible, but now, so close to his goal he wanted nothing more than to die. He wept bitterly at the thought, feeling icy tears course down his hollow cheeks.

'Rise, Darkblade,' the daemon said, and his body responded to the implacable command. Ravaged muscles tautened painfully, propelling Malus upright with a groan of helpless rage. 'Your final hour approaches.'

Malus's body lurched across the clearing towards Spite. His mouth worked silently, trying to utter dark curses from his ruined throat. From somewhere farther up the wooded slope came a chorus of howls and the rolling, mournful notes of horns. The clamour of the battle had reached as far as the beastman camp, and now the herd was on the move.

As he approached the saddle the cold one groaned and cowered, snapping at him fearfully. The daemon lashed the nauglir with its black will, and the cold one whined in submission, allowing the highborn to clamber jerkily onto its back. Still groaning, the nauglir rose wearily onto its feet and was mentally lashed into motion, beginning the last leg of its long, hellish odyssey.

The horn calls faded but the howls of the beastmen drew nearer as the daemon led Spite around the flank of the mountainside. Darkness fell as they rode. Malus swayed in the saddle, his gaze drifting to the black-hilted sword resting by his left knee. With all his might he tried to force his hand to reach for the sorcerous blade, but Tz'arkan's will held him fast.

All for nothing, he thought, as the daemon drove him onward to the temple like a sacrificial lamb. He thought of Hauclir, and the fields of the dead. He thought of the daemon-haunted shade and the soul-shattering screams of his sister. All for nothing.

Hatred and loathing burned like a seething coal in his ravaged chest – and the little finger on his left hand twitched.

Malus scarcely dared to breathe. He couldn't bring himself to hope, but even in the depths of privation and despair there was always room enough for hate. With hate all things are possible, he thought. His bloodied lips trembled in a palsied smile.

Half-formed memories dogged in the highborn's wake as they plunged on through thicket and fern. The echoes of the hunting beastmen called to mind a desperate flight through these same woods exactly one year before. Every now and then they passed a stand of trees or a wooded hollow that seemed familiar to him, though part of him knew that it was only a trick of the mind.

The shouts of the beastman herd were close now – perhaps a half-mile further upslope, hidden by the depths of the forest. Without warning the ground suddenly levelled out, and Malus found himself on a road of pale, snow-covered stones untouched by the passage of millennia. It was a road built for the tread of conquerors, with each stone carved in the shape of a skull and standing stones set at intervals along its length, praising the Ruinous Powers and exalting the deeds of the Chaos champions who ruled there. A year before, the blasphemous runes of the standing stones held no meaning for Malus; now he looked at them through daemon-tainted eyes, and the names carved on the menhirs burned themselves into his brain. Malus could feel his sanity crumbling with each passing moment as they drew nearer to the temple; desperately he turned to his hate, stoking it with all the bitterness and rage his year of servitude had wrought in him. The highborn focused on the hilt of the sword and prayed to every cursed god he could name for the strength to tear the unholy blade from its scabbard.

The air hummed and crackled with unseen energies as the daemon within Malus drew closer to the temple. Unearthly power crackled over his tortured skin, and the black-limbed trees lining the road rattled and shook in an invisible wind. Spite's pace quickened steadily, as though the nauglir was being drawn forward like iron to a lodestone. A strange, buzzing hum began to build in the back of Malus's skull.

By the time they swept around the final bend of the winding road Spite was nearly at a gallop. His drumming feet echoed off the close-set trees, and for a dizzying moment Malus felt as though he'd been cast back in time, riding with a troop of armoured retainers at his back. He thought of Dalvar, the dagger-wielding rogue, and Vanhir, the haughty, hateful knight.

He thought of Lhunara, riding quietly at his side, her fierce smile gleaming in the darkness. Choking back bitter bile, the highborn pushed the memory away.

And then the air trembled with the shout of a hundred furious voices as the beastmen raised their weapons and challenged the lone rider bearing down the road towards them. The herd had guessed where he was headed and had cut him off just short of his goal, exactly as they'd done just twelve months past.

But there were no armoured retainers to open the way for him this time. The beastmen stood in a roaring, bellowing mob that filled the tree-lined avenue before him. Axes, cudgels and rusty two-handed swords were brandished by the light of guttering torches. Spite stumbled to a halt, hissing and screeching in agitation as the mob surged forward.

Malus sensed his chance. The daemon would have to let him draw the warpsword before they were overwhelmed. With all his hate-fuelled will he tried to force his hand to reach for the blade.

But just a few yards short of the cold one the howling mob fell to their knees and pressed their horned heads to the skull-faced stones. In the midst of the mob a shaman with a single red eye gleaming from the middle of his narrow skull bleated: 'The prophecy is fulfilled! The Drinker of Worlds is come! Bow before the blessed Prince of Slaanesh, and let the dirge of Eternal Night be sung!'

Once again the daemon lashed at the nauglir's beleaguered mind, and the warbeast lurched forward, trotting down a path that opened through the centre of the prostrate mob. Malus trembled with impotent rage as they passed unchallenged through the herd and rode on a short way until the trees parted before them. Beyond rose a square, tiered structure of sheer, black stone, windowless and devoid of ornamentation, as cold and soulless as the Abyss itself. Surrounding the temple was a wall formed of similar stone, and a square-arched gateway. A desperate battle had been fought there a year before; skeletons of beastmen and misshapen Chaos beasts still littered the ground where they had fallen to druchii crossbows and swords. They crunched beneath Spite's heavy tread as the cold one walked beneath the gateway and came to a halt within the courtyard beyond.

There were more bones here, speaking of another scene of slaughter. Huge skulls and piles of dark bones that once had been nauglir, and druchii skeletons in rusting armour. They lay in the white snow where he'd slain them almost twelve months before.

He'd killed his own retainers out of shame, unable to bear having them see how the daemon had enslaved him. Now he met their black, empty stares and wished he could grind their grey bones into dust.

Malus's body lurched into motion, sliding awkwardly from the saddle. His face contorted into a rictus of thwarted rage, the highborn could only watch helplessly as his hands unbuckled the warpsword from the saddle and then collected the frayed bag containing the rest of the daemon's relics. As he pulled the sack free, Spite collapsed onto its side, as though unburdened at last of a terrible weight. Its flanks shuddered and heaved, and its breath came in ragged gasps.

'It is time,' the daemon said, its cruel voice reverberating in Malus's skull. 'Quickly now! Carry the relics to the crystal chamber, and soon your curse will be at an end.'

Filled with dread, Malus turned his back on the dying nauglir and marched like a condemned man into the shadow of the daemon's temple.

Chapter Two
THE DOUBLE-EDGED SWORD

The city of Har Ganeth, eight weeks before

SMOKE HUNG LIKE a pall over the City of Executioners, wreathing the broad hill in streamers of grey that tasted of cinders and the grease of cooked flesh. High in the blade-like towers of the temple fortress the sacrificial bells were ringing, calling to the faithful to bare their blades and give thanks for Har Ganeth's deliverance. Tortured screams and the howl of hungry mobs rose like a paean into the cloudy summer sky.

The fighting had raged for more than a week, and the lower quarters of Har Ganeth had suffered the worst. Two days after the riots had ended the narrow, maze-like streets were still choked with corpses and the charred remains of burnt-out buildings. Fresh splashes of vivid red painted the rust-coloured walls of the White City, and the shadowy avenues reeked of the charnel stench of the battlefield. Shopkeepers and tradesmen picked their way carefully amongst the piled debris, looking for useful bits of salvage. Groups of young children ran along the cobblestone streets, brandishing tiny, stained knives and rawhide cords strung with severed fingers decorated with rings of silver and gold. Axes and meat cleavers flashed and *thunked* into dead flesh, separating vertebrae with a wet crackle as the druchii collected severed heads to stack outside their bloodstained doors. Only a few days before, many of those same folk had taken up torch and blade and risen against the priests of Khaine's temple, believing that the apocalypse was at hand. But the would-be Swordbearer of Khaine was revealed to be an impostor, and the leaders of the uprising either driven off or slain, so the people of the city bent their heads and piled skulls outside their shops and homes, praying that the vengeful shadow of the temple executioners would pass them by. At the sound of tramping feet they hunched their shoulders and lowered their gaze to the bloody stones, fearful of attracting the attention of the temple executioners, or worse, the hungry gaze of Khaine's bloodthirsty brides.

Thus, when the heavy tread of a nauglir and the dull clatter of armour echoed down the narrow streets the people of Har Ganeth hid their eyes and paid no heed to the highborn rider – or the black-hilted blade buckled at his side. Only the city's ravens took notice of his passage, raising gore-stained beaks from their bloated meals and flapping great, glossy wings. 'Blood and souls!' they croaked exultantly, regarding Malus Darkblade with lantern-yellow eyes. 'Scourge! Scourge!'

Damned nuisances, Malus thought, his scowl deepening the hollows of his sunken cheeks and drawing dark lines around his thin lips. Spite, sensing its master's irritation, tossed its blocky head and snapped at the capering ravens, scattering venomous drool from its toothy maw. The highborn settled the cold one with an expert tug on the reins and guided the warbeast around the burnt wreckage of an overturned wagon. More black shapes circled overhead, floating like shadows in his wake. The ravens were sacred to Khaine, he'd learned. Is it the sword that stirs them so, he thought, or is it me?

Something cold and hard slithered serpentine around Malus's heart. A voice hissed like molten lead along his bones, setting his teeth on edge. 'A meaningless distinction,' Tz'arkan sneered. 'You and the burning blade are now one and the same.'

The highborn jerked upright in his saddle, armoured fists clenching the thick reins hard enough to make the leather creak as a wave of freezing pressure swelled behind his eyes. He bit back a savage curse, blinking at the black spots that drifted like ashes across his vision. His pulse throbbed turgidly in his temples, veins thick with oily, black ice.

Tz'arkan's hold over him was nearly complete.

It was the daemon's damnable curse that had brought him to Har Ganeth in the first place, seeking one of the five arcane relics that would free Tz'arkan from his crystal prison in the Chaos Wastes – and allow Malus to reclaim his stolen soul. The Warpsword of Khaine was one such relic, but in the millennia since the daemon's imprisonment the weapon had found its way into the possession of the Temple of Khaine, where it was kept in anticipation of the day when the Lord of Murder's chosen one would claim it and usher in the cataclysmic Time of Blood. According to the elders of the temple, that chosen one was none other than Malekith himself, the merciless Witch King of Naggaroth, but Malus knew that to be a convenient fiction, a lie told in the pursuit of temporal wealth and power.

The truth, as it often happened in the Land of Chill, was rather murkier than that.

Malus managed a bitter chuckle. 'Could it be that the great daemon has wound himself up in his own webs of deceit?' he growled. 'Are you sorry now for making me your catspaw? It was your own machinations that put the blade into my hands, after all. My *fate*, as you so gleefully put it.'

He'd learned a lot about fate in the ten months since he'd entered Tz'arkan's chamber in the far north. Fate was the word that puppets used to describe the tugging of invisible strings. It hadn't been fate that had drawn Malus to the north in search of power and wealth; he had been pointed at Tz'arkan's temple and loosed like an arrow, manipulated into undertaking the expedition by his half-sister Nagaira. Yet she herself was being manipulated in turn by Malus's own mother, the sorceress Eldire. Eldire had known of the daemon and its ages-old schemes somehow. She had learned of the prophecy and the Time of Blood, and had spent untold years shaping people and events to bring about their fruition. Not to serve Tz'arkan, but to usurp the daemon's machinations for her own secret purposes. It was an act of towering ambition and ruthlessness that culminated in the birth of her son, Malus. She had shaped him to be the lever that would set the daemon's inscrutable designs into motion.

But prophecies, by their very nature, were slippery, treacherous things.

Others had tried to bend him to their will, or claim the mantle of prophecy for their own. Nagaira had tried to bend him through deception and sorcery, seeking to turn the daemon to her own purposes. Worse still, his twisted half-brother Urial, poisoned in the womb by Eldire herself and given to the temple as a sacrifice, had survived the Cauldron of Blood and been initiated into the mysteries of Khaine's cult. Dissident members of the cult who refused to accept Malekith as Khaine's Swordbearer believed that Urial was the chosen one, and the circumstances of the prophecy fit well enough. He was secretly groomed to claim the sword when the time was right, and after his beloved half-sister Yasmir was revealed as a living saint of the Bloody-Handed God he betrayed Malus and fled to Har Ganeth, where he summoned the temple zealots to cast down the heretical elders of the cult.

For a week the City of Executioners tore itself apart as the zealots led its citizens in a bloody uprising. Urial had come very close indeed to achieving his aims. Too close for comfort, Malus admitted to himself, absently raising a hand to his breastplate where Urial's sword had slipped between his ribs. But for the daemon's power, he would have died.

Tz'arkan had sunk its talons deep into his body, spreading its corruption a little more each time Malus had drawn upon its infernal strength. Even now, his skin felt like ice, his muscles shrivelled and weak, aching for another taste of daemonic power. He had only a few months left to claim the last of the daemon's five artefacts and return them to the temple in the north or his soul would be forever lost, but Malus couldn't help but wonder if he wasn't already too late. Had he fought for the last ten months to reclaim his soul only to become a daemonhost once Tz'arkan was free?

Malus had good reason to believe that had been the daemon's plan all along.

'Foolish druchii,' the daemon spat, 'The warpsword was not meant to be wielded by the likes of you. You see it as nothing more than a sharp blade, but it is a talisman of supernal power. As ever, you trifle with forces beyond your ability to contemplate.'

The highborn caught Spite sniffing at the bloated corpse of a dead horse, still trapped in the overturned wagon's traces. Malus put his spurs to the warbeast's flanks and startled the nauglir back into a heavy-footed trot. 'Oh, but you are mistaken,' he replied. 'I see it as a fine weapon *and* a talisman of great power – one I have every intention of using as I see fit. What do you care, so long as I am doing your damned bidding?'

In truth, Malus suspected he knew the source of the daemon's concern. The warpsword radiated power like a burning brand – even now he could feel its heat, seeping from its scabbard and sinking into his bones. Power enough to supplant the daemon's icy gifts and resist Tz'arkan's will, or so he hoped.

'You imagine that you carry a mere blade on your hip? No. That is Khaine's own hunger given form,' the daemon hissed.

'Then I will see that it is kept well-fed,' Malus replied.

'Of course you will,' Tz'arkan said mockingly. 'You have no choice. The sword has claimed you, and like all those who wielded it before you it will one day turn in your hand when you fail to give its due.'

Something in the daemon's voice gave Malus pause. He glanced down at the warpsword's black hilt and felt a sudden chill.

It's just another lie, he told himself. Malus laid a hand on the sword's black pommel and savoured its warmth. It's the only chance you have against Tz'arkan, and the daemon knows it. 'Best for you then if we part ways before the blade gets the better of me,' the highborn said.

The daemon's laughter etched itself like acid into Malus's bones. 'No, best for *you*, Darkblade. Bad enough that your allotted time is running out – now you trifle with an eldritch artefact that hungers for your life's blood. Don't you understand? Your doom is sealed! The best you can hope for now is to find the Amulet of Vaurog and return to my temple in the north before you are undone. Otherwise your soul will belong to me until the end of time.'

With the daemon's mirth echoing jaggedly in his head Malus kicked Spite into a canter, no longer caring what the cold one caught between its snapping jaws or crushed to paste underfoot. His thoughts roiled like the murderous brew in Khaine's own cauldron as he contemplated his next move.

The farther down the wide hill Malus went the worse the devastation became. The highborn districts around the temple fortress near the summit had been largely untouched; each home was like a small citadel unto itself, ideally designed to fend off all but the most determined assaults. The lowborn districts further down the slope had suffered far more, first at the hands of the temple warriors and then the successive riots that had raged across Har Ganeth for days on end. Many of the stone structures had been blackened by fire and several had collapsed completely, spilling their charred contents onto the streets.

But it was the merchants' quarter and the warehouse districts at the base of the hill that had suffered worst of all. Many shopkeepers had shut their doors and hoped to weather the storm, but as the riots gave way to open warfare between the zealots and the temple loyalists the quarter became a no-man's-land caught between the warring factions. Shops were pillaged or burned in the riots, then had their bones picked clean by scavengers as the fighting wore on.

Beyond the merchants' quarter the slave market and the warehouse district were in ruins. It was here that the fighting raged hottest, once Urial and his zealots seized the temple and trapped the loyalists out on the streets. Large warbands of blood-witches and executioners had been isolated by mobs of frenzied citizens and forced to take refuge in slavekeepers' stables or shipping houses. Fires touched off by the vicious street fighting had raged unchecked for days, and the air around the wreckage was thick with tendrils of turgid, stinking smoke. When the wind shifted Malus could catch glimpses of the city walls, rising untouched above the devastation. If anything the walls had only served to hem in the carnage, turning Har Ganeth's rage back upon itself as the city tore itself apart.

He was still within the warehouse district, less than half a mile from the city gate when he heard the first stirrings of the mob. Their bloodthirsty roar shook him from his bitter reverie, their cries of 'Blood for the Blood God!' echoing weirdly along the ruined streets. The sounds seemed to be coming from just up ahead, though he couldn't be certain of anything in the shifting smoke. For a fleeting moment he contemplated altering his course, but with a flash of irritation he pushed the thought aside. He could guess what the mob was after, and it didn't include the likes of him. The highborn spurred his mount on through the smoke, the nauglir's broad feet crunching cinders and scorched bones with every step.

The sounds of the mob ebbed and flowed, muffled by the wreckage and the shifting wind as he continued down the rubble-strewn avenue, until Malus began to believe that the druchii were heading away from him, moving off to the west. The cries tapered off, and after he'd ridden on in relative silence for a few minutes he finally allowed himself to relax. Just at that moment, as though stirred by the laugh of a capricious god, a gust of wind banished the concealing smoke that surrounded the highborn and the mob erupted in a bloodthirsty cheer less than a dozen yards to Malus's left.

There were thirty or forty of them, filling a broad side street next to the wreckage of a long, single-storey warehouse. Most

of them were lowborn citizens in soot-stained robes, clutching
swords or axes in their grimy hands, but the ringleaders of the
band were a pair of young blood-witches and a handful of
temple executioners. The servants of the temple were standing
on a broad pile of fallen stones to give the crowd a better view
of their efforts. The white stones beneath them were stained in
patterns of red: striations of vivid crimson bled into a dull
brick red, then to a dark reddish-brown where the congealing
gore had settled into crevices and cracks among the stones.
Headless bodies sprawled down the rockslides, spilling their
contents onto the gritty cobblestones.

Several druchii squirmed and hissed in the grip of the mob,
awaiting their turn before the drachms of the executioners. They
had made the mistake of siding with the zealots during the revolt
and had lacked the wit to switch sides again once the uprising
had failed. Or perhaps they had simply been caught in the
wrong place at the wrong time; one of them, Malus noted,
looked more like a trader from Karond Kar, with his indigo-hued
kheitan and a set of slaver's chains hanging from his hip.

For the moment, the hapless prisoners had been granted a
short reprieve. The servants of the temple had far sweeter offerings to occupy their attentions.

Two druchii swayed atop the stone pile, held upright in the
iron grips of the executioners. They had been stripped to the
waist, but Malus noted the filthy white robes and torn sleeves
that were bunched around their hips. Their muscular chests
and arms were severely bruised and blackened; looking at
them the highborn could well believe they'd been hauled
from the rubble of one of the buildings nearby. Tellingly, neither man bore the mark of sword nor axe on their bodies,
despite the days of hard fighting that had raged across the
city.

They were zealots, members of the renegade splinter cult
that worshipped Khaine's true faith. Killers without peer, they
wore no armour in battle and clothed themselves in white to
better show the red favours of their god. Hundreds of them
had flocked to Har Ganeth at Urial's call and had taken a

fearful toll of the temple warriors during the uprising. Once it had become clear that the uprising had failed, most of the survivors had scattered back into the countryside – which made zealot prisoners all the more enticing to the vengeful blood-witches. These two would suffer for weeks under the witches' expert hands before their remains were given to the Cauldron of Blood. It was the worst fate possible for the true believers, who prayed to Khaine daily for a glorious death in battle.

Malus eyed the doomed men coldly and thanked the Dark Mother for the distraction. Better you than me, he thought, then frowned irritably as Spite slowed to a near stop as it caught the scent of fresh blood. The highborn glared at his scaly mount and made to spur the beast back into a canter when suddenly an anguished cry rang out from the rock pile.

'Deliver us, holy one!' the zealot cried to Malus. 'Draw your sword and slay us, in the Blessed Murderer's name!'

Heads turned. Malus felt the predatory stares of the blood-witches against his skin and felt his hair stand on end. All at once the air seemed charged with pent-up tension, crackling with furious energies like the moments before a summer storm. Spite sensed the change, too, and rumbled threateningly at the crowd.

Of all the damnable luck, the highborn cursed. He didn't recognise either of the zealots' pleading faces. Malus had fallen in with the true believers by accident when he'd first made his way into the city, looking for his own secret path into the temple fortress. He had even taken a hand in stirring up the early riots, hoping to distract the temple elders further, and had wound up with far more trouble than he'd bargained for.

The mob eyed Malus like a pack of feral dogs. In his worn robes and scarred plate armour, he had the look of a landless knight or an exiled noble rather than a wild-eyed heretic. The highborn's face was gaunt, emphasising his sharp cheekbones and pointed chin. Eyes the colour of brass shone from sunken eye sockets, marking him as one of Khaine's chosen. More forbidding still was the grey pallor of his face, like a druchii in the grip of a terrible sickness.

'No one is going to save you from your sins, heretic,' Malus spat, wrenching at Spite's reins. 'Khaine has no cold mercies for the likes of you.'

The nauglir shook its massive head and sidestepped, unwilling to turn away from the mob. It clashed its massive jaws and growled menacingly, and the mob hissed in reply.

One of the temple witches levelled her sword at Malus. Lines and loops of fresh blood glistened on her muscular arms and her long, bare legs. 'You are not a temple priest,' she said in a throaty voice, like cold air rising up from a tomb.

'I have never claimed to be,' Malus said tightly, trying to get the cold one under control. Spite circled and stamped, pacing away and then angling back towards the crowd like iron drawn to a lodestone. The tension in the air continued to build, setting the highborn's teeth on edge. What in the name of the Dark Mother was going on?

'Coward! Apostate!' the zealot screamed, surging against the grip of the executioners.

'Seize him,' the witch said coldly.

The mob erupted into lusty shouts, brandishing their weapons as they rushed at the highborn, and Spite lunged at them with an answering roar, nearly jerking Malus out of the saddle.

He could feel the pent-up tension burst in a rush that crackled through the air and sizzled across his bare skin. It was like the seething flare of an open flame or a lash of summer lightning. Malus cried out in bewilderment and anger, struggling to stay upright as Spite tore into the mob. Bones crunched and blood sprayed in the air as the cold one caught a man by the shoulder and bit off his right arm. The druchii's anguished scream set Malus's nerves on fire.

Spite roared and lunged at another man running past the cold one's flank, catching the druchii by the hip and flinging him into the air. Malus cursed and pounded the beast's flanks with his spurs, but the nauglir had gone berserk, tearing at its foes with reckless abandon.

The mob surged hungrily around the snapping beast. A sword blade rang off Malus's breastplate. Pale, blood-streaked faces glared up at him, their dark eyes burning with battle-lust. Bare hands seized his mail fauld and his right leg, trying to pull him out of the saddle. Snarling like a wolf, Malus pulled his leg free and planted his heel in a man's upturned face, but more hands closed about his ankle and dragged him downwards.

He felt himself sliding inexorably from his seat. Rage and desperation seethed through his veins. Without thinking, Malus reached for the warpsword. Its hilt was hot to the touch, and the long, eldritch blade seemed to leap from its scabbard with an ominous hiss.

Roaring blasphemies, Malus raised the ebon blade to the stormy sky. Above the cacophonous shouts of the mob, the highborn heard a horrified shriek from one of the temple witches, then he swept the sword in a vicious arc through the arms and heads of the grasping crowd. Flesh blackened and withered as the sword drank deep of hot blood and mortal pain.

Roars of bloodlust turned to screams of terror and despair. The mob reeled back from the smoking corpses of their brethren, crying out Khaine's name. Malus leapt after them, his face set in a mask of berserk rage.

Overhead, the croaking laughter of ravens echoed across the stormy sky.

THE BLOOD-WITCH's face was oddly serene. Malus admired the alabaster perfection of her high cheekbones and the subtle curve of her elegant jaw. Her brass-coloured eyes were calm, her round lips slightly parted and vivid with the blush of youth. In another time she could have been a violet-eyed princess of lost Nagarythe, about to whisper her secrets into the ear of a lover.

Close enough to kiss those perfect lips, Malus drew a shuddering breath and pulled the warpsword free. The ancient blade scraped against stone as it slid from the pile of rubble at the witch's back, leaving her body to slip from the long blade and slump lifelessly to the ground.

For a moment the highborn blinked drunkenly at the witch's body, as though seeing it for the first time. His skin was hot, as though flushed with fever, and his nerves still sang with fading notes of bloodlust. His gaze drifted to the drooping tip of the warpsword. A faint curl of crimson vapour rose from its razor edge.

With an effort of will Malus raised his head and beheld the trail of slaughter that stretched the length of the long, broad street.

Ruptured bodies and severed limbs lay in a tangled carpet across the cobblestones. Many bore their wounds upon their back, cut down as they tried to escape. Broken weapons glinted in the weak sunlight, showing where others had tried to fight the hunger of a god. Every face Malus could see was twisted in a rictus of terror and pain – all but the two zealot prisoners. Their headless bodies still knelt upright on the cobblestones, their arms outstretched in a gesture of religious ecstasy.

'Blessed Mother of Night,' Malus whispered in horrified awe. 'What have I done?'

'You have slaked the thirst of the burning blade,' Tz'arkan hissed. 'For now.'

Dozens of people, the highborn thought, unable to tear his eyes away from the carnage. *Dozens* of damned people. The last thing he remembered clearly was drawing the sword. After that… only laughter and terrible screams. The thought of such a loss of control terrified him.

Shouts echoed in the distance, back in the direction of the merchant's quarter. The highborn looked for the temple executioners and found their bodies at the base of the rock pile just a few yards away, surrounding the corpse of the second blood-witch. He tried to count the bodies of the lowborn, but gave up in disgust. There was no telling how many there were for certain, or if any might have escaped the slaughter and run for help.

Malus forced his body to work, weaving his way quickly among the fallen bodies. He noted absently how little blood there was – just blackened flesh and shrivelled organs.

Spite was not far from where Malus had dismounted, feeding warily on one of the dead men. The nauglir shied away at the highborn's approach. Malus snarled irritably at the war-beast. '*Stand*, damn you!' he shouted – and caught his hand tightening slowly around the hilt of the warpsword.

Malus froze. Eyeing the black blade warily, he slowly and deliberately slipped the sword back into its scabbard. Twice it seemed to get caught in the scabbard's mouth, forcing him to draw it out slightly and try to sheathe it again. When the weapon finally slid home the highborn breathed a sigh of relief.

Within moments the heat suffusing his muscles began to fade, like an iron plucked from the fire, leaving him feeling wretched and cold once more.

Caught between the dragon and the deep sea, Malus thought, fighting a wave of black despair. Which was the worse fate?

Chapter Three
PORTENTS OF DARKNESS

MOONLIGHT GLEAMED ALONG the gold fittings of the warpsword's scabbard and kindled a dusky fire in the depths of the oblong ruby set at the juncture of hilt and blade. Malus admired the relic fearfully for a moment, holding the sheathed weapon carefully in both hands. He fancied he could feel its heat, pulsing softly like a sleeping heart. He licked his cold lips nervously, then with a deep breath he laid the weapon on the fabric spread across his knees and wrapped it tightly from end-to-end in layers of frayed and dirty sailcloth. With each turn of the cloth he felt a bit colder, a bit smaller and more withered than before. When he was done, Malus tied off the bundle with loops of rough twine and then carried the wrapped weapon over to Spite. The cold one was crouched beneath the trees on the opposite side of the small forest clearing, watching its master warily with its red-ember eyes.

His face set in a mask of grim determination, Malus stowed the warpsword with his saddlebags, securing it tightly to his saddle beside the bag where the rest of the daemon's relics were kept. Reluctantly, he took his hands from the blade and patted the nauglir's flanks. 'No hunting tonight,' he said quietly, eyeing the dark depths of the surrounding wood. 'There's no telling what you might run into.'

It was only a few hours past sundown, and they were almost ten miles from Har Ganeth, deep in the wooded hills north and west of the city. The clearing was one he'd used often in the two months he'd prowled the Slaver's Road outside the City of Executioners. There was even a small lean-to built from pine boughs to provide some shelter from the elements and a store of firewood laid by. Lighting a fire was out of the question, however. The last thing he wanted to do was to advertise his presence, and he doubted the flame would warm his cursed bones anyway.

He'd escaped the city without further incident, though by the time he'd reached the wide city gate he could hear the first cries of alarm from the scene of the massacre. Malus trusted that the citizens would blame the attack on a band of zealots but he had no intention of putting his theory to the test. The highborn had all but galloped through the open gateway, relieved to find the Slaver's Road nearly empty of traffic. For the next few hours he'd worked his way westward along the road, keeping a wary eye out for plumes of dust rising on the horizon.

Malus had a very good reason for wanting to get out of Har Ganeth as quickly as he could: there was every chance that Malekith was on the way to the city with an army at his back, alerted by news of the temple uprising. Though he'd personally ended Urial's coup, the highborn doubted that the Witch King would show him any gratitude. Malus had been a fugitive since early summer after murdering his father at Vaelgor Keep, scarcely twenty miles to the north-east. He'd done it to gain possession of the Dagger of Torxus, another of the daemon's damned relics, not that the motive made any difference according to the laws of the land. Malus's father had been the Vaulkhar of Hag Graef, one of the Witch King's lieutenants, and no one slew one of Malekith's vassals without his leave. He hoped that the Witch King thought him dead, slain along with thousands of druchii in a confused night battle outside Hag Graef several months before, though it wasn't something he was willing to bet his life on. His half-brother Isilvar, now Lurhan's only heir and Hag Graef's Vaulkhar, almost certainly knew the truth. The question was what would he do with the knowledge? Isilvar had very good reasons to want him dead, the least of which was a nasty scar across his throat that Malus had given him in a battle beneath their sister Nagaira's tower a few months ago.

Frowning in thought, Malus combed through his saddlebags and pulled out an oil-stained cloth bag and a small bottle of wine. Then he drew the heavy battle-axe from a loop on the nauglir's saddle and sank wearily to the ground beside the cold one's armoured flank. As he leaned back against the nauglir's side the great beast shifted, its blocky head swinging around to fix him with a beady glare. Malus gave the beast a haughty glare. 'Settle down,' he warned, and tried to get comfortable once more. Again, the nauglir recoiled from his touch, rising to its feet and giving its master a warning hiss.

'All right, all right!' Malus snapped, snatching up his axe and his store of food and stalking to the other side of the encampment. He sat down heavily with his back to a rotting log and fixed the warbeast with a murderous look. 'See if I let you eat the next dead horse we come to.'

After a few moments Spite lowered carefully back onto its haunches and rested its snout on the ground so that it could keep a wary eye on Malus. The nauglir had been acting very strangely ever since they'd returned from the City of the Ageless Kings, far north in the Chaos Wastes. He'd gone there in search of the real warpsword, only to fall into the clutches of the power-mad druchii zealots who'd stolen it. They had intended to kill him and feed upon his life essence, and so they'd crucified him in the broad plaza outside their temple.

He'd had no choice but to call upon Tz'arkan's power to escape. Events after that were somewhat hazy. The next thing he recalled clearly was standing on the bridge of stone outside the Sanctum of the Sword in the temple fortress in Har Ganeth and watching his half-sister Yasmir eating their brother Urial's still-beating heart.

The prophecy of the Scourge maintained that he was destined to marry Yasmir, now considered a living saint of the Bloody-Handed God. After witnessing what she'd done to Urial the very idea of wedding her made his blood run cold. *Perhaps if I'm lucky the warpsword will kill me before that becomes an issue,* Malus thought bleakly.

It was getting colder in the clearing as the moons climbed into the cloudy sky. Even in late summer the Land of Chill was true to its name. Malus unwrapped his meagre bundle of salted fish and yellow sauce and began to eat, chewing doggedly at the tough flesh and washing it down with swigs of vinegary wine. He took his time with the meal; as wretched as it tasted, it was still better than the hardtack that he would be eating come the morrow.

By the time he was done the moons were shining almost directly overhead and his breath made a faint mist in the cold air. Malus doggedly finished off the terrible wine and summoned up his nerve. The other reason he'd chosen such an isolated campsite was because he was in sore need of information, and some conversations were best kept private.

He also had a dreadful feeling that he wasn't going to like what he was about to learn.

Malus wiped his face and put away the cloth and empty flask, then sat cross-legged with his back to the fallen log and his stolen axe within easy reach. The highborn pulled off the armoured gauntlet covering his left hand. A plain silver ring glinted on his finger like a band of purest ice. He held it up to the moonlight, noting with a grimace that the veins on the back of his hand were black with the daemon's corruption.

The highborn made a fist, focusing his remorseless will on a single thought.

Eldire.

A faint, familiar breeze ghosted across Malus's face – and the daemon inside him writhed in anger. His muscles seized and his guts curdled; Malus toppled onto his side with a groan, doubling over with the sudden wave of nausea and pain. Pressure built within his head, as though the daemon had his brain in a vice, causing sparks to dance before his eyes. Malus rolled onto his stomach and vomited his meal onto the cold, hard ground, his breath coming in shallow gasps timed to the pounding in his skull.

The highborn rolled back onto his side, fetching up against the side of the log. He caught the scent of ashes, and then suddenly the pain and sickness was receding like a black, oily tide. The pounding in his skull eased, and Malus thought that he heard the daemon's angry voice receding into an infinite distance. When it was gone he was left trembling with a leaden cold that seemed to radiate from his very bones.

'What have you done?' spoke a woman's voice, hard and cold as carved marble. The words had a peculiar echo to them, as though spoken from deep within a well. 'You fool! Malus, what have you done?'

The highborn's eyes flickered open. Above him loomed a glowing apparition wreathed in pale silver light. 'Hello, mother,' he said, managing a bitter laugh. 'How I've missed your loving voice.'

She was statuesque and regal, clothed in the heavy, dark robes of the witches' convent. Her pale hands were clasped before her and her braided white hair seemed wrought from moonlight, haloing the cruel angles of her face. Her form was insubstantial – the highborn could see through her as though she were made of fog, picking out Spite's sloping form and red-ember eyes on the other side of the clearing. For all that, Malus felt the weight of Eldire's stare like a dagger-point against his skin.

'Impertinent wretch!' Eldire snapped. 'Your body belongs wholly to the daemon now. Your veins pulse with foul energies. I can even see the daemon itself, sliding like a leviathan beneath your pallid skin!'

'Does it coil about my heart like a nest of serpents?' Malus sneered, wiping his mouth with the back of his hand. 'Does it clutch my shrivelled brain in its dripping jaws? Your gifts are wasted in this case, mother. I've known this every minute of every day for nearly a year.'

Eldire's ghostly face blazed with fury. 'This is far worse than mere possession, child! You have taken the final step. I warned you of this, back in the dwarf tombs!'

'Do you imagine I did this by choice?' the highborn shot back. Grimacing against the pain in his guts, he pushed himself wearily upright and rested the back of his head against the moss-covered log. 'The damned warpsword wasn't in the temple after all. I had to go into the Chaos Wastes to claim it.' His gaze fell upon the back of his black-veined hand and his anger faded in a wave of disgust. 'It was either this or death; there were no other choices open to me. For now, I live, and while I live, I can fight.' He met the seer's forbidding gaze. 'And now I have the sword.'

Eldire's dark eyes widened a fraction of an inch. The fury ebbed from her alabaster face. 'You drew the burning blade,' she said, her voice slightly more hollow than before.

'There were very compelling reasons at the time. I won't bore you with the details,' Malus said darkly. 'Tz'arkan was even less pleased than you. It makes me wonder if perhaps the warpsword's power is strong enough to counteract the daemon's influence.'

Eldire frowned at her son. 'Perhaps,' she allowed, with a sigh like a wind seeping from a tomb. 'Khaine's hunger cares little for the schemes of other beings, even daemons as potent as Tz'arkan. In fact,' she said, her expression turning angry again, 'the warpsword is likely the only reason you have any consciousness left. Looking at you, it's a wonder that the daemon isn't able to make you dance like a puppet.'

The idea sent a chill down Malus's spine. His gaze drifted to the wrapped bundle of the warpsword. Could he afford to keep feeding its hunger? Could he afford not to? 'The daemon may possess my body, but I assure you, my will remains intact,' he said. 'I dance for no one, least of all that damnable fiend.' He paused, watching the black veins throb beneath his skin. 'What I want to know is what will happen once the daemon is freed.'

The seer's lips pursed in thought. 'That is an interesting question,' she said. 'By rights, your soul would be snuffed out like a candle flame as Tz'arkan claims your body as its host. Now, however…' After a moment Eldire made a faint shrug. 'I cannot say. It is possible that the sword might counteract the daemon's claim over you, but you may be certain that until the moment arrives Tz'arkan will take whatever steps it can to help decide the matter in its favour.'

Malus gave his mother a hard look. 'So you're saying all is not lost.'

'I'm saying that if you are very clever and very lucky you might manage to trade one doom for another,' the seer replied archly. 'The warpsword will kill you sooner or later, Malus. Now that you've drawn it you can't turn it loose.'

The highborn let out a weary sigh. 'All of us die, mother,' he said, staring into the darkness. 'So it's not much of a price to pay, now is it?'

'Bold words for someone who has never spoken with the dead,' Eldire replied. 'Nevertheless,' she said, raising a hand to pre-empt a retort from her son, 'what's done is done. You have the sword, and that is what is important. That leaves just one relic to reclaim.'

'The Amulet of Vaurog,' Malus said ruefully. 'I've no idea where it is and precious little time to look for it. As near as I can tell I have two months left to return to the temple and set the daemon free, and the trip alone takes almost a month and a half.' He shot Eldire a sidelong glance. 'So unless you've got the power to make me fly, I've only got two weeks left to find the last relic.'

Eldire hitched up the ghostly hem of her robe and bent close to Malus, so that mother and son were almost nose-to-nose. 'Would you like a pair of wings, Malus?' she asked, her voice dangerously sweet.

Malus's sarcastic reply turned to ice at the tone in his mother's voice. 'That's… generous…' he said carefully. 'But perhaps I should worry about finding the relic first and making the trip afterward.'

Eldire smiled a wolf's smile. 'A very wise decision,' she said, straightening once again. 'My time grows short,' she announced. 'Speaking to you in this way is very taxing, especially now that the daemon has grown so strong. Is there aught that you wish of me?'

'I was hoping you knew something about the amulet,' Malus said quickly, forcing himself to sit up straight. 'That was why I called you in the first place.'

'The amulet?' Eldire said. Already her form was losing its nebulous consistency, melting like morning fog. 'It is a potent talisman, wrought from meteoric iron in ages past. No weapon can harm the warrior who wears it.'

'Never mind what it does!' Malus cried. 'Do you know where it is?'

Eldire's image began to blur, dissolving into formless mist. Her answer was little more than a sigh.

'The path to the fifth amulet leads to Naggarond,' the seer replied. 'Seek the amulet in the lightless halls of the Fortress of Iron.'

By the time Malus had recovered his wits, Eldire was gone. He looked to Spite. The nauglir raised its massive head and let out an irritated snort.

'I couldn't have said it better myself,' the highborn said darkly, folding his arms tightly across his chest. 'The Witch King's own fortress. I should have known.'

One doom for another, he thought bitterly to himself, feeling the daemon's corruption rise like a black tide from his bones and spread beneath his skin.

MALUS AWOKE TO aches and pains from head to toe. The clearing was bathed in the pearly light of false dawn, and wisps of fog curled along the ground. He was laying on his side, wrapped tightly in a heavy cloak sodden with morning dew. A few feet away Spite slept with its head tucked behind its long, whip-like tail, hissing like a boiling kettle.

Long fingers teased gently at his scalp, the tips warm against his clammy skin. His sleep-fogged mind savoured the sensation as the fingers brushed against his right ear, sending a trickle of warmth flowing along its curved outer edge.

Another rivulet of heat flowed across his cheek and over the top of his lips. It tasted of salt and iron.

The highborn's eyes went wide. He opened his mouth to speak, but the words were blotted out by a crushing wave of agony that radiated from his skull. Malus writhed within the tight confines of his cloak, but try as he might he could not pull himself free.

Blood ran in a freshet across his face and down his neck. It flowed into his right eye and he gasped at another, fiercer wave of pain.

Helpless, blinking away the drops of blood catching in his eyelashes, Malus turned his head and looked up to find an armoured figure crouching at his shoulder. More blood poured down the back of his head as though his skull were a broken jug of wine.

Bright blood painted Lhunara's pale grey hands, pooling beneath torn black fingernails and running in jagged courses along her wrists. Her blue lips parted in a lunatic smile, and her one good eye shone with a fevered gleam. The other eye, swollen and black with rotting blood, rolled aimlessly in its socket.

'We are of one mind, my lord,' she said, her voice bubbling from liquefying lungs as she raised her hands to the awful wound on the right side of her skull. With a wet, slithering sound she pressed the grey matter in her palms deep into the maggot-infested cavity.

'One mind,' she said, then reached for his face. 'One heart. One eye…'

MALUS AWOKE SCREAMING, thrashing about in slick, dewy loam.

His heart lurched in terror as he found that his arms and legs were wrapped tight. Still half-blind and witless, he writhed and kicked, sputtering and howling like the damned. Then with a convulsive heave he tore one leg free and realised that he was tangled in his heavy cloak.

Panting furiously, Malus forced himself to close his eyes and rest his head against the damp earth. When the hammering in his heart had eased, he slowly and purposefully untangled his limbs and spread the cloak open, heedless of the early morning chill.

Finally, when his breathing had slowed, the highborn opened his eyes. It was well past dawn, and weak sunlight was streaming through the close-set branches of the tree over his head. A thick root bulged up from the ground under his back, pressing hard against his spine.

Frowning, Malus raised his head. He was lying on an animal path between stands of tall oaks. Green, dripping ferns brushed against his cheeks, making him shudder.

He was nowhere near the clearing he'd camped in.

Cursing blearily, he clambered to his feet. The forest stretched away in every direction. Bits of foliage were caught between the plates of his armour, and the palms of his hands were caked with dirt. Blessed Mother of Night, he thought. How did I get here? Memories of the night before were fuzzy at best. He remembered sitting in the darkness, trying to envision a way into Naggarond of all places... and then things became vague. Did I get drunk on that damned vinegary wine, he thought?

He did a slow turn about, casting his gaze frantically about in an attempt to get his bearings. The game trail looked familiar and at least headed south towards the edge of the forest. Rubbing his face with a grimy palm he started walking down the trail, suddenly conscious of the fact that his battle-axe was nowhere to be seen.

Malus followed the trail for nearly a mile through the dense foliage, growing more confused and apprehensive by the moment. As he went he began to notice signs that he might have followed the path previously. From the shallow footprints and broken branches it looked as though he'd been reeling along like a drunkard in the darkness. It was a wonder he hadn't impaled himself on a low branch or cracked open his skull against the side of a tree.

After walking a mile and a half he found himself fighting back a rising tide of panic. Then, off to the south-west, he heard a familiar steam-kettle hiss. With a sigh of relief the highborn left the path and made for the sound, thrashing impatiently through the undergrowth. After about a dozen yards the trees began to thin out, until finally he stumbled onto the edge of his campsite. Spite rose to its feet at his sudden appearance, wide nostrils flaring as it tasted his scent.

Malus stopped dead at the edge of the clearing, scanning the small space warily. His axe was still where he left it. Even the folded parcel of cloth that had contained his evening meal was still where he'd left it. Moving carefully, he crossed the campsite and approached the nauglir. 'Easy, Spite,' he said, reaching for his saddlebags. The cold one snorted at him, one red eye regarding him balefully as the highborn searched through his gear.

The three remaining wine bottles hadn't been touched. He checked each wax seal and found them perfectly intact.

Spite shifted on its broad, taloned feet and grumbled irritably. 'All right, all right,' Malus said, securing the saddlebags and slapping the cold one on the flank. 'Go. Hunt. I need to think.'

The highborn stepped away as the huge warbeast slipped with surprising stealth into the thick undergrowth. Then he turned and once more scanned the ground near where he'd sat. There was no sign of a disturbance. It was as though he'd simply stood up and walked off into the darkness.

Malus settled wearily against the log and tried to clean some of the dirt from his hands. Try as he might, he couldn't remember much of the night after he'd spoken with Eldire. Could she have done something to him? If so, why? He shook his head irritably. The idea made no sense.

Then there was the nightmare. He'd heard of druchii who cried out, even got up and moved about in the grips of a powerful nightmare. Had there been more to the dream that he didn't remember? Had the ghastly vision of Lhunara sent him fleeing into the depths of the forest? 'I may have to start drinking myself to sleep again,' he muttered sourly. 'Or hobbling myself at night like a horse.'

From off to the north came a sudden eruption of frenzied movement – something huge thrashed through the forest, snapping branches and slapping heavily against tree trunks. Malus grunted softly. Spite had already found a morning meal.

Then, as if in answer, came sounds of movement to the south, back in the direction of the road.

Without thinking, Malus snatched up his axe and rolled quietly into a crouch, peering warily over the top of the fallen log. Scarcely daring to breathe, he held perfectly still and strained his senses to the utmost. Moments later he heard a much fainter rustle in the undergrowth, perhaps twenty yards to the south-east. The highborn closed his eyes and tried to picture the surrounding terrain in his mind. Whatever it was, it sounded like it was working its way up the game trail he'd recently been following.

Then came another crackle of broken branches – this time directly to the south. The highborn bared his teeth.

It sounded like a hunting party. And it was coming his way.

Chapter Four
THE ENDLESS

AFTER EVERYTHING HE'D been through in the last ten months, Malus no longer believed in luck. Whoever the hunters were, they hadn't simply stumbled onto him by accident. He doubted they were city folk from Har Ganeth – the camp was too far away and too deep in the woods to catch the attention of a band of refugees. An autarii hunting party was a possibility. The Shades claimed the entire mountain range and hill country north of the Slaver's Road, and it wasn't unheard of for small raiding bands to find their way to the southern foothills to steal from westbound slave caravans. But no autarii worth his salt would be so clumsy as to give away his position, particularly in the deep woods.

That left only one possibility: they were men from Malekith's army.

Malus's hands tightened on the haft of his battle-axe and peered over the top of the log into the shadows beneath the thick trees. It was possible they were just a foraging party, hunting for deer or pheasant to feed the Witch King's warband. It was also possible that they were hunters of a different kind, combing the woods in search of him. But how could they have found me, Malus thought? He reckoned he knew these woods better than any soldier from Naggarond, and he'd been careful to cover his trail the evening before.

Undergrowth rustled off to the highborn's right, still some fifteen yards away. The hunters were moving cautiously and swinging a little further to the west. He turned his gaze to the east, hoping to catch some sign of movement from the second hunting party, but the dense foliage stymied him. Still, he thought, if I can't yet see them, they can't see me.

Then came the sharp sound of a branch snapping near the game trail. Ten yards away, he reckoned, and also a bit farther east. The two groups were swinging around the edge of the campsite. What was more, he suddenly realised that he'd heard no indications of movement from directly south. They know where the campsite is, he thought, feeling the hairs bristle on the back of his neck. They are trying to surround it, cutting me off from fleeing further northward.

He had to move now, before the noose closed around him. Fortunately Spite was somewhere north of him now, feeding on his morning meal. If he could reach the nauglir he was sure that he could outpace whoever was stalking him, fleeing northward into the foothills. Of course, that meant he'd be trespassing on autarii land, but first he had to survive to get there.

Still crouching low to the ground, Malus turned and scuttled across the campsite. As he did, the sounds of movement erupted from east and west. The hunters were making their move.

Malus ducked his head and followed the path that Spite had taken upon leaving camp. At least, he tried – not two feet beyond the edge of the clearing he crashed headlong into a briar thicket that the iron-skinned cold one had simply muscled its way through. Thorny branches lashed at the highborn's face and neck, eliciting a strangled hiss of pain. Malus lashed at the hedge with his axe, hoping that a few good strokes would be enough to hew his way past, but the thin, green branches rebounded from the weapon and lashed back at him like whipcords. Worse, the attempt made considerable noise, causing him to feel dangerously exposed. Malus gave up after a handful of noisy strokes and rushed to the west, looking for a clearer path through the undergrowth.

He heard someone burst from cover and dash into the clearing only a half-dozen yards behind him. Not waiting to see who it was, Malus ducked and dodged past thin saplings and drooping ferns, reaching the end of the thicket and cutting back northward again. His tense gaze scanned left and right, hoping to catch some sign of the nauglir's trail, but the cold one's path was almost invisible to his unskilled eyes. The damn thing is almost thirty feet long and weighs a ton, he thought irritably, yet it can move like an autarii in the woods when it wants to. For a moment he contemplated whistling for Spite – easier to bring the cold one to him than the other way around – but he was certain the hunters would hear him as well. He had no idea what would happen then, and didn't want to find out.

Malus strained his ears for the sound of pursuit and kept to the parts of the wood that offered the least amount of resistance, trading concealment for speed. The ground began to slope gently upward, starting the slow climb to the low foothills that were still more than a mile distant. Within a few minutes he came upon a small wooded hollow and on impulse he headed inside rather than skirt it.

The shadows beneath the close-set trees were deep, but at least it meant that there was less undergrowth to fight through. Almost immediately Malus found a narrow game trail winding through the centre of the hollow and followed it without hesitation. Seconds later he came upon a large pool of fresh blood splashed across the trail and found a pair of large, familiar footprints nearby.

Malus settled into a crouch, breathing heavily. He'd found the spot where Spite had ambushed his prey but the damned cold one was nowhere to be seen. Nauglir, like many predators, preferred to drag their food somewhere more secure before they felt safe enough to eat. Which meant that the warbeast could have gone off in nearly any direction.

A flicker of movement in the shadows to Malus's left brought him around, weapon at the ready. No one was there. The highborn turned in a slow circle, looking for any signs of danger. As near as he could tell, however, he was alone.

Branches crackled perhaps a dozen yards behind him. The hunters had reached the south end of the hollow.

Malus sank into a crouch, quickly sizing up the surrounding terrain. Did he dare make a stand here, or keep running? Now he regretted leaving the warpsword bound to Spite's saddle!

Moving as quietly as he could, Malus swung around the bloodstain so as not to leave a trail his enemies could follow, and sidled into the dense woods to the west of the path. Vines and brambles tugged at his hair and scraped against his steel armour, but he resisted the temptation to swipe them away with his axe. Instead he burrowed deeper, hoping to draw the vegetation behind him like a cloak.

A few yards further on the highborn came to the burnt and blasted trunk of an old oak tree. Clearly felled by lightning years ago, the shell of the old tree rose less than ten feet and terminated in a jagged, moss-covered stump. A cleft in the wide trunk ran from root level up to about waist height. Thinking quickly, Malus hurried to the cleft and carefully wormed his way inside.

Rotten, pulpy wood and squirming insects rained down on him as the edges of his armour plates scraped the inside of the tree. Malus closed his eyes and clamped his mouth tightly shut against the dank-smelling debris and braced his back against the far side of the tree. Then, moving carefully, he raised a foot and felt about for a toehold a few feet off the ground. Within moments his boot found a ridge that would support his weight. Gritting his teeth, the highborn pressed his back against the trunk and heaved upward. As his other foot came off the ground he fumbled quickly for another foothold and found one just above the cleft.

Working quickly, Malus forced his way three more feet up into the hollow trunk and hung there, scarcely daring to breathe.

No sooner had he stopped moving than he heard faint sounds of movement in the woods outside. The highborn stifled a bitter curse. He heard the swish of branches and the crackle of dead wood, and for the first time he heard hushed voices speaking in what sounded like druhir. From what he could tell there were at least three of them, but he couldn't quite make out what they were saying.

The voices drew nearer. The highborn heard the muted rattle of plate harness and the faint clatter of sword scabbards. Malus looked down at the narrow shaft of pale light shining through the cleft. As he watched, a shadow passed across the opening. He held his breath, expecting to see a head peer into the opening at any moment.

For several long moments the conversation continued. The words were strangely muffled; again, Malus couldn't quite divine their meaning, but he could guess from their cadence and tone that they were discussing where to look for him next. At length, one of the hunters seemed to arrive at a decision. With a grunt, the hunters moved off, apparently continuing to head farther west. The highborn let out a slow breath. Once he could no longer hear any sounds of movement he counted slowly to one hundred, then carefully eased himself back to earth.

Getting out of the cleft proved much more difficult than getting in. In the end he was forced to turn about and sink to his knees, then crawl backwards out of the hole. At any moment he expected blades or crossbow bolts to bite into his back, but within a few moments he was free. Brushing rotted wood and insects out of his hair, Malus regained his bearings and headed off east as fast as he could manage.

He hadn't gone more than a few yards when he heard a familiar growl some ways to the north. Now at least he knew which direction the cold one had gone in. The question was whether or not the hunters had heard the same thing, and what they would make of it.

Malus continued west, heading back to the game trail. He could follow the faint trail as far north as he could, hopefully making better time than his pursuers, but if they were now heading in Spite's direction as well he was sure to cross their path. Unless he continued west, crossing the game trail and then doubling back in a wide circle to come at Spite from the east. But doing so would take time. Which risk was more worthwhile?

Caught up in his internal debate, Malus almost missed the flicker of movement to his right. Certain that this time it wasn't his imagination, he fetched up against the bole of a tree and dropped to a crouch, scanning the deep shadows all around him.

Nothing moved. There were no sounds save for the restless wind. Malus waited for ten seconds, seeing nothing, then took a deep breath and started off once more. He went for ten yards and then abruptly stopped, whirling to the right.

There! He saw a shadow flit from the darkness beneath one tree to the next. It was the size of a raven, and darted through the air at shoulder height. The hair on the highborn's neck stood on end. He was being hounded by a shade, no doubt reporting his location back to its master. Even now, Malus imagined the huntsmen he'd encountered were doubling back, following the call of their unearthly hound.

The time for stealth was past. Malus turned and ran for the game trail as fast as he could. With the weight of his armour his footfalls echoed through the dense wood, but all that counted now was speed. Such was his haste that he ran full-tilt into the same thicket he'd encountered earlier. Needle-like thorns raked his face and hands, but with a savage snarl he hacked wildly at the branches with his axe and bulled his way through.

Panting like a dog Malus stumbled onto the game trail – and saw at once that he was not alone.

Three figures stood in a tight group a few yards down the trail to Malus's right. They wore black, woollen robes over breeches and boots, and their torsos were protected by silver steel breastplates engraved with elaborate designs and sorcerous runes. Their bodies were wrapped in heavy, hooded cloaks, and their faces were hidden behind masks of polished silver. Three female faces worked in cold metal regarded him curiously, their polished features seeming to float within the black depths of their hoods. One of the figures raised a black-gloved hand, and Malus turned and ran northward as fast as his feet would carry him.

'Spite!' Malus called, throwing all caution to the wind. Fortunately for him, the game trail twisted and turned, quickly carrying him out of sight of the three shade-casters. Had he run afoul of the autarii after all? The three women he'd seen were witches, of that he had no doubt, but no witches he'd ever seen wore masks and archaic armour over their robes.

Shouts and sounds of movement rang out from Malus's left; the hunters he'd met by the tree were closing in. Off to the north he thought he heard another low growl from Spite. He tried to gauge how far off the sound was when he turned another corner and an armoured figure stepped onto the path directly in front of him.

For a fleeting second Malus thought one of the witches had somehow flown ahead to cut him off. The figure wore black robes and silver steel armour, but the ornate, archaic plates covered the hunter from neck to toe like a proper knight. Two swords hung from the hunter's belt and his face was hidden behind a mask worked in the shape of a leering daemon. A hadrilkar of polished gold glinted from the depths of the man's hood.

The hunter raised a gauntleted hand. Malus was too close to swing the axe, so instead he held the haft out before him and crashed directly into the man. With a crash of wood against steel the masked figure fell backwards and Malus leapt over him without breaking stride.

More shouts sounded behind him, and then he heard a whickering sound slice through the air behind him. Something heavy struck him between the shoulder blades and then a steel web wrapped his chest and arms in a fearsome embrace.

Barbed hooks scraped across his armour and locked inside its crevices, and suddenly Malus was off-balance and stumbling forward. With a furious effort he tried to regain his balance, but then his foot struck a protruding root and he crashed headlong to the ground.

The highborn thrashed and rolled, wrestling with the implacable grip of the net. Footfalls sounded behind him as he struggled, and three masked figures loomed into view over him. One grabbed his ankles, flipping him expertly onto his back, while another grabbed the folds of the net that laid across his chest. The third warrior stood a few feet away and slowly drew his sword.

With a snarl Malus pulled one foot free as the man holding the net began to straighten. On impulse the highborn kicked the warrior in the side of the head, and he fell sideways with a muffled curse. As he did he inadvertently pulled part of the net with him, freeing Malus's right arm. The warrior who had been holding his feet let go and lunged for the highborn, but Malus rolled quickly to his left and unrolled himself from the barbed trap. Driving the second warrior back with a savage sweep of his axe, Malus struggled to his feet – just as the masked swordsman lunged in from the highborn's left.

The warrior's blade was just a silver flicker in the forest gloom. Battlefield instincts alone spared Malus; without thinking he pivoted on his right foot and blocked the sword stroke with the haft of his axe. As it was, the force of the blow nearly drove Malus back to his knees, and before he could recover the swordsman pressed his attack, landing two more solid blows that nearly knocked the highborn off his feet.

Whoever the warriors were, they were tough and skilled opponents. Without a word shared between them the masked men fanned out in a loose semicircle, clearly working to hem him in. The other men kept their swords in their scabbards, however, leaving the lone swordsman to batter Malus's failing guard. The highborn gave ground quickly, retreating further north up the path, but within moments one of the hunters was going to cut behind him and seal off his retreat.

Malus suffered another ringing blow to the haft of his axe and risked a hurried feint at the swordsman's face. The short swing checked the warrior's advance for half a second, but it was enough for the highborn to spin on the ball of his left foot and then lunge at the masked hunter who had circled around behind him. Caught off guard, the warrior tried to retreat, but the highborn charged him with a bestial roar and caught him with a vicious blow that struck sparks from his ornate breastplate. The force of the blow knocked the man from his feet, and the highborn charged past him and continued along the path.

'Spite!' Malus called again, and immediately was answered with a sharp hiss just ten yards off the path to his right. Without hesitation the highborn plunged into the undergrowth, hacking bushes and saplings out of his path with wild sweeps of his axe. If he could just get to the nauglir's side he could turn the tide of the battle in his favour.

Malus caught the sharp smell of spilled blood. Up ahead he caught sight of the nauglir's scaled back and grinned fiercely. The cold one had dragged his kill to another clearing almost a hundred yards farther up the hollow.

'Up, Spite, up!' he cried to the crouching warbeast. Malus could hear the sounds of the masked warriors in close pursuit a scant few yards behind him. As he plunged into the clearing his looked for the wrapped bundle of the warpsword on the cold one's back.

Instead he saw a black-robed figure standing close to the nauglir's saddle. One gloved hand rested on the side of Spite's neck, and the nauglir's eyes were downcast in submission. The witch regarded him impassively from the depths of her silver mask as Malus ground to a sudden halt.

Two more witches glided silently from the shadows to Malus's left and right, attended by two warriors each who advanced with swords in hand. The highborn's three pursuers charged into the clearing directly behind him, completing the encirclement.

Malus turned slowly in place, regarding each of the hunters in turn. His gaze passed from masked face to masked face, dismayed and bewildered by their strange appearance. These were no autarii, he realised. No group of shades would be so regimented.

The highborn stopped in his tracks. Each of the warriors wore the same golden collar. *Gold*, not silver or even silver steel. Peering closely at one of the hadrilkars, Malus saw that it was worked in the shape of a pair of twining dragons.

His breath caught in his throat. These were no mere hunters, Malus realised. He knew who they were, though few had ever seen them face-to-face.

They were the personal bodyguards and agents of the Witch King. They were the Endless.

Chapter Five
FORTRESS OF IRON

Black ice poured from Malus's veins as the seven warriors closed in around him.

The rush of daemonic power shocked him, drawing a horrified cry from the highborn's throat. Time stretched like a bowstring; the movements of the Endless slowed to a turgid crawl, even as Malus's own body seethed with merciless vigour. Inwardly the highborn recoiled in terror and disgust from his unexpected salvation.

'I did not ask for this, daemon,' he hissed. 'You cannot force your damned gifts upon me!'

'Things have changed, Darkblade,' Tz'arkan said. His laughter trembled along Malus's skin. 'I am now free to protect you as I see fit. I would think you would be grateful. Do you imagine that Malekith despatched his chosen with orders to kill you? Had he wanted you dead he could have sent ten thousand spearmen into the woods to root you out like a boar. No, they are here to drag you back to Naggarond in chains, where you will suffer torments that no sane druchii can imagine.'

'Take it back!' Malus snarled. 'Take your cursed ice from my veins. I neither want nor need it!'

'You cannot turn back the seasons,' Tz'arkan replied coldly. 'You had your spring and your summer, little druchii. Soon it will be autumn. Winter cannot be far behind. The ice will come whether you wish it or not.'

Malus clenched his fists around the battered haft of his axe and roared like a wounded beast. The masked warriors were still gliding towards him, poised between one step and the next. Were he able to see their faces he imagined that they would be stretching like melted wax, surprise registering by degrees as the highborn seemed to blur before them. Then, like a butcher, he settled on his first victim and prepared to drown his misery in a tide of hot blood. Yet before he could take a single step a cold, melodious voice spoke in his ear.

'Your sorcery is impressive, Malus of Hag Graef, but in the end it changes nothing.'

The highborn whirled, fear tightening his throat. His axe sang through the air, angling for the witch's neck, but she moved as though he were standing still. She reached forward without apparent effort and touched her fingertips to his armoured chest.

Blue fire exploded behind his eyes. He felt himself falling, the silver face of the witch receding into darkness. Her voice tolled after him like a bell.

'You belong to the Witch King now.'

NIGHT HAD FALLEN by the time he woke again. Malus opened his eyes to the shifting hues of the northern lights in an unsettlingly clear late-summer sky. The stars were cold and pitiless as diamonds, and the twin moons cast strange shadows across the foggy landscape. Black-robed figures moved silently at the corners of his vision, and he heard people speaking in terse, hushed tones.

He was stretched out like a corpse on the hard ground, still cased in his battered armour. He wasn't bound in any way, but his body felt like lead. With a grunt, he tried to sit upright. It was all he could do just to prop himself up on his elbows.

Malus saw at once that he was in the middle of a small camp, somewhere along the Slaver's Road west of Har Ganeth. There were no fires, only small globes of witchlight resting on low, iron tripods, and perhaps a dozen tents set in orderly clusters around the spot where he lay. Masked warriors were busy dismantling and stowing the tents as the highborn watched, while another group saddled a score of coal-black horses hitched to a picket line a dozen yards away. Grey sea fog curled around the steeds' glossy black hooves, and their eyes glowed green in the reflected witchlight.

The Endless went about their tasks all around Malus, paying him as much attention as they might give to a bedroll. A quick check showed that his axe was nowhere to be seen, and they'd plucked his two daggers from his belt. There were no irons to bind his wrists or ankles, which implied a great deal about his captors' capabilities. If he tried to run, the Endless and their witches were certain he would not get far.

'You are awake,' spoke an unearthly, musical voice. It was cold and sweet as a trumpet or a silver bell, and sent shivers down the highborn's spine. He tried to turn his head to glance at the witch, but the effort left him exhausted. Malus sank back to the ground as the masked druchii circled around him and knelt gracefully at his side. She held a narrow decanter of cut red glass in one hand and a polished silver cup in the other. 'That is good. We will be leaving soon.'

She poured a small measure of a black liquid into the cup and held it out to Malus. The highborn studied her eyes warily. They were wide and dark within the gleaming oculars of the mask, and reminded him of nothing so much as the frank, earnest stare of a child. Setting his jaw, he lifted himself up on one elbow and slowly reached for the cup. 'Where is the army?' he asked wearily.

The witch cocked her head to one side. 'Army? There is no army.'

Malus frowned, his dark brows furrowing in consternation. He studied the black liquid at the bottom of his cup and took a small sip. The potent liquor seared his tongue and flowed like molten iron down his throat. Tears sprang to his eyes. 'Then where is Malekith?' he gasped, fighting the urge to cough.

'The Witch King is in Naggarond,' she said, as though it explained everything. 'We have been commanded to bring you to him.'

The liquor seethed inside Malus's guts, but it also returned a small measure of strength to his limbs. Steeling himself, he finished off the cup. 'Reminds me of the time I drank some lamp oil as a child,' he said hoarsely. 'Honestly, the oil had more flavour.'

'It is a dwarf liquor called barvalk,' the witch said, taking the cup from him. 'Dark riders carry it on cold winter nights. It keeps the blood hot and the mind sharp.'

'Probably takes the tarnish off silver as well,' he muttered, but silently admitted that his limbs had begun to loosen and his mind was alert and awake. With a rueful grin he levered himself fully upright and stretched his arms and shoulders.

The witch was well within reach. Her stare was guileless and her manner relaxed. It would take no effort at all to seize her and close his hands around her neck. But what then, Malus thought? Was she the witch that had felled him in the wood with but a single touch? He could not tell. And even if he did slay her, what then? He was surrounded by more than a dozen warriors, and even if he could somehow fight his way free, the Endless had already demonstrated they could track him easily with their magic.

Malus's shoulders slumped within the confines of his armour. Putting him in irons was redundant. There was nowhere he could go, and they knew it.

Then he remembered what Eldire had told him: *the path to the fifth relic leads to Naggarond.*

It was just possible that falling into the clutches of the Endless was a blessing in disguise.

'All right,' Malus said, trying to sound resigned to his fate. 'What next?'

The witch rose to her feet. 'There is food prepared in the tent yonder,' she said, pointing over Malus's shoulder. 'If you are hungry, eat. We will be riding through the night and will not pause again until midday tomorrow.'

Malus nodded. In truth, food was the last thing on his mind at that point, but better to fuel mind and body while he could. 'Where is my mount?'

The witch turned and inclined her gleaming mask towards the line of trees to the north. 'Your cold one is being tended to there, beyond the camp,' she said. 'Go to it after you have broken your fast, and wait for the order to depart.'

Without so much as a farewell the witch began to walk away. 'Wait!' Malus called. 'What is your name?'

The druchii paused. Her head turned slightly, moonlight glinting on one rounded cheek. 'I have no name,' she said, childlike amusement in her voice. 'I am Endless.' Without waiting for a reply she joined a group of figures packing saddlebags nearby. Soon Malus couldn't tell for sure which of the identical figures was her.

The highborn shook his head wearily and clambered to his feet. Malekith's bodyguards continued breaking camp swiftly and efficiently, hardly sparing their prisoner a sideways glance. Not twenty yards to the south a caravan of flesh merchants were driving their wheeled cages northward up the Slaver's Road, heading for Karond Kar. He listened to the drovers curse the stolid oxen as they went, harangued in turn by the slave master and his sons. One of the young druchii slavers looked up at that moment and stared curiously at the small encampment. He saw Malus watching him and raised his coiled scourge in salute.

Malus raised his hand in return, and the young slaver spurred his horse and cantered to the head of the caravan. Still shaking his head, the highborn headed for the tent that the witch had indicated, hoping that the bodyguards had brought some meat and cheese, and perhaps a bit of decent wine.

* * *

ONCE CAMP WAS broken and the baggage packed the Endless set
a gruelling pace as they bore their prisoner back to Naggarond.
Mounted on their preternatural steeds the masked druchii
rode all through the night and half of the following day before
finally calling a halt in the middle of a cold and desultory rain.

Horses snorted and stamped, their breath pluming in the
chilly air as they were led off the road into the tall grass. The
animals paid no heed at all to the cold one in their midst;
sired from thoroughbred stock brought from drowned
Nagarythe, the dark steeds were foaled in the sorcerous stables
of Naggarond itself, and feared neither man nor beast.
Cousins to the dark steeds that the kingdom's messengers
rode, they were fleet as storm winds when given their head,
and could run for days without tiring.

For Spite's part, the nauglir paid little heed to anything,
including Malus himself. Since the encounter with the Endless
near their camp in the woods, the cold one had been strangely
subdued and passive, following commands as meekly as a
whipped slave. On the road the cold one loped along at the
same pace as the rest of the party, ignoring the highborn's subtle commands.

The nauglir followed the horses off the road and settled onto
its haunches, its head perking up a bit at the welcome caress of
the rain. Malus slid from the saddle and tried to stretch the
kinks out of his hips and shoulders. Though no stranger to
hard riding, more than fourteen hours in the saddle left him
feeling as though he'd been beaten with a club.

Masked druchii slid effortlessly from their saddles and
silently inspected their mounts, checking hooves, muscles and
tendons with expert hands. Malus did the same for Spite,
although the highborn was checking for telltales of a very different kind.

He found the cluster of magical runes within moments,
painted with some kind of indigo dye onto the nauglir's bony
skull. The rain had no effect on them, nor did they blur when
he rubbed them with his thumb. Malus patted Spite's neck
resignedly. The Endless had usurped his control over his own

mount and effectively turned Spite into a jailer of sorts. He couldn't spur the cold one to turn on the riders even if he wanted to.

With nothing else to do, Malus leaned against Spite's flank and waited. After a few minutes one of the warriors made his way down the line, holding a bottle of barvalk and half a sausage. Malus steeled himself and took the proffered cup when his turn came, then wolfed down a thick slice of sausage. As soon as the warrior had finished making his rounds he jogged back to the head of the line and without a word the Endless climbed back into the saddle. Their midday break had lasted little more than fifteen minutes.

They rode through the rest of the day and well into the night. Ahead of them went the dragon banner of the Witch King of Naggaroth, and slave caravans travelling in either direction pulled aside and waited with heads bowed as the black riders thundered past. It was nearly four hours past sunset when the Endless finally called a halt, leading their mounts off the road and preparing a cold meal by witch-light. Cold, wet and aching from head to toe, Malus pulled his bedroll from the saddle and fell wearily to the ground beside Spite.

No sooner had he closed his eyes than one of the witches was kneeling beside him with a handful of salted fish and a hunk of bread wrapped in a greasy square of cloth. He took the food without thinking, his exhausted brain only dimly aware that it was close to midnight and the warriors were climbing back in their saddles again. Groaning, the highborn stowed his bedroll and climbed back onto his mount. He ate his meagre rations as they rode.

By the end of the second evening the black riders had reached the western end of the Sea of Malice, and were within a day's ride of the great crossroads where the Slaver's Road met the Spear Road as it headed north to the Wastes. The ration of barvalk at each rest stop had grown more generous, and Malus found himself growing accustomed to the taste. It didn't relieve the aches and pains of the endless ride but it made them slightly more tolerable. As the riders ate and rested, Malus resisted his body's demand for sleep and spent the time carefully arranging his bags. He dug into the pack where three of the daemon's relics were hid and fished out the wrapped bundle that contained the Idol of Kolkuth. He could feel the coldness of the brass figure through the layers of frayed cloth as he set it atop the rest of the bag's contents. During the day's travel he'd worked out a plan of escape. Once the Endless had got him inside the Iron Fortress he would wait until the last moment before seizing the idol and using its power to transport himself away from his captors. He felt certain that once he was inside the fortress he could find ample hiding places from which to begin his hunt for the Amulet of Vaurog.

Providing, of course, that the witches couldn't simply use their shades to locate him once more – and that their sorcerous hold on Spite didn't force the nauglir to turn on his own master.

The Endless rotated their riders through different points in their formation as they travelled; Malus wasn't sure of the reason why, unless perhaps it was to limit their exposure to him as much as possible. After the second day he thought to start a conversation with one of the witches riding beside him, and was surprised when she answered every question he put to her. She told him how the Endless were given to the Iron Fortress as babes, taken as a sort of tithe from each of the highborn families in Naggarond. The witches received training by Morathi herself, while the warriors were taught by a highborn named Lord Nuarc, the finest warlord in the Witch King's warband. They served Malekith until death, at which point their mask and gear were given to a waiting neophyte. There were always a thousand of the Endless, guarding the precincts of the Iron Fortress and marching with the Witch King when the druchii went to war.

From what Malus could determine, the bodyguards wanted for nothing and possessed not a shred of independent thought or ambition. They were essentially incorruptible, a realisation that both frustrated and horrified him at the same time.

Tempted by the witch's loquacity and her apparent lack of guile, Malus asked her how they'd managed to find him. 'It must have been sorcery,' he said offhandedly. 'How else would you have known to look in a nameless clearing in the middle of a vast forest?'

'We are all trained in shade-casting,' the witch replied. Her childlike voice was tinged with surprise, as though it were the most obvious question in the world. 'It is nothing to summon a fetch and have it search for you, providing you have the subject's name.'

'A fetch?' Malus asked.

The witch giggled behind her silver mask. 'The weakest of shades; little more than a fragment of spirit essence, intelligent enough to command but utterly devoid of will or initiative. They can be set to simple tasks, but their reach isn't very long.' She regarded Malus with a condescending shake of her head. 'I'm surprised you know so little, given your demonstration in the forest.'

'My knowledge is... specialised,' Malus replied. 'You say their reach is short?'

She nodded. 'Yes. They have little strength of their own, and must depend upon the energies of the summoner to remain active in the physical realm. A shade-caster can command a fetch over a few dozen miles, perhaps, but no more.'

The highborn looked away, pretending to study the faint line of Dachlan Keep in order to mask his frown of dismay. A dozen miles, he thought? Not much distance for a sorcerer, perhaps, but that would mean he would have to use the idol to leave Naggarond completely in order to escape their reach. Perhaps if he could find a place to hide somewhere in the nearby hills and then use the idol to come and go from the fortress...

Suddenly he straightened in the saddle. Malus turned to the witch. 'You said that a fetch couldn't reach for more than a few dozen miles?'

'Of course,' she replied.

'Then how did you know where to look for me? I could have been in Har Ganeth, or on the road to Karond Kar – I could have been at sea aboard a corsair, for the Dark Mother's sake.'

The witch shrugged. 'We were told to look for you along the Slaver's Road,' she said.

And how did Malekith know that, Malus thought? He was certain that he wasn't going to like the answer.

THEY CAME UPON the crossroads at well past midnight of the fourth day. The air was cool and clear, and the highborn shivered in the saddle from exhaustion as much as dread as the riders slowed their mounts to a walk and passed among the forest of burning souls.

The last time Malus had been this way was at the head of a small army, marching south to conquer Hag Graef in the name of Balneth Bale. The withered figures, wired to tall iron poles all around the crossroads and set alight with sorcerous fire, had held little terror for him then. Now he found himself listening to their faint, maddened cries and dreading the sight of the empty stake that the Witch King had set aside for him. Only those highborn who'd broken Malekith's laws were sentenced to burn at the crossroads, some lingering in agony for years as the elements wore away their bodies inch by inch. As Malus rode among the guttering lamps that used to be powerful men he could not help but tremble at the fate that awaited him. He reached back and checked the bag where the idol was kept, making certain he could reach it quickly when the time came.

On the other side of the crossroads lay a narrow ribbon of road that gleamed ghostly white under the moonlight. The Hateful Road led to Naggarond alone, and was paved with the skulls of a hundred thousand elves. The hooves of the dark steeds clattered hollowly on the magically treated bones and the riders sat straighter in the saddle as they drew closer to home.

The road wound among dark, lifeless hills and through echoing hollows dense with oak and ash, while in the distance the high walls and pointed towers of Naggarond rose ever higher into the indigo sky. Glimmering witchlight shone like a thousand eyes from the buildings of the fortress city, lending it a kind of cold, brooding life. This was not a place built upon ruthless power like Hag Graef, or stained with bloodlust like Har Ganeth – Naggarond was black, eternal hate quarried from cold marble and unyielding iron. It was the implacable heart of the druchii given form.

They travelled the Hateful Road for another hour, until finally they crested a rocky ridge and came upon a flat, featureless plain that stretched between the curving arms of a bleak mountainside. Naggarond curled upon itself like an enormous dragon upon the plain, surrounded by a gleaming wall nearly sixty feet high. Tall towers bristling with iron spikes rose from the wall every mile or so along its length, sited to rain clouds of arrows and heavy stones upon any invader. Ahead, Malus could see a massive gatehouse that was a small fortress unto itself, looming over a double portal wrought from slabs of polished iron nearly twenty feet high. The highborn shook his head in wonder. He'd once thought that Hag Graef's fortifications were fearsome, but nothing compared to Naggarond's forbidding bulk.

The dark riders led their steeds directly across the plain and approached the iron gates. No challenge issued from the gatehouse's jagged battlements; evidently the mere sight of the gleaming silver masks of the Endless was sufficient. With a terrible, echoing groan one of the massive gates swung open and the column trotted down a long, wide tunnel that ran beneath the gatehouse. Darkness pressed in from all sides, and the highborn fought to keep from hunching his shoulders at the thought of the murder holes and oil flues that doubtless pierced the stone overhead.

Malus expected to emerge from the tunnel into a large, open square, much as in the style of other druchii cities. Instead he found himself in a narrow lane overlooked by tall, stone buildings with deep-set oaken doors. Witchlights glowed from sconces hanging over many of the doorways, creating pools of flickering light amid a twisting path of abyssal shadow. The hooves of the dark steeds struck sparks from the grey cobblestones and sent up a thunderous clatter that reverberated from the close-set walls.

All druchii cities were treacherous, labyrinthine places, full of blind alleys and confusing turns designed to entrap and kill the unwary, but Naggarond was unlike any living city Malus had ever seen. Once inside the walls there were no landmarks to navigate by; nearly every street ended at a crossroads that connected to three other narrow lanes, all leading off in unpredictable directions. None of the buildings he saw bore signs or sigils that told what they were, and if there were market squares anywhere he never saw them. Within minutes he was utterly lost, and he knew full well they had only just entered the outer wards of the city.

They rode for more than an hour through the labyrinth, alone but for the echoes of their passage. Malus saw not a single living thing along the way: no citizens or city guards, no drunkards or thieves, penny oracles or cutthroats. It reminded him of nothing more than the houses of the dead, that city of crypts in the east where the ancient dead of Nagarythe were bound fearfully in vaults of stone.

There were three more defensive walls that subdivided the city, closed by three more heavy gates of iron. Tall, silent houses pressed hard against either side of these inner walls; as the first of the six cities, Malus had the sense that it had grown in fits and starts as the kingdom prospered, expanding beyond its own walls again and again until it was ringed like an old, gnarled tree.

Thus, when they paused before a fourth wall of gleaming stone it took several long moments before Malus's exhausted mind registered the narrow, arched gate and the gatehouse formed of blades of forged iron. Witchlights shone from the oculars of iron dragons that rose to either side of the formidable gate, their spread wings formed of hammered iron plates as sharp-edged as swords. Beyond the gatehouse rose a profusion of close-set towers like a thicket of polished spear-blades, pierced by slitted windows that glowed with sorcerous fire. Tendrils of vapour rose from behind the walls of the iron fortress, rising among the towers and reaching for the twin moons with claw-like fingers.

They had come at last to the Fortress of Iron, citadel of the undying Witch King.

Chapter Six
THE WITCH KING

A RATTLING BOOM reverberated from the iron gatehouse, startling Malus from his exhausted stupor, and the arched gate swung inward on ancient, dwarf-wrought hinges. The highborn felt a chill race down his spine as the black gate swung open and he stared into the blackness beyond. He feared to tread any deeper into the Witch King's domain, but he knew that he had to get at least a glimpse at the fortress grounds to allow the Idol of Kolkuth to get him inside. As the first of the riders nudged their dark steeds forward Malus reached back and loosened the flap on the bag where the idol was kept.

The passage through the gate was shorter than he expected, barely twelve feet from one end of the tunnel to the other. Beyond lay a small courtyard paved with flagstones of polished slate and bounded by statues of imposing druchii knights and rearing dragons. Above them loomed the sharp-edged towers of Malekith's citadel and the vassal lords of his warband, casting a deep shadow over the weary travellers. As Malus led Spite into the courtyard he felt the weight of a terrible gaze fall upon him; for a moment he felt like a rabbit

caught in the shadow of a swooping hawk, and cold, unrea-
soning terror seized his heart and turned his muscles to ice.
Even Spite felt it, causing the massive warbeast to sink onto its
haunches and snap its jaws at the empty air. Just as quickly as
it struck, the terrible pressure eased, and Malus caught the hint
of a sinuous shifting amid the thick shadows that lay across
the paving stones. He stole a glance upwards and caught a
faint hint of motion, as though a great serpent were coiling
about one of the citadel's tallest towers. Then he glimpsed the
outline of a long, narrow head silhouetted against the moonlight, and a pair of glowing red eyes that brooded over the dark
city with lordly disdain. A black dragon, Malus realised with a
shudder. His jaw gaped at the terrible sight.

Malus was so caught up with the sight of the fearsome beast
that he paid no heed whatsoever to the highborn that awaited
them in the middle of the courtyard until he spoke. 'Are you
certain you have the right man?' the highborn rasped in a powerful, commanding voice. 'He looks like a corpse.'

The highborn's tone snapped Malus out of his reverie. He
saw the Endless sliding from their saddles and watched the
masked warriors bow their heads respectfully to the druchii
lord, who returned the gesture with a disapproving scowl.
Exhaustion and spite emboldened Malus's tongue. 'Lord
Nuarc, I presume?'

'Did I give you leave to open your damned mouth, boy?'
Lord Nuarc snarled. He was a tall and powerfully built druchii,
clad in enamelled plate armour ornamented with gilt etchings
and potent runes of protection over a skirt of shining ithilmar
mail. His paired swords were masterworks, their pommels set
with rubies the size of sparrow's eggs and resting in scabbards
decorated with ruddy gold, and a cloak of glossy black drag-
onscale hung about his broad shoulders. Even without the
thick gold hadrilkar circling his neck it was clear that he was a
powerful noble and a member of the Witch King's personal
retinue. His sharp nose was scarred in two places by sword-
strokes, and a star-shaped dimple of scar tissue on the side of
his neck spoke of the spear thrust that had ravaged his voice.

The druchii's black eyes shone with keen wit and hinted at a will stronger than steel. His black hair, streaked with grey, was pulled back from his lean face and bound with a band of gold.

'He can be no other, my lord,' said one of the warriors, speaking in a voice eerily identical to the witch Malus had spoken with in their time on the road. 'We found him in the forest near Har Ganeth as you said. By his name the shades knew him.'

Malus leaned back and reached his hand beneath the flap of his saddlebag. The idol's icy surface burned against his fingertips. He tried to visualise a spot back along the road, someplace near woods and hills where he could lie low and plan his next move.

Nuarc looked Malus over again and shook his head. 'I wouldn't have believed it.' He looked the highborn in the eye. 'How did a shrivelled wretch like yourself kill Lurhan of Hag Graef?'

'With a sword. How else?' Malus sneered, his ire getting the better of him. If Nuarc was expecting excuses or snivelling pleas for mercy he was going to be disappointed. 'People have a habit of underestimating me, Lord Nuarc. I tend to make them regret it.'

Nuarc studied Malus for a moment, then nodded appraisingly. 'Brave but stupid,' he declared. 'I suspected as much.' He frowned at the highborn. 'Take your hand out of your bag, boy,' he snapped. 'We didn't bring you all this way to steal your trinkets.'

'No, you brought me here to hang me at the crossroads,' Malus shot back. 'Am I supposed to feel grateful that you won't steal my possessions until after I'm dead?'

'Dead?' Nuarc exclaimed. 'If the Witch King wanted you dead you and I would be having a very different kind of conversation right now.' His lip curled in disdain. 'For the moment, Malekith simply wishes to speak to you.'

Malus had to stop and replay Nuarc's words in his head. 'He wants to speak to me?' he echoed. His exhausted mind couldn't make sense of what he'd been told.

'I'm not in the habit of repeating myself, boy,' Nuarc growled. 'Now get out of that damned saddle. The Witch King knows you've arrived, but I won't send you to the Dragon Court looking like some flea-bitten autarii.'

Nuarc's iron-tinged rasp galvanised Malus's near-senseless body into motion. Before he was fully aware of it he was climbing down from Spite and standing uneasily on the slate paving stones. As if on cue, a pair of beastmasters with ornate kheitans and beast prods appeared from the shadows, ready to take charge of the sullen nauglir.

'Follow me,' the warlord commanded, and turned on his heel. Malus, his mind reeling from the sudden change in circumstances, quickly cinched up the saddlebag containing the relics and stumbled after Nuarc.

What was going on, he thought as he followed the warlord through an ironbound door into the citadel proper. Again, the words of his mother echoed in his mind. *Seek the amulet in the lightless halls of the Fortress of Iron.*

What did she know that he didn't?

NUARC LED HIM to a cold, austere apartment in one of the citadel's towers – it might have been the warlord's own keep, as far as Malus knew – where a trio of silent, efficient servants waited to make him presentable for an audience with the Witch King. They stripped away his battered armour and kheitan, as well as his stained and tattered robes, and laid out food and wine while they drew a steaming bath to wash away the dust of the road. He ate like a wolf while he waited for the hot water to be poured, eyeing the wine wistfully but leaving the bottle untouched. His wits were addled enough as it was.

While he waited a pair of masked warriors slipped silently into the apartment with his bags piled in their arms. Malus masked his fear with a curt nod and quickly checked them after they'd gone. For a wonder, nothing had been disturbed.

Perhaps I've fallen asleep in the saddle and this is all a bizarre dream, he thought. Nothing else makes much sense.

The servants scrubbed him industriously and said nothing about the fresh scars on either side of his torso where Urial's sword had run him through, nor did they show concern for the web work of black veins that ran from his right hand all the way across his shoulder and up the side of his neck. No doubt the servants were spying on behalf of someone – or several someones – but there was little Malus could do about that. Let them make their report. He doubted it could make his situation any more precarious than it already was.

The food and the hot water preyed upon him, making his eyelids droop. Malus splashed a bit of water on his face and tried to concentrate on the facts at hand. In retrospect, his treatment at the hands of the Endless now made a bit more sense. He hadn't been their prisoner at all, just a highborn who had been summoned to the Witch King's court with all dispatch.

And now this, Malus thought, his weary gaze sweeping around the apartment. He wasn't being treated like a guest, necessarily, but certainly as something more than an outlaw. So what could possibly account for that, the highborn thought?

The obvious answer was that Malekith wanted something from him. Something that couldn't be got using the end of a red-hot iron or a torturer's knives.

He waved the servants away and leaned back in the tub. He eyed his bags piled near the door. Was it the warpsword? He tugged thoughtfully at his lip. From all indications it appeared that Malekith had never received word of the uprising at Har Ganeth, so as far as he knew the blade still rested in the Sanctum of the Sword back at the temple. And even if he did know the truth, it wasn't as though the Witch King needed his permission to take it.

Or did he? Since he'd drawn the sword, did that mean no one else could claim until so long as he lived? Malus grinned ruefully. It wasn't as though that would be much of a problem for Malekith either.

What then did he possess that Malekith couldn't simply take from him? He went over everything Nuarc had said in the courtyard outside the citadel, looking for clues as to why he'd been summoned. All Nuarc had seemed to care about was Lurhan's death. The highborn's brows knitted in thought. Could that be it?

Other than his half-brother Isilvar, who now held their father's rank and properties, Malus was Lurhan's only male descendant. And while he was now an outlaw and stripped of any claim to Lurhan's legacy, Isilvar had secretly broken the Witch King's laws as well. Both Isilvar and their sister Nagaira had been members of the cult of Slaanesh; indeed, Malus strongly suspected that Isilvar had been the cult's Heirophant inside the city. After the cult had been exposed and most of its members killed, Malus suspected that Lurhan had discovered his son's involvement and covered it up.

Had Malekith found out? If so, there was no one left who could offer proof... except for him. Malus steepled his fingers beneath his chin. That was an intriguing possibility indeed.

The door to the apartment banged open and Nuarc swept inside like a storm wind, scattering cowed servants like leaves. 'This isn't some damned flesh house, boy,' the warlord growled disdainfully. 'Get dressed. The Witch King is waiting.'

Gritting his teeth, Malus rose from the tub and did as he was told. He heard Nuarc let out a surprised hiss as the warlord got a look at the daemon's handiwork, but the druchii lord asked no awkward questions.

The servants had laid out a fine set of black robes and a court kheitan of soft human hide. Hands plucked at his head; he rounded on the servants with a snarl, belatedly realising the servants were trying to comb his long, tangled hair. Frowning irritably, he let them finish their work and bind the hair back with leather and gold wire.

There was no armour to replace his old harness, and certainly no paired swords to wear at his hip. It was clear that Malekith's interest was entirely conditional. The new outfit he wore would look just as fitting hanging from an iron pole as it would at court. 'All right,' he said grimly, pulling on a pair of new boots. 'Lead on.'

On the way out the door, Malus spared one last look at his piled baggage. He tried to reassure himself that if Malekith wanted him dead the Witch King wouldn't have bothered to give him the opportunity to unpack.

MALUS FOLLOWED NUARC through a maze of dark, empty corridors, each one as silent as a tomb. Witchlamps set in iron sconces cast solitary pools of light along the way, making the darkness seem even deeper and more oppressive. Before long the silence began to prey upon Malus, setting his nerves on edge. There was none of the hectic bustle he was accustomed to at the citadel of Uthlan Tyr, drachau of Hag Graef. Though it was the centre of power for the entire kingdom, the Iron Fortress was cold and still, filled only with echoes.

At first he'd tried to memorise their route, but after a quarter of an hour's worth of twists and turns he gave it up as a lost cause. Like the city outside the fortress, there were no landmarks by which to navigate; only those who belonged there had any hope of finding their way. Malus couldn't imagine how long one had to wander these funereal halls before they gave up their secrets.

Lord Nuarc found his way effortlessly. Within half an hour they passed through an archway into a long, empty chamber lit by massive witchlamps suspended by chains along the arched ceiling. Here Malus began to notice the furtive movements of other druchii: masked Endless, nobles going about the business of state, temple bureaucrats and scarred, nervous servants, all gliding quietly through the shadows to and from the Witch King's court. All made way for the brisk, commanding stride of Lord Nuarc, who swept past them without so much as a nod.

One long chamber led to another. In most druchii cities a drachau's audience chamber was divided into two spaces: the throne room proper and the lower room, where lesser highborn and common folk waited in hopes of a brief audience with their overlord. Here Malus counted no less than four lower chambers, each one large enough to hold a thousand druchii or more. Each room was slightly more ornate than the first; bare walls of polished black marble gave way to statues of druchii princes clad in the raiment of lost Nagarythe, which in turn gave way to titanic columns of red-veined basalt and bas-reliefs of mighty battles between the druchii and their foes. The final lower room was dominated by a tremendous flame that rose in a hissing, seething pillar in the centre of the chamber. The shifting light picked out threads of silver and gold in ancient, enormous tapestries that told of Malekith's suffering in the fires of Asuryan and the Seven Treacheries of Aenarion.

At the far end of the fiery vault stood a pair of iron doors twenty feet high, engraved with the sinuous forms of rearing dragons. The twin drakes seemed to glare down at Nuarc and Malus as they approached the Witch King's throne room. Four of the Endless stood watch at the doors with bared blades in their hands. They bowed as Nuarc approached and gave way before their master. With a single backwards glance at Malus, the warlord placed his hands on the great doors and pushed. The massive iron panels swung open on perfectly balanced hinges, throwing a rectangle of shifting blue light across a floor of gleaming black marble.

Nuarc stepped into the chamber, head held high. As Malus crossed the threshold he felt Tz'arkan contract fiercely around his heart, his power drawing back from his limbs like a swiftly receding tide.

'Step carefully here, little druchii,' the daemon hissed. 'And remember that there are worse things than death.'

Beyond the doorway the Court of Dragons was all but devoid of light. The change brought Malus up short, leaving him near blind and intensely vulnerable in the space of a single step – an effect that of course could only be deliberate. As his vision adjusted to the gloom he saw that he was standing at one end of a surprisingly small octagonal room, barely thirty paces across. Again, after the lofty space of the previous chambers Malus couldn't help but feel the weight of the dressed stone walls pressing in on him. All around the perimeter of the room stood huge dragons carved cunningly from onyx, their wings spread like cloaks as they bowed in obeisance before the tall dais at the far end of the room. There, in shadows as deep as the eternal Abyss, glowed a pair of red-orange eyes that shone with the banked fire of a furnace.

The huge iron doors swung silently shut behind Malus, plunging the chamber into darkness. Malus felt the burning gaze of the Witch King upon him and bowed his head in genuine fear and dread.

Nuarc's voice rang out in the blackness. 'As your dread majesty commands, I have come with Malus the outlaw, formerly of the house of Lurhan the Vaulkhar, late of Hag Graef.'

The voice that replied sounded like nothing formed from a living throat – it was as hard and unyielding as hammered iron, the words rumbling out like the hot wind from a forge. '*I see you, kinslayer,*' the Witch King said. Malekith shifted slightly in the darkness, causing red light to seep from between the seams of his enchanted armour. '*Did you think to escape my wrath, Malus Darkblade? Your father was sworn to my service, and lived and died by my command alone. There can be no forgiveness for such a crime.*'

Silence fell. Malus blinked owlishly as he considered the Witch King's words. Was this some kind of test? He shrugged, wondering if Malekith could see the gesture. 'As you wish,' he replied.

There was the sound of steel rasping against steel, and more ruddy light outlined the segments of the Witch King's form. '*Will you not beg for mercy, kinslayer? Will you not bow down before my throne and treat with me, offering all that you possess if only I would stay my wrath?*'

The suggestion took Malus aback. 'Am I to believe that you would be moved by such a pathetic display? Do I seem so foolish as that?' he said, his tone indignant. 'I think not. You are the Witch King. Who am I to persuade you of anything? If you mean to exact your vengeance upon me, then so be it.'

'*Kneel, then, and show your fealty to me.*'

Malus gave the Witch King a bitter smile. Part of his mind gibbered in terror at his effrontery, but he'd suffered enough humiliation at the hands of Tz'arkan to last a dozen lifetimes. 'Only a vassal bows his knee,' the highborn said. 'But I am a vassal no longer. I am an outlaw now, by your own decree.' He squared his shoulders, drunk on suicidal defiance. 'So I believe I would rather stand.'

The red eyes narrowed, and Malus knew he'd gone a step too far. He drew a deep breath, believing it to be his last – when suddenly a woman's laughter, rich and cruel, rang from the darkness beside the throne.

Pale green light flickered to life across the throne room, kindled in the depths of witchlamps set in iron stands arrayed around the chamber. Again, Malus was momentarily disoriented, his defiance forgotten. Through slitted eyes he dimly perceived a tall, black throne at the top of the dais, and upon that seat of barbed iron he glimpsed the terrible visage of Malekith himself.

But it was the laughter that drew the highborn's eye. A woman was gracefully descending from the dais, clad in black robes as befitted a druchii witch or seer. She was tall and regal, with features that seemed cruel even in the depths of her mirth. White hair fell past her waist, wound with gold wire and delicate finger bones. Her dark eyes flashed with a cold, draconic intellect, her stare cutting through him as cleanly as an obsidian knife.

'Tell me,' she said, her voice belling out in the same cold tones as the witches of the Endless, 'do you come by such reckless courage naturally, or does it come from the daemon curled around your heart?'

Chapter Seven
THE EMISSARY

THE WITCH KING leaned forward upon his barbed throne. Visible heat radiated from the seams of his armour, blurring the air around him. '*Daemon?*' Malekith hissed, his burning eyes narrowing further. Behind Malus, just a few steps from his left shoulder, he heard the cold rasp of steel sliding from its scabbard.

Malus felt sharp talons sink into his heart. It might have been a warning from the daemon or it might have been a sudden rush of fear. Regardless, he took a few moments to master his composure before he answered the seer's question.

'My recklessness is the very reason there is a daemon inside me, Lady Morathi,' he said. He kept his gaze focused straight ahead, fearful of what else the seer might unearth from the depths of his eyes.

Morathi glided past him, circling him slowly. He could feel her icy gaze sweep over him, reminding him of the passing stare of the dragon in the courtyard outside. 'You are no sorcerer,' she declared, 'despite your parentage and the rumours of forbidden practices performed by your siblings.'

'It is a curse, dread lady,' Malus said quickly. 'The daemon entrapped me while I was on an expedition into the Chaos Wastes.'

'Entrapped? To what purpose?' the seer asked, as lightly as if she were inquiring of the weather. Her cold, unnatural voice was sweet, but like any polished tone it was brittle. If it broke, Malus dreaded to hear what lay beneath.

'It is entrapped in turn, dread lady, inside a crystal far to the north. I have been given a year to perform certain tasks to gain its freedom, or else my soul is forfeit.'

'Did one of those tasks involve killing your father?' Nuarc growled.

Malus glanced over his shoulder at the warlord, glad for any excuse to look away from the throne. 'Not directly, no,' the high-born said. 'Lurhan simply got in my way.'

'*The daemon forced you to do this?*' Malekith inquired.

Malus couldn't help but frown. Where was all this leading? 'Forced? Certainly not, dread majesty. I am master of my own fate. But the circumstances were... complicated.' The highborn tried to think of a way to explain things, but gave up with a shrug. 'Let us just say it wasn't my choice. I did what I had to do.'

Lady Morathi appeared on Malus's left side, still studying him intently. They were close enough to touch and the force of her presence was tangible, like a cold razor being drawn delicately across his skin. She radiated power in a way that not even his mother Eldire did. Her face was youthful, her features regal and severe; she was handsome rather than classically beautiful, with a broad face and a rounded chin that was almost square rather than pointed. Her eyes were like windows onto the Abyss, drinking in everything around her. 'Does this daemon have a name?' she asked, her lips quirking in wry amusement.

She knows more than she's letting on, Malus thought. She's testing me, seeing how much I know. Again, he affected a shrug. 'If it does, it hasn't shared it with me,' he said. 'Why would it? Wouldn't that give me power to control it?'

'Daemons go by many names,' Morathi said. 'But only one true name, which they hide as best they can.' She stepped forward, pinning him with her gaze. 'What does this daemon call itself when it speaks to you?'

'Itself? Why, nothing,' Malus replied sourly, 'although it has more than a few choice names for *me*.'

Malus heard a harsh bark of laughter from Lord Nuarc. Morathi stared at him for a moment more, a faint smile quirking the corners of her mouth. 'I have little trouble believing that,' she said, then turned back to the dais. 'It explains much,' she said to the Witch King as she climbed the stairs to take her place beside the iron throne.

The highborn shook his head in consternation. 'From my perspective it explains nothing, dread majesty. Why have I been brought here, if not to answer for my crimes?'

A rumbling hiss escaped from Malekith's horned helmet. *'Oh, you shall answer for what you have done, Darkblade,'* the Witch King said. *'But the payment shall be of mine own choosing.'* Malekith stretched an upturned hand to the ceiling. *'Observe.'*

There was a ponderous groan of machinery overhead. Malus glanced upwards and saw a dark, circular opening in the centre of the domed ceiling. With a thunderous rattle of heavy iron links a spherical shape descended from the opening. First the witchlight picked out curved bars of polished iron, formed into a cage or basket large enough to hold a grown druchii. At first Malus thought the cage was meant for him, but as it sank closer he saw the greenish light reflecting on a huge, uncut crystal held within the iron frame. Suddenly the highborn realised what it was. 'The Ainur Tel,' he hissed.

Malekith nodded slowly. *'The Eye of Fate,'* he said. *'One of the few relics of power brought with us out of Nagarythe millennia ago, carved from the root of the world in aeons past.'*

The great crystal was lowered on four massive chains, sinking into the room until it hung directly before Malus's eyes. With a clash of gears the chains locked in place, and a mote of faint, white light began to glow within the crystal's depths. Slowly the light began to pulse, like the beat of a tremendous heart. The glow intensified with each beat, growing in strength until the huge crystal shone like a pale sun. Malus could feel its energies washing over his skin in turgid waves, setting his nerves on fire. It was all he could do not to recoil from the legendary relic. Only by a supreme effort of will did he manage to still his shaking limbs and look unflinchingly into the light.

Morathi's voice called out to him from the dais. 'Stare into the eye, son of Lurhan,' she said. 'Cast your gaze a hundred leagues to the north.'

Frowning, Malus stared fixedly into the white glare. At first he saw nothing. His eyes grew weak and his lids fluttered – then all at once the harsh light faded and Malus saw blurry images take shape within the crystal. He saw a single, blackened watchtower rising above a bleak and desolate plain. The walls of the keep were blasted and broken and the single gate had been smashed aside, buried beneath a mound of twisted, misshapen bodies. Moonlight shone on the armoured bodies of druchii warriors in the tower's courtyard, and Malus imagined many more in the burnt-out shell of the citadel itself. Hundreds of horned beastmen and savage, tattooed marauders lay among the fallen defenders, struck down by crossbow bolts or pierced by axe or sword. It was clear to him that the watchtower had been taken by storm, its warriors overwhelmed in a single, savage assault.

Within moments the vision blurred and reformed again. The image showed another watchtower, this one standing atop a rocky hill above a swift-flowing river. Again, the walls of the keep were blackened by fire, and the fortifications were gouged and torn as though clawed by monstrous hands. Armoured corpses were splayed across the battlements, and Malus could see a knot of charred corpses where the last of the citadel's defenders made their final stand at the foot of their burning tower.

The image shifted again. Malus was shown another ruined watchtower. His bemused frown deepened into a look of genuine alarm. He glanced worriedly at Morathi – and by the time he looked back at the glowing crystal it was showing yet another border keep that had been put to the torch. This one had been attacked within only a couple of days; tendrils of smoke still rose from the fires smouldering in the wreckage of the tower. Malus's eyes widened as he saw the rubble of the watchtower gate, crushed beneath the weight of a giant whose naked body had been riddled by the tower's powerful bolt throwers.

'What is the meaning of this?' Malus exclaimed. Raiding parties of Chaos-tainted savages riding out of the Wastes was an ever-present threat, which was why there was a line of watchtower keeps along the northern frontier. But raiders went out of their way to avoid the towers as much as possible rather than spend their strength against them. 'I've never heard of a border keep being overrun, much less *four* of them,' he said. A sudden thought sent a thrill down his spine. 'Is this an invasion?'

The Witch King pointed at the relic. *'Behold.'*

This time when the vision cleared Malus saw a sky full of fire. A dark tower stood against the backdrop of a burning forest, and beneath that roiling, flame-shot sky raged a horde of howling monstrosities that crashed in a frenzied wave against the watchtower's battered walls. Spear tips glinted atop the battlements and axes flashed as the beleaguered defenders hacked at scaling-ropes or fended off ladders thrown up by maddened beastmen and furious, blood-soaked barbarians. Crossbow bolts flickered in a black rain from the tall watchtower, wreaking havoc among the ranks of the enemy, but for every attacker that fell it seemed that three more rushed to take its place.

Huge shapes waded through the raging horde: hunched, misshapen trolls and terrible giants dragging clubs made from gnarled tree trunks. As Malus watched, twin streaks of light sped from the top of the watchtower and struck one of the giants squarely in its muscular chest. In an instant the huge creature was wreathed in unnatural green flame – the terrible, liquid dragon's fire both prized and feared by druchii alchemists and corsairs alike. The giant reeled in agony, beating clumsily at the hungry flames consuming its body and throwing off gobbets of sizzling, burning flesh that fell upon the Chaos marauders swirling about its huge feet. Malus imagined the furious cheer that no doubt rose from the battlements as the giant staggered, its face melting and its mouth open in a roar of mortal agony as it toppled onto a herd of onrushing beastmen with an earth-shaking crash.

But the assault did not falter. Other giants lumbered to the watchtower gate and began to batter it with their clubs, seemingly heedless of the stinging bolts that prickled their thick hides. Sorcerous lightning rent the burning sky and flocks of hideous, winged daemons swooped over the battlements, plucking spearmen from the ramparts and dropping them to the stones fifty feet below. Packs of snarling trolls reached the base of the walls and began to climb atop one another to reach the defenders, their beady black eyes glinting hungrily.

Another bolt of dragon's fire arced from the watchtower, striking one of the giants at the gate and setting it alight. The monster dropped its club and stampeded back through the oncoming horde, sowing carnage with every step, but the damage had already been done. Pulverised stone and shattered fittings spun through the air as the remaining giant smote the gate with its club and smashed it to the ground in a cloud of dust and debris. Into the breach swept the tide of savage marauders, and Malus snarled with impotent rage as he saw that the keep was doomed.

'Bhelgaur Keep has fallen,' Morathi declared, and the vision within the crystal faded to darkness.

Malus's mind raced as he tried to make sense of what he'd seen. 'I'm not familiar with Bhelgaur or any of the other keeps you showed me, but if they neighbour one another then that horde has torn a hole in our frontier defences more than *sixty leagues* across,' he said darkly. 'There must be tens of thousands of them.' He shook his head in terrible wonder. 'Such a thing isn't unheard of in the so-called Old World of the humans, but here? It's unimaginable.' The highborn turned to the Witch King, his former defiance and suspicion momentarily overcome by the glamour of war. 'What more do we know of these invaders, dread majesty?'

But it was not the Witch King who replied. 'Their scouts crossed the frontier almost a month ago,' Nuarc said tersely. 'Then came a flood of raiding parties, perhaps twelve or eighteen in number. Four of the watchtowers were struck within days of one another and their defenders put to the sword. Then the raiding parties came together into a single warband and marched on Bhelgaur Keep, the western anchor of our border defences.'

'That puts them within a few days' march of the Tower of Ghrond,' Malus exclaimed. If they made it past the Black Tower then the Chaos host would be at the northern end of the Spear Road and less than two weeks' march from the walls of Naggarond itself.

It was a full-scale invasion the likes of which Naggaroth had never seen before, the highborn realised at once. And it had struck the Land of Chill at the worst possible time, with the campaign season still underway and at least two-thirds of the nobility at sea or away from home. Now Malus understood why the Witch King hadn't marched on Har Ganeth when he'd learned of the uprising. What was more, he knew all too well how badly weakened the armies of the druchii were after the fighting in the City of Executioners and the brief but savage feud between the Black Ark and Hag Graef.

'But why now?' Malus said. 'Other than small raids the tribes of the Wastes have never warred against us. Who is leading this horde, and what does he want?'

Morathi eyed the highborn coldly. 'What, indeed?' she said.

At some unspoken command the doors to the throne room swung open, and Malus heard limping, shuffling footsteps slide across the polished floor. He turned – and his pale face twisted into a grimace of revulsion at the horrid figure lurching towards him.

The highborn's pallid skin was greenish-grey in the witch-light, darkening to a purple-black around the deep wounds in his forehead and neck. His armour had been savaged by blows from axe, sword and talon, scoring deep lines across his breast-plate and tearing his right pauldron completely away. The noble's mail skirt was rent in a half-dozen places, and the robes beneath were stiff with rotting blood. Half of his left hand had been shorn away by a heavy blade, and his right arm ended in a chewed stump just above the elbow. Malus reckoned by the stench that the highborn had been dead for almost a fortnight.

Every inch of the noble's battered armour was covered with intricate runes, apparently inscribed with the druchii's own blood. His eyes were a ghostly white – no pupil or iris could be seen, and they glowed with sorcerous life under the gleam of the witchlights. The corpse, escorted by a pair of masked warriors, shambled towards Malus, apparently heedless of his presence. Hissing in disgust, the highborn backed away – and the revenant stopped, his head turning at the sound. Blind white eyes searched for Malus. The corpse's slack lips twitched as it tried to form words.

Malus's hand went to his hip, reaching instinctively for a blade that was no longer there. He glanced over his shoulder at Nuarc, who glared balefully at the animated corpse. 'What in the name of the Dark Mother is this?' he cried.

'This,' Nuarc growled, 'is Lord Suharc. His watchtower, near as we can tell, was one of the first to fall. Eight days ago a patrol found him stumbling along the Spear Road, and they followed him all the way to the gates of Naggarond itself.' The warlord's hand tightened on the hilt of his drawn sword. 'He came bearing a message from the master of the Chaos horde.'

Before Nuarc could speak further Morathi's voice rang across the hall. 'We have done as you wished, revenant,' she said. 'Malus of Hag Graef has been found and stands before you. Now deliver your message.'

The seer's command left Malus dumbstruck. But the revenant was galvanised by the news. With a sudden burst of energy the corpse stumbled towards him, reaching for the highborn's face with what remained of his ruined hand. Malus recoiled from the creature with a startled cry – only to fetch up against Nuarc, who grabbed the highborn by the back of the neck and shoved him rudely at the oncoming creature.

Cold, stinking flesh closed about Malus's face. He felt the splintered bones of the highborn's hand dig into his cheek as the revenant clumsily studied the shape of his features. With a savage cry the highborn wrenched free of Nuarc's grip and shoved the corpse away. It staggered backwards a few steps but did not fall, turning instead to face the iron throne. Air whistled through the pulped gristle of the revenant's throat as it filled its shrivelled lungs. When the corpse spoke its voice was a bubbling, croaking hiss, and Malus reeled in terror at the hideous sound. Bad enough that the words issued from the throat of a man long dead – worse still was the awful realisation that the voice was one he knew all too well.

'You hold your salvation in your hands, Witch King,' Nagaira said, speaking through the revenant's ruined throat. 'Even now your watchtowers lie in ruins, and my army marches on the Black Tower of Ghrond. The power of the Black Ark is broken, and Hag Graef has been dealt a crippling blow. Your kingdom lies upon the brink of ruin – unless you give this outlaw to me.' The revenant raised its mangled hand and pointed to Malus. 'Deliver my brother, and the war ends in a single stroke. Otherwise the Tower of Ghrond will burn, and Naggarond will follow. Make your choice, Witch King. Naggaroth will burn until you do.'

A rumbling hiss echoed from Malekith's sealed helm. '*I have heard enough.*'

There was a rustle of movement and a flash of steel. The Endless drew and struck the emissary at the same moment, their swords slicing the revenant apart. As the head and the severed limbs struck the floor they burst into hissing flame, filling the chamber with a searing stench.

Malus swayed on his feet, still thunderstruck at all that had transpired. His half-sister had worshipped Slaanesh in secret for many years, but after he'd betrayed her to the Temple of Khaine months before she had escaped and sworn revenge on him. She had made obscene pacts with the Ruinous Powers that had granted her daemonic powers, but now this...

'Now the matter is clear,' Morathi said, fixing Malus with an appraising stare. 'It is not you she wants, son of Lurhan. She is after the daemon inside you. No doubt she believes that she can bend it to her will.'

With supreme effort the highborn got hold of himself. 'No doubt you are right, dread lady,' he said shakily. And who knows, he thought fearfully. Perhaps Nagaira can.

But that mattered little to Malus just then. His eyes darted about the throne room, taking in the position of the Endless and trying to gauge where Nuarc was standing. He had to escape, and quickly. Could he reach the warlord and take the druchii's sword? Could he call upon the daemon's strength to fight his way free? If he could somehow reach Spite he might have a chance…

Malus heard footsteps close behind him, crossing slowly from right to left. 'The Endless can be ready to ride within the hour,' Nuarc said, sounding near enough to be speaking in the highborn's ear. 'Now that we know where the Chaos horde is, we can give this witch what she wants and see them on their way.'

The highborn whirled, reaching for the warlord – only to find Nuarc's sword point less than a finger's width from his throat. Nuarc chuckled cruelly, shaking his head. 'Not so fast, boy,' he said. 'The witch didn't say anything about you getting to her in one piece, so if you want to keep your hands and feet you'll hold as still as a statue.'

Malus glared hatefully at Nuarc, but his reply was directed at Malekith instead. 'You cannot give her what she wants,' he snapped. 'It won't turn aside the horde. Nagaira will simply use me and the daemon to further her own plans of conquest.' He turned slowly to face the throne. 'She means to supplant you, dread majesty. Why else would she have raised so large an army?' How she'd managed to raise such a horde was another question altogether, the highborn thought.

The seer pursed her thin lips thoughtfully. 'Unless we could master the daemon ourselves,' she murmured. 'We could command it to slay the witch, then give Malus to her.'

'You can't control the daemon without its name,' Malus said quickly, trying to keep the desperation from his voice.

Nuarc stepped forward and seized a handful of Malus's hair. 'Then I say we send the witch his head and show her that the daemon will forever be out of her reach!'

'*Enough!*' Malekith roared, his armour flaring like an open furnace. '*No one makes demands of the druchii,*' he rumbled, leaning forward on his barbed throne. His red gaze burned against Malus's skin. '*She will get nothing from us but wrack and ruin.*' He stretched out an armoured hand and pointed imperiously at the highborn. '*You will see to this. When you slew the great Lurhan you deprived me of my rightful property. Now you belong to me instead.* '

Malus tried to tug his hair free, but Nuarc held him fast. 'I live to serve, dread majesty,' he growled through clenched teeth. 'What is your command?'

'*Go to the Black Tower of Ghrond,*' the Witch King said. '*Lord Kuall is the Vaulkhar there. It is he who failed to turn aside the Chaos horde, and you will express to him my displeasure.*' Malekith's armoured gauntlet clenched into a fist. '*Your exploits against Hag Graef are well known, son of Lurhan. Take command of the forces at Ghrond and lead them against the invaders until I arrive with the army of Naggaroth. You will hold them at the Black Tower until I arrive. Do you understand?*'

The highborn took a deep breath. He understood all too well. 'Your will be done, dread majesty,' he said without hesitation. 'I will serve you with all the vigour I possess.' As he considered the situation, his predatory mind saw a possible opportunity. 'There is one matter to consider, however,' he said carefully. 'The people of Naggaroth still consider me an outcast and a criminal. That will make it difficult to speak with any authority.'

Malekith glared implacably at the highborn. '*You are a member of my retinue now, Darkblade,*' he hissed. '*You will ride to Ghrond with the Endless and bear a writ signed with my name.*'

For the first time, Malus essayed a smile. 'Then I may reclaim my rights and status as a highborn?'

The Witch King paused, considering Malus carefully. '*In time, perhaps. Serve me well and you will be rewarded in kind.*'

'Yes. Of course, dread majesty,' Malus said, bowing deeply. 'Then, with your permission, I will return to my chambers and prepare to depart.' The sooner he got away from the iron fortress the better, he thought.

The Witch King dismissed Malus with a wave of his gauntleted hand. The highborn turned on his heel and strode swiftly for the chamber doors, giving Nuarc a defiant glare as he swept past. Already his mind was racing, contemplating all that he had to do when he reached the Black Tower.

For a short while at least, he would command an army again. He never dreamed such a day would come again. *And I have you to thank, dear sister,* the highborn thought with a feral grin.

As he reached the iron doors Morathi called after him. 'The daemon has sunk its roots deep into your flesh,' she said. 'What do you think is going to happen once you set it free?'

The highborn laid his hand on the iron panel. 'If I serve the daemon well it promises to reward me in kind,' he said, and then was gone.

Chapter Eight
THE BLACK TOWER

THE PAIN BUILT steadily as Malus stalked down the echoing corridors of the Witch King's palace, pressing against the backs of his eyes like steam swelling in a kettle. Blood pounded in his temples like a funeral drum, reverberating across his narrow skull until he swore he could feel it in his teeth. The highborn's thin lips pulled back in a feral grimace of pain, drawing uneasy glances from the nobles and state servants who stepped hurriedly out of his path as he swept by.

His limbs worked mechanically as his exhausted mind struggled to come to grips with his latest change of fortune. How had Nagaira managed to take command of an army? It had only been three months since he'd faced her in the tunnels beneath Hag Graef, when she'd attempted to destroy the city in an act of bloodthirsty vengeance. He had given her a terrible wound with the Dagger of Torxus, a magical weapon that severed the tie between body and spirit and pinned the soul to the spot where it was slain, to suffer as a tormented spirit for all time. Yet his half-sister had not died; like Malus, she had no soul for the dagger to steal. She had entered into a blasphemous pact with the Chaos Gods, receiving unimaginable powers in exchange for her service. Perhaps she had used her new-found might to subjugate some of the northern tribes, or perhaps they had been given to her as part of her arcane pact. The Ruinous Powers were free with their gifts, he'd learned bitterly, so long as their own interests were fulfilled as well.

And yet the sheer scope of Nagaira's actions staggered Malus. What were her true motives? It had to be more than mere revenge, surely. Was it Tz'arkan she was after, as Morathi believed? Could the daemon alone be worth so much effort? Malus felt a chill course down his spine as he considered the possibility. No less than five Chaos champions, mighty war-lords and sorcerers all, had combined their fearsome powers to summoning and entrapping the daemon in the temple far in the north. As potent as they were, the champions knew that the daemon would make them more powerful still, and as far as the highborn had been able to determine, Tz'arkan had done just that. For a time the champions had bestrode the earth like gods themselves, causing the world to tremble beneath their feet.

Nagaira would know the tales far better than he, Malus knew. His cold hands clenched into fists as he stalked the twisting corridors. She would understand the awesome poten-tial of the being lurking beneath his skin, and would know how to bend it to her will.

Once I'm in her clutches she'll bargain with the daemon through me, Malus realised. His expression turned bleak. She might even let the daemon take my soul as a token of good will, then use the five relics to bargain with Tz'arkan for even more power. She would have her revenge upon him and grow vastly more potent in the bargain – the very sweetest sort of revenge, as far as he was concerned. And then? Who knew? Perhaps she would march on Naggarond anyway, coming to grips with Malekith himself. With Tz'arkan bound to her, Nagaira might just overthrow the Witch King and claim the Land of Chill as her own.

The pain continued to worsen as he left the Court of Dragons behind. The pressure behind his eyes sharpened into needle-like points that pricked out white pinholes of light at the corners of his eyes. After ten minutes it hurt just to breathe. The air seemed to rasp like a file over his lips and teeth. He staggered, throwing out a hand to steady himself against the bare stone walls as he forced his legs to carry him onward.

He reached the door to his chambers without realising it, fetching up against the oaken panels and fumbling for the iron ring in a blind haze of pain. How he'd found his way back from the court through the maze-like passageways of the fortress was a mystery that he hadn't the wherewithal to consider. The door banged open and he staggered into the brightly lit room, startling a trio of slaves who were busy laying out new clothes and arranging a set of polished plate armour on an arming stand at the foot of the bed. His stolen axe had been cleaned and sharpened, and lay gleaming on a tabletop nearby.

'Out, all of you,' Malus snarled, waving angrily at the blurry shapes that bowed uncertainly on the other side of the room. He staggered to the table and closed his hands on the hilt of the axe. 'I said *out!*' he roared, brandishing the terrible weapon, and the slaves fled from the room in a silent rush, their hands thrown protectively over their heads. As the door thudded shut he let the axe tumble from his hands and lurched to the bed, burying his face in the sheets with a bestial groan.

And then he heard the voice, hissing in his ears like a serpent. *You disappoint me little druchii*, the daemon whispered hatefully, and then he felt the nest of vipers coiled about his heart suddenly contract.

The pain was like nothing he had ever felt before. All the air went out of him; Malus gasped like a landed fish, his eyes wide and his hands clawing futilely at his armoured chest. The highborn slumped to the floor, rolling onto his side in a clatter of steel as he struggled for breath.

'What foolishness is this, bending the knee to that parody of a king and playing at war when you and I have unfinished business,' Tz'arkan continued. 'Have you grown too accustomed to my presence these last few months? Did you forget the bargain you and I made? I assure you, Darkblade, that I have not.'

There was a roaring in his ears, and his vision was turning red, like a tide of blood rising from the edges of his vision. Trembling with effort, Malus drew in a thin gulp of air. 'The relic...' he gasped. 'My... mother...'

The grip on his heart drew sharply tighter; for half an instant Malus was certain that it would burst. All he could see was red; with a faint groan the highborn squeezed his eyes shut.

'What does that witch have to do with this?' the daemon growled. Malus could feel the cold touch of Tz'arkan's anger in his bones. 'Is this another of her pathetic schemes?'

'She said... she said the path to the relic lies here,' the highborn moaned. 'Perhaps... it's... in the Black Tower...'

'Perhaps?' The daemon seethed. 'You would hang your very soul from so slim a thread?'

'For now it's... all I have,' Malus gasped. There was a roaring in his ears, growing stronger by the moment. Darkness beckoned, and he sensed he lay closer to death than he'd ever been before. 'Whatever she plans... I'm a part of it,' he whispered. 'So... she would not lead me... astray. Not yet at least.'

The daemon didn't reply. For a single, agonising instant, Malus felt Tz'arkan's grip continue to tighten – and then without warning it was simply gone. He sucked in air like a drowning man, rolling onto his stomach and biting his lip to keep from crying out. The daemon coiled and slithered within his chest, sliding black tendrils up the back of his neck and across his skull.

'Pray that you are right, little druchii,' Tz'arkan said. 'Whatever her motives, she is not the one you should be wary of. I grow stronger with every beat of your miserable heart. Soon I'll be able to hurt you in ways you can't even imagine. And I will be watching every move you make, Darkblade. Step carefully.'

He could feel the daemon's presence dwindle. The pressure in his head began to fade. It was several minutes before he could push himself upright and blink owlishly in the glow of the pale witchlights. Every muscle in his body ached. With a groan he slowly rose onto his knees. Heavy drops spattered on the stone beneath his head, and he realised that his upper lip was damp. Malus touched it with trembling fingertips, and they came away stained with a cold, black ichor.

There was a looking glass over by the now-empty bathtub. Malus staggered over to it, peering intently into the silvered pane. The face looking back at him was one he only barely recognised. His face was even more drawn and haggard than he remembered, the grey skin pulled tight over corded muscle and fine, white scars to create a fevered mask of cruelty and hate. Streams of ichor ran from his sharp nose, his pointed ears and the corners of his eyes.

His eyes! Malus realised with a start that they were no longer the colour of heated brass – instead the irises were orbs of polished jet, so large that almost no whites were visible. When had Tz'arkan's disguise faded? The thought that the daemon could now alter or change his body at its whim frightened Malus to the core.

Behind him, he heard the chamber door creak open. Hurriedly, Malus snatched up a damp cloth hanging from the edge of the bathtub and pressed it to his face. 'Take another step and I'll split your skull,' he snarled at the intruder.

'You're welcome to try,' came Nuarc's familiar rasp. 'But daemon or no, I think you'd regret it.'

The highborn masked his surprise by scrubbing fiercely at his cheeks. 'Your pardon, my lord,' he said. 'I thought you were one of those damned servants.' After checking to make sure he'd cleaned away the last of the ichor he quickly wadded up the stained cloth and tossed it into the tub. He turned to face the general, gesturing tiredly at the clothes and armour laid at the bed. 'Give me a moment to change and I can leave the fortress at once.'

Nuarc gave Malus a penetrating stare, his expression doubtful. 'You don't look fit to pull off your boots, let alone manage another forced march,' he growled, but then grudgingly nodded. 'Not that I expect you'd let such a thing stop you. You're a hard-hearted, spiteful bastard, right enough.' The warlord pulled a metal plaque from his belt and walked over to the highborn. 'Here is the Witch King's writ,' he said, offering it to Malus as casually as though he were sharing a bottle of wine. 'I'd caution you to use it wisely, but what's the point? With that piece of paper in your hand you can do damn well whatever you please and no one will look sideways at you.'

Malus took the plaque from Nuarc's hand. It was very like the Writ of Iron he'd once been granted by the drachau of Hag Graef. This one was a bit longer, perhaps eighteen inches long, and the protective metal was unpolished silver instead of steel. He opened the hinged plaque and studied the parchment within.

He had expected a lengthy statement detailing his rights and privileges in exacting detail. Instead there were just two simple sentences. *The bearer of this writ, Malus of Hag Graef, belongs to me and acts solely in my name. Do as he bids, or risk my wrath.*

Below the archaic line of druchast was pressed the dragon seal of Malekith, Witch King of Naggaroth.

Malus closed the plaque carefully, savouring the feel of the cool metal on his fingertips. This is what absolute power feels like, he thought. With that writ in hand there was very little he could not do within the borders of the kingdom. Only the highest nobles in the land were immune from his authority, and he answered to no one but the Witch King himself. A slow, hungry smile spread across his face.

'It's a trap of course,' the warlord said, reading the look in Malus's black eyes. 'You realise that I'm sure.'

The highborn paused, his smile fading. 'A trap?' he replied, setting the plaque carefully upon the bed.

Now it was Nuarc's turn to smile. 'Of course it is. Consider the situation,' he said, pacing slowly around the room. 'This sister of yours has attacked the kingdom at a time when we are at our most vulnerable. She knows this – her remarks about Hag Graef and the Black Ark tells us that she is well aware of how weakened we are. The only way to stop her is to keep her occupied long enough for Malekith to scour the cities for every warrior he can lay hands on and form a large enough army to match her.' The general pointed a long finger at Malus. 'And you are the one thing guaranteed to hold Nagaira's attention.'

Malus thought it over. 'If so, why not simply send me to the Black Tower in chains? Nagaira would still tear the city apart trying to get at me, writ or no writ.'

Nuarc gave Malus a sidelong glance. 'Put a druchii in chains and he'll look for the first chance to escape. Put a druchii in power and he'll fight like a daemon to stay there, regardless of the risk.' He crossed the chamber and picked up the writ. 'This piece of parchment is stronger than any chain ever forged,' he rasped. 'You may think yourself clever, but Malekith can see right through you. You are just another pawn to him. He'll use you as a stalking horse to draw Nagaira to the Black Tower, then once she has been beaten back you'll be nothing but an outlaw once more.'

Malus reached up and took the plaque from Nuarc's hand. 'Then why tell me all this? Aren't you betraying your master's secret designs?'

The warlord let out a harsh, rasping laugh. 'Better for the Witch King that you understand the position you are in, and to know that there is nothing you can do to change it! I've heard reports about your generalship in the latest fighting between the Black Ark and Hag Graef; you did passably well against Isilvar's forces. You're young and headstrong, but you've got a sharp mind underneath all that foolishness. What's more, you can be damned unpredictable, and that's the reason I'm here,' he said. 'I want you to understand how tightly Malekith has boxed you in. Don't try anything stupid; it won't work, and it will likely leave us in an even less tenable position than we're in now. The best chance you have of keeping your head on your neck is to follow orders and enjoy the power you've got while you've got it.'

'Until the danger is past,' Malus said coldly. 'And then you'll tie me to a pole at the crossroads.'

Nuarc met the highborn's gaze unflinchingly. 'Would you rather face your sister's tender mercies instead?'

Malus sighed. 'You've made your point, my lord,' he said, tossing the plaque back onto the mattress. He began working at the lacings of his armour. 'I should be ready to ride within the hour.'

'Very good,' the general said with a curt nod, then turned to leave the room. 'I'll send the servants back in to help you change and bring in a good meal. It'll likely be the only one you'll get for the next few days.'

Nuarc stepped into the corridor outside Malus's chamber, barking orders for the servants. Malus jerked the lacings of his breastplate free with sharp, angry movements, glaring balefully at the Witch King's writ as he worked.

THE DARK STEEDS of the Endless swept over the wooded ridge and thundered down the reverse slope, their lathered flanks heaving and their glossy hooves beating upon the packed cinders of the Spear Road as they came at last to the Plain of Ghrond. A light snow was falling, stirred into stinging gusts by a cold north wind that whispered among the dark pines.

At the top of the ridgeline Malus reined in Spite and surveyed the broad plain, baring his teeth at the biting wind. His cheeks and nose were already chapped from the cold, but the pain kept him awake and alert better than any dose of barvalk could. His exhausted, aching body reeled in the saddle; Nuarc had commanded the Endless to bear him to the Black Tower with all dispatch, and their pace had made the trip down the Slaver's Road seem leisurely by comparison. They stopped only once every few days for a cold meal and a ration of the dwarf liquor, and what little sleep the highborn got was on the move. Malus could no longer say for certain what day it was, but to the best of his reckoning they'd covered the week and a half ride to the Black Tower in just four days. Even the dark steeds seemed to be at the limits of their endurance, something the highborn hadn't thought possible.

Below him the lead riders of the Endless stirred up a cloud of pale grey dust as they galloped along the black ribbon of road that crossed the desolate plain. The ashen expanse stretched to east and west as far as the eye could see, while the horizon to the north was edged with a broken, iron-grey line of mountains that marked the edge of the Chaos Wastes. Perhaps a league to the north, rising out of the pale ash like a sentinel's black spear, rose the Tower of Ghrond.

Each of Naggaroth's six great cities served a purpose for the druchii as a whole: Karond Kar built the sleek black ships that corsair captains used on their slave raids, while Klar Karond was the clearing-house for the flesh trade that the corsairs supplied. Similarly, Har Ganeth forged the weapons and armour that armed the warriors of the state, while the Black Tower could be said to be the forge that made the warriors themselves. Every unit of troops raised across the Land of Chill was sent to the Black Tower to be trained in the arts of war. Units of spearmen and cavalry took their turn manning the watchtowers along the northern frontier and blooded themselves on cross-border raids into the Wastes, led by sons of prominent highborn families who were there to learn the rudiments of command. The Black Tower was the lynchpin of the northern marches, built during a time when the druchii feared that an invasion from the Wastes was an ever-present threat.

The nauglir reached the base of the steep slope in a few loping strides, grumbling querulously as the highborn spurred the cold one into a ground-eating trot. What little he knew of the Black Tower had come from books in his father's library; Lurhan hadn't thought it necessary to give his bastard son the customary training that his elder sons had received.

Ghrond was a city only in the sense of its population and density of structures; in reality it was a permanent military camp, its buildings devoted solely to martial pursuits. The fortress city had a hexagonal-shaped outer wall more than forty feet high that was wide enough at the top for a troop of knights to ride their nauglir two abreast along its length. Each corner of the hexagon was further fortified into a triangular-shaped redoubt that was a citadel unto itself, with its own barracks, armoury and storerooms. The redoubts extended some ways out from the walls, so that archers and bolt throwers could fire down their length and catch attackers in a withering crossfire. Like the redoubts, the city's two gates were likewise fortified with imposing gatehouses that could rain death upon any attempt to break through their iron-banded doors.

From the southern gatehouse the sentries could see the entire length of the Spear Road, all the way back to the far ridge. As the Endless drew closer the forbidding wail of a horn rose above the battlements and the massive portal slowly swung open. One look at the silver faces of the riders and their black steeds was enough to convince the sentries of their identity.

Within minutes Malus was riding beneath the arch of the southern gate and into a narrow tunnel lit only by a handful of witchlamps. Heavy stone blocks seemed to press in from every side, and the highborn made out narrow murder-holes and arrow slits along both the walls and ceiling of the space. After about ten yards, the highborn was surprised to find the tunnel angle sharply to the right, then dogleg back to the left again. It made a difficult turn for wagons and an impossible one for a battering ram, he noted with approval. An attacker who managed to penetrate the first gate would find himself stuck in the dark confines of the tunnel and ruthlessly slaughtered by the gatehouse's defenders.

After another ten yards the highborn emerged from the inner gate into a small marshalling square lined with low, stone barracks. Foot soldiers were drilling in formation in the square, and the air rang with the clash of hammers from nearby forges as armourers readied the garrison for battle. The commander of the footmen raised his sword in salute as the riders passed, then resumed bellowing orders to his men.

The space between the outer wall and inner wall of the city was close-packed with barracks, stables, storehouses, forges

and kitchens, organised into fortified districts that could oper-
ate as independent strongpoints in the event the outer wall
was breached. An invader would have to spend precious time
and thousands of lives clearing these buildings and fighting
along the narrow streets before he even reached the inner wall
itself. Malus had read somewhere that each building had been
further built so that the people inside could collapse it when
all hope was lost, further denying its fortifications to their conquerors.

Unlike other druchii cities, the streets of Ghrond were laid
out in neat, orderly lines to facilitate the rapid movement of
troops. Malus and the Endless made good time riding down
the bustling avenues. Ahead of them loomed the black bulk of
the fortress's inner wall, its spiked battlements rising sixty feet
above the city's fortified districts.

Like the outer wall, the inner wall was built in a hexagonal
shape with six small redoubts of its own and a single, solidly
built gatehouse. Beyond rose the black tower itself, supported
by lesser towers like any drachau's citadel and bristling with
spiked turrets fitted with an array of heavy bolt throwers. As
the highborn and the Endless were admitted through the inner
gatehouse he could not help but shake his head in admiration.
All of the power of the watchtowers combined could not equal
the strength built into this fortress. A few thousand druchii
could hold the Black Tower against a force more than ten
times their number. It was an expertly designed death trap,
built solely to ruin an invading army. And he, Malus noted bitterly, was meant to be the bait.

Beyond the inner wall Malus found himself in a small, shadowy courtyard at the feet of the great tower. A troop of Black
Guard stood watch at the courtyard's far end, their white faces
impassive and their wicked-looking halberds held ready.
Attendants in light armour and the livery of the tower's
drachau raced from an adjoining stable as the Endless slipped
heavily from their saddles. Malus did likewise, pausing only to
check the pack containing the daemon's relics and to run a
possessive hand over the wrapped hilt of the warpsword. He

felt its banked heat through the layers of cloth and was sorely tempted to draw it free and buckle it to his harness. Who here would recognise it, after all? But the memory of the slaughter at Har Ganeth forced him to push the temptation aside. He couldn't afford another mindless slaughter here. With a deep breath the highborn pulled his hand away, removing instead the axe from its loop on the nauglir's saddle and then checking to make certain that the writ was securely tucked into his belt. As he did so there was a clatter of steel as a young highborn dashed from the tower into the courtyard.

The young druchii clearly came from a wealthy family. The hilts of his twin swords were chased with gold and set with small rubies, and his lacquered armour was embossed with silver runes of warding and decorated with gold scrollwork. A hadrilkar of silver encircled his slender neck, worked in the shape of twining serpents. His narrow, pointed face was flushed from his quick sprint, and tendrils of black hair had come loose from the band of gold at the base of his neck. He surveyed the assembled riders quickly and sized up Malus as their obvious leader. The young highborn advanced to a proper hithuan and bowed deeply. 'Welcome to the Black Tower, my lord,' he said. 'I am Shevael, a knight in service to the drachau, Lord Myrchas. How may I assist you?'

Malus could well imagine the thoughts going through the young highborn's mind. His new armour was filigreed with gold and wrought with its own powerful spells of protection, and the heavy gold hadrilkar of the Witch King hung about his neck. Yet he bore no swords to mark his station; instead he clutched the worn hilt of a battle-axe in his had. The boy probably thinks I'm Malekith's own executioner, come to pay a call on his lord the drachau, the highborn thought. And, as it happens, he's not far wrong.

'Where is Lord Myrchas and his vaulkhar?' Malus said, his voice hoarse from exhaustion.

Shevael's eyes widened. 'I... he... that is, they are in council at present–'

'Excellent,' Malus replied. 'Take me there.'

The young highborn went pale. 'But… that is, perhaps you would care for some refreshment after your long ride?'

'Did I ask for refreshment?' Malus snapped. He let the axe hang loosely from his hands. 'Take me to your master, boy, or would you rather hear the Witch King's decree yourself?'

Shevael took a step back. 'No, of course not, my lord! That is – I mean – please follow me!'

The young druchii turned on his heel and strode swiftly to the tower. Malus followed, grinning wolfishly, and the Endless fell silently into step around him.

Chapter Nine
THE WITCH KING'S VOICE

THE DRACHAU'S COUNCIL chambers lay near the very top of the tower, which did nothing to improve Malus's mood. The climb, up narrow, twisting stairways and down dimly-lit, bustling corridors, seemed to last for hours. By the time the young knight led him and his Endless bodyguards into the council chamber's anteroom he was entirely out of patience. Pulling the writ from his belt he pushed past the startled Shevael and strode purposefully up to the chamber door. The two Black Guard halberdiers assigned to watch the door glanced from Malus to his silver-masked attendants and stepped carefully aside.

Smiling grimly, Malus put his boot against the door and kicked for all he was worth.

The oaken door swung open, rebounding from the stone wall with a thunderous bang. Nobles and retainers in the room beyond leapt to their feet with startled shouts and wrathful curses. Malus rushed within, catching the recoiling door with the flat of his axe and stopping it with a hollow clang.

Across the large, square chamber lay a broad table, covered with maps, parchment notes, wine goblets and pewter plates littered with half-eaten meals. A dozen armoured highborn and their retainers glared fiercely at Malus's intrusion, many with their hands on the hilt of their blades. Four more Black Guardsmen dashed from the shadows, two on either side of the axe-wielding highborn, the spearheads of their halberds aimed for Malus's throat.

Opposite the chamber door, at the far end of the table, sat an older highborn clad in ornate, enchanted armour. Sigils of coiled serpents were worked in gold across his lacquered breastplate, and his right hand was encased in a taloned gauntlet of a type that Malus knew all too well. It was the literal Fist of Night, the magical symbol of a drachau's authority. Lord Myrchas, the drachau of the Black Tower, studied Malus with small, bright black eyes. His long face, accentuated by a narrow, drooping moustache, was marked by dozens of minor scars from the bite of sword and claw. He reminded Malus somewhat of his late father Lurhan, which blackened the highborn's mood even further.

At the drachau's right hand stood a towering, lanky figure in ornate armour, marked with the sigil of a tower engraved upon his breastplate. He was older than Malus, but not so old as the drachau, and his skin was darkened by years of exposure from campaigning in the field. His sword belt and scabbards were studded with gems, doubtless looted on dozens of raids into the Wastes. The lord was bald as a nauglir's egg, and his face and scalp bore the marks of a great many battles. He might have been handsome once, but that changed the day his nose was broken for the fourth time and his right ear was shorn almost completely away by some foeman's blade. His left cheek was scarred and crumpled, lending his angry scowl a horrid, unbalanced cast. 'What is your name, fool?' the scarred druchii roared. 'I want to know whose head I'll be hanging from the spikes atop the inner gate.'

'I am Malus of Hag Graef,' the highborn replied coldly.

Lord Myrchas straightened. 'Malus the kinslayer?' he exclaimed. 'The outlaw?'

Malus smiled. 'No longer.' He raised the writ for the assembled lords to see. 'His dread majesty the Witch King has seen fit to put my notorious talents to good use.'

The drachau held out his taloned hand. 'Let me be the judge of that,' he declared. 'I've heard of your deeds, wretch. For all I know there's nothing in between those metal plates but a fish-wife's tally sheet.'

Malus bowed his head, genuinely amused by the drachau's accusation, and passed the plaque to the nearest lord, who in turn handed it around the table to Lord Myrchas. As the drachau opened the plaque and studied the parchment within, Malus waved a hand at the Endless. 'I suppose these would be the fish-wife's daughters in disguise?'

Lord Myrchas read the parchment, then scrutinised the seal closely. His face turned pale. 'Blessed Mother of Night,' he said softly, raising his eyes to Malus. 'The world has turned upside down.'

'As it is wont to do from time to time,' Malus said darkly. 'Which is why the Witch King requires the services of people like myself.'

The drachau blanched even further, and Malus couldn't help but feel a rush of cruel glee. This was a role he could come to enjoy, he thought. He turned to the tall lord next to Myrchas. 'Now you have me at a disadvantage, my lord. Who might you be?'

The glint of rage in the druchii lord's eye faltered slightly at the sudden change of events. 'I am Lord Kuall Blackhand, Vaulkhar of the Black Tower.'

Malus's smile widened. 'Ah, yes, Lord Kuall. I've come a long way in a very short time to bring you a message from the Witch King himself.'

A stir went through the assembled nobles. Even the drachau leaned back in his chair and stole a bleak look at the vaulkhar. Lord Kuall straightened at the news, the muscles bunching at the sides of his scarred jaws. Whatever his failings, the vaulkhar of the tower was no coward. 'Very well,' he said, his voice tight. 'Let's hear it then.'

Malus nodded formally. 'As you wish. My lord and master has watched your efforts here in the north since the coming of the Chaos horde, Lord Kuall, and he is displeased with what he has seen. *Very* displeased.'

Worried murmurs passed through the assembled lords, and the drachau's eyes narrowed warily. Lord Kuall, however, went white with rage. 'And what would Malekith have me do?' he cried. 'Meet that damned multitude in the field?' He snatched up a pile of parchments and threw them across the table at Malus. 'Has the Witch King read my scouts' reports? The Chaos horde is immense! When it moves it raises so much dust that you can see it from the sentry posts at the top of the tower. You expect me to form lines of battle and try to defeat such a force? We would be completely overrun!' He banged his armoured gauntlet on the heavy table, causing the goblets to jump. 'I've commanded the army of the tower for two hundred years, and I've lead countless raids into the Wastes. In all that time I've never seen a horde such as this. This fortress – ' Kuall pointed a finger at the ceiling – 'was built to break a Chaos horde against its walls. If you had an ounce of sense you could have seen that just riding through the gates. The only sensible course of action is to conserve our forces and prepare for the coming onslaught, where we can bleed the enemy dry against our fortifications.'

The assembled lords listened and nodded, casting uneasy glances between Lord Kuall and Malus. But the highborn was unimpressed.

'So while you cowered in your hole like a rabbit the enemy has systematically destroyed nearly a third of our frontier watchtowers,' he replied coldly, 'not to mention slaughtered hundreds of isolated troops who stood their ground expecting reinforcements that never arrived. Instead you cowered behind these walls to preserve your own skin, and now the kingdom will be vulnerable to Chaos raids for years to come.'

'The Chaos horde must overcome the Black Tower if they hope to press further into Naggaroth!' Kuall shot back. 'They have no choice but to attack us, and here we are in a position of strength.'

'Are you?' Malus said. 'If I recall correctly, slightly more than half your garrison is made up of cavalry. How useful will they be to you in a protracted siege, unless you plan on putting the cavalrymen on the walls and sending their mounts to the kitchens?' He glared hotly at the vaulkhar. 'You have a powerful, and above all, a mobile force at your command, Lord Kuall, and yet you feared to put it to the test against a mass of ignorant savages. Out of timidity you hoped to fight the enemy with half an army while you sat here in your chair and waited for Malekith to come to your rescue. That is not how our people fight, Lord Kuall. That is not how the state responds to animals that trespass on our domain.'

'You dare call me a coward!' Kuall shouted, tearing his sword from its scabbard. The gathered nobles backed hurriedly away from the enraged lord, knocking over chairs and upending cups in their escape.

'I call you nothing,' Malus sneered. 'When I speak it is with the Witch King's own voice, and he calls you nothing less than a failure.' Malus gestured to the Endless. 'Take this wretch and impale him upon the spikes above the inner gate. With luck he'll live long enough to witness the defeat of the horde.'

The masked bodyguards swept forward in a silent rush, swords suddenly appearing in their hands. With a cry of rage, Kuall gave ground, threatening the implacable Endless with the point of his blade. But the warriors scarcely broke stride, advancing fearlessly into reach of the lord's long sword and trapping it with their own. Two more warriors seized Kuall by the arms, and within moments they were dragging the thrashing druchii across the chamber and out the door.

Malus savoured the shocked silence that fell upon Lord Kuall's sudden exit. His black eyes sought out the drachau and he waited for Lord Myrchas to make the next move.

The drachau met the highborn's stare, and Malus could see that Myrchas was weighing his options. For the moment the drachau was untouchable; as one of the Witch King's personal vassals he was beyond Malus's reach, but the reverse was true as well. Finally his expression softened slightly and the highborn knew he'd won.

'What is our dread majesty's command?' the drachau asked.

'The Witch King is assembling the army of Naggaroth and preparing to march here at once,' the highborn replied, feeling a thrill of triumph. 'Until such time as he arrives I will command the forces of the Black Tower.'

Myrchas bristled at the news. 'Malekith cannot name you vaulkhar without the approval of the tower lords!'

The highborn cut off the drachau's protest with a raised hand. 'I did not claim to be the vaulkhar, Lord Myrchas. I said that I will command the army. It is a fine distinction, but an important one, as I'm sure you'll agree.'

'Very well,' the drachau said darkly, realising that he'd been outmanoeuvred.

'Excellent,' Malus said, then raised his axe and embedded it in the tabletop with a thunderous crash. All of the assembled highborn leapt back with startled oaths, and Malus leaned forward and picked up an empty wine goblet with a fierce grin. 'Now as my first official command I want a bottle of good wine brought out, then you can tell me who you are and report as to the disposition of our forces.'

THE REPORTS LASTED for almost three hours. Malus listened closely to each and every one, forcing himself to stay awake and drinking in every detail he could. His brief time as the lieutenant of Fuerlan's small force had in no way prepared him for the magnitude of commanding the army of the Black Tower.

Malus struggled with the names of the many highborn who came forward to report on one of the many facets of the garrison and the tower's defensive preparations. Lists were presented, detailing the numbers of troops in each regiment, the status of their equipment and their overall readiness, the quantity and quality of their food and the amount of time left in their training period before they were to be sent to their home city. Detailed tallies were given of arrows, crossbow bolts, heavy bolts, spare armour, spare shields, swords, spearheads, arrowheads, catapult stones, gallons of oil, bundles of torches –

'All right, all right!' Malus interjected, waving his goblet at the pair of highborn who were currently reporting on the status of the kitchens. 'I've heard enough.' The two druchii bowed quickly and returned to their seats, grateful to have escaped Malus's notice with their skins intact. Wincing painfully, the highborn shifted in the uncomfortable council chair and drained the dregs of the goblet in a single gulp.

The highborn did his best to collect his scattered impressions as he held out his goblet to be refilled by a waiting attendant. The Endless had taken up positions by the door, watching the council members from behind their implacable masks.

'It is clear to me that the Black Tower has not squandered its time since the appearance of the horde. Your preparations were misguided, but your dedication and effort are to be commended,' he said. The assembled highborn nodded their heads respectfully. Beside Malus, the drachau's high-backed chair stood empty. Lord Myrchas had taken his leave a couple of hours before.

The highborn focused on a druchii noble across the table who had introduced himself as the commander of the cavalry. He was a whipcord-lean figure in dark armour, swathed in a heavy cloak of glossy bearskin. Malus couldn't remember the druchii's name to save himself. 'Let us get back to basics. How many light cavalry did you say we had, lord...'

'Irhaut, dread lord,' the highborn replied smoothly. Lord Irhaut had a long, hooked nose and three gold earrings that glinted roguishly in his left ear, hinting at a successful former career as a corsair. 'We currently muster six thousand light horse, arrayed in six banners.'

Malus nodded. 'Very good.' He turned to the broad-shouldered highborn sitting beside Irhaut. 'And our infantry, Lord Murmon?'

'Meiron, my lord,' the highborn corrected with a pained expression. He had blunt, craggy features and unusually shaggy brows for a druchii. Malus wondered idly if Lord Meiron's mother hadn't mated with a bear to produce such a child. Lord Meiron consulted his reports and drew himself straight. 'We currently muster fifteen thousand spearmen and a thousand Black Guard in sixteen banners, although four of those banners are scheduled to return home–'

'No one is going home until the horde has been destroyed,' Malus said sternly. Lord Meiron blinked beneath his shaggy brows and nodded hesitantly. The highborn scowled. They've been training troops and leading raids for so long that they can't seem to comprehend anything else, he thought. Well, they'd have a chance to revise their thinking soon enough.

Malus realised his goblet was full and took a deep, appreciative draught. He made a mental note to get a tally of the fortress's wine stores when he had a moment. 'Lord Suheir,' he said, turning to the armoured giant on his right. 'How fare the household knights?'

Lord Suheir turned slightly in his chair to face Malus, appearing a bit surprised that his new commander actually remembered his name. Suheir was head and shoulders taller than any other druchii in the room, and looked strong enough to crack walnuts with his hands. If Lord Meiron's mother had mated with a bear, then Suheir's ill-fated dam had lain with a nauglir. He had a wide face and an almost square chin, an unfortunate combination for a druchii lord. 'The household knights are fifteen hundred strong,' he replied in a booming voice. 'As well as five hundred chariots that haven't been used in a single battle as far as I know.'

Malus rolled the numbers over in his mind as he swirled the wine in his cup. Twenty-four thousand troops! It was easily twice the size of any other garrison in Naggaroth, with the possible exception of Naggarond itself. The notion was far more intoxicating than any vintage he'd ever drunk. The amount of power at his disposal was immense. As he contemplated this

his eyes fell to the burnished silver plaque resting on the table before him.

Now he understood Nuarc's words all too well.

The highborn took a deep breath. 'All right. What have we learned about the enemy?'

Heads turned. At the end of the table the oldest druchii present sat up straight in his chair and leaned forward, resting his elbows on the edge of the table. Lord Rasthlan's hair had more grey in it than black, and was pulled back and plaited with plain finger bones and silver wire. Unlike the other highborn he wore only a shirt of close-fitting mail over a kheitan cut in a rustic, almost autarii style. His right cheek was decorated with a swirling tattoo of a snarling hound – a mark of considerable honour among the shades, if Malus's memory served him correctly. Rasthlan certainly looked more at home among the cushions and rugs of an autarii lodge than sitting at a table with civilised folk.

'Our scouts have been tracking the horde since it came together after sacking the majority of the hill forts almost a month ago,' Rasthlan said in a gravelly voice. 'Kuall spoke truly: the army is the largest I have ever seen. Tens of thousands of beastmen, and human tribes besides.'

'Any heavily armoured troops?' Malus asked.

'None that my scouts saw, dread lord,' the scout commander replied. 'But there were giants, and great hill-trolls, and possibly even more terrible things marching along with them in the centre of the host. It appears the horde is led by a very powerful sorcerer or shaman, for the air reeked of dark magic.'

'You may be assured of that,' the highborn replied. 'So, what is your most honest estimate? How large a force are we facing?'

Rasthlan paused, swallowing hard. He looked to the men beside him. 'I could not say for certain, dread lord.'

Malus's dark eyes bored into the older lord. 'Give me your best guess, then. Thirty thousand? Fifty thousand?'

The druchii's gaze fell to the table. 'I wouldn't want to guess…'

'I understand,' Malus said, a hint of steel creeping into his voice. 'So you may take this as an order: tell me, in your best estimate, how large you think the Chaos horde is.'

Lord Rasthlan took a deep breath, then met the highborn's gaze. 'A hundred and twenty thousand, give or take,' he said levelly. 'I've seen them myself. They darken the plains with their numbers. It's like nothing I've ever seen before.'

The rest of the highborn looked uneasily at one another, shock evident in their expressions. Lord Suheir looked at his wide hands. 'Kuall had the right of it,' he said slowly. 'There's no way we can challenge such an army in the field. It would be a massacre.'

Even Malus himself was shocked at such a number, but he kept his face carefully neutral. He studied Rasthlan closely. 'Are you certain of this?' he asked.

The scout commander nodded at once. 'I didn't want to believe it myself, which is why I went and counted their numbers myself.'

Malus nodded slowly, his gaze dropping to the map spread across the table. 'And where are they now?'

Rasthlan rose from his chair and came around the table. 'The horde moves slowly,' he said, 'Less than a dozen miles or so a day. After razing Bhelgaur Keep they turned towards the Black Tower, which means they would be about here.' He pointed to an area of foothills north and west of the Plain of Ghrond, perhaps fifteen leagues distant.

Malus considered the distances and studied the terrain. For the last four days he'd been thinking over all that Nuarc had told him, trying to find a way out of the many snares that had been laid for him. One plan after another had been discarded, until an idea struck him in the early hours of the morning that suggested a possibility of success. Now, looking at the map, he made up his mind. 'Very well. My thanks to you gentlemen. You've given me everything I need to develop a plan of action.' He threw back his head and finished off the contents of the goblet, then set the wine cup carefully on the tabletop. 'It's been a very long day for all of us, I expect. I'm going to find a bed and get a few hours' sleep. We will meet again on the morrow, when I will provide detailed orders for each of the divisions.' Bracing his hands carefully on the arms of his chair, the highborn pushed himself to his feet. 'Until then, you are dismissed. I suggest you all get as much rest as you can. There will be little of it to go around in the next few days.'

The army staff rose to their feet, exchanging bewildered glances as Malus strode purposely towards the door. Finally it was Lord Suheir who summoned up enough courage to speak. 'Dread lord?'

Malus paused, his head swimming with wine and fatigue. 'Yes?'

'Is there something you know that we don't?' he rumbled. 'Lord Rasthlan says that the horde is moving only a dozen miles a day. That means they won't reach the Black Tower for almost a week.'

Malus looked at the captain of knights and gave him a wolfish smile. 'I know. That gives us just enough time to launch our attack.' Then he disappeared from the room, bounded by the swift shadows of the Endless.

Chapter Ten
WARRIOR OF NAGGAROTH

MALUS DREAMT HE was back in the forest near the City of Executioners, racing through the close-set trees beneath the light of the twin moons. Something was following him; he could hear its ponderous footfalls and the brittle crack of the tree boughs as it forced its way through the woods in his wake. And he knew somehow that if whatever it was managed to catch him it would consume his very soul.

His armour and axe were gone, and the brambles tore at his face and clothes. Like razor-edged claws they shredded his thick kheitan and the robes beneath, and peeled away the skin across his cheeks and forehead. Hot blood coursed down his skin, but he felt no pain. He felt nothing but pure, mortal terror that the thing was going to catch him no matter how hard he ran.

And, sure enough, the heavy footfalls sounded closer, as though his pursuer were a giant, covering leagues with every step. Choking back a cry of fear he ran all the harder, the branches and the briars cutting ever deeper into his skin. He longed to find Spite, but the nauglir was nowhere to be seen.

Malus strained to hear the familiar howl of the cold one, thinking it had to be hunting somewhere deep in the wood, but he could hear nothing over the pounding of his heart and the steady *thump* of his pursuer's tread. It sounded as though it was just a few scant yards behind him now; the skin on the back of his neck prickled, but he didn't dare look back, fearful of what might be reaching for him with outstretched talons.

Then without warning he burst into a thickly wooded hollow, finding himself on his knees on a narrow game trail running along its length. With a shudder of relief he realised where he was.

The tree. He had to find the tree. If he could climb back inside his pursuer couldn't find him.

Frantically he leapt to his feet and ran north along the path until he found the bloodstain he remembered on the trail. His heart hammering in his throat he risked a quick glance behind him, and saw that for the moment his pursuer was still just out of sight. Quickly he circled the broad stain and dived deep into the woods on the western side of the path. Thorny vines and brambles cut deep into already bleeding wounds, but he pushed on nonetheless, praying to the Dark Mother that the darkness and the vegetation would conceal him.

Within moments he found himself beside the blasted tree. The old trunk shone softly in the moonlight, like a gift from the goddess. Stifling a cry of relief he forced himself into the dark cleft. Showers of insects and rotten wood rained down on him as he straightened in the darkness, and he took it as a blessing from the goddess.

In his dream the tree was larger inside than without. He turned as the footsteps drew nearer, backing away from the thin slice of moonlight coming through the cleft from outside.

The footfalls were so close now that he could feel the earth tremble with each step. *Thud. Thud. Thud.* He held his breath, his eyes fixed on the thin slant of moonlight before him.

A shadow passed across the cleft. Malus saw a pair of booted feet through the slanted opening, barely a yard away from his hiding place. He took another involuntary step back, deeper into shadow.

The boots shifted left, then right. A voice called out. 'I know you're here little druchii,' Tz'arkan said, his voice slick and deadly as oiled steel. 'It's no use hiding. I can smell you. You're almost close enough to *taste*.'

A shudder passed through Malus at the sound of the daemon's voice. The boots shifted back to the right – then paused. One foot stepped towards the tree.

'Are you in there?' the daemon said. 'Yes, I think you are.'

A scream bubbled up in Malus's throat. He took another step back and fetched up against the uneven bole of the tree. He smelled rot and the wet stink of earthworms. The substance behind him gave slightly beneath his weight, like soft flesh.

Then a hand reached around him and pressed tightly over his mouth and another snaked tight around his waist. Malus smelled the stink of the grave and tasted putrefied flesh on his lips. Worms wriggled from the dead thing's wrist and landed, squirming, on his throat.

'Do not fear, my lord,' a familiar voice breathed in his ear. A cold breath, foul with the stench of rotting meat, lay damply along his cheek. 'The daemon cannot have you. I claimed you first.'

Malus writhed and squirmed in Lhunara's embrace, but her dead limbs held him in an iron embrace. He could smell nothing now but fleshy rot and the bitter smell of grave-dirt. His frantic gaze turned to the shaft of light and he saw the daemon pause outside, suddenly unsure. He tried to scream, to call out the daemon's name. Better to offer up his soul to the daemon's hunger than linger one moment more in Lhunara's foul embrace! But her gelid hand clamped his mouth tightly shut, and he could not get enough air through the reeking miasma that seeped from her decaying skin.

Outside, the boots turned slowly away. 'You can't hide forever, Darkblade,' the daemon called. 'It's only a matter of time before I find you.' Then, to Malus's horror, Tz'arkan walked away. The heavy footsteps receded quickly into the distance.

A cold, slimy tongue traced lightly along the side of Malus's neck. 'You see, I told you I would keep you safe,' Lhunara said, her breath close against his throat. 'No one is going to hurt you but me.'

Then her perfect teeth bit deep into his skin, and for the first time he found the breath to scream.

'My lord! My lord, wake up!'

Malus awoke staring upwards at a starry sky framed by an arch of stone. He lay upon his back, dressed only in a sleeping robe that had somehow tangled around his legs. A cold wind blew against his cheek, tasting of snow. His heart laboured painfully in his chest, hammering like the drumming feet of a charging nauglir.

A dark silhouette hovered over him, backlit by the moonlight. He thrashed violently, still partially in the grip of the nightmare and the figure gripped his arm tightly. 'Be still, my lord! You could throw yourself over the rail!'

The sharp warning penetrated his dulled senses. He blinked away the last vestiges of the dream and realised that he lay on the floor of a narrow balcony, high up on the flank of the Black Tower. Moving slowly and cautiously, he sat upright, helped along by the strong hands of the shadowy attendant. Malus looked out across the white plain, which shimmered faintly in the moonlight. He saw the dark mountains off to the north, limned with the shifting light of the northern aurora. Off to the north-west he could just make out a faint white line of foothills. Beyond them, many leagues north and west, lay Nagaira and the Chaos horde.

'A dream. A terrible dream,' he said to himself, rubbing dazedly at his chin. His body ached and his mouth tasted like a chamber pot. 'I drank too much,' he said absently. 'Never again. Do you hear that Hauclir? Never again, you damned rogue. No matter how much I beg.'

'Hauclir, my lord?' the figure said worriedly. 'It's me, Shevael. The drachau assigned me to serve as your retainer. Don't you remember?'

Malus turned away from the balcony rail and stared closely at the man beside him. 'Ah. Yes. Shevael,' he said in a hollow voice. 'Shevael. Never mind my rambling, lad. It's just wine and memories.'

'Yes, my lord, of course,' the young highborn said, sounding anything but reassured. 'How did you come to be on the balcony in the first place? When I last checked you were sound asleep in your bed.'

Malus rose unsteadily to his feet. The double doors leading from the bedroom to the balcony were wide open; within he could see the banked glow of a pair of braziers, weakly illuminating the wide bed and the tangle of bed sheets that pointed like a trail to where he lay.

'I must have got up in the night,' he said weakly. But he recalled the time in the forest when he'd awoke far from where he'd bedded down. What in the Dark Mother's name is happening to me, he thought? For the first time he found himself missing the constant presence of the Endless. After escorting him safely to the Black Tower and seeing him installed as the commander of the army their duty was done, and they left him to begin the task of preparing a set of chambers for the Witch King's imminent arrival.

The highborn let Shevael lead him back to the bed and pile the sheets and blankets over him. Malus stared at the ceiling. 'What is the hour?'

'It is the hour of the wolf, my lord,' the young highborn answered. 'Dawn will break in another hour and a half. Light comes early this far north.'

'I know, lad, I know,' Malus answered. 'Let me rest here until daybreak, then turn me out. We'll be on the march by midday.'

'Very good, my lord,' the young highborn answered, and retreated from the room. At the door he paused to glance fearfully at the highborn, then slipped out of sight.

Malus paid no heed. He was lost in thought, staring though the open balcony doors at the shifting lights to the north.

* * *

THE THUNDER OF three thousand marching feet reverberated down the length of the marshalling square and vibrated against Malus's ribcage. He felt the measured tramp of boots through the heavy stone of the outer gatehouse, and it brought a feral smile of joy to his pallid face.

He had issued his orders scarcely an hour past dawn, and the forces he'd chosen had assembled in good order barely three hours after that. To their credit, his highborn staff hadn't blinked an eye when he'd laid out his plan. Possibly they'd drunk their fears into submission the night before, much as he had.

The scouts, as always, were the first to depart. They'd left almost immediately after meeting with his lieutenants. Lord Rasthlan had left with them, garbed in dark robes and mail just like the autarii themselves. Glancing up at the midday sun, Malus reckoned that the shades were leagues away by now.

Just an hour before a fanfare of horns sounded from the outer gatehouse, and the first three banners of cavalry left as the army's vanguard. The last few squadrons of those horsemen were just departing through the massive gate, and the regiment of Black Guard were crossing the square next. Their captain raised his sword in salute to Malus as they passed beneath the high arch, and he returned the gesture proudly with his upraised axe.

Beyond the Black Guard waited two more regiments of spearmen, then the household knights and the cold one chariots, destined for the battlefield at last. Farther still waited the remaining three banners of the light cavalry to act as the rearguard. The garrison's entire cavalry force and almost a quarter of its infantry – almost half of the entire army, on balance – were being wagered on a single, desperate gamble. The thought chilled him to the marrow, but anything less would have doomed the expedition to certain failure.

Suddenly a loud commotion arose at the far end of the battlements. Malus heard angry shouts over the heavy tramp of feet and glanced along the walkway to see what was happening. The soldiers of the gate watch who were watching the army alongside him suddenly shifted and dodged about as a single figure stormed down the battlements in Malus's direction. The highborn couldn't see who it was, but he had a fairly good idea.

He straightened and made certain his gleaming armour was presentable as the drachau of the Black Tower burst into view. Lord Myrchas was livid, his entire body trembling with rage.

'What do you think you are doing?' the drachau said in a strangled voice. 'Stop this madness at once and return these troops back to their barracks!'

Malus bowed his head regretfully. 'I cannot,' he replied. 'And you have no authority to command me, even if I were your vaulkhar.'

For a moment it looked as though Myrchas would reach for his sword. His hands trembled with fury... and no small amount of fear, the highborn imagined. 'You cannot defeat the horde in pitched battle!' the drachau cried. 'You're sending these men to certain death and leaving the Black Tower defenceless!'

'Defenceless?' the highborn arched an eyebrow. 'Hardly. I've left you with thirteen thousand well-trained spearmen to defend the fortress walls. That should be more than sufficient to hold the Black Tower against ten times their number. And if my plan succeeds, they will not be needed at all.'

The drachau would not be mollified. 'But the horde–'

'My lord, I have no intention of fighting the Chaos army in a pitched battle,' Malus snapped, fixing Myrchas with a fiery stare. 'A horde like that is not held together by training or dis-cipline. It is a clumsy weapon wielded rather tenuously by its war leader. If the leader dies, the army will turn upon itself like a pack of maddened dogs.' Malus pointed a gauntleted finger northward. 'I am taking the most mobile force I can manage and I plan to launch a night attack aimed right at the horde's beating heart. We're going to cut our way to the war leader's tent and I plan on splitting her skull myself.'

'Her?' the drachau said, momentarily confused.

'Never mind, my lord,' Malus said. 'The point of the matter is that a quick, decisive strike could stop this invasion in its tracks. I need the cavalry's mobility and hitting power, and the spearmen will provide a solid rearguard for the squadrons to rally behind.' He leaned close to the drachau. 'Think of the glory when Malekith arrives with his army to find the war leader's head hanging from a gatehouse spike. They'll sing of your heroism the length and breadth of Naggaroth.'

Myrchas thought it over. A faint gleam of avarice shone in his eyes. 'The rewards for such a victory would be great,' he allowed, then frowned worriedly. 'Are you absolutely certain this will work?'

The highborn shook his head. 'Nothing in war is certain, my lord. But believe me when I tell you that while the Chaos war leader is a mighty sorceress, she has no experience whatsoever as a general. She will not expect an attack like this, which gives us a great advantage. At worst we will be able to inflict tremendous losses and sow terrible confusion on the enemy, which will allow us to retire back to the fortress in good order.'

Malus put every ounce of sincerity he possessed into his argument. He believed in the plan; it was the only one he could conceive that would give him a chance of escaping Malekith's clutches, locating the relic and fleeing northward in time. If he could kill Nagaira before the Witch King arrived with his army then he would be able to use his temporary authority to search for the relic in the Black Tower – and the ruins of the Chaos encampment if necessary – without interference. Then he could slip out of the fortress and disappear into the Wastes with no one the wiser.

The highborn struggled to remain patient while the drachau thought it over. Finally, Myrchas nodded. 'I can find no fault with your plan,' he said at last. 'Go with the Dark Mother's blessing and sow fear and loathing among our foes.' He smiled. 'Naturally I regret not being able to accompany you–'

'Say no more, my lord,' Malus assured him. 'Someone must remain behind to command the garrison and await the Witch

King's arrival. With luck I should return with the army in about five days.'

The drachau smiled. 'We will be awaiting your return,' he said. 'And now that you mention it, there are a great many matters that I must see to before the Witch King arrives, so I will take my leave.'

'Of course, my lord,' Malus said, bowing deeply. He held the bow as the drachau hurried away, hiding the grim smile of satisfaction on his lips.

THE ARMY MARCHED for the rest of the day and well past nightfall. Malus kept the pace brisk but measured; he'd had enough forced marches in the last two weeks to last a lifetime. Spite seemed to have recovered completely from his exertions on the road with little more than a day's rest and half a ton of horseflesh to renew his strength.

On the following day they marched at a cautious pace through the foothills, awaiting the first reports from the far-ranging scouts. Malus kept the army moving at a walk, both to minimise the amount of telltale dust and to avoid running headlong into the oncoming Chaos army. Timing their approach to the horde would be the trickiest part of the attack.

At midday Lord Rasthlan appeared before the vanguard with a pair of autarii in tow. Malus called a halt and met the scouts beneath the shadow of a copse of fir trees on the reverse slope of a low hill.

'Where are they?' the highborn asked as Shevael passed bread, cheese and wine to the tired-looking scouts.

'About five leagues to the north,' Rasthlan said, drinking deeply from his cup. The shades crouched beneath the trees and ate in silence, gazing inscrutably at Malus. Lord Rasthlan tore off a hunk of bread and stuffed it quickly in his mouth, nearly swallowing it whole. 'They've picked up their pace somewhat, but they shouldn't cover more than two or three leagues before nightfall,' he continued.

Malus nodded thoughtfully. The distance would be just about perfect. 'Do you know for certain where the war leader's tent can be found?'

Rasthlan grimaced and shook his head. 'The Chaos savages are thick as flies along the ground,' he said. 'From the edge of their encampment it is nearly three miles to the centre. Too risky to penetrate, even for these ghosts,' he said, indicating the autarii. 'The war leader's tents will lie in the middle of the camp. They should be easy to find, even in the dark.'

The highborn nodded. 'Will your men be ready by nightfall?'

One of the autarii snorted disdainfully. Rasthlan grinned. 'They are ready now, my lord,' he said. 'We will uphold our end of the plan, never fear.'

'Very well,' Malus replied, feeling the first twinges of anticipation. 'Then we wait here until nightfall.' He turned to Shevael. 'Summon the division commanders to attend a war council in three hours to go over final preparations,' he ordered. As the young highborn rushed off, Malus turned back to the scouts. 'And as for you, I suggest you get some rest. It will likely be a very long night.'

THE LARGER OF the two moons was still low on the horizon when the army rose from their temporary camp and began their march to the enemy encampment. During the day they had wrapped their arms, armour and tack in layers of cloth to muffle any telltale noises while they moved. Each regiment and banner marched with a pair of autarii in the lead, holding small, shuttered witchlamps to signal their fellows and act as pathfinders, guiding the army to its objective.

Solitary flakes of snow drifted from a seemingly clear sky, and Malus's breath sent frosty plumes into the air as he rode alongside the household knights. They travelled in remarkable silence for so huge a force, and the highborn could not help but admire the mettle of the troops under his command. A general with sufficient daring could do much with such an army at his back, he mused, and smiled up at the starry sky.

It took more than two hours to travel two leagues across the foothills, then the pathfinders raised their lanterns and called a halt. As the army slowly ground to a stop, Rasthlan suddenly appeared at Malus's side. 'You may form your lines here, my lord,' he whispered, as though the Chaos troops were just on the other side of the hill instead of nearly a mile away. 'We will go ahead from here and deal with their sentries,' he said. 'Wait for the signal.'

Malus nodded. 'The Dark Mother's fortune be with you, Rasthlan,' he said, and the old druchii vanished like a spectre.

Lantern signals were passed all along the column, and slowly, carefully, the army formed line of battle behind the slope of a long, wooded ridge. Once again, the shades and their shuttered lanterns were invaluable, guiding each regiment and banner into the proper position with a minimum of confusion. Still, it was nearly two hours before the army was properly arrayed. After that there was nothing to do but watch the moons creep across the sky and try not to focus too much on the battle ahead.

The wait seemed to last forever. Each moment Malus strained his senses to detect the slightest sign of alarm, even though he knew intellectually that he was too far away from the enemy camp to hear anything short of war horns. Knights shifted uneasily in their saddles, the creak of leather seemingly sharp as a thunderclap to the highborn's strained nerves. Nauglir grunted and stamped. Tiny bits of harness jingled despite every precaution. After almost an hour Malus discovered that his fingertips had gone numb from holding the reins in a nervous, white-knuckled grip. With a deep breath the forced himself to relax and slowly unclenched his aching hands.

Then came the sign they were waiting for. A hunched figure appeared at the top of the hill and flashed open the cover of his shuttered witchlamp: once, twice, thrice. Other pathfinders were sending the same signal all along the druchii line; the shades had done their deadly work and slain the enemy sentries along a one-mile front. There would be no one to give warning to the beastmen and marauders slumbering in their tents until it was far too late.

Malus looked to the left, just spying the edge of the banners of horse that stretched away to his flank; a similar formation waited at the right end of the knight's battle line, their loose formations stretching for more than a mile to either side. To his immediate right, the bristling line of the household knights checked their reins and stirrups and quietly drew their blades. Behind the knights waited the long line of scythe-armed chariots. A torch burned low in the back of each war machine, ready to light the arrows of the archers who waited alongside the charioteers. Still farther back, the highborn could see the three regiments of spearmen, dressing their lines in long ranks of two. Their spearheads glinted cruelly in the moonlight, though if all went well the footmen would never enter the battle at all. They were a veritable wall of silver and steel that disorganised cavalry units could retreat to and shake off any pursuers so they could rally and return to the fight.

Slowly and deliberately the highborn reached down and unhooked the axe from his saddle. He'd been sorely tempted to carry the warpsword into battle instead, but once again the episode at Har Ganeth gave him pause. What if he succumbed to the killing madness again at a time when he needed to be clear-headed and issue orders to the army? There were no guarantees, he finally admitted, and so he'd left the blade – and the bag with the relics – back at the Black Tower. As much as it worried him to leave the artefacts untended, worse still was the thought of them falling into the hands of his half-sister by some awful mischance. She'd already taken the items from him once before; Malus doubted he'd be so lucky as to retrieve them again.

He turned to the household knights, arrayed in a gleaming line two ranks deep that stretched off into the darkness for more than half a mile, well beyond his line of sight. Closest to the highborn were Lord Suheir, the knight-captain and Malus's retainer Shevael. Both eyed him with a mixture of excitement and wary unease. Every man in the small army knew what they were up against; he'd made certain of it before the troops left the Black Tower. If they won, the Chaos threat would be over. If they lost, few if any of them would return home again. They had to win or die.

Malus leaned over in his saddle and spoke quietly to Suheir and Shevael, certain that his words would be repeated on down the line. 'Remember, we are the spear tip,' he said, his expression fierce. 'Leave the chariots and the light cavalry to do most of the butcher's work. Our only task is to cut our way to the Chaos war leader's tent at the centre of the camp, regardless of the cost. Once we're there, I'll put an end to this invasion once and for all. Clear?'

Both men nodded solemnly. Already he could hear the next men in line whispering his words to the comrade beside him.

Lord Suheir raised his curved sword in salute. 'We are with you, my lord,' he rumbled.

Malus nodded and sat up straight. At that moment he realised that twelve thousand men hung on his next word, awaiting the command to unleash a grim slaughter upon their foes. He smiled to himself, savouring the sensation of power. Suddenly the risks inherent in his plan became meaningless. Could any risk in the wide world be great enough to sour the terrible joy he felt?

The highborn turned his gaze to the summit of the wide hill before him and raised his axe high into the air. 'The household knights will advance,' he said in a low voice, then brought the weapon down in a shining arc. 'Forward!'

Spite lurched forward at a steady walk, head lowering as it sensed that a battle was close to hand. The cold ones of the front rank followed suit, rippling forward like the flick of a long, steel whip. Malus spurred the cold one up the hill slope, eager to crest the summit and see what he could of the vast movement occurring around him.

When he reached the top of the hill he looked immediately ahead and found only more rolling terrain stretching off to the horizon, but to left and right the light horse were surging in a black tide over their own series of foothills, moonlight burning coldly on the tops of their long spears. Behind him came the faint rattle and groan of chariot wheels, growing steadily quieter as the war machines picked up speed.

The druchii army swept across the hills like storm clouds, low thunder murmuring in the fall of thousands of shining hooves. Malus raised his axe once more at the top of the next hill and swept it downwards. As one, eight thousand knights and cavalrymen spurred their mounts to a trot.

Now the earth shook with the heavy tread of the cavalry, and the iron wheels of the chariots added their own deep-throated rumble as they picked up speed. The barren hills were flashing past now. The nauglir of the household knights were gliding over the rolling terrain like hunting hounds, venomous drool trailing from their dagger-like fangs. As they rode the wind shifted, and in the distance a herd of northern ponies shrieked in terror as they caught the cold ones' scent. Malus could just catch glimpses of dark tent roofs a half-mile ahead, just beyond a trio of low, broken hills. The highborn swung his axe over his head and put the spurs to Spite's flanks, urging him into a canter.

Spite plunged down the steep slope and bounded swiftly up the opposite hillside, long legs at full extension and a growl rumbling from the cold one's snout as it scented prey just ahead. This time when they streaked over the summit Malus saw that the rolling slopes beyond were carpeted in low, round tents made from crudely sewn hides. The tents of the horde covered everything from horizon to horizon, darkening the hillsides and hollows like a vile disease. The stench of spilled blood and corrupted flesh rolled over him like a cloud, thick enough to hang like a faint haze over the squalid tents of the camp.

The sheer size of the horde struck Malus like an invisible blow. It was one thing to comprehend what a hundred thousand troops represented, but another thing entirely to see it with one's own eyes. We're like a bucket of water being thrown into a furnace, he finally realised. How can we possibly defeat such a foe?

Despair began to seep like poison into his heart – but just then a tent flap opened almost a dozen yards away and a bewildered beastman staggered out into the night air. Its heavy, horned head swung left and right, taking in the oncoming druchii riders and struggling to make sense of what it saw.

Then, in a single moment its expression changed from aggravation to stark panic, and the highborn grinned like a daemon from the Abyss.

One foe at a time, he realised. We beat them one foe at a time.

I'm coming for you, dear sister, the highborn thought with savage joy. Now, after so many months, so many schemes and betrayals, there will finally be a reckoning.

Fixing the terrified beastman with a predatory glare Malus raised his axe and screamed to the heavens.

'Warriors of Naggaroth! CHARGE!'

Chapter Eleven
NIGHT AND FIRE

SHEVAEL RAISED A long, curving horn to his lips at Malus's command and blew a wild, howling note that was answered up and down the druchii line. The household knights roared their bloodlust to the heavens and broke into the Chaos camp in a storm of steel and red ruin.

Malus screamed like a tormented shade, his face alight with daemonic wrath as he drove Spite down a narrow, filth-strewn lane between leaning rawhide tents. Tent ropes parted like threads and poles crackled like kindling as the heavy cold ones smashed headlong through the closely-packed tents. Shouts and screams echoed from within as the nauglir crushed trapped beastmen underfoot or snapped at flailing shapes struggling to escape their collapsed shelters. Geysers of red sparks shot skyward as fires were scattered or stomped by rushing, scaly feet, and orange flames flared brightly where coals landed on brittle hides or oily bedding.

A dark, hulking shape burst from a tent just ahead and to Malus's right. He dropped his reins and raised his axe in a two-handed grip, striking the beastman in the side of the head in a vicious, underhanded swing that shattered the monster's skull. Another beastman erupted from the shadows of his tent ahead and to the left, brandishing a long, rusty sword. The horned fiend swung at Spite's toothy snout, but the nauglir ducked its bony head and bit off the attacker's left leg just above the knee. The beastman's wail of agony swept over the onrushing highborn and was quickly lost behind him as Malus drove ever deeper into the enemy encampment.

Sounds of battle and the thunder of hooves mingled into an echoing roar like the grinding fury of an avalanche. Pandemonium reigned inside the Chaos camp; some beastmen ran for their lives while others lashed out at anything that moved. Swarms of fiery motes traced glowing arcs overhead as the druchii charioteers shot flaming arrows deeper into the camp. Horns blew, horses screamed and marauders shouted hoarse, blasphemous curses to the sky.

Ahead, the reeking path abruptly jogged to the right around a tent festooned with skulls and bloody scraps of freshly skinned druchii hides. Snarling, Malus put his spurs to Spite's flanks and ran right over the rawhide shelter. Something wailed and gibbered within, its cries cut short by one of the nauglir's stamping feet. On the opposite side of the tent a dark shape stumbled out into the open, clutching a curling staff of grey wood. Malus caught a brief glimpse of the bray shaman whirling on its cloven hooves and raising a clawed hand to cast some terrible spell before Spite lunged at the beastman and bit its head off.

The highborn leaned back in the saddle as his mount leapt clear of the collapsed tent. Malus looked frantically to the right, trying to keep track of his knights, but saw only the reeling sides of half-collapsed tents and glimpses of helmeted heads and hacking, red-stained swords rising above the low shelters. Where had his trumpeter gone? 'Shevael!' he shouted, his voice instantly swept away in the maelstrom of battle.

'Here, my lord!' came a faint reply, just on the other side of the tents to Malus's right. One of the shelters burst apart in a cloud of tattered hides and flailing ropes as the young highborn rode his nauglir through it. The knight's pale face was streaked with blood and his eyes shone with battle-lust. 'We have them on the run!' he said, shouting to be heard even though he and Malus were only a few yards apart. 'I've never seen such a slaughter!'

'Stick close to me, lad!' Malus shouted back. 'Sound the signal for the knights to rally! We're getting scattered by these damned tents!' The highborn knew that time was not on their side. For now they had the advantage of surprise, but once the shock wore off the Chaos horde could overwhelm the druchii attackers by sheer force of numbers.

Shevael, wrestling with the reins of his agitated cold one, stared quizzically at Malus. 'What was that about the tents?' he shouted. Then suddenly his eyes went wide. 'Look out, my lord!'

Malus whirled, but Spite had seen the onrushing beast-men first. The cold one spun to the left, nearly throwing Malus out of the saddle, and the axe blow aimed for Malus's neck glanced off his left pauldron instead. The highborn cursed, fighting for balance, and threw a wild swing at the beastman's upturned snout that hacked off part of the mis-shapen beast's left horn.

Four of the goat-headed monstrosities had rushed out of the darkness at Malus, and now they swarmed around the flank of the cold one, aiming blows at both Spite and Malus alike. One of the beastmen thrust a spear at the cold one's snout, gouging a deep furrow just above the warbeast's upper fangs, while another slashed at Spite's neck with a heavy, broad bladed cleaver. The axe-wielder brayed a blasphemous oath and swung again at Malus's chest. Malus anticipated the blow and tried to lean back out of the weapon's reach – but the fourth beastman leapt up and grabbed the highborn's left arm, trying to drag him from the saddle.

Whether by accident or design, Malus was pulled full into the axe's path and the weapon struck him in the chest, just over his heart. A mundane steel breastplate would have crumpled under the savage blow, but the sigils of protection woven into the armour held fast and turned the blade aside with a discordant clang and a shower of blue sparks. Before the beastman could recover and strike another blow Malus shouted a curse and brought down his axe on the warrior's head, striking the beastman right between the eyes. The warrior fell, spilling blood and brains from the cleft in his skull, and the highborn planted a heel in Spite's right side before the creature holding his arm could pull him to the ground. On command the warbeast pivoted right, slashing its powerful tail in an arc to the left. It struck the unwary beastman full in the back with bone-crushing force, tearing the warrior free from Malus and sending its broken body hurtling through the air.

Foam dripping from its fanged snout, the beastman with the cleaver switched targets and charged at Malus, but Spite lunged forward and caught the running warrior in its teeth, shaking the creature like a dog shakes a rabbit. Bones cracked and snapped, and the cleaver spun out of the beastman's lifeless hands. The nauglir took a quick, convulsive bite and the warrior fell in two bloody pieces. That left the lone spearman who turned and ran for its life, bleating in terror as it headed deeper into the camp.

Malus settled himself back in the saddle and grabbed the reins in his left fist. 'Sound the call for the knights to rally and follow me!' he shouted at Shevael, and kicked Spite into a run.

The sky above the Chaos camp glowed a dull orange from the fires of burning tents. Sounds of battle echoed from every side; he wondered how the cavalry was faring to either side of his knights but there was no way to tell from where he was sitting. He cut the straightest path through the camp he could manage, driving Spite over and through any tent in his path. Behind him he heard Shevael sound his war-horn and then distant shouts and thudding feet as the household knights responded.

Trusting that the knights were right behind him, Malus plunged ahead, searching desperately for any signs he was nearing Nagaira's tent. How far into the camp was he? A mile, a mile and a half? There was no way to be sure. The scouts said three miles to the centre of camp, he thought grimly, watching hunched-over beastmen scramble out of the path of the charging cold one. One of the creatures stumbled on a rope, and before it could recover he hacked off its head as he swept by, splashing dark blood against the side of a nearby tent.

Without warning Spite burst into a large, cleared area surrounded by tents. Malus quickly stole a look behind him to see if Shevael and the knights were back there, and the lapse of attention very nearly cost him his life.

Suddenly the air rang with the shrill scream of horses and the bitter oaths of men. Two small objects struck Malus in quick succession, one bouncing off his breastplate and the other ricocheting from his pauldron and scoring a bloody line across his cheek. Startled, the highborn brought his head around just as another hand axe spun by, missing his nose by inches.

He'd ridden right into an improvised picket line where a band of marauders had tied up their horses for the night. The small, grassy space was packed with a dozen screaming, rearing horses and their men, who now turned on the highborn and attacked him with whatever weapons were to hand.

Spite, smelling horseflesh, bellowed hungrily and leapt for the nearest animal. The horse shrieked and reared, slashing at the air with its hooves as its rider shouted vile oaths and struggled to keep his seat. Malus was in a similar predicament, shouting and cursing at the warbeast as it clamped its jaws around the horse's neck and pushed forward on its powerful hind legs, trying to bear the animal to the ground.

Another axe hissed past Malus's head. Shouting, tattooed warriors rushed at him from left and right, brandishing swords and short spears. The highborn jerked at the reins, trying to get Spite to release the squealing horse, but the nauglir refused to give up its prey. The nauglir surged forward, driving the animal over onto its side. Its rider leapt clear, but Malus, caught unawares by the sudden movement was catapulted from the saddle. He flew over Spite's bloodied head and landed just on the other side of the thrashing, dying horse – a few scant feet from its enraged owner.

The marauder was on him in an instant, bellowing a war cry in his barbarian tongue. A rough hand seized the highborn's dark hair and pulled his head up, exposing his throat to the marauder's upraised blade. Malus caught the downward-sweeping sword against the side of his axe, and then drove the end of its haft into the marauder's leg just above the knee. The blunt haft rebounded from the human's thick muscles, but the painful blow staggered him for a moment. Malus jabbed him again, this time in the groin, and the marauder's grip on his hair loosened. The highborn tore himself free and rolled quickly away, scrambling to his feet beside the dying horse to receive the barbarian's charge – and a hurled axe flew out of the darkness and hit Malus in the side of the head.

The axe had been poorly thrown, and struck Malus with the top edge instead of the blade. But the world dissolved in a flash of searing pain, and he dimly felt the impact as his body hit the ground once more. Sounds came and went, and though he could still see, his mind couldn't quite make sense of what was happening. He felt, distinctly, a rivulet of ichor make its way slowly down the side of his head and begin to pool in the hollow of his throat.

He felt the ground shake beneath him, and an awful, low moaning reverberate through the air. The world seemed to grow dark, and for a moment an icy rage galvanised him at the thought that he was about to die.

At that moment, everything snapped back into place – and he saw that the darkness was the shadow of the howling marauder, looming over him with sword upraised.

With a shout Malus tried to roll further away but fetched up against the twitching corpse of the marauder's horse. The sword swept down in a blurring arc and the highborn caught the blow on the haft of his axe. More blows rained down amid a stream of burning curses, several slipping past his guard and ringing off his enchanted armour. Gritting his teeth, Malus threw up his left arm and caught the next blow on his vambrace, then chopped one-handed at the human's right knee. He felt the keen blade split the kneecap and the man fell onto the highborn's lower body, bellowing in rage and pain.

Quick to follow up on his success, Malus sat up and swung hard for the marauder's shaggy head – but the man caught the haft of the axe in his left hand and stopped it cold. Glaring balefully from beneath craggy brows, the marauder let out a lunatic chuckle and flexed his powerful shoulders and arms, forcing the weapon back. Malus cursed and spat, the axe quivering in his hands, but the human's fearsome strength was far greater than his own. Slowly but surely the highborn was pushed backwards and the Chaos warrior dragged himself up the highborn's body, drawing a long, serrated dagger from a sheath at his belt.

Malus's axe was forced past his head and the curved blade driven into the blood-soaked ground. The marauder loomed over him, his scarred lips pulling back to reveal crudely filed teeth. Hot, foetid breath blew in the highborn's face. The marauder whispered something in his bestial tongue and raised his dagger to strike.

Suddenly the highborn's body spasmed and searing ice flowed through his veins. He cried out in shock as needles of pain wracked his eyes. The marauder, seeing what was etched in them, recoiled from Malus with a shriek of wordless terror that ended in a bone-jarring crunch as Spite lunged over the horse's ravaged body and bit the man cleanly in half. Malus was deluged in a shower of blood and spilled entrails as the marauder's lower torso emptied itself onto his chest.

'Mother of Night!' Malus cursed furiously, shoving the steaming remains away and climbing to his feet. Spite had returned to feasting on the horse's innards, and the highborn swatted the nauglir across its bloody snout with the flat of his axe. 'Stop thinking with your damned stomach, you great lump of scales!' he shouted hoarsely. The nauglir flinched from the blow, shaking its gore-stained snout like a large dog, and lowered obediently onto its haunches.

Druchii knights swarmed through the cleared area, and the mangled bodies of horses and marauders lay in bloody heaps all around. Malus staggered over to the nauglir and rested his pounding head against the saddle for a moment before putting his foot in the stirrup and levering himself back into his seat.

'My lord!' Shevael cried from the other side of the cleared area. He hauled on his reins and trotted quickly to his master's side, his bloodstained sword resting against his shoulder. 'I saw you go down, and then the marauders came at me, and – Blessed Murderer! You're wounded!'

The highborn rubbed at the sticky mess covering his face and neck. 'Most of this isn't mine,' he growled, scanning the area quickly. He counted close to fifty knights milling about the picket area, their armour splashed with streaks of gore. Overhead the sky glowed a fierce orange, and the stink of burning hair hung like a pall over the battlefield. There were faint shouts off to the north and the east, but the sounds of fighting had all but tapered away. 'Where are the chariots?' he demanded, spitting bits of human flesh out of his mouth.

Shevael gave Malus a blank look. 'I… don't know,' he said sheepishly. 'We lost sight of them right after I sounded the call to rally. We must have got separated in the confusion.'

Malus cursed under his breath. He had been depending on the chariots to support their withdrawal after they killed Nagaira. The highborn stood as straight in the saddle as he could and tried to see over the leaning tops of wrecked tents, but with the darkness and the columns of smoke rising from nearly every direction it was impossible to see where his troops were. The sea of rough tents was acting against the druchii now, channelling the riders into a dark, twisting maze that worked to separate the banners from one another. 'It's too quiet,' he said uneasily.

'It's been like that for several minutes,' Shevael said. 'The Chaos horde is in full flight. The attack has filled them with panic!' he said excitedly.

But the highborn shook his head worriedly. 'Something's not right,' he said. 'We've got to get moving, Shevael. Where is Lord Suheir?'

Shevael pointed to the north. 'He continued on with most of the knights a few moments ago,' the young highborn replied. 'He said that he caught sight of a cluster of tents on a nearby hill that might be the war leader's pavilion.'

Malus gathered up Spite's reins. 'That's where we need to be,' he snapped. 'Household knights!' he cried, raising his gory axe. 'With me!'

Lord Suheir's knights had blazed broad trails through the jumble of tents, trampling everything in their path as they drove relentlessly north. Malus picked the centre path and led the knights along at a brisk trot, searching the twisting side lanes for enemy activity as they rode. Could the enemy have panicked so completely? If so, would Nagaira still be in her tents? He tried to guess how long it had been since the attack began: five minutes, perhaps? Ten? It was hard to be sure. Time became elastic in the heat of battle, seeming to rush by in some moments and slow to a crawl in others.

They rushed forward into darkness, hearing the roaring of the flames swell around and ahead of them. Fires had leapt out of control among the filthy tents, and the night sky was thickening with stinking smoke. His eyes strained to make out the nearby hill that Shevael spoke of, but he could see nothing in the shifting murk. Worry started to eat at his nerves; his army was no longer under his control, which meant that he had almost no way of pulling them back if something went disastrously wrong. In case they were separated, all of the banner and regimental officers knew a series of locations to retreat to along the route back to the Black Tower, but would they turn back in time? A moment's indecision could cost thousands of lives. For a moment he was tempted to order Shevael to sound a general retreat, then lead the household knights himself on to find Nagaira's tent. But the Chaos horde would hear the horn as well, and once they saw the druchii forces breaking away they would rush in pursuit, leaving Malus and his men advancing right into their teeth. He beat his armoured gauntlet on the cantle of his saddle in frustration. There were no good options that he could determine.

Suddenly a wild shout and the clash of arms echoed through
the murk in the near distance. As if on cue, the wind shifted,
drawing back the veil of smoke and revealing a roughly
circular cluster of low, indigo-hued tents covering a broad hill
less than a quarter mile ahead. A fierce melee had erupted at
the base of the hill; Malus could see Lord Suheir's knights
hacking away at a large force of beastmen, who fought with
ferocious zeal against their better-armed foes. Suheir's larger
force was moving quickly to surround the base of the hill
completely, cutting it off from the rest of the camp. Clearly the
knight-captain believed that he'd found their objective, and
looking up at the cluster of tents, Malus agreed.

'This is it!' he cried to the knights following in his wake. 'Forward up the hill – kill everything that gets in your way!' With
a shout, the knights of the Black Tower spurred their mounts
forward, forming into a wedge formation as compact and
powerful as a spearhead. 'Shevael, sound the charge!'

The young highborn let out a long, howling note from his
horn and like a bolt shot from a crossbow the wedge of
knights hurtled towards the hill. Lord Suheir's knights heard
the horn and saw Malus's approach, and riders scrambled to
open a gap in their lines for the wedge to pass through. Howling, roaring beastmen swarmed into the gap, oblivious to the
doom bearing down on them.

At the point of the wedge, Malus raised his axe above his
head and gave his foes a savage, red-toothed grin. Horned
heads turned at the thunder of the knights' approach. Braying
calls rang out from the knot of beastmen, and the huge creatures hefted clubs, mattocks and axes to receive the highborn's
charge.

The highborn gauged the distance carefully, glaring balefully
at the snarling mob of beastmen. At the last moment, just
before Spite crashed into their ranks, he planted his heels in
the nauglir's flanks and hauled back on the reins. 'Up, Spite!'
he cried. 'Up!'

With a thunderous roar the cold one bent low – and leapt
into the mass of enemy troops. The one-ton warbeast smashed

into the enemy like a hammer, scattering and trampling the beastmen with bone-crushing force. Malus chopped at upturned snouts and chests, alternating blows to his left and his right, inflicting horrific wounds on his stunned foes. Thick, bitter blood burst from ruptured arteries and shattered skulls.

But the rear ranks of the beastmen refused to give way – if anything they redoubled their attack in the face of Malus's charge. A howling beast rushed at the highborn from the right, smashing his club into Malus's hip. His armour turned aside much of the blow, but he roared out in pain and buried his axe deep in the beastman's shoulder. Spite lunged forward and bit off another beastman's head, its skull and horns crunching between the nauglir's jaws like brittle wood. An axe blow glanced from the highborn's left leg. Malus yanked his weapon free from his victim's shoulder and brought it down on the head of his foe to the left. Brains spattered against the highborn's face. Then a surge of armoured figures swept up on Malus's flanks as the rest of the knights cut their way to his side.

'Again, Spite! Up!' he shouted, kicking his heels. The nauglir obeyed, gathering itself and leaping up and through the thin line of beastmen blocking their way. As they landed, Malus pivoted the nauglir hard to the right, using its powerful tail to smash aside a pair of beastmen that had escaped the cold one's rush. Their numbers scattered by the brute force of Malus's manoeuvre, the beastmen became easy prey to the knights following in his wake, and the remaining warriors fighting against Lord Suheir's troops began a fighting withdrawal up the hill. Malus turned to his men and pointed at the beastmen with his axe. 'At them! Into their flanks!' He put his spurs to Spite's flanks and led the knights up the hill at a shallow angle, intercepting the retreating beastmen. Pressed hard from behind and now attacked from the flank, the beastman rearguard collapsed.

Malus kept Spite moving steadily uphill, riding down a fleeing beastman and burying his axe into the warrior's back. Spite lunged forward and caught another in its jaws, biting through its abdomen and letting legs and torso roll bloodily downhill. The nauglir's lashing tail accounted for another foe, breaking its legs with a vicious sweep and leaving the beastman to be trampled by the oncoming knights.

Ahead, a single surviving beastman disappeared inside the shadowy opening of the first tent. Malus reined in Spite outside the enclosure and leapt to the ground, axe at the ready. Within moments he was surrounded by a half-dozen more knights, including Shevael and Lord Suheir. 'Well done, Suheir,' Malus said, saluting the knight-captain, then he addressed the assembled druchii. 'Remember, we're after a potent sorceress. She's no doubt defended by all manner of magical traps and summoned beasts. When we reach her, hold our line of retreat open and let me deal with her.'

Suheir and the knights nodded their helmeted heads, saving their breath for the hard fighting ahead. Malus adjusted his grip on the blood-slick axe haft. You'll not escape me this time sister, the highborn thought grimly. You should have fled while you had the chance.

'All right,' he said. 'Let's go.'

Weapons ready, the druchii entered the gloomy confines of the first tent. The enclosure was dimly lit by a few guttering oil lamps, and the air was thick with a musky incense. Within lay piles of metal that glittered dully in the weak light: fine swords and battered armour, many still marked with dried blood and bits of flesh, as well as silver plates, goblets and other bits of valuable plunder looted from the razed watchtowers. Lord Suheir eyed the piles with some bemusement. 'A funny place for a treasure trove,' he murmured.

'They are offerings to the sorceress,' Malus replied. 'The beastmen and the marauders give her their best plunder as a sign of subservience. It's a statement of power, not greed.'

'It sounds as though you know this sorceress well,' Suheir mused.

'More than I'd like,' the highborn replied, edging across the enclosure.

At the far end of the wide tent lay a heavy hanging of red-dyed canvas. Malus paused before the hanging, uncertain of what lay beyond. Suheir shouldered his way through the group, hefting his shield. 'I'll go first,' he said quietly, stepping carefully up to the covered opening. He studied the cloth and its borders carefully, and finding no strange markings, he slashed his sword across the hanging, revealing the beastman waiting in ambush on the other side.

With a braying roar the horned warrior lunged at Suheir, chopping at the knight's helmeted head. Suheir absorbed the blow against the face of his shield and stabbed low with his sword, catching the beastman in the belly. The warrior staggered, bellowing in rage and pain, and the knight-captain slashed his sword across the creature's abdomen, spilling its guts onto the grassy floor. The beastman collapsed with a groan and Suheir knocked it aside with his shield, then advanced warily into the space beyond with Malus close behind.

The second enclosure was even darker and smokier than the previous one. Huddled shapes knelt in groups of eight in each corner of the space, their heads bowed in supplication as they faced four pathways through the square space. Each pathway led to another cloth hanging, including the one the druchii entered through. Suheir started upon seeing the silhouetted figures, then bent close and prodded one with the point of his sword. 'Dead,' he grunted. 'Looks like mummified beastmen. The incense covers the stink, I suppose.'

Malus nodded silently, gooseflesh racing down his spine as he remembered a similar chamber in the daemon's temple far to the north. 'We're in the right place,' he whispered. 'Head through the opening on the other side of the tent.'

Suheir stepped warily among the mummified corpses and cut down the hanging on the opposite end of the tent. Beyond lay a long, rectangular tent, lit at the far end with two small witch-lamps. Along the length of the tent treble rows of kneeling figures lined both sides of a narrow aisle. 'Blessed Murderer,' Suheir cursed softly, studying the mummified attendants.

They were not beastmen this time, but druchii highborn, clad in battered armour and ragged, bloodstained kheitans. Some had limbs and heads crudely stitched back into place.

Their helmets had been removed, revealing gaping head wounds here and there, and showing the looks of fear and agony frozen on their pallid features.

'More tribute for the war leader,' Malus growled. 'We're close now. Press on.'

Suheir took a deep breath and nodded gravely, then edged his way down the long aisle. At the far end lay a pair of hangings this time, their indigo panels stitched with arcane sigils in gold and silver thread. An invisible nimbus of magic hung about the portal, setting Malus's hair on end.

The highborn turned to the men behind him. 'Wait here,' he said. 'Suheir and Shevael, come with me.'

Steeling himself, he shouldered past the knight-captain and pushed his way past the heavy cloth panels. Everything about this felt wrong. Where were the attendants? The guards? He feared that the pavilion had been abandoned when the attack began, and their bold assault had been for nothing.

Malus stepped past the hangings into a spacious tent set with tables, small bookshelves and chairs, all of which were piled with books, papers and yellowed scrolls. Candles burned on several tables, and a pair of braziers near the centre filled the space with reddish light.

At the far end of the enclosure, on a small dais set with a low-backed chair, sat a solitary figure in a dark, hooded robe.

For a moment Malus was too stunned to react. He could feel the intensity of the figure's gaze smouldering hatefully from the shadows of the wide hood.

'It's a trap,' he declared, and knew with an awful certainty that his intuition was true. He couldn't imagine how Nagaira could have anticipated his attack, but she'd waited here in her tent, knowing that he would come for her.

Grabbing his axe tightly, Malus charged across the room. 'Hear me, Tz'arkan!' he hissed. 'Grant me your gifts!' It was the one and only advantage he possessed, and he'd planned to use it when he came face-to-face with his sister. Now he prayed that if he struck swiftly enough he could forestall whatever ambuscade she'd devised.

Black corruption seethed in Malus's veins, spreading like a cold fire beneath his skin. He crossed the room in an eye blink propelled by a daemonic wind. With a savage curse burning on his lips he struck at the hooded figure with all his strength.

The axe blurred through the air, straight for the figure's head. Quicker than the eye could follow, a pair of long blades swept up from beneath the robes and blocked the highborn's downward stroke with a flare of sparks and a ringing clash of steel. The loose robe fell away and the figure rose, effortlessly pushing Malus backward off the dais.

Instead of Nagaira, Malus found himself face-to-face with an armoured Chaos knight, clad in armour similar to a druchii knight but covered in patterns of blasphemous runes painted in blood. Red light seeped sullenly from gaps in the sorcerous armour, and shone from the oculars of the champion's ornate, horned helmet. Twin druchii longswords held Malus's axe at bay with fearsome strength. Around the champion's neck rested a heavy, red-gold torc.

'The Amulet of Vaurog!' Tz'arkan hissed, roiling inside Malus's chest.

And with that, the trap was sprung.

Chapter Twelve
SHIELDS AND SPEARS

A SECOND CHAMPION, Malus realised with a sense of ominous dread. Suddenly the tremendous size of the Chaos horde made terrible sense. Nagaira hadn't raised the horde alone, but had allied herself with a powerful warlord and won him to her cause.

There was a tremor in the air of Nagaira's tent, like the movement of unseen spirits, and suddenly a chorus of screams and the clash of steel rang out in the antechamber behind the druchii. Then in the far distance Malus heard a roaring, skirling sound that cried out from all along the invisible horizon – it was the wailing of hundreds of war horns, loosing the Chaos horde at last.

With a shriek of rage Malus drew back his axe and hammered the Chaos champion with a storm of vicious strokes at head, neck, chest and arms. Sparks flew and tempered steel sang, but the champion blocked the furious blows with superhuman speed. A return stroke slipped easily past Malus's guard and rang off his pauldron; another struck like an adder and glanced off his right wrist. The champion's twin swords clashed and whirled in a graceful, deadly dance, driving the highborn inexorably backwards in spite of Tz'arkan's potent gifts.

Malus blocked a lightning thrust to his stomach with the haft of his axe and thrust upwards, hoping to catch the champion beneath the chin with the weapon's curved upper edge, but the armoured warrior checked his advance at the last moment and let the axe slide harmlessly by. Without stopping the highborn pivoted smoothly on his heel and swung around and down, aiming for the warrior's right knee, but the champion anticipated the blow and his right-hand sword parried the stroke with ease. At the same time his left-hand blade blurred at Malus's head, and only the daemon's inhuman reflexes drew him back in time. Even so, the sword drew a shallow cut across the highborn's forehead, sending thick streams of ichor down the side of his face.

He'd heard tales of the phenomenal power and skill of warriors chosen by the Chaos gods, but the reality was far more terrifying than he'd imagined. Even the zealots of the cult of Khaine, who worshipped the art of killing, could not compare with the champion's implacable skill. Thinking quickly, Malus retreated from the armoured warrior, desperately looking for some way to turn the battle to his advantage.

The momentary distraction was nearly enough to seal his fate. A sword leapt like lighting at the highborn's face; Malus twisted at the last moment, dodging the blow with a hiss of surprise, but realised, too late, that the attack was a feint. The champion's second sword swung down in a vicious arc and caught his left leg, just above the side of the knee. Fiery pain shot up Malus's leg and it gave way beneath him, toppling him to the matted earth. He fetched up next to an oak table plundered from one of the fallen watchtowers as the champion pressed his advantage and loomed over the highborn like a swooping hawk.

Malus threw a frantic swing at the warrior's midsection, hoping to spoil his attack, but the swing was off-balance and only served to leave him more exposed than before. The champion's right-hand blade rose above his helmeted head and chopped down in a backhanded blow that struck the haft of Malus's axe above his right hand and sheared through it like a sapling. The warrior's left-hand sword plummeted like a thunderbolt, and the highborn raised the severed length of axe-haft and caught the fearsome blow on the seasoned oak between his white-knuckled fists. The keen blade split the haft once again and the sword struck the highborn's breastplate hard enough to drive the air from his lungs.

Then Malus heard a roar like an angry bull and an onrushing shadow swept over him from behind. There was a crash of steel against iron and a shower of fiery orange coals seemed to drift lazily through the air as Lord Suheir smashed aside one of the braziers in a headlong charge at the Chaos champion. The powerfully built knight-captain swung a fearsome stroke at the champion's helm, but the warrior swayed backwards with serpentine grace and let the blade pass harmlessly by, then lashed out with his right-hand sword in a backhanded stroke that struck Suheir's vambrace a glancing blow. Malus saw a spray of blood burst from the point of impact, then watched as the champion thrust with his left-hand sword and stab its reinforced point into the knight-captain's side. The sword punched cleanly through Suheir's breastplate and sank an inch deep, just above the waist. Suheir staggered for just a moment, then lashed out with a backhanded stroke of his own that knocked the champion's stabbing blade aside before rushing the armoured warrior with his steel-rimmed shield held before him. For the first time the champion seemed taken by surprise, and back-pedalled furiously in the face of Suheir's bull-like charge.

Hands grabbed at Malus's shoulders, trying to pull him upright. The highborn looked up to see Shevael's pale, terrified face. The young knight's movements seemed clumsy and slow to the highborn's daemonic reflexes. 'How do we kill him?' Shevael moaned.

The Chaos champion's retreat was swift, but not swift enough. With a roar, Suheir struck the warrior's breastplate with the edge of his shield and set the champion crashing backwards through a small bookcase. Malus grabbed Shevael's arm and staggered upright, biting back a savage curse at the pain in his damaged leg.

Just a few feet away Suheir pressed his attack, hammering at the champion with one fearsome blow after another that tried to batter aside the warrior's defences. The champion blocked each stroke with nimble movements of his left-hand sword. Then, just as Suheir drew back for another punishing stroke, the champion lashed out at the knight-captain's shield arm, knocking it wide so that he could lunge forward with his right-hand sword and strike the side of Suheir's left knee. The knight-captain's armour didn't carry the same enchantments as Malus's did; steel pins snapped, lames and poleyn shattered and the champion's sword carved deep into the knee-joint. The druchii fell onto his good knee with a bellow of pain, covering his wounded leg with his shield as the Chaos warrior sprang to his feet like a hill-cat and levelled his weapons at Suheir's head.

The Chaos warrior was so intent on finishing the knight-captain that he didn't see the table Malus hurled at him until it was far too late. With no time to duck or dodge the solid oaken tabletop the champion could only raise his swords and smash the hurtling furniture to bits with his twin swords.

Above the splintering crash of the thick wood rose a furious roar and the ringing clash of steel on steel. The Chaos champion staggered back half a step – and slowly lowered his head to the length of druchii steel jutting from his midsection. Suheir's fearsome strength had driven his blade clean through the champion's torso, emerging more than a foot from the warrior's steel backplate.

And yet the champion did not fall. For an appalling instant the two warriors were transfixed, each staring at the wound Suheir's sword had made. A line of thick, black ichor flowed heavily down the back of the silver steel blade. Then with a guttural growl the champion's swords flashed and Suheir's head bounced across the matted earth. The knight-captain's body toppled onto its side, pouring a freshet of blood onto the ground, while the champion drove his right-hand sword into the dirt and used his free hand to reach for Suheir's sword, still jutting from his abdomen.

Shevael let out a panicked wail and Malus pushed him away, gritting his teeth at the pain as he limped quickly across the chamber. Flames were climbing the back wall of the tent and licking at several of the bookshelves, kindled by the scattered coals from the upended brazier.

The young highborn staggered, his face a pale mask of terror and rage. With a trembling hand he drew his second sword, and with a deep breath a sense of eerie calm stole across his features. 'Make your escape, my lord,' the young highborn shouted. 'I'll cover your retreat.'

Shevael's grim tone brought Malus up short. 'No, you young fool!' he cried. 'You don't stand a chance–'

But the young highborn wasn't listening. With a furious shout he charged at the struggling champion, his twin swords describing a deadly figure-eight pattern. The Chaos champion lurched backwards in the wake of the sudden attack, stumbling on a pile of spilled books, and Shevael's swords struck the warrior multiple times in the head, chest and leg. But the young highborn's blows were hasty and poorly aimed, and could not penetrate the champion's heavy armour. The Chaos warrior righted himself and with a convulsive motion wrenched Suheir's ichor-stained sword from his body. Still shouting curses at the champion, Shevael pressed his attack, but he underestimated the Chaos warrior's skill. As the young highborn rushed in the champion backhanded Shevael across the face with the pommel of Suheir's dripping blade and in the same motion extended his left arm and stabbed the young knight in the throat. Bright, red blood burst from the awful wound and Shevael collapsed to the ground, gasping and choking for air.

Cursing bitterly, Malus reached his objective. His armoured fingers closed about the iron grillwork of the second brazier, the drying blood on his armoured fingers hissing on contact.

Using his daemonically-infused strength he lifted the red-hot container and hurled it at the champion, catching the Chaos warrior full in the chest. The warrior fell with a resounding clang and a hiss of scorched flesh, his body covered in searing coals and ash. More embers scattered across the enclosure, burning holes in the tent wall and starting more fires among the shredded papers.

Malus leapt to Shevael's side, but already the blood flow from this torn throat was ebbing and his eyes were glassy and unfocused. The highborn shook the young druchii roughly. 'Don't die on me, you damned fool!' the highborn snarled, but it was already far too late. Shevael's eyes rolled back in his head and his body went limp.

Cursing bitterly, the highborn pulled the horn from around Shevael's neck and with a grim look in his eye he pulled off the young highborn's sword belt and buckled it about his waist. The tent by this point was blazing on every side, and waves of heat and choking smoke surrounded him. Coughing furiously, he snatched up the young highborn's swords just as the Chaos champion regained his senses and kicked his way clear of the burning brazier.

Malus fought a tide of black rage as the champion struggled to his feet. He wanted nothing more than to avenge himself upon the foul warrior, but this was not the time. The Chaos fiends had sprung their ambush, and if he didn't get his troops out of the camp they were going to be slaughtered. He'd sooner see his soul lost to Tz'arkan for all time than suffer such a black stain to his honour. With a last, hateful look at the Chaos champion, Malus turned and raced back the way he'd come.

As he pulled back the double hangings however, he was brought up short by a nightmarish scene of carnage. The long, rectangular tent swarmed with the pale figures of the living dead. The druchii corpses that had knelt in supplication along the narrow aisle had sprung to grisly life at some invisible command and attacked the knights Malus had left behind as a rearguard. Many of the stitched-together revenants had been hacked apart, but the rest now hunched over the ruptured bodies of the tower knights, their chalk-white hands slick with blood and torn meat. Several slack-jawed faces turned in Malus's direction as he stood upon the threshold, and the highborn recoiled from the charnel scene with a blasphemous curse.

Behind him the champion lurched to his feet and gathered up his swords. Malus looked quickly about, seeing nothing but flames to left and right, and came to a decision. Taking a deep breath, he raised Shevael's blades and dived headlong through the blazing canvas to his left.

Heat and smoke washed over him for a searing instant, and then he was stumbling through the darkened confines of an adjoining tent, piled high with cushions and sleeping furs. Malus staggered headlong across the tent and slashed at the far wall with both swords. A draught of cool air washed over the highborn's face and he leapt through the shredded cloth, emerging into the night air. Screams and wild howls echoed through the flame-shot darkness all around the hill as the Chaos horde charged out of their hidden positions outside the camp and rushed at the druchii raiders. Knowing that every second counted for the isolated bands of cavalry and footmen, the highborn put Shevael's horn to his lips and blew the general retreat as loudly as he could. He sounded the call three more times, pointing the horn to the east, north and west, then let the instrument fall to his side and headed back to the waiting knights as quickly as he could. As Nagaira's pavilion burned, Malus cut his way through two more tents that lay between him and the mounted warriors, kicking aside piles of skulls and golden plunder as he went.

At last he emerged, bloodied and smoke-stained, before the nervous household knights. They were facing outwards in a large circle, listening to the echoing cries of the enemy and waiting for the onslaught to begin. Even the nauglir sensed the peril approaching, pawing the earth and lowering their heads threateningly.

'Here, Spite!' Malus called as he staggered up to the circle. The knights started at the ghastly apparition of the highborn. 'My lord!' one of the druchii cried out. 'We feared the worst–'

'And you were right to do so,' the highborn said grimly, sheathing his left-hand sword. 'I've led us straight into an ambush.' Without waiting for Spite to sink to his haunches the highborn took a deep breath and hauled himself into the saddle. For good measure he drew the war-horn and sounded the retreat one last time, eliciting a chorus of savage howls from the darkness close by. 'That's it,' he shouted. 'Close order formation! We're falling back to the spearmen and we're not stopping for anyone or anything.' He raised the sword in his right hand.

'Household knights! Forward!' Malus said, and kicked Spite into a run just as the first mobs of beastmen came howling out of the burning night.

MALUS AND THE knights came thundering down out of the charred outskirts of the Chaos encampment with a screaming horde at their heels. True to his word, they'd smashed through or trampled over everything that stood in their path. The highborn's sword streamed thick ropes of blood into the ashen wind, and the nauglirs' snouts glistened with the vital fluids of beastmen and marauders who had been caught before the avalanche of steel and scale.

More than a dozen riderless cold ones loped in the formation's wake, following along with the rest of the pack now that no rider lived to guide them. Knights had been pulled from the saddle by leaping horrors, or felled by flung axes or spears. Each loss was a blow to Malus's pride, a mark of failure that burned worse than any blade and added its weight to the disaster unfolding around him.

As they burst from the smoking confines of the camp Malus looked to the brim of the low hill ahead and his spirits rose as he saw the long lines of spearmen, their shields and spear tips gleaming against the firelight. If they could hold long enough...

Malus pointed his sword to the left and the household knights responded, pivoting smartly and thundering past the spear wall's right flank. The highborn saw the wide-eyed faces of the front ranks as they galloped by, and sensed the fear gripping the young spearmen. No one had told them what was going on, but they knew something wasn't right.

The highborn led the knights down the reverse slope of the hill and called a halt. Off to the right, some fifty yards away, stood a knot of some two hundred cavalrymen. One banner of horse out of six; Malus glanced quickly about and bit back a curse when he could find no more. He turned back to the knights. 'Who is the senior knight now that Lord Suheir is dead?'

Searching glances passed between the assembled warriors. Finally a gruff-looking older knight raised his hand. 'I am, my lord. Dachvar of Klar Karond.'

'Very well, Dachvar. You're in command now,' Malus said. 'Rest your men and see to your mounts. I expect to have need of you again shortly.' Without waiting for a reply he turned Spite about and headed up behind the spear regiments at a run.

The three units stood in close formation, nearly shield-to-shield about a quarter of the way down the hill-slope. Each spearman carried not only his spear, shield and short sword, but also a heavy repeating crossbow and a quiver of black bolts. These were now being loaded by the rear two ranks of each company as the highborn reached the crest of the hill and found Lord Meiron and Lord Rasthlan studying the howling, roaring mob of Chaos troops massing on the far hillside some two hundred yards distant. A short distance down the reverse slope he saw Rasthlan's autarii scouts crouched together in a small group, smoking pipes and speaking to one another in low tones.

Malus reined in beside the two commanders and hastily returned their salutes.

'My compliments on your deployment, Lord Meiron,' the highborn said, using the advantage of height to study the disposition of the spear regiments. 'I'd hoped we wouldn't have need of your spears, but now it appears you'll anchor our rearguard. Has there been any sign of our chariots or the rest of our cavalry?'

'None, my lord,' Meiron replied gravely. 'It's possible the chariots were caught in the fires that swept through the enemy camp – we haven't heard the rumble of their wheels for some time.' He gave the highborn a shrug. 'As to the cavalry, they may be half a dozen leagues away by now. Most of those young bravos are like wolf cubs – they'll chase anything that moves.'

'Lord Irhaut thinks like a hill bandit, my lord,' Rasthlan interjected. 'He has trained his banner leaders to retreat in the face of a superior foe and lead pursuers away from the rest of the army. What Lord Meiron means is that the light horse could be miles away to east and west, drawing off as many of the Chaos forces as possible.'

From the look on Meiron's face it was clear he meant to say no such thing – he was a dyed-in-the-wool infantry commander with nothing but disdain for cavalrymen – but Malus accepted Rasthlan's explanation with a knowing nod. 'Then let us pray to the Dark Mother that he and his men are successful,' the highborn said, his expression grim. 'Because it looks like we have all we can handle right here.'

A cacophonous roar filled the air at the edge of the Chaos encampment. Beastmen threw back their heads and brayed to the smoke-shrouded moon and tattooed humans beat their swords against their shields and howled the names of their blasphemous gods. They swelled in number with every passing moment, spilling like a black tide down the slopes of the far hill. Malus couldn't guess at the size of the mob, but it was certain that the druchii were heavily outnumbered. The noise washed over the spear formations and murmurs of fear could be heard from among the state regiments. The Black Guard, holding the centre of the line, were silent and still as statues, waiting simply for the battle to begin.

Lord Meiron turned to the spearmen and bellowed in a leathery voice that sawed through the raucous din. 'Stand fast, you whoresons!' he snarled. 'Shields up and eyes front! Those degenerate bastards are working up the courage to charge up this hill and throw away their lives! If I were a holy man I would fall to the ground and thank Khaine almighty for foes as stupid as these!'

Cheers and hisses of laughter went up from the ranks, and the spearmen shook their weapons at the swelling horde. Lord Meiron turned back to Malus and smiled proudly. 'Fear not, my lord,' he said. 'We'll see to these animals.'

'I'll hold you to that, Lord Meiron,' Malus said with a nod, then wheeled Spite about and rode downhill to the group of cavalrymen. The light horsemen were stragglers from a number of different banners and were clearly exhausted, their faces and armour stained with layers of smoke and blood. As the highborn approached, the riders sat straighter in the saddle and chivvied their mounts into something resembling a formation. Malus pulled quickly into shouting distance and cried, 'Secure the spears' left flank! The household knights will take the right.' The banner leader acknowledged the order with a salute and began shouting orders to his men, and the highborn turned Spite about and raced back to the waiting knights.

By the time he reached Dachvar the Chaos warriors were on the move. They seethed down the long slope in a ragged, bloodthirsty mass, running, shambling and loping with twisted and slithering strides. They waved crude weapons above their misshapen heads and screamed for the blood of their foes. To Malus's eyes there looked to be more than ten thousand of them, a sight that filled even his black heart with dread. It never should have come to this, he thought bitterly. How had Nagaira anticipated him?

The ground shook to the thunder of thousands of pounding feet. Horned heads and upraised swords stood out blackly against the hellish backdrop of the burning Chaos encampment.

When the first of the enemy warriors were a third of the way from the bottom of the far hill, Malus heard the rough voice of Lord Meiron cry out, 'Sa'an'ishar!' Instantly a rustle ran through the spear regiments as warriors readied their shields and levelled their long spear. Then: 'Rear ranks! Ready crossbows!'

A ripple of armoured forms ran the length of the battle line as druchii warriors raised their repeating crossbows to their shoulders and angled the weapons skyward. Lord Meiron raised his sword. 'Ready... ready... fire!'

Fifteen hundred crossbows thrummed, and a rain of black bolts hissed through the air. Not a one could fail to find a mark as they plunged into the mass of enemy troops, and howls of rage turned to agonised shrieks as the bolts tore through the poorly armoured warriors. Hundreds of humans and beastmen fell, their bodies trampled by their fellows as the rest of the mob ran on.

The charging Chaos troops had reached the bottom of the hill. An oiled rattle echoed up and down the line as the druchii quickly reloaded their weapons. 'Ready!' Lord Meiron cried. 'Fire!'

Another hissing storm of bolts plunged into the Chaos ranks. Hundreds more were wounded or slain, their bodies piling up at the base of the slope. Savage beastmen clambered over riddled corpses or knocked their injured mates aside, some crawling on all fours as they tried to reach the druchii line.

Once again the repeater crossbows rattled, readying another volley. The front ranks of the foemen were less than fifty yards away. 'First two ranks kneel!' Lord Meiron cried, and the spearmen dropped obediently to one knee. 'Rear ranks, fire!'

Black death scythed through the attackers, the powerful bolts punching completely through the closest enemy troops. The first three ranks of the Chaos warriors toppled like threshed wheat, and even Malus shook his head in awe at the scale of the slaughter. In less than a minute the hill slopes had become a killing field, carpeted with the bodies of the dead.

Yet still the Chaos horde came on.

They struck the line of spearmen with a great, rending crash of steel on wood that echoed from the hillsides. Axes, clubs, swords and claws battered against shield and helm, and the druchii line staggered beneath the weight of the enemy assault. It bent backwards a slow step at a time... then stopped. Malus could hear the rough voice of Lord Meiron spitting savage oaths at the troops, and the Black Guard responded with a collective roar. Spears flickered and stabbed into the press of foes, and howls of rage turned to screams of agony as the druchii warriors put their training and discipline to lethal effect.

But would it be enough? Beastmen and marauders were dying by the score, but from Malus's vantage point he could see spearmen pulled from the ranks and torn apart, or dashed to the ground by terrible blows. The flanking regiments were taking the worst of the punishment, their rear ranks rippling like wheat as wounded men were pulled from the line and new men rotated to take their place. The Chaos attack showed no signs of faltering, and more troops were streaming from the camp every minute to add their weight to the battle. If just one of the regiments broke and ran, the other two would be overwhelmed in moments.

They couldn't remain on the defensive for long, Malus saw. Their only option was to attack.

He drew his bloodstained sword and turned to Dachvar. 'We've got to take the pressure off the spearmen,' he said. 'The household knights will form line and we'll charge the Chaos bastards in the flank.'

'Aye, my lord,' Dachvar replied with a nod, then wheeled his nauglir about and trotted the length of the formation. 'Form line and prepare to charge!' he cried, and the knights readied themselves for battle.

Taking the lead, Malus angled Spite to the east and led the formation of knights around the side of the hill, where they could sweep around the slope and strike the Chaos warriors from the left flank. Long minutes passed while the large formation repositioned itself. Malus listened intently to the battle raging on the hilltop, knowing that every passing minute pushed the spearmen closer to the breaking point. Finally, Dachvar signalled at the far end of the line that all was in readiness, and Malus raised his sword. 'Sa'an'ishar! The household knights will advance at the charge!' Then he lowered his blade and the knights let out an exultant roar, kicking their mounts into a run.

There was neither the time nor the distance to work the formation up into a proper charge; the knights swept around the slope like a huge pack of wolves, plunging into the flank of the enemy with a bone-crushing impact of claws, teeth and steel. Spite trampled two beastmen beneath his broad feet and bit the head off another; Malus stabbed a stunned beastman in the back and slashed his sword across a leaping marauder's neck. The mob recoiled at the sudden shock, and the knights forced their way deeper into the mass, their red swords rising and falling and their cold ones flinging mangled bodies high into the air. Meiron's spearmen cheered and redoubled their efforts, reclaiming the few yards of ground they'd lost and pushing the enemy back down the slope.

Axes and clubs battered at Malus's armoured legs. A beastman tried to climb onto Spite's neck, swinging a cleaver-like sword at the highborn's chest. Malus caught the creature's sword-arm with a blow to the wrist that severed its hand, then stabbed the howling fiend in the chest. Its body left a gleaming trail of blood as it slid from the cold one back into the seething mob below, but another beastman literally leapt to take its place. Malus cursed, trading blows with the creature even as he felt another pair of hands to his left trying to pull him from the saddle. The charge had inflicted considerable damage but the mob continued to hold its ground, bolstered by its reinforcements and motivated by fear of its terrible leaders. Now that the knights were stuck in they'd lost their most crucial asset: mobility. Soon the greater numbers of the enemy would tell against them.

Malus feinted a cut at the beastman in front of him, inviting a response. When the creature lunged at him with its sword he was ready, stabbing it in the throat. The beast fell to the ground, coughing blood, and the highborn turned his attention to the braying monster pulling at his left leg. Distantly, he heard an ominous rumble of thunder roll from the depths of the Chaos encampment. What new threat was Nagaira sending his way?

A quick look uphill showed that the spear regiments had ceased their advance, fighting from their original positions at the brow of the hill. To his immediate left, one of the spear units had no foes to contend with at all thanks to the arrival of the knights. Still the enemy mob fought on, surrounding the hard-pressed knights and tearing at them in a frenzy of hate. No sooner had Malus despatched the beastman on his left than a heavy blow smashed into his hip on the right. Desperation began to take hold, and he considered calling a retreat.

Then suddenly the roll of thunder swelled in volume and Malus heard a titanic crash off to his right. Screams and howls of fear rent the air, and it seemed as though the entire enemy mob recoiled like a living thing. Malus heard the spearmen to his left start to cheer, and then he saw that the Chaos warriors were *retreating*, scattering into the darkness to the north-west. The household knights spurred their cold ones in pursuit, cutting down the fleeing foes, until shouted commands from Dachvar brought them to a halt.

A rattling rumble echoed up the slope behind Malus; he turned and saw it was one of the war chariots that had accompanied them from the Black Tower. Standing up in his stirrups, he could see more of the chariots milling about at the base of the hill, their wheels and fearsome scythe blades dripping with blood.

The charioteer behind the highborn reined in his paired cold ones, and the knight standing beside him dismounted and hurried over to Malus. 'My apologies for losing you during the advance, my lord,' the knight said gravely. 'We were forced to stick to those damned, twisting paths, and once we diverged it seemed that we never could head back in the right direction again.'

Malus leaned back in his saddle, breathing heavily and watching the last of the beastmen disappear into the smoke. 'The loss was sorely felt,' the highborn said. 'But your return more than made up for it. Gather your chariots, commander. You are now the rearguard. The spears must fall back to the next rally point with all haste, while we still have a little breathing room.'

The commander of the chariots saluted and headed quickly back to his mount. Malus reached behind him for his war horn, trying to remember how to sound a proper recall and withdrawal. By the grace of the goddess he'd won a momentary reprieve, but he still had to get the remainder of his army back to the tower before they were overrun.

Chapter Thirteen
THE LONG, BLOODY ROAD

'HERE THEY COME again!' one of the spearmen cried, his voice cracking with exhaustion and strain.

The marauder horsemen were pouring back over the ashen ridge, the hooves of their lean-limbed horses kicking up plumes of chalky dust that clung to the bare arms and faces of their riders. Ululating howls rose from the horsemen as they picked up speed down the shallow slope and thundered directly towards the ragged lines of the retreating druchii force.

Spears and shields rattled awkwardly as the exhausted soldiers readied themselves for yet another attack. Lord Meiron took a quick swig of watered wine from a leather flask at his hip and barked out hoarsely. 'No one shoots this time! Conserve your bolts until ordered to fire. Front ranks keep your damned shields up this time!'

Malus leaned back against his saddle and tried to rub the grit and exhaustion from his eyes. The band of horsemen was larger this time – yet another knot of marauders had caught up with the limping druchii raiders. The hit-and-run attacks were getting larger and more frequent. For the thousandth time since dawn he turned in the saddle and looked to the south. They had reached the Plain of Ghrond just at first light, and the sight of the distant tower had renewed their spirits somewhat, but for the last four hours they had only managed half a dozen miles. Chaos horsemen had been harassing them constantly, nipping at their heels like packs of wolves. The attacks had grown so numerous that the spearmen were forced to march in battle formation, limping along in a ragged line six hundred yards across.

They had marched all through the night, probed constantly by hunting parties of Chaos horsemen who struck at the rear columns of the retreating army and faded back into the darkness. For most of the night the surviving banner of light horse had fought hard to keep the enemy cavalry at bay, but now the horses were exhausted. Malus had realised belatedly that this was part of the marauders' strategy, but now it was too late. As the marauders swept down on the waiting spearmen the druchii cavalry could only watch helplessly from their staggering mounts, well behind the lines.

Lord Irhaut and the bulk of the light horse had never reappeared over the course of the night. Malus had kept the retreating force as long as he could at each of the rendezvous points, but there had been no sign of the lost horsemen. Finally, at the last rendezvous, the highborn had been forced to make a difficult decision. He'd summoned Lord Rasthlan and ordered him and his autarii scouts to break off and try to locate the scattered cavalry and link them up with the main body of the force. Rasthlan had accepted the order stoically, though it was clear from his manner that he didn't expect to find anyone still alive. That was the last Malus saw of him and his scouts.

Now he was out of ideas. For the last five hours the only horsemen who'd come riding over the ashen ridges had been painted in crude tattoos and crying for druchii blood.

The marauder horsemen fanned out into a thundering line as they charged at the druchii spearmen. Wild, tattooed faces screamed the names of blasphemous northern gods, and sunlight flashed on the tips of their short spears. The druchii had learned from experience that the marauders would play at pressing home a charge, then launch their spears at nearly point-blank range and wheel away, retreating back up the ridge to prepare for another attack. For the first few attacks the druchii had punished the marauders severely, meeting them with volleys of crossbow bolts that cut down riders and mounts alike. But now their store of bolts was running low. They'd emptied the chariots of all their remaining ammunition, but even so they only had enough for a few volleys left.

The chariots had long since been given over to carrying the wounded. As for the nauglir, they were fearsome shock weapons, but Malus knew better than to pit them in a pursuit against the nimble marauder horses. Like the light cavalry, the knights and the surviving chariots could only sit and watch as the Chaos attack thundered home.

The marauders thundered closer, screaming like tormented shades and wreathed in clouds of ashen dust. At twenty yards the line of druchii spearmen crouched as one, raising their battered shields to cover their exposed faces.

With a furious shout the marauders let fly, hurling a cloud of black spears in a long arc onto the druchii soldiers. They struck the upraised shields with a staccato rattle; some glanced from curved helms or caught on mailed shoulders. Here and there a warrior screamed and fell, clutching at the spear driven deep into his body.

As the last of the spears struck home Malus felt himself relaxing. He could see the spearmen do the same, straightening slightly and lowering their shields a bit as they waited for the horsemen to turn and head back for the ridge.

This time, however, they didn't. In half a second the marauders were past the point where they always turned about, and Malus saw that something was wrong. By the time his exhausted mind realised what was happening it was already too late.

The marauders let out another roaring shout, plucking swords and axes from their belts and crashed full-tilt into the druchii line. By luck or by design the marauders struck one of the battered state regiments, and the spearmen reeled from the impact. Unprepared for the sudden charge, the front ranks of the regiment fell screaming beneath the blows of the howling Chaos warriors. The rear ranks, overcome with shock, began to break away and flee for the illusory safety of the nearby chariots.

'Goddess curse them!' Malus snarled. He turned to his knights. 'Dachvar! We're going in!'

Dachvar wearily drew his sword. 'The household knights are ready, my lord,' he said gravely. The side of his face and neck were black with dried blood from a spear attack during the night. Already, shouted cries were spreading among the surviving knights as they readied themselves for battle. After a night of running they were eager to spill more of the enemy's blood.

The broken spearmen were in full flight now, dropping their weapons and running in terror from the raging marauders. Malus welcomed the black rage that swelled up from his heart and filled his limbs with hateful strength. 'Sa'an'ishar!' he snarled. 'Charge!'

Spite leapt forward with a growl, eager at the prospect of horseflesh. The marauders had possessed enough sense to attack the far end of the battle-line, away from the weary knights, but the charging cold ones covered the few hundred yards in less than ten seconds. The marauders were heedless of their doom, lost in their orgy of slaughter until it was far too late.

Malus gave Spite its head, drawing both of his long blades as the nauglir leapt upon the lead marauder horse. The mangy equine was borne over with a hideous scream, its spine severed by the cold one's snapping jaws. Its rider leapt clear with a savage curse, only to have his skull split as Dachvar thundered past.

'On, Spite! On!' the highborn cried, driving the cold one forward with spurs and knees. Roaring hungrily, the cold one lunged for another nimble horse, catching one out-flung foreleg and biting it off in a spray of bitter blood. The animal fell end-for-end, shrieking and writhing, and the nauglir landed right on top of it, biting and snapping at its back and hindquarters.

The beat of rushing hooves brought Malus's head around – a marauder was racing at him from behind and to the left. The highborn seized the reins with the fingers of his left hand and hauled for all he was worth, pulling the nauglir free of its prey and turning the beast to face the oncoming threat. He only managed it halfway, turning the cold one perpendicular to the charging horseman. The marauder had to choose between swinging wide of the cold one's jaws and passing out of range of Malus, or turning in the opposite direction and risking the cold one's deadly tail for a chance of exchanging blows with its rider. Grinning like a fiend, the marauder chose the latter.

Malus met the oncoming rider with a furious scream, slashing left-handed at the horse's reins and following up with a furious right-handed thrust for the barbarian's eyes. The reins parted like a snapped thread, but the horsemen turned aside the highborn's second blade with the steel rim of his round shield. Laughing, the horseman lashed out with his axe, and Malus felt the blade strike home just above his collarbone. The iron axe head rebounded from his enchanted armour; another six inches higher and the weapon would have slashed his throat open to the spine.

Spite roared and turned in place, snapping at the horse's hindquarters, but the marauder forced his mount tight against the cold one's flank and kept hammering away at Malus's guard. The axe arced down again, aiming for Malus's head, but this time the highborn caught the curving beard of the weapon against the back of his left-hand sword and tried to pull it towards him. But his exhausted limbs were weaker than he imagined, and the marauder seemed to have arms of spring steel. Still laughing, the barbarian snarled something in his bestial tongue and pulled his axe back, neatly dragging Malus from his saddle. The next thing the highborn saw was the scratched iron boss of the horseman's shield as he smashed it into Malus's face. He screamed in rage and pain, blinded by the blow, and swung his right-hand sword in a wild stroke that connected with the horse's ribs and the marauder's leg. Both beasts let out a pained yell, but the marauder continued to pull on the highborn's sword with his axe.

Malus couldn't breathe, his mouth filling with ichor from his broken nose. Blinking away tears of pain, he looked up to see the horseman raising his ichor-stained shield and taking aim at the highborn's outstretched neck. With a shout Malus twisted painfully at the waist and stabbed upwards with his free blade. The point of the sword sank into the marauder's side, just beneath the edge of his broad leather belt. The horseman stiffened, his laughter stilled at last. Red blood ran thickly down the side of the druchii's dark blade; Malus clenched his fist and twisted the sword in the wound. With a convulsive wrench he tore the blade free and the horseman slid lifelessly from the saddle.

As the riderless horse bolted away, Malus levered himself back into his seat and rubbed the back of his left gauntlet over his stinging face. The battle was already over; a bare handful of marauders were racing back to the safety of the ridgeline and the household knights were sitting on their mounts amid a field thick with the bodies of humans and savaged horses. A weary cheer went up from the ranks of the Black Guard, but the sound was lost in the roll and rumble of thunder to the north.

Frowning, Malus looked to the ridgeline and saw that the sky overhead was a roiling mass of black and purple clouds. Streaks of pale lightning crackled in their midst, and a cold wind tasting of old blood stirred the dust and brushed at the faces of the battered druchii host.

Now the purpose of the steady attacks became clear. The marauders had slowed the retreating army to a crawl so that the rest of the horde could press on and catch them.

Lord Meiron was shouting savage curses at the survivors of the broken regiment, chivvying them back into ranks. The household knights turned their mounts back towards the rear of the battle line, casting uneasy glances at the ridge to the north. Malus sat in place for a moment, weighing the odds. He looked to the south, at the distant image of the tower. So close. So damned close.

Lost in his bleak reverie, Malus was startled by the sound of Lord Meiron's voice. 'My apologies, my lord,' he said gruffly. 'The captain of the regiment was one of the first men slain in the charge. I've taken command of the unit personally, and I assure you they won't turn their backs on the enemy again.'

The highborn turned his gaze to the ridgeline. 'There's a storm about to break, Lord Meiron.'

'So I see, my lord,' Meiron answered calmly.

'We don't have much time,' Malus said. 'I reckon we're still a good five miles from the tower. How fast can your men run?'

'Run, my lord?' the infantry commander said. 'We've done all the running we're going to. No, this is where we'll make our stand.'

Malus met Lord Meiron's eyes. 'We can't,' he said. 'We'll be cut to bits. That's the main body of the horde over there.'

'I know, my lord. That's why there's no point running. They've got us. If we run their horsemen will just ride us down.' Lord Meiron drew himself up to his full height. 'And I have never run from a foe in all my life, least of all these animals. I'll not start now.'

Malus narrowed his black eyes. 'I could order you.'

Meiron stiffened. 'Then you'd make me a mutineer, my lord,' he said. 'You'd best get the nauglir and those dandy horsemen moving. I don't expect we have much time now.'

A look of understanding passed between the two druchii. Malus nodded. 'Very well, Lord Meiron,' he said darkly. 'I will not forget this, and I swear to you, neither will the enemy.'

The druchii lord nodded solemnly. 'I'll hold you to that, Malus of Hag Graef. In this life and the next.' Without another word the infantry commander turned on his heel and marched back to his men.

Malus watched him go, his heart bitter. 'In this life and the next,' he said to himself, and drew upon the reins. He kicked Spite to a trot and headed for the waiting knights. With enough of a head start the mounted troops could reach the tower safely, and it shamed him to think that a part of him was glad to be escaping Nagaira's trap.

You will pay for this, sister, he thought. By the Dark Mother I swear it. You will suffer a hundredfold for every man of mine you slay.

He reached Dachvar and the knights and spoke a few, quiet orders, then turned about and rode to the light horse. The cavalry he ordered to move at once, then as they started for the tower he went to the chariots and got them moving as well. The last to go were the knights, and behind them all rode Malus himself.

The black clouds were past the ridgeline now, heading inexorably south towards the tower. Lighting lashed across the sky and smote the backs of the mounted men with blows of thunder.

The last sight Malus had of the battered ranks of spearmen was a line of straight backs and a thicket of spears, aimed towards the storm rolling from the north. He caught sight of Meiron's square-shouldered form standing in the front rank of his regiment, eyes forward, awaiting the coming of the foe.

Along the rear ranks of the spear regiments, young druchii stole quick glances over their shoulder at the retreating cavalry and knights, their faces pale and uncomprehending.

THE STORM CLOUDS paced the dispirited riders all the way back to the tower, dogging their heels with flashes of pale lighting and imprecations of thunder. It took them nearly an hour to reach the high, black walls, and the entire time Malus would catch himself looking back over his shoulder, wondering if Meiron and his men still fought on.

Sombre faces lined the outer walls as the riders made their way to the tower gate. As they came near the gatehouse Malus saw four banners flying from the battlements, their heavy fabrics shifting listlessly in the faint wind. He saw a black crag on a white field surmounted by a silver circlet, and a blue banner with three black masts. Between them was a grey banner with a rearing, dark green nauglir, and above all rose the cloth-of-gold banner of lost Nagarythe, bearing the sign of the dragon and the crown.

Malekith had arrived with his army, and the armies of Clar Karond, Hag Graef and the Black Ark of Naggor rode with him.

On the long ride northward he'd imagined returning to the tower at the head of a victorious army, listening to a fanfare of trumpets from the walls as he bore the head of his sister before him. Now he returned in defeat, with but a broken remnant of the warriors he once led. He felt the weight of each soldier's stare as he led Spite aside and watched the survivors of his army make their way inside the fortress. As the last of his knights disappeared inside the walls, a mournful chorus of horns rose from the gatehouse. The highborn turned in the saddle to see the white plain behind him awash with a black tide of marching troops. Nagaira's horde had reached the Black Tower at last.

With a creak of great hinges the gates of the fortress began to grind shut. Malus took a last look northward before spurring his nauglir inside.

The remainder of his troops waited in the marshalling square beyond the gate, arrayed in parade ranks to either side of the centre path. A single druchii waited in the centre of the square, sitting astride a huge black destrier. Malus approached the old general wearily. Even Spite was too tired to more than sniff in the horse's direction.

Nuarc crossed his hands over the cantle of his saddle and gave the highborn an appraising stare. 'You look like someone dragged you through a butcher's shop,' he said without preamble.

'A *burning* butcher's shop,' Malus corrected, glaring back at the general.

To the highborn's surprise, Nuarc nodded sombrely. 'I know the place,' he said quietly. His expression turned businesslike. 'Malekith wishes to hear your report.'

'Yes, I expect he does,' Malus answered with a sigh. A bitter smile played across his bloodstained face.

Nuarc frowned. 'Something amuses you?'

'I was thinking that a thousand brave druchii just gave their lives so I could safely make it to my execution,' he said. 'Lead on, Nuarc. Let's not keep the Witch King waiting.'

NUARC OFFERED TO give Malus time to clean up, but he declined with a mirthless smile. Better that the Witch King and the assembled lords see what the future held for them, he thought.

The general led the weary highborn through the inner gate and into the high tower. Malus's gait was as unsteady as a babe's. Belatedly he realised that he'd been in the saddle for two days straight. It was a wonder his legs worked at all.

He did notice that he felt no pain from his wounds. Some experimental prodding along his scalp and his knee hinted that the injuries were healing very quickly indeed, thanks to the daemon's black corruption. The highborn wondered perversely how many strokes a headsman would need to take off his head. Would his body keep wriggling for hours afterward, like a snake?

Nuarc cast a curious look over his shoulder at the highborn. Had he laughed aloud? He couldn't recall.

The general led him to a pair of tall doors etched with the tower sigil of Ghrond. A score of black-robed Endless watched Malus impassively as the doors swung open and he was admitted inside.

Malekith studied him with burning eyes from an iron throne no less impressive than the one he presided from at Naggarond. The throne room was larger than the Court of Dragons, built to admit several hundred nobles and their retinues. At the foot of the dais were four ornate chairs, arranged in a semicircle. Four druchii nobles, clad in martial finery, bolted to their feet as Malus and Nuarc made the long walk across the echoing chamber. Malus felt their hot glares like irons against his skin, but the heat made little impression upon him after all the fire he'd recently endured.

He recognised Lord Myrchas at once. The Drachau of the Black Tower was pale with rage, but a glitter of fear shone in his black eyes as Malus was brought before the assembled lords. No doubt he remembers our conversation at the tower, the highborn thought, and he fears that I shall pull him down with me. A not unreasonable assumption.

Then Malus recognised the druchii standing beside Myrchas and felt his heart skip a beat. For a moment he fancied that the vengeful shade of his father Lurhan had risen from the Abyss to torment him. He recognised his father's ornate armour and the great sword Slachyr, the ancient blade of Hag Graef's vaulkhar, but the face of the man wearing the armour looked strange to him. The last time he'd seen his half-brother Isilvar's face it was a pallid green, soft and paunchy from decades of fleshy decadence. Now all that soft skin had melted away, leaving sharp bones and deeply sunken eyes that glittered with almost feral hate. His black hair, still bound in wires with hidden barbs and hooks, was held back with a golden circlet, and his ropy neck was bound by the thick gold hadrilkar of the Witch King's retinue. Malus noted that Isilvar wore his collar of service on the outside of a high collar of supple suede. No doubt to keep the heavy gold from chafing his delicate skin, the highborn thought sarcastically.

Next to Isilvar stood a lanky druchii clad in vivid blue robes and polished silver armour, and of all the nobles in the room only he looked at Malus with something other than anger or hate. Malus supposed he was the drachau of Clar Karond, the one ruler of the six cities he hadn't managed to mortally offend in the last year. The drachau regarded the highborn bemusedly, as if uncertain what all the fuss was about. It took him a moment to realise that the ruler of Clar Karond was somewhat drunk.

On the opposite side of Lord Myrchas stood a tall, narrow-shouldered figure in ornate armour chased with silver and gold. He had a long face and a small, square chin – a handsome man that reminded Malus at once of his mother Eldire. But there was nothing welcoming in Balneth Bale's eyes, only a black gulf of endless hate.

If the assembled lords expected him to quail before their withering stares they were disappointed. He spared them only the briefest of glances, focusing the majority of his attention on the armoured figure upon the throne. When he reached the foot of the dais – surrounded by the circle of hateful lords – he sank slowly to one knee. 'I come at your command, dread majesty,' he said simply.

'*Have you done my bidding, Malus of Hag Graef?*' Malekith asked, his voice seething from his ornate helm like air from a banked forge.

'I live to serve, dread majesty.'

'*Then tell me of all you have done.*'

And so he did, relating his arrival at the Black Tower and his failed attack on Nagaira's camp. He left out no particular – even, to his surprise relating the heroism and self-sacrifice of Lord Meiron and his spearmen. 'It was because of their courage that I stand here to relate these facts, dread majesty,' Malus said. 'I am ashamed that I led so many of your finest warriors to their deaths.'

'There, you see, he freely damns himself!' Lord Myrchas declared, levelling an accusing finger at the highborn. Once it became clear that Malus wasn't going to scapegoat him for the loss of the battle, the drachau's demeanour had reverted to type. 'He deserves the same fate that Lord Kuall suffered! At least Kuall didn't throw away ten thousand of our best men!'

'For all we know, he led those men to their deaths as part of a plan he's worked out with Nagaira herself,' said the new Vaulkhar of Hag Graef. Isilvar's voice, once silken and refined, was now a guttural ruin, worse even than the hoarse growl of Nuarc. The sound brought a smile to Malus's face, though he was careful to keep his face turned to the floor. 'He and my sister have engaged in conspiracies for years, dread majesty. It was she who wrought such ruin in my home city last spring, and it was he who so disfigured our drachau that he remains convalescing to this day. It is clear to me that they were working together to destroy Hag Graef, and I believe they now conspire to destroy the Black Tower and perhaps supplant you as well. He should be slain at once!'

'If he is to die, dread majesty, let it be by my hand!' swore Balneth Bale. The self-styled Witch Lord of the Black Ark stepped beside Malus, his hands clenched into fists. 'He led my son and his army to ruin before the walls of Hag Graef. This is a matter of blood feud!'

'Let Balneth Bale strike him down, dread majesty!' Isilvar declared. 'Let him avenge his son and the feud between our cities will end as well!'

But Malekith seemed not to hear the pleas of his own vassals. '*What of this second Chaos champion?*' he asked.

Malus shrugged. 'I do not know, dread majesty. His appearance in Nagaira's tent was a surprise to me. But he is mighty; he bears tokens of favour from the Ruinous Powers, and his body cannot be harmed by mundane weapons. I suspect that he is the real power behind the horde. The warriors serve him, while he in turn serves Nagaira.'

'*And how large is the host that is arrayed against us?*'

Malus paused. Now he knew how Rasthlan had felt when he'd put the man to the question days earlier. 'I would say that the enemy still numbers around a hundred thousand warriors, dread majesty.'

The number shocked even Isilvar into silence. Malus could clearly hear the scrape of steel against steel as the Witch King turned his head to regard Nuarc. '*How does our own army fare?*'

'We were able to muster forty-four thousand troops, dread majesty: eighteen thousand from Naggarond, two thousand from the Black Ark, and ten thousand each from Hag Graef and Clar Karond, plus two thousand mercenaries scraped from the harbour leavings at the City of Ships. Taking Malus's losses into account that puts the garrison here at around fourteen thousand. So we can muster fifty-eight thousand effectives against Nagaira's host – more than enough to bleed her army dry against these walls. When our additional forces from Karond Kar and Har Ganeth arrive we will be in position to pin the enemy against the walls of the fortress and destroy them.'

'Providing Nagaira employs none of her sorcery,' Isilvar said darkly. 'Or we face no treachery from within.'

Malus could take no more. He was battered and torn, physically exhausted and now his knees were beginning to ache. With painful effort he struggled to his feet. 'If it please your dread majesty to slay me then let us be done with it,' he said. 'I acknowledge my failure in the field. What is your decision?'

For a moment no one spoke. Even Malekith seemed taken aback by the highborn's weary frankness. '*I see no failure here,*' the Witch King said at length. '*You drew Nagaira to the Black Tower as I commanded.*'

'But, dread majesty,' Myrchas exclaimed. 'He lost half the army–'

'*Lost?*' the Witch King said. '*No. He spent them as a warlord must to achieve his aims, fighting an enemy that has invaded our kingdom. Something none of you have done.*'

'But... you can't intend to install him as Ghrond's vaulkhar!' Myrchas cried. 'I won't have it, not with all the offences he has perpetrated against my fellow lords.'

'*No. He will not be Vaulkhar of the Black Tower,*' Malekith said. '*He will no longer command armies in the field.*' The Witch King leaned forward on his throne and stretched out a claw-like hand to Malus. '*Instead, I name him my champion, to confront the enemies of the state and slay them on my behalf.*'

'You can't mean that,' Malus heard someone say. It took a moment to realise it was him.

'*It is my decree, Malus of Hag Graef, that you will be named my champion, and will bear the three golden skulls of Tyran upon your armour so that both friend and foe know that you fight in my name. The honour of the kingdom rests upon your shoulders. Do not forsake it, or the wrath of the Dark Mother shall be upon you.*'

'I... I hear and obey, dread majesty,' Malus replied, bowing before the throne. This wasn't a true reward, he knew, but another facet of Malekith's game. He was just too tired to see what the Witch King's stratagem was. Regardless, it wasn't as though he could refuse.

'How can this be?' said Isilvar, his ruined voice charged with genuine outrage. 'He has committed grave crimes against the kingdom, and against you personally, dread majesty. How is it he not only continues to live, but is deemed worthy of such an honour.'

'He lives because it serves the Witch King's purposes that he do so,' said an iron voice from across the hall. Morathi slid silently out of the shadows, her eyes glittering with cold menace and authority. 'It is a lesson that all of you would do well to learn.'

'*What of my brides, Morathi?*' Malekith asked, referring to the witches cloistered in the Black Tower's convent.

'They are foolish, weak-willed girls,' Morathi replied disdainfully. 'But we may yet get some decent work out of them before the siege is finished. There are gaps in their training I must take steps to rectify.'

'*Make it so,*' the Witch King said, then regarded his vassal lords once more. '*Go now, and prepare for the coming assault. Nagaira's warriors encircle the city even as we speak. Serve me well, and your rewards will be great.*'

None of the assembled lords had any question what the alternative would be.

Chapter Fourteen
THE TEMPLE OF TZ'ARKAN

The Chaos Wastes, first week of winter

BEYOND THE SHADOWY portal of the great temple an inky darkness awaited, pulsing with blasphemous power. It swirled and eddied about Malus as he staggered along the narrow processional, recoiling from the possessed druchii as if in supplication to the daemon that rode within him.

The temple was much changed since he'd last been inside. No, it was *changing* – potent energies coursed through the ponderous stones and prickled invisibly across his icy skin. Tz'arkan swelled painfully within the highborn's tortured frame, and the forces at work within the great building responded, ordering themselves according to the daemon's will.

Malus's body moved of its own volition, driving him forward like one of the risen dead. At the far end of the processional he reached the temple antechamber. More than a hundred figures dressed in ceremonial robes lined the narrow aisle that ran through the large hall. The ancient forms had

knelt in obeisance for so long that the bodies within had long
since crumbled to dust, leaving behind only petrified shells of
leather garments and rune-carved bone. He remembered the
first time he'd seen these wretched figures, and how he'd wondered what sort of awful terror could have inspired the temple
slaves to press their foreheads to the stone floor until they
finally died.

Now he knew all too well.

His boot heels echoed forlornly along the dusty marble floor
as he walked among the ranks of the damned. Suddenly he
heard a rustling sound, like the crumbling of ancient parchment and the crackle of ruined leather, and his heart went cold
as he saw the ranks of the temple servants slowly, jerkily
straighten. Dust swirled within the depths of their drooping
hoods, coalescing in the ghostly shapes of skeletal faces. Green
globes of bale-light shone eerily from their shadowy eye sockets and their spectral mouths moved in silent adoration of their
returning overlord. Ethereal hands brushed against his boots
and the hem of his robes, and Tz'arkan's cruel will measured
his every step, basking in the horrid worship of those agonised
souls. At the far end of the chamber corroded steel creaked
wearily as the armoured shells standing guard over the chamber raised their rusting blades in salute. Green fires burned
within the oculars of the guards' helmets, and the runes worked
into their Chaos armour crawled with sorcerous energies.

'Do you see, Darkblade? This is but a glimpse of the glories
to come. The dead will rise to do my bidding even as the living
give their souls to sate my glorious appetites. These are but the
smallest tastes of the wonders that could have been yours had
you simply chosen to serve me.'

On he went, past the tormented ghosts and into another
large hall containing the altars of the four gods of the north.
Behind each altar rose a horrific idol dedicated to one of the
Ruinous Powers; Tz'arkan led Malus to the idol of Slaanesh
and forced the highborn to his knees before the abominable
figure. His hands made twisting signs in the air and his lips
formed debased words that no mortal was even meant to

speak. Ichor bubbled from his throat and trickled down his pallid cheeks as the daemon forced him to participate in the horrid worship of the Great Devourer. On and on the ritual went, until he feared his teeth would splinter and his lips run like tallow, and his tortured mind screamed for release.

The next sound he recognised was the daemon's laughter, cruel and cold, echoing in his brain. 'You are weak, Darkblade. So weak. This is the so-called hero of Ghrond? Your mind could not even fathom a simple acolyte's benediction. And to think I once saw such potential in you.'

Tz'arkan dragged Malus to his feet and forced him onward, into the great, cavernous space where the bridge of fire waited.

Blistering heat smote the highborn's pallid face; the reek of sulphur stung his nose and caked his aching throat. The earth itself roared angrily in the vast open space, stirred to wrath by the unnatural being trapped in the chamber above. At the far end of the long plaza, some fifty yards away, stood the statue of a winged daemon, crouching on its talons and limned by the sullen, red glow of the lake of fire at its back. The sight of the muscular, human-shaped daemon with its snarling animal face seemed almost comical now after the horrors he had witnessed during the siege of the Black Tower.

With each step the heat beating against his skin increased, and with each step the fearful energies of the daemon seemed to grow as well. Tz'arkan's power radiated from his body; he could feel it seeping from his pores like venom, soaking into the dark, stone walls and tainting them from within.

There was an angry crash, and a plume of molten stone burst from the great chasm that lay beyond the waiting daemon. Malus dimly recalled the last time he'd travelled the floating stair the river of burning stone had lain hundreds of feet below the level of the plaza. Now, it surged and roiled just a few dozen feet from the edge of the square. The heat was unbearable. Malus could feel his skin baking and his lungs ached fiercely with each shallow breath. He tried to close his eyes against the burning air, but the daemon held him in a merciless grip, forcing him onward towards the fire.

Before long he couldn't breathe. Wisps of smoke rose from his tattered robes, and he feared his eyes would burst. He fought against the daemon's control, his efforts growing more and more frantic as he was pressed ever closer to the inferno.

Tz'arkan hissed with delight. 'Your fear is sweet. There is nothing so delicious as a mortal's death throes! But I will not permit you to die Malus, not yet.'

There was a furious hiss and an eruption of steam from the edge of the precipice. Huge boulders rose in serried ranks from the boiling rock, their faceted surfaces glowing with incandescent heat and dripping streams of liquid fire onto the roiling sea below. They formed a floating stairway to a spur of rock that hung from the ceiling of the great cavern. Beyond, Malus knew, lay the chambers of the temple sorcerers and then, the tribute chamber and prison of the daemon itself.

His skin was burning. He could smell his hair singeing in the heat. His lungs clenched, aching for a taste of cool air, and his eyes felt as dry as leather. Yet he was helpless to resist the daemon's iron control.

He seeks to break you, Malus thought. Here, at the very last, he wants to ensure his control over you. Even now he fears you may be able to circumvent his plans. Malus focused on that notion, taking hope from it even as his body was wracked with burning pain and forced to do the bidding of an inhuman will.

The highborn mounted the steps concealed in the daemon statue's flanks, noting the molten glow of heat along the trailing edges of its stone wings. His mind reeled for lack of air, but his body worked like a wood puppet, leaping heavily from one floating stone to the next.

Beyond the rocks curved a stone staircase, intricately carved with dozens of naked figures writhing in eternal torment. He vaguely remembered a body that lay sprawled along the stairs, its forearms slit from wrist to elbow. How he wished he'd taken heed of the corpse's silent warning!

Slowly and painfully the daemon drove him onward, up the stairs and into the charnel house of the sorcerers' sanctums. Here the five Chaos champions had built chambers for themselves and their servants. Those same servants had turned upon one another in the end, their minds broken by the daemon's manipulations as they waited in vain for the return of their masters until they slew one another in an orgy of cannibalism and murder. Looking back, it amazed him how blind he'd been to the dire portents laid right before his eyes. He'd been such a fool – and what ruin had been borne from it!

The daemon drove him past the lifeless, blood-streaked apartments, strewn with crumbling debris from the brutal fights that had raged there. After a few minutes he frowned, his gaze sweeping the floors of the rooms he passed and peering along the dimly lit corridors. Where had all the bodies gone? Had they finally crumbled to dust once the daemon invoked its hideous curse?

Finally he came to the great ramp, worked with hundreds of runes and leering alabaster skulls, and the tall double doors made from solid gold. A nameless dread seized Malus's throat at the sight of them, like a condemned man catching sight of the impaling stake. Beyond those doors lay the entrance to the daemon's chamber and the end of his terrible quest.

And so it comes down to this, he thought bleakly. I've walked alone out of the Chaos Wastes, fought daemon cultists and Chaos-tainted pirates, commanded armies and fleets and fought grim battles for the fate of entire cities. Not long ago a whole kingdom rested in my hands. But this is how it ends, walking like a lamb to slaughter. It was enough to make the fiercest druchii weep tears of rage.

He had nothing left now. Desperately he wracked his brain for some trick, some stratagem to turn the tables on the daemon before it was too late. But how could he fight a creature when he couldn't even master his own wretched body?

Up the ramp the daemon drove him. The golden doors, balanced on perfect hinges, swung open at the touch of invisible hands.

Beyond, Malus heard the skeletal rustle of ancient fabrics and the creak of dried skin. It was the bodies, he realised. The bodies of the dead scholars and servants.

'See? The dead rise and serve the worthy.'

Tz'arkan forced him across the threshold before a bowing assembly of mutilated corpses, worn and withered by time. Heads rose to behold their immortal master, their dried lips smeared against their faces in unctuous, lunatic grins. Skeletal fingers clenched into claws and hollow eye sockets gaped at infernal wonders beyond the ken of mortals.

'Here are your servants, Darkblade,' the daemon declared mockingly. 'They will aid you in what must be done, for there is little time left.'

The undead servants scraped and rustled as the highborn moved stiffly among them. They shambled ahead on the stumps of ruined feet, driven by the same implacable will as he, across the gleaming marble floor and the curving lines of the sorcerous wards that had kept the daemon imprisoned for thousands of years. Their frail robes fluttered in the waves of invisible power that reverberated through the air. They paused before the great, basalt doors, flanked by massive statues of winged daemons, and waited for his approach. In the shadows to either side of the waiting slaves swirled figures of brown dust. They cringed and genuflected to Malus, and he remembered the hideous mummies who'd lain in a torturous half-life before those self-same doors, unable to find release in death thanks to the powers of the binding spells laid like a trap beneath them.

As Malus crossed the first of the arcing silver lines he felt a tremor pass through him. As cold as he'd been before, now he felt as though he were frozen in ice, his spirit wreathed in powers he could barely comprehend. He wondered if he would linger here, trapped within these terrible wards once the daemon feasted upon his soul.

Deep within the bleak despair gripping his brain, the tiny spark of an idea flickered to life. He scarcely dared consider it, half-afraid the daemon would read his thoughts. Malus frowned. Could it be possible? Did he dare?

Did he have any choice?

The undying servants pushed the black doors aside and ushered Malus into the cold radiance of the tribute chamber. The vast hall contained the wealth of dozens of plundered kingdoms now lost to time: coin and gems, plate and graven statues – more wealth than any man could spend in a thousand lifetimes. Even now, despite his dire straits, the sight of the treasure chamber kindled his avaricious heart.

But of all the wonders piled high in the tribute chamber, none could match the enormous crystal that dominated the centre of the room. It was roughly faceted and larger than a man, set in a low tripod of iron. The enormous stone glowed with a softly pulsing blue light, a strangely alluring colour considering the black evil that lay within.

His gaze drifted to the small, unassuming pedestal just a few yards inside the room. It had lain empty for a year now, he thought grimly. Hands trembling, he pulled off his gauntlets and gazed bleakly at the red stone planted on his finger. If he'd had any real courage he would have tried sawing it off rather than leave this place wearing it!

The servants shuffled amid the gleaming splendour, searching for the tools that the daemon desired. Malus's body spasmed as the daemon reasserted its fearsome control. 'The relics, little druchii,' Tz'arkan commanded. 'Lay them out and prepare yourself for the ritual.'

His heart sinking, Malus could only watch as his body obeyed the daemon's commands like a dog. He laid his saddlebag carefully on the stone floor and drew out four of the relics, each one wrapped in dirty cloth. First the Octagon of Praan, then the Idol of Kolkuth and the Dagger of Torxus. Finally he pulled free the Amulet of Vaurog, and his heart went cold at the ordeal he'd gone through to get it. Of all he'd endured to gain Tz'arkan his relics, the price he'd paid for the damned amulet would haunt him for all time. Last of all, he reached for the warpsword at his belt.

'No,' the daemon commanded, forcefully enough to send ichor running from the highborn's eyes and ears. 'The servants will see to the blade.'

Two of the shambling corpses knelt beside Malus and slid the long, black sword from its scabbard. Wisps of smoke rose from their withered hands as they handled the burning blade.

Malus watched the servants lay the blade beside the other relics, while another pair of servants approached from deeper within the chamber. One carried an urn made from gold and etched with spirals of sorcerous runes. The other held a tablet of ancient, weathered stone, carved with dense lines of blasphemous script.

'Take the urn,' the daemon said. 'Remove the cover, and I will show you what must be done.'

He tried to fight it, like the condemned man fights against the grip of his executioners. But for the first time his indomitable will failed him. Malus watched helplessly as his hands took the heavy urn from the corpse's hands and pulled free the lid. Inside was a grey powder that reeked of the crypt.

The highborn could feel the daemon's joy as the urn was opened. 'The bones of my tormentors,' it said. 'Gathered from the far corners of the world. All five of the champions who trapped me were ground up to fill that bowl. All but that scheming fool Ehrenlish – in the end I got all but his skull, but that will be enough.'

Tz'arkan turned Malus bodily and marched him to the crystal. 'Use the dust to lay out the sigil precisely as I command, the daemon said. You must do this alone, Darkblade. I cannot force you. Follow my instructions in every particular. Your soul depends on it.'

All at once he felt the grip of the daemon loosen – the change was so sudden Malus swayed on his feet, stopping his fall only by effort of will. His gaze drifted to the black blade, lying on the stone just a few feet away.

'Do not attempt it,' the daemon said. 'I will stop you before you take a single step, then I will make you suffer in ways you never dreamt possible. Remember the chamber of the altars? That was a gentle kiss compared to what I could do if I were truly displeased. And in the end you would have even less time to save your eternal spirit. Now, begin.'

The instructions flowed like icy filth into the highborn's brain. He gasped at the hideous images flowing through his mind and reached into the urn for a handful of dust.

Chapter Fifteen
THE CORPSE-HANDLERS

The Black Tower of Ghrond, four weeks before

THE CRASH OF thunder smote the walls of the fortress like a hammer blow, causing many of the defenders on the wall to duck their heads and cry out in fear. The earth-shaking roar all but drowned out the high, skirling wail of the horns, crying their shrill warnings from the redoubts. Malus rose to his feet from the base of the battlements and peered out at the lightning-shot blackness. A savage, reeking wind roared in his face and tangled the loose strands of his sweat-streaked hair.

All was darkness upon the ashen plain. He counted the seconds, waiting for a flash of pale lightning. There! A bolt of fire burnt across the heavens, revealing a rushing tide of monstrosities charging for the walls.

'Sa'an'ishar!' he shouted to the spearmen crouching against the battlements beside him. 'On your feet! Here they come!'

Now the roaring of the advancing army could be heard above the raging tempest, and the strobe and flicker of the lightning increased overhead, pushing back the clinging shadows and revealing the oncoming attackers less than twenty yards from the base of the wall. Already the ground there was carpeted with the bodies of marauders and beastmen, and as Malus watched, a black rain of crossbow bolts began to fall upon the screaming horde from the sloping redoubts to the left and right. Horned, half-naked beastmen screamed and stumbled, pierced through by the deadly bolts. Some ran on, while others fell to the blood-soaked earth and died. Still the seething mob charged forward, undaunted by the deadly hail. Long ladders bobbed above lines of grim-faced barbarians; when one of the ladder-men was struck down another marauder ran to take his place. Some men kept going with two or three bolts jutting from their bodies, driven forward by unholy battle-lust and the blessings of their fearful northern gods.

Malus drew his swords and set his jaw in a grim line as the attackers drew closer. Already his armour was splashed with dried blood and stinking ichor, and his arms felt leaden from all the killing he'd done. He couldn't recall if this was the third assault or the fourth. At this point he didn't even know if it was day or night. The clouds that had rolled in before the advancing horde had tightened about the Black Tower like a shroud, blocking out the pale northern sunlight. Once the fighting began, time lost all meaning.

With groans and bitter curses the druchii company assigned to hold this stretch of wall clambered slowly to their feet. They were state troops from Clar Karond, evidenced by their blue robes and the short, lightweight kheitans favoured by druchii corsairs. When the first attack had begun the troops were in high spirits, but now their faces were tired and grim, stained with grime and other men's blood. They looped their arms through battered shields and took up their weapons – one warrior in three hefted a repeater crossbow, while the rest drew their short, stabbing swords. They tested their footing amid the pools of drying blood that stained the paving stones and watched the oncoming mob to see where the ladders would likely land. A young druchii ran down the line, scattering sawdust from a wooden bucket. It would soak up some of the blood once the fighting started in earnest, but there was never quite enough.

Malus leaned back and peered down the length of the wall, checking to make sure all the troops were standing to. He saw a pair of legs still stretched out across the paving stones and jogged down to take a look. 'On your feet, spearman,' the high-born growled, kneeling before the warrior. The warrior was a young woman, called up to fight with the regiment in the wake of Malekith's proclamation of war. There wasn't a mark on her that Malus could see, but her face was white as chalk and her lips were blue. Most likely the blow of a hammer or club had ruptured something beneath the skin and she'd bled to death in her sleep. Taking hold of her mail shirt, Malus dragged her over to the inner side of the wall and rolled her over the edge. Already there were deep drifts of corpses piled on the flag-stones forty feet below. Men were stripping the bodies of armour and weapons and dragging the corpses to the furnaces. Even in these cold climes, the dead could carry pestilence that could decimate the fortress city's defenders.

The rest of the line looked ready, as far as he could see. Each of the eight sections of wall was held by a single regiment, stretching for more than two and a half miles between the hulking redoubts. The regimental commander anchored the far end, while Malus's end had been anchored by the second-in-command. That fellow's brains had been splashed against the side of the embrasure just a few yards to Malus's right. He'd happened to be nearby when the officer died, and with-out thinking had stepped in to take his place. That had been during the second assault, and he'd remained ever since.

Malekith had given him no orders after declaring him cham-pion. With no troops to command – not even a retinue to call his own – it was as though he'd been swept aside in the haste and confusion of the impending attack. He'd found his way to his chambers, found servants to fill a bath and bring him food, and watched as a pair of smiths from the fortress armoury affixed a set of three golden skulls to the breastplate of his armour. The skulls marked him as the Witch King's champion:

Athlan na Dyr, the Taker of Heads. As far as Malus was concerned, they made him a tempting target for every bull-head and barbarian that came over the walls.

Nevertheless, when the horns began to wail he had buckled on his harness and headed for the wall.

He'd hoped that when the attack began it would be led by Nagaira's champion. The warrior, aided by the Amulet of Vaurog, would be a literal engine of destruction atop the city walls, but Malus hoped that with enough spearmen behind him the champion could be pulled down long enough for him to pull the artefact from around his thin neck. After that they could hack the bastard to pieces and hang his helmeted head from the battlements, and Malus would find a way to slip out of the fortress and make his way into the Wastes.

But nothing had gone according to plan so far. The champion had yet to show himself among the screaming throngs, and most of the warriors on the wall regarded Malus with open resentment and hostility. The spearmen of the Black Tower had heard the stories of his disastrous expedition to the north, and blamed him for the loss of their mates and of their commander, Lord Meiron. But they were far from the worst – as Malus walked the battlements he came upon warriors from Hag Graef and the Black Ark, both of whom saw him as the blackest of villains after the ill-fated events of the previous spring. They were just as likely to stab him in the back or throw him from the walls in the middle of an attack, Witch King's champion or no. He'd stayed so long with the regiment from Clar Karond simply because he was just another officer to them.

The crossbows along the battlements were firing now, and Malus could hear the screams of the dying, forty feet below. 'Ladders coming up!' one of the warriors shouted, and the highborn rushed up to the battlements to see how many had landed nearby.

There were only two: one was very close to the redoubt at his right, while the other was almost ten yards to his left. Others going up farther down the line were someone else's problem.

Swift-footed barbarians were already scrambling up the long ladders, many with a throwing-axe gripped in their teeth. More barbarians at the base of the wall were flinging axes up at the defenders, but the druchii paid them little heed.

'Crossbows cover the ladders!' the highborn yelled, although there was little need. The men on this part of the wall knew the routine well by now. Bolts from their crossbows and from the firing slits of the nearby redoubt raked along the line of men climbing hard for the wall. The marauders advanced fearlessly into the storm of black-fletched bolts, pressing on even after being shot multiple times. When they could climb no more they hurled themselves clear of the ladder, screaming or laughing like madmen the whole way to the ground, and those below would redouble their efforts to reach the top.

And reach the top they would. They always did, despite the appalling losses they suffered. The crossbows could only fire so fast, and the Chaos warriors had no fear of death. Slowly but surely the line of warriors inched closer to the battlements.

'Four men on each ladder!' Malus roared, rushing forward to welcome the first foe who came over the battlements. Obediently the troops crowded close around the end of each ladder, ready to strike the attackers from multiple directions at once. This wasn't duelling or elegant swordplay – this was pure butchery, killing men as quickly and efficiently as possible. So long as they kept the enemy warriors from gaining a foothold on the battlements they could almost slaughter the oncoming attackers at will.

Suddenly the air hummed with half a dozen thrown axes, burning through the air in short, glittering arcs as the warriors closest to the top let fly. There was a clash of steel and a warrior beside Malus toppled without a sound; a hurled axe had cleft the spearman's helmet and buried itself in his forehead. 'Shields up, damn you!' the highborn shouted. 'Mind their axes!' He himself reached up and checked the strap on his new helmet. Malus hated wearing the thing, but it was far better than the alternative.

A face appeared at the top of the ladder, grinning like a daemon. Malus leapt at him with a shout, and just missed having
a hurled axe embedded in his face. His sudden move threw the
man's aim off, sending the spinning projectile blurring past
his ear, and before the warrior could drag out his sword Malus
stabbed him through the throat. Blood poured in a flood
down the barbarian's tattooed chest, but the warrior kept coming, forcing his way up the ladder and onto the battlements.
Spearmen dashed in from both sides, stabbing and hacking at
the man, and Malus tucked his shoulder in and crashed into
the reeling man's bloody midsection, sending him flying out
into space.

But the warrior's last seconds bought more time for the man
behind him. A sword thrust slid off Malus's armoured belly,
and then the screaming beastman lowered his horned head
and butted the highborn in the chest. The force of the impact
hurled him back a few feet, and the bellowing warrior leapt
quickly onto the battlements. Druchii warriors pressed in on
either side of the foe, stabbing and slashing with their short
blades. Roaring in fury, Malus leapt back into the fray as well,
catching the warrior in the middle of a turn and hacking
through the side of his neck. Hot blood sprayed across the
spearman as the horned warrior staggered beneath the blow.
One of the spearmen rushed at the warrior, intent on finishing
the creature off, but the beastman was far from finished. With
a braying shout it lowered its broad sword and caught the
onrushing spearman with a thrust to his right thigh that tore
clean through the muscle and cut a major artery. The druchii
fell with a scream, clutching at the mortal wound, while his
companions plunged their blades into the beastman's back.

A barbarian reached the battlements next and leapt over
the dying beastman straight at Malus, his face twisted with
madness and his arms outstretched in a deadly embrace.
Snarling in disdain the highborn ducked clear of the warrior's foolhardy attack, then rushed after the madman's
tumbling body and kicked it off the edge of the inner wall.
The dying druchii was trying to drag his way clear of the

melee, leaving a thick trail of blood through the newly lain sawdust.

Another druchii fell to the paving stones, grappling with a dagger-wielding barbarian. Malus rushed over, planted a foot between the marauder's shoulders and split his skull with a downward sweep of his sword. Two more Chaos warriors had made their way onto the battlements, and a third waited at the top of the ladder, looking for a space to clamber across. Cursing lustily, the highborn dived back into the fray, using his longer swords to telling effect.

One beastman went down, his neck carved to the spine while he traded blows with a nearby spearman, while the marauder to the beastman's left collapsed with the point of the highborn's left-hand sword buried in his kidney. The warrior on the ladder leapt to take their place, but Malus was ready for him. He rushed in as the barbarian jumped, effectively moving in beneath the hulking warrior and stabbing upwards into the man's unprotected belly. The barbarian screamed, bringing his axe down on the highborn's back, but his enchanted plates turned aside the powerful blow. Gritting his teeth, Malus staggered beneath the weight of the dying warrior, but he summoned up his hate and pushed forwards with all his might, unloading the limp form onto the next man scrambling up the ladder. Taken by surprise, both marauders plummeted, screaming, to the ground.

The next warrior up the ladder never reached the top before a crossbow bolt buried itself in the side of his head. For the space of a few seconds the defenders had some precious breathing room. 'Close up ranks!' Malus shouted. He pointed to the limp form of the mortally wounded druchii. 'Someone drag him out of the way. Quickly now!'

A quick check of the other ladder showed that the druchii there had things well in hand; so far none of the attackers had even reached the battlements before dying underneath the defenders' blades.

More spearmen rushed over to surround the ladder next to Malus. Breathing heavily, the highborn stepped back to let the fresh warriors take their turn. He rubbed a gauntleted hand across his mouth, inadvertently smearing his lips with a foeman's blood. Mother of Night, I could use a drink, he thought.

Just then he heard a shrill note sounding from the redoubt to his right. He frowned, trying to puzzle out his meaning – then he heard the guttural roars and agonised screams coming from the next wall over. Spitting a blasphemous curse, Malus turned and ran for the redoubt's iron door, just a few yards to his right. He pounded on the portal with the hilt of his sword shouting imprecations to the druchii on the other side. Within moments the bolts were drawn back and the heavy door opened to admit him.

The highborn brushed past the sentry at the door and ran down the long, narrow passageway that connected to the next wall over. Shouts and commands echoed up and down the corridor from the crossbow and bolt thrower teams firing from inside the fortification, calling out targets and shouting for more ammunition. He passed barrels of water that held long, heavy bolts tipped with glass orbs that glowed a baleful green: they were dangerous and volatile dragonsfire bolts, held in reserve in case the enemy horde sent giants or other huge creatures against the walls.

The passage ran on for almost fifty yards, then angled sharply right. Another fifty yards later and the highborn reached another iron door, watched over by a pair of nervous sentries. Hands and sword hilts were pounding frantically on the other side of the door. The sentries saw Malus coming and snapped to attention. 'The enemy has reached the wall,' one of the warriors began.

'I heard the horn,' Malus snapped. 'Open the door and let me through.'

The two men hesitated – then saw the fearsome look on the highborn's face. As one, the warriors turned to the door and drew back the heavy bolts.

Almost at once there were panicked warriors pushing the door open from the outside. Snarling with rage, Malus drew the iron portal open and roared at the men on the other side.

'Stand to, you worthless dogs!' he said, blocking the doorway with his bloodstained form.

The white-faced spearmen recoiled at the wrathful figure standing before them, and Malus quickly stepped into the space they vacated. Behind him the iron door slammed shut again and the bolts shot home. 'Where do you bastards think you're going?' the highborn raged. 'You're here to defend this wall or die in the attempt. Those were the orders the Witch King gave you!'

But Malus saw at once that the situation was very grave indeed. The battlements near the redoubt were littered with dead and dying spearmen, and marauders were pouring over the battlements. There were fifty spearmen between Malus and the raging battle, all crammed tightly against the side of the redoubt. As far as he could tell the enemy was also pushing hard in the other direction, trying to reach one the ramps that led down into the city proper. If that happened there might well be no stopping them.

There was a ramp just to Malus's right, and the marauders were fighting hard to reach it. Only the sheer press of the panicked spearmen were holding them momentarily at bay. 'Move forward, damn your eyes!' the highborn commanded. 'There's no safety back here! If the foemen don't kill you I surely will!'

The men wavered, weighing their options. One look at Malus showed that the highborn was deadly serious and perfectly capable of carrying out his threat. One of the spearmen, a senior warrior, exclaimed 'Our commander is dead, highborn, and we don't have enough soldiers to drive the enemy back!'

Malus considered calling for reinforcements from the redoubt, but quickly cast the notion aside. Jostling a pair of spearmen aside, he checked the avenue at the base of the ramp and saw no less than two hundred druchii poring through the piled bodies at the base of the wall. 'Who are they?' he demanded, pointing at the corpse-handlers with his sword.

The exasperated trooper glanced down at the druchii band. Despite his panic, his lip curled in distaste. 'Mercenaries,' he replied. 'Harbour scum hired by the drachau of Clar Karond. Captain Thurlayr refused to have them on the wall. Said gulls like them were only fit for picking over the dead.'

Malus shook his head in disbelief. 'That kind of thinking is what got Thurlayr killed, soldier,' he snapped. He grabbed the front of the trooper's mail shirt and pulled him close. 'What's your name?'

The warrior looked into the highborn's black eyes and went pale. 'Euthen, my lord.'

'Well, now you're *Captain* Euthen,' Malus hissed. 'Take charge of these fools and get them back in the battle by the time I return or I'm throwing you off the wall myself. Do you understand?'

'Y… yes sir. Clear sir.'

'Then get to it, Captain,' Malus shouted, pushing the man away. Without waiting for a reply he shoved past another spearman and raced down the long ramp towards the mercenaries.

The harbour rats had the look of corsairs, from what Malus could see at a distance. Tattered robes of different hues, lightweight kheitans and blackened mail were common, and the warriors carried a wild assortment of weapons, including a profusion of daggers and looted throwing axes. Approximately half the mercenaries were poring over the bodies at the base of the wall, stripping them not only of weapons and armour but valuables as well. As he watched, one of the druchii took a dagger to the ring finger of a druchii officer, popping the digit loose with a practiced motion – and then losing it among the pile of corpses beneath him. The rest of the mercenaries sat on the paving stones of the avenue and played at dice or dragon's teeth, seemingly oblivious to the desperate battle being waged on the battlements above.

'Form up!' Malus shouted at the cutthroats. 'The enemy is on the battlements, and it's time you earned your keep!'

The corsairs looked up at the distant figure of the highborn as though he were speaking in a foreign tongue. The looter who'd been groping among the corpses for the officer's severed finger frowned up at Malus. 'We're not allowed,' he shouted back in a bemused voice. 'This one here – ' he pointed at the officer's corpse – 'said we weren't fit to stand 'mongst real soldiers.'

'Besides,' chuckled a female, scooping up her dice, 'it's a good deal safer down here.'

'It won't be for long once the enemy reaches the ramps!' Malus snapped. 'And you can't spend your ill-gotten coin if you're hanging from some beastman's banner-pole! Now get off your arses and get up here!'

The cutthroats looked to one another, considering their options. Malus didn't wait for them to reply – arguing with them would only weaken his already shaky authority, so it was better to act as though he expected them to obey. He turned and ran back up the ramp, and within moments was gratified to hear someone down below start barking orders in a surprisingly professional tone. At least someone down there knows what he's doing, Malus thought.

On the battlements, things looked grim indeed. The Chaos foothold was already more than fifteen yards wide and expanding steadily. Euthen had managed to bully the panicked spearmen back into the fight, but their numbers were too few to accomplish much more than keeping the enemy away from the near ramp.

Malus shoved his way into the crowd. 'Form a wedge!' he shouted, elbowing cursing spearmen into a rough semblance of the formation. 'Wider! All the way to the edges of the parapet!'

Trusting that the soldiers would follow his command, the highborn worked his way to where the tip of the wedge would begin. He found Euthen there, fighting valiantly against a leering Chaos marauder wielding twin axes in his knotty hands. As Malus approached, he watched the marauder carefully, looking for a sign that he was about to strike. Euthen lunged in, attempting a half-hearted swipe at the marauder's leg, and the barbarian tore into the spearman with a terrible howl, hacking into the druchii's left shoulder with one axe while the other sent the captain's short sword spinning off the edge of the parapet. But while the warrior was savaging the hapless Euthen, Malus rushed in and stabbed the barbarian cleanly through the heart.

The warrior sank to the stones with a curse on his lips. Meanwhile, Malus took the injured Euthen by the collar and gave him a gentle shove in the direction of the ramp. 'Warriors of Clar Karond!' he cried, raising his sword. 'Form wedge on me!'

No sooner had he said this than a red-haired barbarian rushed at Malus with a savage yell, his greatsword swinging in a wide arc for the highborn's head. Malus saw the move and hissed disdainfully, ducking and stepping into the stroke so that the wild blow passed harmlessly overhead, then stabbing the warrior in the groin with both of his blades. The man fell with a terrible scream, and Malus quickly stepped past him, deeper into the press of foes. 'Advance!' he ordered.

Miraculously, the spearmen did. Now Malus had foes on three sides, but the men to the left and right aimed their blows at the soldiers in front of them. The warrior before Malus snarled and chopped at him with his axe; the highborn blocked the blow with his left-hand sword and then slashed open the thigh of the warrior to his right. The injured marauder faltered and the spearman in front of him finished the man with a thrust to the neck. When the axe-wielding barbarian attacked again, Malus blocked with his right-hand sword and stabbed his other blade into the marauder on the left. Then he devoted his sole attention to the warrior in front of him, trapping the warrior's axe with a sweep of his left sword and stabbing the marauder in the eye with the blade in his right.

And so the slaughter began. Coldly, methodically, the druchii began to reduce the Chaos foothold. Malus knew that if they could at least fight their way to the enemy ladders then they could cut off their foes' reinforcements, then eventually sheer numbers would eliminate the rest of the marauders that had made it to the walls.

Working together the spearmen made steady progress. Soldiers were struck down to either side of the highborn, only to be replaced by the next spearmen in line. After almost ten yards there were no spearmen left, but Malus saw that the corpse-pickers had taken their place. The mercenaries were clearly in their element in this style of fighting, accustomed as they were to the tight quarters and close sword-work of boarding actions aboard ship. They struck down barbarians with underhanded cuts to their legs, or knives flung into their throats. Sometimes Malus would strike at a man to his flank and then look back to see the foe in front of him collapsing with a throwing axe buried in his skull.

Finally they'd cut off all of the enemy ladders and had cut the marauders down to less than a dozen warriors – and that was when things became truly dangerous. The surviving marauders realised they were trapped, and as one they decided to take as many of their hated foes with them as they could.

A warrior came screaming at Malus with a bloodstained sword in his right hand and a battered shield in his left. Eyes wild and foam flying from the corners of his mouth, he unleashed a flurry of blows that the highborn had to devote all his energy to deflect. He tried to knock the man off his stride with a lightning stroke to his eyes, but the marauder simply caught the blow on the edge of his shield and barrelled on, hammering away at Malus's guard.

So intent was the highborn on this frenzied warrior that he failed to notice when the man on his left slipped in a pool of blood and went to one knee. His opponent crowed in triumph and brought down his heavy warhammer – against the side of Malus's head.

The shock was all-powerful. One moment Malus was locked in a deadly battle with the man in front of him and the next he was hurtling to the ground. He bounced off the paving stones face-first, his brain unable to grasp how he'd got there.

There was a roaring in his ears, like a raging surf that ebbed and flowed just above his head. Everything blurred; the only thing he felt with perfect clarity was a thin trickle of ichor leaking down his cheek.

I'm bleeding, he thought stupidly, and realised that he was likely about to die.

But instead of seeing a sword or hammer descend on his skull, he saw a druchii boot heel come down just inches from his face. The roaring continued, and the boot moved on, to be replaced by another.

He lay there watching boots stamp and slide past him for what seemed like a very long time, and it wasn't until the roaring in his ears tapered away that he realised he hadn't been killed after all.

The next thing he knew there were rough hands pulling at him, trying to roll him over. 'That was the damnedest thing I've ever seen, if you don't mind me saying so, captain,' said a voice. 'Reminds me of this damn-fool highborn I used to know–'

The hands rolled him over, and Malus found himself looking up into a dark-eyed, grinning face. He recognised the scarred features at once, and let out a bemused grunt.

'There you are, Hauclir, you damned rogue,' he said. 'Where is that wine I asked for?' And with that the world went utterly dark.

Chapter Sixteen
DAEMONS AND CUTTHROATS

COLD WATER SPLASHED Malus in the face. He came to, sputtering and coughing, propped up against the hard stone of the battlements. Pools of blood and body parts littered the paving stones around him.

A figure knelt in front of the highborn, holding an upended water bottle. 'Sorry to wake you, my lord,' Hauclir said calmly, 'but it looks like we're about to be attacked again, so I don't have the luxury of allowing you to sleep off that little knock you got on the head. You and I have a bit of talking to do while we're both still able to do it.'

Malus tried to rub the water out of his rheumy eyes. When his vision returned, he found Hauclir to be studying him intently, paying especial attention to his face and neck. The former guard captain was dressed much like the rest of the mercenaries, though the cut of his robes were finer and better kept, and his kheitan was thick, sturdy dwarf-hide. He wore his customary mail hauberk, and his short sword sat in its oiled scabbard. A long, knotted oak cudgel dangled loosely from his right hand.

The highborn shook his head bemusedly. 'I thought I was dreaming,' he muttered thickly. With tentative fingers he reached up and prodded at the side of his head.

'I had much the same reaction,' Hauclir said dryly. His lips twisted in a sarcastic grin, but his dark eyes were cold and hard. 'Now, I'm not going to ask how you somehow went from a closely-hunted outlaw to the Witch King's personal champion; I've seen the way your damned mind works, and nothing you do surprises me any more. Instead, I want you to tell me, in very compelling detail, why you saw fit to betray each and every man in your service after we left you at Karond Kar.'

Malus's own expression hardened. His former retainer's impertinent tone caused the highborn to bristle. 'You were my damned vassal!' he snapped. 'Your life was mine to use as I pleased! I owe you no explanation.'

But Hauclir was far from cowed by the highborn's imperious tone. A slow, dangerous smile spread across his scarred, angular face. 'Look around you, my lord. Do you fancy you're reclining in your high tower back at the Hag? No. You're sitting on a battlefield, surrounded by blood and spilled guts, and the nearest nobleman for two miles is lying at the bottom of the wall with the rest of the rubbish. Right at the moment I own this part of the fortress wall, so you're going to play things by my rules. So let's hear your story, my lord, and it better be a good one, or else I'll chuck you over this damned wall myself.'

The former retainer's tone was light, even cheerful, but Malus looked in his eyes and saw the anger burning there. He had absolutely no doubt that Hauclir meant every word he said. So he shrugged, and told the former guardsman everything.

Or at least he tried to. He hadn't got much past receiving Tz'arkan's curse when the next wave of attackers came howling at the walls. Malus was forced to wait while Hauclir and his men drove off the assault. His weapons had been taken from him, and he wasn't sure he could stand up yet, anyway.

They were interrupted twice more by enemy assaults before Malus finally got Hauclir to the moment their paths crossed once again. The former retainer sat wearily against the battlements beside Malus, picking dried bits of blood from his haggard face. For a long time he didn't speak at all. 'So. A daemon, you say?'

Malus nodded. 'A daemon.'

Hauclir grunted. 'Well, that explains your eyes. And the fact that your head wasn't splattered across the flagstones by that damned hammer.'

The highborn sighed. 'I don't deny there are certain advantages to the situation.'

'And you had no idea it was your father who was at Vaelgor Keep?' the former guardsman asked. 'Who else did you think it could be?'

'It could have been anyone, Hauclir. Lurhan wasn't flying his banner outside the keep, after all. At the time it made more sense that it was Isilvar, working in conjunction with my sister.'

Hauclir grudgingly nodded. 'Yes. I suppose you're right.' He looked sidelong at his former master. 'But you realise that now I have an even more compelling reason to throw you over the wall.'

Malus spread his hands. 'You wanted the truth, Hauclir. Can I have my swords back now?'

'Certainly not. You're a damned daemonhost!'

'For the Dark Mother's sake, Hauclir!' Malus snapped. 'I had a daemon inside me from the moment I returned from the north. Did I ever once try to kill you? No. In fact, I made you a very rich man.'

'Before you broke one of the cardinal laws of the land and I had it all stripped away from me.'

The highborn folded his arms tightly about his chest. 'Shall I beg your pardon, then? What do you want from me, Hauclir? I did what I had to do. Do you think you could have done any better in my place?'

'Gods Below, my lord. I have no idea,' the former guardsman said. He sighed. 'To be honest, it didn't hit me as hard as some of the others. Your man Silar took it the worst, him and Arleth Vann. Dolthaic, he was just angry about losing all the gold.'

Malus nodded thoughtfully. 'Arleth Vann thought that all of you had gone to sea after the battle outside Hag Graef.'

The former retainer shrugged. 'That was Silar and Dolthaic's idea. I just followed along. Couldn't stay in Hag Graef any more, so why not? The two of them put to sea a day after we got there. Looked up the master of the *Shadowblade*; Dolthaic said he knew the captain from a raiding cruise the summer before. They asked if I wanted to go, but I've seen all the ocean I ever want to see. So, I stayed on around the dockyards, picking up the odd work here and there. And then I fell in with these rats,' he said, indicating the mercenaries sitting a discreet distance away. 'We were shaking down bridge travellers for tolls when Malekith's call to arms reached the city. The drachau scooped a lot of the gangs up after that. I'm sure he hopes none of us survive to go back and dirty up his precious city.'

Malus nodded. He reached down and picked up his dented helmet. 'So, it appears I owe you my life.'

'Again.'

The highborn grinned. 'Yes. Again.'

'You don't expect me to serve you again, do you?' Hauclir asked. 'I'm not your man any more, my lord. Not after all that's happened.'

Malus shook his head. 'I'm still technically an outlaw, despite all the finery. I couldn't hold you to your oath if I wanted to.'

'But you still need my help,' Hauclir said.

'Do I?'

'Oh, yes, my lord, you do. And you damned well know it.'

The highborn spread his hands. 'Nothing escapes you, it seems. All right. Name your price.'

Hauclir made a show of thinking things over. 'That Chaos champion has the amulet you need, correct?'

'Correct.'

'And your sister's tent was chock full of loot, correct?'

'Before I burnt it to the ground, yes.'

The former guardsman nodded. 'Well, I expect your path is going to take you back into her vicinity before all is said and done,' he said thoughtfully. 'Me and mine get all the loot we can carry, and we're yours for the asking.'

The highborn looked at Hauclir bemusedly. 'You're a fool. You realise that, I trust?'

'So my mother told me,' he answered. 'Do we have a deal, or not?'

Malus nodded. 'Done.'

'All right then,' Hauclir said, rising to his feet. 'I'll go and explain things to the troops.'

The highborn watched his former retainer go, shaking his head in amazement. For the life of him, he couldn't be certain who was getting the better end of the deal, but all of a sudden he felt much better about his chances of getting the amulet and getting out of the Black Tower alive.

Sometime later Hauclir remembered to return Malus his swords. The rubies in both pommels had been carefully pried away.

It was not long after the twelfth assault that the roiling darkness suddenly receded, leaving the fortress's defenders blinking wearily in the pale light of early morning. Cheers went up from within the city, as the soldiers took the sunlight as a sign the siege had been lifted, but the exhausted warriors holding the battlements saw the enemy encampment for the first time and knew that their ordeal was perhaps only just beginning.

The Chaos horde was camped in a broad band that completely surrounded the fortress city. Cook fires by the hundreds sent thin tendrils of smoke into the sky, and herds of northern horses mingled in great corrals around the camp's circular perimeter. The dusty ground seethed with motion, the dark figures moving about on their errands like a multitude of ravening ants. Malus looked out over the part of the encampment opposite his part of the wall and shook his head in awe. Was there no end to the damned beasts?

If he stood at the far left end of the wall and leaned out far enough to see past the rightward redoubt he could glimpse a pavilion of indigo-dyed tents, just like the ones he'd burned a few days ago. There was a strange distortion in the air above and around the tent, similar to the haze of hot air over a forge. That was where Nagaira and her champion would be found.

His eyes ached and his stomach rumbled, and he hadn't been clean since the Dark Mother alone knew when. Most of the mercenaries were sound asleep, stretched out on the filthy paving stones with their weapons across their chests. Over the last two days he'd got to know many of the sell-swords in the company. None of them had names; only nicknames, to make it harder for the city watch or anyone else to track them down using sorcery. He met a professional killer named Cutter, an unlucky cutpurse named Ten-thumbs, a gambler named Pock-ets and too many others to count. The highborn learned at length that Hauclir's nickname was Knock-knock, which pri-vately amused Malus.

There were nearly a hundred of the cutthroats to begin with, but after throwing back no less than seven attacks their num-bers had dwindled to sixty-five. Almost half that number was wounded to a greater or lesser degree; supposedly there were aid stations and orderlies to patrol the walls and remove injured soldiers, but they'd seen nothing like that since taking charge of their stretch of wall. They had long since run out of bolts for their crossbows as well. Malus had tried to use his authority to get more from the closest redoubt, but the captain in charge had flatly refused, claiming that only Lord Myrchas could authorise such a transfer. The highborn hadn't pursued the matter further. The less he had to deal with that den of snakes in the citadel the better.

He did send some of his more talented foragers into the city in search of food and drink, once it became clear that no one was going to send them anything to eat. In this, the mercenar-ies were singularly successful, returning to the wall with roast fowl, boiled eggs, fresh bread and cheese and several bottles of decent wine. Malus didn't ask any questions, and the foragers were happy to not give any answers.

Three hours into the morning, Malus was sipping from one such bottle when the iron door of the far redoubt swung open and a ramrod-straight figure in gleaming armour strode into the sunlight. Nuarc made his way slowly but purposefully down the length of the wall, eyeing the snoring mercenaries with a look that was somewhere between outrage and bemusement. The few cutthroats still awake returned the general's gaze with the flat stare of hungry wolves.

When the general reached Malus's reclining form his expression of shock only deepened. 'By the Dark Mother!' he exclaimed. 'We were starting to think you'd been killed. No one's seen you at your apartments for days.' Nuarc jerked his head in the direction of the mercenaries. 'What in the Blessed Murderer's name are you doing with this rabble?' he asked. Then his face turned deadly serious and he leaned close to the highborn. 'They aren't holding you for some sort of ransom, are they?'

The notion gave Malus the first real laugh he'd had in a very long time. 'No, my lord. They know very well that I'm not worth the trouble.' He cocked his head at the general. 'Out for a stroll in the sunshine, general?'

Nuarc glowered at the grinning highborn. 'Out to see what the enemy is up to, and to check on things along the wall,' he said darkly. 'And to get away from those caterwauling fools back at the citadel, truth be told.'

Malus held up the pilfered bottle. 'Can I interest you in some wine, general?' Much to the highborn's surprise, Nuarc accepted the offer and took a deep draught before handing it back. The gesture sobered Malus at once.

'How bad is our situation, my lord?'

On reflex, the general glanced at the mercenaries some feet away to make certain they were out of likely earshot. 'Things could be better,' he admitted. 'We've held the walls for almost three days now, but the regiments have taken a bad beating. The hardest hit units have been rotated off the walls, but our reserves are being stretched thin.'

'Rotated?' Malus exclaimed. 'We've been up here for two days! No one's brought us food or ammunition, and no one's sent orderlies for our wounded.'

'That's because no one knows you're here,' the general answered grimly. 'None of the mercenary companies are part of the army's muster list, and no one back at the citadel is capable of thinking past their own damned agendas.'

The thought shocked Malus. 'You mean to tell me no one is in command?'

Nuarc shook his head. 'Each drachau thinks of nothing but his own honour and prestige. They intrigue against one another constantly, and no one will cooperate towards the city's defence. They've staked out which walls belong to each drachau, and they spare no thought for the others.'

'But... but that's absurd!' Malus cried. 'What does the Witch King say about this?'

The general shrugged. 'He watches and waits to see which lord will assert himself. It's his way. But Myrchas is too timid, Isilvar is too inexperienced, Balneth Bale is too weak and Jhedir of Clar Karond is too drunk. About the only consensus Myrchas, Isilvar and Bale have reached is that you have to be put to death at the first available opportunity. Fortunately for you, they can't decide what manner of execution to use.'

Malus shook his head in stupefied wonder. 'What about our reinforcements, then?'

Nuarc took a deep breath. 'Any forces from Karond Kar would have a long way to travel, even if they commandeered every available boat and sailed them to the western shore of the Sea of Malice,' he said. 'They aren't expected for a week or more. Troops from Har Ganeth, on the other hand, should have been here by now. No one knows what could have caused their delay.'

Malus could venture a guess, but thought it wiser not to say. He took a long draught from the bottle and rolled it around his tongue. 'I regret that I cost the army a further ten thousand troops,' he said bitterly.

'Nonsense,' the old general barked. 'I might have done the same thing. It was a good plan, but you assumed too much.'

The highborn considered this, and nodded. 'All right. What do you think we should do now?'

'Me?' Nuarc replied, a bit surprised at the question. He looked out at the enemy encampment for a moment before replying. 'I would pull the army back to the inner wall.'

Malus blinked. 'But then we'd be trapped.'

'We're trapped *now*, boy,' the general shot back. 'The inner wall is higher, and there's less ground to have to defend. We could rotate units more often and still make the enemy pay a steep price every time they tested us. We're very well supplied, so Nagaira can't starve us out, and ultimately time is not on her side. Our warriors at sea are returning home even now, and within a month she would be facing a powerful army of highborn marching up from the south.' The general shrugged. 'But no one has asked my thoughts on the matter.'

The highborn took another drink and turned his face to the sky. 'Well, at least the sun is shining.'

'I know. That's what worries me the most,' the general said.

'And how is that, my lord?' Malus asked.

'Because up until now your sister has put a great deal of effort into keeping the city locked in darkness. According to Morathi, the cost of such effort is considerable, especially in the face of opposition from her and the city's convent.'

'Morathi has been fighting against Nagaira? I hadn't noticed.'

'Did you imagine all that lightning was your sister's doing?' Nuarc asked. 'It doesn't make much sense when one is spending all that energy to keep things dark, now does it?'

'No, I suppose not,' Malus replied peevishly.

'So there you are. She pits her strength against Morathi and the witches for three days – and now this.' Nuarc raised his head slightly, almost as though he were sniffing the air. 'Something's up, boy. She's changing tactics.'

That was when they heard the sound. Malus had no words for it; it was a horrible, wailing, tearing noise that seemed to reverberate through the air and yet not be a part of it. One thing Malus was certain of – it came from the direction of Nagaira's tent.

Tz'arkan reacted immediately, its daemonic energies rippling along Malus's skin. 'Your sister's gifts are potent indeed,' it hissed. 'She has opened a great doorway between the worlds.'

'Between the worlds?' Malus muttered. Then he understood. 'Chaos,' he said to Nuarc. 'Nagaira is calling upon the storms of Chaos. She's summoning monsters to send against the walls!'

At that same moment the alarm horns howled from the redoubts. The mercenaries were awake at once, scrambling warily to their feet. 'We need crossbow bolts,' the highborn said. 'Quickly!'

The old general nodded. 'I'll see to it,' he said, and hurried back to the nearby redoubt.

Malus drew his swords. 'Stand to, you wolves!' he called to the cutthroats. 'The bastards are going to try their luck again!'

Hauclir came striding swiftly down the line, barking commands to his men. 'What's going on now?' he asked, his sword and cudgel ready.

The highborn gave him a bleak look. 'Remember the Isle of Morhaut?'

'Oh, damnation,' Hauclir said, his face turning pale.

At the far end of the line the redoubt door opened and a pair of soldiers were all but hurled out onto the parapet by Nuarc, each one carrying a barrel full of crossbow bolts. 'Load the crossbows! Quickly now!' Malus yelled. 'We haven't much time.'

And indeed, he was right. No sooner had he spoken than he heard the heavy *bang* of the redoubt's bolt throwers, and something not of the mortal world screamed and gibbered just out of sight around the redoubt's sloping flank. Everyone on the parapet turned in the direction of the sound, their faces full of dread.

Chapter Seventeen
MOVE AND COUNTERMOVE

THE SLITHERING THING that lurched into view from around the corner of the redoubt was a hideous knot of roiling muscle and misshapen bone as large as a nauglir. Mouths that were little more than muscular tubes lined with dagger-like teeth writhed and gaped like serpents above the fleshy mass, and great, scythe-bladed arms lashed and stabbed at the air, reaching madly for prey. The abomination had been pierced by a bolt from one of the redoubt's bolt throwers, and its body was wreathed in seething green sorcerous flame. It lurched a few more steps towards the wall, shrieking an agonising, lunatic wail, then collapsed into a shrivelling, burning mass.

The cutthroats' cheer of relief was short-lived however, as it became clear the otherworldly creature was far from alone.

A huge pack of smaller creatures came racing around the end of the redoubt, loping, slithering, bounding and scuttling with hideous, predatory grace. They flowed past the burning Chaos creature and charged straight for the fortress wall, throwing back their bald heads and screeching hungrily at the defenders above. Behind them lurched three more of the larger, more powerful monstrosities, bellowing angrily as they dragged their bulk across the ashen ground.

Hard-bitten cutthroats screamed like frightened children as the seething pack of Chaos beasts reached the wall and began to scuttle up its sheer height like spiders. 'Stand to, you dogs!' Malus roared. 'Crossbows! Don't just stand there! Open fire!'

Galvanised by the steely tone in Malus's voice the handful of crossbowmen stepped to the battlements and leaned over the edge and fired at the monsters rushing up the fortress wall. Two bolts struck home, dislodging a pair of the screeching fiends and sending them plummeting to the ground, where they struck hard and curled in upon themselves like dead insects. Reassured by the knowledge that the monsters could die like any other living thing, the mercenaries regained some of their lost courage and readied their weapons as the beasts drew nearer.

The heavy bolt throwers in the redoubt banged once more, and twin streaks of green fire plunged down at the shambling behemoths still crawling towards the wall. One of the dragons-fire bolts missed, splashing a pool of searing fire along the ground, but the other struck home. The blazing monster continued to shamble forwards even as it died, its wails adding to the cacophony of noise assaulting the defenders' senses.

More war horns blared, and cries of battle echoed all across the northern quadrant of the fortress. Cursing under his breath, Malus dashed to the inner edge of the parapet and leaned out as far as he dared, peering at the section of wall on the other side of the redoubt to his right. The next wall over was the scene of a desperate battle as the spearmen there grappled with a furious pack of Chaos beasts. On the other side of these spearmen lay the north gatehouse. Malus had no doubt that was where the monsters would go. If the gatehouse fell then the whole outer wall was lost.

Screeching and roaring, the first of the Chaos beasts came scrambling over the battlements and threw themselves at the waiting mercenaries. A druchii went down with a multi-legged monster wrapped around his torso, his sword driven clean through the beast's midsection. Another creature crouched on the battlements and lashed at two of the cut-throats with whip-like tentacles lined with tiny, fanged mouths. Malus saw Hauclir block a lunging beast's charge with his heavy cudgel and hack the thing open with his short sword. Ten-thumbs levelled his crossbow and shot another point-blank, the heavy bolt punching clean through the monster's body. Another mercenary shrieked in agony as a monster drove its blade-like forelegs into his eyes.

More and more of the creatures were swarming over the wall every moment. Blood and ichor stained the parapet in equal measure. Malus saw Nuarc standing by the redoubt's open door, slicing a charging monster neatly in half with his rune-marked sword. 'We need reinforcements!' the highborn yelled over the din. 'We can't keep this up for long!'

But Nuarc shook his head. 'They'll never get here in time,' he cried, rushing forward and stabbing another beast that had fastened onto a mercenary's throat. 'We hold the wall with what we have or not at all!'

Damn those fools in the citadel, Malus thought! Their petty intrigues were doing Nagaira's work for her.

Just then a fierce wind rushed over the top of the redoubt and buffeted Malus's face. He smelled brimstone and old blood, and heard a vast rushing of wings. Instinct spurred Malus into motion even before the wave of flapping figures burst overhead. 'Get down!' he yelled at Nuarc, crashing into the older druchii and driving him back against the redoubt wall just as a swarm of winged monsters came roaring down the length of the parapet. The creatures lashed at the struggling druchii with their long, saw-bladed tails; a few snatched up unsuspecting mercenaries in their talons and flung them screaming from the wall. Under assault now from two sides, the defenders' courage began to waver, and they started to give ground to the snarling beasts.

Malus pushed away from Nuarc with an angry snarl. 'Not another step back!' he roared at his men. 'You can stand and fight or run and die! Kill these bastards before they kill you!'

To the terrified crossbowmen he yelled, 'Shoot those damned flying beasts out of the air!'

Once again the defenders redoubled their efforts under the lash of Darkblade's tongue, but Malus knew that he couldn't keep things going for long. Another major reversal and the battle could turn into a rout.

A long, lean shape with six legs and a gaping, tooth-lined orifice in place of a head clawed its way up the body of the mercenary nearest Malus and then launched itself at the highborn. Roaring an oath, he caught the monstrosity on the point of his blade and threw it screaming over the battlements. The winged creatures came rushing in again, but this time several tumbled from the sky with crossbow bolts buried in their pale bodies. Malus sliced off another's wing as it shot past, sending it careening full-tilt into the side of the redoubt. Another of the mercenaries was plucked from the parapet, but this time both druchii and monster went tumbling to the ground with the cutthroat's dagger buried in the creature's chest.

Malus sensed that the tide of battle was starting to turn in the defenders' favour. No more of the swift creatures were appearing over the battlements, at least, and the mercenaries were rallying themselves and ganging up on the monsters that remained.

Then he heard the wailing cry from the other side of the wall and his heart lurched in his chest. He'd forgotten about the two behemoths.

Malus dashed to the battlements and peered over – then ducked his head back just as quickly. One of the monsters was almost within arm's reach, trailing a slick of yellow slime as it slithered its way up the wall. The second creature had flattened against the wall of the redoubt to avoid the punishing fire of the bolt throwers and was nearly to the top of the wall as well. Malus pounded on the edge of the battlements in frustration. He couldn't imagine anything less than a dragonsfire bolt being able to destroy the huge creatures.

His gaze drifted to the open redoubt door. Maybe he didn't need the bolt throwers at all.

Malus dashed inside the redoubt. The two sentries who normally stood watch at the door had evidently fled, or perhaps been killed out on the parapet when the Chaos beasts first attacked. He ran down the long corridor for another few yards, until he came to a water barrel holding a pair of the long, glass-tipped dragon's breath bolts. He pulled the long, spear-like bolts from the water, taking great care not to knock them together, then turned and hurried back the way he came.

Nuarc was waiting for him just as he emerged from the doorway. The general recoiled from the highborn with a startled hiss. 'What in the name of the Murderer are you doing with those!' he exclaimed.

'Taking care of some pests,' Malus replied, just as the first of the behemoths appeared at the edge of the battlements with a wailing roar.

'Get back!' Malus yelled at the mercenaries nearby – who were already falling over one another trying to escape the monster's thrashing limbs. Then he hefted one of the long bolts like a javelin, took two quick steps and hurled it at the monster's side.

The bolt wobbled in the air as it flew the short distance to the target. Faster than Malus thought possible, the beast saw the projectile coming and smashed it out of the air with the sweep of a scythe-like arm, breaking the glass globe at the bolt's tip and showering itself with liquid flame. Shrieking and flailing in agony, the monster sizzled like fat dropped in a fire, then fell away from the battlements and tumbled like a comet to the ground.

Even as the first monster was plummeting to earth Malus took up his second bolt and peered cautiously over the battlements. Instantly a pair of scythe-arms lashed at him, missing his face by scant inches. The behemoth was only perhaps a dozen feet below, clashing its multiple jaws and undulating inexorably upwards. With a cruel grin the highborn held his ground and took deliberate aim. All he really had to do was drop the bolt onto the creature, and within moments it too was burning in a greasy heap at the base of the wall.

The last of the smaller Chaos beasts took another of the mercenaries with it when it died – farther down the wall one of the druchii fell from the battlements with a scream, still stabbing at the beast that was burrowing its way into his chest. Malus watched beast and victim fall to their deaths and said a silent thanks to the Dark Mother that it was the last of them.

Leaning against the battlements, Malus took in the scene of carnage that stretched the entire length of the long wall before him. Bodies and pieces of bodies lay strewn everywhere, amid puddles of congealing blood and stinking ichor. The mercenaries were pulling their wounded comrades to their feet, but there were too few of them. Not three minutes ago there had been sixty-five mercenaries fighting alongside him, and now he was hard-pressed to count more than thirty that were still breathing. He scanned the battered cutthroats for a glimpse of Hauclir, and found the former guard captain at the far end of the line, working hard to get the mercenaries ready in case of another attack.

Nuarc stood just a few feet away with his back to the redoubt wall, wiping dark fluid from the length of his blade with a coarse piece of cloth. 'A near run thing,' the general said, 'That was an inspired piece of lunacy, fetching those dragon's breath bolts. Never seen that done before.'

Malus grinned tiredly and was about to reply when a warhorn wailed a shrill, insistent note from the gatehouse. Nuarc stiffened, and Malus saw the briefest flicker of fear in his dark eyes. 'What is it?' he asked.

Cursing under his breath, Nuarc dropped his cleaning cloth and dashed a few yards down the wall. Malus joined him, following the warlord's gaze to the scene of slaughter unfolding along the neighbouring wall.

Chaos beasts were swarming over the battlements in a glistening flood, racing over the torn corpses of the defenders and pouring down the long ramps into the city beyond. At the far end of the wall where it met the gatehouse, two of the huge Chaos monsters were hammering and prying at the iron door leading into the gatehouse proper.

Behind the monsters, bloodstained swords in hand, stood Nagaira's Chaos champion.

The armoured figure was surrounded by lesser Chaos beasts, which circled his heels like hunting hounds. Worse still, more than a dozen armoured Chaos warriors stood ready on the battlements behind the champion, waiting for the door to come down. As Malus watched, a half-dozen of the winged nightmares flapped heavily up from the base of the wall, each one clutching another armoured warrior in its talons.

Malus's heart sank. The attack on their wall had just been a feint, aimed at keeping them occupied so that they couldn't come to the gatehouse's defence. They'd outsmarted him again! 'Hauclir!' he barked. 'Form up your wolves! Now! We've got to get to the gatehouse–'

'There's no damn time,' Nuarc said, his voice tight with anger. 'Your men are spent and the enemy has a secure foothold. You'd be pulled apart before you even got close to the gatehouse.'

'I can get more of the dragon's breath–'

'And do what? Throw it at the enemy and then advance into the flames? Use some sense, boy!' Nuarc snapped. 'Remember what I said about the inner wall being easier to defend? We have to fall back now, before those bastards get the outer gate open, or we'll never make it at all. Come on!'

Without waiting for a reply, Nuarc broke away and hurried down the length of the wall, calling for the mercenaries to follow. The harbour rats, already at the limits of their endurance, were all too eager to escape. Malus took a moment to glare hatefully at the enemy champion, who wore the one thing the highborn needed to reclaim his soul and seemed capable of thwarting him at every turn.

As he glared at the armoured fiend, the champion straightened, and as though he were able to read the highborn's thoughts, the helmeted head turned and looked his way.

Malus raised his sword and levelled it at the champion. 'This isn't over yet,' he said to the baleful warrior, then he swallowed his bitter fury and turned to follow quickly in Nuarc's wake.

* * *

'FIRST HE COSTS us ten thousand men, and now he's cost us the fortress's outer wall!' Isilvar shouted, pointing an accusing finger at Malus. 'I tell you, he's in league with Nagaira, somehow. How else can one explain such incompetence?'

The vaulkhar and the three drachau were seated in high-backed chairs with velvet cushions, in a lesser audience chamber than the grand court chamber at the base of the Black Tower. A large, marble topped table before them was set with the remains of a sumptuous lunch, now all but forgotten in the wake of the day's disaster. Lord Myrchas studied Malus coldly, rolling a Tilean grape between his pale fingers. The Witch Lord, Balneth Bale, made a show of studying the parchment map of the inner fortress laid out on the table, but how much of it he could see amid the platters, goblets and bits of food was open to discussion. Lord Jhedir of Clar Karond chuckled at Isilvar's tirade and took another sip of wine.

Sitting in the shadows behind the four lords sat Malekith himself, fingers steepled and red light seeping from the oculars of his horned helm. The Witch King hadn't said a single word since Malus had been called to make his report. The highborn stood defiantly beyond the end of the long table, with Nuarc standing close behind him. Retainers and servants shuffled quietly about the room's perimeter; on the north end of the chamber stood a high, arched entryway that opened onto a narrow balcony which looked down over the inner wall and the city beyond. Hauclir stood by the open archway, idly cleaning his nails with a small knife and dividing his attention between events without and within.

'I wasn't aware that I'd been placed in personal command of the outer wall defences,' Malus hissed. Unlike the richly attired nobles, he'd come to the audience chamber after finding a place in the citadel for the surviving mercenaries. He was still clothed primarily in steel, blood and black ichor. 'Perhaps that explains why no one along the outer wall had the faintest idea what was happening, nor were they given any leadership or direction once the north gate fell. It would certainly explain why my section of the wall received no food, ammunition or medical orderlies in the entire two days I and my men stood guard there. Why, if only I'd known, dear brother. Perhaps I could have saved the wall and the Dark Mother only knows how many of our men!'

The retreat to the inner wall had begun well enough; the Black Tower's garrison was familiar with the plans for such a manoeuvre, as laid down by Lord Kuall, the previous vaulkhar, and they had even drilled for it regularly. But once the gate fell and the Chaos horde came swarming into the city, confusion and panic quickly took hold. With no clear chain of command there was no one to organise a rearguard to hold the attackers at bay so the rest could get to safety. Worse, the regiments from Malekith's army had to deal with their own set of conflicting orders from their individual drachau, commanding them to think of themselves first and everyone else second, if at all. The retreat quickly became a free-for-all. Regiments from the same city stuck together and left their rivals behind. Entire regiments were isolated in the city and wiped out, while there were rumours that there were at least three instances of druchii regiments fighting one another for the chance to escape the enemy.

Nuarc and Malus had done what they could, gathering up stray units and forming an ad hoc rearguard that managed to hold the central avenue outside the inner gate for some three hours before finally being forced to retreat. At this point Malus had no idea whether they'd done any good or not. Now night was drawing in, and the highborn found it hard to believe he'd been standing on the outer wall just eight hours before. He was more tired than he'd ever been in his life, and at that moment he wanted nothing in the world so much as the chance to reach over and tear out his brother's throat with his bare hands.

Isilvar met Malus's burning gaze without flinching. 'The fact remains that you were on the wall – in fact, according to your own report, you were adjacent to the main enemy attack all along. Yet you did nothing to stop it, interestingly enough.'

'I was in the middle of a *battle*,' Malus shot back. 'Where were you? In the bath? Having your teeth filed? You're the damned

Vaulkhar of Hag Graef, the most powerful warlord of the most powerful city in Naggaroth. Do you even know how to use that sword you're carrying?'

Isilvar leapt to his feet, his dark eyes glittering. 'I could show you if you like.'

'You had your chance to show me in the cult chamber beneath Nagaira's tower,' Malus replied with an evil grin. 'But you ran like a frightened deer, then. Did you tell yourself you were escaping for the sake of Slaanesh and her cult, or did you save the self-serving excuses for later?' He leaned over the edge of the table. 'I should think that if anyone here is familiar with conspiring with Nagaira, it would be you.'

The vaulkar went pale – with rage or fear Malus wasn't entirely sure. 'You… you have no proof of such a thing!' he rasped, his hand rising unconsciously to his throat.

'Care to put that to the test, dear brother?' Malus said, a cruel smile playing at the corners of his mouth. He noticed Myrchas, Bale and even Jhedir casting long looks at the trembling figure of the vaulkhar.

Across the marble-floored chamber, Hauclir cleared his throat. When Malus didn't respond, he tried again, louder this time.

The highborn turned to regard Hauclir. 'Are you well?' he said icily.

'Well enough, my lord,' he said, straightening. The former guard captain gestured to the balcony with his knife. 'I think there's something out here you might want to see.'

'Do I look busy to you, Hauclir?' Malus snapped, indicating the assembled nobles with a sharp sweep of his hand.

'Of course, my lord, but–'

'Can it wait?'

Hauclir frowned. 'Well, I suppose it can,' he said.

'Then trouble me with it later!' the highborn said with a look of exasperation.

The former guardsman folded his arms, glowering at his one-time master, then shrugged. 'As you wish,' he said, turning back to the open archway.

Malus turned back to Isilvar, trying to recapture his train of thought. Isilvar still glared at him from across the table, his hand in the hilt of his blade. His face seemed a bit calmer now, the highborn noted with a frown.

But before he could continue there was a thunderous boom that rolled through the open archway beside Hauclir. Everyone except Malekith jumped at the sound.

Malus glanced worriedly at Hauclir. 'What in the Outer Darkness is that?' he cried.

The former guardsman gave the highborn a sardonic glare. 'Evidently nothing of any import,' he said peevishly.

Snarling, Malus rushed to the archway with Nuarc in tow. Even Isilvar and the drachau rose from their chairs and made their way warily across the room.

With a passing glare at his impertinent former retainer, Malus stepped onto the balcony and looked down from a dizzying height at the top of the inner wall and the glittering ranks of the troops massed to defend it. Beyond lay the corpse-choked streets and the smouldering buildings of the outer city, teeming with looting bands of beastmen and drunken marauders.

In a wide square a few hundred yards from the inner gate however was a sight that made Malus's heart skip a beat. Long lines of straining beastmen were pulling a pair of enormous catapults down the long avenue and into firing positions alongside a third siege engine whose throwing arm was already being winched back for another shot. A pall of stone dust hung in the air above the gatehouse, indicating the catapult's intended target.

Beside Malus, Nuarc let out a low curse. 'They must have been assembling them under cover of that damned darkness,' he muttered. 'Your sister is more resourceful than I imagined.'

'She lacks martial experience, but she's well read,' Malus said grimly. 'Do you think they can knock down the gatehouse with those things?'

The warlord grunted. 'Of course they can. All they need is time and ammunition, something they seem to have in abundance.'

Malus fought down a swell of frustration. Nagaira wasn't giving him a chance to catch his breath for a single moment. He didn't have to consider the situation very long before he realised what must be done. Turning on his heel he strode back into the chamber. Isilvar and the drachau retreated as he swept inside, as though he carried some kind of plague.

The highborn turned to Lord Myrchas. 'Is there a tunnel?'

'Tunnel? What do you mean?'

'Is there a tunnel leading from the citadel into the outer city?' Malus snapped. 'Surely there must be some way to launch raids in the event the outer wall is breached.'

The drachau of the Black Tower started to speak, then paused. He frowned in bemusement.

'For the Dark Mother's sake, Myrchas! Don't you know?'

Before the drachau could embarrass himself further, Nuarc spoke up. 'There is such a tunnel. I saw it once when I was studying the plans of the citadel.'

The highborn nodded curtly. 'All right then. Lead on, my lord,' he said to Nuarc, then gestured at Hauclir. 'Let's go and get the men.'

But an armoured figure stepped into Malus's path. Isilvar stood nearly nose-to-nose with his half-brother. 'And where do you think you're going?' he said, hand on the hilt of his sword.

Furious, Malus stepped forward, catching Isilvar's sword arm and the wrist with one hand and shoving him hard with the other. The vaulkhar fell in an undignified heap, his scabbarded sword tangled beneath him.

'While the rest of you sit here peeling grapes and squabbling like children I'm going to take care of those catapults,' he snarled. 'No doubt by the time I return you'll have invented some other set of excuses to explain away your clean hands and faint hearts.'

Isilvar's face turned white with fury, but he made no reply. Malus gave his half-brother a mocking salute, then, glaring angrily at the assembled drachau, he motioned for Nuarc to take the lead and followed him from the room.

Meanwhile, in the shadows, the Witch King watched Malus go and kept his own silent counsel.

Chapter Eighteen
THE DRAGON'S BREATH

'Oh, for the Dark Mother's sake!' Hauclir hissed in exasperation, holding open the small burlap bag so the mercenaries could see the clinking contents within. 'Which one of you halfwits thought it was a good idea to let Ten-thumbs carry the incendiaries?'

The cutthroats exchanged sheepish looks. In the light of the single witchlamp in Malus's hand, the three mercenaries looked like mischievous shades. Pockets smirked at the former guard captain. 'Ten-thumbs only drops stuff he's trying to steal,' she said, her voice pitched just loudly enough to carry down the line of waiting troops. 'Besides, we figured if he went up in flames no one would miss him.'

Thin hisses of laughter echoed up and down the line. Even Malus found it hard not to grin. They were twenty feet underground, at the far end of a mile-long tunnel that ran from the citadel into the outer city, right in the midst of the bloodthirsty Chaos horde. The tunnel seemed well-made, its square stones slick with dark patches of moss and dripping slime, but everyone eyed the tarred black cross-beams holding up the low ceiling with evident worry. Even weak attempts at humour were welcome.

'Easy for you to say, Pockets. He doesn't owe you any coin,' Hauclir replied. Working carefully, he reached into the bag and pulled out the globes of dragon's breath one at a time. Each glass sphere was wrapped in thick wads of rough cotton to conceal the distinctive green glow and keep the volatile contents safe. He parcelled out the incendiaries among the group, handing one to Pockets, one to Cutter, one to Malus and keeping one for himself, then – with a look of pure trepidation – handing one back to Ten-thumbs. The young cutpurse accepted the deadly orb with as much aggrieved dignity as he could manage.

'I'll take the extra one,' Malus said, holding out his hand. 'And never mind what I may or may not owe you.'

'Very good, my lord,' Hauclir said, handing the orb over. The highborn set the incendiaries carefully at the bottom of a carry-bag tied to his belt, then looked over the raiding party one last time. There were only seven mercenaries, counting Hauclir; Malus felt that a smaller group had a better chance of getting close enough to the siege engines to hit them with the orbs and then slip away again in the confusion. Three of the cutthroats carried crossbows, and Malus had managed to appropriate one for himself from the citadel armoury. Hauclir had further assured him that both Cutter and Pockets were light on their feet and good with their knives.

'All right,' the highborn said, turning and raising the witch-lamp to illuminate the narrow shaft at the end of the tunnel. Rusting iron staples had been hammered into the packed earth, providing a ladder to reach the surface. 'According to Nuarc, this opens into a warehouse in the armourer's district. Once we're on the surface, no lights or unnecessary talking.'

Pockets gave Malus a slow wink and a feline smile. Her alabaster skin and sharp features reminded the highborn of a maelithii. The black eyes and filed teeth didn't help. 'No worries, my lord,' she said in her rough harbour accent. 'We've a bit of experience in this sort of thing.'

'Except usually we're breaking into the warehouses instead of breaking out of them,' Ten-thumbs said. He was the youngest of the mercenaries, with a long, lean face and large, nervous eyes.

'Let's get on with this,' growled Cutter, flexing his gloved hands. The assassin was shorter than the average druchii, and slightly darker of skin, giving him an exotic appearance. His face was scarred by a pox he'd had as a child, and his right ear looked like it had been chewed by rats. As near as Malus could tell he was also unarmed; he couldn't see a knife anywhere on the druchii's body.

Malus took a deep breath and nodded. 'Cutter, Pockets, you first. See what's up there and report back.'

Cutter went right for the rungs and climbed swiftly up the shaft. Pockets moved with a bit more caution, following slowly in the assassin's wake. As the two cutthroats climbed the shaft, Malus snuffed out the witchlamp and set it carefully on the tunnel floor. He turned his head in Hauclir's direction. 'Now we just hope that there isn't a crate of iron bars sitting atop the trap door,' he muttered.

They waited in silence and utter darkness, breathing softly and listening for the slightest sound. Above them, Malus thought he heard the faint scrape of a door, and distant, muffled noises – voices, perhaps? He held his breath. Were there Chaos warriors in the warehouse?

The tiny noises faded, leaving only silence.

As the darkness and silence enfolded him like a shroud, Malus was left with only his thoughts – and the presence of the daemon.

Devoid of sensory distractions, the highborn was hyperaware of his physical form. All at once he felt the weight of fatigue bearing down upon his shoulders and blurring his mind. He felt hunger, and pain from a half-dozen minor wounds, but as sensations they were cold and somehow distant, as though sensed from the other side of a wall of stone.

He flexed his hands, feeling them brush against the insides of his armoured gauntlets, but again, the sensation was diffused.

Alarmed, he reached up and touched his face, feeling the cold steel fingertips of the gauntlet as a dull pressure against his cheek. His heart quickened fearfully, and he felt the daemon shift slightly in response. This time, however, it wasn't a sensation of snakes coiling in his chest – he felt the daemon move through his entire body, like a leviathan sliding beneath his skin.

It wasn't a barrier that separated Malus from his own body – it was Tz'arkan itself. The daemon's hold upon him was more complete than he'd dared imagine. It was as if their roles had been reversed, and now he was the dispossessed spirit lurking in a form not his own.

Immediately the daemon's presence subsided, like a predator pausing warily in mid-stride. Gritting his teeth, Malus forced himself to calm down, to slow the ragged beating of his heart. Tz'arkan was paying close attention to his reactions. Clearly the daemon did not want him to know the extent of its control. But why?

The answer suggested itself immediately. The warpsword. It had the power to counter the daemon's influence. No doubt Tz'arkan feared that if he knew how much control the daemon truly had over him, it would drive him to take up the burning blade again. So long as the warpsword remained in its scabbard on Spite's back the daemon had the upper hand – and, the highborn realised with growing horror, more freedom of action than it would have otherwise.

The nightmares, he thought. What if I wasn't stumbling about in my sleep? What if it was the daemon, moving me about like a puppet?

Suddenly there was a muffled shout from above, and the sound of running feet. Malus heard a choking cry that sounded almost directly overhead – then something metal came rattling and clanging all the way down the twenty-foot shaft, striking sparks from the iron rungs as it fell. Malus and the cutthroats spat muted curses as the object struck the floor of the tunnel next to the highborn's boot with a muted thud.

Malus bent down and groped around for the object. His armoured fingertips rang faintly on metal, then his hand found the hilt of a sword.

Faint movement sounded overhead. 'All clear,' Pockets whispered.

The highborn frowned up into the darkness. 'Is there any point whispering now?' he asked in a normal voice.

'I don't know. Maybe.' The gambler sounded defensive. 'Can't be too careful, right?'

'Evidently not,' Malus growled back. 'We're coming up. Try not to drop anything on our heads in the meantime.'

The highborn took the lead, reaching for the first of the iron rungs and then slowly working his way upwards in the cave-like darkness. His hands seemed to find the rungs effortlessly, and he wondered now if the daemon was subtly guiding his hand, using senses beyond the highborn's ken.

As he neared the top, Malus found the darkness lessened somewhat by a faint, orange glow that etched hard lines and black silhouettes out of the greater gloom. He found the top edge of the shaft and levered himself up out of the hole, finding the dark shape of Pockets waiting for him a few feet away. Large crates, many filled with what looked like metal bars or sheet stock, stood in orderly rows around the hidden trapdoor. Next to Pockets sprawled the body of a marauder, his scarred hand seemingly outstretched towards the open shaft.

'We found a group of these animals cooking meat over a small fire on the other side of these crates,' the druchii cutthroat whispered. 'Cutter and I got the lot of 'em, but this one must have been off taking a piss somewhere. It was his sword went down the shaft.'

Malus straightened and looked about. They were near the front of the building, and the orange glow he'd seen earlier came from the marauder's small fire and the shifting light of much larger fires streaming in through the building's large, open doorways. The highborn moved quietly across the cluttered space and peered warily outside. As night had fallen the Chaos horde had started fires all across the outer city, and pillars of flame and smoke billowed into the air from the warehouses scattered across the city's districts. A warm, hungry wind whispered through the eaves of the warehouse, stirred to life by the churning columns of fire, and Malus thought he could hear the faint cries of the horde borne aloft on the hot air as they celebrated their victory.

For the moment the nearby streets appeared to be empty. Malus breathed a sigh of relief. He glanced back at Pockets. 'How many marauders were there?'

'Five, counting this one,' she said.

The highborn nodded. 'Strip them of their cloaks and furs. We'll need them.'

As Pockets went to work the first of the mercenaries began appearing from the shaft. Malus kept watch in the meantime, going over his battle plan one last time and looking for possible weak points. After the debacle in the north he was determined not to tarnish his honour with yet another costly defeat.

Within minutes Hauclir was standing beside him. 'We're ready, my lord,' he said quietly.

Malus nodded and went back to join the assembled troops. He reached down and picked up the first set of stained furs atop the pile that Cutter and Pockets had gathered. 'Hauclir, you and the crossbowmen put these on,' he said, wrapping the stinking hide around his shoulders. 'Pockets, Cutter and Tenthumbs will stay in the middle of the group.'

Hauclir's lip curled in disgust, but he obediently bent down and picked up a bloodstained cloak. 'This isn't going to fool anyone.'

'If we keep our distance it should suffice,' Malus said. 'We just have to look similar enough in the darkness that we don't raise any suspicions until we reach the square.'

Once Hauclir and the crossbowmen were wrapped in marauder attire the raiding party set off, creeping stealthily down the dark, corpse-laden streets. The exit point of the tunnel was to the south of the citadel, so they were forced to spend almost three hours in a circuitous route around the inner city until they could come within striking distance of the siege engines.

The Chaos horde had completely surrounded the inner fortress, filling the outer city like a swarm of maddened locusts. Fires burned out of control in parts of the city, and howling bands of beastmen and marauders rampaged through the once-orderly districts, looting and destroying everything in their path. Screams of terror and pain rent the night; the enemy had taken hundreds of prisoners after the outer wall had fallen, and now they sated their bestial appetites on their captives in every horrific manner possible. The small raiding party went all but unnoticed amid such pandemonium; only once did a band of marauders come close enough to get a good look at the shadowy group, and they were shot dead before they could shout an alarm. Pockets, Cutter and Ten-thumbs took their furs and the raiding party continued on.

Finally, just past midnight, the raiders found themselves north of the broad square containing the siege engines. The massive catapults had been firing without pause for hours; each siege engine was the size of a town house, resting on massive ironbound wheels and held together with iron pins as thick as shinbones. Almost a hundred slaves per engine were used to crack the massive arms into firing position, and another fifty more were put to work loading the siege engine with boulders or hunks of masonry weighing hundreds of pounds. Already the thick walls of the inner gatehouse and the tall gates themselves were showing signs of damage. Nuarc had been right; given enough time the Chaos engines would dash the fortifications to the ground.

Unfortunately for them, Malus thought with a vicious smile, their time was nearly up.

The raiding party had gone to ground in a looted barracks some two blocks north of the square, close enough to hear the crack of the taskmasters' whips and the bang of the catapults as they fired. One last time Malus considered the final stages of his plan. Everything seemed to be in place. It's all going according to plan, the highborn thought. Obviously there's something I'm missing. After a moment's thought he motioned Cutter over.

'My lord?' the cutthroat said, settling quietly into a crouch beside the highborn.

'I want you to scout around the square,' Malus said. 'We've had good fortune so far, but I'm starting to wonder how much of it we have left. Go and see if there's anything out of the ordinary.'

'Right you are, my lord,' Cutter growled, and vanished into the darkness. In the meantime the raiders settled down in the shadows and did what they could to rest.

Another hour and a half went by. The night grew steadily colder as the night passed into early morning, and the paving stones outside glittered with a thin layer of frost. Malus was reminded of the passing of the seasons and the last few grains of sand remaining in the daemon's hourglass. Was he fighting the wrong battle, he wondered? Here he was risking his life for the defenders of the fortress when he needed to be finding a way to get the Amulet of Vaurog and escape to the north. As it was, he only had a few days left before he began cutting into the time necessary to reach Tz'arkan's distant temple.

For the moment, his plight and the fortress's plight was one and the same. So long as Nagaira and her champion were surrounded by an army they were safe. That was going to have to change.

Hauclir and several of the cutthroats were sleeping in their filthy cloaks when Cutter finally returned. He settled down beside Malus. 'It's an ambush,' the pox-marked druchii said. 'There's a hundred marauders waiting in a barracks to the west of the square, with lookouts posted on the roof.'

Startled murmurs passed among the cutthroats. Suddenly Hauclir was wide-awake. 'They expect us to hit the catapults?'

'Of course they would,' Malus said, nodding to himself. 'They know we can't afford to let them pound us at their leisure.' *It's possible that they even expect me to lead the raid,* Malus suddenly realised. *It is, obviously, the sort of thing I* would do. He rubbed his pointed chin thoughtfully. 'We still hold the advantage, though.'

'Because now we know where the ambushers are,' Hauclir said.

'Exactly,' the highborn replied. He glanced back at Cutter. 'All of the ambushers are in a single building?'

The assassin nodded. 'If it hadn't been for their lookouts I'd have never known they were there. No lights, no fires – they're a clever bunch of animals.'

Malus thought it over. A crucial decision had to be made. 'All right,' he said at length. 'Hauclir, take Cutter and the crossbowmen and circle around to the west. When you're in position, kill the lookouts and then hit the ambushers with your dragon's breath. That will be our signal to attack the siege engines.'

'*Our* signal?' Pockets said, looking to Ten-thumbs. 'What, the three of us?'

'A hundred marauders cooking alive should provide an ample distraction,' Malus replied coolly. 'Enough for us to get into the square and employ our own orbs. Then we break away in the confusion and return to the tunnel.'

The female druchii shook her head in horror. 'There's no way. It's suicide.'

But Malus smiled. 'Not at all. If there's one thing I know well, it's that you can get farther on pure audacity than anything else. Just do what I do, and we'll get through.' Without waiting for any further protests, he nodded to Hauclir. 'Get your men and get moving,' he said. 'We'll give you half an hour to get into position.'

Without a word, Hauclir rose to his feet and motioned to the crossbowmen. Within minutes Malus watched them disappear across the narrow street and down a shadowy alley to the west.

Pockets and Ten-thumbs gathered their weapons and met Malus at the doorway. 'He's as mad as you are, my lord,' she said, nodding in the direction Hauclir had gone.

Malus grinned ruefully. 'He served a highborn once who was fond of foolish risks. A complete madman. I suppose it left its mark on him.'

The female druchii frowned. 'Really? I should have guessed. What a liar!'

Malus gave her a bemused look. 'What are you talking about?'

She shrugged. 'He told us his old master was a hero, as vicious and clever as they came.'

The highborn's grin faded. 'He couldn't have been more wrong,' he said, suddenly uncomfortable. 'Come on. We've got to get closer to the square.'

Keeping to the shadows, the three druchii sidled down the long avenue towards the siege engines. Lines of slave workers came and went, dragging wagons loaded with boulders to feed the great catapults. Marauders on horseback lashed at the slaves and urged them on with savage curses. Whenever one of the riders drew close Malus led the cutthroats inside the closest building until the horseman passed.

It took nearly twenty minutes to work their way down the two blocks to the edge of the square. A small band of marauders waited there, ostensibly guarding the avenue entrance, but they were passing looted wineskins back and forth and grunting to one another in their bestial tongue. The highborn led the two mercenaries into the deep shadow of a nearby alley. 'We wait here,' he whispered. 'Get your orbs ready. When the commotion starts, I'll take the catapult to the left. Ten-thumbs, you take the one in the middle, and Pockets will go to the one on the right. Aim for the winding drums; even if they have some sorcerous means of dousing the flame, it should burn through the ropes quickly enough to knock the catapults out. We'll meet on the other side of the square and head for the tunnel.'

As it happened, they didn't have long to wait. Off to their right they heard a great *whoosh*, and a chorus of wild screams, and suddenly the marauder horsemen were racing past, heading for the square as fast as their mounts would take them. 'Now!' Malus hissed, and he dashed into the street, running along behind the horsemen. He could see a shifting green glow to the west, in the direction of the sounds, and knew that Hauclir and his men had been brutally successful.

The marauders guarding the entrance to the square were swaying on their feet and howling like the angry dead, torn between their orders and their instinct to race to the fight. They paid no attention to the horsemen or the small band of warriors trailing in their wake. The slave crews for the siege engines had been driven into three groups by their furious taskmasters and herded to the back of the square, away from the waiting siege engines. Malus turned and nodded to the cutthroats and headed straight for the catapult on his left, fishing one of his orbs of his carry-bag.

As he loped past one of the slave-gangs a whip-wielding taskmaster turned to look at him as he sped past and shouted a question in his barking tongue. Malus continued on, picking up speed. Green light shone between the fingers of his right hand.

The taskmaster yelled again, his tone sharper this time. Malus bared his teeth in a snarl. Just a dozen more yards to go.

As fast as he was, Pockets was faster. At the far end of the square bedlam erupted as the first of the catapults burst into flame. Angry cries of alarm echoed back and forth among the marauders. Throwing caution to the wind, Malus ran for his target as fast as he could.

A furious shout sounded behind the highborn, and he heard the thunder of hobnailed boots pounding after him. He reached the rear of the catapult and kept going, running for the huge winding mechanism in front. Off to the right, the second catapult was bathed in a sheet of hissing flame.

Just as he reached the far end of the catapult a chaos marauder leapt around the corner into his path, two short axes held ready. He shot the snarling man in the face with his crossbow, then half-spun on his heel and threw the green orb at the cable-wound drum looming above him.

The glass shattered and the liquid inside ignited with a roar and a dazzling green flash. Air rushed past Malus like a giant's indrawn breath, and for a terrifying moment he felt himself pulled *towards* the blaze. He staggered, then regained his footing and raced for the far end of the square as fast as his feet would carry him.

By now the entire square blazed with green light. A thrown axe whirred past his head, and he worked the reloading lever on his crossbow as quickly as he could. The shadows beckoned to him from twenty yards away. At the moment it felt like twenty miles.

Hoof beats clattered across the paving stones to the highborn's right. A horseman was spurring his wild-eyed mount right at him, a short spear held ready to throw. The crossbow's bolt racked home in the firing trough with a loud *clack*, and Malus stopped just long enough to raise his weapon and shoot the marauder high in the chest. The Chaos warrior threw his spear at the same moment, and the weapon struck Malus in the right shoulder, glancing off his enchanted armour. The blow hit hard enough to spin the highborn half-around, and he found himself stumbling backwards and facing almost a score of screaming marauders, closing fast with the burning catapults blazing at their backs.

At the sight of his face the two men in the lead drew back their axes and let fly. The first one went wide, but the second smashed into the highborn's left arm with enough force to knock the crossbow from his hand. Malus shouted a curse and tried to fumble in his bag for the second orb, but gave up in a moment and simply hurled bag and all at the oncoming enemies.

The bag sailed through the air and landed at the lead marauder's feet but swathed in cotton and the thick burlap, the orb refused to break! Malus cursed and groped for his sword – just as the lead marauder tried to knock the bag aside with a savage kick.

Whump. The marauder band disappeared in a fierce explosion, sucking away even their screams in a rushing torrent of air. Teeth bared in a feral grin, Malus turned about and all but dove into the deep shadows of an alley beyond the square.

Swallowed up by the welcoming darkness, Malus listened to the furious shouts of the enemy echo all around him. Sword and axes clashed as warriors of the horde turned on one another in confusion. The sound was sweet to the highborn's ears.

Above the sound of the enemy's disarray rose another noise, high and sharp like the whistle of a razor-edged blade. The warriors of the Black Tower were cheering.

Chapter Nineteen
GHOSTS OF THE DARKNESS

MALUS DREAMT HE was falling into darkness. Cold wind, damp and mouldy as a tomb, blew against the back of his neck and tangled his black hair as he plummeted downwards. From moment to moment his toes and fingertips would brush the packed earthen walls of the narrow shaft. Every so often he felt gnarled roots slip past his fingers, but never in enough time to snatch at them and save himself.

Slow, daemonic laughter echoed in his ears as he plunged into the Abyss.

The impact, when it came, startled him. It reverberated like thunder in the noisome blackness, and it felt as though every bone in his body shattered like glass. And yet there was no pain; just a creeping coldness, spreading through him like oil.

He could not guess how long he lay there. Malus could feel cold ichor seeping from his shattered skull and spreading across the earth beneath him. He lay there, waiting to die, but his body refused to submit to its injuries.

Then another wind brushed his face – this time from above. It reeked of blood and sickness and bodily vice, of every

depravity Malus could imagine and more. And then he heard
the laughter once more, and realised what was coming for him.

He rolled onto his knees, feeling bones cutting through his
insides like jagged glass. His stomach spasmed, and he vomited a soup of black liquid and pulverised organs onto the
unseen earth. The wind tickled at his neck like a lover, and
with a groan he staggered to his feet and began to run.

Laughter echoed after him. 'I love it when you run!' the daemon's voice said behind him. 'Look over your shoulder,
Malus! I'm right here behind you!'

But he didn't dare look. If he turned around, even for an
instant, he knew Tz'arkan would catch him. As long as he ran,
he was free.

Malus lurched and stumbled blindly down a long corridor,
hands flung out before him. He crashed left and right into
walls of packed earth as hard as stone and smelling of the
grave. Splinters of bone pressed against the insides of his skin,
burst through and then fell away in spurts of black fluid. Yet
still he ran on, his body wired together by nothing more than
galvanic fear and icy madness.

Then without warning he reached the end of the line,
crashing headlong into an unyielding wall of earth. Malus was
hurled to the ground by the impact, but the laughter of the
daemon drove him back to his feet in an instant. He beat at
the wall with his ragged fists; he clawed at the stone-like earth
until the flesh of his fingertips was torn away. The laughter
grew louder in his ears, and the air grew cold around him –
and then his flailing hand closed around something hard and
metallic jutting from the earthen wall.

An iron rung. He recognised it at once, and feverishly began
to climb upwards, reaching frantically for the next iron staple
and grabbing it with an almost hysterical wave of relief. Was
he in the tunnel beneath the Black Tower? He had to be! The
knowledge sped his climb even further, until it seemed that
the laughter behind him was starting to fade. Tz'arkan, it
seemed, didn't know how to climb. A lunatic giggle escaped
his stained lips.

The trapdoor was exactly where he reckoned it would be. Malus pushed against it and it flew open, allowing a flood of warm, orange light to spill down from the space above. Now it was his turn to laugh as he struggled upwards, desperate for the glow of an honest fire.

That was when the hand closed about his ankle. 'You and I are not finished yet, Darkblade,' the daemon hissed. 'You have given yourself to the darkness, remember?'

He cried out, kicking and pulling at his leg, but the daemon was far stronger. Slowly, inexorably, he was pulled back down into the shadows.

Until he felt a strong pair of arms circle his chest and pull him upwards as though he were a child. Tz'arkan held on for a moment, struggling vainly, then the iron grip about his ankle gave way. It might have taken his foot with it, but at that moment Malus didn't care.

Strong hands hauled him upwards into the light. He hung there like a babe, laughing and weeping with relief. A shadowy figure stepped towards him, limned with fire. A cold hand caressed his cheek, tracing lines through the thick sludge coating his skin.

'There you are, beloved,' Nagaira croaked. She smiled, and rivulets of filth oozed over her ruined lips as she bent close to him. Her pale skin was marbled with pulsing, black veins, and there was only blackness where her eyes ought to be. Malus looked into their depths and realised that there were *things* living there, beings older and vaster than time. He screamed and tried to struggle, but the Chaos champion held him from behind, his armoured hands tightening around Malus's arms until black ooze ran from between his steel-clad fingers.

'We've come a very long way to find you,' Nagaira said. Her breath was cold and putrid, like air escaping from a corpse. The icy nothingness in her eyes pulled at him. 'There's so much I want to show you. So much that you need to see.'

Then her lips covered his, and he tasted icy, squirming rot against his tongue as the ancient things behind Nagaira's eyes took notice of him for the first time and the world exploded in pain.

WHEN MALUS OPENED his eyes he was lying on a cold, stone floor and his kidneys were aching like they'd been kicked.

'I apologise for that, my lord,' he heard Hauclir say. 'But you gave me little choice.'

He tried to move, and found himself tangled in something heavy and voluminous. With a groan he rolled onto his back and found himself wrapped in a bed sheet and blanket. Hauclir stood over him with a grim look on his face, holding his cudgel in his scarred hands. Five livid scratches ran down the right side of his face.

'Do you know who I am this time?' the former guardsman said. 'Or do I have to jog your memory again?'

'Jog my organs is more like,' Malus said with a grimace. 'Help me up, you damned rogue.'

With a grunt, Hauclir bent and pulled the highborn awkwardly to his feet. Malus looked about and realised he was standing in the hallway outside his quarters. He hissed a bitter curse. 'Again,' he muttered.

'You mean this isn't the first time you've walked in your sleep and assaulted people?' Hauclir grumbled.

'No. Not the first time,' Malus replied, entirely oblivious to Hauclir's impertinent tone. 'What in the Dark Mother's name is happening to me?'

'If I didn't know you, I'd say you were going mad,' Hauclir replied. 'Unfortunately, I *do* know you.' He glanced about quickly, ensuring that they were alone. 'Is it the daemon?' he whispered.

Malus frowned. 'I don't know. It's possible. I've lately wondered the same thing myself.' He pulled irritably at the sheets wound around his legs. 'Let's get out of this corridor before someone sees me like this. What is the hour?'

'A bit past midmorning, my lord,' Hauclir answered, setting aside his cudgel and bending to help unwind the highborn. 'Lord Nuarc told us that we were to stand down and get some rest while we could. Do you remember?'

Malus stepped out of the sweat-stained sheets and tried to focus his thoughts. 'The last thing I remember clearly is crawling across the floor of my room and climbing into bed.' He registered a familiar taste in his mouth and winced. 'There was wine involved, wasn't there?'

'Just a bit,' Hauclir agreed.

'I think I could stand some more,' Malus said, and staggered back through the open door into his apartments.

The doors to the balcony were open again, letting in a long rectangle of pale sunlight that stretched halfway across the room. His shuffling feet sent dark bottles clinking and spinning across the floor. 'Gods Below, Hauclir,' the highborn cursed, looking over the array of empty bottles. 'How much did we drink?'

'*We*, my lord?'

There wasn't a single bottle left with so much as a drop of useful liquid inside it. Growling irritably, the highborn staggered towards the balcony. A terrible disquiet lurked at the back of his mind, and he couldn't quite say why.

Or perhaps better to say I'm having a hard time being specific, the highborn thought ruefully. The Dark Mother knows I have more than enough to vex me at the moment.

Malus shaded his eyes with his left hand and squinted into the morning light. A muted clamour rose from the inner wall, and from his high vantage point he could see that the Chaos horde was assaulting the inner fortress. The sight filled him with apprehension, for reasons he couldn't explain.

'How long has the attack been going on?' Malus asked.

'Started right at dawn,' Hauclir replied, joining Malus at the balcony. 'They've been at it ever since.' He eyed the highborn. 'Good thing we're up here resting and drinking wine instead of down there fighting,' he said pointedly 'Isn't that right, my lord?'

'Wine,' the highborn said thoughtfully. 'Right. Fetch another bottle will you? And something to eat. Bread, cheese – whatever you can find. I've got to get into my armour.'

The former guardsman opened his mouth to protest, but gave it up for a lost cause. 'As you wish, my lord,' he grumbled.

MALUS FOUND LORD Nuarc giving orders by the inner gatehouse, directing three regiments of spearmen against seemingly endless waves of Chaos warriors. A battering ram still burned fitfully a few yards short of the gate, surrounded by the charred bodies of its operators, and warriors continued to repel long siege ladders cast up by swarms of enemy troops. Crossbow bolts filled the air like swarms of flies, surrounding the ladders nearest the gatehouse with dark clouds of death. A steady rain of bodies fell on either side of the high wall as marauders and beastmen were slain upon the battlements or shot through as they clung to the sixty-foot ladders.

Heads turned as the highborn reached the battlements. Spearmen from Hag Graef and the Black Ark raised their weapons in salute as he passed, and a ragged cheer followed Malus and Hauclir all the way to the gatehouse itself. The daring raid on the catapults – now just a trio of charred hulks in the square to the north – had turned Malus and the cutthroats into heroes overnight. It was a small victory, in the grand scheme of things, but it was the first of its kind for the weary defenders, and they celebrated it as only desperate soldiers can.

Even Nuarc's customary glare was tempered with a modicum of respect as the highborn joined him above the gatehouse. 'I thought I told you to get some sleep,' the warlord shouted over the din.

'I tried, but you're making too much noise down here,' the highborn shouted back. 'I don't suppose you could keep it down a bit?'

The general laughed. 'I can't help it if the bastards won't die quietly,' he replied.

Shaking his head, Malus studied the battle raging along the walls. 'How bad is it?' he asked.

'We're actually doing well so far,' Nuarc replied. 'We've got twice as much manpower here than we had at the outer wall, and it's a higher and more difficult climb. Also, the enemy attacks are fierce, but uncoordinated this time. I think you must have stirred something up when you destroyed those siege engines last night.'

'Stirred something up,' the highborn echoed thoughtfully, looking out at the wreckage in the square. 'Has there been no sign of Nagaira or her champion?'

'None,' the general said. 'I don't know why, but I've learned long ago not to question good fortune when it comes my way.'

But the more Malus thought about it, the more troubled he became.

'Something wrong, my lord?' Hauclir inquired.

'I don't know,' Malus answered. 'Wait – no. Something's not right. I just can't figure out what it is.'

Hauclir surveyed the activity on the walls and shrugged. 'Everything looks in order from up here.'

'That's part of the problem,' Malus said. 'Nuarc thinks we stirred something up last night when we attacked the catapults, but I don't think so. They were expecting a raid, and had troops waiting to ambush us.'

The former guard captain thought it over. 'They laid their trap and we blew it up in their faces. That would be enough to stir anyone up, don't you think?'

A spark of realisation struck Malus. 'The catapults were bait,' he said, a look of dread dawning on his face.

Hauclir's frown deepened. 'I suppose so,' he said. 'But we foiled the trap.'

'No!' Malus cried. 'That's not the point. They knew we would have no choice but to attack those catapults. In fact, they counted upon it!'

'To what purpose?'

'What else? Now they know we have another way out of the castle.'

Hauclir's jaw dropped. 'And if we can get out, they can get *in*. Gods Below, my lord. Could they be that clever?'

'This is Nagaira we're talking about. Of course they can be that clever,' Malus growled. Suddenly his dream took on an awful clarity that sent a chill down his spine. 'Let's go.'

'Go where?' Hauclir asked, though the tone in his voice suggested he already knew the answer.

'To gather your cutthroats and see how clever my sister truly is,' the highborn replied.

THE ENTRANCE TO the long tunnel lay in the bowels of the Black Tower itself, on the same level as the fortress's vast cisterns. Holding aloft a half-dozen witchlamps on long, slender poles, Malus, Hauclir and all thirty mercenaries rushed though the cavernous, arched chambers, passing broad, stone-capped basins that held the tower's water supplies. Their weapons were ready and they cast wary glances into every shadowy corner they passed. Malus led the way, fearful that they were already too late.

'Even supposing your theory is correct,' Hauclir said breathlessly, 'the beasts would still have to find the entrance to the tunnel, and I know for a fact we weren't followed.'

'They don't need to see us to be able to track us,' Malus said grimly. 'They could set hounds on our scent; they could set *beastmen* on our scent, for that matter. We're just fortunate they haven't found their way into the fortress yet.'

Pockets, jogging along behind the two druchii, piped up. 'I don't suppose either of you brought some more of those terrible little orbs with you?'

Malus shook his head. 'We've few enough left as it is, and if we tried to use one in the tunnel it would eat through the wooden supports and bring the thing down on our heads. And I don't want to cut off our only escape route unless it's absolutely necessary.'

The druchii loped along to a dark alcove at the far end of the cistern network. There, some ways off from the rest of the storage containers, lay a circular, wooden cover similar to the ones that sealed the tower's real cisterns. At Malus's direction two of the cutthroats pulled the cover aside to reveal a spiral staircase winding down into darkness.

'Crossbows up front,' Hauclir ordered, then the former guard captain turned to Ten-thumbs. 'You stay up here,' he said. 'If you hear fighting, you head upstairs as fast as you can and get reinforcements. I don't care who they are.'

'Yes, Captain,' the young thief said, his eyes wide and fearful.

Malus plucked a crossbow from a nearby cutthroat's hands and quickly loaded it. Cutter cleared his throat and spoke. 'We should douse the lights,' he said.

The mercenaries shared anxious looks. Pockets frowned. 'You want us to go down there blind?'

'Better to go in dark than lit up like daybreak,' the assassin replied. 'If those animals have found their way in, they're likely carrying torches, which gives us easy targets.'

The highborn saw the wisdom of it at once. 'Do as he says,' he commanded. When all of the lights had been extinguished, the small band of warriors were swallowed by absolute darkness. 'The two men with lamps farthest back will bring theirs along,' he said. 'The rest, leave yours aside. When I call for light, you ignite your lamps. Understood?'

Murmurs of assent rose from the back of the party. Malus nodded, feeling his heart hammering in his chest. 'All right, let's go.'

They descended the winding staircase totally blind, shuffling along one shallow step at a time. Men stumbled against one another, whispering curses, and occasionally a scabbard or sword tip would clink against the stone. The air turned chill and dank by slow degrees. Malus held his crossbow levelled, listening for the slightest sound of footsteps coming up to meet him.

At length, Malus felt his boot scrape against earth. A wisp of cold air caressed his cheek and he shuddered at the memory of the dream he'd had, little more than an hour before. Men shuffled into place on either side of him. 'Hst!' he whispered, just loud enough for keen druchii ears to hear. 'We'll walk forward slowly for a few yards and stop. Listen for my signal.' Quiet grunts to either side and behind him acknowledged the order.

They edged forward down the long tunnel, careful to make as little noise as possible. The blackness was total, infinite. The mercenaries could hear nothing but the sound of their own breath, hissing between clenched teeth. Finally, after Malus reasoned that nearly all of the troops had reached the bottom of the stairs, he whispered, 'Halt. Front rank, kneel.'

He and the two men beside him sank slowly to one knee, clutching their crossbows tightly. They peered into Abyssal blackness and listened for the slightest sound on an oncoming foe.

Minutes passed. Malus saw no hint of light in the darkness or heard any sounds of movement. There was an unmistakeable tension in the air, but his own troops could easily account for that.

Time dragged slowly on. Warriors shifted uncomfortably, drawing hissed warnings from Hauclir. Malus bared his teeth. They were out there. He was certain of it.

The warrior immediately behind Malus bent low and whispered in the highborn's ear. 'Message from Hauclir. He wants to know if we should advance down the tunnel.'

'No,' the highborn whispered. 'The enemy will have to come to us, and we're better situated here–'

He froze. Was that a faint scuff of a foot somewhere ahead? Malus listened, not daring to breathe. Another sound – perhaps the tiny rattle of a buckle or chain. Or it could be his imagination, stoked by tension and absolute blackness.

Malus thought the situation over and reached a decision. He raised his crossbow to his shoulder, aimed at waist height, and fired.

The thump of the crossbow was loud enough to startle the warriors behind Malus – but nothing like the agonised scream that rent the darkness farther down the tunnel.

'Both ranks, open fire!' Malus ordered, quickly reloading his crossbow. More bowstrings thumped, and heavy bolts thudded into shields or glanced from steel armour with glints of bright blue sparks. Some of the bolts sank into flesh, drawing more bloodcurdling screams, and then the tunnel echoed with the thunder of running feet as the Chaos troops began their charge.

The close confines of the tunnel rang with frenzied shouts and blasphemous war cries. It sounded like a thousand warriors were bearing down on Malus and his meagre force. There was no real way to tell how close they were in the bedlam of shouts and screams echoing all around him. 'Keep shooting!' he shouted into the din. 'Aim low. They can't get to us if we block the tunnel with their bodies!'

Fire. Reload. Fire. For almost a minute Malus's arms worked in deadly rhythm, working the loading lever of his repeater crossbow and firing into the darkness. Marauders screamed and stumbled with a clatter of mail and steel-rimmed shields. The sharp smell of blood and voided bowels thickened the subterranean air.

Malus fired again, and this time his victim's agonised scream sounded almost directly in front of him. 'Front rank, pass your crossbows back and draw steel!' he roared. He shoved his own weapon back to the warriors behind him and yelled back at the mercenaries as he drew his twin blades. 'Lights!' he called.

The order came just barely in time. Cold, green light flooded the narrow tunnel and revealed an axe-wielding barbarian not three feet from Malus. The human's face was twisted in a rictus of rage and pain, and a crossbow bolt was buried to the fletchings in his muscular left shoulder. The sudden glare from the witchlamps blinded the warrior for an instant, and the highborn lunged forward and thrust his right-hand blade through the muscles of the marauder's upper thigh. A fountain of arterial blood poured from the wound, and the warrior staggered, howling in pain. But before he could recover he was dashed against the side of the tunnel by the warrior behind him as his frenzied tribe-mate rushed to come to grips with his foes.

'Stay on your knees!' Malus ordered the men to either side of him. The howling barbarian came right at the highborn, his shield held low. Malus feinted with his right-hand sword and blocked a sweeping axe-stroke with his left – and then the druchii behind Malus shot the warrior point-blank in the face. The steel bolt punched clean through the warrior's skull and struck the marauder behind him in the throat.

Yet no sooner had both men collapsed than their tribe-mates were clambering over them to hack at the hard-pressed druchii line. Malus and the men in the front rank fought like rats, stabbing at exposed knees, feet, thighs and groin. They slit men's bellies where they could, and where the enemy's guard was too strong they held the barbarian off long enough for a druchii crossbow to fell him.

And yet there seemed to be no end to the bastards. Bodies began to pile so high in front of the druchii that the marauders had to drag them aside in order to reach their foes. Malus's knee was sodden with spilled blood. He soon lost count of the number of men who died trying to force their way down the tunnel, and his arms began to burn with exhaustion from near-constant battle.

The fight seemed to rage for hours, but Malus knew that it was most likely only a handful of minutes. The druchii exhausted their ammunition before long, and the second rank drew their own blades and joined in the swordplay. The marauders were able to press them more closely after that, but they still faced the difficult task of fighting two swordsmen at once.

Exhaustion began to take its toll. The druchii to Malus's right faltered for only a moment and a barbarian axe dashed out his brains. Instantly another warrior leapt forward and knelt in his place as Malus cut the barbarian's hamstring with a quick flick of his wrist. Other druchii died behind him, struck down by flung axes or the thrust of saw-edged blades. Their formation contracted slightly, falling back a few feet towards the stairs. Malus began to wonder when the reinforcements were going to arrive.

And then suddenly a horn wailed down the tunnel from out of the darkness, and the marauders fell back at once. They dragged away as many of the dead as they could, something Malus had never known the marauders to do before. A ragged cheer went up from the surviving druchii, but Malus cut them off with a sharp wave of his hand. Something wasn't right.

Then he heard it. The heavy tread of armoured feet, rolling like thunder towards the battered druchii warriors. Suddenly he realised that the enemy had used the barbarians to wear them down and soak up their ammunition, preparing them for the hammer blow.

'Mother of Night,' he cursed. 'On your feet!' he called to the men beside him. 'Get ready!'

But by then it was already too late.

The figure that loomed before them in the witchlight had once been a man. In some sense he still was, but now his body was swollen with corruption. Muscles as thick as a nauglir's threatened to burst from the warrior's taut skin, and his eyes shone like embers from behind a massive, horned helmet of dark iron. The Chaos warrior was clad in heavy armour from head to toe, adorned with jagged spikes and curling horns, heavy chains and cruel hooks festooned with shrivelled heads. His massive hands gripped a pair of hand axes that looked too large for a sane man to wield, and yet wield them the warrior did, tearing into the surprised druchii with a bloodcurdling roar.

The mercenary to Malus's left died without a sound, the front of his head shorn away by a flickering sweep of an axe. The druchii to Malus's right leapt forward with a shout, thrusting at a gap in the warrior's armour just above his thigh. But the blade missed the gap and skated harmlessly off polished iron, and the warrior punched the haft of his left-hand axe through the mercenary's skull.

Seeing an opening, the highborn lunged forward, chopping down on the warrior's left wrist and half-severing it in a spray of blood. To Malus's horror, the warrior laughed and smashed his right-hand axe into the highborn's side. It was only the enchantments woven into his armour that saved the highborn from the fearful blow; as it was, the impact knocked him from his feet and smashed him against the side of the tunnel wall.

Screaming a wild war cry, Pockets charged at the towering Chaos warrior, clutching a sword and dagger in her small hands. The warrior snarled contemptuously and swatted at her with his axe. But the nimble druchii ducked beneath the blurring sweep of the blade and then leapt onto the warrior's massive chest. Before the surprised warrior could react she howled like a mountain cat and buried her dagger to the hilt in the warrior's right eye.

With a gurgling cry the warrior fell to his knees, and Pockets sprang clear barely an instant before a heavy axe crashed into the warrior's neck and hacked away his head in a spray of hot gore. The warrior behind the headless corpse kicked the body over with a booming curse and leapt for the girl's retreating form, his axes blurring and moaning in the reeking air.

Druchii leapt at the monster from three sides, and were mown down like wheat. The charging mercenary to the warrior's right was flung back against the wall in two pieces. Dead ahead a cutthroat rushed forward, trying to cover Pockets as she retreated, and got his head struck off for his trouble. Malus ducked beneath the warrior's deadly swing and lunged in from the right. His right-hand sword crashed against the side of the warrior's armoured knee and his left-hand blade snaked upwards, catching the warrior beneath the chin and driving upwards into his fevered brain.

But the resolve of the cutthroats had collapsed before the onrushing Chosen, and a terrified flight began. Malus pulled his sword clear of the toppling warrior just as the witchlamps wobbled crazily and then abruptly dwindled as the retreating troops bore the two men back around the turn of the staircase.

More Chaos warriors howled for blood in the sudden darkness. Swearing lustily, Malus raced for the staircase after his men. The climb upwards was a frantic pursuit of crazily swinging light; the lamp men always seemed just at the verge of the turn in the stair, so the highborn could only catch wild glimpses in the shifting glow before it vanished once more. He saw terrified faces and wide, dark eyes, fearful glimpses thrown past narrow shoulders and stumbling forms practically crawling up the stairs as fast as their hands and feet could carry them. Behind Malus the darkness echoed with wild, bestial shouts as the Chosen warriors gave chase.

Then, without warning the close confines of the staircase opened up into the arched space of the cistern vaults, and the panicked retreat came to an abrupt halt. Witchlights bobbed and swung in the open space above, shedding narrow streams of pale light. All Malus could see were the backs of four or five struggling druchii trying to get off the stairs, but he clearly heard Hauclir's voice, rolling over the mercenaries like thunder. 'Any one of you takes another step forward I will split your skull myself!' he roared. 'Stand your ground! The enemy will advance no further into the citadel! We have to hold at all costs until reinforcements arrive!'

The reinforcements aren't here yet, Malus thought? Blessed Mother of Night!

He didn't know whether to thank Hauclir or kill him. On the one hand, he's stopped the rout in its tracks, but on the other hand the highborn was now trapped on the staircase at the tail end of the line with a howling Chaos horde heading his way!

Vicious oaths and bloodthirsty cries echoed crazily up the staircase. Malus turned about, levelling his swords. 'Turn and face the enemy!' he cried to the men behind him. 'They can only come at us one at a time on the stair. We can hold here for a long while if we keep our nerve!'

Thankfully the men listened. He felt them shuffling about, and blades appeared above his head. He steeled himself and crouched low, waiting for the inevitable assault.

He heard the onrushing warriors climbing the staircase, their shouts growing louder and louder. It was all but impossible to see more than a few feet down the staircase – the damned witchlamps kept swinging as though caught in a gale, creating wild patterns of light and shadow along the stairs.

Then, just as it appeared that the warriors were almost at the next turn of the staircase, the howling stopped. Silence fell like a shroud. Malus heard mercenaries gasping for breath above him. Someone moaned fearfully. He bared his teeth and tightened his grip on his blades.

There was the faint scratch of a boot heel on the stone stairs below Malus. A faint ring of harness. Then the shifting light picked out the gleaming tip of a rust-stained druchii sword. The highborn caught the scent of rot and wet earth, like a recently opened grave.

Slowly, gracefully, the Chaos champion rose into the wavering light, his helmet upturned to Malus and the Amulet of Vaurog glinting at his neck.

Chapter Twenty
MIDNIGHT ALLIANCES

THE CHAOS CHAMPION fixed Malus with a gaze like a viper, filling his veins with dread. The armoured warrior seemed to float up the stairs towards Malus, swords outstretched like a lover's waiting arms.

'Mother of Night,' Malus cursed desperately, raising his own twin blades. 'Daemon!' he hissed. 'Attend me! Lend me your strength!'

The daemon stirred, shifting disconcertingly beneath the highborn's skin – but the customary rush of icy power did not come. Malus had barely enough time to register Tz'arkan's treachery before the champion struck.

Silver steel blades darted and slashed at the highborn's legs and abdomen, striking sparks where the keen blades slipped past Malus's guard and glanced from his enchanted armour. He parried furiously, roaring with anger at the daemon's betrayal, because he knew that, even without the terrible power of the Amulet at the champion's disposal, he was no match for the warrior's Chaos-fuelled abilities.

He took a glancing blow to the side of his knee and barely parried a swift thrust at his groin. The champion was not only skilled but well versed in the art of sariya fencing. His technique matched Malus's almost perfectly, and the realisation only enraged the highborn further. Malus channelled all his hatred and fury into his blows, allowing certain attacks through his guard in order to strike back at his foe. Powerful blows rained down on his breastplate and fauld, turned aside time and again by the potent sorceries of the armourers of Naggarond. In return he struck at the champion's arms and neck, hoping to sever a sword-hand, or better yet strike off the warrior's helmeted head. But the champion's speed was such that most often Malus's blows cut through empty air or struck a glancing blow on the champion's armour. It was as though the warrior could anticipate his every move.

There was a furious commotion among the mercenaries behind Malus, but he couldn't spare even a momentary glance over his shoulder to see what was going on. Then a dagger whirred past his head and struck the champion with such force that it penetrated his breastplate just beneath the collarbone. A normal warrior would have been staggered by the blow, but the champion scarcely noticed. It did cause the warrior to hesitate a fraction of an instant, giving Malus the chance to sweep aside the champion's left-hand sword and stab his foe through the throat. Dark blood coursed down the flat of the highborn's blade, but the warrior pulled himself off the tip of the sword as a man recoils from the prick of a thorn, and then immediately renewed his attack.

A figure brushed past Malus, charging down the staircase towards the champion. Hauclir caught the champion's right-hand sword against the side of his scarred cudgel and hacked at the warrior's wrist with his short, heavy sword, but the blade could not penetrate the champion's iron armour. Quick as a snake, the champion pivoted and lunged at Hauclir with his left-hand blade, and it was all Malus could do to knock it off-track with a blow from his own sword.

Moments later Cutter joined in the fight as well, throwing another dagger that rang off the champion's armoured leg. The

Chaos warrior responded with a lightning-quick cut at the assassin's neck, but the druchii evaded the blow with astonishing speed. Seeing his opportunity, Hauclir lunged in and smashed his cudgel against the champion's right arm. The blow would have broken the bones of a lesser man, but the champion simply staggered slightly and forced the former guardsman back with a lunge at his throat.

Now, with three skilled opponents pressuring him from different angles, the Chaos champion was forced onto the defensive. Malus pressed his attack, raining blows on the warrior's left arm and shoulder. Sparks flew and fragments of iron armour were hewn away by the force of the highborn's blows, but the champion held his ground, countering each attacker in turn with swift parries and deadly feints. Malus was starting to think that they were gaining the upper hand – and then Hauclir stepped in on the champion's left, smashing his cudgel against the warrior's right knee and then reversing the blow to swing at the champion's head. The Chaos champion appeared caught off guard, thrusting his blade at Cutter's neck, but the attack was only a feint. Like a thunderbolt the champion's sword plunged down, slicing through Hauclir's right thigh. The former guard captain fell with a curse, and Cutter lunged forward with a yell, thrusting for the champion's eyes – only to have the Chaos warrior's left-hand sword bury itself deep in his right shoulder.

Seeing both druchii fall in the space of a single second filled Malus with terror and rage. Unleashing a terrible war-scream he put all of his strength and speed into a single cut that smashed into the champion's temple. Sparks flew, and the force of the blow whipped the champion's head around. Still shrieking his rage, the highborn followed up with a backhand blow that smashed into the warrior's helm right at eye level. Iron snapped with a discordant clang, and the champion's helmet burst asunder.

The warrior's head snapped back from the force of the blow. Black hair, matted with filth and old blood fell loosely to the champion's shoulders. Pallid skin, gleaming with sickness and shot through with pulsing black veins, shone greenish-white in the witchlight. A single, black eye fixed Malus with a glare of implacable hate. The other eye was sightless and glowed with grave-mould. A terrible sword wound cleft the warrior's skull above that ruined eye, its ragged edges black with corruption and squirming with parasitic life.

Malus looked into Lhunara's face and cried out in terror and anguish. 'Gods... oh Gods Below!' he cried. 'You can't be...'

Lhunara's black lips pulled back in a lunatic grin. Unlike his dreams, her teeth were still perfect and white. Her muscular body trembled, and a terrible, bubbling sound rose from her throat. It was the foulest, most vile laughter Malus had ever heard.

'With hate... all things are possible,' she croaked, drawing back her dripping blades. 'With hate... and the Dark Gods' blessing.'

She took a step towards him, and Malus looked in her ruined eyes and knew he was about to die.

He was saved by a thin, reedy voice that echoed from the top of the staircase. 'Dragon's breath!' Ten-thumbs shouted. 'Stand clear!'

Malus turned and saw the young thief standing less than ten yards away, holding a glowing green orb in his upraised hand. Hauclir shouted up at the boy through gritted teeth, 'No, you fool! You'll kill us all!'

'Throw it, boy!' Malus shouted. 'Do it now!'

But Lhunara was already gone, dashing fleet as a deer down the staircase until she was lost in darkness. Malus cursed bitterly and slumped onto the stairs, the vision of her hateful face lingering like a ghost before his eyes.

Mercenaries rushed down the stairs to grab Hauclir and Cutter and pull them clear. Hauclir glared up at Ten-thumbs. 'Who in the Dark Mother's name gave you that orb?' he snarled.

Ten-thumbs grinned. 'What? This?' he tossed the glowing ball above his head – to the horrified shouts of everyone nearby – and snatched it deftly out of the air. 'I've had this for quite a while. It's my little ace in the hole.' He tossed the orb from hand to hand.

And missed.

Ten-thumbs let out a horrified squawk and lunged for the glowing orb. The slick glass bounced through his fumbling fingers and plunged towards Malus, Hauclir and the horrified mercenaries. Dozens of hands grabbed for the orb, slapping the glowing ball this way and that, until finally it bounced free and smashed against the wall about four feet above Malus's head. Cutthroats scrambled in every direction, screaming in terror.

The small witchlamp burst with a sharp *pop* and a smell like a lightning storm. Small fragments of glass rained down on Malus's head.

'Oh, damn,' Ten-thumbs groaned. 'My mother gave me that light. I've had it since I was a child.'

Silence hung heavy in the air. The cutthroats, who moments before had been convinced they were about to burn alive, reeled like drunkards, overcome with relief. Hauclir leaned back against the outer wall of the staircase and glared up at the morose thief. 'By the Dark Mother, I don't know whether to kiss you or skin you alive.'

Nervous chuckles broke out among the cutthroats, quickly turning into gales of loud, hysterical laughter as they came to grips with their unexpected salvation. A pair of mercenaries helped Hauclir and Cutter up the staircase. Hands reached for Malus, but he pushed them away. Slowly, awkwardly, he staggered upright. His limbs felt like cold lead, and his head was cased in bitter ice.

He was the last to climb the curving stair into the cold shadows of the cistern vault. By the time he made it to the top the echoing space was full of angry warriors. Lord Isilvar stood at their head, his expression pale with fury. The cutthroats had drawn together in a tight knot around their wounded leader, glaring balefully at the sneering faces of Hag Graef's spearmen

'What is going on here?' Isilvar grated.

'A battle, dear brother. What else?' Malus shot back. He hadn't expected Ten-thumbs to be quite so successful at drumming up reinforcements. In the back of his mind he realised that they were sorely outnumbered and far from any reliable witnesses should Isilvar suddenly decide to murder the lot of them. The knowledge did nothing to blunt his impertinent tongue. 'I realise you don't see much of these, what with your duties as vaulkhar.' Before Isilvar could reply, Malus plunged onward. 'The Chaos forces have discovered the tunnel. We managed to hold them off until you arrived, but they could be massing for another assault even as we speak.' The highborn grinned mockingly. 'I yield the honour of repelling the next wave to you, as is only fitting to your rank.'

Muscles bunched furiously at the corners of Isilvar's jaws. 'We will have to fire the tunnel and collapse it,' he said. 'The Chaos horde has redoubled its assault on the walls, and every available man is needed at the parapet.'

'Then if you will excuse me, brother, I must hasten to my duty,' Malus replied. Without waiting for Isilvar's leave, he motioned to his men and made to depart. For a brief moment it looked as though the ranks of Hag Graef spearmen would refuse to let them pass, but Malus met the gaze of an older spearman who nodded curtly and stepped aside. The druchii behind the spearman followed suit, and suddenly there was a long, clear path through the spear company leading across the cistern vault. Helmeted heads, both veteran and conscript, nodded respectfully to Malus and his troops as they limped past.

Hauclir, shored up by Pockets on one side and Cutter on the other, came up alongside the highborn. 'That Chaos champion,' he began, 'she looked as though she knew you. Who is she?'

'A nightmare,' Malus said in a dead voice.

AT FIRST, ALL he could hear were voices. They were muffled and echoed strangely, as though heard from beneath the surface of a deep, dark lake.

'My time runs short,' Nagaira said. The sound of her voice was powerful, vibrant and utterly wrong, full of discordant tones like shattered glass. 'I have obligations to fulfil, mighty one. Obligations that will not be denied.'

'Do not speak to me of time,' Tz'arkan hissed. 'Mine runs short as well. But he knows the way, now. He knows what must be done.'

'But will he act? That is the question.' There was the faint chime of finely hammered silver, and the sound of a knife cutting through meat.

'Who can say?' the daemon growled. 'Nothing you mortals do makes any sense to me.'

The blackness began to fade. Shapes formed to either side of him. He was lying on his back, tangled in sheets. Cold air caressed his bare chest. Nagaira and the daemon spoke above his prone form like adults talking over a sleeping child.

'I fail to see why all this is necessary,' Nagaira said. 'Your scheme is overly complicated to my mind.'

'As complicated as your revenge at Hag Graef?' the daemon retorted.

'Point taken,' she said with a sigh. There was another faint ringing of metal, and this time Malus watched the blurry form of his sister lift a goblet to her lips and drink. 'Yet couldn't you simply deliver Malus to me yourself?'

Suddenly Malus was very alert. The shapes resolved further. He could see Nagaira clearly now. She was sitting in a chair, tucked close to a banquet table, turning a silver goblet in her black-veined hands. Her touch left lines of black tarnish across the gleaming curve of the metal. A knife and fork rested at the edges of the plate set before her, which was piled with steaming cuts of bloody meat. She took no notice of Malus at all, fixing the black emptiness of her gaze upon the being sitting opposite her.

'It is not so simple as that,' the daemon replied. Malus turned his head to look upon the daemon, but its shape was concealed in deep shadow. A plate of bloody meat sat untouched before it. 'You are thinking in such immediate terms, my child. Consider the implications of my plan in their full measure, and what it will mean for you once we have returned from the north.'

'Then he must be persuaded to act,' the druchii witch said. She carefully set the goblet on the table before her.

'Of course,' Tz'arkan replied. 'Do as you think best.'

Malus tried to move, but the sheets pulled tight, trapping him fast. Nagaira looked down at him, reaching to touch his cheek with a long, claw-like nail. 'How much of my brother will remain, after all is said and done?'

'Enough,' the daemon said at length. The shadowy figure reached forward and dipped a clawed hand into Malus's chest. The highborn glanced down, past his chin, to see Tz'arkan lift his still-beating heart from the gaping cavity of his chest. 'You see? It is still quite strong. So is his mind. He should satisfy your appetites for some time to come.' The daemon leaned back in his chair and gestured expansively at the highborn's ravaged body. 'Will you take any more for your plate, child?'

Nagaira leaned forward, peering thoughtfully at Malus's face. 'I should like his eyes,' she said. 'I've always loved them, you know.'

A strong hand clamped down on Malus's forehead, pressing it to the table. Another figure entered his field of vision, looming over him from above. Lhunara bent over him, her ravaged face lit with a lover's smile. Wriggling maggots fell onto his cheek from the gaping wound in her head.

She pressed a cracked thumbnail to the corner of his eye and he began to scream.

HANDS WERE PRESSING him down onto the bed. Malus kicked and thrashed, screaming in rage and fear. He heard low voices cursing above him, and for a dizzying instant he wasn't sure if he was waking or still trapped in the dream. With a wild effort he tore his arms and shoulders free, shoving away the shadowy figures looming over his bed, and rolled to its edge just in time to vomit a large quantity of rancid wine onto the stone floor.

'I told you those last two bottles were mostly vinegar,' Hauclir said from across the room. 'But you wouldn't listen. Of course, you might have been too drunk to hear me at that point, but I thought it was worth a try.'

Early morning light filtered in through the bedchamber's open window. Hauclir sat in a chair near the balcony entrance, his wounded leg propped up on a low table dragged over for just that purpose. Vague figures moved quietly about in the darkened chamber, patching armour or sharpening their weapons. Pockets and Ten-thumbs were roasting meat over a brazier near the foot of the bed, whispering to one another in low voices.

Malus writhed his way out of the sodden bed sheets and staggered onto his feet. His mind swam from the aftereffects of wine and shock. The dream still hung in his mind with dreadful clarity. Was it real? Was the daemon consorting with Nagaira now? How could he know for certain? He looked to Hauclir, but what could he say that the daemon wouldn't also hear? 'What is the hour?' he asked blearily.

'Early morning,' Hauclir said. 'Too early, in fact. And thank you for asking about my wound. It's not nearly as bad as I feared.'

'We have to get to the nauglir pens,' the highborn interjected. 'Now.'

Hauclir studied Malus carefully. 'You're still drunk, my lord.'

'Since when has that ever made a difference? Help me get into my armour,' the highborn replied, tugging at his stained nightshirt.

BUTCHERS' CLEAVERS ROSE and fell outside the nauglir pens within the citadel's expansive inner compound, and vast lakes of blood glittered in the early morning sun. As Malus and Hauclir approached the low stone structure a group of young servants were pulling the bodies of beastmen and marauders from the back of a wagon and lining them up for the cutters to inspect. Several hundred nauglir consumed a great deal of meat in a given day, and the druchii saw no reason to waste anything that came their way.

The roar of battle from the inner wall, less than half a mile distant, had continued unabated since the day before. Chaos warriors were hurling themselves in endless waves against the high walls. Hauclir said that soon they wouldn't need ladders at all, but could scale the walls over the piles of their own dead.

The former guard captain was limping painfully along beside Malus, using an improvised crutch made from a pair of spear hafts. 'Why the sudden rush to visit your cold one?' he asked, a glint of suspicion showing in his dark eyes. 'If you're planning on a quick ride into the country I don't think you're going to get very far.'

'I need to get something from my saddlebags,' the highborn said curtly. His mind was still churning over the implications of his dream. In retrospect, he should have expected this, he thought angrily. Now that he'd enlisted the aid of his mother Eldire and then bound himself to the warpsword, Tz'arkan was bound to try and find ways to outmanoeuvre him and retain the upper hand. He had no idea that the daemon could speak to Nagaira through his dreams. Was it also responsible for his many nightmares about Lhunara? The thought both terrified and enraged him.

He'd been a fool to put the warpsword away, risk or no risk. That was going to change.

Malus rushed past the bloodstained butchers and down the ramp into the pens. The chamber was dark and the air dank and acrid with the scent of scores of the huge warbeasts. Each nauglir had its own pen, not unlike a horse's stall, but made of dressed stone rather than wood and secured by a stout gate of iron.

It took several minutes before the highborn found the pen where Spite was kept. The nauglir was dozing on the sandy floor, snout tucked behind its curved tail. The warbeast stirred as Malus quickly unshackled the gate and slipped inside the pen. Hauclir, his clothes still stained with fresh blood, wisely chose not to follow.

'There you are, beast of the deep earth,' Malus said. At the sound of its master's voice the cold one rose quickly to its feet. Force of habit led the highborn to check the cold one's claws, teeth and hide for signs of illness. 'It looks as though these imbeciles are treating you well,' he muttered, eyeing the blood-stained sand nearby. 'And your appetite is good.'

Malus moved his inspection to his saddle and tack, then to the saddlebags still strapped to the cold one's back. The bag containing the relics was still safely secured, and next to it lay the long, wrapped bundle of the warpsword. He fancied he could already feel the heat of the burning blade, like a brazier of banked embers waiting to be stirred to life. Taking a deep breath, the highborn reached for the sword.

Instantly a spasm of burning pain shot through Malus's body. He doubled over with an agonised groan, his hands clenching into trembling claws. Spite started at the sound, glancing back at Malus with a warning growl.

The daemon shifted and tensed beneath the highborn's skin. 'Oh, no, little druchii,' Tz'arkan purred. 'I don't think so.'

'My lord?' Hauclir cried. 'Are you all right?'

But the highborn couldn't speak; indeed, he could scarcely breathe for the pain that wracked his chest and arms. He dimly saw Spite slinking slowly away from him, and his experienced eye immediately recognised that he was in dire trouble. Beyond the roaring in his ears he heard the cold one rumble deep in its throat.

He forced every iota of his will into forcing words past his gritted teeth. 'Re… lease me,' he grated.

'Oh, I shall, little druchii,' the daemon said. 'But first, perhaps I'll let this beast of yours bite off your sword arm. I can make you stick your hand in its mouth if I wish. Would you like to see?'

A violent tremor wracked the highborn's body… and his right arm slowly, haltingly, began to rise.

'My lord!' Hauclir cried. 'What in the name of the Outer Darkness are you doing?'

Across the pen, Spite let out an angry bellow. Immediately the other nauglir in the pens took up the roar, shaking the air with their thunderous cries.

'Such weak, crude flesh you have, Darkblade,' the daemon said. 'It's no great loss if a part of it is torn away. In fact, I'm entirely happy to let your stinking beast bite both of your arms off, if that's what I must do to keep you away from that sword. I have new allies now, you see. They can finish the job you started and give me what I want.'

A thin, despairing wail rose from Malus's lips as he watched his right arm fully extend. His body moved like a children's doll, turning jerkily towards the cold one. Spite's head was lowered, its powerful tail lashing tensely across the sandy floor. The cold one was about to strike.

Suddenly a robed form lurched across the sand and knocked Malus to the floor just as the nauglir struck. Its blocky jaws clashed shut, scattering sprays of venomous drool right where Malus had been standing moments before.

'Back, you damned lump of scales!' Hauclir roared, lashing at the beast's face with his crutch in one hand and trying to drag Malus clear with the other. Spite snapped at the offending stick and ground it to splinters, but it bought Hauclir enough time to drag Malus halfway across the pen. The highborn's legs flailed at the sandy floor, trying to help push them along. The cold one let out another furious bellow, its talons digging furrows in the sand, but before it could gather itself to charge, Hauclir pulled the highborn through the gate and slammed the iron barrier closed.

'Gods Below, my lord, what was that all about?' Hauclir demanded, his breath coming in ragged gasps. Fresh blood spotted the bandage wrapping his thigh.

Before Malus could speak, the daemon whispered warningly in his ear. 'Be very careful what you say, Darkblade,' he warned. 'Or the next time you wake you'll find every one of your precious servants with their throats cut.'

The highborn gritted his teeth. 'I... was just checking on my belongings,' he said. 'The damned beast just didn't care for my scent. Too much wine, as you said.'

The former guard captain frowned. 'Are you certain that's all?' he said, his dark eyes scrutinising his former master.

'What else could it be?' Malus snapped, his voice bitter. Before Hauclir could reply he cut the druchii off with a wave of his hand. 'No more questions. I want to go to the wall and check on the state of the siege. I've got a terrible suspicion that something big is about to happen.'

Chapter Twenty-One
BETWEEN THE LIVING AND THE DEAD

COLUMNS OF GREASY, black smoke rose from behind the inner wall of the fortress, and the air was thick with the smell of roasting flesh. Every half-mile along the avenue behind the wall rose a pyre for the druchii dead, each one tended by a score of exhausted servants and a couple of hollow-eyed officers who noted down each soldier given over to the flames. The orderly removal of corpses to the funerary furnaces had been abandoned days ago. The dead were piling up far faster than the removal crews could handle, and most of the men had been pressed into service on the battlements besides.

The piles of the enemy dead were vaster still, rising in stinking heaps more than twelve feet high in places and running the entire perimeter of the wall. Malus was awed by the sheer scope of the slaughter and more than a little disturbed at the Chaos horde's near-suicidal zeal. They will bury us in their own dead if they must, he realised with a mixture of worry and admiration. All that matters to them is victory and ruin, and they will keep coming at us until their leaders are dead or the last barbarian has been cast from the walls.

He caught himself wondering what sorts of things he might accomplish with such an army at his back and ruthlessly forced such thoughts aside.

With Hauclir limping along in his wake he made his way up the long, bloodstained ramp to the battlements alongside the northern gatehouse. Bodies and bits of armour plunged past the two druchii in a grisly hailstorm as the troops on the parapet cleared away the detritus of the latest assault. The most recent attack had been seen off as the highborn had crossed the inner compound from the nauglir pens, and the sudden silence along the battlements was eerily disturbing after what seemed like hours of screams and bloodshed.

The highborn was appalled at the scene of carnage atop the wall. The dark stone parapet was mottled with a thick layer of blood, sawdust and viscera, and druchii spearmen sat or slept amid the filth, too exhausted and numbed to even notice. Broken weapons, bits of armour and pieces of flesh littered the entire length of the wall. Great ravens hopped and croaked at one another as they sought for choice morsels among the motionless bodies of the living. Even Malus, who had recently walked the blood-soaked streets of Har Ganeth, was stunned by what he saw. He glanced back at Hauclir and saw that the former guard captain's face was pale and grim.

Beyond the walls the outer city was a wasteland of burnt buildings and rude tents. Exhausted Chaos warriors sprawled like packs of wild dogs along the filth-strewn avenues, and hundreds upon hundreds of dead bodies carpeted the killing ground before the inner wall as far as Malus's eyes could see. Howls and gibbering cries rose and fell among the ruins, barking curses in a language none of the defenders could understand, but whose meaning was utterly clear. Soon, all too soon, the killing would begin once more.

There was a commotion ahead as Malus neared the door to the gatehouse. A trio of spearmen were struggling with a fourth warrior, who was shouting and struggling wildly in their grip. 'They won't stop! They won't stop coming!' he cried, his dark eyes wide in a face covered in dried blood and grime.

'We can't stay here! We can't!' The warriors struggling with the panicked druchii exchanged frightened glances. One of the soldiers drew his stabbing sword.

'What's all this?' Malus snapped, the sharp tone in his voice surprising even himself. The struggling warriors started at the barked command, and even the panicked druchii subsided in their arms.

The troops looked to one another, and the most senior man cleared his throat and replied. 'It's nothing, dread lord. We're just taking this man off the wall. He's unwell.'

'There's nothing wrong with this soldier,' Malus snarled, stepping forward and pushing his way into the knot of spearmen. He grabbed the panicked druchii by the scruff of the neck and forced him to stand. 'You've got both your eyes and all of your limbs,' he snapped. 'So what's wrong with you?'

The spearman trembled in the highborn's grip. 'We can't stay here, dread lord,' he moaned. 'It's been days, and they just keep coming–'

Malus shook the man like a rat. 'Of course they keep coming, you damned fool,' he growled. 'They're *animals*. It's all they know how to do.' He shoved the man against the battlements, forcing his body in the direction of the enemy camp. 'Listen to them! What do you hear?'

'Howls! Black curses!' the druchii shouted angrily. 'They never let up! It goes on and on for hours!'

'Of course it does!' Malus shot back. 'Every single one of those beasts are sitting out there in the muck and cursing your name loud enough that all the Dark Gods can hear it! Do you know why? Because they want nothing more than to get past these walls and slaughter every living thing they can reach, but *you won't let them*. They're the biggest damned army that's ever marched against Naggaroth, and you are standing up here on the wall with your spear and keeping them from the one thing they desire.'

The highborn dropped the man onto the filth-encrusted parapet. 'It's ridiculous! Absurd! They rise from their stinking tents each day and caper like fools before their twisted altars, working themselves into a blood-soaked frenzy that nothing on earth could stand against – and every day they slink back to their tents with their tails between their legs and lick their wounds in the shadow of these black walls. Of course they curse your name! The very thought of you burns like a coal in their guts because you've beaten them every time they've come against you. Every damned time.' He pointed out at the enemy camp. 'You should savour those sounds, soldier, because they are a lament. They're the sounds of fear and desperation. And it's all because of you.'

The spearman stared at Malus in shock. The highborn looked down at him and smiled. 'Victory is in your grasp, soldier. Are you going to let it slip away now, or will you beat these bastards once and for all?'

'You can count on us, dread lord! We'll kill every last one of the beasts!' cried a spearman just a few yards away. Malus was startled by the outcry; looking over, he realised that most of the warriors had risen to their feet while he spoke, and now they hung on his every word. Their dirty, bloodied faces beamed with fierce pride.

The panicked spearman rose shakily to his feet. He swallowed hard and looked Malus in the eye. 'Let them come, dread lord,' he said. 'I'll be waiting for them.'

A cheer went up from the assembled troops. Malus grinned, a little uncomfortably, and waved to the survivors of the regiment. 'Get some rest,' he shouted, and waved in the direction of the enemy camp. 'Enjoy the music while you can.' The warriors laughed, and Malus turned away, striding swiftly for the gatehouse.

Nuarc was waiting for him at the entrance to the fortification. The general's face was as filthy as any common soldier, its lines deepened by exhaustion and hunger. Nevertheless, he gave Malus an admiring grin. 'That was well done, boy,' he said quietly. 'I probably would have just let his file mates take care of the problem.'

The highborn shook his head. 'Then we'd just be doing the enemy's work for them,' he said. 'I'm spiteful enough to want to make those beasts work for every single one of us they kill.'

Nuarc chuckled. 'Well said.' He motioned to the highborn. 'Come inside. You look like you could stand to eat something.'

He led Malus and Hauclir into the gloomy corridors of the gatehouse, passing through deserted rooms and corridors lined with barrels of heavy bolts, until they reached a long room pierced with firing slits that looked out onto the killing ground before the gate. Perhaps a dozen weary-looking druchii soldiers, male and female alike, looked out over the corpse-strewn approach with their crossbows close to hand. A brazier in the centre of the low-ceilinged chamber provided a modicum of warmth, and upon a nearby table sat a couple of loaves of bread, some hunks of cheese and dried fish, along with a half-dozen leather jacks and several bottles of wine.

'Help yourself,' Nuarc said, waving at the contents of the table. The troops on watch cast predatory glances at the two interlopers who had been welcomed into their midst, like a pack of dogs suddenly forced to share their meat. Malus's stomach roiled at the sight of food, but Hauclir nodded his head respectfully to the warlord and helped himself to the food.

Nuarc poured some wine into one of the jacks and took a small sip. 'Word of your exploits has been spreading among the men. First the raid on the siege engines, and now the battle in the tunnel. You're fast becoming the hero of the hour.'

Malus let out a disdainful snort. 'Never mind the fact that the battle in the tunnel wouldn't have happened if I hadn't fallen for Nagaira's stratagem,' he growled. 'If those poor fools think me a hero, then things are desperate indeed.'

Hauclir chuckled around a mouthful of dried fish, but Nuarc stared into the depths of his wine jack and frowned. Malus caught the gesture and sobered at once. 'How bad is it?'

'We're barely holding on at this point,' Nuarc said gravely. 'As best we can tell, we lost just over a third of our troops in the debacle at the outer wall, and the rest are worn out. We don't lack for food or weapons, but the constant attacks have taken their toll. If we have another day of attacks like yesterday we could lose the inner wall by mid-afternoon.'

The revelation stunned Malus. 'What about the reinforcements from Har Ganeth and Karond Kar?'

Nuarc shook his head, his expression grave. 'There's been no word. At this point I doubt they will arrive in time, if at all.'

'And what of those damned lords in the Black Tower?' the highborn snarled. He began pacing the long room like a caged wolf. 'Have they any bold plans to save us from disaster?'

Nuarc reached for the wine bottle once more. 'I've heard rumours,' he said. 'Are you sure you won't take some wine?'

'Gods, no, general,' Malus said. 'I've had enough of that vinegar to last me a while.'

The warlord poured himself a healthy draught. 'There are indications that your brother the vaulkhar is contemplating a plan that will end the siege in a single stroke.'

Malus chuckled bitterly. 'He plans to lead the garrison against the Chaos horde?'

Nuarc shook his head. 'He intends to turn you over to Nagaira.'

The highborn's weak humour faded. 'You can't be serious.'

'I wish I wasn't,' Nuarc admitted. 'But you embarrassed Isilvar and the other nobles in front of the Witch King – and what's worse, your exploits are winning the admiration of the troops. That makes you very dangerous, as far as they are concerned.'

'Malekith would never allow such a thing!'

The warlord shrugged. 'I've served Malekith for more than three hundred years, boy, and I can't say what he will or won't allow. It's clear to me that he's testing Isilvar and the other lords, but to what end I can't begin to guess. The thing is, they are beginning to realise this as well, and it's making them nervous. They want the siege to end, and giving Nagaira what she wants is the quickest and easiest way to do it.'

'If Isilvar actually believes that, he's an even bigger fool than I imagined,' Malus said, torn between murderous rage and cold panic. 'If Nagaira believes that she can take the Black Tower – and humble the Witch King in the bargain – she won't hesitate to do so.'

Nuarc grimaced. 'I was afraid you were going to say something like that,' he replied. 'Then we'd best figure out another way of ending this siege before Isilvar and the other lords decide to take matters into their own hands.'

Malus bared his teeth in frustration. 'I believe I'll have a bit of that wine after all,' he said.

At that moment an earth-shaking rumble swelled up from the north, causing the oaken table to rattle and the wine bottles to wobble and clink against one another. A strange peal of thunder rent the air, like the sound of a hammer on glass. The druchii at the firing slits were suddenly alert. One of them turned to Nuarc with a frightened look on her face. 'You'd better come see this, my lord,' she said. 'Whatever it is, it can't be good.'

Nuarc and Malus rushed to the firing slits, shouldering aside wide-eyed druchii warriors. The old warlord's expression turned grim. 'Damnation,' he hissed.

Outside, beyond the far curve of the outer wall, a huge column of swirling smoke rose into the cold, clear sky. Green threads of lightning pulsed and rippled through the roiling murk, and even from almost six miles away Malus could feel the winds of sorcery tingling in waves across his skin. As they watched, the column of dark magic rose more than a thousand feet into the air and poured out its energies across the sky. Blackness spread outwards from the column in an inky, turbulent pool, casting a dreadful pall across the war-torn land beneath. More tortured thunder squealed beneath the tainted sky, and a sudden gust of cold, dank wind beat against the face of the inner wall.

'Damnation is right,' Malus said. 'I don't like the looks of this at all.'

Nuarc turned to one of the warriors. 'Sound the call to stand to,' he ordered. 'Unless I miss my guess, the enemy is about to hit us hard.' The warrior nodded, his face white with fear, and dashed from the room.

The wind picked up, skirling eerily through the narrow firing slits and filling the druchii's nostrils with the smell of damp earth. Green lightning strobed through the black sky overhead, glinting on the swords and shields of beastmen and marauders who were starting to trickle down the narrow lanes towards the killing ground before the inner fortress. Thunder keened overhead, and fat, greasy drops of rain began to spatter against the battlements. Above them, on the roof of the gatehouse, horns began to wail, their cries all but lost in the rising wind.

Within seconds the rain became a drenching downpour, tinged green by constant flashes of lightning. Cold air billowed through the firing slits; the druchii warriors recoiled with a curse, gagging on an overpowering stench of corruption. Malus cursed as well, but for a different reason entirely. A moment before he could clearly see the Chaos army massing for another assault, but now they were hidden completely by sheets of oily rain. They could be halfway across the killing ground by now.

The highborn turned to Nuarc. 'Will Morathi and her witches intercede against this awful rain? This could cost us the inner wall if we can't see the enemy until they're standing on the battlements!'

Nuarc shook his head helplessly. 'She is even harder to predict than her son. If Malekith orders her to do so, then perhaps she will.'

'Then you've got to get back to the citadel and speak to the Witch King!' The highborn turned to Hauclir, who was busy stuffing parcels of food and a bottle of wine into the sleeves of his robe. 'Hauclir! Put that down and escort Nuarc back to the Black Tower. Quickly!'

The former guard captain hurriedly folded his arms, causing the pilfered food and wine to disappear. 'As you wish, my lord,' Hauclir grumbled.

Nuarc snapped off a series of commands to the warriors, naming a half-dozen who would accompany him back to the citadel. Malus took the opportunity to join Hauclir and lead him towards the chamber doorway, out of earshot. 'When you've got Nuarc back to the citadel, round up the harbour rats and get back here as quick as you can,' he said quietly. 'We may have to do something drastic in the next few hours if we're both going to get what we want from Nagaira.'

'Drastic? Like what?' Hauclir whispered.

'Honestly? I haven't the faintest idea,' Malus replied, managing a roguish grin. 'Just like old times, eh?'

Hauclir winced. 'Old times? The ones where we nearly got drowned, or burnt up, or eaten by daemons?'

Malus glared at his former retainer. 'Now see here – what about all the good times?'

'Those *were* the good times.'

The highborn bit back a retort as Nuarc and his escorts approached. 'Just get back here as quick as you can, you damned rogue,' he said quietly.

Malus followed the small party to the rear of the gatehouse and left them at a spiral staircase that would deposit them at an iron door set beside the inner gate. Then he drew his twin blades and made his way to the outer wall.

Moments later he reached the exit leading out onto the battlements and saw the heavy oaken door rattling in its frame, buffeted by a howling wind. Shouts and screams echoed faintly from the other side. Gathering his courage, the highborn pulled open the rattling door – and found himself standing upon the brink of hell.

Druchii warriors reeled beneath the lash of reeking wind and noisome rain, many crouching and pressing the tops of their helmets against the battlements to get some relief from the hideous storm. Forks of green lightning rent the skies overhead, seemingly close enough to touch. Malus saw pale faces lit with absolute terror and heard cries of fear all up and down the struggling line of spearmen. To the highborn's horror he saw almost a dozen ladders already rising above the edge of the wall, their wooden rails quivering with the tread of hundreds of feet.

Less than twenty yards away half a dozen warriors were struggling with a thrashing figure lying on the paving stones. Malus heard shouts of anger and fury and saw a long dagger plunge again and again into the prone figure. A black rage boiled up from his heart.

'Stand and face the enemy!' he roared into the howling wind. Swords in hand, he strode out onto the parapet, heedless of the sheets of stinking water that blew into his face and into the crevices of his armour. 'The warriors of Naggaroth do not cower in the face of the storm! They fight or they die! Make your choice!'

Heads turned to Malus as he passed by. Lightning flared, lending his face a daemonic cast. Slowly but surely the spearmen of the regiment gripped their weapons and rose to the feet. Whether they did it out of honour, or shame, or fear of what he might do to them, Malus neither knew nor cared.

The brawl was still raging when Malus reached it, and with a furious shout he took to kicking the spearmen who were punching and stabbing at their victim. Fearful shouts rose in response to his angry blows. One knife-wielder even turned on Malus for a brief instant, his bloodstained knife ready, until he realised who he faced and recoiled with a frightened shout.

Now Malus could see the thrashing, snarling warrior at the bottom of the pile. Each flicker of lightning revealed ghastly wounds to the druchii's chest, belly and legs – horrible rents torn by knife, sword and axe. The warrior had his pale hands around the neck of another spearman, and was trying to pull his struggling victim within reach of his torn lips and broken, bloodstained teeth.

Malus realised how little blood there was around the snarling warrior, and then a cold knot of realisation turned his guts to ice.

The druchii was dead. He'd been dead for hours.

With a horrified shout, Malus slashed down with his blades, severing the revenant's right arm at the elbow and then shearing half its skull away. The creature recoiled and his screaming victim pulled himself free – but the revenant tried to lunge for the warrior yet again, even as his brains spilled out onto the paving stones. The highborn stepped in quickly and with a backhand swing he severed the creature's head from its shoulders. Only then did the wretched thing flop lifelessly onto the stone.

Thunder roared close to Malus's ear. Warriors cried out in terror. One of the spearmen looked up at Malus, bleeding freely from a line of deep scratches carved into his face and neck. The highborn recognised him as the panicked soldier he'd spoken to only minutes before.

'It's the rain, dread lord!' he shouted over the wind. 'It got onto Turhan's face and it brought him back to life!'

'Blessed Mother of Night,' Malus whispered, suddenly realising Nagaira's plan. He strode quickly to the inner edge of the parapet and looked down into the deep shadows at the foot of the wall.

Lightning burnt through the air overhead and Malus glimpsed the heaving mounds of rent and smashed corpses – hundreds, perhaps thousands of them – clawing their way free of the tangled piles that lined the inner avenue and staggering towards the long ramp leading to the top of the wall.

The scene was the same as far as Malus could see, all along the sections of the inner wall. His sister's infernal sorceries had trapped the defenders between two armies: one living and the other dead. *And I just sent Hauclir and Nuarc down into the midst of that nightmare,* he thought.

Horns began to wail all along the wall. Whether it was a cry of warning or a call to retreat, Malus could not tell. He couldn't begin to guess how such a plague of revenants could be stopped in time – all he could do was hold his part of the wall with the troops and the resources he had at his command.

Thinking quickly, Malus turned to the bleeding warrior. 'You! What's your name, spearman?'

'Anuric, dread lord,' the soldier stammered.

'You're Sergeant Anuric now,' Malus snapped. He swept his stained sword in an arc, indicating the druchii who'd struggled with the revenant. 'Take these men and get to the gatehouse as fast as you can. Grab all the dragon's breath bolts you can find and hurl them onto the ramp! Do you understand?'

The warrior nodded. 'Understood, dread lord!'

'Then why are you still sitting there? Go!' He shouted, and the warriors scrambled to obey. Shouts and screams of battle were already sounding up and down the line as the first of the Chaos attackers reached the top of the wall. As the spearmen ran back for the gatehouse Malus turned and dashed in the opposite direction, racing the shambling corpses to the top of the steep ramp.

The eight segments of the inner wall were each about three-quarters of a mile in length, but now it seemed to stretch for leagues in the flickering, chaotic darkness. Malus slipped and staggered across the oily paving stones, dodging frantic battles between screaming spearmen and howling Chaos marauders and buffeted by fierce winds that threatened to hurl him from the parapet and plunge him into the mass of shambling revenants below. Frenetic glimpses of desperate fights came and went as the highborn ran past. A spearman went down with a beastman tearing at his throat, blood bursting from the druchii's mouth even as he drove his sword again and again into his attacker's muscular chest. Another spearman crawled blindly across the paving stones, bawling like a babe from the ruined pulp that had once been his face. A pair of spearmen dragged a flailing marauder off the battlements by his braided hair and threw him face-first onto the parapet, where one of them reached down and expertly slit his throat from ear to ear. The flood of steaming blood lapped at Malus's feet as he raced past.

He was twenty yards from the end of the ramp and he could see that he was going to lose the race. The first of the revenants were almost at the top, and none of the warriors at that end of the line had any idea what was coming up behind them.

'End of the line! Look to your backs!' Malus shouted at the top of his lungs, but his words were all but lost in the roaring storm and the maelstrom of battle. Snarling in frustration, Malus started to shout again – but a figure tackled him from behind, driving him face-first into the paving stones.

Malus heard a beastman's snarl just above his head and felt its hot, foetid breath against the back of his neck. Then a sharp blow and a searing pain lanced down the length of his right jaw, and he felt hot, thick ichor splash against his cheek. Roaring like a beast himself, the highborn tried to twist beneath his attacker, driving his armoured elbow into the side of the Chaos warrior's bony snout. The beastman roared and tried to stab Malus again with his jagged knife, but the blade glanced off the highborn's backplate. Driven by pure instinct, Malus twisted back fully prone and reversed his grip on his right-hand sword with a quick flick of his wrist, then brought the sword around behind him with all the strength he could muster. The blade sank deep into the beastman's side, and Malus continued to roll, forcing the stunned and bleeding warrior off the inner edge of the parapet.

Breathing heavily, Malus clambered to one knee and saw a pair of revenants rushing towards him with grimy hands outstretched.

The undead monsters had reached the top of the wall, and already the druchii at the end of the line were being overwhelmed. Malus saw two spearmen attacked from behind and dragged down beneath a mob of tearing hands and clashing jaws. The rest were retreating with horrified screams, yielding still more of the parapet to the shambling fiends.

Malus leapt at the oncoming revenants with a fierce warscream, his twin blades weaving a whistling pattern of dismemberment and death. Two quick swipes and the monsters' hands were chopped to jagged stumps; then the highborn darted a step to the left and with two quick blows chopped off an arm and the leftmost revenant's head. Before the body had even hit the paving stones Malus reversed his stance and lashed out at the creature to his right, decapitating it cleanly with a single, blurring sword-stroke. 'Aim for their heads!' he shouted at the reeling warriors. 'Follow me!' And laughing like a madman, he threw himself into the press.

The undead warriors knew neither pain nor fear, but their only weapons were claws and teeth and unnatural vigour. Fuelled by rage and spiteful hate, Malus carved a fearsome swathe through the oncoming revenants. He knew that if he could reach the top of the ramp and stem the tide of creatures that reached the parapet then they could still hold the top of the wall. He sliced away fingers and parts of hands, lopped off arms and hacked away skulls. Marauders, beastmen and druchii all fell before his flickering blades.

He fought his way along twenty yards of blood-soaked parapet, felling everything that rose before him. The battle seemed to go on for hours, until the slaughter became a kind of terrible dance. Malus heard the furious shouts of the warriors behind him as they followed in his wake, and howled like a wolf loose amid the sheep. For the first time since the march on Hag Graef, many months past, he felt truly alive.

When he reached the far end of the wall it took the highborn by surprise. A pair of headless revenants slumped to the paving stones and his blades struck sparks against the wall of the far redoubt just behind them. More of the undead were trying to force their way onto the parapet, but now a solid knot of druchii spearmen at Malus's back had reached the top of the ramp and were hacking at the monsters with murderous efficiency. The highborn fetched up against the wall of the redoubt and tried to shake off the battle-madness as best he could.

Just then there was a crackling *whoosh*, and a sheet of green flame shot skyward along the back of the inner wall. Cheers went up among the druchii as the dragon's breath ignited among the shambling horde. Malus turned and saw Anuric staggering towards him, a look of weary relief plain on the young druchii's face. The spearman raised his hand in salute, then his eyes rolled back in his head and he collapsed face-first onto the parapet. A pair of marauder throwing axes jutted from the spearman's back.

Beyond the spearman's prone form the druchii line was a seething mass of fierce battles as waves of Chaos warriors poured over the battlements and leapt at the defenders. The druchii were holding on by their teeth, but there seemed to be no end to the furious assault.

Leaving the spearmen to hold the ramp, Malus advanced on the wavering line. As he passed Anuric's body he paused, then after a moment's consideration he knelt and rolled the young druchii's body off the edge of the wall, giving him over to the ravening flames as befitted a son of Naggaroth. Then he opened himself once more to the battle-madness and leapt howling into the fray.

Chapter Twenty-Two
THE BLOOD OF HEROES

THERE SEEMED NO end to the killing.

As the corrupting rain fell and the wind howled its fury Malus stalked like a mountain cat along the length of the embattled druchii line, falling like a thunderbolt on the Chaos attackers and then passing on to the next desperate battle, leaving hewn limbs and twitching bodies in his wake. Always he struck the enemy from an unexpected angle, sliding a quick thrust into an unsuspecting warrior's ribs or slicing his hamstrings as he focused on the druchii in front of him. His deadly efforts had nothing to do with honour or glory; it was cold, calculated slaughter, repeated again and again all along the length of the blood-soaked wall.

The druchii fought back like the cornered animals they were. With the seething green fires raging at their backs, the spearmen knew there was nowhere to run, and so the harder they were pressed the more vicious they became. Marauders and beastmen were seized and thrown bodily into the hungry flames that raged along the ramp, or set upon from every angle like a deer beset by a pack of wolves. The druchii fought on despite grievous wounds, falling only after the last of their blood had been spilled onto the paving stones. It was as if Malus's battle-madness had infected them as well, and little by little the tide began to turn back in their favour. The knots of struggling Chaos warriors dwindled, driven further and further back towards their rain-slick ladders, then before long the defenders were standing at the ladders themselves and raining blows down on the heads of anyone who tried to scale them.

Malus could not say how long they fought. The storm raged on and on, showing no signs of slacking, and time lost all meaning, measured in lunatic flashes of green light. Again and again he caught himself searching among the struggling warriors, looking for a glimpse of Lhunara. Strangely, Nagaira's champion made no appearance during the desperate battle.

When the final wave broke against the battlements he was back at the far end of the line beside the gatehouse, standing behind a trio of roaring, blood-drenched spearmen who were crouched like snakes beneath the battlements opposite the last of the scaling ladders. For a long time they'd lurked there and ambushed each warrior that had come over the wall, stabbing upwards into the man's legs, belly and groin and then throwing the screaming victim into the fire. They had slain so many men this way that it had become a kind of routine, and so when a massive, bull-headed beastman came roaring up out of the darkness the spearmen were caught completely off-guard.

With a furious bellow the minotaur leapt over the battlements in a single bound, landing amongst the startled spearmen and laying about with a pair of enormous hand axes. One druchii was cleft in twain from shoulder to hip with a single blow; another took a splintering blow to the chest that hurled her broken body end-for-end over the inner side of the wall. The third druchii, still consumed with bloodlust, leapt at the towering beast with a fierce shout, burying his stabbing sword in the minotaur's side. But the blade penetrated barely a finger length in the monster's thick hide, and the minotaur struck the spearman a desultory blow with the back of one axe that tore the druchii's head from his body. Malus bared his teeth at the monster before him and rushed in with both swords flashing.

His first stroke slashed across the monster's enormous, muscular thigh, drawing a pained roar and the whistling stroke of a bloodstained axe. Malus tried to twist out of the way of the blow, but the weapon still caught the trailing edge of his right pauldron and the impact hurled him back against the gatehouse wall as though he'd been kicked by a nauglir. The impact knocked the breath out of him and his head struck the stones with a resounding crack that left him momentarily blind. His hearing, however, worked just fine, and he could hear the minotaur's furious bellow as it rounded on Malus and moved in to finish the highborn off.

Acting on pure instinct, Malus threw himself forward, rolling between the minotaur's legs as the beast's twin axes carved furrows in the gatehouse's stone wall. Still blinking stars from his eyes, the highborn rose to his feet and slashed his swords across the cable-like tendons behind the minotaur's knees. The crippled beast collapsed with an agonised roar, and Malus brought his swords down in a scissor-like motion that sliced open both sides of the creature's thick neck almost to the spine. Red blood sprayed in steaming arcs across the stone wall of the gatehouse, and Malus spun on his heel in search of more foes.

And that was his mistake. He'd finished with the minotaur, but the minotaur wasn't finished with him.

The highborn heard a furious bellow at his back, then a tremendous impact smashed into his left shoulder and hurled him to the paving stones. Fiery pain spread in a red wave down the left side of his back, but Malus had little time to appreciate the extent of his injury. Still roaring, the minotaur launched itself at Malus, half-leaping, half-dragging its huge bulk after him.

Cursing in pain, Malus rolled onto his back as the bull-headed monstrosity loomed over him. A heavy axe smashed into his breastplate; Malus cried out as ribs cracked beneath the ensorcelled steel, but the axe-head glanced aside from the curved plate. The minotaur drew back its weapon for another strike, but Malus lashed out like a viper, severing the creature's hand with a deft stroke of his right-hand blade. Roaring, maddened by blood loss, the monster smashed the jagged stump of its wrist into Malus's face. Splintered bone gouged the highborn's cheek and hot blood poured thickly into his eyes.

Screaming in rage, Malus lashed out blindly with his sword and connected with something as resilient as a young sapling. He struck again and sheared through – and the minotaur's head fell free, smashing the highborn in the face.

Then the heavy body, still spurting blood, collapsed on top of him.

Hot liquid flowed over the highborn's face and neck, filling his nostrils and pouring into his gasping mouth. I'm going to drown on a castle parapet in the middle of a plain of ash, he thought wildly. Coughing and sputtering, he tried to push the minotaur's heavy body aside, but the dead weight refused to budge.

After what felt like hours, the flood of gore tapered away. Dimly, Malus heard pounding foot steps and muffled shouts. The body of the minotaur shifted slightly, then suddenly rolled free. Cold rain lashed at the highborn's face – not the foetid corpse-rain of before, but honest, clean water. Malus gaped like a fish, greedily drinking it in. He rubbed thick ooze out of his eyes and blinked at the stormy sky. Green lightning still raged overhead, but the darkness had thinned somewhat, paling to an iron-grey.

Hands pulled at the highborn's arms. Silhouettes crowded at the corners of his vision. Lightning flashed, and he made out the thin, worried face of Ten-thumbs and Hauclir's cynical grin. 'I can't leave you alone for a minute without you getting into some kind of mischief, can I, my lord?' the former guard captain said.

Malus flopped about in their arms like a drunkard, wincing in pain no matter which way he turned. 'Perhaps if you'd actually been here for the battle this might not have been necessary,' the highborn snarled.

'Well, we'd have been here sooner – mind the leg, my lord! – but some fool set fire to the ramp.'

Malus found himself on his knees, using Hauclir like a ladder to haul himself upright. A black handprint stood out prominently on his bandaged thigh. Peering past Hauclir's shoulder, Malus saw the spearmen rolling the last of the enemy dead off the forward edge of the battlements. The dragon's breath had finally exhausted itself, having run out of fuel to burn. The survivors of the spear regiment staggered about in a weary daze, their bloodstained faces slack with shock and exhaustion. Malus was stunned at how few of them were left. He counted less than three score where just a short while ago there had been almost a thousand.

No one cheered. There were no celebrations of victory. The few survivors were glad enough to still be alive. That was all the glory that mattered to them.

Malus pushed himself away from his former retainer. Already the pain was subsiding, and an icy knot in the side of his chest spoke of the daemon's power knitting his broken bones back together. He looked about at the dozen cutthroats that had followed Hauclir back from the citadel. Cutter and Pockets were busy looting the enemy dead; the wounded assassin had a bloodstained bandage plastered to his shoulder and was busy pointing out places for Pockets to search. Tenthumbs was chasing a bouncing gold earring along the parapet, his young face a mask of exasperated determination.

Malus shook his head wearily. 'Did Nuarc make it back to the citadel?'

Hauclir nodded. 'We got out just before those damned revenants started to stir and made damned good time getting back to the tower,' he said. 'Getting back here was a different story. There are packs of those revenants all over the inner compound now.'

'Did we hold the rest of the wall?'

The former guard captain nodded. 'Khaine alone knows how, but we did. For now, at least.'

Malus frowned. 'What's that mean?'

Hauclir looked back over his shoulder at the exhausted troops, then nodded his head at the gatehouse. 'Let's talk inside,' he said quietly.

A sense of foreboding crept over the highborn. Nodding wordlessly, he led the cutthroats into the gatehouse. Out of the rain, however, the stink of spilt blood and the oily residue of Nagaira's sorcerous rain rose like a cloud around the highborn, half-choking him. 'Upstairs,' he gasped. 'We'll talk on the roof.'

They found the spiral staircase leading to the top of the gatehouse and emerged once again into the howling wind and rain. Cloaked druchii huddled together around the four large bolt throwers mounted along the battlements, paying little heed to the small band of warriors at the far end of the broad, flat space.

Malus pulled off his armoured gauntlets and tried to clean them in a large puddle of rainwater. 'All right, what's going on?' he said quietly.

Hauclir knelt beside the highborn. 'Nuarc ordered me to remain once we'd reached the citadel in case he needed to relay any messages back to you. He was in talking to the Witch King for quite a while, and when he came out he wasn't alone. Your half-brother left first, looking like he'd been made to swallow a live coal, and then came a whole flock of messengers. Nuarc came out last of all, and had some interesting news.'

Malus splashed water on his face and rubbed it through his matted hair. 'Well, what did he say?'

'He said that the Witch King is getting ready to make his move,' Hauclir replied. 'Malekith is pulling the best regiments from the inner wall and bringing them inside the citadel even as we speak, as well as all the nauglir from the pens.'

Malus thought the news over. 'So we're letting the Chaos horde take the inner wall?'

Hauclir shrugged. 'At this point I'm not certain we could stop them if we wanted to. The Witch King's leaving behind enough of a rearguard to slow down the next assault, but no more.'

All at once Malus felt wearier than he'd ever felt in his life. He glanced down at the layers of blood and ichor coating the scarred surface of his armour and shook his head in frustration. 'And what does Nuarc and the Witch King ask of me?'

'Well, that's the interesting thing,' Hauclir replied. 'I'm to return you to the citadel at once.'

Malus frowned. 'And did Nuarc say why?'

'Not in so many words,' the former guard captain said. 'All Nuarc told me was that he thought Isilvar had failed the Witch King's test... and that put you in an interesting position.'

The highborn let Nuarc's words sink in for a moment. 'Are... are you telling me that Nuarc thinks the Witch King is going to name me Vaulkhar of Hag Graef over Isilvar?'

'Frankly I have no idea what I'm telling you,' Hauclir replied. 'Nothing you highborn do makes any sense to me. I'm just relating to you what Nuarc said.'

Malus nodded to himself. Would Malekith do such a thing? Why not? He'd already made Malus his champion – was it so far a leap to hand him the rank of vaulkhar? The thought of it quickened his pulse. How sweet a victory that would be: to humble Isilvar before the assembled lords and see him humiliated in the court of Hag Graef!

Only Tz'arkan stood in his way. The highborn's hands clenched into fists. Was there a way to claim his due from Malekith and still ride into the north to put an end to the daemon's infernal curse?

Perhaps, he thought. If he saw to it that the siege was broken and Nagaira destroyed.

Malus said, rising swiftly to his feet. 'I'll go straightaway to the citadel, but I want you and your warriors to get to the nauglir pens and make certain that Spite is brought into the tower.'

Hauclir chuckled. 'I'm sure the beast can take care of itself, my lord.'

'It's not Spite I'm worried about so much as the gear on its back,' the highborn said. 'There are... relics amid my saddlebags that must not fall into Nagaira's hands. Do you understand?'

The former guard captain gave Malus a searching look. 'Yes, my lord,' he said carefully. 'I understand clearly.'

'Then get moving. I don't want to keep Nuarc waiting.'

But just as the highborn and his cutthroats headed for the gatehouse stairs the air reverberated with the sullen rumble of drums.

The sound came from the broad square at the edge of the outer city. Malus hesitated, torn between a desire for haste and the need to know what the enemy was up to. Finally he turned and shouldered his way through the mercenaries, cursing under his breath as he strode swiftly to the gatehouse battlements.

His keen eyes saw a throng of bare-chested beastmen filling the square, their chests and arms painted in blood. They brandished bloody axes and bundles of severed druchii heads, still streaming trails of fresh gore. Malus could just make out the sound of a guttural chant weaving in and out of the rhythm of the great drums.

Behind the beastmen came a long line of stumbling, naked figures, spurred on by the barbed lashes of a dozen marauder overseers. Each of the druchii prisoners had suffered brutal tortures at the hands of their captors, their bodies marked with crude strokes of knife and iron.

Hauclir joined Malus's side and sneered disdainfully at the procession. 'If they think to break our will with a little torture they've come to the wrong place.'

'No,' Malus said warily. 'This is something else.'

The prisoners were herded into groups of eight and made to kneel at specific points in a rough circle at the centre of the square. Then came a band of beastmen wearing brass tokens and necklaces of skulls, each carrying a wide brass bowl and a longhaired brush. Filling the air with savage yells and barking cries, the beastmen dipped their brushes in the gleaming bowls and began to trace a complicated symbol across the stones of the square.

As they worked, Malus saw a figure clad in a dark robe and gleaming armour plate approach the edge of the square. It was no beastman or hulking marauder; Malus recognised the commanding stride of his half-sister at once.

He turned to the druchii gunners nearby. 'Can you hit those bastards from here?'

One of the warriors shook his head. 'Not a chance.'

'What if you used dragon's breath?'

The gunner let out a disgusted snort. 'We're out. Some damned officer came and took them all during that last attack.'

Nagaira walked gracefully into the centre of the expanding sigil, accompanied by a pair of hulking minotaurs who carried another druchii prisoner between them. The wretched figure had suffered the attentions of Nagaira's torturers far more than any of the other prisoners. His pale skin was covered with deep scars or fresh brands that stretched over almost every inch of his exposed skin, and his arms were bound in chains of brass. The prisoner's head rose at the sound of the drums, and even from so great a distance Malus recognised the druchii's face.

'Mother of Night!' he exclaimed. 'That's Lord Meiron!'

With a crash of drums the sigil was completed. A thousand beastmen threw back their horned heads and roared at the raging sky. Nagaira spread her arms and cried out a series of guttural words in a foul tongue that caused the assembled prisoners to writhe in fear and pain. Invisible waves of power radiated from the witch, distorting the air around her.

Something in her incantations disturbed Tz'arkan, causing the daemon to tense threateningly beneath Malus's skin. 'The little bitch has forgotten where her true allegiance lies,' the daemon hissed.

Before Malus could wonder what Tz'arkan meant, Nagaira's chant reached a crescendo. Lightning flared and a peal of thunder split the sky like the fist of an angry god. As one the beastmen raised their axes with a furious shout and turned upon the helpless prisoners, hacking them to pieces in an orgy of slaughter.

Fiery light burst from the bloody lines etched upon the stone. Lord Meiron stiffened, then screamed. The air around the druchii blurred, and his ravaged body started to swell. Malus felt his blood turn cold. 'Blessed Mother of Night,' he whispered, his voice full of dread.

Hauclir turned to Malus, his expression fearful. 'What would you have us do, my lord?' he asked.

'Run,' the highborn said. 'Run!'

Out in the square, Meiron's body continued to expand. The highborn's back was arched in agony and his muscles bulged until the skin split like an overcooked sausage, revealing the gleaming meat within. Meiron's face fell away from the dripping, shrieking skull, and a long pair of new limbs rose like blades from the highborn's back. As Malus watched, those limbs unfurled into a pair of gleaming, leathery wings.

The daemon continued to grow, wreathed in the boiling blood of the hundreds of sacrificial victims murdered in the square. Light and heat coalesced around the infernal creature's hands, taking the shape of a long, gleaming axe and a fearsome, barbed scourge.

Towering over the howling beastmen in the square, the bloodstained daemon raised its distended skull and roared a challenge at the defenders of the Black Tower.

The druchii manning the bolt throwers screamed in terror and several of the warriors ran for the stairs, hot on the heels of the fleeing mercenaries. Malus watched Hauclir and the cutthroats begin descending the spiral stair and knew that they would never reach the ground alive unless something was done to hold the daemon at bay.

He turned back to the towering fiend and met the daemon's brass eyes, raising his twin blades in challenge. Tz'arkan recoiled inside Malus's chest, sending a spasm of pain through the highborn's heart. 'What are you doing, Darkblade?' the daemon snarled.

'Do you not want Nagaira to see the error of her ways?' Malus declared.

The blood-soaked daemon spread its wings and leapt into the sky with a bloodthirsty roar. Malus threw back his head and laughed like one of the damned, and Tz'arkan's black vigour coursed through his veins.

Frantic commands echoed around Malus as the druchii still manning the bolt throwers wrestled their heavy weapons around to aim at the winged terror. The daemon seemed to fill the sky before them, its brass eyes and curved tusks gleaming in the dim light. Heavy cables banged, and four bolts streaked skyward. One missed the plunging daemon's head by less than a yard; another punched a neat hole through the creature's right wing. The last two bolts smashed full into the daemon's broad chest, their iron heads digging deep through iron-like layers of muscle and bone.

The twin impacts staggered the daemon in mid-flight. Bellowing in rage, it crashed against the edge of the gatehouse battlements, shattering the stone merlons to bits and sending a web-work of cracks along the building's thick roof. Malus was hurled backwards by the impact, throwing him beyond the sweeping arc of the daemon's fearsome axe. The blow meant for him hissed through the air and smashed a bolt thrower to splinters instead; blood and body parts of the three crew scattered in a wide arc from the impact. Snarling, the daemon lashed out at a bolt thrower to its left with its barbed scourge, wrapping it and two of its crew in a net of woven cables. Wood crackled and metal groaned as the daemon used the scourge to pull its massive bulk the rest of the way onto the battlement. The screams of the bound crewmembers turned to liquid shrieks as the barbed tendrils pulled taut and ground them into pulped flesh and bone.

Uttering a bestial roar of his own, Malus leapt back onto his feet and flew like an arrow at the axe-wielding daemon. With Tz'arkan's power burning in his limbs, the highborn was a blur of black armour and sharpened steel. He crossed the groaning roof in an eye blink, darting within the reach of the daemon's weapons and slashing fiercely at its axe arm. The keen blades rang from iron-hard muscle and bone, and then Malus felt the daemon's hot, foetid breath against his face as it snapped at him with its powerful jaws.

Malus sensed the daemon's lunge and tried to twist out of the way at the last moment, so instead of biting off his right arm the daemon's jaws closed on his armoured shoulder instead. Its fangs could not penetrate his enchanted plate but the highborn let out an agonised shriek as the metal plates compressed, twisting his arm from its socket and snapping his collarbone like a dry twig. The daemon lifted him off the ground and bit down hard once again, grinding broken bones together in Malus's chest, then it tossed him aside like a hound would a dead rat. He hit the stone roof hard, shrieking in pain once more, and skidded more than a dozen feet until he stopped near one of the last two bolt throwers at the far edge of the gatehouse roof.

Even as he ground to a halt the daemon was moving within him. Muscles spasmed and twisted of their own accord, dragging his mangled arm back into position with a crackling of sinew and bone. Malus screamed and thrashed, his eyes wild with pain, but Tz'arkan's terrible will prevented him from losing consciousness. The highborn's lunatic gaze fell upon the two bolt thrower crewmen just a few yards away, cowering in terror behind their weapon. '*Shoot… it!*' he snarled at them past ichor-flecked lips. The wide-eyed druchii took one look at Malus and leapt back into action, feverishly working at the twin cranks that drew back the weapon's steel bow.

The daemon rose to its full height, yanking its bloodied scourge loose from the mangled bolt thrower in a shower of splintered wood and steel. At the far end of the gatehouse the other surviving bolt thrower team lost their courage and ran for their lives, but their screams caught the winged fiend's attention. It lunged for the fleeing druchii, slicing one in half with a sweep of its axe and trapping the other in the barbed tails of its scourge. The daemon whirled towards Malus, swinging the scourge in an arc that sent the trapped crewman tumbling and screaming through the air. The flailing druchii missed the last bolt thrower by just a few feet before plunging into the darkness beyond the gatehouse.

With a loud *click-clack* the bolt thrower's cable locked into firing position. The crew scrambled to load another bolt in the firing channel just as the gatehouse roof trembled beneath the daemon's thundering footfalls. Malus gritted his teeth and once more surged to his feet, working the life back into his right sword hand, then rushed to meet the charging fiend.

He anticipated the lash of the daemon's scourge and ducked beneath its whistling tails, then cut to his right and drove the points of both his blades into the monster's left thigh. The weapons bit deep, drawing tendrils of black smoke from the daemon's bloodstained flesh. Roaring angrily, the winged fiend checked its pace and spun, slashing out at Malus with its axe. As fast as the highborn was, he could not move fast enough to avoid a glancing blow to the chest that broke ribs and smashed him aside like a child's toy.

As Malus tumbled once again along the gatehouse roof the last bolt thrower fired, and another iron-headed bolt punched into the daemon's abdomen. The monster staggered beneath the blow, then lashed at weapon and crew with its scourge. Both of the druchii weapon handlers were shredded in the passage of the barbed tails, and the bolt thrower itself was torn from its mount.

Baring its teeth in a feral grin, the daemon turned back to Malus, but the highborn was already on his feet again, fuelled by rage and pain as his shattered ribs were drawn back into place by Tz'arkan's will.

Malus ducked a sweeping blow of the daemon's axe, then stabbed out with his sword and raked a long, ragged gash along the length of the fiend's muscular arm. Snarling like a wolf, he nimbly dodged the fiend's backhanded swipe – and then the barbed tails of its scourge wrapped tightly around his legs.

He was pulled off his feet and dashed hard against the unyielding stone. It was Tz'arkan's power alone that allowed him to roll aside just as the daemon's axe smashed down beside him. Stone splintered, and a huge section of the gatehouse's roof collapsed in a shower of dust and debris, plunging Malus and the daemon into the space below.

Malus hit the tumbled stones hard and rolled against the side of the daemon's chest. Before the fiend could react he raised his left-hand blade and drove it with all his might into the daemon's shoulder, burying the weapon to the hilt. Roaring with rage, the daemon tried to pull Malus away with its scourge, but the highborn held on for dear life and drove his other blade into the fiend's muscular throat.

With a furious roar the daemon unfurled its wings – and suddenly more black smoke poured in a flood from its many wounds. Heat radiated from the fiend's body like a banked forge. Screaming in thwarted rage the daemon leapt skyward, and exploded in a clap of thunder and a blast of light.

Malus was hurled end-for-end through the air, striking the broken edge of the roof and bouncing along its length. The highborn fetched up hard against the line of battlements that looked over the citadel's inner compound, his skin scorched and his ears ringing from the blast. His swords were gone, lost when the daemon was banished. Gathering up his courage and trusting in Tz'arkan's power he rose to his feet and leapt over the battlements, plunging like a stooping hawk to the pavement sixty feet below. He hit the ground hard enough to crack the paving stones, but his body absorbed the blow with supernatural resilience.

It was hard not to smile. Terrible as Tz'arkan's gifts were, they could be exhilarating at times.

Guttural howls shook the air along the battlements of the inner wall. Nagaira's daemon might have lost its challenge, but it had put the druchii defenders to flight, and now the Chaos horde had seized the inner wall at last. Already, shadowy figures were racing down the long ramps into the inner courtyard itself, hard on the heels of the retreating druchii spearmen. Snarling like a wolf, Malus rose to his feet and raced off into the darkness. The siege was quickly coming to a head, and within the Black Tower the Witch King was preparing to make his move.

Chapter Twenty-Three
LORD OF RUIN

WITHIN THE WALLS of the inner keep the air reverberated with screams of terror and the guttural howls of the dead. The courtyards were full of panicked druchii racing for the safety of the Black Tower. Empty-handed soldiers, their spears cast aside, clambered over one another and stumbled along the cobblestones, fleeing for their lives. Craftsmen, apprentices, servants and slaves fled along with them. Like fear-maddened animals they turned upon one another in their frenzy to escape. Malus saw soldiers drawing their stabbing swords and lashing out at anyone in their path. A druchii wearing a blacksmith's apron fell with a scream, groping at the bloody wound in his back; his apprentice whirled and dashed out a spearman's brains with a heavy mallet, spattering his mates with a spray of gore. The highborn came upon a regimental officer facedown on the paving stones, a pool of dark blood spreading from his slashed throat. A sword with a jewelled pommel rested in his lifeless hand and a puddle of gold coins spilled beneath him from his torn coin-purse. It was more wealth than most low-born druchii saw in a lifetime, but no one spared it a second glance.

White faces etched with fear glimmered in the unnatural darkness, swirling like a cloud of panicked birds around Malus. Most of the panicked troops were looking back the way they'd come, listening to the exultant roars and wailing horns of the Chaos warriors swarming over the inner walls. It made them easy prey for the monsters stalking like wolves through the deep shadows of the inner compound. Nagaira's revenants dragged men down like panicked deer, tearing out their throats with claw-like fingers and feasting upon their steaming entrails. More than once Malus was forced to race past a screaming druchii buried beneath a knot of snarling, clawing monsters.

Once, a pair of pale, withered arms reached for him out the shadows of a nearby doorway. The revenant had once been a druchii spearman, his face half shorn away by the blow of a northman's axe. Cracked nails clawed at his throat; with a snarl Malus grabbed the hissing creature by the neck and tore its head from its shoulders. By the time the headless body clattered to the ground the highborn was long gone, running as fast as he could down the long avenue towards the citadel.

His body still felt cold and swollen. Muscles slid like steel cables beneath his skin, coated in thick, oily corruption. The daemon's gifts he'd summoned at the gatehouse had not ebbed, a realisation that both comforted and disturbed him at the same time.

With the daemon's unnatural speed he slipped like a ghost through the chaos of the rout. Caught between the Chaos horde and the waiting revenants, Malus feared that not one man in five among the fleeing druchii would reach the safety of the Black Tower. Malekith had been wise to pull his best troops from the walls in advance of Nagaira's attack.

He could guess the Witch King's intentions. The Chaos horde would be scattered and disorganised after the bloody pursuit, drunk with slaughter after destroying the exhausted remnants of the routing spear regiments, and Nagaira's sorceries would be depleted as well. When Malekith launched his counterattack, bolstered by the magical prowess of Morathi and the witches of the Black Tower's convent, the tables would well and truly turn. More than half of the enemy army would find itself trapped within the confines of the inner courtyard, facing fresh, disciplined infantry and the Witch King's battle-hungry knights. The slaughter would be awesome to behold, Malus reckoned, worth even the hundreds of druchii being sacrificed around him.

If Nuarc was correct about the Witch King's intentions, then it could be he who led the charge, as befit the Vaulkhar of Hag Graef. Malus smiled hungrily at the thought. After he finished massacring the troops within the inner compound he would rally the army and lead them into the outer city and beyond. They wouldn't stop until Nagaira's head dangled from one of Spite's trophy hooks.

Another of his half-sister's revenants lurched out of the shadows towards him, arms outstretched. Malus grabbed the creature's shoulder and the side of its neck and tore it down the middle like a sheet of wet parchment. He flung the dripping pieces aside and laughed lustily at the dark sky, anticipating the glories to come.

A few moments later he reached another wide courtyard that lay at the foot of the tower itself. Green fire flickered balefully from two large pyres to either side of the highborn, casting a riot of reaching shadows across the cobblestones and limning the polished helms of the two spear regiments formed up outside the doors of the great citadel. Bodies littered the broad square: revenants shot through the skull by sharp-eyed crossbowmen and a few unlucky druchii who'd been caught in the crossfire.

Malus slowed his pace somewhat as he loped into the square, showing his open hands as he approached the twin regiments. To his surprise, a ragged cheer went up from the spearmen as he strode forward. The sound quickened what little blood remained in his shrivelled veins, and he acknowledged the accolades with a raised fist and a wolfish grin.

He passed down the narrow gap between the two regiments and found a mounted officer waiting for him on the other side. The highborn raised his sword in salute. 'It is good to see you, dread lord,' the officer shouted over the thunderous din. 'The Witch King commanded me to watch for you, and bid you to attend him at his war council without delay.'

Malus's grin widened. 'I'll not keep his Dread Majesty waiting,' he shouted back. 'Has a group of infantry passed through here in the last quarter-hour with a cold one in tow? I sent my retainers to the pits to fetch my mount just before the gatehouse was attacked.'

The officer shook his head. 'We've only had a handful of troops pass through so far,' he cried. 'None of them with a nauglir.'

Malus's smile soured. He looked back the way he'd come, gauging the distance between the citadel and the nauglir pits. Where in the Dark Mother's name were they?

Something had gone wrong, he thought. They might have run afoul of a pack of revenants or been overtaken by a band of panicked troops. He fought against a tide of despair. Hauclir would get them back in time, he told himself. The insolent rogue is no end of trouble sometimes, but he's never failed me when it mattered. The highborn turned to the officer. 'Keep an eye out for them, and make certain they get inside,' he shouted. There was nothing more he could do. The officer nodded and turned his horse about, heading back to his waiting troops. Malus spared a final look at the tumult raging beyond the fires, and ran on to the tower.

Beyond the battle-line the black doors of the citadel yawned wide, ready to receive the lucky few who survived the flight from the inner wall. The green glow of witchlamps held back the darkness in the cavernous halls within, and the air rang with a different sort of clangour. Formations of spearmen stood ready, their scarred faces set in masks of concentration as they checked weapons and harness, while knights and their squires tended their wargear and the needs of their scaly mounts. The air was taut with coiled tension, like a crossbow ready to fire. Malekith had drawn back his mailed fist and now merely waited for the proper moment to strike.

Malus paused just inside the doorway, momentarily uncertain of where to proceed. Would the Witch King hold his council in the throne room, or the less formal chambers near the top of the tower? Just as he'd resolved to find a page or tower servant to ask, one appeared at his elbow.

'If you would follow me, dread lord,' the page said, bowing low. 'I am to conduct you to the council chambers.'

The highborn nodded curtly. 'Lead on, then,' he said absently, his mind awhirl. Malus fell into step behind the page, his mind immersed in drawing up hasty battle-plans for the Witch King's small army.

He followed the page upstairs, climbing the tall tower to the upper council rooms. Malus scarcely noticed the climb, buoyed by the daemon's cold strength and thoughts of the glory that awaited him. We'll have one last reunion, dear sister, the highborn thought grimly. And then I'll send you screaming into the Abyss where you belong.

Two guardsmen stood with bared blades outside the door to the council chamber. They saluted as Malus approached, and the page retreated with another deep bow. At the door, the highborn paused, suddenly realising how filthy he was. Every inch of his enamelled plate armour was coated with dust, grime and blood, and his face only slightly less so. Then he shrugged, allowing himself a grim smile. The Witch King wanted a warrior to lead his armies, he thought. A warrior he shall have. He laid his gauntleted hand on the door and pushed it wide, striding swiftly within.

The small room was dimly lit, bathed in the sullen glow of a pair of banked braziers. Maps and parchments were scattered across the broad table, just as Malus had last seen it. Retainers moved quietly among the shadows, attending upon the seated lords who watched the highborn approach. Balneth Bale glared coldly at Malus from his right, while Lord Myrchas scowled at him from the left. Lord Jhedir was conspicuously absent, Malus noted at once. Likely facedown in a puddle of wine somewhere, the highborn thought disdainfully.

As he stopped before the table the retainers retreated back to the far walls of the room, and Malus realised with a frown that none of the silver-masked Endless were present either.

His gaze fell upon the shadowy figure reclining at the far end of the table and his heart went cold.

'All hail the conquering hero,' Isilvar sneered, his ruined voice dripping with hate. He straightened in his chair and leaned towards Malus, until the red glow of the braziers painted his cheeks the dull colour of dried blood. 'You see, my lords? I told you he would reach the citadel safely. My half-brother has a talent for escaping the disasters he creates.'

'Where is Malekith?' Malus demanded, fighting a slowly rising tide of panic.

Isilvar smiled cruelly. 'Below, in the audience chamber. He is calling a council of war. Didn't you hear?'

Malus bared his teeth in a wolfish snarl, angry at having been outwitted so easily. 'I heard. He has commanded me to attend upon him.' The highborn coldly surveyed Isilvar and his allies. 'I suppose Jhedir is there as well. Interesting that the Witch King values the counsel of a drunkard over the likes of you, don't you think?'

He turned on his heel – and saw four of Isilvar's men barring his path to the door. Steel glimmered in their hands. Suddenly Malus was acutely aware of the empty scabbards at his hip.

'We have little need of councils, brother,' Isilvar replied. 'Our plan has already been set into motion. This siege begins and ends with you, Darkblade. As much as I would love to see you dragged back to the Hag in chains and taken apart one piece at a time, the needs of the moment demand that I give you to our dear sister instead.' The vaulkar's smile widened. 'I'm certain she has something very special in mind for you.'

Malus's mind raced as he tried to think of a way out of his half-brother's trap. He looked to Lord Myrchas and Balneth Bale and wondered how strong their alliance truly was. 'You thrice-damned fool,' he said to Isilvar. 'I'm the Witch King's champion. Do you think you can just march me out through the citadel's doors and hand me to Nagaira?'

Isilvar chuckled. 'Certainly not. Thanks to you, however, we won't need to.' He beckoned to the shadows with one long-fingered hand.

A hooded figure glided silently into the crimson light, dressed in druchii robes and a worn kheitan of dwarf hide. Grave mould glowed faintly from the depths of the hood where one of the figure's eyes should have been.

Malus turned and threw himself at the druchii guarding the door. Fuelled by the daemon's power he crossed the distance between them in an instant. In a blur of motion he snatched the sword from one of the stunned warriors and smashed the druchii to the floor with an open-handed blow to his chest. The sword flickered in Malus's hand and another of the guards fell back, clutching at the gushing wound in his throat.

The highborn reached for the iron ring of the chamber door – and his entire body convulsed with a wave of icy pain. Gritting his teeth, Malus forced his hand to close about the ring, but his muscles rebelled. Tremors wracked his armoured frame as he bent every iota of will towards his escape, but it was as though flesh and bone had been transformed into solid ice.

A groan slipped past his thin lips. Inside, the daemon chuckled maliciously.

'Your sister is waiting, little druchii,' Tz'arkan said. 'We wouldn't want to disappoint her, would we?'

Slowly, achingly, his body turned away from the door. The stolen sword fell from his hand. Across the room, Isilvar watched Malus's body betray him with a mix of cruel delight and bemused wonder. He turned to Lhunara. 'I trust my sister understands the nature of the exchange?'

The hooded figure nodded. *'You will have your victory, Isilvar,'* she said, her voice bubbling up from dead lungs. *'Slay all within the inner wall, and the rest will retreat to the north. Harry the rearguard as long as you wish. We will slip away when night falls.'*

Isilvar nodded. 'Excellent.' He smiled to his fellow lords. 'By nightfall we shall all be heroes, and the Witch King will reward us well.' The vaulkhar glanced at Malus, who still trembled with thwarted rage. 'By tomorrow the Witch King will have forgotten all about my lost brother.' He gestured dismissively to Lhunara. 'Take him down the hidden stair to the cistern tunnel,' he said. 'We are late for the Witch King's war council.'

Lhunara bowed stiffly to Isilvar, then stretched out her hand to Malus. The daemon within him stirred, and to the highborn's horror his legs began to move. Slowly at first, then with gathering strength, he crossed the room like an obedient dog and fell in beside his former lieutenant.

The lords rose from their seats and filed past Malus. Balneth Bale fixed the highborn with a hateful stare and spat full in his face. 'My only regret is that I cannot slay you myself,' he growled. 'I will pray tonight that this sister of yours prolongs your suffering for a great many days.'

Lord Myrchas came next. He eyed Malus up and down, shaking his head in frightened wonder. 'You are an even greater fool than I imagined,' he said, then walked away.

Isilvar was last. He leaned close to Malus's immobile face. 'I wish you could have seen the look on your face when you walked into this room,' he said, his voice sweet poison. 'Did you honestly think I would sit meekly by and let you take my title from me? I won't see you die, brother, but I did watch your dreams turn to ash in a single instant. I will savour that moment for centuries to come.'

And then he was gone. The door swung shut, and attendants busied themselves with removing the body of the druchii Malus had killed. Lhunara turned to her former lord. Her cold breath stank of mould and corruption. She raised a gloved hand and traced a fingertip along Malus's jaw.

'*Mine at last,*' the revenant said, and her body trembled with terrible, bubbling laughter.

Chapter Twenty-Four
THE AMULET OF VAUROG

THERE WAS A hidden stair at the far end of the council chamber
that wound its way down the length of the tower and into the
lower levels. Malus followed his former retainer as obediently
as a hound, raging inwardly as Tz'arkan manipulated his limbs
like a master puppeteer. From time to time the highborn heard
voices and shouted orders emanating from the other side of
spyholes and hidden doors along the stairwell. At one point he
could have sworn that they passed within a scant few yards of
Malekith's war council itself. Malus fought every step of the
way, praying to every god and goddess he knew for someone
to hear their passage or stumble onto their escape. But Lhunara's luck held out, and Tz'arkan's iron grip kept Malus
helpless as a babe.

Before long a chill settled against Malus's skin, and he knew
that they had descended below ground. A few minutes later
Lhunara led him through a narrow door and into the cistern
vaults. They walked through utter darkness, picking their way
past the deep wells with unnatural ease. Malus found himself
wishing with every step that the daemon would put a foot

wrong and send them plunging into cold, brackish water. With all his armour he would sink like a stone. A watery death was preferable to remaining a slave in his own skin!

Isilvar had never set fire to the secret tunnel as he'd claimed. In the heat of battle it had never occurred to Malus that his half-brother would try to use it for other purposes. In retrospect, however, he was probably the one person in the tower who could treat with Nagaira effectively, owing to their ties to the Cult of Slaanesh.

They emerged into the wasteland of the outer city, now all but deserted with the bulk of the horde howling at the foot of the Black Tower. Lhunara led him down the corpse-choked lanes, past burnt-out buildings covered in obscene sigils and squares filled with victims of sacrifice and debased revelry. Ghrond had been transformed into a city of the dead; the carnage beggared anything Malus had seen in the bloody streets of Har Ganeth. The Black Tower had been transformed by the terrible siege into a city of ghosts, and there was still more hard fighting yet to come.

Beyond the outer gate waited the rude tents of the Chaos encampment. No sentries challenged Lhunara as she led Malus across the ashen plain; camp followers and wretched slaves clad in tattered rags peered warily from behind tent flaps or scattered like rats down the twisting lanes as the Chaos champion led the highborn to the pavilion of indigo-dyed tents that Malus had first spied days before. The air still roiled and seethed about the seat of Nagaira's power; the closer Malus got to her tents the more he felt a curious pressure building behind his eyes, as though something unseen was pressing insistently against the inside of his skull. Tz'arkan reacted to it as well, swelling painfully within the highborn's chest until Malus felt he was about to burst.

Huge, horned figures stood guard outside Nagaira's tent: more than a score of minotaurs, clad in crude iron armour and hefting fearsome double-bladed axes. They bellowed a challenge at Lhunara as she approached, until the Chaos champion pulled back her hood and showed them her face. At the sight of her terrible visage the monsters bent their ponderous heads as one, their nostrils twitching as Malus marched stiffly past.

The pavilion of indigo tents wasn't the elaborate, interlinked affair that Nagaira's previous abode had been. Rather, Malus counted nine smaller tents, festooned with arcane sigils and constructs of freshly cleaned druchii bones, arrayed around a larger, central enclosure. The highborn reckoned the smaller tents were given over to Nagaira's personal retainers; he wondered which one was Lhunara's. Did a creature such as she even feel the need for sleep, or to take refuge from the elements?

As they approached the central tent Malus could feel the air roiling about him, churned by otherworldly energies emanating from within. The heavy hide flaps covering the entrance billowed open at their approach, crackling like whips in an invisible wind. Faint screams and cries of terror rose and fell within.

Lhunara and the daemon led Malus inside. He could no longer tell who was leading whom, for Tz'arkan seemed to gain strength and urgency from the obscene energies seething about the tent. Beyond the entrance the large enclosure was subdivided by heavy canvas hangings, reminding the highborn of his sister's tent during the march on Hag Graef. In this case, however, the chambers were arranged in a crude spiral, leading them along a labyrinth of sorts around the circumference of the witch's tent. Along the way they passed through a succession of dimly lit spaces, each one marked with complex sigils formed of powdered gold, silver and crushed bone. The powders were the only signs of material wealth Malus could see. So much for Hauclir's visions of plunder, Malus thought bleakly.

Before long Malus could not say whether he walked in the mortal world or trod upon the threshold of another, far more terrible realm. The darkness about him stirred like ink, sliding over his skin like smoke, and strange whispers of horror and madness echoed in his ears.

Behold your future, Malus heard an unreal voice whisper to him. Whether it came from Lhunara, or Tz'arkan, or himself, he could not rightly say.

The chambers narrowed as they went. Canvas hangings pressed in about Malus, thick with oily darkness and sorcerous energies. Fear built within him, but his limbs were no longer his to command. The daemon bore him onwards through the suffocating blackness, until they rounded a final turn and the highborn found himself at the heart of Nagaira's sanctum.

There was no light. Instead, the air itself seemed leeched of shadow, creating a grey sort of gloom that hurt the eye to look upon. Malus saw no walls, or roof. A horrid, atonal chanting filled the tortured air, uttered from the twisted throats of nine beastmen shamans. They knelt in a broad circle, their horned heads thrown back and the muscles of their necks etched in taut relief in the strange half-light. Within the circle formed by the warped figures of the beastmen lay nearly a dozen shrivelled corpses, sprawled in an untidy heap before a figure that left Malus's tormented mind reeling in terror.

It was formed of inky layers of darkness and hues of smoke and shadow, swirling in the silhouette of a druchii-like figure standing with arms outstretched as though beckoning like a lover to the wailing victim floating helplessly before it. The victim was an autarii, his naked body unblemished save for dozens of ritual tattoos snaking across his muscular arms and shoulders. His body was stretched as though upon an invisible rack; each muscle tensed and twisted like ropes beneath his skin.

As Malus watched, wisps of steam began to rise from each of the autarii's tattoos, glittering like melting frost and swirling in thin tendrils about the Shade's agony-wracked form. The wisps of sorcerous power flowed towards the shadowy figure, as though drawn in by a hungry inhalation; the surface of the figure's body shifted, and Malus saw scores of horrific faces take shape along the being's limbs and torso. The obscene visages drank in the Shade's magical bindings, until the mist began to turn a pale shade of pink, then bright crimson. The autarii's body began to shrivel, his muscles softening like wax and his skin growing ashen. His screams bubbled and his eyes burst, and his tongue split apart. Within moments it was over. Another smoking, shrivelled husk clattered to the floor beside its fellows, and the beastmen's horrid chanting devolved into a chorus of joyous, barking cries.

The beckoning figure was swathed in crimson mist, swirling and mingling with the shifting currents of darkness until it smoothed into a patina of dusky skin that Malus knew all too well. The body shifted slightly, taking on beguiling curves and long, black hair. Between one heartbeat and the next the monster took the shape of his half-sister, naked and perfect.

Nagaira did not have the hollow eyes Malus saw in his dreams. They were dark orbs of jet, just like his. Her thin lips curved into a cruel smile. When she spoke, however, her voice was the same whispering chorus from his worst nightmares.

'The autarii are a bestial breed, but they understand the nature of spirits and how to bind them,' she said. 'Their souls are strong and sweet, like wine. Even that highborn fool who led them held enough power to make him savoury.' Her catlike smile widened. 'They were a fine gift, brother. I have saved them until last.' She beckoned to him with a taloned finger. 'Now you're here, and the final moves of the game are at hand.'

Within the confines of his mind, Malus snarled like a trapped wolf, but his body moved to the daemon's bidding. He and Lhunara stepped within the circle, and the beastmen bowed deeply, pressing their horned heads to the floor. Tz'arkan made no attempt to step over the piled bodies of the Black Tower's scouts. Bones snapped like twigs and grey skin turned to ash beneath Malus's boots.

The very air constricted about Malus like a fist. The air he breathed was hot and curdled, searing his lungs. When Nagaira moved towards him, the awful pressure only increased. Her vortex of power didn't emanate from her sorcerous circle, but from Nagaira herself; it seeped like acid from her skin, etching itself onto the fabric of reality around her. To the highborn's surprise, even Tz'arkan subsided as she approached, and Malus thought of the scores of unnatural voices intermingled with her own. How many pacts had she sealed with the Ruinous Powers for the strength she now possessed, and how could he hope to overcome it?

Nagaira stepped close, her eyes glittering like a serpent's. 'Have you no kiss for me, dear brother?' she said in her unearthly voice. She leaned in to him, her power rippling through his armour and sending waves of pain through his flesh. Her lips pressed lightly against the side of his neck and his heart skipped a beat at the touch. When she stepped away her lips glistened with black ichor.

Malus's jaw worked, but it was the daemon who spoke. 'Have a care, witch,' Tz'arkan said. 'This is my body now, not your brother's! I have invested too much in it for the likes of your caresses.'

Nagaira inclined her head. 'I forgot myself, oh Drinker of Worlds. It has been some time since my brother and I were together. There is much I wish to share with him.' She turned to Lhunara. 'Where are the relics?' she snapped, as though speaking to a slave.

The demand caught Lhunara unawares. She was staring intently at Malus, as though she were mapping the course of each black vein woven beneath his sickly skin. Her ruined face turned to Nagaira, blinking away her reverie. '*Relics?*' she said, a momentary frown of consternation twisting her festering brow. '*Relics? There were no relics, witch. Only him.*'

Nagaira struck the revenant with the back of her hand, swifter than a serpent. The blow echoed through the unearthly space, hard enough to break the neck of a living druchii. The witch snarled, 'Fool! Without the relics we cannot proceed! Have the maggots eaten so much of your brain that you cannot understand this?' She pointed to Malus. 'Until the great Tz'arkan has been freed, Malus is *his*. Do you understand? We must find these relics, or you will never have the vengeance you seek.'

Lhunara rocked back on her heels from the force of the blow. Her one eye was bright with fury. '*I searched his quarters and found nothing,*' she hissed.

For a moment, Malus dared to hope. Here was an opening he might exploit. But then his lips moved, and the daemon answered them. 'He keeps the four relics on the back of his cold one,' Tz'arkan said. 'He sent his retainers to fetch it from the nauglir pits near the citadel, but they never returned.'

Lhunara's cold fists clenched at the sound of the daemon's voice. '*Then we shall find these trinkets among the dead once we've completed the destruction of the Black Tower,*' she said contemptuously.

'Prepare yourself, then,' Nagaira replied coldly. 'The Witch King is stirring in his tower, and the true battle for the city will soon begin. Do not fail again, revenant. The eyes of the Dark Gods are upon you.'

If Nagaira meant to unnerve the revenant with her threats, they came to nothing. Lhunara bowed curtly, and with a possessive glance towards Malus, she turned on her heel and strode swiftly from the chamber.

Nagaira watched her go with narrowed eyes. 'You made a grave mistake when you betrayed that one,' she said to Malus. 'She is as fierce and as implacable as a winter gale. Who knows how long she lay in the shadow of Tz'arkan's temple with that terrible wound in her head? Yet she refused to die. She lay there and prayed to the darkness with every last shred of her will, until the Gods Who Wait finally answered as she drew her last breath. They would have given her anything she asked, but she wanted one thing, and one thing only. Not wealth, nor power, nor even a whole skin. No, she wanted nothing more than pure, bloody-minded revenge.' Nagaira smiled in grudging admiration. 'By the time I found her she had already raised a sizeable army from the beastmen and the human dregs that surrounded the mountain. Once I realised how much she wanted you, it was easy enough to forge an alliance and place the Amulet of Vaurog around her neck.' She laughed coldly. 'I think the fool must have loved you, brother. Is that not rich? What else could have birthed such terrible hate?' The witch smiled at her brother. 'Sometimes, when she thinks she is alone, she whispers to herself all the terrible things she dreams of doing to you. So gloriously vicious and single-minded,' Nagaira said with a terrible sigh. 'It makes her easy to control, much like you once were. Who knows? If she serves me well in the battle to come I might even give you to her as a reward. If we triumph here I can afford to be magnanimous.'

'So you intend to betray Isilvar,' Tz'arkan said.

The witch snorted derisively. 'Betray? That implies we had an agreement in the first place,' she said. 'He came crawling to me, looking for a way out of the trap he'd fallen into. I knew from the moment the siege began that he'd try something like this. All I had to do was apply pressure and wait.'

'And the Witch King?'

Nagaira shrugged. 'Malekith grew more predictable as the siege wore on. He would never abandon the Black Tower without a fight, and once we were past the outer wall it made a counterattack inevitable. By now, Morathi's colossal arrogance has led her to believe that I have exhausted my energies during that last attack, so now is the time to strike. Do you imagine I could pass up such an opportunity?'

The daemon chuckled. 'I imagine you have little choice. You have your own masters to serve, witch. Such power does not come without fearsome promises of repayment.'

Nagaira's expression froze. 'There were… agreements… that were made,' she allowed. 'Malekith and his mother will make fine gifts for the Gods Who Wait, and they have never been as vulnerable as they are now. I should think you would be pleased,' she said haughtily. 'An ally upon the Iron Throne would make your plans much easier, I should think.'

'Plans?' the daemon said.

'You are the Scourge,' she said simply. 'The prophecy was written by you in aeons past to pave the way for your rise to power. You mean to use the druchii as the agents of your ambition in this universe.'

'And you?' the daemon asked.

The witch smiled faintly and bowed. 'I live to serve the Prince of Pleasure,' she said in her unearthly voice.

Tz'arkan smiled. 'You amuse me, witch,' it said. 'But there is little time for battle. My time grows very short. Malus will have to ride that nauglir of his to death in order to reach the temple as it is.'

'Ride? Great Tz'arkan, once I've offered the Witch King and Morathi to the Dark Gods and seized the Iron Throne, we will fly to your temple on dragon wings,' she said. 'There is time enough for the vengeance I seek.' She cocked her head, as though listening to some faint sound. 'I must take my leave of you, dread lord. Already the winds of magic are stirring. Morathi and her pitiful novices are readying themselves for the attack.' She made to leave, then paused, looking thoughtfully at Malus. The witch stared intently into his eyes, as though trying to find the highborn amid the darkness that was the daemon. 'Are you so attached to this body?' she asked, touching Malus's breastplate with a curved talon. 'Once you are freed you may take any form you like.'

'That is so,' the daemon allowed, 'but the prophecy has attached itself to his name. I must continue to be Malus for a time, once I have been set free.' Inwardly, Malus could feel the daemon's amusement. 'Of course, if you could ensure that the real Darkblade were to vanish from sight...'

Nagaira laughed. 'Be assured, dread lord. That would be no trouble whatsoever.'

'Then we will speak of this again at the temple in the north,' Tz'arkan replied. 'Go and claim your vengeance, witch. I will wait here until you return, and savour your brother's despair.'

Nagaira bowed again, and stepped from the circle. As one, the beastmen rose and followed her into the darkness.

Outside, a warhorn wailed. Malus sensed movement about the Chaos encampment, as the last reserves of the horde were called to battle. Did Nagaira truly have the power to trap and destroy the Witch King himself? After what he'd seen, the highborn thought it possible.

Still as a statue, the highborn was left to wonder as the kingdom of the druchii teetered on the edge of ruin. Despair threatened to overwhelm him.

Curled like a serpent in the darkness, Tz'arkan drank deep from the well of Malus's pain.

MALUS SOON LOST all track of time. Few sounds penetrated the chambers of Nagaira's tent, and once she was gone there was no relief from the darkness. He might have lingered for mere minutes, or hours, or even days. Each moment was more agonising than the next, as Nagaira's stratagem inched towards completion.

He didn't notice the sounds at first. They slowly impinged on his awareness as a kind of faint scratching, like rats scampering in the walls.

Malus focused his attentions on the noise. It came and went, but always from the same general direction, off to the highborn's left.

After a time, the scratching became faint, raspy sawing. Then he heard a harsh whisper.

'How many damned compartments can one tent have?'

'Shut up and keep sawing,' hissed a familiar voice. 'We've got to be close to the centre now,' Hauclir said

'You said that the last two times,' the first voice shot back. Malus thought it sounded like Pockets.

Within Malus, the daemon stirred. He felt Tz'arkan's cold, cruel smile. 'The Dark Gods are generous,' the daemon murmured. 'We shall have pleasant diversions to occupy us while we await your sister's return.'

Tz'arkan turned Malus about and stalked across the inner chamber. His hands reached out and found the canvas wall. Moments later something sharp poked the fabric from the other side.

Malus's lips worked. 'Hauclir?' the daemon whispered, using the highborn's voice.

'My lord?' the former retainer responded. 'It's good to hear your voice! Are you bound, or injured?'

'No, I'm well,' the daemon replied. 'But Nagaira's sealed this chamber with some spell. I can't get out.'

'We'll see to that, my lord,' Hauclir answered. The object poked hard against the canvas. After a moment the needle tip of a dagger poked through.

'Gods Below,' Pockets hissed. 'This is like cutting through stone.'

'Keep at it,' Hauclir ordered. As Pockets continued to work her knife through the ensorcelled fabric, the former retainer whispered to Malus. 'We'll have you out in just a moment, my lord.'

The daemon smiled. 'What about the relics?'

'We have them as well,' Hauclir replied. 'Spite is close by.'

'That's excellent news,' Tz'arkan said. Malus could only watch in horror as his hand slid down to the dagger at his belt. Slowly, quietly, the daemon drew the weapon free.

Pockets drove her knife through the canvas wall and began sawing downward. After a few moments she'd cut a slit large enough for a man to wriggle through. The daemon raised Malus's dagger. 'Come inside,' he said. 'There are statues of gold and silver in here. It's time you got your reward.'

Malus raged helplessly within the confines of his own body, trying to regain control of his own limbs, but the daemon's grip was stronger than iron. He could see the slaughter that was about to unfold the moment Hauclir poked his head inside the chamber.

'That's the best news I've heard all day,' the former retainer answered. 'Give me your hand.'

'Of course,' the daemon replied, shifting the knife to Malus's left hand and extending the right one through the torn fragment. He reached for Hauclir blindly, groping about with Malus's armoured fingers.

Then all at once his hand found something and closed around it. Malus felt the smooth hilt of a sword – and a torrential rush of heat that poured through his hand and set his veins afire.

The daemon let out a furious shout as the Warpsword of Khaine took Malus in its burning grip. Tz'arkan tried to let go of the blade, but the highborn's fingers would no longer obey. Hungry fire seared Malus from head to foot, and he cried out in agony and triumph as the daemon's hold was broken.

After a moment Malus realised that Hauclir was hissing urgently at him. He forced himself to take a deep breath and answer. 'What is it?'

'I said, could you possibly scream a little louder? I'm pretty sure there are a few scattered tribes on the other side of the Chaos Wastes that didn't hear you.'

Malus laughed quietly, flexing his fingers around the hilt of the blade. 'Step away, you damned rogue,' he said, and sliced carefully at the tent wall. The canvas peeled back with a hiss of burnt fabric.

Hauclir, Pockets and Cutter rushed into the chamber, holding small witchlamps in their hands. The former retainer looked about the space and frowned. 'I don't see any gold or silver,' he said.

'No,' Malus replied breathlessly, holding the sword aloft. 'That was an utter lie.'

'I should have known,' Hauclir said with a sigh.

The highborn looked at the cutthroats in wonder. 'What in the Dark Mother's name are you doing here?'

Hauclir shrugged. 'Blame it on your cold one, my lord,' he said. 'It took us forever to fight our way to the nauglir pens. There were packs of those damned revenants lurking in every doorway, it seemed. Once we finally got there and let Spite loose, the damned thing sniffed at the air and just went loping off. We couldn't stop it, so we decided to follow the beast and see where it was going,' he said. 'It led us out through the south gate, then outside the city itself. We thought for sure someone would challenge us, but the camp is deserted. Nagaira's called all her troops into the city. At any rate, after a bit we worked out that the nauglir was hunting for something, and we figured it might be you.'

Malus nodded. 'But this?' he asked, showing Hauclir the sword.

'Oh. That was easy,' he replied. 'It was obvious you were trying to get it from Spite back in the nauglir pits, and the daemon managed to stop you. I figured that if you were to be found out here then the daemon must have had a hand in it, so I thought that bringing the sword along was a wise move. Was I right?'

'You have no idea,' Malus answered. 'In fact, you may have saved Naggaroth.' He quickly told the cutthroats about Nagaira's plans. 'She believes she has the power to bring down Malekith and Morathi both,' he said at last.

The cutthroats looked to one another fearfully. 'Can she?' Hauclir asked.

'After all I've seen… yes. I think she can.'

'Then I think we need to get your mount and run for our lives,' Hauclir replied.

But Malus shook his head. 'No. Malekith may be vulnerable, but so is Nagaira. She might have enough strength to master the Witch King and Morathi, but not all three of us at once,' he said. 'And she has to be destroyed.'

'For the sake of the kingdom?'

'Don't be stupid,' Malus snapped. 'For my sake. The witch knows too much.'

'Ah, of course. Your pardon, my lord,' Hauclir said dryly. 'Well, then. What would you have of us?'

Malus's hand tightened on the burning blade. He could feel its hunger now, seething like coals in his gut. 'Follow me,' he said to the cutthroats. 'And when the killing starts, stay out of my way.'

THEY WERE JUST emerging from the Chaos encampment when the Witch King launched his attack.

War horns screamed from the tall tower, and Malus watched as a dark form raised its serpentine neck atop the citadel and roared a challenge at the sky. With a powerful sweep of leathery wings, Malekith's dragon Seraphon launched into the dark sky. At the same moment, green lightnings smote the darkness, rending it and driving it back. In the searing flashes of light, the highborn spied an armoured figure on the dragon's back, brandishing a glowing sword at the Chaos horde.

The sword swept down and Seraphon dove with a thunderous roar, filling the inner compound with a hissing stream of

dragon flame. Shouts and screams rose from the dying warriors, and the final battle was joined.

Malus, Hauclir and the cutthroats came to a halt a quarter
mile from the open city gates. Spite paced alongside the small
band, sniffing the air warily. The former retainer turned to the
highborn. 'We're going in there?' he said, pointing to the city.
Pillars of fire and smoke were already wreathing the Black
Tower, and the clash of swords and armour could be heard
from where they stood.

'Only so far as the square outside the inner gate,' Malus
replied. 'That's where we'll find Nagaira, I expect.'

'And how do you plan on stopping her?'

'Don't worry,' Malus said. 'I have a plan.'

'Do I want to know what the plan is?' Hauclir asked.

The highborn shook his head.

'You're probably right,' Hauclir agreed. 'Lead on.'

With Malus in the lead, the small band raced through the
ruins of the outer city. Forks of green lightning lashed down
from the boiling skies, plunging like knives again and again
onto the square outside the inner gate. Seraphon continued to
swoop low over the inner compound, scouring the area with
ravening bursts of fire as the outnumbered druchii army
fought their way from the citadel. Somewhere ahead, in the
thick of the fight, Lhunara would be wreaking bloody havoc
on the Witch King's troops.

Malus expected that the Chaos horde would fall back, drawing the druchii host out past the inner gate and up to the great
square. That's when Malekith would take the battle directly to
Nagaira, and she would spring her trap.

They got to within less than a hundred yards of the square
before their path was blocked by a herd of waiting beastmen.
For the moment their attention was focused solely on the sorcerous battle being waged nearby.

Malus led the group into the shadow of a burnt-out barracks.
'Here is where we part ways,' he said. 'I must face Nagaira
alone.'

'What do you want us to do?' Hauclir said.

The highborn looked his former retainer in the eye and drew a deep breath. 'I want you to circle around the square and wait,' he replied. 'When I attack Nagaira it's only a matter of time before Lhunara comes running. You will have to hold her off long enough for me to deal with my sister.'

'Blessed Murderer,' Cutter said. 'She nearly killed me the last time.'

'And me as well,' Hauclir replied.

Malus nodded. 'How is your leg?' he asked.

'Fine, oddly enough,' the former retainer said. He reached down and pulled his stained bandages aside. Only a dull, black scar showed where Lhunara's blade pierced his leg. 'I can't explain it.'

Malus noted the ichor stains darkening the bandages. It was the daemon's energies, he thought. I bled onto your bandages, and it seeped into the wound. He set his jaw. 'That's fortunate,' he said. 'Because you'll need all the luck you can get. Just hold her off long enough for me to deal with Nagaira. That's all I ask.'

The cutthroats looked to one another. Hauclir shrugged. 'We've come this far,' he said. 'We'll see this through.'

Malus nodded, clapping Hauclir on the shoulder. 'Go, then. I'll see you all shortly,' he said, hoping that it would be true.

The cutthroats moved off to the east. Malus laid a hand on Spite's snout. 'Stand,' he said, rubbing the nauglir's scales appreciatively. 'Wait until I call, beast of the deep earth. You've done enough for me already.'

Then, sword in hand, he stepped into the street and started to run.

The herd of Chaos warriors filling the street outside the square was unaware of the danger bearing down on them until it was far too late. Distracted by the pillars of lightning and deafened by the thunderous explosions, they did not notice the dark blur racing down the debris-strewn avenue until he was upon them. Half a dozen beastmen fell dead, glowing wounds smoking in their chests, before the enemy could even react.

Malus tore into the enemy with a savage howl, the warpsword carving through the tight-packed ranks like a scythe. Weapons snapped and armour melted at the blade's touch; arms and legs tumbled across the cobblestones and heads were shorn away. The highborn grew stronger with every blow, and the movements of his enemies seemed to slow, until they appeared to be standing still. He slipped past their feeble blows and slaughtered them by the score, until finally the enemy could take no more and melted away in every direction. Those who tried to run through the square itself were cut apart by the angry slashes of lightning that raged within.

Covered in steaming gore, Malus staggered drunkenly to the edge of the open space. In the centre of the square shone a hemisphere of green light more than sixty paces across. Lightning flared and rebounded from this sorcerous shield, maintained by Nagaira's shamans, who sat in their customary circle and chanted arcane phrases skyward. Within the circle, Nagaira floated a few feet off the ground. Once again she was no more that the black shadow-shape that he'd seen in the tent, surrounded by curling tendrils of black smoke that wove about her like a net of serpents.

Beyond, Malus could see fighting atop the inner wall. Malekith's counterattack had pushed the besiegers almost to the inner gate itself. Very soon the Witch King would reach the square and fall into Nagaira's clutches. Malus was running out of time.

Brandishing the burning blade, Malus charged at the shamans' glowing sphere. Lightning seemed to drip lazily from the air, splashing against the ward and playing about the square. He struck the glowing ward with the warpsword, and a web of red cracks spread across its surface. Instantly the beast-men were aware of him, shouting magical chants and pointing fetishes of bone at the damage to the sphere. The cracks faded as he drew back his blade, but he struck the surface again and again. Slowly but surely, the damage spread.

More lightning arced down, as though Morathi sensed the change in the nature of the ward and had redoubled her efforts. The green glow began to dim as its energies were strained to the utmost. Across the square, Malus saw huge figures approaching the ward at a dead run – they were Nagaira's minotaur bodyguard. Undaunted, the highborn continued his punishing assault.

Within the hemisphere, Nagaira slowly turned to face him. Her night-haunted face was devoid of expression, but he could feel the cold pressure of her furious stare.

Another barrage of lightning bolts hammered at the ward. Malus timed his strokes with the thunderclaps, adding to Morathi's assault. Then, without warning, the shield collapsed, shattering like glass beneath a hammer blow. There was a flare of light, and several of the beastmen collapsed, blood streaming from their ears. Several more were immolated in bolts of green lightning, leaving charred husks sprawled across the paving stones. A bolt of lightning even struck Nagaira herself, momentarily staggering her.

With the shield broken, the minotaurs charged across the intervening space at Malus, axes held ready. The highborn rushed at them with a ferocious cry, and the burning blade sang through the air. One of the huge warriors swung wide and was cut in half as the highborn raced past. Another lunged at the highborn with a sweeping cut and had both hands sliced away.

An axe crashed into Malus's pauldron; the highborn spun and drove his sword through the minotaur's abdomen, boiling its guts. Another axe struck him full in the breastplate. Laughing, Malus tore his sword free and cut the legs out from under the enemy champion.

Lightning raged among the howling minotaurs, blasting warriors to the ground. A bolt struck Malus and flung him skyward, dropping him in a heap several yards away. Still smoking, he lunged back onto his feet and returned to the fray. Only three of the huge champions were left, stunned and shaken by the blast. Malus cut them down.

Then a strange buzzing filled the air, like a swarm of angry hornets, and Nagaira struck him with a bolt of pure darkness.

It passed through his armour as though it wasn't there, and he felt his organs melt at its touch. A spear of pure agony lanced through Malus's chest, and he spat sizzling ichor onto the stones. His sister loomed above him almost a dozen yards away, wreathed in tendrils of darkness. Pure rage emanated from her in palpable waves.

'You disappoint me,' Nagaira thundered. A bolt of lightning lashed at her, but his sister paid it little heed. 'I had thought you were wiser than this.' Suddenly she lunged at him, crossing the space between them in an eye blink. Her fist crashed into Malus and flung him across the square like a toy. He crashed into the wall of a warehouse fifteen yards away, striking the stone hard enough to crack it before rebounding back onto the pavement.

'A wise man would have waited in the darkness for his doom to find him,' Nagaira said. 'But you? You seek it out.'

She swept down on him again. This time Malus brought the warpsword up in a hissing arc and sliced through the witch's midsection. Nagaira staggered with a scream of countless tortured souls, but she recovered almost immediately. Her fist closed about his throat and she flung him headlong through the air.

This time he crashed against the burnt hulk of one of the Chaos catapults. Oaken timbers shattered under the impact, and he landed hard at the siege engine's base.

Nagaira stalked after him. Lightning lashed at her smoky figure again and again, slowing her flight. Still she pressed on, undeterred.

'I could swat you down like a fly, dear brother,' she seethed. 'By all the gods I should! But Tz'arkan must be freed, and so I must content myself with merely crippling you.' She swept down and slapped the highborn's chest with the flat of her hand, cracking his ribs like eggshells.

Malus screamed in agony and buried his sword in Nagaira's chest. The blade burst from the witch's back, drawing a scream of rage. Black ichor smoked from the tip of the blade. She drew back her hand to strike him again – and another bolt of sorcerous lightning struck her, blowing the two druchii apart.

Malus landed hard on his back, biting back a wave of intense pain. Nagaira landed in a heap some yards away. Her body had a grey cast now, and the tendrils of smoke that enshrouded her were all but gone. With a furious oath, she spoke an incantation that rent the air around her and her form regained a portion of its power.

Then a shadow swept over her from above. Nagaira looked up just as Seraphon bathed her in a pillar of dragon fire.

Malus could see her black form wreathed in angry fire. She screamed, spreading her arms wide within the flame, and magical power pulsed from her body. The dragon banked away, but Nagaira's ruined form turned to track it. She pointed a smoking finger at the sky, and a chorus of daemonic howls filled the air. Tendrils of smoke leapt like whipcords from her body, reaching for the armoured form riding atop the swooping dragon.

Summoning his rage, Malus staggered to his feet and charged across the square. At the last moment she saw him, and with a word sent another bolt of black fire through him. He staggered, feeling his guts turn to mush, but the blade sustained him, driving him on. Malus raised the burning blade and chopped it deep into Nagaira's chest.

She howled and writhed around the blade, her unearthly form hissing and sizzling under the weapon's touch. Still she drove the tendrils skyward, reaching for the Witch King. 'You cannot slay me!' she cried. 'The Dark Gods themselves fill me with their power!'

Malus spat a mouthful of ichor into his sister's face. 'And they do not countenance failure,' he said, twisting the blade in her body.

Nagaira screamed again – and the smoking tendrils faltered, just short of their goal. Her body turned grey, once more. Gibbering with rage, she hissed a litany of curses, calling upon the gods for more power. But she had already drawn far too much, and the patience of the fickle Chaos gods was at an end.

Like snakes, the tendrils turned, seeking easier prey. They plunged like arrows, burying themselves in Nagaira's skull.

Malus hurled himself clear of his sister, drawing the burning blade after him. As he watched, daemonic faces took shape all over her body, the mouths working hungrily as they devoured his sister from within. Still screaming, she shrank in the air before him.

The last things to go were her eyes. Nagaira glared at Malus with a look of purest hate. Then she was gone in a clap of terrible thunder.

'Enjoy the favour of the gods, dear sister,' Malus said darkly. And then, like a black wind, Lhunara was upon him.

He never heard her approach. Only the warpsword saved him; it seemed to turn in his hand, reaching skyward just as her bloodstained blades came slicing for his throat. His body moved without conscious thought, striking the twin swords aside in a shower of sparks.

There was no time for fear, or curses, or clever stratagems. She fell upon him like a storm, and it was all Malus could do just to survive.

Her glowing eye gleamed balefully from the depths of her helmet as she drove Malus across the square. The warpsword was a blur, meeting her every stroke with a ringing block that just barely kept death at bay. Already ichor was seeping from a score of shallow cuts on his face and neck.

After several long moments, Malus regained his wits in the face of Lhunara's maddened assault. She said not a word, slashing and thrusting at him with an urgency born of desperation and madness. Where Nagaira emanated rage and power, his former retainer was driven by nothing more than bitter pain and despair. Now he sensed that she knew her chance for vengeance was slipping away.

Her urgency made her sloppy. Lhunara swung for Malus's neck and he ducked beneath the blow, slicing the warpsword through her midsection. The blade parted her armour like paper, the edges turning molten from the sword's heat. Ichor poured from the wound and she groaned... but still she fought on.

The sight stunned Malus. I can't kill her, he thought. Not even the warpsword could slay her!

Lhunara leapt at the highborn and he planted his feet, blocking her twin swords and stopping her rush until she stood nearly nose-to-nose with him. He smelt her foul breath and saw burn scars etched in pale lines along her throat. Within the depths of her helmet Malus could see the deformed cheekbone that had broken beneath Nagaira's blow.

Suddenly he understood. No blade could kill the bearer of the Amulet of Vaurog.

He knew what he had to do. Gritting his teeth, he let go of the burning blade.

At once, Tz'arkan's power tore through his body, filling him with strength and wracking his body with pain. Roaring in agony, he clapped his hands against the side of Lhunara's helmet and squeezed. Face to face, he heard her scream as the steel deformed and bent inwards. She tried to pull away, but there was no room to land a blow, and the daemon's strength was irresistible. He felt Tz'arkan's power growing and wondered how long he had before the daemon regained control of him once more.

Lhunara moaned. Her body spasmed, and bone cracked. Black ichor sprayed across his face.

She drew a wracking breath. 'I… loved you,' she hissed. The words came out like a curse.

'I know,' Malus said, and crushed the helmet flat.

Lhunara's headless body collapsed to the ground. Lightning flickered on the red-gold surface of the Amulet of Vaurog as it rolled free of her body.

Stooping quickly, Malus snatched up the warpsword. For a moment he feared that the daemon would resist him; his fingers trembled, but with an effort of will he seized the hilt and felt the sword's fire hold the raging daemon at bay. Then he grasped the amulet and placed the torc around his neck.

Malus turned his face to the sky, seeking the Witch King. Seraphon was swooping low over the battlements of the inner wall, plucking beastmen from the parapet and flinging them to their deaths. More were racing down siege ladders, seeking to escape the death trap within the inner compound. Already, fleeing figures were running headlong through the darkness to either side of the square. The siege had been broken at last.

Malus wanted to roar his triumph to the heavens, but then he caught sight of a lone figure limping onto the square. The warpsword twitched in his fingers, but then he recognised who it was. Cursing under his breath, he loped across the corpse-choked space just as Hauclir collapsed onto the stones.

His short sword and trusty cudgel were gone, and his mail was soaked in blood. Lhunara had stabbed Hauclir through the chest not once, but twice. His skin was pale, and his breath was coming in shallow gasps. He blinked dully as Malus stood above him. 'I… I think we failed, my lord,' he said.

'No,' Malus replied bitterly. 'You did well, you damned rogue.'

'We held her as long as we could,' Hauclir said. 'Damn, but she was fast. She got Cutter first, then Ten-thumbs. Then she got me. I don't know what happened to Pockets. When I came to, she and that bitch were gone.'

'I'm sure she got away,' Malus said, not believing a word. 'Just rest easy. The troops will be here any minute, and we'll get you to the healers.'

Hauclir looked up at Malus. 'That's about the worst lie you've ever told,' he said. 'You're going to leave me. I can see it in your eyes.'

Malus bit back his anger. 'I have to go, Hauclir,' he said softly. 'I'm out of time.'

Suddenly Hauclir's face turned solemn. 'I know,' he said. 'So am I.' Then he turned his face away, and closed his eyes.

Malus looked down at his former retainer for a long moment, then slowly turned away. Bitterness burned like a coal in his gut. There was nothing he could do. The dire warning of the daemon still rang in his mind. *He'll have to ride that mount of his to death to make it to the temple in time.* It might already be too late to reclaim his soul, he realised.

And now I'm throwing away the last of my honour as well, he thought.

A dozen paces away he ground to a halt. Slowly he returned the warpsword to its scabbard. As its heat ebbed, he felt the daemon's strength slowly return.

'Damn me to hell,' Malus muttered, then turned and ran back to Hauclir. Gritting his teeth, he knelt by his former retainer's side and unbuckled his sword belt. Quickly he set the sword aside, and the power of the daemon surged.

Malus looked down at his ichor-stained palms and pressed them to Hauclir's wounds. 'Get up, damn you,' the highborn growled. 'Did you hear me, you damned rogue? Get up! You've vexed me for most of a year, and I'll be damned if you're going to die on me now!' Dread filled the highborn, but he focused his will and summoned Tz'arkan's power, trying to force it into Hauclir's wounds.

Hauclir gave a convulsive heave and began to cough. Malus recoiled from the druchii's body, seeing the wounds scabbing over with a dull, black crust.

Malus managed a nervous smile. 'There's your reward. You can thank me later,' he said, and lunged for the safety of the warpsword.

He fell just six inches short. In mid-leap the daemon gripped him in an invisible fist, halting his flight. He landed hard, his fingers outstretched, but salvation was just out of reach.

Agony coursed through him as Tz'arkan swelled into his brain. The pain went on and on, cutting into the depths of his heart and mind.

'Pray your precious honour gives you succour on the long ride to come,' the daemon hissed triumphantly. And the world dissolved in a haze of madness and pain.

Chapter Twenty-Five
THE END OF TIME

The Chaos Wastes, first week of winter

THE DUST OF ancient warlords slipped from Malus Darkblade's hands, laying out the last segments of the arcane circle that surrounded the daemon's massive crystal prison. Nearly an hour had passed since he'd begun; his skull throbbed with the daemon's blasphemous knowledge and his limbs ached with strain. He'd measured his steps with exacting care, shaping the sorcerous symbols as precisely as he could. Now the great urn was empty, and the complicated ward nearly complete.

As the powdered bone ran through his fingers he felt the final moments of his life slipping away along with it. It slid from his grasp on a tide of inevitability, driven by the daemon's implacable will. As the sorcerous circle took shape around him, Malus glimpsed the vast skein of intrigues and bloody deeds wrought by the daemon down through the millennia, all leading up to these final moments. Empires had come and gone, sorcerers and kings risen to glory and trampled into the dirt and thousands, perhaps *millions* of lives destroyed, all so that he would find himself in this chamber, at this hour, pouring the bones of conquerors upon the stone floor.

He saw what the future held. Tz'arkan had shown him hints of the world to come in the fires of Hag Graef, in the blood-soaked streets of Har Ganeth and the horrific siege of the Black Tower. An age of darkness and ruin was at hand. The daemon would walk among the druchii in the guise of the Scourge and reshape them into a weapon that would drown the world in blood.

Malus looked down at the last threads of fine powder trickling from his hand. We are all nothing but dust in the eyes of the gods, he thought, surprised to feel no sense of rage at the realisation. All the heat had gone out of him. His heart was cold and heavy as stone.

Time had run out. All of his schemes had, in the end, come to naught. Tz'arkan had millennia to lay his webs, testing their strands and pulling them taut. Now there was nothing left for him but to take the last few steps left to him.

It was time for Tz'arkan to rise from his ancient prison, and time for Malus Darkblade to die.

The last of the dust trickled through his fingers, landing in precisely the right spot to close the vast and intricate circle. The highborn felt a tremor in the air, as though the final piece of a terrible, cosmic puzzle had finally slipped into place.

'That's it,' the daemon hissed. It pressed against Malus's bones like a beast pushing at the bars of its cell. 'Now the tablet. Read the incantation inscribed upon it. Hurry!'

Stepping carefully, Malus stepped outside the circle and took his place at the foot of the mighty ward. The temple servants rose as one and moved to the five relics waiting nearby. Their ancient bodies creaking and crackling under the strain, the revenants picked up the artefacts and arranged them around the circle, then knelt beside them. The last artefact laid in place was the warpsword itself. The ancient servant placed the long blade nearly at Malus's feet.

The next thing he knew, the servant with the stone tablet was kneeling beside him, hands raised in supplication. As though in a dream, Malus reached out and plucked the tablet from the revenant's hands. He turned to the nearby pedestal and rested the tablet upon its surface. Writing older than Naggaroth, perhaps older than the very world itself, burned their angular lines into his brain. The blasphemous incantation meant nothing to the highborn, but their strange consonants came easily to his lips, thanks to the daemon's brutal tutelage.

The words burned his lips and scarred his throat, but the more he spoke, the faster they burst free. Crackling energies filled the vast treasure vault. A hot wind swirled about the gleaming crystal, pulling at Malus's hair and plucking at the servants' ancient clothes. Agony tore through Malus's chest, but the highborn had no breath to spare for tortured screams. Instead, he spoke the words before him, unravelling the ancient bindings laid upon Tz'arkan thousands of years past.

The wind grew, howling like a tormented ghost in the echoing space. He could feel the nest of snakes uncoil themselves from around his heart and begin forcing their way up his throat. Smoke seeped from Malus's mouth and nose, drawn into the cyclone like oil poured upon the surface of a turbulent sea. It spread like a black stain in the air, hovering before the crystal as the incantation reached its inevitable climax.

As the last lines of the ritual were spoken, the wind grew to a thunderous cyclone. The foul wind buffeted the undead servants, ripping at their rotten clothes and flaying their desiccated skin as it forced them to their knees. The inky smoke writhed and pulsed, lit from within by arcs of pellucid flame as it contracted into an amorphous mass before the highborn's eyes.

Then the last word burst from Malus's throat with a spray of black ichor, and it felt as though his body was being torn apart. The stone tablet shattered into razor-sharp fragments as the daemon broke its bonds at last.

With a rushing sound like an indrawn breath, the cloud of Abyssal smoke contracted further, assuming a terrible, towering form that loomed over Malus's hunched body. The daemon's body was shaped like a druchii's, only broader and far more muscular; it was beautiful, so far beyond the apex of perfection that it was maddening to look upon. Only its broad, malformed head and burning eyes betrayed its birth in the storms of Chaos. Taloned hands reached skyward, and Tz'arkan opened long, misshapen jaws and roared like a newborn god.

'FREE!' The daemon thundered. Not from the stone, but from Malus himself. The realisation did not surprise him. Indeed, a part of him had suspected it all along.

The icy touch of the daemon's power disappeared from the highborn's body in an instant, leaving behind nothing but terrible pain. Malus doubled over in agony, knocking the slim pedestal onto its side.

He knew what had to happen next, and a strange calm settled over him. 'I've done what you asked,' the highborn croaked. 'Now you must fulfil your bargain, daemon. Give me back my soul.'

Tz'arkan, Drinker of Worlds, looked down upon the highborn's pitiful form and showed triple rows of needle-like fangs. 'You shall have all you deserve,' the daemon said with a hateful laugh. 'But first, I must *feed*!'

Too fast for the eye to follow the daemon lunged forward, pressing its massive palm against Malus's breastplate. Deep inside his chest, Malus felt something give way, like a thread breaking, and he felt his heart stop at last. Pain ebbed like a swift tide, leaving only a cold emptiness in its wake.

The daemon drew back, pulling a stream of dark substance through the surface of the highborn's ensorcelled armour. Malus watched Tz'arkan pull his soul from his body and draw it to its gaping mouth. Dying, he sank slowly towards the floor.

Dying, but not yet entirely dead. The ancient sorceries of the temple wards slowed the passage of time in the great chamber. In this one place, a druchii's last breath could take a thousand years to escape.

Lost in its triumph, Tz'arkan began to feed upon the highborn's withered soul. The Drinker of Worlds failed to see Malus's hand reaching for the dark hilt of the warpsword just a few feet away.

His fingers touched the hilt of the burning blade, and felt its warmth kindle the embers of hate in Malus's dead heart. His stained lips pulled back in a bestial snarl.

With hate, all things are possible, he thought, in death as in life. The Warpsword of Khaine seemed to leap into his hands of its own accord, and he swung it in a hissing arc at Tz'arkan's towering frame.

The warpsword tore across the daemon's midsection, igniting its sorcerous shape. A howl of pain and fury tore through the treasure vault, buffeting Malus like a storm wind. It was answered by thin shrieks and wails of terror as Tz'arkan's undead servants cowered before their master's rage.

It was a gamble, perhaps the greatest wager he'd ever made. His calculations pitted the will of Khaine against the hunger of the daemon. The black blade and the sigil in the treasure vault had given him the idea; would the warpsword surrender his soul to Tz'arkan so easily? He believed it wouldn't, not if there was even the slightest hope that he could triumph against the daemon before him.

And if he was wrong, so be it, he thought, drawing back the smoking blade for another blow. He wasn't going into the Outer Darkness without putting up a fight.

The highborn's body felt light and swift as he lunged for the daemon, riding a wave of battle-hunger bequeathed by Khaine's fearsome blade. But before he could strike Malus saw the daemon's blazing eyes fix upon him, and Tz'arkan's thunderous voice spoke words of power that seared the air between them. The daemon's taloned fist clenched around Malus's night-dark soul, trapping it in a cage of crooked lightnings – then it thrust its other hand, palm out, right at the highborn's chest.

Malus felt the air between him and the daemon crackle with invisible power, and he hurled himself to the side a split-second before the bolt of power erupted from Tz'arkan's hand. The black bolt parted the air with a sound like tearing cloth and left a congealed mist of blood and bile in its wake. It licked like a dragon's tongue little more than a hair's width past the highborn's arm, and his skin recoiled from its passage, even within the confines of his enchanted armour. The bolt lashed through the wailing crowd of servants, dissolving their rotted forms with its merest touch. Gold coins melted and ran like tallow. Diamonds and rubies darkened and shattered at the energy's entropic touch. The ravening black fire burned across the length of the treasure vault and scored the thick wall with a crackle of splintering stone.

Tz'arkan still burned as well, the edges of the wound across its midsection curling and blackening like parchment as flickering yellow flames guttered and spat within its unnatural, perfect flesh. The daemon cackled insanely, its voice trembling in pitch between amusement and murderous rage as it pivoted to face Malus once more. Black vapour curled from its outstretched hand. It reached for him as though offering a benediction.

The ebon fire leapt out at Malus again. On instinct, he threw himself flat, his armoured form crashing to the polished stone floor, and once again he barely escaped the spell's all-consuming touch. It withered the pedestal where the stone tablet had rested, then scored a deep furrow along the floor as it tracked through still more of the hapless servants. Their thin screams bubbled and hissed as their bodies collapsed into steaming ash.

But the daemon wasn't finished yet. Tz'arkan continued to turn, lashing the arc of sorcerous fire at Malus like a whip. Pillars exploded at its passing touch, showering the vault with pulverised dust and whizzing fragments. Clay urns burst with sharp bangs as their contents boiled in the blink of an eye. Stands of ensorcelled armour crumpled like foil. Then the ravening fire played back across the floor, blackening the gleaming curves of the huge containment wards and then arcing against the squat, iron tripod that held the daemon's crystal prison. The dark metal sagged like hot wax, and the huge, faceted stone tipped and fell ponderously forward. Tz'arkan's entropic lash struck the gleaming crystal, and for a heart-stopping moment the facets sent tendrils of destructive power in all directions, slashing through the huge room like a storm of irresistible knives. A moment later the crystal blackened from within, a canker growing in its core with frightening speed that swelled until it reached the edges of the stone and burst it apart with an earth-shaking explosion. Malus was hurled forward by the blast, his armoured body pummelled by shards of crystal the size of a druchii's fist.

I can't keep this up, he realised. I can't get close to Tz'arkan now, and any moment my luck is going to run out. For half a moment he contemplated bargaining with the daemon – Tz'arkan needed his body to dwell in so it could return to Naggaroth, didn't it? But even as he considered it, he knew that the time for intrigues were long past. He had to think of something else, and fast.

Ears ringing, Malus cast about for somewhere to take cover from the daemon's ebon fire – and then his eyes caught a glint of brass just a few yards away, resting at the edge of the summoning circle. Of course, he thought! Gathering his legs beneath him he scrambled desperately towards the nearby relic, even as the air behind him crackled with building power.

The highborn's questing fingers closed about the brass octagon even as the daemon's sorcerous power leapt at him. Malus spun, raising the Octagon of Praan before him, and the bolt of ebon fire exploded against its surface. Jagged streaks of energy ricocheted from the amulet, deflected by its power and burying themselves like thunderbolts in the ceiling, walls and floor. Malus felt waves of heat radiate from the relic, and to his horror, he saw sizzling teardrops of molten brass running from the surface of the artefact. The daemon's full power was more fearsome than he'd imagined.

It was clear the amulet wouldn't survive another bolt. Malus tossed the damaged relic aside and sought out the next artefact along the rim of the great circle. The highborn's face turned grim. He was only going to get one more chance, and he had to make it count.

Malus lunged across the smoking floor, reaching for the relic. On the other side of the summoning circle, Tz'arkan's laughter faded. The flames licking at the tear in his chest guttered and went out.

'You insignificant little worm,' the daemon hissed. 'I've torn the life out of you, and still you wriggle. Everything you ever were, everything you ever dreamt of, I have taken all away. And yet still you refuse to accept your wretched fate! It is over, Malus Darkblade. You have been a troublesome servant indeed; at times I despaired that we would ever reach this glorious moment. But no matter how hard you fought against me, in the end you still did my bidding, whether you knew it or not.' The daemon uttered a poisonous chuckle. 'Once I have consumed your soul I will take your disgusting shape and return to Naggaroth, and the reign of the Scourge will begin,' the daemon said. Arcs of dark power crackled along its taloned fingers. 'And I could not have done it without you, Darkblade, weak as you were. And now you shall reap your reward.'

Malus closed his hand about the relic. 'Here's a token of my esteem as well,' he growled, rolling onto his back and hurling the Dagger of Torxus left-handed at the daemon.

The dagger was a dark blur, spinning end-for-end across the battered circle and burying itself in Tz'arkan's chest. There was a thunderous crackling of thwarted energies as the power the daemon was about to unleash was disrupted by the force of the relic itself. Fierce arcs of ebon fire lashed at the jutting hilt of the terrible dagger, carving gruesome wounds across the daemon's own unnatural flesh. The Dagger of Torxus began to blacken as well, its pommel and hilt vaporising under the sorcerous chain reaction. 'No!' Tz'arkan roared, clawing desperately at the dagger's hilt. Tz'arkan's body began to unravel under the onslaught, skin dissolving and flesh turning to liquid beneath. The daemon's howl of fury grew wilder by the moment. 'You cannot stop me, wretch! This world is mine, now! Hear the words of Tz'arkan and despair! The time of ruin is come! And in time you will–'

The rest was lost in a rising crescendo of concussive blasts, as the daemon's power and the energies of the Dagger of Torxus tore one another apart. With a final effort, Tz'arkan ripped the smoking weapon from its chest – and then daemon and dagger both vanished in a flare of white light and a clap of deafening thunder.

A GROAN BROUGHT Malus back to his senses. He had somehow risen to his knees, the burning blade still clutched in his right hand. Tendrils of smoke rose from his battered armour, and clouds of pulverised stone and metal hung heavy in the dimly lit vault.

Tz'arkan was gone. Destroyed or banished back to its goddess-forsaken realm, the highborn neither knew nor cared. Malus took a deep breath, heedless of the reek of burnt metal and scorched flesh that thickened the air. He felt light, almost weightless within his armour. He'd never realised how much of a burden the daemon's presence really was.

A soft chuckle escaped his torn lips. I won, he thought. *I won*.

His gaze fell to the gauntlet covering his right hand. Setting the warpsword across his thighs, Malus pulled the armoured glove away to reveal the ruby cabochon ring that had mocked him for so many months. With trembling fingers he gripped the ring and pulled. It slid easily from his finger, tumbling from his grasp and ringing faintly as it bounced along the floor. The highborn smiled in triumph. Another weary chuckle turned to a wild laugh of joy. 'I won!' he cried.

Something tugged at the side of his face. Absently, Malus reached up with his free hand to pluck it free. His cheek was cold to the touch.

Frowning, the highborn's fingers closed around a small, jagged shape buried in his skin. There was a dull twinge of pain as he tugged it free and held it out before him.

It was a piece of crystal the size of a gold piece, its edges sharper than any knife. He hadn't even felt it bite into his skin.

Worse, there was no blood on it. There wasn't even a dark stain of ichor. Malus's throat went dry.

He reached up once again and gingerly pressed against the side of his throat. Try as he might, he could feel no pulsing of blood in his veins. 'Oh, no,' he breathed. 'Oh, you damned, infernal bastard. You took it. You took my thrice-damned soul!'

The highborn's cry of rage was drowned out by another ominous groan. There was a crackle of breaking stone, then a thunderous crash as part of the treasure vault's ceiling collapsed. The heavy slabs of obsidian struck the already weakened floor and broke through, pouring a rain of ruined treasure and tons of debris into the level beneath.

Suddenly the air above Malus echoed with ominous groans and sharp cracks as well. 'Mother of Night,' Malus growled. The daemon might yet succeed in bringing the entire damned temple down around his ears.

The highborn eyed the open doorway. What would happen once he passed beyond the reach of the containment wards? Would death claim him at last?

There was sharp report just above Malus, and a chunk of obsidian the size of his torso crashed to the floor just a few feet to his left. That decided the highborn. If he stayed where he was he was as good as dead anyway. He gathered up his gauntlet and the warpsword and ran for his life.

He hadn't taken more than a dozen paces when the rest of the ceiling gave way in a long, grinding roar. Gusts of pulverised stone washed past him, swallowing the highborn for an instant in a smothering, black fog. Gritting his teeth, Malus ran on, aiming for the spot where he knew the doorway to lie. The floor shook beneath him as tons of rubble poured down from the temple ceiling.

Suddenly the floor seemed to fall away from him and he was stumbling headlong through empty space. He fell for a long, dizzying instant, then crashed face-first on a canted stone floor. Again the pain felt like a strange echo of true sensation; he knew he was hurt, but he wasn't certain how badly. Malus felt himself skid half a dozen feet before fetching up against a stretch of level floor. He tried to clear his head with a savage shake, belatedly realising that he'd stumbled down the long ramp leading into the living quarters on the level below the vault.

The air was still thick with dust and smoke. Malus staggered back to his feet, coughing as he struggled to breathe in the grey-brown murk. The floor continued to tremble beneath his feet, and the sounds of collapsing stone had mingled together into one long, muffled roar. Holding the warpsword out before him he ran on into the haze, navigating by memory as he sought the top of the curving stairs.

Stone fell all around him as he went; he smashed against piles of debris scattered across his path, but each time he picked himself up and drove on. The minutes stretched interminably, until he thought he'd got turned around in the murk and was hopelessly lost. Just as he began to lose heart, however, a gust of air smote his face, and he stumbled into a cleared space kept open by a furnace-like updraft of air. The spiral staircase lay before him, its curving wall lit by an ominous orange glow. 'Mother of Night,' he cursed, hesitating at the top step. Malus shook his head helplessly. 'No way out but down,' he said at last. 'If this doesn't warm my bones, nothing will.'

Taking a deep breath, he rushed down the twisting stair. The heat pressed against his flesh like a wall, but he only felt the dimmest echo of warmth. The air rippled and shimmered like a desert mirage as he descended ever lower towards the lake of fire.

He emerged upon a threshold of melting stone, at the mouth of a seething dragon's maw. Magma raged a hundred feet below; as Malus watched, chunks of rock from the cavern's ceiling plunged into the churning sea, raising plumes of molten stone dozens of feet high. The wings of the daemon at the edge of the plaza glowed white-orange along its bottom edges, dripping streams of melting rock into the lake below.

Malus sheathed the warpsword and pulled on his right-hand gauntlet, then hurried quickly down the stairs. As he stepped on the first of the floating boulders, however, the stairway shifted wildly beneath him. The multi-ton boulder wobbled – and began to sink, picking up speed.

'Blessed Mother of Night!' Malus cried, his dark eyes widening in alarm. He took a running start and leapt for the next boulder in line, and it began its death-plunge as well. Scarcely daring to stop, the highborn increased his pace, leaping from one plunging rock to the next and drawing ever closer to the lake of magma below. Behind him the massive boulders struck the lake and exploded into fragments, hurling enormous pillars of molten stone into the air.

The last section of stairs was little more than ten feet above the lake of fire. When his boots touched it the boulder plunged beneath him, striking the magma almost at once. Jets of steam burst from fissures in the stone, and the boulder burst apart beneath the highborn's feet. Screaming every oath he knew, Malus hurled himself forward and leapt the last few feet to the shimmering stones of the plaza. He landed hard on his knees and elbows, hearing the steel hiss against the burning stone.

The plaza began to tremble beneath Malus, and an ominous rumble started to build above his head. Clambering to his feet, he charged across the broad plaza, and through the chamber of the Chaos Gods that lay beyond. The faces of the Ruinous Powers leered at him from their pedestals as he passed through their midst. Had he the time he would have gladly dragged each and every one across the plaza and fed them headfirst to the lake of fire.

The rumbling was increasing. Malus felt a wind growing in strength behind him as the temple's collapse accelerated. By the time he reached the temple antechamber he was howling like a madman, expecting the roof to fall in on him at any moment. The ghosts, still trapped in the chamber by the force of their ancient vows, regarded him in silent horror as he abandoned them to their fate.

Malus burst into the snowy night air with a desperate howl, just as the temple completely caved in behind him. The ground shook as though it had been struck by the hammer of a god, throwing the highborn forward onto the frozen ground. The sounds of splintering stone and settling earth went on behind him for many long minutes. When it finally stopped, the silence that stretched though the surrounding forest was deafening.

Slowly, carefully, Malus rose to his feet. He turned, and saw that the temple of Tz'arkan was no more. The huge edifice had fallen in upon itself, settling into the ravenous lake of fire. All that was left were tumbled piles of obsidian stone, wreathed by noxious vapours from the raging magma beneath. He looked upon the devastation and was surprised that he felt no relief at having escaped. Indeed, he felt nothing at all.

Small sounds of movement by the temple gate brought Malus around. Groups of beastmen were approaching, their twisted faces rapt with awe as they viewed the destruction of the great temple. Their leader, the one-eyed shaman, sank to his knees before Malus. 'What does this mean, great prince?' he croaked in his bestial tongue.

The highborn's gaze took in the swelling mob, then came to rest upon the awestruck shaman. His rage was gone. His body felt empty, his bones as cold as stone. Victory, he mused, was not supposed to feel like this.

'What does this mean?' he echoed in a dead voice. 'The end of the world, of course. For you, I mean.'

He drew Khaine's burning blade and showed it to the milling herd. Then he showed them what it could do.

MALUS DARKBLADE SQUEEZED the last drops of the blood from the beastman's heart into the side of Spite's fanged mouth, then tossed it onto the heap with the rest. Frowning thoughtfully, he pulled off his blood-soaked gauntlet and pressed his hand against the side of the cold one's snout. He couldn't tell if the nauglir's body heat was improving or not. 'Come on, damn you,' he whispered. 'There's enough meat here now to feed a squadron of cold ones. You just have to raise that scaly snout of yours and eat.'

The nauglir made no move to the pile of severed limbs Malus had stacked scant inches from its jaws. The war beast regarded him with one large, red eye. Shaking his head, the highborn rose to his feet. 'I've done all I can for you, you great lump of scales. If you're going to die on me now, get on with it. It's up to you. But if you're going to get me back for all the punishment I've inflicted on you in the last few weeks, you're going to need to get your strength back.'

Sighing to himself, the highborn turned away and strode to the roaring fire he'd built from molten stone and piles of severed logs. The ground surrounding the bonfire and for scores of yards in either directions had been transformed to churned, red-tinged mud. Bodies and pieces of bodies littered the earth as far as Malus could see. He'd managed to keep enough self-control to spare the last few dozen beastmen and put them to work butchering their companions and gathering logs for the fire. He'd intended to cut them down as soon as they were done, but while he busied himself feeding Spite they'd slipped away into the darkness. He doubted he would see them again.

For the next hour he busied himself by gathering the bones of his fallen retainers and feeding them one by one to the raging fire. He owed them that much, he believed, though he felt nothing as he delivered them to the flames.

I've become dead inside, he thought, watching the bones blacken in the flame. Dead within, dead without, he thought. A lord of ruin in truth.

Tz'arkan had spoken truly. The daemon had taken everything from him, just when it seemed his deepest desires lay within his grasp. I could return home, he thought. I'm still the Witch King's champion, and after the bitter victory at Ghrond he will have need of strong hands to help secure the kingdom. He could still have his reckoning with Isilvar. He could find Hauclir, if he still lived, and set about rebuilding once more.

And yet… and yet he felt nothing. No hunger. No sense of anticipation, even at the prospect of sweet revenge against his last surviving brother. No hatred for the last, treacherous blow the daemon had dealt him.

No hatred, he thought, shaking his head. This is no way for any druchii to live.

Malus stared into the flames for a long time, watching the molten stones char his retainers' bones to dust. As the night waned, more flakes of snow began to fall. By the time that dawn was paling the sky, he'd decided what must be done.

He turned back to Spite to find the nauglir on its feet, nosing hungrily through the piles of beastman flesh laid before it. The sight brought a grim smile to the highborn's face. While the war beast ate, the highborn checked Spite's feet and tail for signs of sickness or strain. Spite watched its master at work and growled ominously between bites. Malus met the nauglir's red gaze with a feigned scowl. 'I was starting to think you'd given up,' he said. 'Good to know I named you Spite with good reason.'

He let the nauglir rest until well past noon while he formulated his plan and gathered up pieces of meat for the journey ahead. He'd heard that the seer of the Black Ark of Naggor possessed a potent relic that would show the location of whatever the owner wished to find, no matter where – or in what realm – it lay. He would need such a tool if he was going to find where Tz'arkan had gone.

He was going to get his soul back. Malus had no idea how such a thing could be done, but he would do it, or die in the attempt. Wherever the daemon had fled to, even if it lay within the very storms of Chaos itself, Malus was going to find him and reclaim what was his. Naggaroth and Hag Graef could wait. What was the point of revenge, after all, if he had no means of savouring it?

By mid-afternoon, Spite was ready to travel. Malus checked his frayed bags and his fresh rations, and then swung heavily into the saddle. He led the nauglir to the square gate, past scores of snow-covered corpses, and reined in at the site of the long road dwindling into the distance.

'You're out there somewhere, daemon,' Malus whispered into the icy wind. 'And if you can hear me, you'd best prepare yourself. The Lord of Ruin is coming for you.'

Malus Darkblade rested a gloved palm against the side of Spite's scaly neck. 'On, beast of the deep earth,' he said. 'To the

Black Ark, to the daemon realms, to the Abyss itself if that is where the trail leads. Our journey is over. Now the hunt begins.'

AFTERWORD

If I'd had the faintest idea what I was getting myself into, I might never have written the Darkblade books.

By the summer of 2004 I'd been a professional writer and game designer for going on eight years. I'd worked on dozens of role-playing games and supplements, and published about a half-dozen short stories, but I'd never written a novel in my life. This wasn't for lack of trying, mind you; in fact, the reason I'd gotten into RPG's in the first place was because of a failed novel pitch. I'd approached White Wolf Games Studio with a proposal for a trilogy of novels based on their popular *Werewolf: the Apocalypse* role-playing game, but the pitch had fallen victim to a case of bad timing. The company wasn't interested in publishing game-related fiction at that point, but they did like my writing enough to offer me a job working on their games. Of course I said yes, figuring that I'd get some valuable experience and, sooner or later, I'd get another shot at writing a novel. Turns out I was only half-right. I learned a lot about writing, editing and publishing, but, ironically enough, I was so busy writing game-related material that I never had the time for anything else.

After eight years of writing about monsters and urban horror, I was feeling restless and looking to branch out into other genres. One of my best friends had got me interested in Warhammer 40,000 the year before, and on a whim I submitted a Space Wolves story to *Inferno!* magazine, edited at that time by the estimable Christian Dunn. I was still a complete novice when it came to the game's setting, but to my great surprise Christian bought the story and worked very patiently with me to polish off the rough spots and get it fit for publication. Unfortunately, the magazine was discontinued less than a month later, before the story could see print. Once again, my timing was impeccable.

All was not lost, however. That summer I received an email from Lindsey Priestley, senior editor at Black Library. Lindsey had read my story, and wanted to know if I might be interested in submitting pitches for their novel line. I had a series of pitches – three for Warhammer Fantasy, three for Warhammer 40,000 – on her desk within the week.

Lindsey and I went back and forth over the pitches for the next several weeks. She wanted me to try my hand first at a fantasy book, dashing my hopes of a trilogy of Black Legion stories set just after the events of Abaddon's 13th Black Crusade (some day, though, some day…). We'd settled on one story in particular – although, to be perfectly honest, I can't remember which one it was at this point – and I was just starting on the outline when, one morning, I got a mysterious email from Lindsey. Marc Gascoigne, then-publisher of the company, wanted to chat over the phone about a special project he had in mind.

Marc Gascoigne? Special project? *Me?* Nervously, I waited by the phone. When he rang up, half an hour later, I tried not to sound too overawed. In retrospect, I probably failed.

'We're looking to do a series of novelisations based on Dan Abnett's *Malus Darkblade* comics,' Marc told me. 'There would be five books, one for each of the comic stories, and you'd be co-writing them with Dan. Do you think you might be interested in the project?'

You'd be co-writing them with Dan.

I distinctly remember my eyes going wide as saucers when Marc said those words. I tried to sound detached and glib, as though I were asked to co-write novel series with phenomenally talented authors every day of the week. I think the words that actually came out of my mouth were something like, 'OhmyGodohmyGodohmyGodYESPLEASE.'

Cool and sophisticated. That's me.

'Brilliant,' Marc said. 'So, have you read *Born in Blood*?'

'Er. No,' I said.

'But you're familiar with Malus Darkblade, right?' he said.

'Um. Actually, no.'

'Ah,' Marc said. 'Well, we'll send you some material to read over, then we can talk about working out a proposal for the series.'

'Sounds great!' I babbled. 'Can't wait to get to work!'

We talked for a bit more about deadlines and other particulars. At the end of the call, he said how glad he was to have me on the project. 'We tried six other authors before you, and none of them worked out,' he said cheerfully. 'But I'm sure you'll do just fine.'

Sure. I'd never written a novel before, much less *five*, and I didn't have the faintest idea who or what Malus Darkblade was, and I would be following in the footsteps of one of Black Library's best-loved authors. How hard could it be?

I got my first hints about a week later, when I received a packet in the mail containing a copy of *Born in Blood* and a lot of pages photocopied out of the first and second editions of the Dark Elf army book.

To my surprise, it turned out that Malus Darkblade was a total bastard. He was duplicitous, violent, self-centred and breathtakingly ruthless, and those were his *better* qualities. His people were pointy-eared, slave-taking sociopaths who worshipped a God of Murder. Their idea of fun was to torture people to death or hack them up in blood-drenched religious festivals. Midway through Dan's story, he has Malus murder his own father, for heaven's sake! How in the world was I going to write five entire *novels* about a protagonist that was so utterly, unapologetically evil?

And then there were the graphic novels themselves. *Born in Blood* told a single story in five very short instalments, that being Malus's quest to find the five magical relics that would free his soul from the daemon Tz'arkhan. Dan's story was punchy, fast-paced and brilliantly realised, with every episode focusing on whatever final challenge Malus had to face in order to claim each of the relics. So I started out with a novel structure that was basically one large story, but had to be broken down into five individual tales that each more or less stood on its own merits – and I had to build them *backwards*, starting with the endings of each one and working back to the beginning.

The first thing I started working on was developing the civilisation of the druchii themselves. The lore in the army books gave a rough introduction to how their society functioned, but for the purposes of the books I had to flesh them out a lot further. I needed to know *why* they did what they did. I needed to know how they managed to be so vicious and cruel, yet work together as a people. I wrote a background file about twenty pages long, drawing on my background as an RPG designer, and fleshed out the broad strokes of their civilisation. From there, I began to create the list of characters that would populate the stories, starting with Malus's family and then sketching out his retainers. Once I had this foundation in place, I was able to start outlining *The Daemon's Curse*.

What I didn't have yet was a handle on Malus himself. How could I take someone so villainous and actually make him appealing?

Naturally, it was Dan himself who provided the answer. At San Diego Comic-Con in 2004, I sat down with him and Marc and talked about Malus and the series as a whole. Well. They talked. I did a lot of listening. At one point, Dan turned to me and said, 'The thing you have to remember about Malus is that he isn't necessarily the smartest, or the quickest, or the most powerful bloke out there. What makes him dangerous is that he just doesn't quit. No matter what happens to him or who he's up against, he just won't stop until he gets what he wants.'

Looking back, that thirty-minute conversation pretty much charted the course of the entire series and laid the foundation for other stories to come. Dan's brilliant like that.

I went back home after the convention and thought about what Dan had said, and slowly but surely, the pieces started to fall together. My focus changed. Malus was no longer *just* a murderous, sociopathic highborn. He was the illegitimate son of a father who hated him and a mother who saw him as nothing more than a pawn to serve her own world-shaking agenda. His brothers and sisters alternated between using him and trying to kill him, just because he was weaker than they. Even his name, *Darkblade*, was an epithet, implying that he was worthless and easily broken.

But he was going to prove them all wrong, by the Dark Mother. He didn't care what it took. He didn't have wealth or power. He wasn't the strongest, or the most handsome, or the best swordsman in Hag Graef. He was the underdog, struggling to survive against foes that were far more deadly than he. As bad as Malus was, the world he lived in was much, much worse.

Of course, that was just the beginning. The story grew in the telling, sometimes taking things in unexpected directions that turned out to be much better than what I had originally planned. Hauclir was supposed to die at the end of the second chapter of *Bloodstorm*, but instead he went on to become Malus's sardonic but faithful sidekick through much of the series. Originally, Yasmir was my least favourite of Malus's treacherous siblings; she was meant to lose her mind over the course of *Bloodstorm* and ultimately die at Malus's hand, but she became a living saint of Khaine instead, and an integral part of Darkblade's ultimate destiny.

These books were, hands down, the hardest things I've ever done. Each and every book was more complicated, more challenging, than the one that came before it. Thankfully, I didn't have to do it alone. Dan was much more a mentor than a collaborator: perceptive, patient and unfailingly generous with both his time and his hard-won expertise. Forget what he told you in his introduction; he was just being his usual, classy self. These books couldn't have been written without him. (And I'm not just saying that because he made me cry like a little girl at Baltimore Games Day.)

I also couldn't have done my part without the help and support of my editor Lindsey, who provided sage advice and copious amounts of encouragement throughout the entire process. As each successive book took longer and longer to complete, she kept her cool and somehow managed to avoid strangling me. For that I am eternally grateful.

Last, but far from least, I owe my wife Janet an enormous debt of gratitude for her support and patience during the years it took to write this series. She was always there to listen when I'd managed to write myself into a corner, and always managed to offer a solution that put me back on track. Frankly, she's pretty much the only reason I didn't turn into a quivering blob of goo by the middle of book three. Janet and Dan's wife, Nik (a very lovely and classy lady herself, who copy edited most, if not all of the books in the series) are contemplating forming a 'Wives of Writers Support Group'. God knows I wish them both the best. They need all the help they can get.

Malus's story, you see, is far from over. This book merely represents the culmination of the first of Darkblade's epic adventures. Dan went on to write several more volumes detailing the highborn's quest to regain his soul from Tz'arkan, and his eventual return to Naggaroth, and there are even further hints of his future sprinkled throughout the series.

This is the end of the beginning, as it were. Darkblade's adventures will continue. It will be a while yet, as Dan and I both have a number of projects waiting in the queue, but I can't see Malus sitting idle for long. We're not finished with Darkblade – and I suspect he's not quite finished with us, either.

Mike Lee
Nashville, May 2009

Next - The Treasure of the Beastmen.

...W HEAR MORE OF THE TALE OF *MALUS DARKBLADE*, DARK ELF, CURSED BY DAEMONS.

HEAR OF HIS UNWILLING QUEST TO RETRIEVE FIVE RELICS OF UNHOLY POWER FOR THE BESTIAL ABOMINATION *TZARKAN*.

HEAR NOW, THE STORY OF THE *FIRST* RELIC ...

BRRRAAAARGHHHH!

DarkBlade

PART TWO

SCRIPT: DAN ABNETT   ART: KEV HOPGOOD

NEXT- THE LABYRINTH

HEAR TOLD MORE OF THE TALE OF *MALUS DARKBLADE*, CURSED WARRIOR, DARK ELF, PUPPET OF CHAOS.

HEAR HOW HE WAS *ENSLAVED* TO SEARCH FOR FIVE RELICS OF UNHOLY POWER, ENSLAVED BY THE FOUL DAEMON *TZARKAN*.

AND HEAR NOW, THE STORY OF THE *THIRD* RELIC...

AT THE EDGE OF THE WASTELAND LIES *VAELGOR KEEP*, A WAY STATION FOR DARK ELF RAIDING PARTIES.

ONE BITTER NIGHT IN WINTER, A RETURNING WARBAND WERE CELEBRATING THEIR TRIUMPHS.

DRINK DEEP, MY KIN ! THE FABLED *DAGGER OF TORXUS* IS OURS ! OUR NAMES WILL BE INSCRIBED ON THE ROLL OF HONOUR IN KHAINE'S OWN TEMPLE ON OUR RETURN !

NEXT- HELLFIRE

DarkBlade
Part Five

LISTEN AS THE DREAD STORY OF *MALUS DARKBLADE* NOW UNFOLDS.

WHOEVER LIVES HERE, DAEMON ... HAS QUITE AN APPETITE.

KNOW FIRST THAT HE WAS *CURSED* TO SEEK OUT FIVE RELICS OF UNHOLY POWER FOR THE FILTHY DAEMON *TZARKAN*, WHO LIVES INSIDE HIS SOUL.

THEN LET'S HOPE HE'S SLEEPING, MALUS.

THEN HEAR THE TALE OF THE *FOURTH* RELIC.

SOMEWHERE IN THESE DARK GULLIES LIES THE LOST WARPSWORD OF KHAINE. WE'RE NOT LEAVING UNTIL YOU'VE FOUND IT.

SCRIPT: DAN ABNETT ✳ ART: KEV HOPGOOD

WINTER HAD COME AROUND AGAIN, AS COLD AND BITTER AS THE WINTER BEFORE WHEN MALUS DARKBLADE'S ARROGANCE HAD LED HIM TO THE RESTING PLACE OF THE BOUND DAEMON T'ZARKAN...

... AND THE *CURSE* HAD COME UPON HIM.

HE HAD BEEN GIVEN FOUR SEASONS TO RECOVER *FIVE RELICS OF DARK POWER*, AND RETURN WITH THEM OR HIS LIFE WOULD BE FORFEIT.

THOSE FIVE TASKS HAD BEEN DEMANDING, BUT NOW THE *HARDEST* TASK OF ALL REMAINED...

... THE JOURNEY BACK ACROSS THE FROZEN WASTES TO FIND THE DAEMONS' PRISON BEFORE THE LAST FEW DAYS OF THE YEAR TICKED AWAY AND TOOK HIS *LIFE* WITH THEM.

BY THE TIME HE REACHED THE DARK GORGE THAT LEAD TO THE OLD TEMPLE WHERE THE DAEMON WAS BOUND, ONLY A *SINGLE DAY* REMAINED OF HIS ALLOTTED TIME.

THE BONES OF HIS KINSMEN LAY WHERE HE HAD LEFT THEM.

COLD WINTER GALES SLICED DOWN FROM THE LATITUDES WHERE ICE NEVER MELTS.

IT TOOK MOST OF THAT LAST DAY TO PREPARE THE RITUAL ...

... SIGILS WERE INSCRIBED, PUNGENT FIRES LIT...

LITANIES RECITED FROM STONE TABLETS SMOOTH WITH AGE...

... AND THEN THE LAST CONJURINGS, CHANTED IN A TONGUE THAT HAD NOT BEEN SPOKEN FOR *NINE COLD CENTURIES.*

THE MAGICAL SHACKLES THAT HAD BOUND TZ'ARKAN FOR SO LONG WERE NOW WORKING LOOSE.

SOMEHOW, MALUS WAS NOT SURPRISED THAT THE DAEMON WAS ESCAPING FROM HIM, AND NOT THE STONE.

TZ'ARKAN WAS FREE ONCE MORE.

DREADFULLY WOUNDED BY THE VERY RELICS THAT HAD FREED HIM, THE DAEMON FLED.

MALUS WAS ALONE AT LAST.

BUT EVEN AS HE ROSE, MALUS KNEW THERE HAD BEEN A PRICE TO PAY. HE FELT AN EMPTINESS, A *HOLLOWNESS...*

THE DAEMON HAD FLED, TAKING PART OF THE *DARK ELF'S SOUL* WITH HIM.

NOW MALUS DARKBLADE HAD A *NEW* QUEST, ONE HE KNEW MIGHT TAKE HIM TO THE ENDS OF THE WORLD AND THE EDGES OF HIS LIFESPAN.

HOWEVER, HE SWORE HE WOULD NOT FAIL. TZ'ARKAN WOULD NOT ESCAPE.

B
THAT
OF COURS
ANOTHER TA
ENTIRE

END OF BOOK ONE.

ABOUT THE AUTHORS

Dan Abnett lives and works in Maidstone, Kent, in England. Well known for his comic work, he has written everything from the *Mr Men* to the *X-Men*. His work for the Black Library includes the best-selling Gaunt's Ghosts novels, the *Eisenhorn* and *Ravenor* trilogies, and the acclaimed Horus Heresy novel, *Horus Rising*. He's also worked on the popular strips *Titan* and *Darkblade*, and, together with Mike Lee, the *Darkblade* novel series.

Mike Lee was the principal creator and developer for White Wolf Game Studio's *Demon: The Fallen*. Over the last eight years he has contributed to almost two dozen role-playing games and supplements. His Black Library novels include *Nagash the Sorcerer* and *Fallen Angels*. An avid wargamer and devoted fan of pulp adventure, Mike lives in the United States.

WARHAMMER

THE CHRONICLES OF

MALUS DARKBLADE

VOLUME ONE

Omnibus contains
The Daemon's Curse,
Bloodstorm and
Reaper of Souls

DAN ABNETT
& MIKE LEE